# ENGLISH-ARABIC CONVERSATIONAL DICTIONARY

*Richard Jaschke*

With a Grammar, Phrases,
an Arabic-English Vocabulary
and a
**SUPPLEMENT**
**of New Words and New Phrases**



HIPPOCRENE BOOKS
*New York*

**The Arabic translations in the supplementary New Words and New Phrases are by PHILIP KAE of the Arab-American Business Service Bureau, New York.**



First Hippocrene edition, 1987

For information, please address:
Hippocrene Books, Inc.
171 Madison Ave.
New York, NY 10016

ISBN 0–87052–494–1

Printed in the United States of America.

# ABOUT THIS BOOK

THIS LITTLE book, one of the best pocket guides to Arabic ever published, has been out of print for too long a time. The present publishers are happy to reissue it in an enlarged edition, with a supplement of new words and the addition of several new phrase groups covering up-to-date fields like flying, traveling by car, using a camera, etc.

Travelers and students of the language will find the dictionary particularly useful in achieving proficiency in the spoken language. The manual contains both the Syrian and Egyptian dialects, thus doubling its value for the user.

A large number of representative phrases is included in this volume, starting on page 32. Copious references are made to them at the foot of every page of the main dictionary starting on page 150. Many colloquial expressions are grouped together for convenience under special headings such as "Asking a Favor," "In the Café," "Arrival and Departure," etc., besides such general groupings as affirmative phrases and asking a favor, among others. For obvious reasons such words as "lion," for which the Arab has some four hundred expressions, and "sword," for which he has double that number, are rendered only by the usual equivalent, but those who take the trouble to familiarize themselves with the grammar (pp. 7 to 31) will seldom be at a loss for the right colloquial word or phrase.

An unusual amount of helpful material is packed into this concise pocket dictionary. Despite the somewhat old-fashioned flavor of some of the phrases, the reader will find the book, with its new supplement, a thoroughly reliable aid in acquiring a basic knowledge of conversational Arabic.

# NOTE

**Both the Syrian and Egyptian dialects are given, the latter in italics ; e.g. in the Dictionary : evening** masa *mise*, **i.e. 'evening' is** masa **in Syrian and** *mise* **in Egyptian. Where there is no Arabic in italics, the Syrian and Egyptian are alike, as in : fire** nâr, **where 'fire' is** nâr **both in Syrian and Egyptian.**

**The Arabic is transcribed in English letters, and can be read as such, but :**

> â, ê, î, ô, û **must always be pronounced respectively as in far,** eh **(as a in fame), fatigue,** no, **rude (oo in moon) :** kâr, shê, shî, rôsto, *gûwa*.
>
> ä **sounds like a in fare :** mäkin **; it occurs in Syrian only.**
>
> a, e, i, o, u **are always short as in fat (or rather as the French a in la),** end, **till, not, full :** maḥall′, lezze, kizib, oḳḳa, muḥâl.

**The diphthongs** ai **and** au **sound respectively as ai in aisle (or y in my) and as ou in out :** maidân, maus.

**Final** e **is not silent, but pronounced as the e's in tenement :** tâze, *tezkire, we, zekîbe, mise*.

> *g* **is hard as in get, give :** *gindi*.
>
> j **sounds as in the French je, jamais :** jindi.
>
> kh **sounds as the Scotch ch in loch :** khiṭâb.

**The vowels and diphthongs as above have been adopted because they correspond better with the Arabic, and because they are simpler and more uniform than the representation of those sounds, for instance, by** ah, **ay,** ee, **etc.**

**Accentuation.—The syllable on which the stress falls is marked by a following accent, e.g.** filbait′ **: stress on** bait, ḍarab′to **: stress on** rab. **Where no accent is marked the stress is always on a long vowel (â, ä, ê, î, ô, û) if present ; in other cases it falls on the first syllable, e.g.** ʿumûmi **: stress on** mû, masa **: stress on** ma.

## Note

**Regard being paid to the rules concerning the vowels on the opposite page, the Arabic may be read as if it were English. Appended is fuller information on the other letters:**

b **as in ball:** bela.
d **has a soft dental sound:** daura.
ḍ **is a strongly pronounced palatal** d**:** ûḍa.
f **as in fife:** faras.
g **always hard as in gift, God:** *gedîd, gifn, gûwa, sign.*
h **as in house:** hî.
ḥ **is a very hard aspirate:** ḥâli, rûḥ.
j **like the French j in jour:** jâj, sijn, wajad, yûjaʿ.
k **as in kill:** kumruk, knîsi.
ḳ **like ck in luck:** daḳḳ; **the Bedouins sound it a hard g; in some parts of Syria and in and around Cairo it is almost imperceptible:** ḳunṣul **nearly like** unṣul.
kh **as Scotch ch in loch, or Spanish j in viaje:** khaukh, wakhm.
l **as in lily:** laili.
m **as in mat:** mismâr.
n **as in noon:** naulûn.
r **as in river:** rafrâf.
ṛ **like the 'thick' r as sounded by many Parisians, or like the Northumbrian r:** ṛarîb, baṛl.
s **is always sharp as in seven:** krâsi, ḥasab.
ṣ **is more hissing than** s**:** ṣarṣûr.
sh **as in shop:** shâkûsh', *ushhur.*
t **as in titbit:** tutun.
ṭ **is very hard, almost as if preceded by u:** ṭafa.
w **as in will:** waṣl.
y **as in year:** yâ, yzûr, zaiy, walâyim.
z **as in zeal:** zaṛzaṛ.
ʿ **is a soft guttural vowel:** ʿaraḳ.
≠ **shows the place where a slight pause must be made, or where at least the word must be suddenly interrupted:** sa≠al, *as≠ili.*

**Each letter must be distinctly sounded; the** th, **therefore, in** muthim **as** t-h, **not as in mathematic. Exceptions to this rule are, however,** kh **and** sh, **because they represent one letter (sound) only.**

# CONTENTS

## Contents

# GRAMMAR

## THE ARABIC ALPHABET AND ITS TRANSCRIPTION

| Number. | Character. | Name and numerical value. | Transcription. | Remarks. |
|---|---|---|---|---|
| 1. | ا | Alif 1 | =, â | Is expressed by the sign =, (1) when it stands in the middle of a word at the beginning of a syllable, e.g. is=al I ask, bil=izn' with the permission, which must never be pronounced i=sal or bi=lizn', (2) when at the end of a syllable it is the prop for a hamza, i.e. a breathing-out, distinctly perceivable as hiatus, e.g. ma=mûl hoped, ista='zin *asta='zin* I ask permission, where after the a a slight pause should be made. The Alif is rendered by â when it is the mark of prolongation of the vowel a. |
| 2. | ب | Bê 2 | b | |
| 3. | ت | Tê 400 | t | |

| Number. | Character. | Name and numerical value. | Transcription. | Remarks. |
|---|---|---|---|---|
| 4. | ث | Thê 500 | t, s | Some of the peasants and most of the Bedouins of Syria give it the original sound as th in think; but it is generally sounded as t; in some words, however, as s, e.g. tâni *tâni* second, sabbat to prove. |
| 5. | ج | Jîm *Gîm* 3 | j *g* | In some parts of Northern Syria and by the Bedouins it is sounded as j in jar; but in Syria proper and in Palestine as the French j, i.e. as z in glazier; in Egypt always a hard g as in get; e.g. jabal (the j as in French) *gebel* (the *g* hard as in god) mountain. |
| 6. | ح | Ḥê *Ḥâ* 8 | ḥ | Is a very strong aspirate, spoken in the larynx, something like h in haul —there is no exact European equivalent. |
| 7. | خ | Khê *Khâ* 600 | kh | Like ch in loch, or in the German ach, and like Greek χ. — In the few cases where kh does not represent No. 7, but Nos. 22, 26 they are separated by a hyphen: k-h; cf. No. 13. |
| 8. | د | Dâl 4 | d | |

| Number. | Character. | Name and numerical value. | Transcription. | Remarks. |
|---|---|---|---|---|
| 9. | ذ | Zâl 700 | d, z | By those who pronounce No. 4 as in think, No. 9 is sounded soft as in this; elsewhere as z or d in dizzy, e.g. iza if, dîb wolf. |
| 10. | ر | Rê 200 | r | |
| 11. | ز | Zain *Zê* 7 | z | As in zenith. |
| 12. | س | Sîn 60 | s | As in hiss. |
| 13. | ش | Shîn 300 | sh | In the few cases where sh does not represent No. 13, but Nos. 4, 26 or 12, 26, they are separated by a hyphen: s-h; cf. No. 7. |
| 14. | ص | Ṣâd 90 | ṣ | Emphatic s, produced in the upper palate, as in sat. |
| 15. | ض | Ḍâd 800 | ḍ | Emphatic d, the tongue being closely pressed against the palate. |
| 16. | ط | Ṭâ 9 | ṭ | Emphatic t, the tongue being closely pressed against the palate. |
| 17. | ظ | Zâ 900 | z, ḍ | Generally as 11, sometimes as 15. |
| 18. | ع | ‘Ain ‘*En* 70 | ‘ | A peculiar guttural sound produced by the emission of air through the tightly compressed throat. |
| 19. | غ | Ṛain *Ṛên* 1000 | ṛ | r sounded well down in the throat, resembling the French r grasseyé, and |

| Number. | Character. | Name and numerical value. | Transcription. | Remarks. |
|---|---|---|---|---|
| | | | | somewhat like the German ch. (It is in some other manuals rendered by gh.) |
| 20. | ف | Fê 80 | f | |
| 21. | ق | Ḳâf 100 | ḳ | k or g sounded well down in the throat; in the greater part of Syria and in some parts of Egypt (as in Cairo and neighborhood) it is silent at the beginning of a word, e.g. ḳâḍi judge, pronounced âḍi, ḳauwâṣ consular policeman, pronounced auwâṣ; in the middle of a word, at the beginning or end of a syllable, it has the pronunciation of the Alif rendered by ⸗ (cf. 1., remark), e.g. muḳad'das saint, like mu⸗ad'das, ʿaḳrab scorpion, like ʿa⸗rab; also in the middle of monosyllables it appears as this strong breathing, e.g. waḳt time, like wa⸗t; as this pronunciation is very difficult a slightly audible semivowel is often heard between the ⸗ and t: almost dissyllabic wa⸗it. |

| Number. | Character. | Name and numerical value. | Transcription. | Remarks. |
|---|---|---|---|---|
| 22. | ك | Kâf 20 | k | |
| 23. | ل | Lâm 30 | l | |
| 24. | م | Mîm 40 | m | |
| 25. | ن | Nûn 50 | n | |
| 26. | ه | Hê 5 | h | Always as in hand. |
| 27. | و | Wau 6 | w, u, û | Rendered by w, as in war, at the beginning of a syllable; by u when following an a, with which it forms the diphthong au or the vowel ô; by û when it marks the prolongation of the vowel u. |
| 28. | ى | Yê 10 | y, i, î | Rendered by y, as in yard, at the beginning of a syllable; by i when following an a, with which it forms the diphthong ai or the vowel ê; by î when it marks the prolongation of the vowel i. |

The doubling of a consonant, which in written Arabic is indicated by a ّ placed over it, must, in pronunciation, always be marked by a prolongation of the sound, e.g. illi *elli* who, which, but ili to me. This doubling always takes place when the definite article precedes words beginning with certain letters, as shown on page 7.

## THE VOWELS AND DIPHTHONGS

In the written Arabic the short vowels are indicated not by special letters, but by signs (points) placed above or below the consonants, the long vowels and diphthongs being expressed with the aid of the letters Alif, Wau, Yê, which, like all the other Arabic letters, are in reality consonants.

—The short vowels are :

a, in Syria generally sounded purely, i.e. as the short Italian and French a ; between the two last consonants of a word, except when one of them is an emphatic (14, 15, 16), or a guttural letter, or an r, its sound mostly inclines towards e, e.g. samek fish ; as, however, in Syria this latter pronunciation is not general, and the original a is everywhere understood, it has in our transcription been only adopted where a distinct e is generally sounded instead of a, as in diheb gold. In Egypt the a is pronounced purely only before and after certain consonants ; it mostly inclines to the English a in hat, or e.

e, in Syria seldom, in Egypt very frequently, found, arising from a dull pronunciation of a, e.g. *beled* (Syr. balad) district, town.

i, e.g. bint girl.

o, e.g. ḍarab'to I struck him.

u, e.g. ruḥt I went, mush not.

—The long vowels are :

â, e.g. nâr fire.

ä (in Syria only), e.g. bäb door, ktäb book.

î, e.g. bîr well, fountain, îd hand.

ê and ô take in Egypt regularly, in Syria seldom, the place of ai and au, e.g. *bêt* (Syr. bait) house, *fôḳ* (Syr. fauḳ) above.

û, e.g. hû *hûwa* he, rûḥ spirit, soul.

—The diphthongs are :

ai and au, e.g. bait house, fauḳ above ; in Syria almost everywhere pronounced as y in my and ou in out, the sounds inclining to ê and ô in a few districts only. In Egypt, on the contrary, these two diphthongs are replaced by ê and ô (see above), except before y or w, e.g. ṭaiyib good, auwal first, where they occur as in Syria.

**Note.—The diphthong** oi, **which one seems to hear in** moi **or** moiyi *moiye* **water, does not exist; as, however, this transcription corresponds better than** mwai *muwai'ye*, **as it ought to be spelled, with the sounds as heard by the foreigner, it has been adopted.**

## THE ARTICLE

**The indefinite article is commonly omitted, e.g.** bait *bêt* **a house,** ktâb *kitâb* **a book.**

**The definite article is** il *el*; **it remains the same for all genders, numbers, etc., and is combined with the following word, e.g.** ilbait' *elbêt* **the house,** ilku'tub *elku'tub* **the books.**

**If the word following the definite article begins with a** d, ḍ, t, ṭ, s, ṣ, sh, z, n, r, **or** j *g*, **the** l **of** il *el* **is not pronounced, but the first letter of the following word is doubled, e.g.** iddau'li *eddôle* **the empire, the dynasty,** ishshams' *eshshems'* **the sun,** innâr *ennâr* **the fire,** ijja'bal *egge'bel* **the mountain, i.e. the** l **of the article is assimilated to the first letter of** dauli *dôle*, shams *shems*, nâr, jabal *gebel*.

## THE NOUN

### GENDER

**The following substantives are of the feminine gender:**

**(1) Those denoting females, e.g.** maryam **Mary,** umm **mother,** faras **mare.**

**(2) The names of countries and towns, e.g.** maṣr **Egypt,** bairût *bêrût'* **Beyrout.**

**(3) A few names of such parts of the human body which are duplicated, e.g.** ʿain *ʿên* **eye,** ijr *rigl* **foot,** îd **hand.**

**(4) Those ending in** a **or** i *e*, **e.g.** jarra *garra* **water-jar,** kilmi *kilme* **word; to which class belong the feminine appellatives formed from their masculine by adding** a **or** i *e*, **e.g.** fallâḥa *fellâḥa* **peasant-woman, from** fallâḥ *fellâḥ* **peasant,** kalbi *kelbe* **bitch, from** kalb *kelb* **dog. The same endings serve for forming a unitary name out of a collective one, e.g.** shaʿr **hair:** shaʿra **a hair,** ward **roses:** wardi *warde* a rose. In this formation the ending a is used if the substantive ends in an emphatic or a guttural letter, and generally when it ends with an r; otherwise i *e* is used.

(5) A limited number of other nouns, for whose feminine gender custom has decided, the most common of which are: arḍ earth, nafs *nefs* soul, shams *shems* sun, rîḥ wind, rûḥ spirit, nâr fire, sullam *sellim* stairs, ladder, darb way, dâr house, hall, ṭâḥûn′ mill, sama heaven, jahan′nam *gahan′nam* hell, nâs *nâs* people, men.

All the other nouns are masculine.

FORMATION OF THE DUAL AND PLURAL

The dual is formed by adding ain *ên*, e.g. il=îd *el=îd* the hand, il=îdain′ *el=îdên′* both hands; bait *bêt* a house, baitain′ *bêtên′* two houses. Words ending in a or i *e* form their dual by adding tain *tên*, but in the Syrian the original ending is then dropped, e.g. marra once, marrtain′ *marratên* twice; kilmi *kilme* word, kilmtain′ *kilmetên* two words, a couple of (a few) words.

The plural is either regular, formed by the addition of a syllable, or irregular, formed by internal transposition. With masculine nouns the latter is by far the more usual formation.

The regular plural of masculines is formed by the addition of în, that of feminines in a or i *e* by the addition of ât (or ât) after elision of the ending a or i *e*, e.g. khîyâṭ′ *khaiyâṭ* tailor, plur. khîyâṭîn′ *khaiyâṭîn′*; shajra *shagara* tree, plur. shajrât *shagarât* trees; âli *âle* instrument, plur. âlât′ *âlât′*.

The ending ât (or ât), however, is in the Syrian-Arabic dialect sometimes affixed to masculine appellative nouns, and then implies an accessory notion of sort or quality, sometimes that of a portion, e.g. nbîdât′, from nbîd wine, as in hannbîdât′ ṭaiybîn ktîr this sort of wine is very good.

The rules on the formation of the irregular or broken plural are too complicated to be given here. The broken plurals have therefore been given in the Vocabulary. Practice only can teach the correct use of this plural, of whose most common forms we give a few examples:

bait *bêt* **house, pl.** byût *biyût*; shâhid **witness, pl.** shuhûd **(or, Syr. only**: shhûd); fûṭa **towel, pl.** fuwaṭ; ktâb *kitâb* **book, pl.** kutub; mdîni *medîne* **town, pl.** mudn *mudun*; ḳiṭ'a **piece, cut, pl.** ḳiṭa'; dîb **wolf, pl.** dyâb *diyâb*; waḳt **time, pl.** auḳât; shuṛl **business, work, pl.** ishṛâl **(or, Syr. only**: shṛâl); kâtib *kâtib* **writer, clerk, pl.** kuttâb *kuttâb*; nafs *nefs* **soul, person, pl.** infus *nufûs*; raṛîf **loaf of bread, pl.** irṛifi *arṛife*; ḳâlib **form, pl.** ḳwâlib *ḳawâlib*; 'ajûz *'agûz* **old woman, pl.** 'ajâyiz *'agâ-iz*; nâr **fire, pl.** nîrân'; faḳîr **poor, pl.** fuḳara; shâ'ir **poet, pl.** shu'ara; ṛani **rich, pl.** iṛnya *aṛniye*; arḍ **earth, land, pl.** arâḍi; laili *lêle* **night, pl.** lyâli *leyâ'lî*; hadîyi *hedîye* **present, gift, pl.** hadâya *hedâya*; ḥmâr *ḥumâr* **ass, pl.** ḥamîr; 'amm **uncle (father's brother), pl.** 'umûmi *a'mâm*; ḥajar *ḥagar* **stone, pl.** ḥjâra **and** aḥjâr *aḥgâr*; kursi **chair, pl.** krâsi *karâ'sî*; shibbâk *shibbâk* **window, pl.** shbâbîk' *shebâbîk'*; miftâḥ *muftâḥ* **key, pl.** mfâtîḥ' *mefâtîḥ'*; maskîn **poor, pl.** msâkîn' *mesâkîn'*; usḳuf **bishop, pl.** asâḳfi *asâḳife*; muṛrabi *maṛrabi* **Magribian, pl.** mṛârbi *maṛâribe*; bairûti *bêrû'ti* **Beyroutian, pl.** byârti *bayârite*; maṣri **Egyptian, pl.** maṣârwi *maṣâware*. — **Words denoting nationality, sect, class, etc., which generally end in** i, **form their plural mostly by affixing the feminine termination** a **or** i *e* **respectively** yi *ye*, **e.g.** ḳauwâṣ **consulate-policeman, pl.** ḳauwâṣa; frinsâwi *feransâwi* **Frenchman. pl.** frinsâwî'yi *feransâwî'ye*; baḥri **sailor, pl.** baḥrîyi *baḥrîye*.

**Irregular plurals**: rijjâl *râgil* **man, pl.** rjâl *rigâle* **men**; insân **man, human being, pl.** nâs *nâs* **mankind**; mara *mar-a* **woman, pl.** nisa **or** niswân *niswân*; ab **father, pl.** âbâ' **or** abhât *abhât*; umm **mother, pl.** ummhât *ummehât*; bint **daughter, girl, pl.** bnât *banât*; akh **brother, pl.** ikhwi *ikhwe* **or** ikhwân; ukht **sister, pl.** akhawât *ikhwât* **(or, Syr. only**: khaiyât); îd **hand, pl.** iyâdi *ayâdi*; khawâja *khawâga* **Mr., mister, pl.** khawâjât' *khawâgât'*; bâsha, âṛa, bêk **(titles), pl.** bashawât, aṛawât, bakawât *bêkawât'*.

**Many substantives have several plural forms at the same time, e.g.** baḥr **sea, has** buḥûr, biḥâr, abḥur, abḥâr, **etc.**

## DECLENSION

**In Arabic the substantive and the adjective do not change their forms according to the different positions they occupy with regard to other substantives or to the verb. In the nominative, accusative, and genitive they appear in their simple forms, e.g.** irrijjāl râḥ *errâgil râḥ* **the man went,** ana shuft irrijjāl *ana shuft errâgil* **I saw the man,** bint irrijjāl *bint errâgil* **the daughter of the man. The vocative is indicated by a preceding** yâ, **e.g.** yâ rijjāl *yâ râgil* **Oh man! The dative is marked by the preposition** la *li* **(with the article:** lil), **e.g.** a'ṭai'to lafaḳîr *a'ṭêto lifaḳîr* **I gave it to a poor man;** lilfaḳîr **to the poor man.**

**This applies to the singular and plural. However, the simple form of the substantive may be used for the genitive case only when both parts of the genitival relation are either definite or indefinite; in the first case the governing noun is, in Arabic, written without the article, e.g.** bint ilma'lik *bint elme'lik* **the daughter of the king,** bint malik *bint melik* **a (the) daughter of a king. In all other cases the phrase must be rendered circuitously, e.g., a daughter of the king** bint (or wâḥdi) min bnāt ilma'lik *bint* (or *waḥde*) *min banât elme'lik* **a daughter of the daughters of the king. The periphrasis may also be used when both parts are definite; but then the governing noun takes the definite article, and the word** taba' *betâ'*, **fem.** *betâ'et*, **pl.** *betû'* **is placed between the governing and governed substantive, e.g.** ilbint' taba' ilma'lik *elbint' betâ'et elme'lik* = bint ilma'lik *bint elme'lik* **the daughter of the king.**

**If the governing noun is a feminine with the ending a or i** *e*, **it takes instead of the above the ending** it *et* **or** t, **e.g.** ḳannînit nbîd *ḳananîyet nebîd* **a flask of wine,** mart ittājir *mirât ettâgir* **the wife of the merchant,** jnaint ilbâsha *genênet elbâsha* **the garden of the pasha.**

**Compound words are expressed by means of the genitive, e.g.** bāb ilmdîni *bâb elmedîne* **the town-gate; the same is the case with such expressions as Ascension Day** yaum iṣṣu'ûd *yôm eṣṣu'ûd* = **Day of the Ascension.**

# THE ADJECTIVE

## FORM

**The forms of the adjectives are manifold; the following are a few examples of frequent use:** ṣa'b **difficult,** nijis *nigis* **impure,** kbîr *kebîr* **large,** ṭawîl **long,** ḥilu **sweet,** ṣabûr **patient,** aḥmar **red,** a'war **one-eyed,** sikrân *sakrân* **drunk,** jû'ân *gî'ân* **hungry,** maskîn **poor,** kwaiyis *kuwai'yis* **handsome,** zṛaiyir *zuṛai'yar* **little.**

**For the forms of the different participles frequently used as adjectives, see the verb (pp. 21 to 31).**

**By the addition of** i, **occasionally** wi **or** ni, **a noun becomes an adjective denoting origin, descent, a belonging to, e.g.** shmâli *shemâli* **northern, from** shmâl *shemâl* **north;** bairûti *bêrû'ti* **Beyroutian, from** bairût *bêrût'* **Beyrout;** frinsâwi *feransâwi* **French, from** fransa *feran'sa* **France;** barrâni **outer, from** barra **outside.**

**Many adjectives, especially those denoting nationality, may also be used as substantives.**

**Adjectives are strengthened by the following words placed after them:** ķawi **strong,** ktîr *ketîr* **much,** jiddan *giddan* **much,** khâliṣ **altogether, entirely, e.g.** illai'li laṭîfi jiddan *ellêle laṭîfe giddan* **the night is very pleasant.**

## GENDER

**The simple form of the adjective always represents the masculine; the feminine is formed by adding** a **or** i *e*, **e.g.** shnî' *shenî'* **ugly, fem.** shnî'a *shenî'a*; jdîd *gedîd* **new, fem.** jdîdi *gedîde*; **only such adjectives as** aḥmar **red, and** a'war **one-eyed, denoting color, or bodily malformation or defects, form their feminine irregularly:** ḥamra, 'aura.

**Adjectives of relation or connection, ending in** i, **and derived from substantives, form their feminine in** îyi *îye*, **e.g.** shmâli *shemâli*, **fem.** shmâlî'yi *shemâlî'ye*; frinsâwi *feransâwi*, **fem.** frinsâwî'yi *feransâwî'ye.*

FORMATION OF THE PLURAL

**The adjectives have no dual, the plural form being employed instead.**

**The plural of most adjectives as well as participles is formed by the ending** în **for both genders, e.g.** ṭaiyib **good, pl** ṭaiybîn *ṭaiyibîn*; sikrân *sakrân* **drunk, pl.** sikrânîn' *sakrânîn'*; ḥilu **sweet, pl.** ḥilwîn; ḥâḍir **ready, pl.** ḥâḍrîn' *ḥaḍrîn*.

**Some classes of adjectives have a broken plural and use the same form for both genders; thus** kbîr *kebîr* **large,** ṭawîl **long, and the other adjectives of this class, form their plural:** kbâr *kubâr*, ṭwâl *ṭuwâl*, **etc.;** aswad *iswid* **black becomes** sûd, abyaḍ **white has** bîḍ, aḥmar **red has** ḥumr, aṣfar **yellow has** ṣufr: a'ma **blind has** 'imyān *'amyân*, a'war **one-eyed has** 'ûr, **and** a'raj *a'rag* **lame has** 'urj *'urg*.

**Adjectives often use their regular feminine form as a plural; this is the rule with those of relation ending in** i **(for their feminine see foot of p. 11);** ikhtyâr *ikhtiyâr* **old (used adjectively or substantively) has in the plural** ikhtyarîyi *ikhtiyarîye*.

DECLENSION

**The rules for the declension of substantives apply also to adjectives, but the latter have no special mark in the dative, e.g.** larijjāl fakîr *lirâgil fakîr* **to a poor man. Of course, when used substantively, it has this mark, e.g.** lafakîr *lifakîr* **'to a poor,' i.e. to a poor man.**

CONJUNCTION WITH SUBSTANTIVES

**The adjective always follows the substantive which it qualifies, and agrees with it in gender and number. It receives the article only if its noun is also determined by the article or by a genitival relation, or is a proper name, e.g.** ilbait' ilkbîr *elbêt elkebîr* **(instead of which, however, with improper elision of the first article, one often hears** bait ilkbîr *bêt elkebîr*) **the large house,** bint ilma'lik izzrîri *bint elme'lik ezzuṛai'yere* **the little (youngest)**

**daughter of the king,** yûsuf iṭṭawîl *yûsuf eṭṭawîl* **the tall Joseph; but** bait kbîr *bêt kebîr* **a large house,** bint zṛîri *bintè*[1] *zuṛai'yere* **a little girl.**

COMPARISON

**For the comparative and superlative the Arabic adjective has one form only, paying no regard to gender or number, e.g.** aṣʿab **more difficult, harder, and** ilaṣʿʿab *elaṣʿʿab* **the most difficult, the hardest, from** ṣaʿb **difficult, hard;** akbar **greater, etc., from** kbîr *kebîr* **great;** aktar **more, etc., from** ktîr *ketîr* **much.** Shedîd **powerful,** ḳalîl **little (with identical second and third radicals) form** ashadd' **and** aḳall'.

# THE PRONOUN

## THE PERSONAL PRONOUN

| | Sing. Nominative. | Plur. |
|---|---|---|
| **1. Pers.** | **I** ana | **we** niḥna *iḥna* **or** *iḥne* |
| **2. Pers. m.** | **thou** int *inte* | **you** intu |
| **2. Pers. f.** | **thou** inti *enti* | |
| **3. Pers. m.** | **he** hû **or** huwa *hûwa* **or** *hûwe* | **they** hinni *hum* **or** *huma* |
| **3. Pers. f.** | **she** hî **or** hiyi *hîya* **or** *hîye* | |

**The accusative of the personal pronoun is mostly joined immediately to the governing verb as suffix, these suffixes being the same as those of the possessive adjectives (p. 15), except that of the 1st pers. sing., which is** ni **instead of** i, **e.g.** ḍarab'ni **he struck me,** ḍarab'to **I struck him. If the accusative is to be emphasized, the suffix is followed by the nominative form, e.g.** ḍarabak int *ḍarabak inte* **he struck thee (thee emphasized).**

**Besides this conjunctive form there is a disjunctive one, of which in Syrian that for all persons is in usage, in the**

---

[1] **For the intermediate vowels, used in the Egyptian dialect only, to avoid the meeting of more than two consonants, we use these marks** *è, ì, ù, à.*

Egyptian dialect that for the 2nd and 3rd pers. sing. only. It is:

| | Sing. | Plur. |
|---|---|---|
| 1. Pers. | me yăyi (Syr. only) | us yăna (Syr. only) |
| 2. Pers. m. | thee yăk *îyâk'* | you yăkon (Syr. only) |
| 2. Pers. f. | thee yăki *îyâ'ki* | |
| 3. Pers. m. | him yăh *îyâh'* | them yăhon (Syr. only) |
| 3. Pers. f. | her yăha *îyâ'hâ* | |

If, however, in Syrian, this isolated form follows a w 'and,' it is joined to the latter and composes the forms wîyă'yi, wîyăk', wîyă'ki, etc., with a nominative meaning, e.g. ana wîyăk' I and thou, hû wîyă'ha he and she. In the Egyptian dialect *wayâ* has become a preposition: 'with.'

There is no genitive of the personal pronoun.

The dative is formed by adding the possessive suffixes to the preposition la *li*, which latter also indicates the dative of substantives; the forms thus composed are the following (for the possessive suffixes see next page):

to me li or *lîye*, or Syr. only: ili
to thee m. lak, or, Syr. only: ilak
to thee f. lik, or, Syr. only: ilik
to him lo or *loh*, or, Syr. only: ilo
to her liha or *luha*, or, Syr. only: ilha
to us lina, or, Syr. only: ilna
to you ilkon or likon *lukum*
to them ilhon or lihon *luhum*.

Through these suffixes the personal pronoun is also expressed when in conjunction with other prepositions, the latter then sometimes undergoing small modifications, e.g. fî in, with regard to: fîyi (also fîni) *fîye*, fîk, fîki, fîh, fîha, fîna, etc.; ʿala up, up to: ʿalai'yi *ʿalêye* (also *ʿalai'ye*), ʿalaik' *ʿalêk*, ʿalai'ki *ʿalêki*, ʿalaih' *ʿalêh*, etc.; maʿ or maʿa with: maʿi *miʿâye*, maʿak *miʿâk*, maʿik *miʿâki*, maʿo *miʿâh*, maʿaha *miʿâha*, etc.

## THE REFLEXIVE PRONOUN

The reflexive pronoun is formed by the substantives nafs *nefs* or zăt *zât*, or, Syr. only: ḥâl, with the corresponding possessive suffixes, e.g. jaraḥt' ḥâli *garaḥ'tè nefsi* I wounded myself, ḳauwas ḥâlo *ḳauwas nefso* or *rûḥoh* he shot himself.

The same substantives also serve for expressing 'I myself,' etc. e.g. int zâtak *inte zâtak* or int nafsak *inte nefsak*, or, with the preposition b *bi*, int bzâtak *inte bizâtak* thou thyself.

### THE POSSESSIVE PRONOUN AND ADJECTIVE

The possessive adjective is expressed by the following suffixes joined immediately to the substantive:

| Sing. | Plur. |
|---|---|
| 1. Pers. my i (after consonants), yi *ye* (after vowels) | our na |
| 2. Pers. m. thy ak (after consonants), k (after vowels) | your kon *kum* or *kû* |
| 2. Pers. f. thy ik (after consonants), ki (after vowels) | |
| 3. Pers. m. his o (after consonants), h (after vowels) | their hon *hum* |
| 3. Pers. f. her ha | |

e.g. ktâb *kitâb* book: ktâbi *kitâbi* my book, ktâbo *kitâbo* his book, ktâbha *kitâbha* her book; shifa healing, cure: shifâyi *shifâye* my cure, shifâk thy cure, etc. Substantives whose singular or plural ends in a or i *e*, change this ending into t before the suffixes of the singular, and it *et* before the suffixes of the plural, e.g. mara woman, wife, marti *imrâti* or *mirâti* my wife; baḳara cow, baḳarit'na *baḳaret'na* our cow; as꞉ili *as꞉ile* questions (pl. of su꞉âl *su꞉âl*), as꞉il'ti my questions, as꞉ilit'na *as꞉ilet'na* our questions.

ab (or, Syr. only: bai) father, takes the following forms with the suffixes: abi or abûyi *abûye* (or, Syr. only: baiyi) my father, abûk (or, Syr. only: baiyak) thy father, abûh (or, Syr. only: baiyo) his father, abûna (or, Syr.

**only:** baina) **our father, etc.; akh (or, Syr. only:** khai) **brother, has forms corresponding to those of** ab, **thus:** akhi **or** akhûyi *akhûye* **(or, Syr. only:** khaiyi) **my brother, etc.**

**Instead of this simple formation of the possessive one may make use of the word** taba' *betâ'*, **fem.** *betâ'et*, **pl.** *betû'*, **just as with the genitival relation of the substantive on p. 10; only in the latter case it must have the definite article, which it never has with the possessive suffixes; thus:** ilktâb taba'i *elkitâb betâ'i*=ktâbi *kitâbi* **my book,** ilûlâd' taba'o *elûlâd' betû'o* = ûlâ'do *ûlâ'do* **his children.—Possession is also expressed by** mâl **property,** ḥaḳḳ **right,** metâ' **goods, e.g.** eṣṣandûḳ mâli **the box my property=my box.**

**The possessive pronoun used substantively is always formed with this auxiliary word, thus:** taba'i *betâ'i* **mine.**

## THE DEMONSTRATIVE PRONOUN AND ADJECTIVE

**This** hâda **or** haida *da* **or** *di*, **fem.** hâdi **or** haidi *di*, **pl.** hadôl **or** haudi *dôl*.

**That** hadâk **or** haidâk *dik-hâ* **or** *duk-hâ* **or** *duk-hau'wa*, **fem.** hadîk **or** haidîk *dik-hâ* **or** *dik-hai'ya*, **pl.** hadolîk **or** haudîk *duk-ham'ma*.

**The noun defined by one of these demonstrative adjectives always has the article.**

**In the Syrian Arabic, instead of these full forms for 'this,' etc., the shortened form** ha **is generally used, regardless of number and gender, being joined to the article of the following noun; in which case the full form is frequently repeated after the substantive, e.g.** harrijjâl haida **this man,** hølbint' haidi **this girl,** hanniswân hadôl **these women. The shortened form, however, must never be used if this pronoun is used substantively, e.g.** haida irrijjâl **this is the man.**

**In the Egyptian Arabic the demonstrative adjective is almost always placed after the noun, e.g.** *errâgil di* **this man,** *elbin'tê dik-hâ* **that girl,** *enniswân dôl* **these women. When used as pronouns these words are frequently strengthened by having** *â* **placed before them, e.g.** *âdi' errâgil* **this is the man.**

## THE RELATIVE PRONOUN

**If the relative pronoun 'who, which, that' refers to a substantive not determined, it is left out in Arabic, e.g. I know a man who can do this** baʿrif rijjâl byiḳdir yaʿmil haida *baʿrif râgil beyiḳ'dar yiʿmil di.*

**After determined substantives the relative pronoun is** illi *elli* **for both genders and numbers. When it stands in the nominative it has, of course, the simple form, e.g. the steamer which left to-day** ilwâbûr' illi sâfar ilyaum' *elwâbûr' elli sâfir ennahar'da*; **when it stands in the genitive the governing noun receives the corresponding possessive suffix, e.g. the woman whose child I saw** ilma'ra illi shuft walad'ha *elmar'-a elli shuftè waled'ha*; **when it stands in the accusative the governing verb receives the corresponding possessive suffix, e.g. the man whom I saw** irrijjâl illi shufto *errâgil elli shufto*; **the people whom thou hast struck** innâs illi ḍarabt'hon *ennâs elli ḍarabt'ûhum*; **when it stands in the dative, i.e. with the preposition** la *li*, **or when it is governed by another preposition, the dative or the other preposition receives the corresponding possessive suffix, e.g. the merchant to whom I wrote** ittâjir illi katabti'lo *ettâgir elli katabti'lo* **(the** l **in** katabti'lo **is the dative preposition); the house in which thou livest** ilbait' illi btiḳʿud fîh *elbêt elli betiḳ'ʿud fîh* (fîh **= in it).**

## THE INTERROGATIVE PRONOUN AND ADJECTIVE

**Who** mîn, **to whom** lamîn *limîn*, **whom** mîn; **but it should be noted that the verb governing the accusative receives the corresponding possessive suffix, e.g. whom didst thou see?** mîn shufto? **What (nom. and acc.)** shû **or** aish *ê* **(always placed after) or** *êsh*, **e.g.** shû bitḳûl? *bitḳûl ê?* **what sayest thou? What, which, what kind of (sing. and plur.)** aina *aiy* **or** *en'hû*, **fem.** *en'hî*, **pl.** *enhum*, **e.g.** min aina shikl bitrîd? *min aiyi* **or** *en'hû shikl ʿâis?* **of what sort wishest thou? what kind dost thou want?**

### INDEFINITE PRONOUNS

**somebody, anybody** hada *ḥad* **or** *ḥadd*
**nobody** mâḥa'da *mâ ḥadish* **or** *mâ ḥaddish*
**something** shî *shê* **or** *ḥâge*
**nothing** mâshi *mush ḥâge*
**a few, some** kam *kâm*
**everybody** kullwâḥid *kulli wâḥid*
**one** ilwâḥid *elwâhid*, ilinsân *elinsân* ; **or expressed by the third pers. plur. of the verb, e.g.** bîḳû'lu *biḳûlu* **one says (they say).**

## NUMERALS

### CARDINAL NUMBERS

**1** wâhid, **fem.** wâḥdi *waḥde*
**2** tnain *etnên* **(fem., Syr. only :** tintain′)
**3** tlâti *telâte* **or** *talat*
**4** arbʻa *arbaʻ* **or** *arba′ʻe*
**5** khamsi *khamse*
**6** sitti *sitte*
**7** sabʻa
**8** tmânyi **or** tmâni *temen* **or** *teman′ye*
**9** tisʻa
**10** ʻashra *ʻeshara*
**11** ḥdaʻsh *ḥadâsher*
**12** ṭnaʻsh *etnâsher*
**13** tlaṭṭaʻsh′ *telatâsher*
**14** arbaṭaʻsh′ *arbaʻtâsher*
**15** khamsṭaʻsh′ *khamastâsher*
**16** siṭṭaʻsh′ *sittâsher*
**17** sabaṭaʻsh′ *sabaʻtâsher*
**18** tminṭaʻsh′ *temantâsher*
**19** tisaṭaʻsh′ *tisʻatâsher*
**20** ʻishrîn *ʻeshrîn*
**21** wâḥduʻishrîn′ *wâḥidweʻeshrîn′*
**22** tnainuʻishrîn *etnênweʻeshrîn′*
**23** tlâtiuʻishrîn′ *telâteweʻeshrîn′*
**24** arbʻa=uʻishrîn *arbaʻaweʻeshrîn*
**30** tlâtîn′ *telâtîn′*
**40** arbʻîn *arbaʻîn*
**50** khamsîn
**60** sittîn
**70** sabʻîn
**80** tmânîn′ *temânîn′*
**90** tisʻîn
**100** mîyi *mîye* **or** mâyi *mâye*
**101** mîyiuwâ'ḥid *mîyewewâ'ḥid*
**102** mîyiwitnain′ *mîyewetnên′*
**103** mîyiwitlâ'ti *mîyewetelâ'te*
**104** mîyiuar'bʻa *mîyewear′baʻa*

| | | |
|---|---|---|
| 200 | mîtain′ | *mîtên′* |
| 300 | tlātmî′yi | *tultemîye* |
| 400 | arb‘amîyi | *rub‘emîye* |
| 500 | khamsmîyi | *khumsemîye* |
| 600 | sittmîyi | *suttemîye* |
| 700 | sab‘mîyi | *sub‘emîye* |
| 800 | tmänmîyi | *tumnemîye* |
| 900 | tis‘mîyi | *tus‘emîye* |
| 1000 | alf | |
| 2000 | alfain′ | *alfên* |
| 3000 | tlättālāf | *telât âlâf* |
| 4000 | arba‘tālāf | *arba‘t âlâf′* |
| 5000 | khamstālāf | *khamast âlâf* |
| 6000 | sittālāf | *sitt âlâf* |
| 7000 | sab‘tālāf′ | *saba‘t âlâf′* |
| 8000 | tmäntālāf′ | *temant′ âlâf′* |
| 9000 | tis‘tālāf′ | *tis‘at âlâf′* |
| 10000 | ‘ashrtālāf′ | *‘esharet âlâf′* |
| 11000 | ḥda‘sharalf | *ḥadâsher alf* |
| 12000 | tna‘sharalf | *etnâsher alf* |
| 100000 | mîtalf or karra | |
| 200000 | mîtainalf or karrtain′ | *mîtên′ alf* |
| 1000000 | malyûn | *milyûn* |
| 2000000 | malyûnain′ | *milyûnên′* |
| 3000000 | tlāt mlâyîn′ | *telât milyûn* |

**wâḥid is always placed after the substantive, e.g.** rijjāl wâḥid *râgil wâḥid* **one man;** ilwâḥid *elwâḥid* **'the one' is used in the sense of 'one, you, they' (see p. 18 top).**

**Instead of** tnain *etnên* **with the substantive the latter is generally used in the dual form, e.g.** sā‘atain′ *sâ‘atên′* **two hours. But one says** issā‘a tintain′ *essâ‘a etnên* **at two o'clock.**

**After the numbers from three to ten the substantive follows in the plural; but then the former drop their endings, except when the noun begins with a vowel, in which case the ending is changed into** t**; thus:** tlāt rjāl *talat rigâle* **three men, but** khamst infus *khamast infus* **five persons. After the other numbers the substantive follows in the singular, but the Syrian forms of the numbers 11 to 19 have** ar **added, e.g.** ṭna‘shar marra *etnâsher marra* **twelve times. In compound numbers the larger ones always stand first, only the units precede the tens, e.g. 879** tmänmîyi utis‘a usab‘în *tumnemîye tis‘a wesab‘în.* **If a date is to be expressed** sint *senet* **'year' is placed before the number, e.g. 1908** sint alf utis‘mîyi utmānyi *senet alf wetus‘emîye weteman′ye.*—**For the numerical value of the letters see the Alphabet (pp. 1 to 5); see also: 'epitaph' in the Vocabulary.**

### THE ORDINAL NUMBERS

**first** auwal or aulâni *auwalâni*, **fem.** ûla *auwale* or aulânî'ye *auwalânî'ye*
**second** tâni *tâni*, **fem.** tânyi *tanye*
**third** tâlit *tâlit*, **fem.** tâlti *talte*
**fourth** râbiʿ, **fem.** râbʿa *rabʿe*
**fifth** khâmis, **fem.** khâmsi *khamse*
**sixth** sâdis *sâdis*, **fem.** sâdsi *sadse*
**seventh** sâbiʿ *sâbiʿ*, **fem.** sâbʿa *sabʿe*
**eighth** tâmin *tâmin*, **fem.** tâmni *tamne*
**ninth** tâsiʿ *tâsiʿ*, **fem.** tâsʿa *tasʿe*
**tenth** ʿâshir, **fem.** ʿâshra *ʿashre*

**From eleven upwards the ordinals have no distinguishing forms; in their stead the cardinals are used with the article.**

### ADVERBIAL NUMBERS

**Once** marra, **or, if the oneness is emphasized,** marra wâḥdi *marra waḥde* **one single time.**

**Twice** marrtain' *marratên.* **From thrice upwards the adverbial numbers are formed regularly with** marra **and the preceding cardinal, thus: four times** arbʿa marrât *arbaʿa marrât*, **twelve times** ṭnaʿshar marra *etnâsher marra*, **etc.**

### DISTRIBUTIVE NUMBERS AND FRACTIONS

**The former are simply indicated by the repetition of the cardinal number, thus: one at a time, one each** wâḥid wâḥid, **two at a time, in pairs** tnain tnain *etnên etnên*, **etc.**

**There are special forms for the fractions from** $\frac{1}{2}$ **to** $\frac{1}{10}$**:**

| | | |
|---|---|---|
| $\frac{1}{2}$ nuṣṣ | $\frac{1}{5}$ khums | $\frac{1}{8}$ tumn |
| $\frac{1}{3}$ tult | $\frac{1}{6}$ suds | $\frac{1}{9}$ tusʿ |
| $\frac{1}{4}$ rubʿ | $\frac{1}{7}$ subʿ | $\frac{1}{10}$ ʿushr *ʿoshr* |

**These words, which are substantives, form the dual regularly, and the plural by the elision of the vowel and insertion of an** â *â* **between the second and third con-**

**sonants (together with the prefixing of an *i* or *a* in the Egyptian dialect), thus:** rubʿain′ majîdi *rubʿên megîdi* **two-fourths megeeds,** tlât rbâʿ *telat irbâʿ* **three-fourths, etc.**

**From $\frac{1}{11}$ upwards the fractions are expressed by** wâḥid min **with the following cardinal, thus: $\frac{1}{11}$** wâḥid min ḥdaʿsh *wâḥid min ḥadâsher*, **etc.**

## THE VERB

**The root of the Arabic verb, under which it appears in all dictionaries, and therefore also in the vocabulary at the end of this book, is the third person singular masculine of the preterite tense.**

**The verb is called strong, if its root has three different, or more than three, consonants, provided that in the former case the first consonant is not a** w; **it is weak, if the root has three consonants, the first of which is a** w, **or if it has less than three different consonants.**

**New verbs are deduced from the simple verb by inner formation, especially by the addition of one or more letters; these derivatives imply a modification of the meaning of the primitive verb.**

**The primitive verb as well as the verbs derived from it have special simple forms for the following tenses and moods: (1) preterite, (2) imperative, (3) participle. Besides these, the Arabic possesses another special simple tense form called the aorist. On the use of the latter for expressing other tenses see next page.**

**The written language possesses an active and a passive voice for each of these tenses and moods; but in the vulgar tongue this old passive voice is only uniformly found in the participle; in the preterite it occurs with a few strong verbs only, e.g.** *ḳitil* **he has been killed,** *ṛilib* **he has been conquered. Otherwise, for the expression of the passive voice, the vulgar language uses one of the derivative forms, preferably forms VII and VIII (p. 30).**

**There is no special form for the subjunctive.**

**The infinitive is generally expressed by the aorist.**

**Arabic has no infinitive in our sense, its infinitive being rather a pure substantive.**

**The tenses for which Arabic has no special simple forms are rendered in the following way:**

**(1) The present generally by the participle, e.g. I am going** ana râyiḥ *ana râ-iḥ* **; or by the aorist with preceding** ʻammâl *ʻammâl* **or** ʻam, **e.g.** ʻammâl yiktub *ʻammâl yiktib* **or** ʻam byiktub *ʻam beyik'tib* **he is writing;**

**(2) the imperfect (indicative and subjunctive) by the present or the aorist with preceding** kân *kân*, **e.g.** kân râyiḥ *kân râ-iḥ* **he was going, he went, he were going, or** kân (ʻammâl) yiktub *kân (ammâl) yiktib*, **or** kân (ʻam) byiktub *kân (ʻam) beyik'tib* **he was writing, he wrote, (if) he were writing;**

**(3) The pluperfect (indicative and subjunctive) by the preterite with preceding** kân *kân*, **e.g.** kân katab *kân katab* **he had (or would have) written;**

**(4) the future, when expressing the idea that a person intends, or is about, to do something, by the aorist with preceding** râyiḥ *râ-iḥ* **or** raḥ *râḥ* **or** *ḥa*, **e.g.** râyiḥ iktub *râ-iḥ aktib* **or** raḥ iktub *ḥa aktib* **I am going to write, I will (shall) write. To express a real future time the simple aorist is used, or the aorist (without** b**) with preceding** badd *bidd* **with the possessive suffixes, e.g.** baddo yiktub *biddo yiktib* **he will or shall write.**

## THE PRIMITIVE VERB

### The Strong Verb

**The root, i.e. the third pers. sing. of the preterite, of the triliteral strong verb has either an a or an** i **between the first and second, and second and third consonants, e.g.** katab **he wrote, he has written,** shirib **he drank. For brevity's sake we will now call the verb with two a's simply** katab, **that with two i's** shirib.

**The root of the quadriliteral verb (the colloquial has no verbal roots with more than four consonants) always has an** a **as first vowel between the first and second consonants, and another** a **as second vowel between the third and fourth consonants. For brevity's sake we will now call the quadriliteral verb after its paradigm** zakhraf.

### *The Preterite*

**There are special forms for the masculine and feminine of the second and third pers. sing. only. The endings for the different persons are :**

| | Sing. | Plur. |
|---|---|---|
| **1. pers.** | —t | —na |
| **2. pers. m.** | —t | —tu |
| **2. pers. f.** | —ti | |
| **3. pers. m.** | — | —u **or** —*um* |
| **3. pers. f.** | —it *et* | |

katab **undergoes no change when these endings are affixed, thus :** katabt' **I wrote,** katabt' **thou m. didst write,** katab'ti **thou f. didst w...,** katab **he wrote,** katabit *katabet* **she wrote,** katab'na **we wrote, etc. ;** shirib **loses in Syrian its first** i **before consonantal endings, in Syrian and Egyptian its second** i **before vocal endings or before one of the personal suffixes** ak, ik, o, **thus :** shribt *shiribt'*, shribti *shirib'ti*, shribna *shirib'na*, shribtu *shirib'tu*, **but** shirbit *shirbet*, shirbu, shirbo.

### *The Aorist*

**In the aorist of the triliteral verb the first vowel of the root is elided ; the second is of** katab u **or** i **(but see rule at foot of page), of** shirib a, **except** ʿirif **to know and** ʿimil **to do, which have** i ; ḳidir **to be able has** i **in Syrian and** *a* **in Egyptian. Verbs whose second or third consonant is a guttural, i.e. a** h, ḥ, kh, ʿ, **or** ṛ, **generally have an** a.

**The aorist forms its different persons with the following prefixes and endings :**

| | Sing. | Plur. |
|---|---|---|
| **1. pers.** | i *a* **or** bi *ba*— | ni **or** mni *beni, meni*— |
| **2. pers. m.** | ti **or** bti *beti*— | ti **or** bti *beti*—u |
| **2. pers. f.** | ti **or** bti *beti*—i | |
| **3. pers. m.** | yi **or** byi *beyi* **or** *bi*— | yi **or** byi *beyi, bi*—u |
| **3. pers. f.** | ti **or** bti *beti*— | |

**Before the endings** i **or** u **as well as before the personal suffixes** ak, ik, o, **(whose initial sounds are vowels)** katab **drops in the Syrian also the second vowel.**

**Examples:** biktub *baktib*, **I write, may, will or shall write,** btiktub *betik'tib* **thou m. writest,** btiktbi *betikti'bi* **thou f. writest,** byiktub *beyik'tib* **or** *biktib* **he writes,** btiktub *betik'tib* **she writes,** mniktub *menik'tib* **we write,** btiktbu *betikti'bu* **you (ye) write,** byiktbu *beyikti'bu* **or** *bikti'bu* **they write.**

**The form without prefixed** b: iktub *aktib*, tiktub *tiktib*, **etc., is usually employed when another verbal form precedes the aorist.**

**Note.—In the Syrian and frequently in the Egyptian Arabic, the verbs** ʻirif **to know and** ʻimil **to do have the vowel a instead of** i **in the prefixes of the aorist, thus:** byaʻrif *beyaʻʻraf* **he knows,** byaʻmil *beyaʻʻmil* **he does.**

*The Imperative*

**As to the vowels of** katab **and** shirib **the rules for the imperative are the same as those for the aorist. The following are the prefixes and endings:**

| | Sing. | Plur. |
|---|---|---|
| **2. pers. m.** | i or u— | i or u—u |
| **2. pers. f.** | i or u—i | |

**e.g.** imsik **seize,** uskut **be silent,** ishrab **drink.**

**In Syrian this prefixed vowel is sometimes omitted altogether, but then the** i, u, **or** a **is lengthened, e.g.** msîk = imsik, shrâb = ishrab.

*The Present Participle*

**It has** ā *â* **between the first and second consonants, and an** i **between the second and third, e.g.** kātib *kâtib* **writing,** shārib *shârib* **drinking. On the formation of the feminine and of the plural see the adjective pp. 11, 12; in both cases, however, the** i **is dropped, and in the Egyptian Arabic the** *â* **is generally shortened into** *a*, **e.g.** kātbi *katbe*, kātbîn' *katbîn* **from** kātib *kâtib*.

*The Past Participle*

**It is formed by prefixing** ma; **the first vowel is dropped, the second is** û, **e.g.** maktûb **written,** mashrûb **drunk.**

**The Weak Verb**

**A verb is called weak if the root, i.e. the 3rd person singular of the preterite, has three consonants, the first of**

which is a w, or if it has less than three different consonants. There are five classes of the weak verb—distinguished by the differences of the verbal root:

(a) the first consonant is a w, e.g. waʿad to promise;

(b) the sceond and third consonants are the same and, after elision of the second vowel, form a double consonant, e.g. madd to stretch;

(c) the first or second consonant is missing, e.g. akal or *kal* to eat, sa⸗al to ask;

(d) the third consonant is missing, e.g. rama to throw, riḍi to be content;

(e) an â (or, Syr. only: ā̂) stands between two consonants, e.g. ḳâl to say, râd to wish, bâʿ to sell, nā̂m *nâm* to sleep.

The flexion of class (c) of these weak verbs is little different to that of the strong verb. The aorist of such as akal has the prefixes bā̂ *bâ*, btā̂ *betâ*, byā̂ *beyâ*, mnā̂ *benâ* or *menâ*, e.g. bā̂kul *bâkul* I eat. Such as sa⸗al have an a as second vowel in the aorist, e.g. bis⸗al *bas⸗al* I ask. The imperative has the same vowels as the aorist.

Note.—akal or *kal* to eat, and akhad or *khad* to take, form the imperative irregularly, viz.:

| | Sing. | Plur. |
|---|---|---|
| 2. pers. m. | kôl *kul*, khôd *khod* | kulu, khudu |
| 2. pers. f. | kuli, khudi | |

The other four classes show more irregularities.

### (a) *The Verbs with* w

The preterite and the two participles are regular; in the aorist the second vowel follows the general rule; the w is blended with the prefixes as follows:

| | Sing. | Plur. |
|---|---|---|
| 1. pers. | û *au* or bû *bau*— | nû or mnû *menû* or *be-nû*— |
| 2. pers. m. | tû or btû *betû*— | tû or btû *betû*—u |
| 2. pers. f. | tû or btû *betû*—i | |
| 3. pers. m. | yû or byû *beyû*— | yû or byû *beyû*—u |
| 3. pers. f. | tû or btû *betû*— | |

e.g. bûʿid I promise, btûʿid *betûʿid* thou promisest, etc.

The imperative has the same vowels as the aorist, and the w is changed into û, e.g. ûʿid promise, ûḳaf stand.

### (b) *The Surd or doubled Verbs*

**In the preterite these have the following endings:**

| | Sing. | Plur. |
|---|---|---|
| **1. pers.** | —ait *ét* | —aina *êna* |
| **2. pers. m.** | —ait *ét* | —aitu *étu* |
| **2. pers. f.** | —aiti *éti* | |
| **3. pers. m.** | — | —u |
| **3. pers. f.** | —it *et* | |

**e.g.** maddait' *maddêt* **I have stretched,** maddait' *maddêt* **thou m. hast stretched,** maddai'ti *maddêti* **thou f. hast stretched,** madd **he has stretched,** maddit *maddet* **she has stretched,** maddai'na *maddêna* **we have stretched, etc.**

**In the aorist they have** u **or** i, **seldom** a. **The prefixes are:**

| | Sing. | Plur. |
|---|---|---|
| **1. pers.** | ..*a* **or** b *ba*— | n *ne* **or** m n **or** *bin*— |
| **2. pers. m.** | t *te* **or** bit— | t *te* **or** bit—u |
| **2. pers. f.** | t *te* **or** bit—i | |
| **3. pers. m.** | y *ye* **or** bî *bi*— | y *ye* **or** bî *bi*—u |
| **3. pers. f.** | t *te* **or** bit— | |

**e.g.** bmidd *bamidd'* **I stretch,** bitmidd' **thou stretchest, etc.**

**The imperative has the same vowels as the aorist and no prefixes, e.g.** midd **stretch.**

**The two participles are regular, e.g.** mâdid *mâdid* **stretching,** mamdûd **stretched.**

### (c) *See above* (*p.* 25).

### (d) *Verbs with no Radical after the Second Vowel*

**Example for such verbs with two a's:** rama **to throw; example for such verbs with two i's:** riḍi **to be content.**

**In the preterite these verbs receive the following endings after elision of the a and i respectively:**

| | Sing. | Plur. |
|---|---|---|
| **1. pers.** | —ait *ét*, —ît | —aina *êna*, —îna |
| **2. pers. m.** | —ait *ét*, —ît | —aitu *étu*, —îtu |
| **2. pers. f.** | —aiti *éti*, —îti | |
| **3. pers. m.** | — | —u, —u |
| **3. pers. f.** | —it *et*, —it *yet* | |

**Note that in all cases where in Syrian the first vowel of the strong verb** shirib **is dropped, it is also dropped here.**

**Examples :** ramait' *ramêt* **I threw (have thrown),** ramait' *ramêt* **thou m. hast thrown,** ramai'ti *ramêti* **thou f. hast thrown,** rama **he has thrown,** ramit *ramet* **she has thrown,** ramai'na *ramêna* **we have thrown,** ramai'tu *ramêtu* **you have thrown,** ramu **they have thrown, ;** rḍît *riḍît* **I was (have been) content, etc.**

**In the aorist the prefixes are as usual ; the first vowel is always dropped. The verbs with two a's have** i **as last vowel, those with two i's have** a **; but in the second and third persons plural this last vowel is always** u**, e.g.** birmi *barmi* **I throw,** btirmi *betir'mi* **thou throwest,** btirmu *betir'mu* **you throw,** byirmu *beyir'mu* **they throw;** birḍa *barḍa* **I am satisfied,** mnirḍa *benir'ḍa* **we are satisfied,** btirḍu *betir'ḍu* **you are satisfied, etc.**

**In the imperative the prefix is always** i**, the vowels being as in the aorist, e.g.** irmi **(or, Syr. only :** rmî**) throw, etc.**

**In the present participle the first vowel is** â **(or, Syr. only : ā), the second is always** i**, e.g.** râmi **throwing,** râḍi **being content, agreeing.**

**In the past participle** mi *ma* **is prefixed, the first vowel is elided, the second is always** i**, e.g.** mirmi *marmi* **thrown.**

**The irregular verb** ija *gi* **or** *gâ* **'to come' conjugates its preterite as follows :**

**Sing.**

**1. pers.** jît *gît* **I came or have come**
**2. pers. m.** jît *gît* **thou camest or hast come**
**2. pers. f.** jîti *gîti* **thou camest or hast come**
**3. pers. m.** ija *gi* **or** *gâ* **he came or has come**
**3. pers. f.** ijit *gat* **she came or has come**

**Plur.**

**1. pers.** jîna *gîna* **we came or have come**
**2. pers.** jîtu *gîtu* **you came or have come**
**3. pers.** iju *gum* **or** *gâ=u* **they came or have come**

**The aorist is** biji *bagi* **I come, and is conjugated analogously with** birmi *barmi* **I throw (see above).**

**The imperative is borrowed from quite another verb, and is:**

| Sing. | Plur. |
|---|---|
| **2. pers. m.** ta'âl **or** ta'a *ta'âla*<br>**2. pers. f.** ta'âli **(or, Syr. only:** ta'i) | ta'âlu **(or, Syr. only:** ta'u) |

**The participle is** jâyi *gâ=i* **coming.**

(e) *Verbs having a long* â *or* â *between two radicals*

**In the preterite the long** â **(or, Syr. only:** â**) is changed into** u **or** i **before endings commencing with a consonant, e.g.** ḳult **I (have) said,** ḳult **thou m. saidst,** ḳulti **thou f. saidst,** ḳâl **he said,** ḳâlit *ḳâlet* **she said,** ḳulna **we said,** ḳultu **you said,** ḳâlu **they said; likewise** ridt **I wished,** bi't **I sold, etc.**

**In the aorist, those having** u **in the preterite take** û**, those having** i **in the preterite take** î**; a very few only retain** â **(or, Syr. only:** â**). The prefixes are the same as those for the doubled verbs, e.g.** bḳûl *baḳûl* **I say,** bitḳûl **thou sayest,** bîrîd' *birîd* **he wishes,** bînâ'mu *binâmu* **they sleep.**

**The imperative has the same vowels as the aorist, and no prefixes, e.g.** ḳûl **say,** rîd **wish (command),** nâm *nâm* **sleep.**

**Present participle:** ḳâyil *ḳâ=il* **saying,** râyid *râ=id* **wishing,** nâyim *nâ=im* **sleeping.**

**Past participle not in usage; in its stead the participle of one of the derived forms is used.**

THE DERIVATIVE VERBS

**As already mentioned, from each primitive verb new verbs can be deduced implying a modification of the meaning of the primitive form. The primitive verb is marked I, and the derived verbs generally being reckoned nine in number, the latter are marked II to X. Some roots are to be met with in one form only, most are in several, none in all forms; form IX is used of colors only, as** iḥmarr'**, aorist** yiḥmarr' **to become red.**

**In the following description of the other forms the general character only of their formation and meaning can**

be stated. The formation of the tenses and moods has been illustrated by examples after the paradigm katab. We had to desist from the delineation of the rules for the formation of the weak verbs; but have, however, given the form of the preterite of each class after the above paradigms, so that the formation of the other tenses and moods may easily be seen by comparison with the strong verb.

II. Doubling of the second radical. Meaning: strengthening or repetition, sometimes causation (i.e. change from the intransitive into the transitive) of the primitive form, e.g. kassar to break (trans.) in small pieces, from kasar to break (intrans.); dakhkhal to cause some one to enter, introduce, from dakhal to enter.

| | preter. | aor. | imp. | pr. part. | past p. |
|---|---|---|---|---|---|
| strong v. | kattab | ykattib *yikat'tib* | kattib | mkattib *mekat'tib* | mkattab *mekat'tab* |
| | *a* | *b* | *c* | *d* | *e* |
| pret. of weak v. | wa‘‘ad | maddad | akkal | ramma raḍḍa | ḳauwal baiya‘ |

III. First vowel â, second vowel a *i*. Meaning: reciprocal action among two or more, e.g. ḳâtal *ḳâtil* to fight with some one, from ḳatal to kill.

| | preter. | aor. | imp. | pr. part. | past p. |
|---|---|---|---|---|---|
| strong v. | kâtab *kâtib* | ykâtib *yikâtib* | kâtib *kâtib* | mkâtib *mekâtib* | mkâtab *mekâtab* |
| | *a* | *b* | *c* | *d* | *e* |
| pret. of weak v. | wâ‘ad | mâdad | âkal sâ:al | râma râḍa | ḳâwal bâya‘ |

IV. Prefix a; the first vowel is dropped, the second is a. Meaning: change from the intransitive into the transitive, thus giving a causal signification, e.g. as‘ad to make happy, from si‘id to be happy.

| | preter. | aor. | imp. | pr. part. | past p. |
|---|---|---|---|---|---|
| strong v. | aktab | yiktib | iktib | miktib *muktib* | miktab *muktab* |

Of the weak verb no such form exists, and even of the strong verb it is seldom found.

V. Prefix: ta or t *it* before II. Meaning: partly passive, partly reflexive signification of II, e.g. tkassar *itkas'sar*

**to be broken into small pieces,** t'al'laḳ *it'al'laḳ* **to attach oneself, adhere to.**

**VI. Prefix:** ta or t *it* **before III. Meaning: reciprocal signification, or mutual striving to carry out III, e.g.** tḳâtal *itḳâtil* **to fight with each other, or to seek to kill.**

**VII. Prefix:** in; **both vowels are always a. Meaning: passive, reflexive, or permissive signification of the primitive verb, e.g.** inka'sar **to break (intrans.),** inṭa'raḥ **to throw oneself,** insâḳ **to let oneself be conducted.**

| | preter. | aor. | imp. | pr. part. | past p. |
|---|---|---|---|---|---|
| **strong v.** | inka'tab | yinktib<br>*yinki'tib* | inktib<br>*inki'tib* | minktib<br>*menka'tib* | — |
| | *a* | *b* | *c* | *d* | *e* |
| **pret. of weak v.** | inwa''ad | inmadd' | ina'kal<br>insa'-al | inra'ma | inḳâl<br>inbâ' |

**VIII. Prefix:** i, **and insertion of a** t **after the first radical (in Egypt it is sometimes prefixed); both vowels are a. Meaning: passive or reflexive signification of the primitive verb.**

| | preter. | aor. | imp. | pr. part. | past p. |
|---|---|---|---|---|---|
| **strong v.** | ikta'tab<br>or<br>*itka'tab* | yikttib<br>*yikti'tib*<br>*yitki'tib* | ikttib<br>*ikti'tib*<br>*itki'tib* | mikttib<br>*mekta'tib* | — |
| | *a* | *b* | *c* | *d* | *e* |
| **pret. of weak v.** | itta''ad | imtadd'<br>or<br>itmadd' | ittâkal | irta'ma<br>irta'ḍa or<br>*itra'ma* | iḳtâl<br>ibtâ'<br>or *'itbâ* |

**IX. See p. 28, bottom.**

**X. Prefix:** ista; **the first vowel is dropped, the second is a, in Egypt frequently** *i*. **Meaning: to wish for something for oneself, to ask for or demand something, to take some one or something for something, e.g.** ista-'zan *ista-'zin* **to ask permission,** istaḥ'san *istaḥ'sin* **to take to be beautiful, to take as good, to approve, allow of.**

| | preter. | aor. | imp. | pr. part. | past p. |
|---|---|---|---|---|---|
| **strong v.** | istak'tab | yistak'tib | istak'tib | mistak'tib<br>*mustak'tib* | mistak'tab<br>*mustak'tab* |
| | *a* | *b* | *c* | *d* | *e* |
| **pret. of weak v.** | istau''ad | istamadd' | ista-'kal<br>istas'-al | istar'ma<br>istar'ḍa | istaḳâl<br>istabâ' |

### THE QUADRILITERAL VERB

The preterite is conjugated like katab, thus: zakhraft' I have adorned, zakhraft' thou m. hast adorned, zakhrafti thou f. hast adorned.

The aorist takes the same prefixes and endings as class (b) resp. (e) of the weak verb; its first vowel remains a, its second becomes i or *a*, thus: bzakhrif *bazakh'raf* I adorn, etc.

The imperative has the same vowels as the aorist, thus: zakhrif *zakhraf* adorn.

The participle is formed with the prefix m or mu *me*; the second vowel is in the present participle i *a*, in the past participle a, thus: mzakhrif *mezakh'raf* adorning, mzakhraf *mezakh'raf* adorned.

## THE PARTICLES

As most of these find their place in the dictionary, a few general remarks will suffice here.

The adverbs usually do not differ in form from the adjectives, e.g. ṭaiyib 'good' and 'well,' ktîr *ketîr* 'much' and 'very.' Some are formed from substantives or adjectives by adding an or *en*, e.g. abadan *ebeden* never, dâyman *dâ-iman* always. Others have very peculiar forms, e.g. haun *hene* here.

The use of prepositions is only learned by practice; for their conjunction with the personal pronoun see p. 14.

# PHRASES

**Note.—In the English portion of the following phrases the usual forms of address 'you' and 'your' have been adhered to for obvious reasons, but these have of course been rendered by the second person singular in the Arabic (except where the plural is required, in which case it is indicated by (plur.), as on p. 74), and the traveller must carefully remember to use the 'thou' and the 'thy' in Arabic. There are numerous periphrases for the second person singular, the most common being:** ḥadrtak *ḥaḍretak* **(literally, thy presence),** janâbak *genâbak* **and** siyâdtak *siyâdetak* **(lit., thy excellency, mostly used towards persons of authority, especially the clergy). The tourist, however, seldom needs the same; even the native rarely makes use of them towards the traveller; the simple 'thou' and 'thy' suffices; if, however, one wishes to be particularly polite, one may make use of the plural, as in English.**

**All the phrases are given in both dialects, although some are less applicable in Egypt.**

## GENERAL PART

### GREETINGS AND INQUIRY AFTER THE HEALTH, ETC.

| | **Syrian.** | **Egyptian.** |
|---|---|---|
| **Good morning** | ṣabâh ilkhair' or ṣabbḥak bilkhair'[1] | *ṣbâḥ elkhêr* or *yiṣab'baḥak bilkhêr*[1] |
| ″ **Answer:** | yis'id ṣabâḥak | *yis'id ṣabâḥak* |

**1 Abbreviation of** Alla yṣabbḥak bilkhair' *Allâh yiṣab'baḥak bilkhêr*, **lit., God give thee a happy morning! This full form is used in order to give more solemnity to the greeting and to show more complaisance.**

| | | |
|---|---|---|
| **Good day** | nhârak sa'îd or aukâtak sa'îdi | *nehârak sâ'id* or *aukâtak sâ'ide* |
| **" Answer:** | nhârak mbârak or yis'id aukâtak | *nehârak mubârak* or *nehârak sâ'id mubârak* |
| **Good evening** | masalkhair' or massîk bilkhair'[1] or lailtak sa'îdi[2] | *misalkhêr* or *massîk bilkhêr*[1] or *lêltak sâ'ide*[2] |
| **" Answer:** | yis'id masâk or lailtak mbâraki[2] | *lêltak sâ'ide wumbârke*[2] |
| **Good night** | lailtak sa'îdi | *lêltak sâ'ide* |
| **" Answer:** | lailtak mbâraki | *lêltak mubârake* |
| 4 **Greeting! Hail!** | mar'habâ! or il-'awâfi! | *mar'habâ!* or *el-'awâf!* |
| **" Answer:** | mar'habâ! or Alla y'âfîk'! | *mar'habâ!* or *Allâh ye'âfîk'!* |
| **How are you?.** | kîf hâlak? or kîf khâtrak? or kîf sahhtak? or kîf şâyir fîk? | *kêf hâlak?* or *ezaiyi khâţrak?* or *ezaiyi şiḥhetak?* or *ezai'yak?* |
| **Quite well, I hope?** | inshal'la mashrûh? or inshal' la mabsûţ? | *inshallâh tekûn mashrûḥ?* or *mabsûţ?* |
| 7 **Answer: Quite well (lit., thank God, well)** | ilham'dilla bkhair or ilham'dilla mashrûh or ilham'dilla mabsûţ | *elḥam'do lillâh bikhêr* or *elḥam'do lillâh mashrûḥ* (or *mabsûţ*) |
| **or:** | | |
| **We thank God, or, Under your looks well** | nishkur Alla b=anzârak(bnazarak) fî khair | *nishkur Allâh bi=anzârak (bina'zarak) fî khêr* |
| **And you, how are [you?** | w=int kîf hâlak? | *winte kêf hâlak?* |
| 10 **I do not feel well** | mâli kêf or mâni mabsûţ | *mâlish kêf* or *mânish mabsûţ* |

[1] **Abbreviation of** Alla ymassîk bilkhair' *Allâh yimassîk bilkhêr* **lit., God give thee a happy evening! For the use of this form** **see p. 32 note.**

[2] **The latter expression (lit., 'good night' q.v.) can be used in Syrian Arabic at an advanced hour only, say from three o'clock after sunset.**

| | | |
|---|---|---|
| **I am sorry** | tkaddart' ktîr or ṣi'ʿib ʿalai'yi | *itkaddart'ê ketîr* or *ṣuʿb ʿalêye* |
| **What has befallen you, or : what is the matter ?** | shû ṣâyir'lak ?, shû jârî'lak ?, shû ḥâṣil'lak ?, shû bâk ?, shû mâlak ? | *garâlak ê?, ḥaṣallak ê?, mâlak?* |
| **I caught a cold (lit., je suis enrhumé)** | murash'shaḥ | *ana mazkûm* |
| 4 **I have a cold** | ṣâyir'li rashḥ or ṣâyir'li nazli | *ḥaṣal'-li zukâm* or *ḥaṣal'-li nazle* |
| **I have a headache** | râsi byûja'ʿni | *râsi btûgaʿni* or *râsi wagaʿetni* |
| **I have had a fever** | ṣarli ḥimmi or inḥammait' | *ʿaiyân bilḥimme* or *itḥammêt* |
| 7 **I was unwell** | kint ḍ'ʿif | *kuntê ḍaʿif* |
| **I had an attack of illness** | ṣarli skhûni | *kuntê sukhn* |
| **I did not sleep this night** | mâ nimt fi hal-lail' | *mâ nimtish el-lêlâ' di* |
| 10 **I did not close my eyes all night** | kull illail' mâ ṛa-maḍ'li jifn or illail' uṭûlo mâ ṛamaḍit ʿaini | *kull el'lêl mâ ṛam-maḍ'lish gifn* or *ellêl kullo mâ ṛamaḍet'shi ʿêni* |
| **Since when have you been ill ?** | min aimta maríḍ? or ḳaddaish' ilak ḍaʿîf? | *min imte ʿaiyân?* |
| **Since the day on which I returned from the journey** | min yaum illi rjiʿt mnissa'far | *min yôm' elli ri-giʿtê min essa'-far* |
| 13 **Since then (lit., since that time)?** | min haidâk' il-waḳt' ? | *min elwaḳ'tê dik-hâ ?* |
| **Do you take medicine ?** | ʿammâl tâkhud idwyi ? or ʿam btitḥak'kam ? or ʿam btitʿâlaj ? | *betâkhod adwiye ?* or *betiddâwi ?* or *betitʿâlig ?* |
| **I hope it is nothing** | inshal'la mâ hî shî | *inshallâh mâ yekun'she ḥâge* |
| 16 **It is temporary, I hope** | ʿaraḍîyi inshal'la | *shiddê wetzûl in-shallâh* |

| | | | |
|---|---|---|---|
| | **I hope we shall soon see you in good health (again)** | inshal'la ʼmin-shûfak ḳarîb bkhair | *inshallâh neshûfak ḳarîb bikhêr* |
| | **I hope you will soon get well** | inshal'la ḳarib bitṣiḥḥ' (or btit-ʿâfa) | *inshallâh ḳarîb teṭîb* |
| | **Many thanks, obliged** | kattir khairak mamnûn | *kattar khêrak memnûn* |
| 4 | **How is the lady (wife)?** | kîf ḥâl (or ṣaḥḥt) issitt'? | *kêf ḥâl (or ṣiḥ-ḥet) essitt'?* |
| | **How is your wife?** | kîf ḥâl bint ʿam-mak? | *kêf ḥâl bintê ʿammak?* |
| | **She inquires after your health** | btis-al khâṭrak | *betis'-al ʿalêk* |
| 7 | **She greets you** | bitsal'lim ʿalaik' | *bitsal'lim ʿalêk* |
| | **She is quite well** | ṣaḥḥit'ha ktîr mlîḥa | *ṣiḥḥet'ha taiyibe* |
| | **She enjoys perfect health** | bṣaḥḥt ilkâmli | *biṣṣi'ḥe elkâmile* |
| 10 | **Thank God** | ilḥam'dilla | *elḥam'do lillâh* |
| | **We thank God** | nishkur Alla | *nishkur Allâh* |
| | **Convey her my salutation, my respects** | ihdîha salâmi, wâjbâ'ti | *ihdîha selâmi* |
| 13 | **Inquire for me after her health** | is-al'li khâṭir'ha | *is-al ʿan khâṭir'ha* |
| | **Greet her from me** | sallim'li ʿalai'ha | *sallim'li ʿalêha* |
| | **Is (his presence or lordship) the father still ill?** | ḥadrt ilwâlid baʿ-do marîḍ? | *ḥadret elwâlid lissa ʿaiyân?* |
| 16 | **Is your father still unwell?** | abûk (or baiyak) baʿd mâlo kêf? or abûk baʿdo mshauwash? | *abûk lissa mâ-lôsh' kêf?* or *abûk baʿdo mi-shau'wish?* |
| | **He is better, thank God** | ṣâr aḥsan (or rav-waḳ) ilham'dilla | *ṣâr aḥsan elḥam'-do lillâh* |
| | **And (her ladyship) the mother, how is she?** | waḥadrt' ilwâldi kîf ḥâlha (or kîf ṣâyir fîha)? | *weḥad'ret elwâ-lide kêf ḥâlha?* |

| | | |
|---|---|---|
| **And how is your mother?** | w=ummak kîf ḥâlha? | *we=um'mak kêf ḥâlha?* |
| **She is well** | mashrûḥa or mabsûṭa | *ṭaiyibe* or *bikhêr* |
| **As usual** | ḥasab ʿâdit'ha or mitl ilʿâdi | *ʿala ḥâletha* |
| 4 **My mother cannot leave the house** | ummi mâ fîha tiṭlaʿ mnilbait' | *ummi mâ betiḳ'darshi tiṭlaʿ min elbêt* |
| **I had no knowledge that she was ill** | mâ kân ʿindi khabar inna marîḍa | *mâ kânshi ʿandi khabar inneha ʿaiyâne* |
| **Your brother always seems well** | akhûk (or khaiyak) bîbai'yin dâyman mabsûṭ | *akhûk bâʿin dâ=iman mabsûṭ* |
| 7 **Do me the favor of inquiring for me after his health** | iza kint bitrîd, is=al'li khâṭro | *in shi=t is=al'li ʿalêh* |
| **Convey him my salutation** | ballṛo salâmi | *ballaṛo selâmi* |
| **Greet him from me** | sallim'li ʿalaih' | *sallim'li ʿalêh* |
| 10 **I shall not fail, willingly, with pleasure** | wuṣil, ʿarrâs wilʿain', ʿala râsi | *yaṣil, ʿarrâs walʿên, ʿala râsi* |
| **God be with you (lit., God keep you)** | Alla ysallmak | *Allâh yisal'limak* |

VISIT

| | | |
|---|---|---|
| **Some one is knocking at the door** | ʿam bîduḳ'ḳu ilbâb | *elbâb beyikh'baṭ* |
| 13 **There is some one ringing** | ʿam byindaḳḳ' ijja'ras | *biduḳḳ egga'ras* |
| **Go, see who (it is)** | rûḥ shûf mîn | *rûḥ shûf mîn* |
| **Go, open the door** | rûḥ ftâḥ ilbâb | *rûḥ iftaḥ elbâb* |
| 16 **It is Mr. N. N.** | hâda ilkhawâja.. | *di elkhawâga..* |
| **Let him come in** | khallîh yfût or khal'li fût | *khallîh yekhushsh'* |
| **Ask him in** | iʿzi'mo | *dakhkha'lo* |

| | | |
|---|---|---|
| **Welcome, a hundred (Eg. a thousand) times welcome** | ahlan wasah'lan, mît ahlan wasah'lan | *ahlan wasah'lan alf ahlan wasah'lan* |
| **The blessing has entered (viz. by your coming)** | ḥallit ilba'raki | *ḥallet elba'rake* |
| **Answer: God bless you** | Alla ybârik fîk | *Allâh yebârik fîk* |
| 4 **I have not seen you for a long time** | min zamân mâ shuftak | *min zemân mâ shuftak'shi* |
| **You have distressed us, or, you left us in grief, in solitude (by a friend's absence)** | auḥasht'na | *auḥa h'tina* |
| **Answer: May God not leave you desolate** | Alla lâ yûḥshak or lâ auḥashak Allâh or Alla lâ yûḥish minnak or auḥash'na insak | *lâ auḥash Allâh minnak* or *Allâh lâ yûḥish minnak* |
| 7 **I have a great longing for you** | ana ktîr mushtâḳ laik | *ana mushtâḳ ilêk ketîr* |
| **Answer: And we still more** | wniḥna bil=ak'tar | *wiḥne bil=ak'tar* |
| **We always have the greatest (lit., we are always in the extreme of) longing to see you** | niḥna dâyman fî ṛâyit ishshauḳ' lashauf'tak | *iḥne dâ=iman fî ṛâyet eshshôḳ liru'=yetak* |
| 10 **We are obliged for your visit** | mamnûnîn' tishrîfak | *memnûnîn' min teshrîfak* |
| **Pray rest a little** | tfaḍḍal istrîḥ | *itfaḍ'ḍal isterai'yaḥ* |
| **Please sit down** | tfaḍḍal uḳ'ud | *itfaḍ'ḍal uḳ'ud* |
| 13 **Offer the gentleman a chair** | ḳaddim kursi lilkhawâja | *ḳaddim kursi lilkhawâga* |
| **Will you not take off your cloak?** | mâ tishlaḥsh' issâko mtâ'ak? | *mâ ti=la'sh' elbâlṭo betâ'ak?* |

| | | |
|---|---|---|
| **Please (take a seat) on the divan** | tfaḍḍal ʿaddîwân′ | *itfaḍ′ḍal ʿaddîwân* |
| **Will you not sit down a minute (or : a little)?** | mâ bitrîd tiḳʿud′lak daḳîḳa (or shwaiyi)? | *mush ʿâ-iz tuḳʿud daḳîḳe* (or *shuwai′ye*) *?* |
| **We seldom see you** | ḳalîl tanshûfak | *neshûfak ḳalîl* |
| 4 **Why do we not (why do we no longer) see you with us?** | laish mâ ʿammâl nshûfak ʿindna? | *lê mâ neshûfak′shi ʿandi′na?* |
| **I feared that I might not find you at home (lit., in the house)** | khift inni mâ blâḳîk′ filbait′ | *khuft inni malteḳîkshe filbêt* |
| **I came yesterday to see you, (but) I found you gone out** | jît mbâriḥ tâ shûfak, lâḳai′tak ruḥt | *gêt embâreḥ ʿala shân ashûfak, leḳêtak ruḥt* |
| 7 **They said nothing to me (about it)** | mâ ḳâlû′li shî | *mâ ḳâlûlî′sh* |
| **They did not inform me** | mâ khabbarûni | *mâdunîsh′ khabar* |
| **I have no knowledge (of it)** | mâ ʿindi khabar | *mâ ʿandîsh khabar* |
| 10 **I am sorry (lit., it is my misfortune) that I was not at home** | min sû ḥazzi inni mâ kint filbait′ | *min sû ḥazzi mâ kuntish filbêt* |
| **Answer: We are sorry (lit., it is our misfortune)** | min sû ḥazzna niḥna | *min sû ḥazzina iḥne* |
| **Mr. N. will be here directly (lit., will come in this moment)** | ilkhawâja (**Mohamm.:** issai′yid) .. hallaḳ bîji | *elkhawâga* (**Mohamm.:** *essai′yid*) .. *dilwa-′ti yîgi* |
| 13 **With your master's leave give me a drink of water** | ʿan izn (**or** ʿan amr) mʿallmak aʿṭîni shirbit moi | *ʿan izn* (**or** *ʿan amr*) *meʿal′limak aʿṭîni sharbet moiye* |

| | | |
|---|---|---|
| **Quickly! a glass of water for the gentleman** | ḳawâm kubbâyit moi lilkhawâja | *ḳawâm kubbâyet moiye lilkhawâga* |
| **Yes, or: at your service (lit., on my head)** | ʿala râsi | *ʿala râsi* |
| **At once!** | ḥâḍir! | *ḥâḍir!* |
| 4 **If you please, Sir** | tfaḍḍal yâ khawâja | *itfaḍ'ḍal yâ khawâga* |
| **Thanks (lit., God make your good, i.e. fortune great)** | ykattir (or kattir) khairak | *kattar khêrak* |
| **Thanks (God save your hands)** | ysallim (or sallim) daiyâtak | *sallim ayâdîk* |
| 7 **May you be much the better for it** | hanîyan [1] | *hanî-an* [1] |
| **Answer: God prosper you** | hannâk Allâh or Alla yhannîk | *Allâh yehannîk* |
| **We hope you will honor us for supper** | mnitraj'ja innak bitsharrif'nalil-ʿa'sha | *nitrag'ga tesharraf'na lilʿa'sha* |
| 10 **Will you not eat with us (lit., share our salt)?** | mâ bitrîd tmâliḥ'na? | *mush ʿâ-iz tâkol wayâna?* |

**1 This is said by those who preserve the old customs to him who has drunk, whereupon the latter replies as above whilst raising his hand to the forehead as in greeting. This custom obtains only, however, with water, lemonades, etc. When the visitor has taken the coffee, which in Arabic houses is always offered, he says, after placing the cup beside the little saucer (Arab.** zarf**):** dâyimi *dâ-ime*, **lit., continually, i.e. may coffee never be wanting in your house!, whereupon the host replies:** Alla ydîm ḥayâtak *Allâh yedîm ḥayâtak* **or** *Allâh yedîm ʿalêk elkhêr* **God give you a long (lit., continuous) life (or prosperity). The host then frequently adds, after placing the cup on the tray, which of course he always does last:** sharraf'tu **you have honored (us), then the visitor:** tsharraf'na *itsharraf'na* **we have honored ourselves. When pledging wine, etc. the usual form is:** lasir'rak **to your health!**

| | | |
|---|---|---|
| **Will you not stay a little to lunch with us, to lunch at ours (chez nous), that we may lunch together?** | mâ bitrîd iḍḍall' shwaiyi tâ titṛad'da ma'na, tâ titṛad'da 'indna, tâ nitṛad'da sawa? | *mush 'â=iz tifḍal shuwai'ye titṛad'da mi'âna, titṛad'da 'andi'na, nitṛad'da sawa?* |
| **I am obliged by your kindness, but I cannot, do not take it amiss** | mamnûn faḍlak, lâkin mâni ḳâdir (or mâ biḳdir), lâ twâkhid'ni | *memnûn minfaḍlak, lâkin mânish ḳâdir (or mâ baḳdarsh'), mâ tiâkhiznîsh'* |
| **I am invited elsewhere** | ma'zûm fî ṛair maṭraḥ | *ma'zûm fî maṭraḥ tâni* |
| 4 **I pray you to excuse me** | bitrajjâk ti'zir'ni | *batraggâk tu'zur'ni* |
| **I cannot stop** | mâ biḳdir it'au'waḳ (or iddah'ḳan) | *mâ aḳdarsh' at=akh'khar* |
| **I have come (for just) a moment to see you** | jit laḥza tâ shûfak | *gêt laḥza 'ala shân ashûfak* |
| 7 **I will do myself the honor another time** | bitshar'raf ṛair marra | *atshar'raf marra tâniye* |
| **Obliged by your visit** | mamnûn tishrîfak | *memnûn min teshrîfak* |

TAKING LEAVE

| | | |
|---|---|---|
| **What? you will leave us (already)?** | kîf? baddak iddashshir'na? | *ê? terauwaḥ?* |
| 10 **You have just this moment come** | hallaḳ shî wṣilt | *dilwaḳ'ti gêt* |
| **It is still early** | ba'd bakkîr | *lissa bedri* |
| **Stay a little longer** | ḳ'udlak shwaiyit lukhra | *uḳ'ud kemân shuwai'ye* |
| 13 **No, I must (will) go** | lâ, baddi rûḥ | *lâ, biddi arûḥ* |
| **It is late** | ṣâr laḳḳîs | *baḳa wakhri* |

| | | |
|---|---|---|
| **It is dark (lit., it has become dark)** | ṣâr ʿatm; ʿattamit iddi'ni | *baḳa ḏalme; ed-din'ye ḏallimet* |
| **It is night (lit., it has become night)** | ṣâr lail | *baḳa lêl* |
| **I lingered (am late); cf. No. 13.** | t=akhkhart'; t au-waḳt'; tdah-ḳant'; tlaḳḳast' | *it=akhkhart'; it-ʿauwaḳt'* |
| **4 My time is up (I have made myself late)** | fât waḳti; fât il-waḳt' ʿalai'yi | *fât waḳti; fât el-waḳt'i ʿalêye* |
| **It seems you are in a hurry** | mbaiyin, mustaʿʿ-jil **or** mrau-wij | *bâyin innak mu-staʿʿgil* |
| **I am very busy to-day** | mashṛûl ktîr il-yaum' | *ana meshṛûl ke-tîr ennahar'da* |
| **7 I have much to do to-day** | ʿalai'yi shuṛl ktîr ilyaum' | *ʿalêye shuṛlè ketîr ennahar'da* |
| **I have important business** | ʿalai'yi shṛâl mhimmi | *ʿalêye ashṛâl mu-him'me* |
| **I have urgent business** | ʿalai'yi shṛâl lâzmi | *ʿalêye ashṛâl lâ-zime* |
| **10 I have a long way to go** | ʿalai'yi mishwâr bʿîd | *ʿalêye mishwâr beʿîd* |
| **I have to go many ways (I have many walks to take)** | ʿalai'yi mshâwîr' ktîri | *ʿalêye meshâwîr' ketîre* |
| **A meeting has been arranged between me and some one on business** | fî mîʿâd' baini wbain wâḥid la-shuṛl' | *fîh mîʿâd' bêni webên wâḥid li-shuṛl'* |
| **13 I fear I tarried (I fear I am late); cf. No. 3.** | bkhâf inni it=-akh'khar | *bakhâf at=akh'-khar* |
| **I fear I shall not arrive in time** | bkhâf inni mâ ûṣal filwaḳt' | *bakhâf mauṣal'-shi filwaḳt'* |
| **I fear I shall be late (lit., the time passes by me)** | bkhâf yfût il-waḳt' ʿalai'yi | *bakhâf yefût el-waḳ'tè ʿalêye* |
| **16 It is time for departure** | ḥall waḳt irra-wâḥ | *ḥall waḳt erra-wâḥ* |

| | | |
|---|---|---|
| **I hope I shall see you (again) shortly** | inshal'la bshûfak ʿan ḳarîb | *inshal'lâh bashûfak ʿan ḳarîb* |
| **I will do my utmost to come to-morrow** | baʿmil juhdi tâ iji bukra | *baʿmil guhdi agi bukra* |
| **I will not disturb you any longer (lit., we have disturbed you too much, enough of this disturbance)** | taḳḳal'na ʿalaik' ktîr or ḥâjtak tiḳli or bîkaf'fi tiḳli | *taḳḳal'na ʿalêk ketîr* |
| 4 **When will you honor us?** | aimta bitshar'rif laʿand'na? | *imte teshar'raf ʿandi'na?* |
| **When shall we have the pleasure of seeing you again?** | aimta mnit=ânas bimshâhat'tak? | *imte nit=ânis bimushah'detak?* |
| **Very soon (in the shortest time), please God** | fî aḳrab waḳt inshal'la | *fî aḳrab waḳt inshal'lâh* |
| 7 **As soon as I possibly can** | auwil marra illi byimkin'ni | *auwal marra elli yimkin'ni* |
| **By your leave** | bi=iz'nak | *bi=iz'nak* |
| **With permission** | bil=izn' | *bil=izn'* |
| 10 **I beg leave (viz.: to absent myself)** | bista='zin | *asta='zin* |
| **Your (plur.) mind be with us** or: | khâṭirkon ʿalai'na | *khâṭirkum ʿalêna* |
| **Remain (plur.) in the custody of God** | tammu fî ḥirâset allâh | *tammu fî ḥirâset allâh* |
| 13 **Farewell, good-bye** | audaʿnâk or khâṭrak | *istaudaʿnâk Allâh* |
| **We wish you a good morning** | ṣabbaḥnâk | *neṣab'baḥ* |
| **Good day** | auḳâtak saʿîdi | *auḳâtak sâʿide* |
| **Good evening** | massainâk | *nimas'si* |
| **Good night** | lailtak saʿîdi | *lêltak sâʿide* |

| | | |
|---|---|---|
| **Answer: Farewell** | maʿassalāmi or maḥmûlissalāmi or biḥa'faḍ Allâh or fî amānillâh' | *maʿassalâme* or *maṣḥûb bissalâme* or *fî amânillâh'* or *bilamân* |
| **Answer: God save you!** | Alla ysallmak! | *Allâh yisal'limak!* |
| **God keep you!** | Alla yiḥfazak! | *Allâh yiḥfazak!* |

ON SPECIAL OCCASIONS

**To one returning from the bath or barber:**

| | | |
|---|---|---|
| 4 **May it do you good** | naʿîman | *naʿîman* |
| **Answer: May God favor you** | Alla yinʿam ʿalaik' | *Allâh yinʿim ʿalêk* |

**To one setting out on a journey:**

| | | |
|---|---|---|
| **May God let you arrive in safety, or:** | Alla ywaṣṣlak bissalāmi | *Allâh yiwaṣ'ṣalak bissalâme* |
| 7 **Please God you may arrive well, or:** | inshal'la tûṣal bkhair | *inshal'lâh tûṣal bikhêr* |
| **Farewell! or:** | maʿasslāmi! or maḥmûl issalāmi! | *maʿassalâme!* or *maṣḥûb bissalâme!* |
| **God be with you!** | Alla ykûn maʿak! | *Allâh yekûn miʿâk!* |
| 10 **Answer: God keep you!** | Alla ysallmak!; Alla yiḥfazak! | *Allâh yisal'limak!; Allâh yiḥfazak!* |
| **I hope we shall see you back in good health** | inshal'la nshûfak bkhair | *inshal'lâh neshûfak bikhêr* |
| **Answer: And you (too will then be) in good health** | w-int bkhair | *winte bikhêr* |

**To one returning from a journey:**

| | | |
|---|---|---|
| 13 **Thank God for (your) well-being, or:** | ilḥam'dilla ʿassalāmi | *elḥam'do lillâh ʿassalâme* |

| | | |
|---|---|---|
| **Thank God for your return in good health** | ilḥam'dilla ‘ala rujû‘ak bkhair | *elḥam'do lillâh ‘ala rugû‘ak bikhêr* |
| **Thank God we see you (back) well** | ilḥam'dilla illi shifnâk bkhair | *elḥam'do lillâh elli shufnâk bikhêr* |
| **Answer: God keep you!** | Alla ysallmak!; Alla yiḥfazak! | *Allâh yisal'limak!; Allâh yiḥfazak* |

**To a beggar to whom you give nothing:**

| | | |
|---|---|---|
| 4 **God give you (something)! or:** | Alla ya‘ṭîk! | *Allâh yi‘ṭîk!* |
| **God send you (something)! or:** | Alla yib‘at'lak! | *Allâh yib‘at'lak!* |
| **God provide (for) you! or:** | Alla yirzḳak! | *Allâh yirzuḳak!* |
| 7 **God open to you (viz. the gates of sustenance), or:** | Alla yiftaḥ ‘alaik' | *Allâh yiftaḥ ‘alêk* or *allâh yiḥan'nin ‘alêk* |
| **It is not present (i.e. I have nothing with me)** | mush ḥâḍir | *mâ fîsh khorde* |

**Congratulations for Festivals and New Year.**

| | | |
|---|---|---|
| **May you prosper every year** | kull sini w=int sâlim or kull sini w=intu sâlmîn' (or bkhair) or kull ‘âm w=intu ṭaiybîn | *kulle sene winte ṭaiyib* or *kulle sene wintu ṭaiyibîn* (or *bikhêr*) or *kulle ‘âm wintu ṭaiyibîn* |
| 10 **Answer: And you likewise** | w=int sâlim or w=intu sâlmîn' (or bkhair) or w=intu ṭaiybîn | *winte ṭaiyib* or *wintu ṭaiyibîn* (or *bikhêr*) |
| **May many years repeat themselves for you, or:** | tin‘âd ‘alaik' snîn ‘adîdi | *ti‘îsh liamsâlo fî khêr* |
| **May many such (years) repeat themselves for you** | yin‘âd alaik' min imtâlo | |

| | | | |
|---|---|---|---|
| | **Answer: And for you** | wʻalaikʼ or wʻala ḥaḍrtak or wʻal-ḳâyil | *we=in'te* or *we=in'tû* |

## INTERROGATIVE PHRASES

| | | | |
|---|---|---|---|
| | **Who?** | mîn? | *mîn?* |
| | **Who is this man?** | minû haida? | *mînhu' di?* |
| 4 | **Who is this woman?** | minî haidi? | *mîn dî?* |
| | **What is that?** | shû haida? | *di ê di?* |
| | **Who are you?** | mîn int? | *mîn inte?* |
| 7 | **Where are you?** | wain int?; fainak?; wainak? | *fên inte?* |
| | **What are you doing?** | shû ʻammâl taʻmil? (or ʻam btaʻmil?) | *betiʻʼmil ê?* |
| | **What are you going to do?** | shû râyiḥ taʻmil? | *râḥ tiʻmil ê?* |
| 10 | **Where are you [going?]** | lawain' râyiḥ? | *ʻala fên râ=iḥ?* |
| | **Whence come you?** | mnain jâyi? | *min ên gâ=i?* |
| | **What do you command?** | shû bit=âmir? | *betu='mur ê?* |
| 13 | **What is your pleasure, Sir?** | naʻam yâ sîdi?[1] | *naʻam yâ sîdi?*[1] |
| | **How did you say?** | kîf ḳult? | *ḳult ezai'?* |
| | **What are you saying?** | shû ʻammâl tḳûl? | *bitḳûl ê?* |
| 16 | **What do you say (to it)?** | shû bitḳûl? or mâ ḳaulak? | *bitḳûl ê?* or *ḳôlak ê?* |
| | **What is the news?** | shû fî jdîd? | *fîh khabar gedîd?* |
| | **What new tidings are there?** | shû fî akhbâr jdîdi? | *fîh akhbâr gedîde?* |
| 19 | **Have you tidings from ..?** | ʻindak akhbâr ʻan ..? | *ʻandak akhbâr ʻan ..?* |
| | **Do you know this (for) certain?** | btaʻrif haida akîd? | *betiʻʼraf di akîd?* |

**1 In this meaning the phrase must be pronounced with a strong interrogatory accentuation, that it may not be understood in its original meaning: 'Yes, Sir' (see foot of p. 47).**

| | | |
|---|---|---|
| **What is the question?** | shû ilmas'=ali? or shû ilḳaḍîyi? | *elmes'=ale ê?* **or** *elḳaḍîye ê?* |
| **What are they talking about (lit., about what the speech)?** | ʿala aish ilkalâm? | *elkelâm ʿala ê?* |
| **What has happened to you?** | shû ṣarlak? | *ḥaṣal'lak ê?* |
| 4 **What has befallen you?** | shû jarâlak? | *garâlak ê?* |
| **What (is the matter) with you?** | shû bâk? | *mâ lak?* |
| **How old are you?** | ḳaddaish' ʿumrak? or ibn kam sini? | *ʿumrak kâm sene?* |
| 7 **Are you hungry?** | jûʿân'? | *gâʿân'?* |
| **Are you thirsty?** | ʿiṭshân? | *inte ʿaṭshân?* |
| **Have you meat?** | ʿindak (or maʿak) laḥm? | *ʿandak* (**or** *miʿâk*) *laḥm?* |
| 10 **Have you bread?** | ʿindak (or maʿak) khubz? | *ʿandak* (**or** *miʿâk*) *ʿêsh?* |
| **Is the breakfast ready?** | ilfṭûr ḥâḍir? | *elfuṭûr ḥâḍir?* |
| **Is the supper ready?** | ilʿa'sha ḥâḍir? | *elʿa'sha ḥâḍir?* |
| 13 **Did you hear?** | smiʿt? | *simiht'?* |
| **Did you understand** | fhimt? | *fihimt'?* |
| **Did you understand me?** | fhimt ʿalai'yi? | *fihimti'ni?* |
| 16 **Are you speaking seriously?** | ʿam btiḥki ṣaḥiḥ? (or min jadd?) | *betiḥ'ki ṣaḥîḥ?* |
| **Where did you alight (get down)?** | wain nzilt? | *nizilt'i fên?* |
| **Where is your house** | wain baitak? | *bêtak fên?* |
| 19 **Where do you live?** | wain sâkin? | *ḳâʿid fên?* |
| **Will you go out this evening?** | btiṭlaʿ illai'li? | *betiṭ'laʿ ellêle?* |
| **Where were you this morning?** | wain kint ilyaum' ʿala bukra? | *kunti fên ennahar'da eṣṣubḥ'?* |
| 22 **How far is it from here to Tantah, Damietta, Saida, Tripoli?** | ḳaddaish' min haun laṭan'ṭa, ladimyât, laṣai'da, laṭrâblus? | *ḳaddi ê min hene liṭan'ṭa, lidumyâṭ, liṣai'da, liṭarâbulus?* |

| | | |
|---|---|---|
| **Which (lit., from where) is the road to.. ?** | mnain iṭṭarîk la ..? | *min ên essik'ke li ..?* |
| **For whom are you looking?** | ʿala mîn ʿam bit-fat'tish? | *biddauwar ʿala mîn?* |
| **For what are you looking?** | ʿala aish ʿam bit-fat'tish? | *biddauwar ʿala ê?* |
| 4 **What do you think of it?** | shû fikrak fîh? or shû btiftkir fîh? | *fikrak fî ê?* or *betifti'kir fîh ê?* |
| **What are you thinking of?** | biaish' ʿammâl tiftkir? | *betif'tikir bi-ê?* |
| **Do you understand Arabic?** | btifham ʿarabi? | *betif'ham ʿarabi?* |
| 7 **Do you speak English, French, Italian, German?** | btiḥki inglîzi, frinsâwi, ṭilyâni, nimsâwi? | *betiḥ'ki ingelîzi, feransâwi, iṭal-yâni, nemsâwi?* |
| **Can you read?** | btaʿrif tiḳra? | *betiʿ'raf tiḳra?* |
| **Can you write?** | btaʿrif tiktub? or btaʿrif ilktîbi? | *betiʿ'raf tiktib?* or *betiʿ'raf elki-tâbe?* |
| 10 **How much for this?** | biḳaddaish' hai-da? | *bikâm di?* |
| **What price?** | ḳaddaish' tama-no (or ḥaḳḳo)? | *temeno kâm?* |
| **Do you smoke tobacco?** | btishrab du-khân? | *betish'rab du-khân?* |
| 13 **Do you smoke a nargileh** | btishrab argîli (or nafas)? | *betish'rab shî-she* (or *nefes*)? |
| **How goes the nar-gileh (lit., does the n... work well)?** | il-argili btishtril ṭaiyib? | *eshshîshe betisha'-ral ṭaiyib?* |
| **Is the pipe alight?** | inna'fas shâʿil? | *eshshîshe miwal'-[laʿ?]* |
| **What is his name?** | shû ismo? | *ismo ê?* |
| 16 **What is her name?** | shû isma? | *ismaha ê?* |

AFFIRMATIVE PHRASES

| | | |
|---|---|---|
| **Yes, Sir** | naʿam (or aiwa or bala) yâ sîdi | *ai naʿam* (*aiwa* in Cairo, *îwa* in Alex-andria, *aiwallâh* is strengthening) |

| | | |
|---|---|---|
| **That is right (true)** | haida ṣaḥîḥ | *di ṣaḥîḥ* |
| **That is so** | haida haik | *di kide* |
| **It is I** | ana hû | *dana* |
| 4 **That is he, that is it** | haida hû | *âdi' hûwe* |
| **I believe you** | ana bṣaddḳak | *ana baṣad'daḳak* |
| **You are right** | ilḥaḳḳ' ma'ak (or fî îdak) | *elḥaḳḳ'ê bîdak* |
| 7 **I am convinced that..** | ana mut=ak'kid in.. | *muḥaḳ'ḳaḳ 'andi in..* |
| **You are wrong (in error)** | int ṛilṭân | *inte ṛalṭân* |
| **You are in the wrong** | int maḥḳûḳ ; int mukhṭi | *inte maḥḳûḳ; inte mukhṭi* |
| 10 **It is your fault** | ilḥaḳḳ' 'alaik' | *elḥaḳḳ'ê 'alêk* |
| **I promise you that..** | ana bû'adak in.. | *ana au'idak in..* |
| **It is time to..** | ṣâr ilwaḳt' tâ.. | *dilwaḳ'ti..* |
| 13 **His name is** | ismo | *ismo* |
| **Her name is** | isma | *ismaha* |
| **It is long since..** | min zamân.. | *min zemân..* |
| 16 **A short time ago** | min muddi ḳaṣîri (or ḳarîbi) or mâ fî zamân or ḳabl shwaiyi | *min mudde ḳalîle* (or *ḳarîbe*) or *ḳablê shuwai'ye* |
| **Shortly** | 'an ḳarîb or ba'd shwaiyi | *shuwai'ye we..* |
| **That is good** | haida ṭaiyib | *di ṭaiyib* |
| 19 **It suffices, enough** | byikfi, ḥâji | *bess, bikaf'fi* |
| **That satisfies me, enough for me** | haida byikfîni (or bîkaffî'ni) or ḥâjti | *di bikfîni* (or *bikaffîni*) or *biziyâde* |
| **I am busy** | ana mashṛûl or 'alai'yi shuṛl | *ana meshṛûl* or *'andi shuṛl* |
| 22 **That is much** | haida ktîr | *di ketîr* |
| **That is little** | haida ḳalîl | *di shuwai'ye* |
| **I am hungry** | ana jû'ân' | *ana gâ'ân'* |
| 25 **I am thirsty** | ana 'itshân | *ana 'atshân* |
| **My head aches** | râsi byûja''ni | *râsi betûga''ni* |
| **I am feverish** | ana sâkhin | *ana sukhn* |

| | | |
|---|---|---|
| I am very feverish | ana sâkhin ktir | *ana sukhnê ḳawi* |
| I am unwell | mâlî kêf **or** ana mshauwash | *mâlish kêf* **or** *ana mishau'wish* |
| I am tired | ana tiʿbân | *ana taʿbân* |
| 4 I am sleepy | ana niʿsân | *ana niʿsân* |
| I am cold | ana birdân | *ana bardân* |
| I am warm | ana mshauwib | *ana mishau'wib* |
| 7 I am obliged to you | ana mamnûnak | *ana memnûn minnak* |
| I will tell you something | baddi iḥkîlak kilmi | *biddi aḥkîlak kilme* |
| I am satisfied with you | ana mabsûṭ minnak | *ana mabsûṭ minnak* |
| 10 I am very angry with you | ana ktir ziʿlân minnak **or** ana msaudin minnak ktîr | *ana zaʿlân ketîr minnak* **or** *ana maḳhûr minnak ḳawi* |
| I am offended with you, take it amiss | âkhid ʿala khâṭri minnak | *wâkhid ʿala khâṭiri minnak* |
| I am quite at your service (lit., every service is incumbent) | kull khadâmi tilzam | *kulli khidme tilzam* |
| 13 Yours to command (lit., under the order) | taḥt il-amr' | *taḥt el-amr'* |
| I should like to go for a walk to-day | ili khâṭir shimm ilha'wa ilyaum' | *aḥibb' ashimm' elha'wa ennahar'da* |
| That is what I want | haida illi brîdo | *di elli ʿâizoh* |

NEGATIVE PHRASES

| | | |
|---|---|---|
| 16 No, Sir | lâ yâ sîdi **or** khair yâ sîdi | *lâ yâ sîdi* |
| That is nothing | haida mâ hû shi | *di mush ḥâge* |
| There is nothing | mâ fî shî | *mâ fîh shê* |
| 19 It is nobody, there is nobody | mâ fî ḥada | *mâ fîsh hadd* |
| I have (possess) nothing | mâ ʿindi shî | *mâ ʿandîsh ḥâge* |

| | | |
|---|---|---|
| **I have nothing (there is nothing the matter with me)** | mâ bini shî | *mâ lîsh ḥâge* |
| **I heard nothing** | mâ smiʿt shî | *mâ simiʿ'tish* |
| **I did not understand** | mâ fhimt or mâ dârit'li | *mâ fhim'tish* |
| **4 I say no** | ana bḳûl lâ | *ana baḳûl lâ* |
| **I do not know** | mâ baʿrif | *mush ʿârif* |
| **What do I know!** | shû biʿarrif'ni! | *ana ʿâraf!* |
| **7 I cannot** | mâ biḳdir or mâni ḳâdir or mâ fîni | *mâ baḳdarsh'* |
| **You are not right** | mâ maʿak ḥaḳḳ or ilḥaḳḳ' ʿalaik' | *mâ lakshè ḥaḳḳ* or *elḥaḳḳ'è ʿalêk* |
| **You are not wrong** | ilḥaḳḳ' mâ hû ʿalaik' | *elḥaḳḳ'è mush ʿalêk* |
| **10 It is not your fault** | mâ ʿalaik' ḥaḳḳ | *mâ ʿalêkshì ḥaḳḳ* |
| **That is not enough** | haida mâ byikfi or haida mâ bîkaf'fi | *di mâ yikfîsh* or *di mâ bikaffîsh* |
| **It is not yet time to ..** | baʿd mâ ṣâr il-waḳt' tâ .. | *lissa mâ gâsh el-waḳ'tè li ..* |
| **13 I cannot read** | mâ baʿrif iḳra | *mâ aʿraf'shì aḳra* |
| **I cannot write** | mâ baʿrif iktub | *mâ aʿraf'shì aktib* |
| **It is not far, it is not unlikely** | mâ hû bʿîd | *mush beʿîd* |
| **16 It is not necessary** | mâ hû lâzim or mush lâzim or mâ fî lazûm | *mush lâzim* or *mâ fîsh luzûm* |
| **That will not do** | haida mâ bîṣîr' | *di mâ yiṣaḥ'ḥish* |
| **That will never do** | mâ bîsîr' abadan | *mâ yiṣaḥ'ḥish ebeden* |
| **19 It does not matter, no matter** | mâ bîsâ'yil or mâ bîḍurr' or lâ bâs or lâ ba₌s | *mâ ʿalêsh* |

## ORDERS AND PROHIBITIONS

| | | |
|---|---|---|
| **Please** | tafaḍ'ḍal | *it₌faḍ'ḍal* |
| **Come here** | taʿ'â lahaun' | *taʿâla hene* |
| **22 Come nearer** | ḳarrib | *ḳarrab* |

| | | |
|---|---|---|
| **Sit down beside me** | uḳʿud jambi | *uḳʿud gambi* |
| **Stand up** | ḳûm | *ḳûm* |
| **Come in** | fût **or** fût lajûwa | *khushsh* **or** *khushshê gûwa* |
| 4 **Go out** | iṭlaʿ **or** iṭlaʿ labar'ra | *iṭlaʿ* **or** *iṭlaʿ barra* |
| **Go, hurry** | rûḥ staʿjil **or** rûḥ rauwij | *rûḥ istaʿ'gil* |
| **Follow me closely** | ilḥaḳ'ni min ḳarîb | *ilḥaḳ'ni min ḳarîb* |
| 7 **Follow me at a distance** | ilḥaḳ'ni min bʿid | *ilḥaḳ'ni min beʿîd* |
| **Walk (or go) before** | imshi ḳuddâm; isbaḳ | *imshi ḳuddâm; isbaḳ* |
| **Do go away** | rûḥ baḳa | *rûḥ baḳa* |
| 10 **Open the door** | iftaḥ ilbâb | *iftaḥ elbâb* |
| **Open the window** | iftaḥ ishshubbâk | *iftaḥ elḳizâze* |
| **Open the windows** | iftaḥ ishshbâbîk' | *iftaḥ eshshebâbîk'* |
| 13 **Open the blinds** | iftaḥ ilkhashbât **or** iftaḥ iddarfât | *iftaḥ elkhashabât* |
| **Listen to me** | smaʿli | *ismaʿ'ni* |
| **Give heed to me (attend to me)** | ismaʿ minni **or** khôd minni | *ismaʿ minni* **or** *khod minni* |
| 16 **Eat** | kôl | *kul* |
| **Drink** | ishrab **or** shrâb | *ishrab* |
| **Look at it** | tfarraj ʿalaih' **or** iṭṭal'liʿ fîh | *itfar'rag ʿalêh* |
| 19 **Put it in your pocket** | ḥuṭṭo fî jaibtak | *ḥuṭṭo fî gêbak* |
| **Put it on the table** | ḥuṭṭo ʿaṭṭau'li | *ḥuṭṭo ʿaṭṭarabêze* |
| **Begin** | ballish | *ibtidi* |
| 22 **Go on, continue** | kammil | *kammil* |
| **Stop, cease** | baṭṭil | *ikhlaṣ* |
| **Mind, take care** | dîr bâlak **or** aʿṭi bâlak | *khalli bâlak* |
| 25 **Forward, go it, go** | yalla | *yalla* |
| **Stop, halt!** | waḳḳif **or** ʿindak | *waḳḳaf* **or** *ʿandak* **or** *uṣbur* |

| | | | |
|---|---|---|---|
| | Turn back (trans.) | dauwir | *dauwar* |
| | Turn round (intrans.) | dûr | *dûr* |
| | Quickly | ḳawâm or bil'a'-[jel] | *ḳawâm* |
| 4 | Slowly, gently | 'ala mahl or shwai shwai | *shuwai'ye shuwai'ye* |
| | Answer me | ridd 'alai'yi | *ruddè 'alêye* |
| | Speak to me | ḥâkî'ni | *ḥâkî'ni* |
| 7 | Be silent | uskut | *uskut* |
| | Go away from here | rûḥ min haun | *rûḥ min hene* |
| | Go away from me | rûḥ 'anni | *rûḥ 'anni* |
| 10 | Come down, descend | inzil | *inzil* |
| | Take away | shîl | *shîl* |
| | Prepare everything | ḥaḍḍir kull shî | *ḥaḍḍar kulli shê* |
| 13 | Compose yourself | rauwiḳ; raiyiḥ bâlak | *raiyaḥ bâlak* |
| | Be quiet | khallîk murtâḥ | *khallîk mirtâḥ* |
| | Do not occupy your mind, do not be uneasy | lâ tsharril fikrak or lâ yinshril bâlak | *mâ tishril'shi fikrak* or *mâ yinshiril'shi bâlak* |
| 16 | Take this letter to Mr. N. N., and do not deliver it to any one else but him | khôd halmaktûb lilkhawâja .., wlâ tsallmo laḥa'da rairo hû | *khod elmektûb di lilkhawâga .., wemâ tisallimûsh liḥad'di rêro* |
| | Don't do this | lâ ta'mil haida | *mâ ti'mil'shi di* |
| | Don't do this a second time | lâ ta'mil haida tâni marra | *mâ ti'mil'shi di tâni marra* |
| 19 | Don't do it again | lâ t'ûd ta'mil'ha | *mâ ti'milhâsh tâni marra* |

## ASKING A FAVOR

| | | |
|---|---|---|
| Do me the favor | a'mil ma'rûf; ikrim 'alai'yi; tfaḍḍal 'alai'yi; tkarram 'alai'yi | *i'mil ma'rûf; krimni; itfaḍ'ḍal 'alêye; itkar'ram 'alêye* |
| Will you have the goodness to tell me? | byiḥsin 'indak tḳulli? | *yikhal'laṣak teḳul'li?* |

| | | |
|---|---|---|
| **If you will do me the favor you will greatly oblige me** | iza kân bitrîd taʿmil maʿi halmaʿrûf, bitṣaiyir'ni mamnûn ktîr | *iza kuntê tiʿmil miʿâye elmaʿrûf di, tikhallîni memnûn ketîr* |
| **Do you permit me to ..** | btismaḥ'li or bti=zin'li or bitrakhkhiṣ'li in .. | *tismaḥ'li* or *ti=zin'li ..* |
| **If you deny my request I shall be much vexed** | in khaiyabt' ṭalabi bitkad'dar ktîr | *in khaiyib'tê ṭalabi batkad'dar ketîr* |
| 4 **It will grieve me greatly if you do not grant my request** | byiṣʿab ʿalai'yi ktîr, in kint mâ btismaʿ rajâyi | *biṣʿab ʿalêyeketîr, iza kuntê mâ betismaḥ'shê ragâye* |
| **I ask you** | bitrajjâk or bitraj'ja min luṭfak or dakhîlak or dakhlak | *batraggâk* or *batrag'ga min luṭfak* |
| **I implore you** | biḥyâtak or bʿar-dak | *wiḥyâtak* or *fiʿar'ḍak* |
| 7 **I adjure (entreat) you** | billâh ʿalaik' or bḥakki ʿalaik' | *billâhi ʿalêk* or *biḥyâti ʿalêk* |
| **I know your courtesy is very great** | baʿrif maʿrûfak zâyid | *maʿrûfak zâ=id ʿalêye* |
| **No doubt your kindness is very great** | lâ shakk faḍlak kbîr (or ʿazîm) | *min gêr shekk faḍlak kebîr* |
| 10 **I ask you but this one favor** | bitrajjâk bhashshî mâ bitlub minnak ṛairo | *batraggâk bishshê di mâ aṭlubshê minnak ṛêro* |
| **This request for a thousand** | halṛa'rad b=alf ṛarad [1] | *elmarûʿa di bial'fê marûʿa* [1] |
| **Excuse my disturbing you** | lâ twâkhid'na ʿajjaznâk | *mâ ti=âkhiznâsh' ʿaṭṭalnâk* |

[1] **A genuine Arabic expression implying: the grant of this single favor is worth to me that of a thousand others.**

| | | |
|---|---|---|
| **God will reward you for it** | Alla bî'au'wiḍ 'alaik' | *Allâh yi'au'waḍ* or *yikhlif 'alêk* |
| **God will reward you instead of me** | Alla bîkâfîk' 'anni | *rabbi'na yikfîk 'anni* |
| **I expect this of your generosity** | haida ilma=mûl fî karam akhlâḳak | *di elma=mûl min karam akhlâḳak* |
| 4 **I shall be obliged to you** | bkûn mamnûnak or bkûn mamnûn lafaḍ'lak or bkûn maḥsûbak | *ḥakûn memnûn* or *akûn memnûn lifaḍ'lak* or *akûn maḥsûbak* |
| **I can rely on you, can I not?** | bittkil 'alaik', mush haik? | *a'tamid 'alêk, mush kide?* |
| **I shall not forget your kindness for the whole of my life** | mâ binsa jamîlak (or ma'rûfak) kull 'umri | *mâ ansâsh gemîlak* (or *ma'rûfak*) *ṭûl 'umri* |

OFFERS

| | | |
|---|---|---|
| 7 **I do not know what to offer to give you pleasure** | mâ ba'rif shû baddi ḳaddim'lak tâ irḍi khâṭrak | *mâ a'rafsh' aḳaddim'lak ê yirḍi khâṭrak* |
| **I beg you to accept this trifle from me** | bitrajjâk tiḳbal minni hashshî ijjiz'=i | *atraggâk tiḳbal minni eshshê di ezzuṛai'yar* |
| **Take it out of love to me** | khudo min shân khâṭri or iḳba'lo kirmâl khâṭri | *khudo 'ala shân khâṭri* or *iḳba'lo ikrâman likhâṭri* |
| 10 **Accept this slight token of my gratitude** | iḳbal hal'alâmit izzhîdi 'an mamnûnîy'ti | *iḳbal el'alâme ezzehîde di 'an memnûnî'yeti* |
| **I have nothing that does not belong to you (my all is in your purse)** | kullni 'ala kîsak | *ḥagti ḥagtak* |
| **I offer it to you with all my heart** | bḳaddim'lak yâh min kull ḳalbi | *addîlak di bikul'li riḍa* |

REFUSALS

| | | |
|---|---|---|
| 13 **That won't do, or: that is im-** | haida mâ bîṣîr' or mâ byimkin or | *di mâ yiṣaḥ'ḥish* or *mâ yimkinsh'* |

| | | |
|---|---|---|
| **possible, or : that cannot be done** | muḥâl or musta-ḥîl | or *muḥâl* or *mustaḥîl* |
| **It grieves me very much, but what shall I do?, I cannot (or : it is impossible for me)** | biṛimm'ni ktîr, lâ-kin shû ba'mil (or shû baddi a'mil)? mâ biḳdir (or mâ byimkin'-ni) | *biṛum'mini ketîr, lâkin a'mil ê? mâ aḳdarsh' (or mâ yimkinnîsh)* |
| **That does not depend on me, or : that is not in my power** | mâ hû fî îdi or haida fauḳ îdi or mâ hû râji' la-꞊am'ri (or mâ ili yaddîyi 'alaih') | *mush fî îdi or di fôḳ îdi or amro mush râgi' lîye* |
| **That does not concern me** | haida mâ bî-khuṣṣ'ni | *di mâ yikhuṣṣi-nîsh* |
| **4 I cannot do what you wish** | mâ biḳdir a'mil illi baddak yâh | *mâ aḳdarsh' a'-mil elli 'âizo* |
| **I regret that I must refuse your request** | byiṣ'ab 'alai'yi inni ṣuddak | *yis'ab 'alêye inni arag'ga'ak* |
| **Be assured that it is not my fault** | t꞊akkad inno mâ 'alai'yi ḥaḳḳ | *it꞊ak'kid innê mâ 'alêyâsh' ḥaḳḳ* |
| **7 I cannot now** | mâ biḳdir hallaḳ | *mâ aḳdarsh' dil-waḳt'i* |
| **The moment is not opportune** | ilwaḳt' mâ hû mnâsib (or mlâ-yim) | *elwaḳ'tê mush munâsib* |
| **Excuse me** | i'zir'ni or ṛiḍḍ in-na'zar or lâ twâkhid'ni | *mat꞊âkhiznîsh'* |
| **10 I hope you will excuse me** | bitraj'ja tiḳ-bal 'uzri or bi-traj'ja 'adam ilmwâkhidi | *batraggâk tiḳbal 'uzri or batrag-gâk 'adem elmu-âkhaze* |
| **God willing, another time** | inshal'la ṛair marra or mar-rit lukhra in-shal'la | *inshal'lâh marra tâniye* |
| **Be patient** | uṣbur | *uṣbur* |
| **13 Patience is the key to gladness** | iṣṣabr' miftâḥ ilfa'raḥ | *eṣṣabr' muftâḥ elfa'raḥ* |

| | | |
|---|---|---|
| **Do as you like, or: please yourself** | aʻmil ishshî illi bitrîdo; ʻala kêfak; ʻala châṭrak | *iʻmil elli ʻâ=izo; ʻala kêfak; bi-khâṭrak* |

## CONSENT

| | | |
|---|---|---|
| **I consent, good!** | birḍa or râḍi or biḳbal or ḳâbil or mlîḥ or ṭaiyib | *ana râḍi* or *aḳbal* or *ḳuwai'yis* or *ṭaiyib* |
| **Willingly** | ʻala râsi or ʻarrâs wilʻain' or tikram or marḥabâbak | *ʻala râsi* or *ʻarrâs walʻên* or *marḥabâbak* |
| 4 **With all my heart** | min kull ḳalbi or min kull khâṭri | *min ʻênê'ya* |
| **Ready; at command** | ḥâḍir; taḥt il=amr' | *ḥâḍir; taḥt el=amr'* |
| **As you wish** | mitl mâ bitrîd | *zê mâ terîd* |
| 7 **Reckon on me** | ʻalai'yi fîha lâ tiftkir | *di ʻalêye mâ tiftikirsh'* |
| **I cannot refuse you anything** | mâ biḳdir ṣuddak fi shî | *mâ akdarsh' aʻârḍak fî shê* |
| **You anticipate my thoughts, my wishes** | sabaḳt' ifkâri or ʻirift' (or ḥzirt) illi bfikri | *sabaḳti'ni* or *ʻirift' elli fi bâli* |
| 10 **I would gladly render you a greater service** | brîd ḳaddim'lak khadâmi akbar (or tiḥriz aktar) | *ʻâ=uz aḳaddim'lak khidâme akbar* |
| **I do for you what I would not do for another** | baʻmil min shânak illi mâ baʻmlo laṛai'rak | *aʻmil ʻala shânak elli mâ aʻmilôsh lirêrak* |
| **Your wishes come before those of others** | ṛaraḍak mḳaddam ʻala ṛaraḍ ṛairak (or ṛairo) | *ḥagtak ḳablê ḥâget ṛêrak* |
| 13 **Out of love for you** | min shân khâṭrak or kirmâl khâṭrak | *ʻala shân khâṭrak* or *ikrâman likhâṭrak* |
| **I have done it with great pleasure** | ʻamalt'hu min zât khâṭri | *ʻamalt'hu min zât khâṭiri* |
| **Certainly** | akîdan | *akîdan* |

RETURNING THANKS

| | | |
|---|---|---|
| **Thanks** | kattir khairak or bishkur faḍlak or bishkur afḍâlak | *kattar khêrak* or *bashkur faḍlak* or *bashkur afḍâlak* |
| **Much obliged** | mamnûn or ṛarîḳ ihsânak or bṛâyit ilmamnûnî'yi | *memnûn* or *birâyet elmemnûnî'ye* |
| **I do not undervalue your goodness (lit., I do not ignore the value of your goodness)** | mâ bijhal ḳîmit afḍâlak | *mankirshè faḍlak* |
| 4 **I do not know how I shall reward you** | mâ ba'rif kîf baddi kâfîk' | *mâ a'rafshi biê akâf=ak* |
| **God reward you for me** | Alla ykâfîk' 'anni | *Allâh yikfîk 'anni* |
| **You shame me by your kindness** | khajjalt'ni bima'rûfak | *khaggil'tini bima'rûfak* |
| 7 **Oh what a shame to have caused you this trouble** | yâ 'aibishshûm min hattiḳ'li | *yâ 'êbeshshûm' min ettuḳ'le di* |
| **Excuse the inconvenience, the trouble** | az'ajnâk or 'ajjaznâk or 'imilnâlak tiḳli or taḳḳal'na 'alaik' or kallaf'na khâṭrak or kallaf'tu ilkhâṭir | *akhkharnâk* or *'aṭṭalnâk* or *taḳḳal'na 'alêk* or *kallif'na khâṭrak* |

RECEIVING THANKS

| | | |
|---|---|---|
| **It is not worth mentioning** | haida mâ byihriz or haida shî mâ byizkar (or mâ hû ḥirzân) | *di shê ma yinzikirsh* or *yuzkarsh* |

| | | |
|---|---|---|
| **Don't mention it** | istarfrallâh [1] or ukhai'rak [2] | *astarfirullâh* [1] or *wekhêrak* [2] |
| **You are welcome (lit., I did it with pleasure)** | 'amalt'hu min zât khâtiri | *'amalt'hu min zât khâtiri* |
| **There is no ceremony between us** | mâ fî bainna taklîf | *mâ fîsh teklîf* |
| 4 **That was my duty** | khadâmtak wâjbi 'alai'na or fard 'alai'na or wâjib 'alai'na | *khidmetak wâgibe 'alêna* or *fardê 'alêna* or *wâgib 'alêna* |
| **To serve you is an honor** | khadâmtak sharaf | *khidmetak sharaf* |

ADMIRATION, SURPRISE

| | | |
|---|---|---|
| **What a wonder!** | mâshallâh'! or shû hal-amr' il-'ajîb! | *mâshallâh'!* or *yâ salâm!* |
| 7 **Strange thing!** | shî 'ajîb! or shî rarîb! or shî mustar'rab! | *shê 'agîb!* or *shê rarîb!* or *asta'gib!* |
| **There is nothing better, finer than that** | mâ fî ahsan minno or mâ fî akwas minno or mâ fî ajmal minno (or wala ajmal) | *mâ fîsh ahsan minno* or *mâ fîsh akwas minno* or *mâ fîsh agmal minno* |

---

1 **Properly: 'I beg God's pardon,' viz. for my sins, my faults. This expression is used on very many and different occasions; here it implies: 'I have so few merits that on the contrary I must ask pardon of God for my faults; you have, therefore, no reason to thank me.' One frequently uses this expression as a mark of modesty when being praised. Sometimes this** istarfrallâh *astarfirullâh* **serves as an ironical non-acceptance of an incredible or impossible assertion; in this case, of course, it has the corresponding accentuation.**

2 **Answer to** kattir khairak *kattar khêrak* **(see p. 57). Sometimes** kattir salâmtak **is used instead.**

| | | |
|---|---|---|
| There is nothing like it | mâ fî mitlo | *mâ fîsh zêyo* |
| Very fine ! | ktîr mlîḥ ! or ktîr kwaiyis ! or ktîr laṭîf ! | *kuwai'yis ketîr !* or *kuwai'yis ḳawi !* or *laṭîf ḳawi !* |
| How beautiful that is ! | mâ aimalo ! or mâ akwaso ! | *mâ agmalo !* or *mâ akwaso !* |
| 4 That is astonishing | haida shî bî-ʿaj'jib or amr ʿajîb | *di shê yiʿgib* or *amrè ʿagîb* |
| Is it possible ? | bîṣîr' ? or byimkin ? | *biṣîr* or *ṣaḥîḥ ?* |
| Is it a dream ? | filyaḳ'za willa filmanâm ? | *filyaḳ'za walla filmanâm ?* |
| 7 What is that ? | shû haida ? | *di ê di ?* |
| Impossible, incredible | muḥâl or shî muḥâl or shî mâ byitṣad'daḳ or mâ byirkab ʿala ʿaḳl or mâ byidkhul ilʿaḳl' | *muḥâl* or *shê muḥâl* or *shê mâ yikhushshish elʿ akl'* or *mâ yiṣaddaḳûshè el ʿaḳl'* |
| Who would have believed that, who would have thought that | mîn kân bîṣad'diḳ or mîn kân byiftkir or mîn kân yikhṭur fî bâlo or ʿala bâl mîn kânit haidi or mîn kân bîshan'kish hashshinkâsh | *mîn ḳân biṣad'daḳ* or *mîn kân biftikir* or *mîn kân yikhṭur fî bâlo* |
| 10 Would anyone have expected that ? | kân byikhṭur fî bâl insân ? or kân byiji bifikr' ḥada ? | *kân yikhṭur fî bâl insân ?* or *kân yigi fi fikrè ḥadd ?* |
| By God this is a strange affair | wallâhi haida faṣl | *wallâhi di ʿagîb* |
| How ?, really ? | kîf ?, ṣaḥîḥ ? or akîd ? | *ezai' ?, ṣaḥîḥ ?* |
| 13 That is beyond comprehension | haida fauḳ ilʿaḳl' | *min wara elʿuḳûl* |

## REGRET, AFFLICTION, AVERSION

| | | |
|---|---|---|
| It is a pity! | yâ ḍî‘â'no![1] or yâ ḥain! or yâ ḥarâm![2] | *yakhsâre!* |
| What a misfortune! | shû halmṣîbi! or shû halblîyi! or shû halwaḳ'‘a! or shû haḍ dar'bi[3] | *êsh elmuṣîbe dî!* or *êsh elbelîye dî!* |
| I regret it very much | tḥassart' ktîr or inṛammait' ktîr or ana ktîr zi‘lân min hashshî (or min hal-amr') | *itḥassart'ê ketîr* or *itṛammêt ketîr* or *ana za‘lân ketîr min esh-shê di* (or *min el-amr'ê di*) |
| 4 That is very unpleasant, annoying | shî bîkad'dir or shî byiz‘il or shî byinki or shî byiḳhar | *shê mukad'dir* or *shê yiza‘‘al* or *shê yinki* or *shê yiḳhir* |
| That grieves me from the bottom of my heart (properly: to the last degree) | haida shî bîṛimm'ni la-âkhir daraji or haida shî bîwaj'ji‘ il-kalb' | *di shê yiṛum'mini li-âkhir darage* or *di shê yûga‘ elḳalb'* |
| That goes against one, or: that is disgusting, or: | shî btinfur minnunnafs' or shî bîḳar'rif or shî | *shê tun'fur minno ennefs'* or *shê yiḳar'raf* or |

[1] Lit., 'Oh, the pity of it!' the o is the possessive suffix of the 3rd pers. sing. masc.; its place is taken by ha or hon *hum* when the 'of it' refers to a fem. sing. or to a plural.

[2] This expression more especially implies pity for a sick or poor person, etc.

[3] Besides these expressions the women in Syria make use of a good many others, all of them meaning: 'how unfortunate I am!', for instance yâ ḥasrti, yâ dilli, yâ kasrti, yâ ta‘tîri, yâ muṣîbti, yâ balwati, ilwail'li, ulî; the latter especially when lamenting the dead.

| | | |
|---|---|---|
| **that is abominable, repugnant** | bishiʿ or shî karîh | *shê bishiʿ* or *shê karîh* |
| **That is horrible, dreadful** | shî mahûl or shî fazîʿ or shî byirʿib or shî bîkhau'wif | *shê mahûl* or *shê yikhau'wif* |
| **That makes one's hair stand on end** | shî bîwaḳ'ḳif (or bîḳab'bib) shaʿr irrâs | *shê yiwaḳ'ḳaf shaʿr errâs* |
| **I can no longer stand it** | mâ baḳa fîyi (or fîni) or mâ bḳît iḳdir or mâ ʿâd fîni haddi ḥâli or mâ ʿâd fîni iḥtmil or mâ ʿâd ʿindi ṣabr | *mâ baḳêtsh aḥtamil* or *mâ beḳêtish aḳdar* or *mâ baḳâsh fîye aḥtamil* or *mâ ʿandîsh ṣabr* |

SATISFACTION

| | | |
|---|---|---|
| 4 **I am very glad of it** | ana mabsûṭ (or masrûr) minno ktîr | *ana mabsûṭ minno ketîr* |
| **I am very happy (properly: Oh my good luck!)** | yâ saʿdi or yâ saʿd bakhti | *yâ saʿdi* or *yâ saʿdê bakhti* |
| **Everything, thank God, is going well with me (lit., to my mind)** | kull shî ilḥam'dilla ʿala khâṭri or kull shî mâshi mitl mâ brîd | *kulli shê elḥam'do lillâh ʿala khâṭri* or *kulli shê mâshi zê mana ʿâ=iz* |
| 7 **I bring you good news** | minbash'shrak or ilbshâra ilak | *nibashsha'rak* or *elbishâra lak* |
| **I congratulate you with all my heart** | bhannîk (or bârik'lak) min kull ḳalbi | *bahannîk min kulli ḳalbi* |
| **What (good) luck** | shû halḥazz' or shû hassaʿâdi | *êsh elḥazz'ê di* |
| 10 **What an honor** | shû hashsha'raf | *êsh eshssha'raf di* |
| **How glad I am** | ḳaddaish' ana mabsûṭ or ḳaddaiḥ' ḥazzi kbîr | *ḳaddi ê ana mabsûṭ* or *ḳaddi ê ḥazzi kebîr* |

| | | |
|---|---|---|
| **Excellent** | ʿattamâm or tamâm or bṛâyit ilmnâsabi | *ʿattamâm* or *tamâm* or *biṛâyet elmunâsabe* |
| **Bravo** | mâshallâh′ or mâshal′la ʿalaik′ or ʿâfîtain′ or ʿâfâk′ or âfâ′rîm or yiṣlaḥo or Alla ykattir min imtâlak or brâwo | *mâshallâh′* or *mâshallâh′ ʿalêk* or *afârim* or *berâwo* |

DISSATISFACTION AND REPROACHES

| | | |
|---|---|---|
| **Fie, what is that?** | tfû (or uff[1]), shû haida? | *tfû* (or *iff*[1]), *di ê di?* |
| 4 **It is a shame** | htîki or faḍîḥa or ʿâr or ʿaib[2] | *hetîke* or *faḍîḥa* or *ʿâr* or *ʿêb*[2] |
| **Are you not ashamed?** | mâ btistḥi? or mâ btikhjal? | *mâ tisʾtiḥîsh?* or *mâ tikhgalsh′?* |
| **That is shameful** | shî ḳabîḥ or shî shanîʿ or shî ʿaib | *shê ḳabîḥ* or *shê shenîʿ* or *shê ʿêb* |
| 7 **That is abominable** | shî mamḳût or shî makrûh or shî karîh | *shê yinat′tik* or *shê karîh* |
| **Why do you always play me such stupid tricks?** | laish tâ taʿmil′li dâyman haik fṣûl? | *lê tiʿmil′li dâiman kide?* |

---

[1] The first of these two expressions indicates more the aversion mixed with contempt, for instance: tfû ʿalaik′ *tfû ʿalêk!* fie upon you!; the second is an expression of impatience, of inability to stand something any longer, and only in a wider sense of the aversion arising from same.

[2] To all these expressions ʿalaik′ *ʿalêk!* (it is a shame) 'for you' can be added. Stronger is ḥaif ʿalaik′ *ikhs ʿalêk!* shame upon you!, which, however, is sometimes used playfully with the meaning of 'You are mistaken.' Simple disapproval of an action is expressed by ḥarâm ʿalaik′ *ḥarâm ʿalêk!* it is forbidden to you, i.e. you are not allowed.

| | | |
|---|---|---|
| **How could you do such a thing as this ?** | kîf ṭilʿit maʿak haidi ? | *ezai' ṭiliʿet maʿak elḥâga dî ?* |
| **Why this wickedness, i.e. how could you be so wicked ?** | mnain hashshaḳâwi ? or mnain harradāwi ? or mnain jibt halkhabāsi ? | *min ên eshshaḳâwe dî ?* or *min en erradâwe dî ?* or *min ên gibt elkhabâse dî ?* |
| **I am very dissatisfied with you** | aṇa ktîr ziʿlān minnak (or ʿalaik') | *ana zaʿlân ḳawi minnak* (or *ʿalêk*) |
| 4 **Leave off at last, stop that** | khalliṣ yâ or khalliṣ'na baḳa or baddna nikhlaṣ | *khallaṣ yalla* or *khallaṣ'na baḳa* or *biddina nikhlaṣ* |
| **Keep still, quiet** | ihda or kinn or lâ tḥarrik sākin | *ihda* or *kinnê nafsak* or *mâ teḥar'rakshê sâkin* |
| **Be silent** | uskut or ikhras | *uskut* or *ikhras* |
| 7 **What kind of talk is this ? What is (all) this chatter ?** | shû halʿalk' or shû halḥa'ki or shû halfshâr or shû ʿam bitkhab'bis | *êsh elʿar'kê di* or *êsh elḥa'ki di* or *êsh elfash'rê di* |
| **I lose all patience** | mâ baḳa fîni or ḍâḳ ṣidri | *mâ baḳâsh fîye rûḥ* or *ḍâḳ ṣadri* |
| **Beware a second time** | îyāk' marra tānyi or iṣḥa (or ûʿa) min shān ṛair marra or marrit lukhra farjîk | *îyâk' tâni marra* or *iṣḥa* (or *ûʿa*) *ʿala shân marra tâniye* |
| 10 **Another time you will not forget it** | mâ btinsa taʿmit'ha | *mâ tinsâsh ḥalâwet'ha* |
| **Say no more, not a word** | lâ tiḥki walâ kilmi | *mâ tiḥkîsh welâ kilme* |

OF THE WEATHER

| | | |
|---|---|---|
| **How is the weather ?** | kîf iṭṭaḳs' ? | *elha'wa ezai' ?* |
| 13 **The weather is fine** | iṭṭaḳs' ṭaiyib | *elha'wa ṭaiyib* |

| | | |
|---|---|---|
| **The weather is bad** | iṭṭaḳs' radi (or makhbûṭ) | *elha'wa baṭṭâl* |
| **It is warm** | fî shaub or ṣâyir shaub | *fîh ḥarr* |
| **It is very warm** | fî shaub ktîr | *fîh ḥarrê ketîr* |
| 4 **Outside it is very cold** | barra bard ktîr | *barra bardê ketîr* |
| **It will rain** | badda tshatti or baddo yṣir maṭar | *biddiha tishti* or *biddiha tunṭur* |
| **It is going to rain** | raḥ tshatti | *râḥ tishti* |
| 7 **Is it raining ?** | iddin'yi shâtyi? or ʿam bitshat'ti ? | *betish'ti ?* |
| **Yes, it is raining** | aiwa ṣâyir shiti or ʿam bitshat'ti | *aiwa betish'ti* |
| **There is a drizzling rain** | ṣâyir maṭar rafîʿ or ṣâyir bakhkh maṭar | *bitnad'daʿ* or *en-na'ṭara bit-bukhkh'* |
| 10 **The earth needs much rain (lit., thirsts greatly for rain)** | il-arḍ' ʿiṭshâni lama'ṭar ktîr | *el-arḍ'ê ʿaṭshâne ketîr lina'ṭar* |
| **There will be a sudden downpour of rain** | bîṣîr' maṭar syûl | *enna'ṭara gaiye zê essêl* |
| **It rains in torrents** | iddin'yi kâbsi ; nâzli kabs | *eddin'ye mishtîye* |
| 13 **The clouds are dispersing (lit., it is being widened)** | ʿam bitfas'siḥ or ʿam btifrij | *bitfat'taḥ* |
| **The sun begins to shine** | badit tishriḳ ish-shams' ; balla-shit tshammis | *ibta'det tishriḳ essems'* |
| **It is clearing up** | ṣârit ʿammâl tiṣ-ḥa or ʿam byir-jaʿ iṣṣa'ḥu | *yirgaʿ eṣṣa'ḥu* |
| 16 **The sky is clear** | ijjau' ṣâḥi (or ṣâfi) or issa'ma ṣâfyi | *elgau' ṣâḥi* or *es-sa'ma ṣâfiye* |
| **The sky is over-clouded** | muṛai'ymi or il-ṛaim' fî kull issa'ma ; ṭabaḳ ilṛaim' | *eddin'ye meṛai'yi-me* or *elṛêm fî kull essa'ma* |

| | | |
|---|---|---|
| **The weather is mild** | iṭṭaḳs' laṭîf or iṭ-ṭaḳs' mu'tadil | *elha'wa laṭîf* or *mi'tidil* |
| **The wind is boisterous** | ilha'wa ḳawi or irrîḥ shedîd | *elha'wa shedîd* |
| **The wind has shifted** | ṭraiyar ilha'wa or ḳalab irrîḥ | *iṭrai'yar elha'wa* or *inḳa'lab errîḥ* |
| 4 **It is extremely hot** | ṣâyir shaub muf-riṭ (or fauḳ il'âdi) | *fîh ḥarrè shedîd ḳawi* |
| **The sun has hidden himself** | ishshams'inḥa'ja-bit or ishshams' muṛai'ymi | *essems' inḥa'gabet* or *eddin'ye me-ṛai'yime* |
| **The wind is getting up** | nafakh ilha'wa or ṭili' hawa | *ṭili' elha'wa* |
| 7 **It is thundering** | 'am btir'ad (id-din'yi) | *betir''ad (eddin'-ye)* |
| **It is lightning** | 'am btibriḳ (id-din'yi) | *betib'ruḳ (eddin'-ye)* |
| **It is hailing** | ṣâyir barad or 'am byinzil barad | *beyin'zil telg* |
| 10 **The lightning has struck (lit., fell)** | nizlit zâ'iḳa or waḳa'at zâ'iḳa | *nizil elbarḳ'* |
| **Do you see the rainbow ?** | shâyif ḳaus ilḳa'-daḥ ? | *shâ-if ḳôs elḳa'-zaḥ ?* |
| **It is snowing** | ṣâyir talj or nâzil talj (or 'am btit-lij) | *beyin'zil telg* |
| 13 **What a storm !** | milla zauba'a ! | *malla zôba'a !* |
| **There will be a storm** | baddo yṣîr zau-ba'a | *betîgi zôba'a* |
| **There will be a frost** | baddo yṣîr jlîd | *biddo yeṣîr gelîd* |
| 16 **I am very cold** | ana birdân ktîr | *ana bardân ke'îr* |
| **The air is very damp** | ilha'wa riṭib ktîr or fî ṛtûbi ktîr filha'wa | *fîh ruṭûbe ketîr filha'wa* |
| **Much dew is falling** | ṣâyir nidi ktîr or nâzil nidi ktîr | *nâzil nade ketîr* |
| 19 **The snow is melting** | ittalj' 'am bîdûb' | *ettelg' bidûb* |
| **The sky is lowering** | ijjau' 'itim (or mu'tim) | *elgau' 'itim* or *me'attim)* |

| | | |
|---|---|---|
| **There is a fog** | ṣâyir ḍabâb | *fîh ḍabâb* |
| **It is dusty** | ṣâyir ṛabra **or** ʿam bitṛab'bir | *fîh turâb* **or** *beyitṛab'bar* |
| **The weather does not remain steadfast a moment** | ijjau' mâ byibḳa daḳîḳa ʿala ḥâlo | *elha'wa mâ bibḳâsh daḳîḳe ʿala ḥâle wâḥide* |
| 4 **The weather is changeable** | iṭṭaḳs' mutḳal'lib | *elha'wa mitṛai'yar* |
| **I will not go out in this weather; it is too uncertain** | mâ brîd iṭlaʿ fî haṭṭaḳs'; bîkhau'wif | *mush ʿâ-iz aṭlaʿ filha'wa di? yikhau'wif* |
| **The wind is in the north, east, west, south** | ṣâyir hawa shmâli, sharḳi, ṛarbi, ḳibli | *elha'wa baḥri, sharḳi, ṛarbi, ḳibli* |
| 7 **There is much mud in the streets** | fî waḥl ktîr fiṭṭurḳât **or** iṭṭurḳât mûḥli | *fîh waḥlê ketîr fissi'kak* **or** *essi'kak muwaḥ'ḥale* |

DIVISION OF TIME[1]

| | | |
|---|---|---|
| **What are the names of the months of the solar year?** | shû asâmi shhûr issint' ishshamsîyi? | *êsh asmâ shuhûr esse'ne eshshemsîye?* |
| **January, February, March, April,** | kânûn' ittâni, shbâṭ, adâr, nî- | *yanâ-ir, febrâ-ir, mârs, abrîl,* |

[1] **All the Christians of Syria and Egypt reckon after the European era, the Mohammedans after the Mohammedan era, which has retained the lunar year. The months of the latter are:** muhar'ram, ṣafar, rabîʿ ilau'wal *rebîʿ elau'wal*, rabîʿ ittâni *rebîʿ ettâni*, jumâdi ilau'wal *gamâd elau'wal*, jumâdi ittâni *gamâd ettâni*, shaʿbân *shaʿbân*, rajab *ragab*, ramaḍân, shauwâl, zilḳaʿdi *zilḳiʿde*, zilḥij'ji *zilḥig'ge*. **Official documents generally bear a double date: the Greek and the Mohammedan, or the Mohammedan and that of the Turkish state-year which goes by the Julian calendar. On the 1st of February 1908 the year 1326 of the** hijra, **and on the 14th of March 1908 the state-year 1324 began.—The Christian era** ta-rîkh ilmesîḥi *elmesîḥe*, **the Mohammedan era** ta-rîkh ilhijrîyi *elhijrîye*.

| | | | |
|---|---|---|---|
| | **May, June, July, August, September, October, November, December** | sân', îyâr' (or nûwâr'), ḥazîrân', tammûz, âb, ailûl, tishrîn ilau'wal, tishrîn ittâni, kânûn' ilau'wal | *mâ'yô, jûniye, jûliye, aṛoss'tôs, sebtem'ber, okto'ber, novem'ber, dessem'ber* |
| | **What are the names of the four seasons?** | shû asâmi ilar'baʿ fuṣûl? | *asmâ elfuṣûl elar'baʿa ê?* |
| | **Spring, summer, autumn, winter** | irrabîʿ, iṣṣaif', ilkharîf, ishshi'ti | *errebîʿ, eṣṣêf, elkharîf, eshshi'te* |
| | **Last year** | sint ilmâḍyi or ʿamlau'wal | *esse'ne elli fâtet* or *ʿamenau'wal* |
| 4 | **For one (the last) year** | min sini or min zarf sini | *min sene* |
| | **For (the last) six months** | min nuṣṣ sini or min sitt ishhur | *min nuṣṣê sene* or *min sitt ishhur* |
| | **It is a month, a fortnight, a week ago** | ṃin shahr, min khamsṭaʿshar yaum, min jumʿa | *min shahr, min khamasṭâsher yôm, min gumʿa* |
| 7 | **In a month** | baʿd shahr | *baʿdê shahr* |
| | **Shortly** | ʿan ḳarîb | *ʿan ḳarîb* |
| | **In an hour** | baʿd sâʿa | *baʿdê sâʿa* |
| 10 | **After a while** | baʿd burha or baʿd shwai | *baʿdê shuwai'ye* |
| | **Yesterday** | ams or mbârḥa or mbâriḥ | *embâreḥ* |
| | **Last night** | ams ʿashîyi or lailt imbârḥa | *lêlt embâreḥ* |
| 13 | **The day before yesterday** | auwal ams or auwilt' imbârḥ | *auwal embâreḥ* |
| | **To-day** | ilyaum' or hannhâr | *ennahar'da* |
| | **To-night** | halma'sa or hallai'li | *ellêle dî* or *ellêlâ'-di* |
| 16 | **This morning** | haṣṣabâḥ or ilyaum' ʿalabukra | *eṣṣubḥ'* or *ennahar'da fiṣṣubḥ'* |
| | **In the morning** | ʿala bukra or ʿabbuk'ra | *eṣṣubḥ'* |
| | **In the forenoon** | ḍaḥwit nhâr | *ḳabl eḍḍuhr'* |

| | | |
|---|---|---|
| **At noon** | iḍḍuhr′ or ʿind iḍḍuhr′ | *eḍḍuhr′* or *fiḍ-ḍuhr′* |
| **In the afternoon** | baʿd iḍḍuhr′ | *baʿd eḍḍuhr′* |
| **In the evening** | ʿind ilma′sa or ʿashîyi | *elʿi′she* |
| 4 **At night** | fillail′ | *fillêl* |
| **To-morrow** | bukra or ṛadi | *bukra* |
| **The day after to-morrow** | baʿd bukra | *baʿdê bukra* |
| 7 **This year** | hassi′ni or issi′ni | *esse′ne dî* or *es-sanâ=di* |
| **Next year** | sint ijjāyi | *esse′ne eggâ=iye* |
| **Next week** | jumʿit iṭṭâlʿa | *eggum′ʿa eggâ=iye* |
| 10 **Early; it is still early** | bakkîr; baʿd bakkîr or lissa waḳt or baʿd waḳt | *bedri; lissa bedri* or *lissa fîh waḳt* |
| **Late** | laḳḳîs | *wakhri* |
| **Sometimes** | aḥyânan or aḥyân or baʿḍ ilauḳât | *baʿdê sâʿât′* or *baʿḍ elauḳât* |
| 13 **From time to time** | min waḳt lawaḳt′ or kull waḳt baʿd waḳt | *min waḳt liwaḳt′* or *kulli waḳt baʿdê waḳt* |
| **Every day** | kull yaum | *kulli yôm* |
| **Every other day (two days)** | kull yaumain′ | *kulli yômên′* |
| 16 **Every hour** | kull sāʿa | *kulli sâʿa* |
| **Sooner or later** | ilyaum′ yâ bukra | *ennahar′da yâ bukra* |
| **As soon as possible** | bi=aḳ′rab waḳt or bi=aḳ′rab mâ ykûn or bi=aḳ′rab mâ yimkin | *bi=aḳ′rab waḳt* or *bi=aḳ′rab mâ yekûn* or *bi=aḳ′rab mâ yimkin* |
| 19 **What o'clock is it?** | ḳaddaish′ issāʿa? | *essâʿa kâm?* |
| **Look at your watch** | kshifli sāʿatak or shufli bsāʿatak | *shûfli essâʿa kâm* |
| **It has stopped** | wâḳfi | *waḳfe* |
| 22 **It is not wound up [watch]** | mâ hî mdauwara | *mâ hîyesh medau′wara* |
| **Wind up your [watch]** | dauwir sāʿatak | *dauwar sâʿatak* |
| **Does your watch go well?** | sāʿatak māshyi ṭaiyib (or mlîḥ)? | *sâʿatak mashye ṭaiyib?* |

| | | |
|---|---|---|
| **What is it by your watch?** | ḳaddaish′ issâ'a 'indak? | *essâ'a 'andak kâm?* |
| **It is 1 o'clock** | issâ'a wâḥdi[1] | *essâ'a waḥde*[1] |
| **It is just striking 7** | hallaḳ 'am bit-dukk′ sab'a | *dilwaḳ'ti bit-dukk′ sab'a* |
| 4 **It is past 8** | ṣârit issâ'a aktar min tmânyi | *essâ'a teman'ye weziyâde* |
| **It is a quarter past 8** | issâ'a tmânyi uru'ba' | *essâ'a teman'ye weru'ba'* |
| **It is half past 9** | issâ'a tis'a unuṣṣ′ | *essâ'a tis'a we-nuṣṣ′* |
| 7 **It is a quarter to 11** | issâ'a ḥda'sh illa ruba' | *essâ'a ḥadâsher illa ruba'* |
| **It is ten minutes to 11** | issâ'a ḥda'sh illa 'ashra | *essâ'a ḥadâsher illa 'ashara* |
| **It is not quite 2** | mâ ṣârit tintain′ 'attamâm | *lissa essâ'a mâ ṣâret'shi etnên* |
| 10 **It will soon be 5** | ḳarîb tṣîr issâ'a khamsi | *essâ'a tîgi khamse* |
| **It will soon strike 3** | mâ baḳa illa tdukk issâ'a tlâti | *dilwaḳ'ti tedukk′ essâ'a telâte* |
| **3 o'clock** | tlât sâ'ât′ or issâ'a fî tlâti | *telât sâ'ât′* or *essâ'a fî telâte* |

---

[1] **When travelling in Syria it must never be forgotten that the natives (Christians as well as Mohammedans, except the 'civilised ones,' i.e. those who have accepted European externals) have throughout retained the old division of the day, and begin the counting of hours from sundown. As in Syria the sun sets on the longest day at 7.10, and on the shortest day at 5 o'clock, twelve o'clock Arabic time corresponds to these hours, in the evening and in the morning; twelve o'clock European time, midnight or noon, corresponds therefore on the longest day with 4.50, on the shortest day with 7 o'clock Arabic time. Although this mode of reckoning causes the greatest inconveniences, because, of course, the time of sunset differs according to the shortness and length of the days, it obtains generally, as stated, in Syria, and there as everywhere in the Turkish empire is in use with the Turkish authorities, both administrative and judicial.**

| | | |
|---|---|---|
| **It has not yet struck 4** | lissa mâ daḳḳit issâ'a arb'a | *lissa mâ daḳḳet-shi essâ'a ar-ba'a* |
| **It is not yet noon** | lissa mâ ṣâr iḍ-ḍuhr' | *lissa mâ gâshî eḍḍuhr'* |
| **It is 12 o'clock (Frank), it is noon, it is midnight** | issâ'a ṭna'sh (franjîyi), ṣâr iḍḍuhr', ṣâr nuṣṣ lail | *essâ'a etnâsher (ifren'gi), eḍ-ḍuhr', nuṣṣ ellêl* |
| 4 **It is 12 o'clock (Arabic), in the evening, in the morning** | issâ'a ṭna'sh ('arabîyi), 'al-mur'rib, 'ala bukra | *essâ'a etnâsher ('arabi), 'al-mar'rib, 'aṣṣubḥ'* |
| **It is 8 minutes past 5** | issâ'a khamsi witmân daḳâyiḳ | *essâ'a khamse wa-teman'ye daḳâ-iḳ* |
| **It is half past 12** | issâ'a ṭna'sh unuṣṣ' | *essâ'a etnâsher wenuṣṣ'* |
| 7 **It is 12 (noon) at the latest** | 'alktîr issâ'a ṭna'sh | *essâ'a etnâsher bil-ak'tar* |

**The Muslim's five daily prayers are:** ṣalât iṣṣubḥ' **prayer before and during sunrise,** ṣalât iḍḍuhr' **prayer at noon,** ṣalât il'aṣr' **prayer about nine o'clock (before sundown),** ṣalât ilmar'rib **prayer after sunset,** ṣalât il'ishâ **night prayer.**

## SPECIAL PART

### ARRIVAL AND DEPARTURE

| | | |
|---|---|---|
| **Ho there! you! boatman! put me ashore** | hê! int! yâ baḥri! khudni ʿalbarr' | *hê! inte! yâ baḥri! khudni ʿalbarr'* |
| **Have you luggage, Sir?** | maʿak ʿafsh yâ mʿallmi? | *miʿâk ʿafsh yâ sîdi* |
| **Yes, I have three portmanteaus, two travelling bags, and some small luggage** | naʿam, maʿi tlât ṣanâdîḳ' ushanṭtain' wishwai'yit ʿafsh | *aiwa, miʿâye telât ṣanâdîḳ' weshanṭatên weshuwai'yet ʿafsh* |
| 4 **What do you want for putting me ashore?** | ḳaddaish' baddak ḥatta twaṣṣil'ni ʿalbarr'? | *bikâm tiwaṣṣal'ni ʿalbarr'?* |
| **I shall want half a pound** | baddi nuṣṣ lîra | *ʿâ-iz nuṣṣè bintu* |
| **That is far too much** | haida zyâdi ktîr | *di ketîr khâliṣ* |
| 7 **Any one else would take me for a franc, at the utmost for two francs** | ṛairak byâkhid'ni bifrank' uʿalktîr bifrankain' | *ṛêrak beyâkhud'ni bifrank' weʿalketîr bifrankên* |
| **That is too little, Sir** | haida ḳalîl yâ mʿallmi | *di ḳalîl yâ sîdi* |

| | | |
|---|---|---|
| **Well, I will give you 2½ francs, but mind you must take no other people but me in the boat** | ṭaiyib, baʿṭîk frankain' unuṣṣ', lākin dîr bālak mâ btākhud hadan ṛairi bilflûkya | *ṭaiyib, aʿṭîk feranken wenuṣṣ', lâkin khalli bâlak mâ tâkhud'shi ḥaddi ṛêri filfelûke* |
| **I give you nothing, not even a single para, if you do not take me alone** | mâ baʿṭîk shî ulâ bârit ilfard' iza mâ akhatt'ni waḥdi | *mâ aʿṭîkshe walâ bâra waḥde in mâ kuntish tâkhod'ni liwaḥ'di* |
| **As you will, Sir** | mitl mâ bitrîd yâ mʿallmi | *zê mâ terîd yâ sîdi* |
| 4 **Go on, take (plur.) the luggage down into the boat** | yalla, nazzlu ilʿafsh' lilflûkya | *yalla, nazzilu elʿafsh' filfelûke* |
| **How many portmanteaus have you (plur.) taken down?** | kam ṣandûḳ nazzal'tu? | *kâm ṣandûḳ nazzil'tu?* |
| **Two portmanteaus only** | ṣandûḳain' bass | *ṣandûḳên' bass* |
| 7 **Where is the third portmanteau?** | wain iṣṣandûḳ ittālit? | *fên eṣṣandûḳ ettâlit?* |
| **Look (plur.) for it** | fittshu ʿalaih' | *dauwarum ʿalêh* |
| **Have you (plur.) found it?** | lâḳaitûh'? | *lâḳêtûh'?* |
| 10 **Is this the portmanteau, Sir?** | haida iṣṣandûḳ yâ mʿallmi? | *di eṣṣandûḳ yâ sîdi?* |
| **Yes, carry (plur.) it quickly down together with these two travelling bags** | ainaʿam, ḳawām nazzlûh maʿhashshanṭtain' | *îwa, ḳawâm nazzilûh maʿashshanṭatên dôl* |
| **Take (plur.) also this bundle of sticks, and the umbrella, and this wool rug** | khudu kamān harrab'ṭit ilʿiʿṣi washshamsîyi whalḥrām | *khudu kemân rabṭat elʿuʿṣi dî washshemsîye walḥirâm di* |
| 13 **Take (plur.) good care that nothing is broken** | dîru bālkon ṭaiyib ḥatta mâ yinksir shî | *khallu bâlkum ṭaiyib ʿala shân mâ yinkisir'shi ḥâge* |

| | | |
|---|---|---|
| Fear nothing, Sir | lâ tkhâf yâ m'allmi or mâ 'alaik' yâ m'allmi | *mâ tekhâfshi yâ sîdi* or *mâ 'alêsh yâ sîdi* |
| Please, Sir, step into the boat | tfaḍḍal, yâ khawâja, nzîl lilflûkya | *itfaḍ'ḍal yâ khawâga, inzil filfelûke* |
| Have you (plur.) got everything ready? | khallaṣ'tu kull shî? | *khallaṣ'tu kulli shê?* |
| 4 Yes, ready | na'am ḥâḍir | *na'am ḥâḍir* |
| Give (me) your hand that I may descend | hait îdak tâ inzil | *hât îdak 'ala shân anzil* |
| I cannot jump if the boat is so far off | ana mâ biḳdir fizz wilflûkya b'idi halḳadd' | *ana mâ aḳdarshi anuṭṭ walfelûke be'îde ḳaddi kide* |
| 7 Bring the boat nearer | ḳarrib ilflûkya bijjâyi | *ḳarrab elfelûke* |
| Go on, pull (plur.), we shall see | yalla, ḳaddfu tanshûf | *yalla ḳaddifu ḥaneshûf* |

---

| | | |
|---|---|---|
| It seems the sea runs high | bibân ilbaḥr' kbîr | *bibân elbaḥr' kebîr* |
| 10 The wind is boisterous | irrîḥ shedîd (or ḳawi) | *elha'wa shedîd* (or *ḳawi*) |
| I am giddy | ana dâyikh | *ana dâ-ikh* |
| I am going to be sick | raḥ bistaf'riṛ | *râḥ astaf'raṛ* |
| 13 Slowly! | 'ala mahlkon! or shwai shwai! | *bishwêsh!* or *shuwai'ye shuwai'ye* |
| There is a big wave coming | jâyiṭ'na mauji ḳawîyi | *gâ-iyâ'na môge ḳawîye* |
| Take (plur.) care we are not drowned | dîru bâlkon lâ niṛraḳ or iṣḥu niṛraḳ | *khallû bâlkum mâ niṛraḳshi* or *û'a niṛraḳ* |
| 16 Use (plur.) the oars more | kattiru ilmaḳâdîf | *kattaru elmaḳâdîf* |

| | | | |
|---|---|---|---|
| | **Mind (plur.) the boat is not thrown on the rocks** | iṣḥu tulṭam il-fiûkya biṣṣkhûr | *iṣḥu tulṭum el-felûke biṣṣukhûr* |
| | **Are we still far from the land?** | lissâna b'âd 'an ilbarr'? | *lissa iḥne be'îdîn' 'an elbar'?* |
| | **We have arrived at the custom-house** | wiṣil'na lilkum'-ruk | *wiṣil'na lilgum'-ruk* |
| 4 | **Bring (plur.) out all the cases and all the luggage** | ṭaili'u iṣṣanâdîḳ' willa'bash kull-hon | *ṭalla'u eṣṣanâdîḳ' wal'af'shè kullo* |
| | **Leave (plur.) nothing in the boat** | lâ tkhallu shî bil-flûkya | *mâ tekhal'lûsh ḥâge bilfelûke* |
| | **Have you (plur.) nothing else?** | mâ biḳi shî 'ind-kon? | *mâ lîsh ḥâge 'an-dukum?* |
| 7 | **Give (us) the pay** | hât ilij'ra | *hât elug'ra* |
| | **Here is your (plur.) pay** | hai ijrit'kon | *âdi' ugrat'kum* |
| | **Only this?** | bass haudi? | *bessè dôl?* |
| 10 | **Did you not see how great labor we had on the way?** | mâ shift ḳad-daish' t'ibna fiṭ-ṭarîḳ? | *mâ shuftish ḳad-dî ê ti'ib'na fiṭṭarîḳ?* |
| | **Eh! that is enough** | ê! bîkaf'fu | *ê! bîkaf'fu* |
| | **Give us a few piastres bakh-sheesh** | a'ṭîna kam ḳirsh bakhshîsh | *a'ṭîna kâm ḳirsh baḳshîsh* |
| 13 | **Take (plur.) this!** | khudu haida! | *khudu di!* |
| | **What have you with you?** | shû fî ma'ak? | *mi'âk ê?* |
| | **That is all I have with me** | haida kull illi ma'i | *di kull elli mi'âye* |
| 16 | **I have nothing dutiable** | mâ ma'i shî lil-kum'ruk | *mâ ma'ish shê lilgum'ruk* |
| | **I have nothing but clothes, and books, and travel-ling utensils** | mâ ma'i illa tjâb uku'tub wilwâ-zim lissa'far | *mâ ma'ish ḥâge ṛêr hudûm we-ku'tub welawâ-zim essa'far* |

| | | |
|---|---|---|
| You must open the boxes that we may inspect them | lâzim tiftaḥ iṣṣa-nâdîk′ḥatta nik-shif ʿalai′hon | *lâzim tiftaḥ eṣṣa-nâdîḳ′ ʿala shân nikshif ʿalêhum* |
| Such is the law | haida innazâm | *elḳânûn′ kide* |
| It cannot be avoided | mâ bîṣîr′ bala | *ṛêr kide mâ yi-ṣaḥ′ḥish* |
| 4 It is absolutely necessary | lâ budd minno | *lâ buddê minno* |
| There is nothing to inspect | mâ fî shî lil-kashf′ | *mâ fîsh ḥâge lil-kashf′* |
| Take this[1] | khôd haida | *khod di* |
| 7 Good, go, Sir | mlîḥ, rûḥ, yâ kha-wâja | *ṭaiyib, rûḥ, yâ khawâga* |

---

| | | |
|---|---|---|
| Where is the passport? | wain ittiz′kri (or ilbazabort′)? | *fên ettez′kire (or elbazabor′to)?* |
| Here is my passport | hai tizkir′ti (or haida ilbaza-bort′) [yâh) | *âdi′ tezkir′ti* |
| 10 Give it to me | aʿṭîni yâha (or | *idîhâ′li* |
| No, I keep my passport | lâ, bazabor′ti byibḳa maʿi | *lâ, tezkir′ti tibḳa miʿâye* |
| You have seen it; why will you take it? | int shifto; shû lâzim tâkhdo? | *inte shufto; lâ-zim ê takhdo?* |
| 13 Give the passport, fear nothing | hait ilbazabort′, lâ tkhâf | *hât ettez′kire, mâ tekhâfshi* |
| We give it to the authorities, and the authorities send it to the consulate, and you fetch it then from there | mnaʿṭîh lilḥkûmi, wilḥkûmi bit-waddîh lilḳunṣ-lâto, wabtib′ḳa tâkhdo min hau-nîk | *nidîha lilḥukû-me, walḥukûme tiwaddîha lil-ḳunṣulâto, wa-tib′ḳa takhdo min henâk* |
| What am I to do under all these circumstances! | shû baddi min kull halla′baki! | *êsh biddi min kull elkarka′be di* |

---

1 Viz. a gratuity; according to the number of packages, a franc or more is (in Syria) given to the customs-officer.

| | | |
|---|---|---|
| Fetch porters to carry the cases and the other things to the hotel | jîb ʿittâli yiḥmlu iṣṣanâdîḳ' ubâki ilawâʿi yâkhdû'hon lillukan'da | *hât shaiyâlîn' yiḥmilu eṣṣanâdîḳ' webâḳi elhawâ-ig yeshîlû'hum lillokan'da* |
| How much do you (plur.) want for a portmanteau? | ḳaddaish' baddkon ʿaṣṣandûḳ? | *kâm ʿâ-izîn' ʿaṣṣandûḳ?* |
| A franc | frank | *ferank'* |
| 4 I pay only sixty paras | mâ baʿṭi illa sittîn miṣrîyi | *mâdîsh' illa sittîn faḍḍa* |
| Nobody carries a portmanteau from here to the hotel for this pay | mâ ḥada byiḥmil ṣandûḳ min haun lillukan'da bhalij'ra | *mâ ḥaddish biḥmil ṣandûḳ min hene lillokan'da bilug'ra dî* |
| I procure a porter for thirty paras | ana bdabbir ʿittâl bitlâtîn' miṣrîyi | *ana agîb shaiyâl bitelâtîn' bâra* |
| 7 I carry them, Sir, and pay me what you will | ana biḥmil'hon yâ khawâja wiʿṭîni ḳadd mâ bitrîd | *ana aḥmil'hum yâ khawâga waʿṭîni zê mante ʿâ-iz* |
| Have done, carry them for a piastre | khalliṣ'na, ḥmil-hon bḳirsh | *ikhlaṣ, iḥmil'hum bikirsh'* |
| Which (lit., from where) is the way to the hotel? | mnain darb illukan'da? | *sikket ellokan'da min ên?* |
| 10 That is the hotel man, he will take you there | haida zalmit illukan'daji bîwaṣṣ'lak | *di khaddâm ellokan'da yewaṣ'ṣalak* |
| Is the hotel far from here? | illukan'da bʿîdi min haun? | *ellokan'da beʿîde min hene?* |
| No, it is near | lâ, ḳarîbi | *lâ, ḳuraiyi'be* |
| 13 Is it inside the town or outside? | dâkhil ilba'lad yimma khârij'ha? | *dâkhil elbe'led wala khârigha?* |
| At the end of the market-place | fî âkhir issûḳ | *fî âkhir essûḳ* |
| Take me to the best hotel in the town; it must be airy, clean, | dillni ʿala aḥsan lukan'da fî halba'lad; tkûn shirḥa, nḍîfi, | *dilini ʿala aḥsan lokan'da filbe'led dî; tekûn shirḥa, naḍîfe, ʿâliye,* |

| | | |
|---|---|---|
| **high(ly situated), the food good, in short, a decent hotel** | ʿâlyi, aklha ṭaiyib, lukan'dit akâbir | *aklâha ṭaiyib, lokan'dat nâs ṭaiyibîn* |
| **We have arrived, Sir** | wiṣil'na yâ sîdi | *wiṣil'na yâ sîdi* |

---

| | | |
|---|---|---|
| **I will start by the first steamer** | baddi sâfir fî auwal wâbûr' | *biddi asâfir biau'wal wâbûr'* |
| **When is the first steamer due which leaves for Alexandria (for Constantinople, for Marseilles, for Beyrout, for Jaffa, for Smyrna)?** | aimta mîʿâd' auwal wâbûr' bîsâ'fir liliskandrîyi (listambûl, lamarsîlya, labairût, layâ'fâ, lizmîr)? | *imte mîʿâd' auwal wâbûr' bisâfir liskenderîye (listambûl, limarsîlya, libêrût', liyâ'fâ, lizmîr)?* |
| 4 **The steamer has arrived** | wuṣil ilwâbûr' | *elwâbûr' gi* |
| **At what time will it start?** | aina sâʿa bîsâ'fir? | *aiyi sâʿa bisâfir?* |
| **At 8 o'clock in the evening it will start, but the passengers must be on (board) the steamer at 5 o'clock** | issâʿa tmânyi ʿashîyi byimshi, lâkin irrukkâb lâzim ykûnu bilwâbûr' issâʿa khamsi | *essâʿa teman'ye min ellêl bimshi, lâkin elmesâfrîn lâzim yekûnu filwâbûr' essâʿa khamse* |
| 7 **Load the luggage and take it to the custom-house** | ḥammil ilawâʿi, khudhon ʿalkum'ruk | *ḥammil elḥawâ-ig, khudhum ʿalgum'ruk* |
| **Can we not clear the baggage through the customs without these formalities?** | mâ mnikdir nkhalliṣ ilawâʿi mnilkum'ruk min dûn halla'baki? | *mâ nirdarshi nikhal'laṣ elḥawâ-ig min elgum'ruk min rêr elker-ke'be di?* |
| **We request the customs to send some one here to examine the baggage** | niṭlub mnilkum'ruk yibʿat hadan lahaun' yikshif ʿalawâʿi | *nuṭlub min elgum'ruk yibʿat ḥaddi hene yikshif ʿalḥawâ-ig* |

| | | |
|---|---|---|
| **You can satisfy the mind of the custom-house officer with a trifle** | tirḍi khâṭir ilkumruk'ji b=ash mâ kân | *tirḍi khâṭir elgumruk'gi bi-ai'yi ḥâge* |
| **That is your business; do the needful** | hashshurl' shur-lak; a'mil il-mwâfik | *di shuṛlak; i'mil elmuwâfiḳ* |
| **At 3 o'clock some one will come and examine the baggage, and at 4 o'clock you will go in the boat with the baggage from the hotel direct to the steamer** | issâ'a tlâti byiji wâḥid yikshif 'alawâ'i wissâ'a arb'a btinzil bil-flûkya ma'al-'afsh' mnillu-kan'da râsan lil-wâbûr' | *essâ'a telâte yîgi wâḥid yikshif 'alḥawâ=ig wassâ'a arba'e tinzil bilfelûke ma-'al'afsh' min ellokan'da dugri lilwâbûr'* |

STAYING AT A PLACE

*At a Hotel*

| | | |
|---|---|---|
| 4 **I wish to speak with the proprietor of the hotel** | brîd iḥki ma'-ṣâḥib illukan'da | *biddi akal'lim waya ṣâḥib ello-kan'da* |
| **Have you rooms to let?** | 'indak uwaḍ (or maḥallât) lil-ij'ra? | *'andak uwaḍ (or maḥallât) lilug'-ra?* |
| **Yes, Sir** | na'am, yâ sîdi | *aiwa yâ sîdi* |
| 7 **I want two rooms for a few days** | lâzim'li ûḍtain' min shân kam yaum | *lâzim'li ôḍatên' 'ala shân kâm yôm* |
| **I want a room on the upper story** | baddi ûḍa fiṭṭâ-biḳ ilfûkâ'ni | *biddi ôḍa fiddôr elfôḳâ'ni* |
| **Bring the luggage into the room** | jibli ilḥawâyij lilûḍa | *hâtli elḥawâ=ig lilôḍa* |
| 10 **I want a room on the lower story leading to the garden** | baddi ûḍa fiṭṭâ-bikittiḥtâni tik-shif 'albustân | *biddi ôḍa fiddôr ettaḥtâni teṭull' 'albustân* |

| | | |
|---|---|---|
| **I want a room on the upper (floor) facing (Syr. opening to, Eg. overlooking) the sea (the mountains)** | baddi ûḍa filʿâli kāshfi ʿalbaḥr' (ʿajja'bal) | *biddi ôḍa filʿâli teṭull' albaḥr' (ʿagge'bel)* |
| **What is the rent of this room per day?** | ḳaddaish'. ijrit halûḍa filyaum'? | *kâm ugrat elôḍa dî filyôm?* |
| **The rent of the room only (is) four francs, with breakfast and dinner, eight francs** | ijrit ilûḍa waḥdha arbaʿ frankāt, maʿalṛa'da wilʿa'sha tmān frankāt | *ugrat elôḍa waḥdiha arbaʿ ferank', maʿalṛa'de walʿa'she teman'ye ferank'* |
| **4 As I shall not always take meals in the hotel I will rent the room only** | min ḥais inni mâ bākul temel'li fillukan'da bista='jir ilûḍa waḥdha | *min ḥês inni mâ âkulshi temel'li fillokan'da asta='gir elôḍa waḥdiha* |
| **The sheets are not clean** | ishsharâshif mush nḍâf | *elmilâyât' mush nuḍâf* |
| **Bring us others** | jiblna ṛairhon | *hâtlina ṛêrhum* |
| **7 Change them** | ṛaiyir'hon | *ṛaiyar'hum* |
| **Bring me matches and a light and put them on the table** | jibli shiḥḥâṭa usham'ʿa uḥuṭṭ'hon ʿaṭṭau'li | *hâtli kibrît washam'ʿa waḥuṭ'ṭuhum ʿaṭṭarabêze* |
| **Wipe this chest of drawers, it is quite dusty** | imsaḥ halbirô, kullo wasakh | *imsaḥ eddulâb di, kullo wisikh* |
| **10 Hurry up with the arranging of the room; we are tired, we want to sleep** | ʿajjill'na bitartîb ilûḍa; niḥna tiʿbānîn', baddna nām | *istaʿʿgil bitertîb elôḍa; iḥne taʿbânîn', ʿâ=izîn' nenâm* |
| **Bring water and towels** | jîb moi wimnāshif | *hât moiye wamenâshif* |
| **Bring cold water to drink** | jîb moi bārdi lishshirb' | *hât moiye bâride lishshurb'* |
| **13 I will wash my feet; warm some** | baddi ṛassil ijrai'yi; sakh- | *biddi arsil rigleye; sakhkhan'li* |

| | | |
|---|---|---|
| **water and bring it me in a bowl** | khin'li moi ujîb-ha fî waʿa (or maʿjini) | *moiye wehâtha fî ṭâse* |
| **At what time do the guests breakfast (dine)?** | aina sâʿa byitṛad'du (byitʿash'shu) ilmsâfrîn'? | *aiyi sâʿa bitṛad'du (bitʿash'shu) elmesâfrîn'?* |
| **This serviette is not clean** | halfûṭa mâ hî nḍîfi | *elfûṭa dî mush naḍîfe* |
| **Change me this serviette** | ṛaiyir'li halfûṭa | *ṛaiyar'li elfûṭa dî* |
| 4 **Bring me another knife (another fork)** | jibli ṛair sikkîni (ṛair shauki) | *hâtli sikkîne tâniye (shôke tâniye)* |
| **Bring me another spoon** | haitli malʿaḳa ṛair haidi | *hâtli maʿlaḳa tâniye* |
| **Bring me something to eat and (some) tea up to my room** | jibli lilûḍa shî lilakl' ushai' | *hâtli shê lilakl' weshây lilôḍa* |
| 7 **Do me the favor, send quickly for a laundress** | kallif khâṭrak, ibʿât ḳawâm wara ṛassâli | *iʿmil maʿrûf, ibʿat ḳawâm waḥde ṛassâle* |
| **I must have my linen washed, and I shall not stay here long** | baddi ṛassil tyâbi umâ bitʿau'waḳ ktîr haun | *biddi aṛsil hudûmi wemâ aḳʿoji ketîr hene* |
| **Call me to-morrow morning at six o'clock** | faiyiḳ'ni bukra ʿala bukra issâʿa sitti | *ṣaḥḥîni bukra bedri essâʿa sitte* |
| 10 **Knock loudly at my door early to-morrow until I awake** | duḳḳ ilbâb ṛadi bakkîr daḳḳa ḳawîyi ḥatta fîḳ | *ikhbaṭ elbâb bukra bedri khabṭa ḳawîye liḥadd' aṣḥa* |
| **Mind my (legged) boots must be readv, cleaned, and dry** | dîr bâlak lâzim tkûn jazmti ḥaḍra mamsûḥa nâshfi | *khalli bâlak lâzim tekûn gazmâti ḥaḍra mamsûḥa nashfe* |
| **There is no towel, no soap** | mâ fî fûṭa, ṣâbûn' | *mâ fîsh fûṭa, ṣâbûn'* |

| | | |
|---|---|---|
| **Serve me the coffee with milk at six o'clock punctually** | ḥaddir'li ilkah'wi bilḥalîb issâ'a sitti tamâm | *hâtli elkah've bille'ben essâ'a sitte tamâm* |
| **I want a needle and thread** | lâzim'li ibri u-khaiṭ' | *lâzim'li ibre we-khêṭ* |
| **Send me the barber; I want to get shaved and to have my hair cut** | ib'at jîb ilḥil-lâk; baddi iḥluk ukuṣṣ' sha'ri | *ib'at'li elmezai'-yin; biddi aḥlaḳ waḳuṣṣ' sha'ri* |
| 4 **Are there any newspapers here?** | haun fî jurnâlât'? | *fîh gurnâlât' he-ne?* |
| **Where is the closet?** | wain ilmustarâḥ (or bait ilmoi')? | *fên bêt errâḥe* (or *elkanîf*)? |
| **How much is my bill?** | ḳaddaish ḥsâbi? | *ḥisâbi kâm?* |
| 7 **How much have I to pay?** | ḳaddaish' 'alai'yi tâ idfa'? | *kâm 'alêye adfa'?* |
| **Bring me the bill** | jibli ilḥsâb | *hâtli elḥisâb* |
| **Give me a detailed account** | a'ṭîni ḳâymi mfaṣṣali | *a'ṭîni ḳâ-ime mu-faṣ'ṣale* |

*Various Inquiries*

**(Sights, Walks, Consulates, Post-Office, Doctor, etc.)**

| | | |
|---|---|---|
| 10 **What is there in this place that is worth seeing?** | shûfi fî halba'-lad yistḥikk' il-fir'ji? | *êsh filbe'led dî yistaḥikk' elfur'-ge?* |
| **Are there any fine promenades?** | fî muntazahât kwaiysi? | *fîh muntazahât kuwai'yise?* |
| **I want some one to take me to the places of note** | baddi wâḥid ydillni 'alma-ḥallât ishshahî-ra | *biddi wâḥid ye-dill'ini 'alma-ḥallât eshsha-hîre* |
| 13 **What shall I give him per day (per hour)?** | ḳaddaish' ba'ṭîh ijra 'alyaum' ('assâ'a)? | *kâm adîh ugra 'alyôm('assâ'a)?* |
| **Does he know English, French?** | yifham inglîzi, frinsâwi? | *yifham inglîzi, feransâwi?* |

| | | |
|---|---|---|
| Is he ready? I wish to go at once | ḥâḍir? baddi rûḥ hallaḳ | *hûwa ḥâḍir? biddi arûḥ dilwaḳt'* |
| Where is the English Consulate? | wain ḳunṣlâto (or kinshlârî'yit) ingiltar'ra | *fên ḳonṣolâto (or kanshellârî'yet) ingiltar'ra* |
| Does the consul reside in the Consulate? | ilḳun'ṣul sâkin bilḳunṣlâto? | *el'ḳon'ṣul sâkin filḳonṣolâto?* |
| 4 Conduct me to him | waṣṣil'ni la'an'do | *waddîni 'ando* |
| Is he at home? | hû filbait'? | *hûwe filbêt?* |
| Tell him Mr. N. N. wishes to see him | ḳullo musyû .. baddo yshûfo | *ḳullo musyû .. biddo yeshûfo* |
| 7 I wish to walk in the open air (open country) | baddi shimm il-ha'wa filbarrîyi | *biddi ashimm' elha'wa filkhale* |
| Where is the English (German, Austrian, French, Russian, Turkish) post-office? | wain busṭat ilinglîz (ilalmâ-nî'yi, innam'sa, ilfrinsâwî'yi, ilmis'kob, il'os-man'li)? | *fên busṭat elinglîz (elalmâ-nî'ye, ennem'se, elferansâwî'ye, elmoskôf el'os-man'li)?* |
| Take me there | waṣṣil'ni lahaunîk | *waddîni henâk* |
| 10 Are there any letters for me (with my name)? | fî mkâtîb' min shâni (bi=is'mi)? | *fîh gawâbât' 'ala shâni (bi=is'mi)?* |
| What is the postage of a letter to ..? | ḳaddaish' ijrit ilmaktûb la...? | *kâm ugrat elga-wâb li...?* |
| Which is the best post for Europe? | aina busṭa aḥsan la=ûrob'ba? | *aiyi busṭa aḥsan li=ûrob'ba?* |
| 13 The best post is that which leaves on Tuesdays at five o'clock in the afternoon by the English steamer | aḥsan busṭa hî illi bitsâfir yaum ittlâti issâ'a khamsi ba'd iḍḍuhr' ma-'alwâbûr' ilinglîzi | *aḥsan busṭa hîye elli bitsâfir yôm ettelâte essâ'a khamse ba'd eḍ-ḍuhr' ma'alwâ-bûr' elinglîzi* |
| Where is the telegraph-office? | wain bait ittil-grâf? | *fên bêt ettelegrâf?* |
| What is the charge for a telegram of twenty words to ..? | ḳaddaish' ijrit tilgrâf 'ishrîn kilmi la...? | *kâm ugrat tele-grâf 'eshrîn kil-me li...?* |

| | | |
|---|---|---|
| **Where can I change a few lire into small money?** | wain biḳdir iṣrif (or ṣarrif) kam lîra biḳi'ṭa'? | *fên aṛdar aṣrif (or aṣar'raf or afukkê) kâm bintu?* |
| **Where is there a money-changer (banker)?** | wain fî ṣirrâf (bankêr)? | *fên wâḥid ṣarrâf?* |
| **I do not feel well, I wish to see a doctor** | mâli kêf, baddi shûf ḥakîm | *mâlîsh' kêf, biddi ashûf ḥakîm* |
| 4 **Take me to an English (German) doctor** | waṣṣil'ni la'and' shî ḥakîm inglîzi (almâni) | *waddîni 'andê ḥakîm inglîzi (almâni)* |
| **Where is there a pharmacy?** | wain fî ijzâ-î'yi (or farmashîyi)? | *fên waḥde agzakhâne?* |

*Renting a Room or a House*

| | | |
|---|---|---|
| **Find me a well situated room in a decent house** | shufli ûḍa fî bait awâdim mauka''ha mlîḥ | *shûfli ôḍa fî bêt nâs awâdim mauḳi''ha melîḥ* |
| 7 **They tell me you have rooms to let** | ḳâlû'li inno 'indak uwaḍ lilki'ri | *ḳâlû'li innê 'andak uwaḍ lilki're* |
| **Yes, Sir, I have several rooms** | na'am, yâ sîdi, 'indi jimlit uwaḍ | *aiwa, yâ sîdi, 'andi gumlet uwaḍ* |
| **I want a furnished room** | lâzim'li maḥall' mafrûsh | *lâzim'li maḥall'ê mafrûsh* |
| 10 **I can only give you an unfurnished room (I cannot ..unless without furniture)** | mâ biḳdir a'ṭîk illa ûḍa bala farsh | *mâ aḳdarsh' a'ṭîk illa ûḍa min ṛêr farsh* |
| **I want no costly furniture** | mush lâzim'li farsh tamîn | *mush lâzim'li farshê temîn* |
| **The necessary suffices me: a bed, a table, a few chairs, and a chest of drawers** | byikfîni iḍḍrûri: farshi, ṭauli, kam kursi ubirô | *yikfîni eḍḍarûri: serîr, ṭarabêze, kâm kursi wadulâb* |

| | | |
|---|---|---|
| **I ask you to put these things into the room for me; otherwise I will not take it** | bitrajjâk tḥuṭṭli halish'ya bilûḍa; willa mâ bâkhid'ha | *batraggâk teḥuṭṭ'li elash'ye dôl filûḍa; walla mâ âkhud-hâsh'* |
| **Show me the apartment to let** | farrij'ni (or farjîni or warrîni) maḥall' ilij'ra | *warrîni maḥall' elug'ra* |
| **These two apartments are disengaged** | halmaḥallain' fâḍyîn' | *elmaḥallên dôl faḍyîn* |
| 4 **One of them suffices me** | wâḥid minhon byikfîni | *wâḥid minhum yikfîni* |
| **Choose** | naḳḳi or ikhtâr | *naḳḳi* or *ikhtâr* |
| **Perhaps I will take them both** | byimkin bâkhid'hon tnainhon | *yimkin âkhud eletnên* |
| 7 **This apartment seems damp; its air is heavy** | mbaiyin halmaḥall' ruṭib, hawâh tḳîl | *elbai'yin elmaḥall'ê di riṭib, hawâh teḳîl* |
| **This apartment is much exposed to the sun** | halmaḥall' maḥkûm lishshams' ktîr | *elmaḥal'lê di meḥakkim lishshem'sê ketîr* |
| **Do the doors and the windows close well (lit., are .. in order)?** | ilibwâb wishbâbîk' maḍbûṭîn'? | *libwâb washebâbîk' mazbûṭîn'?* |
| 10 **This pane is broken, you must repair it** | halḳizâz maksûr, baddak tṣallḥo | *elḳizâz di maksûr, lâzim tiṣal'laḥo* |
| **I shall not give you a para of the rent until everything is repaired** | mâ ba'ṭîk miṣrîyi mnilij'ra ḳabl mâ yitṣal'laḥ kull shî | *mâ adîkshê ḥâge minelug'ra ḳablê mâ yiṣṣal'laḥ kulli shê* |
| **The walls, too, must be whitewashed before I move into the house** | kazâlik ilḥîṭân' lâzim'hon ṭarsh ḳabl mâ idkhul liddâr | *kezâlik elḥîṭân' lâzim'hum biyâḍ ḳablê mâ adkhul elbêt* |
| 13 **The large room on the ground-floor** | ilman'zara | *elman'zara* |
| **.. upstairs** | ilḳâ'a | *elḳâ'a* |

| | | |
|---|---|---|
| **I want a somewhat larger apartment (the lower story or the upper story of a house, a small house)** | lâzim'li maḥall' kbîr shwaiyi (iṭṭâbiḳ ittiḥtâni yimma iṭṭâbiḳ ilfûḳâ'ni, bait zṛîr) | *lâzim'li maḥall'ê kebîr shuwai'ye (eddôr ettaḥtâni walla eddôr el-fôḳâ'ni, bêt zu-ṛai'yar)* |
| **You had better instruct an agent to get you such an apartment** | ilau'faḳ twaṣṣi samsâr tâ ydab-bir'lak haik ma-ḥall' | *elau'faḳ tiwaṣ'ṣi simsâr yeshûf-lak maḥall'ê zê-yi di* |
| **Find me lodgings (a dwelling-house)** | dabbir'li maḥall' lissa'kan (ḥâra) | *shûfli maḥall'ê lissa'kan (bêt)* |
| **4 How many rooms must there be?** | kam ûḍa lâzim ykûn fîh (**if referring to** ḥâra; fîha)? | *kâm ôḍa tekûn fîh?* |
| **I want a house with three (four, five, six, seven, eight, nine) rooms, also a kitchen and a larder** | lâzim'li bait (or dâr) tlâtt (arba'‘t, khamst, sitt, sa-ba‘t, tmânt, ti-sa‘t) uwaḍ umaṭ'-bakh ubait' lil-mûni | *lâzim'li bêt telât (arba‘, khamas, sitt, saba‘, te-mân, tis‘a) uwaḍ wemaṭ-bakh wekerâr* |
| **I have found a house for you** | shuftil'lak (or dabbartil'lak) bait | *shuftil'lak bêt* |
| **7 Well, come to me to-day in the afternoon at five o'clock that we may go to see it** | ṭaiyib, ta‘ala‘an'-di ilyaum' ba‘d iḍḍuhr' issâ‘a khamsi tanrûḥ nshûfo | *ṭaiyib, ta‘âle ‘an-di ennahar'da ba‘d eḍḍuhr' es-sâ‘a khamse ne-rûḥ neshûfo* |
| **Send for the proprietor of the house or his agent** | waddîlna wara ṣâḥib ilbait' yim-ma wakîlo | *ib‘at liṣâḥib elbêt walla wekîlo* |
| **Without doubt this house is damp** | lâ shakk halbait' ruṭib | *mâ fîsh shekk elbêt riṭib* |
| **10 This house is close (suffocating); it has neither air nor light** | haddâr mṛimmi (or fiṭsa); mâ ilha hawa ulâ ḍau | *elbêt di muṛimm' (or fiṭis); mâ lôsh hawa wala nûr* |

| | | |
|---|---|---|
| **I want an open (detached) and airy house** | baddi bait maṭlûḳ ushi'riḥ | *biddi bêt ṭiliḳ washi'riḥ* |
| **The kitchen is very small** | ilmaṭ'bakh zrîr ktîr | *elmaṭ'bakh zuṛai'yar ḳawi* |
| **Has this house no stable and no coachhouse ?** | haddâr mâ liha yâkhûr' ulâ maḥall' lilʿarabîyât' ? | *elbêt di mâ lôsh iṣṭabl' walâ arbakhâne ?* |
| 4 **What is the rent of this house ?** | ḳaddaiṣh' ijrit haddâr ? | *kâm ugrat elbêt di ?* |
| **For how long do you want it ?** | ʿala ḳaddaish' baddak yâha ? | *ʿala kâm ʿâ-izoh ?* |
| **For three months, for six months, for a year** | ʿala tlâtt ishhur, ʿala sitt ishhur, ʿala sini | *ʿala telât ushhur, ʿala sitt ushhur, ʿala sene* |
| 7 **I cannot let it for less than (lit., unless for) two years** | mâ biḳdir ikrîha illa ʿala sintain' | *mâ aḳdarsh akrîh illa ʿala senetên* |
| **The rent per year is two thousand (four thousand five hundred) piastres** | kirâha bissi'ni alfain' (arbaʿtâlâf' ukhamsmît) ḳirsh | *kir'weto bisse'ne alfên (arbaʿt âlâf' wekhumsmîyet) ḳirsh* |
| **The payment for the two years (to be made) in advance** | idda'faʿ ʿassintain' salaf | *edda'faʿ ʿassanatên muḳad'dam* |
| 10 **That is a hard condition** | haida sharṭ ḳawi | *di sharṭê ḳawi* |
| **That is the custom here** | hai ʿâdit ilba'lad | *di ʿâdet elbe'led* |
| **I accept on condition that I have the right to renew the lease at the same price, even if it (the house) could bring in more** | biḳbal bsharṭ in ykûnli ḥaḳḳ jaddid ajârha bihalij'ra wlau jâbit aktar | *aḳbal bisharṭ' in yekûn lîye ḥaḳḳ agad'did el-igâr bilug'ra dî welau' gâbet aktar* |

| | | |
|---|---|---|
| **All repairs which may be necessary whilst you occupy it are at your charge** | kull ittiṣlîḥât' il-lāzmi muddit illi tiskun fîha ʿala ḥsābak | *kull ettaṣlîḥât' el-lâzime muddet ma tiskun fîh ʿala ḥisâbak* |
| **But you must hand over the house to me in good repair** | lākin bitsallim'ni iddâr ṣâṛ salîm | *lâkin tisallim'ni elbêt ṣâṛ salîm* |
| **You must have the rooms white-washed and all the doors and windows repaired before I enter** | lāzim tiṭrush ilu'waḍ witṣal'-liḥ kull ilibwāb wishshbābîk' ḳabl mā idkhul | *lâzim tibai'yaḍ elu'waḍ wati-ṣal'laḥ kull lib-wâb washshe-bâbîk' ḳablê mâ adkhul* |
| 4 **Has this house no garden?** | haddâr mā liha jnaini? | *elbêt di mâlôsh genêne?* |
| **No, Sir, the garden belongs to the neighbors** | lâ, yâ sîdi, ij-jnai'ni lijjîrân' | *lâ, yâ sîdi, egge-nêne betâʿ eggî-rân'* |
| **Is there water in the house?** | iddâr fîha moi? | *elbêt fîh moiye?* |
| 7 **In the yard there is a well with very good water (there is a cistern with rain water)** | fîlḥaush' fî bîr moiyto ṭaiybi ktîr (fî ṣahrîj moiyt maṭar) | *filḥôsh bîr moi-yeto ṭaiyibe ḳawi (fîh ṣahrîg moi-yet maṭar)* |
| **I will consider it and give you a decisive (last) answer the day after to-morrow** | bifti'kir ubaʿṭîk ijjawāb ilḳaṭ'ʿi (or ākhir jawâb) baʿdbuk'ra | *afti'kir weaʿṭîk eggawâb elḳaṭ'ʿi (or âkhir gawâb) baʿdêbuk'ra* |

## *Engagement of a Servant*

| | | |
|---|---|---|
| **Can you recommend me a good servant?** | btiḳdir twaṣṣîni ʿala khâdim mlîḥ? | *tiṛdar tiwaṣṣîli ʿala khaddâm melîḥ?* |
| 10 **Yes, Sir, my (male) cousin serves well** | naʿam, yâ sîdi, ibn ʿammi byikh-dum ṭaiyib | *aiwa, yâ sîdi, ibnê ʿammi bikhdim ṭaiyib* |

| | | |
|---|---|---|
| **Go, fetch him that I may see him** | rûḥ jîbo tâ shûfo | *rûḥ hâto ʿala shân ashûfo* |
| **I hear from the proprietor of the hotel that your honor wants a servant** | smiʿt min ṣâḥib illukan'da in janâbak lâzmak khâdim | *simiʿt'ė min ṣâḥib ellokan'da innė genâbak lâzim'lak khaddâm* |
| **Yes, I am looking out for some one to serve me** | naʿam, ʿammâl fattish ʿala wâḥid yikhdum'ni | *aiwa, badau'war ʿala wâḥid yikhdim'ni* |
| 4 **What is your name?** | shû ismak? | *ismak ê?* |
| **Abdalla** | ʿabdal'la | *ʿabdal'la* |
| **How old are you?** | ḳaddaish' ʿumrak? | *ʿumrak kâm sane?* |
| 7 **Eighteen years** | tmanṭaʿ'sharsini | *temantâsher sane* |
| **Have you been in service before?** | khadamt' ḳabl halwaḳt'? | *khadam'tė ḳabla?* |
| **With whom were you hitherto?** | ʿind mîn kunt laḥadd' ilyaum'? | *ʿandė mîn kuntė liḥadd' el=ân?* |
| 10 **Why did you leave your master?** | laish dashshart' mʿallmak? | *saiyibt'ė meʿal'limak lê?* |
| **I did not leave him; he went away** | ana mâ dashshar'to; hû sâfar | *ana mâ saiyibtûsh; hûwe sâfir* |
| **Have you served in a European house?** | khadamt' fî bait franj? | *khadamt'ė fî bêt ifren'gi?* |
| 13 **Do you know how to serve well?** | btaʿrif tikhdum ṭaiyib? | *betaʿ'raf tikhdim ṭaiyib?* |
| **Tell me what you know** | ḳulli shû btaʿrif | *ḳulli betaʿ'raf ê* |
| **I know how to serve in the chamber and at table** | baʿrif ikhdum filûḍa uʿassuf'ra | *baʿraf akhdim filûḍa waʿassuf'ra* |
| 16 **Can you cook?** | btaʿrif tiṭbukh? | *betaʿ'raf tiṭbukh?* |
| **No, Sir, I cannot cook** | khair, yâ sîdi, mâ baʿrif iṭbukh | *lâ, yâ sîdi, mâ aʿraf'shi aṭbukh* |
| **But then I must have a cook** | lâkin ṣar lâzim'ni ʿashshi (or ṭabbâkh) | *lâkin yilzam'li ʿashshi* (or *ṭabbâkh*) |
| 19 **I can cook in Arabic fashion;** | ana baʿrif iṭbukh ʿarabi; min | *ana ʿâraf aṭbukh ʿarabi; min eṭṭa-* |

| | | |
|---|---|---|
| of the European cooking I know only a few dishes | ṭabkh ilfran'ji mâ baʿrif illa baʿḍ ishkâl | *bîkh elifren'gi mâʿaraf'shi illa baʿḍ ashkâl* |
| That suffices me | haida byikfîni | *di yikfîni* |
| Every morning you will sweep the house and the rooms, and dust the furniture | kull yaum ʿala bukra bitkan'nis iddâr wil-u'waḍ ubitnaf'fiḍ ila-wâʿi (or ilfarsh') | *kulli yôm fiṣṣubḥ tuknus elbêt wal-u'waḍ watinaf-faḍ elfarsh'* |
| Every Saturday you will scrub (scour) the house | kull yaum sabt tishṭuf iddâr | *kulli yôm essebt' tishṭuf elbêt* |
| 4 Look for a woman to scrub the house | dauwir ʿala mara tishṭuf iddâr | *dauwar ʿala mar-a tishṭuf elbêt* |
| Take care nothing in the house is broken and everything is always clean and in order | dîr bâlak lâ yink-sir shî filbait' wiykûn kull shî dâyman nḍîf wimrat'tab | *khalli bâlak mâ yinkisir'shi ḥâge filbêt wayekûn kulli shê dâ-iman naḍîf wa-murat'tab* |
| Every morning you will shake the clothes and brush them | kull yaum ʿala bukra bitnaf'fiḍ ittyâb ubitfar-shîha | *kulli yôm fiṣṣubḥ' tinaf'faḍ elhu-dûm wetfar-rash'ha* |
| 7 In the forenoon you will go to the market and buy all that is necessary for the house | ḳabl iḍḍuhr' bit-rûḥ lissûḳ wib-tish'tri kull mâ yilzam lilbait' | *ḳabl eḍḍuhr' te-rûḥ lissûḳ wa-tish'tiri kulli mâ yilzam lilbêt* |
| The supper must be ready every day at six o'clock | ilʿa'sha baddo ykûn ḥâḍir kull yaum issâʿa sitti | *elʿa'she yekûn ḥâ-ḍir kulli yôm essâʿa sitte* |
| What wages would you like? | ḳaddaish' bitrîd ijra? | *kâm ʿâ-iz ugra?* |
| 10 What you will, Sir | ḳadd mâ bitrîd, yâ sîdi | *zê mâ terîd, yâ sîdi* |
| I will give you a hundred piastres and board | baʿṭîk mît ḳirsh bilmûni (or mmauwan) | *aʿṭîk mît ḳirsh bilmûne (or mu-mau'wan)* |

## *Service in the House*

| | | | |
|---|---|---|---|
| | **What do you command, Sir?** | shû bit=âmir, yâ sîdi? | *betu='mur ê, yâ sîdi?* |
| | **I will dress (put on my clothes)** | baddi ilbis tyâbi | *biddi albis hudûmi* |
| | **Give me the clothes** | a‘ṭîni ittyâb | *a‘ṭîni elhudûm* |
| 4 | **These trousers are covered with (lit., are all) mud; why did you not shake and brush them properly?** | halbanṭalûn kullo waḥl; laish mâ naffaḍ'to ufarrash'to ṭaiyib? | *elbanṭalûn di kullo waḥl; lê mâ naffaḍtôsh wafarrashtôsh ṭaiyib?* |
| | **Bring me a shirt and a collar** | jibli ḳamîṣ uḳab'bi | *hâtli ḳamîṣ wayâḳa* |
| | **Give me my pants, my socks, and my trousers** | a‘ṭîni lbâsi ukilsâti ubanṭalûni | *a‘ṭîni libâsi washarabâti wabanṭalûni* |
| 7 | **These socks are torn** | halkilsât nâḳbîn' | *eshsharabât dôl manḳûbîn'* |
| | **Mend them (or have them mended)** | ḳaṭṭib'hon | *ḳaṭṭab'hum* or *irfîhum* |
| | **Bring another pair** | hait jauz ṛairo | *hât gôz tâni* |
| 10 | **Bring me the slippers** | haitli ilḳaltshîn | *hâtli elbâbûg'* |
| | **Bring water for washing** | jîb moi lilṛasîl | *hât moiye lilṛasîl* |
| | **Bring water for drinking** | jîb moi lishshirb' | *hât moiye lishshurb'* |
| 13 | **Fill the jug** | malli ilbrîḳ (or ishshar'bi) | *imla el=ebrîḳ* |
| | **Pour hot water in the wash-hand basin** | ḥuṭṭ moi sukhni billa'kan | *ḥuṭṭê moiye sukhne fiṭṭîsht* |
| | **I want to shave** | baddi iḥluḳ | *biddi aḥlaḳ* |
| 16 | **This razor is of no use; it is full of notches** | halmûs mâ byinfa‘; munsa'lim | *elmûs di mâ binfa‘sh'; munsa'lim* |
| | **The razors will not cut** | ilmwâs mâ bitḳuṣṣ | *elamwâs mâ biḥlaḳûsh* |

| | | |
|---|---|---|
| **Give them to the barber to grind** | aʿṭîha lilḥillâḳ yjallikh'ha | *aʿṭîha lilmezai'yin yigallakh'ha* |
| **Where is the soap and my looking-glass?** | wain iṣṣâbû'ni wilmrâyi? | *fên eṣṣâbû'ne walmirâye?* |
| **This water is too hot** | halmoi' sukhni ktîr | *elmoi'ye di sukhne ketîr* |
| 4 **Put cold water to it** | zîd ʿalai'ha moi bârdi | *zid ʿalêha moiye bâride* |
| **Bring me a towel** | aʿṭîni fûṭa | *aʿṭîni fûṭa* |
| **Have you cleaned the boots (i.e. half-boots) for me?** | masaḥtil'li illastîk? | *masaḥti'ni ellastîk?* |
| 7 **Why have you not yet cleaned the (legged) boots?** | laish lahal'laḳ mâ masaḥt' ijjaz'mi? | *lê lidilwaḳt' mâ masaḥ'tish eggaz'me?* |
| **What laziness is this!** | shû halka'sal! | *êsh elka'sal di!* |
| **Brush my hat** | farshîli ilburnai'ṭa | *farrash'li elburnêṭa* |
| 10 **Give me the brush** | aʿṭîni ilfirshâyi | *aʿṭîni elfur'she* |
| **I cannot find it** | mani shâyif'ha | *mânish shâ-if'ha* |
| **Give me my handkerchief, gloves, and umbrella** | aʿṭîni maḥrami wilkfûf wishshamsîyi | *aʿṭîni mandîl wal - eldiwân washshemsîye* |
| 13 **Give me the purse (the book) which is on the table in the study (in the drawing-room, in the dining-room, in the bedroom)** | aʿṭîni ilkîs (ilktâb) illi ʿala ṭaulit ilmak'tab (ilḳâʿa, ûḍit issuf'ra, ûḍit innaum') | *aʿṭîni elkîs (elkitâb) elli ʿala ṭarabêzet elmak'tab (eṣṣalûn, ôḍat essuf'ra, ôḍat ennôm)* |
| **Empty the wash-hand basin (the bucket, the chamber)** | kubb illa'kan (issaṭl', ilardîyi or ilmustaʿmali) | *kubb eṭṭisht' (essaṭl', elḳaṣrîye)* |
| **Wash my feet, my head** | naṭṭil ijrai'yi, râsi | *naṭṭil riglêye, râsi* |

| | | |
|---|---|---|
| **Bring me a few jugs of water; I wish to have a bath** | jibli kam jarrit moi; baddi it-ṛas'sal | *hâtli kâm abrîk moiyi; biddi astaḥam'mê* |
| **Give me a glass of water** | a'ṭîni shirbit moi (or kubbâyit moi) | *a'ṭînî shurbet moiye* (or *kubbâ-yet moiye*) |
| **This glass is dirty; wash it** | halkubbâyi wus-kha; ṛassil'ha | *elkubbâye dî wis-kha; iṛsil'ha* |
| 4 **Bring me the coffee (the tea, the milk, the bread, the butter, the cheese, the sugar)** | jibli ilḳa'hwi (ishshai', ilḥa-lîb, ilkhubz', iz-zib'di, ijjibn', issuk'kar) | *hâtli elḳah'we (eshshây, elle'-ben, el'êsh, ez-zib'de, eggibn', essuk'kar)* |
| **Why did you not get (look for) fresh butter this morning?** | laish mâ fat-tasht' ilyaum' 'ala bukra 'ala z bdi ṭarîyi? | *lê mâ dauwar'-tish ennahar'da fiṣṣub'ḥê 'ala zib-de tâza?* |
| **Put water on the fire and let it boil quickly** | ḥuṭṭ moi 'annâr ukhallîha tiṛli ḳawâm | *ḥuṭṭê moiye 'an-nâr wekhallîha tiṛli ḳawâm* |
| 7 **Make the bed** | sauwi ilfar'shi | *sauwi elfar'she* |
| **Every morning you will raise the mosquito curtain and in the evening before I go to sleep you will lower it** | kull yaum 'ala bukra tirfa' in-nâmûsî'yi w'a-shîyi ḳabl mâ nâm tnazzil'ha | *kulli yôm eṣṣub'ḥê tirfa' ennâmû-sî'ye wal'i'she ḳablê mâ anâm tinazzil'ha* |
| **Why did you not sweep the house?** | laish mâ kannast' ilbait'? | *lê mâ kanas'tish elbêt?* |
| 10 **Brush the room, the drawing-room** | kannis ilûḍa, iṣṣâlya | *kannis elôḍa, eṣṣâle* |
| **Sprinkle a little water in the house and before the door** | rishsh shwaiyit moi biddâr uḳuddâm ilbâb | *rushshê shu-wai'yet moiye fil-bêt weḳuddâm el-bâb* |
| **The table (i.e. the dining-table) must be ready in half an hour** | issuf'ra lâzim tkûn khâlṣa ba'd nuṣṣ sâ'a | *essuf'ra tekûn khalṣa ba'dê nuṣṣê sâ'a* |

| | | |
|---|---|---|
| **Lay the table** | mudd issuf'ra | *midd essuf'ra* |
| **Clear the table** | shîl (or ḳîm) issufra | *shîl essuf'ra* |
| **This bread is not good (lit., not conducive to health); fetch it from another baker in future** | halkhubz' mâ byiswa shî (or mâ byinfa' shî); ibḳa ishtri min 'ind ṛair khibbâz | *el'êsh di mâ binfa'sh'; ibḳa ishtiri min 'andê khabbâz tâni* |
| 4 **Bring tobacco (cigarettes, a nargileh)** | jîb tutun (sîgarât', argîli) | *hât dukhân (sigâra, shîshe)* |
| **Light the fire** | sha''il innâr | *walla' ennâr* |
| **Light the candle (the lamp)** | ḍauwi ishsham''a (ilḳandîl) | *walla' eshsham''a (ellam'da)* |
| 7 **Cut (trim) the wick and put in a little more paraffin** | ḳuṣṣ ilftîli uḥuṭṭ' kamân shwaiyit kâz | *ḳuṣṣ elfetîle weḥuṭṭ'ê kemân shuwai'yet gâz* |
| **Place the table beside the bed and put the light and the matches on it** | ḥuṭṭ iṭṭau'li jamb ilfar'shi uḥuṭṭ' 'alai'ha ishsham''a wishshiḥḥâṭa | *ḥuṭṭ eṭṭaraḃêze gamb elfar'she weḥuṭṭ' 'alêha eshsham''a walkibrît* |
| **Bring a night-light** | jîb nûwâ'si | *hât ḳauwâme* |
| 10 **Make (lit., spread) the bed** | ifrush ilfarsh' | *ifrish esserîr* |
| **Take off the coverlet and leave the sheet only** | ḳîm illḥâf ulâ tkhalli illa ishshar'shaf | *shîl elliḥâf wemâ tekhallîsh illa elmilâyât'* |
| **The coverlet is too thin; put (yet) the travelling-blanket over the bed-cover** | ilṛa'ṭa khafîf; ḥuṭṭ kamân ilḥrâm fauḳ illḥâf | *elṛa'ṭa khafîf; ḥuṭṭê kemân elḥirâm fôḳ elliḥâf* |
| 13 **Close the window and the shutters** | sakkir ilḳizâz wilkha'shab | *iḳfil eshshibbâk walkha'sheb* |
| **Leave one window and the door open** | khalli ṭâḳa wâḥdi wilbâb maftûḥîn' | *khalli shibbâk wâḥid walbâb maftûḥîn'* |
| **Lock the door** | sakkir or uḳful ilbâb | *sakkir* or *uḳful elbâb* |

| | | |
|---|---|---|
| **The bed is very hard** | ilfar'shi ķâsyi ktîr | *elfar'she gamde ketîr* |
| **Leave the light; if I cannot sleep at once I shall read** | khalli iḍḍau'; iza mâ ķdirt nâm ḥâlan biķra | *khalli ennûr; iza mâ ķidir'tish anâm aķra* |
| **Go to bed now** | rûḥ nâm hallaķ | *rûḥ nâm dilwaķt'* |
| 4 **Put the light out** | iṭfi iḍḍau' | *iṭfi ennûr* |
| **Do not forget to put the lamp out** | lâ tinsa tiṭfi ilķandîl | *mâ tinsâsh tiṭfi ellam'da* |
| **Do not forget to call me to-morrow morning at 6 o'clock** | lâ tinsa tfaiyiķ'ni bukra issâʿa sitti | *mâ tinsâsh tiṣaḥḥîni bukra essâʿa sitte* |
| 7 **Sew this button on my trousers and sew up this seam (tear)** | rakkib'li hazzirr' lilbanṭalûn u-khaiyiṭ'li halfitķ' | *rakkib'li ezzurâr di lilbanṭalûn wekhaiyaṭ'li elfat'ķe di* |
| **Buy (some) needles (thread, pins, buttons, shirt-buttons)** | ishtri ibar (khîṭân', dabâbîs', zrâr, zrâr lilķumṣân) | *ishtiri ibar (khîṭân', debâbîs', zurâr, zurâr lilķumṣân)* |
| **Order me a carriage for three o'clock in the afternoon** | waṣṣîli ʿala ʿarabîyi lissâʿa tlâti baʿd iḍḍuhr' | *waṣṣîli ʿala ʿarabîye lissâʿa talâte baʿd eḍḍuhr'* |
| 10 **But it must be at the door at three o'clock punctually** | lâkin lâzim tkûn issâʿa tlâti tamâm ķuddâm ilbâb | *lâkin lâzim tekûn essâʿa telâte tamâm ķuddâm elbâb* |
| **Settle (fix) the price per hour with the proprietor of the carriage** | ifṣul ilij'ra ʿassâʿa maʿ ṣâḥib ilʿarabîyi | *ifṣil elug'ra ʿassâʿa maʿa ṣâḥib elʿarabîye* |
| **Bridle the horse; I will ride** | iljim ilḥṣân; baddi irkab | *laggim elḥuṣân; biddi arkab* |
| 13 **Stay in the house until I return** | khallîk filbait' tâ irjaʿ | *khallîk filbêt liḥadd' argaʿ* |
| **Stay here until he comes** | uķʿud ila an yeji | *uķʿud ila an yegi* |

| | | |
|---|---|---|
| **Woe to you if you go out of the house during my absence** | îyâk' tiṭlaʿ mnil-bait' bṛaibti | *îyâk' tiṭlaʿ min elbêt biṛêbeti* |
| **Let no one enter the house** | lâ tkhalli ḥada yfût lilbait' | *mâ tikhallîsh ḥad yekhushsh' elbêt* |
| **If any one asks for me tell him that I am not at home** | iza ḥada saʾal ʿanni, ḳullo minni filbait' | *iza saʾal ḥad ʿalêye, ḳullo inni mush filbêt* |
| 4 **Do not forget to lock the house securely if you go out** | lâ tinsa tiḳful (or tsakkir) il-bait' mlîḥ iza ṭliʿt labar'ra | *mâ tinsâsh tiḳfil* (or *tesukk*) *elbêt ṭaiyib iza ṭiliʿt'ê barra* |
| **Water the flowers (the garden)** | isḳi izzhûr (ij-jnai'ni) | *isḳi elʾazhâr (eg-genêne)* |
| **Take this flower-pot (flower-pots) out** | khôd hashshaḳ'fi (shiḳaf) labar'ra | *shîl elḳaṣrîye dî (elḳaṣâri dôl) barra* |
| 7 **You must obey me instantly (without questioning)** | lâzim ṭâwiʿ'ni fiddaḳîḳa (min ṛair mrâjaʿa) | *lâzim tiṭâwiʿ'ni fiddaḳîḳa (min ṛêr murâgaʿa)* |
| **Why do you not do what I tell you?** | laish mâ btaʿmil ishshî illi bḳul-lak ʿanno? | *lê mâ betiʿmil'shi elli baḳul'lak ʿalêh?* |
| **If you continue so with this laziness (if this laziness continues) I shall deduct something from your wages** | iza kân biddall' ʿala halka'sal, bikhṣum ʿalaik' min ijrtak | *iza kân tibḳa ʿalke'sel di, akh-ṣim ʿalêk min ugretak* |

*With the Laundress*

| | | |
|---|---|---|
| 10 **Can you recommend me a woman who washes and irons well?** | btiḳdir twaṣṣîli ʿala mara tṛassil utik'wi mlîḥ? | *tiṛdar'shi tiwaṣ-ṣîli ʿala marʾa tiṛsil wetik'wi ṭaiyib?* |
| **Are you the laundress of the house (of the hotel)?** | inti ṛassâlit il-bait' (illukan'-da)? | *enti ṛassâlet elbêt (ellokan'da)?* |

| | | |
|---|---|---|
| **Do you know how to wash and iron well?** | bta'rifi trassli utik'wi mlîḥ? | *beti'rafi tirsi'li wetik'wi ṭaiyib?* |
| **I have linen to be washed** | 'indi tyâb lilṛasîl | *'andi hudûm lil-ṛasîl* |
| **Wash it (Arab. plur.) well** | ṛassilîhon ṭaiyib | *iṛsilîhum ṭaiyib* |
| 4 **When will you bring me the washing?** | aimta bitjîbî'li ilṛasîl? | *imte tegîbî'li el-ṛasîl?* |
| **The next week** | jum'it iṭṭâl'a (or ijjâyi) | *eggum''a eggâ-iye* |
| **I want it in three days** | byilzam'ni ba'd tlâtt îyâm' | *yilzam'li ba'dê telât aiyâm* |
| 7 **I will do my utmost to bring it to you** | ba'mil juhdi tâ jiblak yâh | *ba'mil guhdi lam-ma agibuh'lak* |
| **Do not keep me waiting long (do not make me tarry for it); I have no linen left** | lâ tit'au'waḳi 'alai'yi fîh; mâ biḳi 'indi tyâb | *mâ tit-akhkha-rîsh 'alêye; mâ baḳatshi 'andi hudûm* |
| **You will darn the torn socks and sew on the missing buttons** | tibḳi tirtîli ilkil-sât innâḳbîn' witrakk'bi iz-zrâr innâḳṣîn' | *tibḳi tirfîli esh-sharabât elman-ḳûbîn' waterak-ki'bi el-az'rire ennaḳṣîn* |
| 10 **In a word, all that needs repairing must be repaired** | ilḥâṣil kull shî byilzamo tiṣlîḥ lâzim yitṣal'laḥ | *elḥâṣil kulli shê yilzamo taṣlîḥ lâzim yiṣṣal'laḥ* |
| **To mend the garments** | ṣallaḥ or raḳḳa' issiyâb (or ittyâb) | *ṣallaḥ or raḳḳa' essiyâb (or etti-yâb)* |
| **Here is the washing-bill** | hai ḳâymit ilṛasîl | *âdi' ḳâ-imet elṛa-sîl* |
| 13 **I will read it to you, and you will see if it is right (exact)** | biḳrâlik yâha witshûfi iza kânit ṣaḥîḥa (maḍbûṭa) | *baḳrâhâ'lik wa-teshûfi iza kânet ṣaḥîḥa (mazbû-ṭa)* |
| **But you must bring me this list again (with you)** | lâkin baddik trajji'i hal-ḳâymi ma'ik | *lâkin lâzim ti-rag'ga'i elḳâ-ime dî mi'âki* |

| | | |
|---|---|---|
| **Whatever is missing (of the things) will be charged its full price** | illi bîkhîṣ' mnilawâ'i byinḥsib ḥaḳḳo bittamâm | *elli yekhissê min elḥawâ=ig yinḥisib ḥaḳḳo bittemâm* |
| **How much do you charge (lit., take) for the dozen ?** | ḳaddaish' btâkhdi 'addazzîni? | *ḳaddî ê betakh'di 'addasta ?* |
| **Twelve piastres, Sir** | ṭna'shar ḳirsh, yâ khawâja | *etnâsher ḳirsh, yâ khawâga* |
| 4 **I have heard that everybody pays only ten piastres for the dozen** | smi't inn ilkull' mâ byidfa'u illa 'ashr ḳurûsh 'addazzîni | *simi't' innê kullî nâs mâ yidfa'ûsh illa 'ashara ḳurûsh 'addaste* |
| **Pay what you will, Sir** | idfa' ḳadd mâ bitrîd, yâ sîdi | *idfa' ḳaddê mâ terîd, yâ sîdi* |
| **Washing-bill** | ḳâymit ilṛasîl | *ḳâ=imet elṛasîl* |
| **Six shirts** | sitt ḳumṣân | *sitte ḳumṣân* |
| 7 **Four shirts with collars** | arba' ḳumṣân bḳabbât | *arba'at ḳumṣân biyâḳât'* |
| **Two nightshirts** | ḳamîṣain' linnaum' | *ḳamîṣên' linnôm* |
| **Six pairs of socks** | sitt ijwâz kilsât | *sittigwâz sharabât* |
| 10 **Two flannel pants** | lbâsain' fanel'la | *libâsên' fanel'la* |
| **Three white trousers** | tlât banṭalûnât' bîḍ | *telât banṭalûnât' bîḍ* |
| **Two woollen vests (waistcoats)** | ṣidrîytain' ṣûf | *ṣidêriyên' ṣûf* |
| 13 **One white vest** | ṣidrîyi baiḍa | *ṣidêri abyaḍ* |
| **Two nightcaps** | 'arḳîytain' linnaum' | *'araḳîyetên' linnôm* |
| **Six silk pocket-handkerchiefs** | sitt maḥârim ḥarîr | *sitte menâdîl' ḥarîr* |
| 16 **Six white pocket-handkerchiefs** | sitt maḥârim bîḍ | *sitte menâdîl' bîḍ* |
| **Six neckties** | sitt rabṭât raḳbi | *sitte rabṭât raḳabe (karawât)* |
| **One neckcloth** | miḥramet irraḳ'bi | *miḥramet erra'ḳabe* |

| | | |
|---|---|---|
| Two gowns (robes) | fuṣṭânain' | *fuṣṭânên'* |
| Three petticoats | tlât tanânîr' | *telâte tenânîr'* |
| Twelve serviettes (cloths) with a red border | ṭna'shar fûṭa bi-ḥawâshi ḥumr | *etnâsher fûṭa bi-ḥawâshi ḥumr* |
| 4 Six plain cloths | sitt fuwaṭ sâda | *sitte fuwaṭ sâde* |
| Six towels | sitt mnâshif | *sitte menâshif* |
| Three aprons | tlât wazrât | *telâte wazrât* |
| 7 Four sheets | arba' sharâshif | *arba'a milâyât'* |
| Four pillow-cases | arba' ṛashâwât' mukhad'di | *arba'tikyâs mekhad'de* |
| Another time I will ask you to come earlier | ṛair marra bit-rajjâki tiji bakkîr | *marra tâniye bat-raggâki tigi bedri* |
| 10 This collar is not well folded | halḳab'bî mâ hî maṭwîyi mlîḥ | *elyâḳa dî mush maṭwîye ṭaiyib* |
| This waistcoat and these cuffs are not sufficiently starched | haṣṣidrîyi uhalk-mâm mâ hinni mnashshâyîn' bilkfâyi | *eṣṣidêri dî weluk-mâm dôl mush munashshâyîn' bilkifâye* |
| This is not well ironed | haida mâ hû mikwi mlîḥ | *di mush makwi ṭaiyib* |
| 13 Take this robe and wash it over again (lit., anew) | khudi halfuṣṭân urass'lîh min auwil wijdîd | *khudi etfuṣṭân di wersilîh min auwal wagedîd* |

*In the Bath*

| | | |
|---|---|---|
| The water for bathing | ilmoi' li=ttaṛas'-sul | *elmoi'ye li=ttaṛas'sul* |
| The proprietor of the bath | iṣṣâḥib ilḥam-mâm | *eṣṣâḥib elḥam-mâm* |
| 16 Cloak-room attendant | nâṭûr' | *nâṭûr'* |
| Take me into a special room that I may take off my clothes [shoes] | khudni la=ûḍa makhṣûṣa tâ ishlaḥ tyâbi | *khudni li=ôḍa makhṣûṣe aḳla' hudûmi* |
| Bring the wooden | jîb ilkibkâb | *hât elkubkâb* |
| 19 Bring cloths | jîb fuwaṭ | *hât fuwaṭ* |

| | | |
|---|---|---|
| **Hold me that I may not fall; I am not accustomed to walking in wooden shoes** | imsik'ni tâ mâ ûḳa'; mani m'auwad 'ala mashi ilḳibḳâb | *imsik'ni 'ala shân mâ ḳâ'-shi; mânish mit'au'wid 'ala mashi elḳubḳâb* |
| **Take me first into the intermediate room that I may rest a little and afterwards go into the innermost (room)** | khudni bilau'wal lilwasṭâni tâ irtâḥ shwaiyi uba''do idkhul l'jjûwâ'ni | *khudni bilau'wal lilwusṭâni artâḥ shuwai'ye we-ba''dên adkhul elgûwâ'ni* |
| **Bring us a cup (bowl) of lemonade** | jiblna kâsit lai-mûnâ'ḍa | *hâtlina kubbâyet lêmûnâ'ta* |
| **4 I will enter the innermost** | baddi fût lij-jûwâ'ni | *biddi akhush'shê elgûwâ'ni* |
| **In there it is very hot** | jûwa ḥâmi ktîr | *gûwa ḥâmi ḳawi* |
| **Attendant! come, rub me down** | yâ mkaiyis! ta'a kaiyis'ni | *yâ mekai'yis! ta-'âle kaiyis'ni* |
| **7 If you will perspire freely, sit down on the hot stone** | iza kân baddak ti'raḳ ktîr, uḳ'ud 'ala bait innâr | *iza kân biddak ti'raḳ ketîr, iḳ-'ud 'ala bêt en-nâr* |
| **The water is too hot** | ilmoi' sukhni | *elmoi'ye sukhne* |
| **Open the tap and let in cold water** | iftaḥ ilḥanafîyi ubarrid'ha | *iftaḥ elḥanafîye webarrad'ha* |
| **10 Enough, I will go out** | ḥâji, baddi iṭla' | *bess, biddi aṭla'* |
| **These cloths are not clean** | halfu'waṭ mâ hî ndîfi | *elfu'waṭ dôl mush nuḍâf* |
| **Bring others** | jîb ṛairhon | *hât ṛêrhum* |
| **13 Give me my clothes** | a'ṭîni tyâbi | *e'ṭîni hudûmi* |
| **Bring the looking-glass** | jîb ilmrâyi | *hât elmirâye* |
| **Here is the money for the bath** | hai ijrit ilḥam-mâm | *âdi' ugrat elḥam-mâm* |
| **16 Too little, Sir** | ḳalîli, yâ khawâ-ja | *shuwai'ye yâ kha-wâga* |

| | | |
|---|---|---|
| **Take this, and all the other gratuities are to be settled by you** | khôd haudi wibkîyit ilbakhshîsh ‘alaik′ | *khod dôl wabaḳiyet elbaḳshîsh ‘alêk* |

**See phrases 16 and 17 on next page.**

*At the Barber's*

| | | |
|---|---|---|
| **Take me to a barber (hairdresser)** | khudni la‘and′ ḥillâḳ | *waddîni ‘andê mezai′yin* |
| **Please to enter** | tfaḍḍal fût | *itfaḍ′ḍal khushsh* |
| **4 I wish to be shaved** | baddi iḥluḳ | *biddi aḥlaḳ* |
| **Ready (i.e. at your service), Sir** | ḥâḍir, yâ sîdi | *ḥâḍir, yâ sîdi* |
| **The water is not hot** | ilmoi′ mâ hî sukhni | *elmoi′ye mush sukhne* |
| **7 The water is too hot; add cold to it** | ilmoi′ sukhni; barrid′ha | *elmoi′ye sukhne; barrad′ha* |
| **The razor is no good** | ilmûs mâ byinfa‘ | *elmûs mâ binfa‘sh′* |
| **Take care (not) to cut me** | twaḳḳa (or û‘a) tijraḥ′ni | *û‘a tigraḥ′ni* |
| **10 Fear nothing** | mâ ‘alaik′ or lâ tkhâf | *mâ ‘alêsh or mâ tekhafsh′* |
| **Your hand is light, but your razors are bad** | îdak khafîfi, lâkin mwâsak ‘âṭlîn′ | *îdak khafîfe, lâkin amwâsak ‘aṭlîn* |
| **Sharpen them** | jallikh′hon (or khudhon ‘alḳâyish) | *gallakh′hum* |
| **13 My hair is hard** | sha‘ri ḳâsi | *sha‘ri ḳâsi* |
| **Wet it well** | billo mlîḥ | *billo ṭaiyib* |
| **Use plenty of soap** | kattir iṣṣâbûn′ | *kattar eṣṣâbûn′* |
| **16 This soap has a dreadful smell** | haṣṣâbû′ni rîḥit′ha bish‘a | *eṣṣâbû′ne dî rîḥit′ha bish‘a* |
| **Oh! what have you done?** | akh! shû ‘imilt′? | *akh! ‘amalt′ ê?* |
| **You have cut me** | jaraḥt′ni | *garaḥti′ni* |

| | | |
|---|---|---|
| **I am bleeding** | ṭiliʿ iddam | *ṭiliʿ eddamm'* |
| **Do not shave off too much** | lâ tkarriṭ ʿash-shaʿr' | *mâ tiḳarwaṭsh' eshshaʿr'* |
| **Shall (lit., will you that) I trim your moustache?** | bitrîd khaffif'lak shwârbak? | *ʿâ=iz akhaffif'lak shenabak?* |
| 4 **Shave the whole beard** | iḥluḳ'li daḳni kullha | *iḥlaḳ'li daḳni kulliha* |
| **Leave the moustache only, and shave the rest** | dashshir ish-shwârib bass w=iḥluḳ ilbâḳi | *khalli eshshe'nab bess wa=iḥ'laḳ elbâḳi* |
| **(the possessor of a fine moustache is:)** | â'bû shwârib | *â'bû shenab* |
| **Trim my beard a little** | khaffif'li iddaḳn' shwaiyi | *khaffif'li eddaḳ'-nê shuwai'ye* |
| 7 **Cut my hair; cut it short behind** | ḳuṣṣli shaʿri; ḳaṣṣro min wara | *ḳuṣṣê shaʿri; ḳaṣ-ṣaro min wara* |
| **Your scissors do not cut** | maḳaṣ'ṣak mâ bîḳuṣṣ' | *maḳaṣ'ṣak mâ bi-ḳuṣ'ṣish* |
| **Cut my hair a little shorter on both sides at the temples** | ḳaṣṣir'li ishshaʿr' shwaiyitlukhra ʿajjambain' ʿind ilmaṣâdiṛ | *ḳaṣṣar'li esh-shaʿr'ê kemân shuwai'ye ʿag-gambên ʿand eṣṣudûṛ* |
| 10 **Do not use much pomatum** | lâ tkattir ilbû-mâ'ḍa | *mâ tiktarshi el-bumâḍa* |
| **Put no pomatum at all (on my hair)** | lâ tḥuṭṭli bûmâ'-ḍa abadan | *mâ teḥuṭṭ'ish bu-mâḍa ebeden* |
| **Wash my head** | ṛassil'li râsi | *iṛsil râsi* |
| 13 **Make haste, finish** | ʿajjil, khalliṣ | *istaʿ'gil, khallaṣ* |
| **Enough!** | byikfi (or ḥâji)! | *bikaf' fi* (or *bess*)! |
| **Brush my clothes** | farshîli tyâbi | *farrash'li hudû-mi* |
| 16 **To one returned from the barber or bath: May it do you good!** | naʿîman! | *naʿîman!* |
| **Answer: May God favor you!** | Alla yinʿim ʿalaik'! | *Allâh yinʿim ʿalêk!* |

## *In the Café*

| | | |
|---|---|---|
| **Let us go into this café** | tanfût lahalḳah'wi | *nekhushsh' elḳah'we dî* |
| **We can talk there at our leisure** | mniḳdir nitḥad'das haunîk ʿala mahlna | *niḳdar nitḥad'dit henâk ʿala kêfna* |
| **Capital! I am all in a heat** | mnâsib! ana mshauwib ktîr | *munâsib! ana meshau'wib ketîr* |
| 4 **I am dying of thirst** | maiyit mnilʿa'ṭash | *maiyit min elʿa'ṭash* |
| **I must cool off** | baddi baurid | *yibrad gismi* |
| **I will take something refreshing** | baddi âkhud shî mraṭṭib | *biddi âkhud shê meraṭ'ṭab* |
| 7 **Boy! Bring a chair (two chairs)** | yâ walad! jîb kursi (kurstain') | *yâ waled! hât kursi (kursiyên)* |
| **What do you order, gentlemen?** | shû bit=âmru, yâ khawâjât'? | *betu'=muru ê, yâ khawâgât'?* |
| **Have you lemonade (ice)?** | ʿindak laimûnâ'da (bûza)? | *ʿandak lêmûnâ'ta (bûza)?* |
| 10 **I will drink only a cup of coffee** | ana mâ bishrab illa finjân ḳahwi | *ana mâ ashrabsh' illa fingân ḳahwe* |
| **Bring us two cups of coffee** | aʿṭina finjânain' ḳahwi | *eʿṭîna fingânên' ḳahwe* |
| **With or without sugar?** | bsukkar willa bala sukkar? | *bisuk'kar walla min ġêr sukkar (sâde)?* |
| 13 **Make (lit., give) it sweet** | haitha* ḥilwi | *hâtha* ḥilwe* |
| **Make (lit., give) it bitter** | haitha* murra | *hâtha* murra* |

* **Pronounce** hait-ha *hât-ha.*

| | | |
|---|---|---|
| 16 **I want a bowl of barley-water** | baddi kâsit bzûrât' | *biddi kubbâyet buzûrât'* |
| **Have you any English (Austrian) beer?** | fî ʿindak bîra inglîzî'yi (nimsâwî'yi)? | *ʿandak bîra inglîzî (nemsâwî)?* |
| **Bring us a bottle of English beer** | jiblna ḳannînit bîra inglîzî'yi | *hâtlina ḳizâzet bîra inglîzî'ye* |
| **Pale (white) ale** | bûze | *bûze* |

| | | |
|---|---|---|
| **A glass of water!** | kubbâyit moi! | *kubbâyet moiye!* |
| **Have you tobacco?** | ʿindak tutun? | *ʿandak dukhân?* |
| **Bring us a little tobacco (cigarette-paper, matches, a live coal)** | jiblna shwaiyit tutun (warḳit sîgâ'ra, shiḥḥâṭa, baṣṣit nâr) | *hâtlina shuwai'yet dukhân (waraḳat sîgâ'ra, kabrît, wilʿa)* |
| 4 **Make me a nargileh; but it must be clean and well prepared** | ʿabbîli argîli; lâkin tkûn nḍîfi unafas'ha mlîḥ | *ʿabbîli shîshe; lâkin tekûn naḍîfe wanefes'ha melîḥ* |
| **This tube is very dirty; it causes it to breathe, i.e. it is not air-tight** | hannabrîj wusikh ktîr; bînaf'fis | *ellai' di wisikh ḳawi; binaf'fis* |
| **Bring another tube** | jîb nabrîj ṛairo | *hât lai tâni* |
| 7 **Bring a live coal, i.e. a light** | jîb jamra (or nâra) | *hât wilʿa* |
| **This nargileh is no good** | halargîli mâ btinfaʿ | *eshshîshe dî mâ betinfaʿsh'* |
| **Uff! At the first draught my head swims** | uff! min auwal shaḥṭa dâkh râsi | *iff! min auwal shafṭa dâkhet râsi* |
| 10 **The tembek[1] is not well squeezed out** | ittim'bek mâ hû madʿûk mlîh | *ettumbâk mush madʿûk ṭaiyib* |
| **Make me a new nargileh** | ʿabbîli râs jdîd | *ʿabbîli râs gedîd* |
| **This nargileh will not work** | halargîli mâ btishtṛil | *eshshîshe dî mâ betishtiṛilsh'* |
| 13 **There is too much (too little) water** | ilmoi' ktîri (ḳalîli) | *elmoi'ye ketîre (shuwai'ye)* |
| **The tembek is bad** | ittim'bek ʿâṭil | *ettumbâk ʿâṭin* |
| **Is there no story-teller in this café?** | mâfi ḥakawâti fî halḳah'wi? | *mâfîsh râwi filḳah'we dî?* |
| 16 **Story, tale** | ḥikâyi or ḳiṣṣa, pl. ḳiṣaṣ | *ḥikâye* or *riwâye* |

[1] The tembek is a kind of Persian tobacco smoked in a hookah-pipe only.

| | | |
|---|---|---|
| **There is, but he comes in the evening** | fî, lâkin byiji fil'ashîyi | *fîh, lâkin bigi el'i'she* |
| **There is a puppet-player** | fî karakûzâ'ti | *fîh ḳaragôz* |
| **There is a European (Egyptian) band** | fî naubit franj (mṣârwi) | *fîh nôbet ifreng' (maṣârwe)* |
| 4 **What do we owe you?** | ḳaddaish' bad-dak minna? | *kâm 'â-iz minna?* |
| **The cup of coffee costs twenty paras and the nargileh ten paras** | finjân ilḳah'wi bi'ishrîn faḍḍa winna'fas bi-'ash'ra faḍḍa | *fingân elḳah'we bi'eshrîn faḍḍa wanne'fes bi'a'-shara faḍḍa* |
| **The tembek (comes) from us; charge the coffee only** | ittim'bek min 'indna; ḥâsib 'anilḳah'wi bass | *ettumbâk min 'an-dina; iḥsib el-ḳah'we bess* |
| 7 **This time I shall pay** | halmar'ra 'alai'yi | *elmar'ra dî 'alêye* |
| **Another time you shall settle the account** | ṛair marra bit-ḥâsib int | *marra tâniye ḥâ-sib inte* |
| **As you will, Sir** | amrak, yâ sîdi | *amrak, yâ sîdi* |

*At a Money-Changer's (Banker's)*

| | | |
|---|---|---|
| 10 **Here are two bank-notes, of 500 francs each** | haudi warḳtain' bank, kull wâḥ-di bkhamsmît frank | *âdi' waraḳatên bank, kulli waḥ-de bikhumsmît ferank'* |
| **Give me their value in gold** | a'ṭîni ḳîmit'hon diheb | *e'ṭîni ḳîmet'hum dahab* |
| **Give me one half in French gold and the other half in coin of the country** | a'ṭîni innuṣṣ' 'imli frinsâwî'yi diheb winnuṣṣ' ittâni irrâyij filblâd | *e'ṭîni ennuṣṣ' 'um-le feransâwî'ye dahab wannuṣṣ' ettâni errâ-ig filbilâd* |
| 13 **How much is the French (English, Turkish) pound worth, or: what** | ḳaddaish' btiswa lîrit ilfrinsâwi (ilinglîz, il'os-man'li) **or:** shû | *kâm beyis'wa el-bin'tu (elginê el-inglîzi, elginê el-istambûli)* **or:** |

| | | | |
|---|---|---|---|
| | **is the rate of exchange of the French (English, Turkish) pound?** | si'r lîrit ilfrinsâwi (ilinglîz, il'osman'li)? | *si'r elbin'tu elginê elinglîzi, elginê elistambûli) ê?* |
| | **How many piastres is the megeed worth in this place** | kam ḳirsh byiswa fî halba'lad ilmajîdi? | *kâm ḳirsh biswa filbe'led dî erriyâl?* |
| | **What commission (lit. cutting, retrenchment) have you charged?** | ḳaddaish'ḥasabt' ḳaṭ'? | *ḳaddi ê ḳaṭaḥt'?* |
| | **We generally charge 2 per cent** | 'âdit'na niḳṭa' bilmîyi tnain | *'âdet'na niḳṭa' bilmîye etnên* |
| 4 | **We discounted (cut) the pound by thirty paras** | ḳaṭa''na 'allîra tlâtîn' faḍḍa | *ḳaṭa''na 'adda'hab telâtîn' faḍḍa* |
| | **It seems there is a difference** | izzâhir fî farḳ | *ezzâhir fîh farḳ* |
| | **The difference is thirty paras for the purse** | ilfarḳ' tlâtîn' bâra 'alfrâṛa | *elfarḳ'ê telâtîn' faḍḍa 'alkîs* |
| 7 | **The account is correct** | ilḥsâb tamâm | *elḥisâb temâm* |
| | **Only these two pound pieces do not please me** | bass hallîrtain' mâ hinni 'âjbîn'ni | *bess ellîretên' dôl mush 'agbînni* |
| | **One is sweated and the other deficient (in weight)** | ilwâḥdi mamsûḥa wittânyi nâḳṣa | *elwaḥ'de mamsûḥa wattan'ye naḳṣa* |
| 10 | **This lira looks bad** | shaufit hallîra mazṛûli | *shôf ellîra dî mazṛûle* |
| | **Give me another [instead]** | baddil'li yâha | *ṛaiyarhâli* |
| | **Have you a pair of scales?** | 'indak mîzân'? | *'andak mîzân'?* |
| 13 | **Let us weigh this [one]** | tanzîn haidi | *nûzin dî* |
| | **It weighs three grains short** | khâyṣi tlât ḥabbât | *bitkhissê telâte ḥabbât* |
| | **Have you a touch-stone?** | 'indak mḥakk? | *'andak meḥakk'?* |
| 16 | **Rub it on the touch-stone** | ḍrubha 'almḥakk' | *iḍrab'ha 'almeḥakk'* |

| | | |
|---|---|---|
| **Give it here, we will test it with aqua-fortis** | hait tanjarrib'ha bmoiyt ilfaḍ'ḍa | *hât nigarrab'ha bimoi'yet elfaḍ'-ḍa* |
| **It is pure gold** | hî diheb khâliṣ | *hiye dahab khâliṣ* |
| **I have a bill on you** | ili ʻalaik' warḳit ḥwâli | *lîye ʻalêk ḥawâle* **or** *kimbiâle* |
| 4 **Be so good as to (lit., if you please) pay it to me** | iza kân bitrîd idfaʻʻli yâha | *iza kuntê terîd idfaʻhâli* |
| **What sort of money will you have ?** | aina jins ʻimli bitrîd ? | *en'hû gins ʻumle ʻâ=iz ?* |
| **Half silver and half gold** | innuṣṣ' fiḍḍa winnuṣṣ' diheb | *ennuṣṣ'ê faḍḍa wannuṣṣ'ê dahab* |
| 7 **Give me a little small change** | aʻṭîni shwaiyit ḳiṭaʻ (**or** frâṭa) | *eʻṭîni shuwai'yet takâsîr'* |
| **Change me this megeed into small money** | ṣarrif'i halma-jîdi biḳi'ṭaʻ zṛîri | *iṣrif li erriyâl di biḳi'ṭaʻ zuṛai'-yare* |

*At a Watchmaker's*

| | | |
|---|---|---|
| **This is a watch-maker's shop** | haida dikkân sâ-ʻâ'ti | *di dukkân sâʻâ'ti* |
| 10 **Let us enter** | tanfût laʻan'do | *nekhush'shê ʻan-do* |
| **Master, look at this watch, what is the matter with it ?** | yâ mʻallim, shûf hassâʻa, shû ṣâ-yir'la ? | *yâ meʻal'lim, shûf essâʻa di, ga-râlha ê ?* |
| **It stops from time to time** | bitwaḳ'ḳif baʻḍ ilauḳât | *bitûʻa baʻḍ el-auḳât* |
| 13 **It dropped on the ground** | waḳaʻit ʻal=arḍ' | *wiḳiʻet ʻal=arḍ'* |
| **It is fast** | bitsab'biḳ **or** btishṭaḥ | *betis'baḳ* |
| **It is slow** | bit=akh'khir **or** bitḳaṣ'ṣir | *bit=akh'khar* |
| 16 **It is out of order** | mukhar'baṭa | *melakhba'ṭa* |
| **It does not go** | mâ temshîsh **or** mâ teshta'ṛilsh | *ma temshîsh* **or** *mâ teshta'ṛilsh* |

| | | |
|---|---|---|
| Something must be broken in it | baddo ykûn maksûr fîha shî | *lâzim yekûn maksûr fîha shê* |
| It must be repaired | lāzim'ha tiṣlîḥ | *lâzim'ha taṣlîḥ* |
| It must be cleaned | lāzim'ha masḥ | *lâzim'ha masḥ* |
| 4 Its spring is broken | zumbarak'ha maksûr | *zambalik'ha maksûr* |
| Repair this watch for me | ṣalliḥ'li hassā'a | *ṣallaḥ'li essâ'a dî* |
| How much will the repairs cost? | ḳaddaish' bikal'-lif tiṣlîḥha? | *kâm bikal'lif taṣ-lîḥha?* |
| 7 Do it quickly | 'ajjil'li fîha | *ista''gil fîha* |
| I must have it the day after tomorrow, in three days at the latest | baddi yāha ba'd-buk'ra u'alktîr ba'd tlātt îyām' (or ba'd min bukra) | *'â-iz'ha ba'dê bukra we'alketîr ba'dê telat îyâm'* |
| The glass is broken | ballaurit'ha mak-sûra | *ḳizâzet'ha mek-sûra* |
| 10 Have you a glass its size? | 'indak ballau'ra 'ala ḳaddha? | *'andak ḳizâze 'ala ḳaddiha?* |
| See what is needful (to it) and do it | shûf shû lā-zim'ha wi'mi'lo | *shûf ê lâzim'ha wi'mi'lo* |
| I will pay what you like provided you repair it thoroughly | ba'ṭîk ḳadd mâ bitrîd bsharṭ in-nak tiḍbuṭ'ha | *a'ṭîk ḳaddê mâ terîd bisharṭ' innak tuzbuṭ'ha* |
| 13 If any part of it is weak, replace it | iza kān fîha āli ḍ'ifi ṛaiyir'ha | *iza kân fîha âle ḍa'ife ṛaiyar'ha* |
| If it is no good at all, take it and give me a good watch and I will pay the difference | iza kān mâ btinfa' bilkul-lîyi khudha wi'ṭîni sā'a mlîḥa ubidfa''-lak ilfarḳ' | *iza kân mâ betin-fa'sh' ebeden khudha wi'ṭîni sâ'a ṭaiyibe we-adfa''lak el-farḳ'* |
| What is the matter with the clock that it does not strike? | mâ lahâ issā'a inha lâ teduḳḳ'? | *mâ lahâ essâ'a innâha lâ te-duḳḳ'?* |
| 16 Perhaps it is full of dust | rubbama ykûn milyān min ilṛubâr | *rubbama yekûn malyân min elṛubâr* |

## *At a Shoemaker's*

| | | |
|---|---|---|
| **I want (a pair of) shoes (half-boots, Wellingtons)** | lāzim'li tāsû'mi or kundra (lastîk, jazmi) | *lâzim'li tâsû'me or kundu'ra (lastîk, gazme)* |
| **Have you anything ready?** | ʿindak shî ḥâḍir? | *ʿandak shê ḥâḍir?* |
| **Show me the kinds you have** | farjîni ilishkāl illi ʿindak | *warrîni el-ashkâl elli ʿandak* |
| **4 Show me a few pairs of each kind and size** | warrîni kam jauz min kull shikl wiḳyās | *warrîni kâm gôz min kulli shikl waḳiyâs* |
| **I will try them on** | baddi jarrib'hon | *biddi agarrab'hum* |
| **They are too wide** | wās'în' ktîr | *was'în ketîr* |
| **7 This pair is not the size for my foot (does not fit me)** | hajjauz' mâ hû ʿala ḳadd ijri (mâ bîlāyim'ni) | *eggôz di mush ʿala ḳaddê rigli (mâ yinâsib-nîsh')* |
| **Give us another pair** | aʿṭîna jauz ṛairo | *eʿṭina gôz ṛêro* |
| **They are too tight** | ḍaiyḳîn ktîr | *ḍaiyaḳîn ḳetîr* |
| **10 They hurt my toes** | byijraḥûli ṣâbîʿ ijrai'yi | *bigraḥûli ṣawâbiʿ riglêye* |
| **They pinch me (lit., they hurt me my feet)** | bîʿuṣṣû'li ijrai'yi | *yiznu'ḳu riglêye* |
| **They will stretch in wearing** | byû'saʿû ʿallibs' | *beyû'saʿû ʿallibs'* |
| **13 I cannot walk in them** | mâ fîyi (or fîni) imshi fîhon | *mâ aḳdarsh amshi fîhum* |
| **My foot must be easy in them** | ijri lāzim tirtâḥ fîhon | *rigli lâzim tirtâḥ fîhum* |
| **You must make me another pair of shoes** | baddak taʿmil'li tāsû'mi ṛairha | *lâzim tiʿmil'li tâsû'me ṛêrha* |
| **16 Take the measure of my foot** | khôd ḳyās ijri | *khod ḳiyâs rigli* |
| **These boots are too narrow at the heel** | hajjazmāt ḍaiyḳîn min ʿind ilkaʿb' | *elgazmât dôl ḍaiyaḳîn filkaʿb'* |

| | | |
|---|---|---|
| **Help me to take them off** | sâ'id'ni tâ ish-laḥ'hon | *sâ'id'ni aḳlaḥ'-hum* |
| **Make me (such) boots as (you can) get ready quickly** | a'mil'li jaz'mi tiṭla' ḳawâm | *i'mil'li gazme tiṭ-la' ḳawâm* |
| **The leather must be good** | ykûn sakhtyânha mlîḥ | *yekûn gildêha ṭai-yib* |
| 4 **Make me a pair of half-boots with a single sole (with a sole and a half, with a double sole)** | a'mil'li jauz las-tîk bna'l wâḥid (bna'l unuṣṣ' or bnuṣṣ na'l, bna'-lain') | *i'mil'li gôz lastîk bina'l'ê wâḥid (bina'l' wenuṣṣ' or binuṣṣ'ê na'l, bina'lên)* |
| **Make me a pair of cloth half-boots** | a'mil'li jauz las-tîk kittân | *i'mil'li gôz lastîk kittân* |
| **Make them wide in front** | wassi''ha 'ind râs-ha | *wassa''ha 'andê râs-ha* |
| **I have corns** | ijrai'yi fîhon msâmîr' | *riglêye fîhum 'êne samak* |
| 7 **Work them carefully** | ishtril'hon shurl mutḳan | *ishtiril'hum shurlê matḳûn* |
| **In any case get them ready in three days** | min kull budd khallis'hon ba'd tlâtt îyâm' | *min kullê bidd khallaṣ'hum ba'-dê telat îyâm'* |

*At a Carpenter's and Upholsterer's*

| | | |
|---|---|---|
| 10 **I want to buy (some) furniture for the house** | baddi ishtri atât lilbait' | *biddi ashti'ri farsh elbêt* |
| **I want furniture that is handsome and durable, and whose price is moderate** | baddi atât ykûn kwaiyis umâkin wiykûn tamano mhâwad | *biddi farsh yekûn kuwai'yis wemâ-kin wayekûn te-meno mehâwid* |
| **First I want wooden frames for divans, a bedstead, tables, chairs, a chest of drawers, and a book-case** | auwalan baddi dawâwîn' kha-shab utakht' uṭaulât wikrâsi ubîro wikhzâni lilku'tub | *auwalan biddi de-wâwîn' khasheb weserîr weṭara-bêzât' wakerâsi webarô wadû-lâb' lilku'tub* |

| | | |
|---|---|---|
| I have nothing ready (of) that you require | mâ ʿindi shî ḥâḍir min maṭlûbak | *mâ ʿandîsh ḥâge ḥâḍre min maṭlûbak* |
| Then make me what is necessary for a drawing-room and a bedroom | fa-i'zan ishtṛil'li illâzim laḳâʿa ula-ûḍit naum | *ṭaiyib ishtiṛil'li ellâzim lisalûn weli-ôḍat ennôm* |
| Make me a square table of 1½ metre in length and ¾ metre in width | aʿmil'li ṭauli murab'baʿa ṭûlha mitr unuṣṣ' uʿarḍ'ha tlâtt rbâ ilmitr' | *iʿmil'li ṭarabêze merab'baʿa ṭûlha metr wenuṣṣ' weʿarḍ'âha telat irbaʿ metr* |
| 4 Make me a round table of 1½ metre in diameter | iṣhtṛil'li ṭauli ındauwara ḳaṭrha mitr urubʿ' | *ishtiṛil'li ṭarabêze medau'wara ḳuṭrâha metr weru'baʿ* |
| Make a dining-table (washing-stand, kitchen-table, console, a sideboard with a marble slab) | aʿmil ṭauli lissuf'ra (ṭauli lilṛasîl, ṭauli lilmaṭ'bakh, konsôl, bîro ilo blâṭa rukhâm) | *iʿmil ṭarabêze lissuf'ra (ṭarabêze lilṛasîl, ṭarabêze lilmaṭ'bakh, raf, barô birukhâm)* |
| Have you any ordinary chairs (rocking-chairs, sofas)? | ʿindak krâsi iʿtyâdî'yi (krâsi hizzâzi, kanabâyât')? | *ʿandak kerâsi iʿtiyâdî'ye (kerâsi hazzâze, kanabîhât')?* |
| 7 Make me a book-case with six shelves and two glass doors | ishtṛil'li khzâni lilku'tub bsitt ṭabaḳât uli'ha darftain' ḳizâz (or wibwâjhit ḳzâz) | *ishtiṛil'li dûlâb' lilku'tub bisit'te ʿuyûn walo darfetên zugâg (or wabiwish'shê zugâg)* |
| I want a writing-table with a drawer in the middle, two cupboards at the sides, and above, two shelves for books | lâzim'li ṭauli lilktibi bjirrâr filwaṣṭ' wikhzântain' ʿajjambain' ufauḳ'ha ṭabaḳtain' lilku'tub | *lâzim'li ṭarabêze lilkitâbe bidur'gê filwusṭ' wadûlâbên' ʿaggambên wefôkha ṭabaḳatên lilku'tub* |

| | | |
|---|---|---|
| **You must make me all these things as soon as possible, and send them ready into the house** | baddak ta'mil'li halish'ya kullha bi=ak̥'rab wak̥t utib'at'ha khâl-ṣa lilbait' | *biddak ti'mil'li elish'ye dôl kul-lûhum bi=ak̥'rab wak̥t watib'at'-ha khalṣa lilbêt* |
| **I want an Arabian divan** | lâzim'ni dîwân' 'arabi | *lâzim'li dîwân' 'arabi* |
| **I want a mattress of straw (of sea-weed)** | lâzim'ni firâsh min k̥ashsh (min k̥ashsh franji) | *lâzim'li marta'be min k̥ashsh (min k̥ashsh ifren'gi)* |
| **4 I want a quilt (pillows, divan-cushions)** | lâzim'ni lihâf (mu-khaddât, msâ-nid liddîwân') | *lâzim'li lihâf (makhaddât, me-sânid liddîwân')* |
| **The covering of the cushions and of the divan must be woollen cloth or thick calico** | baddo ykûn wij ilmsânid widdîwân' jûkh yimma shît smîk | *lâzim yekûn wishsh elmesâ-nid waddîwân' gûkh walla shît tekhîn* |
| **Make me curtains of some pretty material** | a'mil'li birdâyât' k̥mâsh kwaiyis | *i'mil'li setâ=ir k̥umâsh kuwai'-yis* |
| **7 Bring me a sample of it first** | jibli 'ainîyto (or masṭar'to) k̥abl | *hâtli 'aiyinto k̥abla* |
| **Buy some wooden rods and rings for the curtains** | shtiri k̥udbân khashab uha'-lak̥ lilbirdâyât' | *ishtiri k̥udbân khasheb weha'-lak̥ lissetâ=ir* |
| **I want a mattress stuffed with wool for the winter, and another mat-tress stuffed with cotton for the summer** | baddi farshi mih-shîyi ṣûf lish-shi'ti ufar'shi ṛairha mihshîyi k̥uṭn liṣṣaif' | *biddi farshe mah-shîye ṣûf lish-shi'te wefar'she ṭâniye mahshîye k̥uṭn liṣṣêf* |

*At a Draper's and a Tailor's*

| | | |
|---|---|---|
| **10 I want some (wool-len) cloth** | lâzim'ni jûkh | *lâzim'li gûkh* |
| **What sort of cloth do you want?** | aina jins jûkh baddak? | *en'hû gins gûkh 'â=iz?* |

| | | |
|---|---|---|
| **Show me patterns** | warrîni (or farjîni) msâṭir | *warrîni a'iyinâṭ* |
| **I want uncolored (colored) cloth** | baddi jûkh sâda (mlauwan) | *'â=iz gûkh sâde (melau'wan)* |
| **Show me the best you have** | farjîni aḥsan (or a'la) mâ 'indak | *warrîni aḥsan mâ 'andak* |
| **4 I do not like this color** | mâ bḥibb hallaun' | *mâ aḥib'bish el-lôn di* |
| **This color pleases me** | hallaun' bya'jib'-ni | *ellôn di bi'gib'-ni* |
| **This cloth seems dyed** | hajjûkh mbaiyin maṣbûṛ | *eggûkh di bâyin maṣbûṛ* |
| **7 I want cloth of dyed origin (i.e. dyed in the wool)** | ana baddi jûkh min aṣlo maṣbûṛ | *ana 'â=iz gûkh maṣbûṛ min aṣlo* |
| **This color will fade** | hallaun' byijrud (byibjur) | *ellôn di yugrud* |
| **This cloth is thin (light)** | hajjûkh rḳîḳ (khafîf) | *eggûkh di rufai'-ya' (khafîf)* |
| **10 How much the drah?** | bḳaddaish' id-drâ'? | *bikâm eddirâ'* |
| **Thirty piastres** | bitlâtîn' ḳirsh | *bitelâtîn' ḳirsh* |
| **That is dear** | haida ṛâli | *di ṛâli* |
| **13 That is the lowest price** | haida âkhir taman | *di âkhir temen* |
| **I do not like haggling** | mâ bḥibb sâwim | *mâ aḥib'bish anâhid* |
| **Can you give it for five and twenty piastres?** | bta'ṭîh bkhamsi u'ishrîn ḳirsh? | *tidîh bikham'se wa'eshrîn ḳirsh?* |
| **16 No, Sir, it will not deliver (or clear) me, i.e. it would not pay** | khair, yâ sîdi, mâ bîkhalliṣ'ni | *lâ, yâ sîdi, mâ bikhallaṣnîsh* |
| **We will split the difference (by halves), and I will give you 27½ piastres** | mniḳsim ilfarḳ' mnâṣafi uba'ṭîk sab'a u'ishrîn ḳirsh unuṣṣ' | *niḳsim elfarḳ' menâṣfe wea'ṭîk saba' wa'eshrîn ḳirsh wenuṣṣ'* |
| **Good!** | ṭaiyib! | *ṭaiyib!* |

| | | |
|---|---|---|
| **Cut me off four drahs** | ḳuṣṣli arba‘ tidru‘ | *ḳuṣṣili arba‘t idru‘* |
| **I want some material for a waistcoat, good in the yarn (i.e. fine-spun)** | lāzim'ni wij ṣidrîyi, jeyyid innesj' | *lâzim'li wishshè ṣidêri, gayyid ennesg'* |
| **This cloth is too light (too dark)** | hajjûkh fātiḥ ktîr (ṛâmiḳ ktîr) | *eggûkh di fâtiḥ ketîr (ṛâmiḳ ketîr)* |
| 4 **I want a material that will wash** | baddi ḳmāsh yinṛsil | *‘â=iz ḳumâsh yinṛisil* |
| **Send for the tailor** | rûḥ wara ilkhîyâṭ' (or indah lilkhîyaṭ') | *shaiya‘ lilkhaiyâṭ (or indah lilkhaiyât)* |
| **I sent for you to take my measure and make me a suit** | ba‘att' warâk tâ tākhud ilḳyās witfaṣṣil'li badli | *ba‘tt'i lak ‘ala shân tâkhud elḳiyâs watifaṣṣal'li bedle* |
| 7 **Make me a complete suit (coat, waistcoat, trousers)** | a‘mil'li badli kāmli (sitra, ṣidrîyi, banṭalûn) | *i‘mil'li bedle kâmile (sutre, ṣidêri, banṭalûn)* |
| **Cut the suit after the usual fashion** | faṣṣil ilbad'li mitl izzai' iddārij | *faṣṣal elbed'le ‘alalmôda* |
| **The buttons must be covered (bone, metal)** | izzrâr baddhon ykûnu ṃlabbasîn (‘aḍm, ma‘din) | *el=az'rire yekûnu melabbisîn (‘aḍm, ma‘den)* |
| 10 **Use good lining** | khôd bṭâni mlîḥa | *khod biṭâne ṭaiyibe* |
| **The pockets must be of strong linen cloth, and wide** | ijjyāb ykûnu ḳmāsh kittān mākin uwās‘în' | *egguyûb yekûnu ḳumâsh kittân mâkin wewas‘în* |
| **This coat does not fit me** | hassit'ra mâ btiji ‘alai'yi | *essut're dî mâ bitgîsh ‘alêye* |
| 13 **This coat does not suit (become) me** | hassit'ra mâ btilbuḳ'li | *essut're dî mâ tilbaḳ'shè lîye* |
| **Its sleeves are too long** | kmāmha ṭwâl | *kmâmha ṭuwâl* |

| | | |
|---|---|---|
| **It is tight under the shoulders** | ḍaiyḳa min taḥt ilbâṭâṭ' | *ḍaiyaḳa min taḥt elbaṭâṭ* |
| **The trousers are good, but the waistcoat is too open** | halbanṭalûn mlîḥ, lâkin iṣṣidrîyi maftûḥa ktîr | *elbanṭalûn di ṭaiyib, lâkin eṣṣidêri maftûḥ ketîr* |
| **Alter it (or make it fit)** | ṣalliḥ'ha or jallis'ha | *ṣallaḥ'ha* |

*At the Dealer's in Oriental Objects*[1]

| | | |
|---|---|---|
| 4 **I will go to look at the market and buy some oriental objects, as old weapons, silks from Damascus, articles of wool from** | baddi rûḥ itfar'raj 'assûḳ wishtri tuḥaf sharḳîyi, mitl isliḥa ḳadîmi, wiḳmâsh ḥarîr shuṛl ishshâm. u=ish'ya min ṣûf | *biddi arûḥ atfar'rag 'assûḳ washtiri ḥâgât' sharḳîye, zê asliḥa ḳadîme, waḳumâsh ḥarîr shuṛl eshshâm, we=ash'ye min ṣûf* |

[1] **When purchasing oriental articles the greatest precaution should be exercised. These dealers are almost without exception the craftiest of the crafty Orientals. Above all do not be misled by the mien of simplicity and honesty displayed in a masterly manner, nor by the numerous asseverations and oaths supporting the look. Unless the traveller has a penetrating and experienced eye, or some knowledge of goods and antiquities, he will do well not to make purchases by himself: the Oriental at once knows the inexperienced buyer and will take as much advantage of him as possible. Not that it is much safer to choose as companion one of the numerous 'dragomans' and 'commissionnaires' lolling about the hotels and their neighborhood, for these people receive their percentage from the dealer according to the support they have given him in draining the tourist's purse. (If the intending purchaser offers one third of the price demanded, it will enable him to raise it when the seller lowers it.) But there are also certain reliable persons to be found out by inquiry on the spot; for instance, by application to one of the English mercantile establishments in some of the larger towns of Syria or Egypt.**

| | | |
|---|---|---|
| **Zûk,[1] old vessels of earthenware, etc.** | shuṛl izzûḳ, u-꞊awâni ḳadîmi min fikhkhâr uṛai'ro | *shuṛl ezzûḳ, we-꞊awâni ḳadîme min fukhkhâr weṛêro* |
| **What do you wish, Sir?** | shû bitrîd, yâ khawâja? | *'âiz ê, yâ kha-wâga?* |
| **Have you any silken (men's) shawls?** | 'indak kaffîyât' ḥarîr? | *'andak kuffîyât' ḥarîr?* |
| **I have all kinds** | 'indi min kull ilijnâs | *'andi min kull el꞊agnâs* |
| **4 I want something heavy** | baddi shî tḳîl | *biddi waḥde tekîle* |
| **I want some ladies' shawls** | baddi kaffîyât' kharj niswân | *biddi kuffîyât' khargê niswân* |
| **Show me the kinds you have** | farjîni ilishkâl illi 'indak | *warrîni el꞊ash-kâl elli 'andak* |
| **7 Where are these made (lit., work from where these)?** | shuṛl wain hau-di? | *shuṛli fên dôl?* |
| **Work from Damascus** | shuṛl ishshâm | *shuṛl eshshâm* |
| **Is this shawl entirely of pure silk or is there cotton in it?** | halkaffîyi kullha ḥarîr 'alhill' yimmadâkhil'ha kuṭn? | *elkuffîye dî kulli-ha ḥarîr khâliṣ walla dâkhil'ha kuṭn?* |
| **10 Have you any silk burnooses of Zûk manufacture?** | 'indak brânis ḥarîr shuṛl iz-zûḳ? | *'andak berânîs' ḥarîr shuṛl ez-zûḳ?* |
| **Have you any table-covers?** | 'indak irṭyit su-fra (or wujûh sufra)? | *'andak ṛuṭyân sufra (or wugûh sufra)?* |

**Special care should be taken in bu-ing antîkât' (plur. of antîka, implying all kinds of antiquities, including coins and curiosities), for the country abounds with numerous falsifications and imitations which are chiefly made in Europe, though old coins are also forged in the East with great skill.**

1 zûḳ mîkâ'yil, **situated about four hours from Beyrout in the Kesrawan, is celebrated for its textile fabrics.**

| | | |
|---|---|---|
| **I want some purses and slippers with embroidery in gold** | baddi ikyâs uban- tuflât bḳaṣab | *ana ʿâ-iz akyâs webâbûg' biḳa'- ṣab* |
| **These do not seem to be the manufacture of this country** | mbaiyin hadôl mush shuṛl halblâd | *elbâyin dôl mush shuṛl elbilâd dî* |
| **No, these are Stamboul make** | lâ, haudi shuṛl stambûl | *lâ, dôl shuṛl istambûl* |
| 4 **I want a complete suite to furnish a drawing-room: some large and small cushions, divan - covers, small mattresses, curtains, and a table-cover** | baddi ṭaḳm kâmil lafarsh' ḳâʿa: min msânid u- tikkâyât', uwu- jûh dawâwîn', wiṭrârîḥ' lilarḍ' ubirdâyât' u- wij' ṭauli | *ʿâ-iz ṭaḳmê kâmil lifarsh' essa- lûn: min mesâ- nid wetakkâyât', wewugûh dewâ- wîn', weyânât lil- arḍ' wesatâ-ir wewish' ṭarabêze* |
| **Everything must be of one kind: of wool, red foundation with colored embroidery** | kullo baddo ykûn min shikl wâ- ḥid: min ṣûf, il- arḍîyi ḥamra winnaḳ'shi mlauwani | *kullo yekûn min shiklê wâḥid: min ṣûf, elarḍîye ḥamra wannaḳ'- she melau'wane* |
| **Take me to a carpet shop** | dillni ʿala makh- zin sijjâdât' | *dillinî ʿala duk- kân siggâdât'* |
| 7 **Have you any carpets?** | ʿindak sijjâdât'? | *ʿandak siggâdât'?* |
| **I want a Persian carpet** | baddi sijjâdi ʿaja- mîyi | *ʿâ-iz siggâde ʿa- gemîye* |
| **This carpet [1] which is smooth (lit., without flocks) is Turkoman make** | halbsâṭ [1] illi bala guzbara shuṛl itturkmân | *elbusâṭ [1] di elli min ṛêr wabara shuṛl etturke- mân* |

[1] bsâṭ *busâṭ*, **plur.** busṭ **or** busuṭ, **is the name of any large carpet, also of those thick wool fabrics made in Zûk and Damascus and used for divan-covers, portières, and curtains ;** sijjâdi *saggâde* **is first of all the carpet of about five feet in length and two feet six inches in width, on**

| | | |
|---|---|---|
| **I wish to buy some old swords** | baddi ishtri syûf ḳadîmi | *biddi ashtiri siyûf ḳadîme* |
| **Here is a fine blade of good workmanship**[1] | hai naṣli kwaiysi mjauhara | *âdi' naṣle kuwai'-yise megau'hara* |
| **These are Indian sabres** | hai syûf hindîyi | *âdi' siyûf hindîye* |
| 4 **Here is an old dagger with an inscription** | hai khanjar ʿalaih' ktîbi | *âdi' khangar ʿa-lêh kitâbe* |
| **Here are muskets of all kinds** | hai bwârîd' min kull ilishkâl | *âdi' banâdiḳa min kull el=ashkâl* |
| **Have you any pistols inlaid with ivory or mother-of-pearl?** | ʿindak ṭaban-jât khashab'ha mnazzal ʿâj yimma ṣafad? | *ʿandak ṭabangât khasheb'ha me-naz'zil ʿâg walla ṣadaf?* |
| 7 **We have not yet seen any old pottery** | mâ shifna baʿd fikhkhâr kadîm | *lissa mâ shuf-nâsh fukhkhâr ḳadîm* |
| **Have you any Chinese porcelain?** | ʿindak awâni ṣî-nî'yi? | *ʿandak awâni ṣê-nî'ye?* |
| **Here is an old Chinese flower-vase** | hai mazharîyi ṣî-nî'yi ḳadîmi | *âdi' mazharîye ṣê-nî'ye ḳadîme* |
| 10 **This dish does not ring; it seems to be cracked** | haṣṣaḥn' mâ bî-ṛinn'; ka=in'no mashʿûr | *eṣṣaḥn'ê di mâ yi-ṛinn'ish; ke=in'-no mashʿûr* |

**which the Mussulman says his prayers; it is then in a general sense used for any carpet. Other names for carpets are** ṭunfuse **or** ṭinfise, **pl.** ṭanâfis; farsh, **pl.** furûsh; iklîm, **pl.** akâlîm'; zerâbi **is a small carpet. To cover with carpets is** farash, **which is originally 'to spread', as the bed, and in a wider sense, to furnish a house.**

**1 In Syria 'genuine Damascus blades' are offered to the tourist in large quantities. They are all made in—Germany, chiefly in Solingen, and a very experienced eye is required to discern genuine goods, which, needless to say, only fall into the hands of strangers after long and careful search, or by mere chance.**

| | | |
|---|---|---|
| **There appears no sign of a crack** | mush mbaiyin fîh atar kasr | *mush bâyin fîh asar kesr* |
| **Have you nothing enamelled?** | mâ ʿindak shî ilo mîna? | *mâ ʿandak'shi mîna?* |
| **Let us settle (decide) the price** | tâ nitfâṣal ʿatta'man | *nitfâṣil ʿatte'men* |
| 4 **What is the price of this piece?** | ḳaddaish' taman halḳaṭ'ʿa? | *ê temen elḳiṭ'ʿa dî?* |
| **Its price is ninety piastres** | ḥaḳḳha tisʿîn ḳirsh | *temen'ha tisʿîn ḳirsh* |
| **That is too dear** | ṛâli ktîr [manoḷ | *ṛâli ketîr* |
| 7 **Take it for nothing** | khudo bala ta-ʃ | *khudo balâsh* |
| **Last word, how much?** | âkhir kilmi, ḳad-daish'? | *âkhir kilme, kâm?* |
| **Three silver megeeds in specie** | tlât riyâlât' ma-jîdi ʿain (or bwij-hon) | *telâte riyâl* |
| 10 **How much is this carpet?** | hassijjâdi bi-kâm? | *essiggâde dî bi-kâm?* |
| **Without bargaining and haggling its price is a hundred francs** | min dûn mfâṣali ulâ mkâsara ta-man'ha mît frank | *min ṛêr mufâṣale welâ mukâsara temen'ha mît fe-rank'* |
| **I will give you 80** | baʿṭîk tmânîn' | *adîk temânîn'* |
| 13 **That will not p y (lit., deliver) me** | mâ bîkhalliṣ'ni | *mâ yikhallaṣ'nîsh* |
| **Its cost price is 95 francs** | rismâlha kham-siutisʿîn frank | *rasmâlha khamse wetisʿîn ferank'* |
| **Here are 5 pounds Turkish; deduct what is yours and give me the rest** | hai khams lîrât' ʿosman'li; ikh-ṣum illiilak wiʿ-ṭîni ilfâdil (or ukammil'li) | *âdi' khamse ginê stambûli; ikhṣim elli lak weʿṭîni elfâdil (or el-bâḳi)* |
| 16 **Send these things to the hotel for me** | ibʿat'li halawâʿi lillukan'da | *waddî el-ash'ye dôl ellokan'da* |

*Hire and Purchase of a Horse*

| | | |
|---|---|---|
| **I will go for a ride to-morrow** | baddi bukra shimm ilha'wa brâkib | *biddi bukra ashimm' elha'-wa wana râkib* |

| | | |
|---|---|---|
| **Take me to a livery-man (also muleteer)** | dillni ʿala mkâri | *dillini ʿala mukâri* |
| **Have you any horses for hire?** | ʿindak khail lil-ij'ra? | *ʿandak khēl lil-ug'ra?* |
| **Yes, Sir, I have good horses** | naʿam, yâ sîdi, ʿindi khail ṭaiybi | *aiwa, yâ sîdi, ʿandi khêl ṭaiyibe* |
| 4 **Where are the horses?** | wain ilkhail'? | *fên elkhêl?* |
| **Will you be pleased (to go) to see them or shall we bring them to you at the hotel?** | titfaḍ'ḍal tshûf-ha yimma min-jîblak yâha lillukan'da? | *titfaḍ'ḍal teshûf-ha, walla negib-hâlak ellokan'-da?* |
| **Procure me some horses (stallions), strong and hardened (viz., to fatigue)** | dabbir'li kam ḥṣân mâknîn' umadʿûkîn' | *shûfli kâm ḥu-ṣân gamdîn we-madʿûkîn'* |
| 7 **Here is a black horse the like of which there is not in the whole place, and here is a red mare, strong, with firm step** | hai ḥṣân adham mâfi mitlo fî kull ilba'lad, uhai' fa-ras ḥamra ḳa-wîyi daʿsit'ha mâkni | *âdi' ḥuṣân adham mâfîsh zêyo fî kull elbe'led, we-âdi' faras ḥamra ḳawîye daʿset'ha makne* |
| **Here is a bay horse, and these are grey horses** | hai ḥṣân ashḳar uhau'di iḥṣini zurḳ | *â li' ḥuṣân ash-ḳar wedôl aḥṣine zurḳ* |
| **Choose which you will** | naḳḳi illi bitrîd-hon | *naḳḳi elli ʿâ-iz'-hum* |
| 10 **I want strong horses that are unblemished, do not limp, in short are free from all wounds and defects** | baddi khail ḳa-wîyi, lâ hî maj-rûḥa, ulâ btiʿ-ruj, wilḥâṣil khâlyi min kull ʿaṭab ʿuaib' | *biddi khêl ḳawîye, mush magrûḥa, welâ teʿrag'shi, walḥâṣil khalye min kulli ʿaṭab weʿêb* |
| **He drops his head** | râs-hu nâzil | *râs-hu nâzil* |
| **He is lame** | yaʿraj | *yaʿrag* |

| | | |
|---|---|---|
| **The horses must** | ilkhail′ baddha tkûn | *elkhêi tekûn* |
| **be trained** | mrauwaḍa | *merau′waḍa* |
| **have a good action** | ishkînha mlîḥ | *mashyâha ṭaiyib* |
| **not jump and not prance** | lâ tnaṭniṭ utir′ṭuz | *mâ tenaṭṭat′shi welâ til‘ab′shi* |
| **not shy** | lâ tijfal | *mâ tigfalsh′* |
| **not be wild** | lâ tkûn shmûs | *mush mutawaḥ′ḥishe* |
| **not take the bit in their teeth (i.e. not bolt)** | lâ tâkhud illjâm bisnânha | *mâ tâkhuj′ elligâm bisnânha* |
| **not lash out** | lâ tilbaṭ | *mâ turfuṣṣ′* |
| **not bite** | lâ tikdush | *mâ te‘uḍ′ḍish* |
| **I want a tame mare** | baddi faras hâdyi | *biddi faras hadye* |
| **Saddle this horse and bridle him, and bring him to me that I may try him** | isruj halḥṣân wilji′mo ujib′li yâh tâ jarrbo | *sarrag elḥuṣân di walaggi′mo wehâtuh′li agar′rabo* |
| 4 **Take off the saddle that I may see that your mare is not wounded** | ḳîm issarj′ tâ shûf lâ tkûn farasak majrûḥa | *shîl essarg′ ashûf mâ tekûnshi farasak magrûḥa* |
| **This is a stallion, no mare** | hai ḥṣân, mâ hû faras | *di ḥuṣân, mush faras* |
| **Did I not tell you I want a mare?** | mâ ḳultil′lak baddi faras? | *mâ ḳulti lakshê biddi faras?* |
| 7 **(To judge) by the look this horse has bad habits** | shaufti fî halḥṣân mkhaṣṣal | *elbâyin fîlḥuṣân′ di mekhaṣ′ṣal* |
| **We will try him** | tanjarr′bo | *nigarra′bo* |
| **It seems he is restive** | mbaiyin byiḥrun | *elbai′yin byeḥran* |
| 10 **You have drawn in the reins too tightly** | shaddaitil′lo illjâm | *shaddêt elligâm* |

| | | |
|---|---|---|
| **Loosen his reins a little** | irkhîlo shwaiyit illjâm | *ir'khî elligâm shuwai'ye* |
| **This horse has a strong chest and powerful forefeet** | halḥṣân ṣidro ḳawi wîdaih' mâknîn' | *elḥuṣân di ṣadro ḳawi we=îdêh' gamdîn* |
| **How is he in going down-hill?** | kîf hû binnzûl? | *ezai' hûwe binnuzûl?* |
| 4 **Down-hill and up-hill and on the plain, his action is unequalled (lit. his walk has not its equal)** | binnzûl wiṭṭlû'u-bissah'li mashyito mâfi mitlha | *binnuzûl waṭṭulû' webissah'le mashyeto mâ fîsh zêyiha* |
| **The harness of the horse must be complete: saddle, bridle, girth, and stirrups** | lâzim ṭaḳm ilḥṣân ykûn kâmil: bsarjo wiljâmo wiḥzâmâ'to wirkâbâ'to | *lâzim ṭaḳm elḥuṣân yekûn kâmil: bisar'go weligâmo weḥizâmâ'to werikâbâ'to* |
| **Have you not a European saddle?** | mâ 'indak sarj franji? | *mâ 'andak'shi sarg ifren'gi?* |
| 7 **This saddle is no good; (it is) torn, patched up, dirty** | hassarj' mâ byinfa'; mkhazzaḳ, muraḳ'ḳa', mwassakh | *essarg'è di mâ binfa'sh'; mekhaz'zaḳ, meraḳ'ḳa', mewas'sakh* |
| **It is a shame to ride (lit., one rides) on it** | 'aib wâḥid yirkab 'alaih' | *'êb elwâḥid yirkab 'alêh* |
| **This bridle is old; it will break with us on the road** | halljâm 'atîḳ; byinḳṭi' ma'na fiddarb' | *elligâm di ḳadîm; binḳiṭi' mi'âna fissik'ke* |
| 10 **We want a horse for the servant** | baddna ḥṣân lilkhiddâm | *biddina ḥuṣân li!khaddâm* |
| **Let him choose at his will** | khallîh ynaḳḳi 'ala kêfo | *khallîh yenaḳ'ḳi 'ala kêfo* |
| **We want mules for the luggage** | lâzim'na barl lil-'afsh' | *lâzim'na barlè lil-'afsh'* |
| 13 **Procure us some good mules** | dabbir'lna kam barl ṭaiybîn | *shûflina kâm barlè ṭaiyibîn* |
| **Padded saddle for donkeys and mules** | jull or jlâl | *gilâl* |

| | | |
|---|---|---|
| **You must send a man with us to tend the beasts** | lāzim tib'at zalami ma'na ysûs iddwābb | *lâzim tib'at ḥad mi'âna yikhdim eddewâbb* |
| **How do you let your horses, for the day or to a certain place (for the journey)?[1]** | kîf tikri khailak, 'alîyām' yimma lamaḥall' makhṣûṣ?[1] | *ezai' tikri khēlak, 'alyôm walla limaḥall'ê makhṣûṣ?[1]* |
| **We want the beasts for our disposal at will (lit., revolving hoof)[2]** | baddna iddwābb ḥâfir dûwâr'[2] | *'â=izîn' eddewâbb ḥâfir dauwâr* |
| 4 **I will have nothing to do with the feeding and tending of the horse: I ride only, and see how much you want a day** | ana mâ bîkhuṣṣ'ni ilḥṣân u'alîḳo wisyāsto: ana ba'rif irkab ushûf kaddaish' baddak 'alyaum' | *ana mâ bikhuṣṣinîsh elḥuṣân we'alîḳo wesiyâseto: ana bess arkab weshûf kâm biddak 'alyôm* |
| **Thirty piastres** | tlātîn' ḳirsh | *telâtîn' ḳirsh* |
| **You are making it too much** | kattart'ha | *kattart'âha* |
| 7 **The horses are on the green to-day[3]** | ilkhail' ilyaum' birrabî' | *elkhēl ennahar'da firrebî'* |

[1] Especially for short journeys it is well to agree upon tûṣî'li, corresponding to our 'for the journey,' properly 'arriving,' 'taking there.' In this case you need not trouble about anything, neither about fodder nor the return of the animal.

[2] According to the custom prevailing and generally acknowledged in Syria the hirer of an animal is liable for compensation when an accident happens to the beast elsewhere but on the direct road to, or in, the place for which it has been hired. If therefore you do not intend to betake yourself to a certain place by the direct route you will do well to hire the animals ḥâfir dûwâr' 'for any employ,' properly: 'revolving hoof.'

[3] In spring the horses are fed on grass only for six or eight weeks, and for this purpose most of them are driven to pasture outside the town. As during this time few

| | | |
|---|---|---|
| **Barley is expensive in these days** | ishsha'îr ṛâli bhalîyâm' | *eshsha'îr ṛâli lîyâm'dôl* |
| **But the man whom you send with us, his catering concerns you** | lâkin izza'lami illi baddak tib'ato ma'na mûnto 'alaik' | *lâkin el-insân elli biddak tib'a'to mi'âna ma-ûneto 'alêk* |
| **This horse we have tried at pacing; but does it also trot and gallop?** | halḥṣân jarrabnâh ishkîn; yâtara bîrûḥ' kamân khabeb wikhyûli? | *elḥuṣân di garrab'na mashyo; yâtara birûḥ kemân khabeb warahmḥ'?* |
| **4 Of course it gallops** | [yilḥ ma'lûm bîkhai'- | [*maḥ ma'lûm beyir'-* |
| **How much food do you give your horse?** | ḳaddaish' bit'al'-liḳ liḥṣânak? | *ḳaddi ê ba'al'laḳ 'ala ḥuṣânak?* |
| **I give him in the evening half a mudd and in the morning a quarter of a mudd** | b'alliḳ'lo min 'ashîyi nuṣṣ mudd umin' 'ala bukra rub'îyi (in **Syria 1 mudd = 18 litres or 4 rubiye)** | *ba'al'laḳ 'alêh el'i'she rub' weṣṣubḥ' nuṣṣê rub'* **(in Egypt 1 ruba = 8½ litres)** |

*Eating and Drinking*

| | | |
|---|---|---|
| **7 Is there a restaurant in this place?** | fî lukan'da fî hal-ba'lad? | *fîi lokan'da filbe'led dî?* |
| **There are many restaurants here** | fî lukandât ktîr haun | *fîh lokandât ketîr hene* |
| **What have you to eat and to drink?** | shû fî 'indak lil-akl' wishshirb'? | *êsh 'andak lilakl' washshurb'?* |
| **Soup** | shorba | *shorba* |
| **Boiled meat (from which soup is made)** | maslûḳ | *maslûḳ* |

---

**horses remain in the towns the prices for hire go up. This is, of course, also the case on the arrival of many travellers and when the fodder is expensive. In Syria the average hire for a horse with food, stabling, and boy is six shillings a day.**

| | | |
|---|---|---|
| **Fish** | samek | *samak* |
| **Beefsteak** | biftâk | *biftek* |
| **Baked meat** | laḥmi miḳlîyi | *laḥme maḳlîye* |
| **Roast meat** | mishwi or rôsto | *mashwi* or *rôsto* |
| **Vegetables** | mṭabbaḳât | *khoḍâr* |
| **Ragout** | yakhni | *yakhni* |
| **(Various) kinds of sweets** | ishkâl ḥulwîyât' | *ashkâl ḥalawîyât'* |
| **Fruits** | fuâki | *fewâkih* |
| **Commandaria-wine** | nbîd kummandâri | *nebîd kummandâri* |
| **Cyprus-wine** | nbîd ḳubrsi | *nebîd ḳubrusi* |
| **Lebanon-wine** | nbîd shuṛl ijja'bal (or baladi) | *nebîd shuṛl egge'bel* (or *beledi*) |
| **Claret** | bordô | *bordô* |
| **Irak (brandy)** | ʿaraḳ | *ʿaraḳi* |
| **Cognac** | kunyâk | *kunyâk* |
| **and other dishes and drinks** | uṛai'ro mnilmwâkîl' wilmashrûbât' | *weṛêro min elmâkûlât' walmashrûbât'* |
| **This soup is too highly seasoned (lit., too salt and peppered); it is not eatable** | hashshor'ba mâlḥa ktîr wibhârha ktîr; mâ btittâkil | *eshshor'ba dî mâliḥa ḳawi wabuhârha ketîr; mâ titâkilsh'* |
| **This boiled meat is lean** | halmaslûḳ ḍʿîf | *elmaslûḳ di ḍaʿîf* |
| 4 **This meat is overdone** | hallaḥm' mishwi ktîr | *ellaḥm'ê di mashwi ketîr* |
| **This roast meat is still raw (i.e. underdone)** | harrôsto baʿdo nai | *elmash'wi di lissa nai* |
| **Give me a piece of roast meat which is good** | aʿṭîni shaḳfit rôsto tkûn mlîḥa | *idîni ḥiṭṭet rôsto tekûn melîḥa* |
| 7 **You have laid me neither knife, nor fork, nor spoon, nor serviette** | mâ ḥaṭṭaiti'li lâ sikkîni ulâ shauki ulâ malʿaḳa ulâ fûṭa | *mâ ḥaṭṭêtilîsh' lâ sikkîne welâ shôke welâ maʿlaḳa welâ fûṭa* |

| | | |
|---|---|---|
| **Bring a small glass for the wine** | jîb ḳadaḥ zṛîr linnbîd | *hât kâs zuṛai'yar linnebîd* |
| **Give me a glass (tumbler)** | a'ṭîni kubbâyi | *e'ṭîni kubbâye* |
| **This piece of meat is tough** | hallaḥ'mi 'âsyi | *ellaḥ'me dî gamde* |
| 4 **This is leather, not meat** | hai jildi, mâ hî laḥmi | *di gilde, mush laḥme* |
| **I do not like fat** | mâ bḥibb iddihn' | *mâ aḥibb'ish eddihn'* |
| **Bring me a piece which is not fat** | jibli shaḳfi mâ hî midhini | *hâtli ḥiṭṭe mush midhi'ne* |
| 7 **This (piece of) meat is dry, it must have a little sauce** | hallaḥ'mi nâshfi, baddhashwaiyit salsa | *ellaḥ'me dî nâshife, lâzim'ha shuwai'yet salsa* |
| **Give me another piece of bread** | a'ṭîni shaḳfit khubz ukhra | *e'ṭîni kemân ḥiṭṭet 'êsh* |
| **Bring the salt-cellar** | hait ilmam'laḥa | *hât elmallâḥa* |
| 10 **Bring some vinegar and oil** | jîb khall uzait' | *hât khall wezêt* |
| **Bring some mustard** | jîb khardal | *hât mustarda* |
| **Is this table-wine?** | haida nbîd sufra? | *di nebîd sufra?* |
| 13 **This wine is mere water** | hannbîd kullo moi | *ennebîd di kullo moiye* |
| **Have you cheese?** | 'indak jibn? | *'andak gibne?* |
| **Have you no Frank (European) bread?** | mâ 'indak khubz franji? | *mâ 'andak'shi 'êsh ifren'gi?* |
| 16 **What fruit have you?** | shû 'indak fuâki? | *êsh 'andak fewâkih?* |
| **We have summer and winter fruit** | 'indna fuâkit iṣṣaif' wishshi'ti | *'andina fewâkih eṣṣêf washshi'te* |
| **Hand me the dish with the grapes (the figs, apricots, peaches, apples, pears, bananas, melon, fresh dates)** | nâwil'ni ṣaḥn il'i'nib (ittîn, ilmish'mish, iddurrâḳ, ittiffâḥ, innjâṣ, ilmauz', ilbaṭṭîkh, ilba'laḥ) | *nâwil'ni ṣaḥn el'i'neb (ettîn, elmish'mish, elkhôkh, ettiffâḥ, elkummit'ra, elmûz, elbaṭṭîkh, elbe'leḥ)* |

| | | |
|---|---|---|
| **Bring the coffee and give me a glass of cognac** | jîb ilḳah'wi wi'-ṭîni ḳadaḥ kun-yâk | *hât elḳah'we wi'ṭî-ni kâs kunyâk* |

TRAVELLING IN THE INTERIOR

*Inquiries before Starting*

| | | |
|---|---|---|
| **How is the road from here to . . ?** | kîf iṭṭarîḳ min haun la...? | *ezai' essik'ke min hene li...?* |
| **Is the road good?** | iddarb' mlîḥa? | *eddarb'ê ṭaiyib?* |
| **4 How many beasts do I want for this journey?** | ḳaddaish'lâzim'lî dwâbb lahas-safra? | *kâm lâzim'li de-wâbb lissa'far di?* |
| **A horse for your-self, another horse for your servant, and two mules for the luggage** | ḥṣân ilak, ḥṣân âkhar lakhâd-mak ubarlain' lil'afsh' | *ḥuṣân 'ala shâ-nak, ḥuṣân âkhar 'ala shân khad-dâmak webarle-tên lil'afsh'* |
| **Will one mule for the luggage not do?** | mâ bîkaf'fi barl wâḥid lil'afsh'? | *mâ yikaffish bar-la wâḥide lil-'afsh'?* |
| **7 Yes, if you take no tent with you** | na'am, iza mâ akhatt' ma'ak ṣîwân' | *aiwa, iza mâ kuntish tâkhod khême wayâk* |
| **Are there not every-where (lit., in every part) on the road places in which one can spend the night?** | mâfi 'aṭṭarîḳ fî kull maṭraḥ ma-ḥallât yiḳdir il-wâḥid ybât fîha? | *mâfîsh' fissik'ke fî kulli maṭraḥ maḥallât beyir'-dar elwâḥid yi-bât fîha?* |
| **Do we always find on our way people with whom we can descend (i.e. put up)?** | minlâḳi 'ala ṭa-rîḳna dâyman nâs niḳdir ninzil 'indhon? | *binlâḳi 'ala sik-ketna dâ-iman nâs nirdar nin-zil 'anduhum?* |
| **10 Are the houses in the villages clean?** | ilbyût fiḍḍi'ya' nḍîfi? | *elbiyût filbilâd naḍîfe?* |

| | | |
|---|---|---|
| **Not always, Sir** | mush dâyman, yâ sîdi | *mush tamalli, yâ sîdi* |
| **It is then necessary to take a tent with us** | fa-i'zan lâzim nâkhud ma'na ṣîwân' | *baḳa lâzim nâkhud mi'âna khême* |
| **If you will travel to Palmyra you cannot do without a tent** | iza kân baddak trûḥ latad'mur, lâ budd lak min ṣiwân' | *iza kân biddak terûḥ litad'mur, lâ buddê lak min khême* |
| 4 **Is there danger on the road?** | fî khaṭar 'ad-darb'? | *fîh khaṭar fid-darb'?* |
| **Is the road safe?** | iddarb' amîni? | *eddarb' amîn?* |
| **Yes, Sir, this road is much frequented** | na'am, yâ sîdi, haddarb' maṭrûka ktîr | *aiwa, yâ sîdi, ed-darb' di maṭrûḳ ketîr* |
| 7 **No, Sir, there is fear of thieves (of Bedouins)**[1] | khair, yâ sîdi, fî khauf mnilḥaramîyi (mnil'a'rab)[1] | *lâ, yâ sîdi, fîh khôf min elḥarâmîye (min el-'a'rab)*[1] |
| **Can we not get two or three horsemen (i.e. mounted policemen) to accompany us?** | mâ mniḳdir ndabbir'lna khîyâlain' tlâti yrâfḳû'na? | *mâ niṛdarsh nâkhod khaiyâlên' telâte yerâfiḳû'na?* |
| **How much does one give the horseman per day?** | ḳaddaish' bya'ṭu lilkhîyâl' bilyaum'? | *kâm yiddu lilkhaiyâl bilyôm?* |
| 10 **Four or five francs** | arba' khams frankât | *arba' khamse ferank'* |
| **Is a guide necessary?** | lâzim dâlûl'? | *lâzim dalîl?* |
| **Head of a caravan** | shêkh ilḳâfili | *shêkh elḳâfile* |

1 **While in Syrian parlance** il'a'rab, **when standing alone, implies 'the Bedouins' only, the Arabic-speaking Syrians call themselves** ûlâd' il'a'rab, **or** bnât il'a'rab **(i.e. sons or daughters of the Arabs), and the individual** ibn 'arab **or** bint 'arab. **The Mohammedan Syrians are by the Christians generally but improperly called** atrâk **'Turks'; see also p. 134 note 2.**

| | | |
|---|---|---|
| **We will find guides when necessary (lit., if in need)** | minlâḳi dwâlîl' iza kân fî luzûm | *benilti'ḳi dulala iza kân fîh luzûm* |
| **Must we not take food with us?** | mush lâzim nâkhud alk ma'na? | *mush lâzim nâkhud akl mi'âna?* |
| **No, Sir, everywhere you will find food; but it is better (lit. more convenient, more proper for the purpose) to take cooking apparatus with you** | lâ, yâ sîdi, wain mâ kunt bitlâḳi akl; amma ilau'faḳ tâkhud ma'ak âlât' ṭabkh | *lâ, yâ sîdi, fi kulli maḥal'lê tiltiḳi akl; amma el-au'faḳ tâkhud mi'âk âlât' eṭ-ṭabîkh* |

*Preparations for the Journey.—Departure.*

| | | |
|---|---|---|
| 4 **Go seek a tent to hire or to buy** | rûḥ dauwir 'ala ṣîwân' bilij'ra yimma bḥaḳḳo | *rûḥ dauwar 'ala khiyam bilug'ra walla bitta'man* |
| **We want mats and carpets and cushions and a mattress** | lâzim'na ḥuṣr usijjâdât' wimṣânid ufar'shi | *lâzim'na ḥuṣr wesiggâdât' wamesânid wefar'she* |
| **Pack the things all together, and load them on the mule** | iḥzum ilawâ'i kullhon uhammil'hon 'albaṛl' | *ḥazzim elḥawâ-ig kullûhum weḥammil'hum 'albaṛl'* |
| 7 **Take care to forget nothing** | a'ṭi bâlak lâ tinsa shî | *khalli bâlak mâ tinsâsh ḥâge* |
| **Did you put the little box and the provisions in the saddle-bag?** | ḥaṭṭait' iṣṣandûḳa wizzûwâ'di bilkhurj'?[1] | *ḥaṭṭêt eshshan'ṭa wazzûwâ'de bilkhurg'?*[1] |

[1] The khurj *khurg* **consists of two large and wide pockets joined to each other; it is placed in such a way across the saddle behind the rider, that the two bags hang down the sides.**

| | | |
|---|---|---|
| Put the box in one pocket, and the provisions, the knife, fork, spoon, and the glass in the other | ḥuṭṭ iṣṣandûḳa fî ʻaini wizzûwâ'di wissikkîni wishshau'ki wilmal'ʻaḳa wilkubbâyi fî ʻaini | *ḥoṭṭ eshshan'ṭa fî ʻên wazzûwâ'de wassikkîne washshôke walmaʻʻlaḳa walkubbâye fî ʻên* |
| Strap the saddle-bag behind you | sammiṭ ilkhurj' warâk | *khaiyaṭ elkhurg' warâk* |
| Take care of the little box; there are things in it that break, and perish, and would spoil the others | twaḳḳa iṣṣandûḳa; fîha ishya byitkas'saru wibyaʻʻṭalu wibyin'zaʻu ṛairhon | *ûʻa ʻashshan'ṭa; fîha ashye titkisir wetinfi'sid wayikhas'saru ṛêruhum* |
| 4 There are fine instruments in it, as a thermometer, and drawing (painting) materials, and oil-colors | fîha âlât' rafîʻa mitl mîzân' ilḥarr' wilbard' uâlât' ittaṣwîr udihânât' | *fîha âlât' rufaiʻyaʻe zê tirmometr we=âlât' ettaṣwîr wedihânât'* |
| There are medicine-bottles and phials in it | fîha ḳanânit idwyi ukhanâjîr' | *fîha ḳazâ=iz adwiye wekhanâgîr'* |
| Up to the present the horsemen of the authorities have not arrived, and the time is up we will start | lissa khîyâ'lit ilḥkûmi mâ wuṣlu uṣâr ilwaḳt': baddna nsâfir | *lissa khaiyâlîn' elḥukûme mâ wiṣlûsh walwaḳ'tê râh: biddina nisâfir* |
| 7 Is my horse ready, saddled? | ḥṣâni ḥâḍir, masrûj? | *ḥuṣâni ḥâḍir, mesrûg?* |
| Saddle my horse | usruj (or shidd) ḥṣâni or ḥuṭṭ issarj' liḥṣâni | *usrug (or shidd) ḥuṣâni or ḥuṭṭ essarg' liḥuṣâni* |
| To mount the horse, to mount the crupper | rakib ʻalalḥṣân, rakib ʻala kafal ilfa'ras | *rakib ʻalalḥuṣân, rakib ʻala kafal elfa'ras* |
| 10 Did I not tell you to look to the horse half an | mâ ḳultil'lak, lâzim tdabbir ilḥṣân ḳabl shrûḳ | *mâ ḳulti lakshi, lâzim tiḥad'dar elḥuṣân ḳable* |

| | | |
|---|---|---|
| hour before sunrise ? | (or ṭlû‘) ish-shams' bnuṣṣ sâ‘a ? | *shurûḳ (or ṭulû‘) eshshems' binuṣṣ'ê sâ‘a ?* |
| This is not the horse which they showed me yesterday | haida mush ilḥ-ṣân illi farjûni yâh mbâriḥ | *di mush elḥuṣân elli warrûhli embâreḥ* |
| Take this horse back to his master and tell him that I will only accept the horse which I tried yesterday | rajji‘ halḥṣân laṣâḥbo uḳul'lo inni mâ biḳbal illa ilḥṣân illi jarrab'to mbâriḥ | *ragga‘ elḥuṣân di liṣâḥibo weḳul'lo inni mâ aḳbalsh illa elḥuṣân elli garrab'to embâreḥ* |
| This is the horse of which we spoke (lit., about which the compact) | haida hû ilḥṣân illi ṣâr ishsharṭ' ‘alaih' | *âdi' hûwe elḥuṣân elli ḥaṣal esh-sharṭ' ‘alêh* |
| 4 But this is not his saddle | lâkin haida mâ hû sarjo | *lâkin di mush sargo* |
| This saddle is no good at all; riding on it is bad; it is hard, besides being old and torn | hassarj' mâ byinfa‘ abadan; rikbto radîyi; ḳâsi, ‘ada inno ‘atîḳ wimkhaz'-zaḳ | *essarg'ê di mâ binfa‘sh' ebeden; rukûbto baṭṭâle; gâmid ma‘inno ḳadîm wemekhaz'zaḳ* |
| The girths are rotten | ilḥizâmât' mihri-yîn | *elḥizâmât' mahrî-yîn'* |
| 7 Change the saddle and the bridle | ṛaiyir issarj' willjâm | *ṛaiyar essarg' willigâm* |
| The stirrups are too short, make them longer | irrkâbât' ḳuṣâr, ṭauwil'hon | *errikâbât' ḳuṣai-yara, ṭauwil'-hum* |
| The stirrups are too long, make them shorter | irrkâbât' ṭwâl, ḳaṣṣir'hon | *errikâbât' ṭuwâl, ḳaṣṣar'hum* |
| 10 Tighten the girth | shidd ilḥizâm | *shidd elḥizâm* |
| Is everything ready ? | kull shî ḥâḍir ? | *kulli shê ḥâḍir ?* |
| Does nothing more detain us ? | mâ baḳa fî ‘âḳa ? | *mâ baḳâsh fîh shê yi‘akh'kharna* |
| 13 Have we forgotten nothing ? | mush nâsyîn' shî ? | *mush nasyîn ḥâge* |

| | | |
|---|---|---|
| **Hold the stirrups that I may mount** | haddi irrkâb tâ irkab | *imsik errikâb 'ala shân arkab* |
| **We will go on before you (plur.)** | niḥnanisbuḳ'kon | *iḥne nisbaḳ'kum* |
| **We cannot walk with you (plur.)** | mâ fîna nmâshî'-kon | *mâ niṛdarshi nimâshî'kum* |
| 4 **We will wait for you (plur.) at the spring ..** | mninṭur'kon 'al-'ain' il... | *nistannâkum 'al'ên el...* |
| **Go on! do not stop (plur.)!** | sûḳu[1], lâ tit'au'-waḳu! | *sûḳu[1], mâ tit=akhkharûsh!* |
| **Go (plur.) on before us to the village..and pitch the tents for our arrival** | rûḥu ḳuddâmna liḍḍai''a il... winṣu'bu iṣṣwâ-wîn' labain'ma nûṣal | *rûḥu ḳuddâmna lilbe'led el...winṣu'bu elkhiyâm lamma nûṣal* |

*Night's Quarters in a Village*

| | | |
|---|---|---|
| 7 **We will pass the night in the first village to which we come** | baddna nbât fî auwal ḍai'a nû-ṣal laiha | *biddina nebât fî auwal beled nûṣal liha* |
| **How far is it from here to the first village on our road?** | ḳaddaish' min haun la=au'wal ḍai'a fî darbna? | *kâm min hene li=au'wal beled fî darbina?* |
| **About half an hour, an hour, two hours, three hours** | taḳrîban(bkham-min) nuṣṣ sâ'a, sâ'a, sâ'atain', tlât sâ'ât' | *bakham'min nuṣṣê sâ'a, sâ'a, sâ'atên', telât sâ'ât'* |
| 10 **The sun is near setting; we must hurry that we may arrive before dark** | ishshams' ṣârit 'alṛurûb; lâzim nista''jil (or nrauwij) tâ nûṣal ḳabl mâ t'attim | *eshshems' ḳarrabet 'alṛurûb; lâzim nista''gil 'ala shân nûṣal ḳablê mâ ta'at'tim* |

---

[1] *sâḳ* **is to drive, urge on, to gallop, ride quickly; e.g.** *sûḳ!* **ride quickly, look sharp!** suḳna mlîḥ *suḳna ṭaiyib* **we galloped well.**

| | | |
|---|---|---|
| **We have arrived (here we are)** | wuṣil'na (or wuṣul'na) | *wiṣil'na* |
| **Ho there, people of the house!** | yâ iṣḥâb ilbait'! | *yâ aṣḥâb elbêt!* |
| **Who (is there)?** | mîn haida? | *mîn di?* |
| **4 Where is there a place at which we can spend this night?** | wain fî shî maṭraḥ nbât fîh hallai'li? | *fên maṭraḥ nebâṭ fîh ellêlâ'-di?* |
| **Please (step in) to us** | tfaḍḍal la'and'na | *itfaḍ'ḍal 'andina* |
| **Where is the sheik's (priest's) house?** | wain bait shaikh iḍḍai''a (ilkhûri)? | *fên bêt shêkh elbe'led?* |
| **7 Can we not enter (lit., descend or alight at) the priest's house?** | mâ fîna ninzil fî bait ilkhûri? | *mâ nirdarshi ninzil fî bêt elkhûri?* |
| **As you wish, Sir** | mitl mâ bitrîd, yâ sîdi | *zê mâ terîd, yâ sîdi* |
| **Take us to the house of the priest** | dillna 'ala bait ilkhûri | *dillina 'ala bêt elkhûri* |
| **10 Good evening, father!** | Alla ymassîkon bilkhair', yâ abûna![1] | *Allâh yimassîkum bilkhêr, yâ abûna![1]* |
| **Have you room for us this night?** | bîsâ''na 'indak illai'li? | *tisâ'na 'andak ellêle?* |
| **Welcome! the blessing has entered!** | ahlan wasah'lan! ḥallit ilba'raki! | *ahlan wasah'lan! ḥallet elba'rake!* |

[1] Properly 'our father'; it is the usual address to all that wear a clerical coat. These people, especially the monks, rank almost always very low: they are dirty and amazingly ignorant. Laudable exceptions are sometimes met with among the Maronite (the name is derived from the monastery of St. John Maro) secular priests in the Lebanon. Indeed, the entire Maronite population is intelligent, industrious, and more honest than the orthodox Greek.

| | | |
|---|---|---|
| **Abdallah, bring in the saddle-bag** | yâ ʿabdal'la, jîb ilkhurj' lajûwa | *yâ ʿabdal'la, shîl elkhurg'è gûwa* |
| **Provide a place for the animals** | dabbir maṭraḥ liddwâbb | *ḥaddar maṭraḥ liddawâbb* |
| **Feed and water them** | ʿallik'lon wis-ḳîhon | *ʿallaḳ ʿalêhum wasḳîhum* |
| **4 Whence come you (plur.)?** | mnain jâyîn'? | *intû gâ-iyîn' min ên?* |
| **Where do you (plur.) intend to go?** | lawain' ḳâṣdîn'? | *intû ḳaṣdîn ʿala fên?* |
| **We are travellers** | niḥna sûwâḥ' | *iḥne sûwâḥ'* |
| **7 You (plur.) are surely very tired** | bitkûnu tiʿbânîn' ktîr? | *intû taʿbânîn' ke-tîr?* |
| **I am a little tired** | ana tiʿbân shwai-yi | *ana taʿbân shu-wai'ye* |
| **Will you have re-freshing drinks?** | bitrîd sharbât? | *ʿâ-iz sharbât?* |
| **10 Will you have water and wine?** | bitrîd moi win-bîd? | *ʿâ-iz moiye wane-bîd?* |
| **A glass of lemon-ade, if I may ask** | kubbâyit laimû-nâ'ḍa in ḥisin | *kubbâyet lêmû-nâ'ta iza kân yimki'nak* |
| **To-morrow we will stay here** | bukra baddna niksir haun | *bukra biddina nukʿud hene* |
| **13 I will start from here to-morrow morning at seven o'clock European time (see p. 69 note)** | baddi sâfir min haun bukra ʿala bukra issâʿa sabʿa franjîyi | *biddi asâfir min hene bukrabedri essâʿa sabʿa i-frengî* |
| **Get the horses ready for 6.30** | ḥaḍḍir ilkhail' lis-sâʿa sitti unuṣṣ' | *ḥaḍḍar elkhêl lis-sâʿa sitte wenuṣṣ'* |
| **Have you (plur.) eaten?** | akal'tu? | *kaltu?* |
| **16 Will you (plur.) sup?** | bitrîdu titʿash'-shu? | *ʿâ-izîn' titʿash'-shu?* |
| **We will provide you (plur.) with what is ready: bread, and cheese, eggs, and curdled milk** | mindabbir'lkon mnilḥawâḍir: khubz ujibn' ubaiḍ' ula'ban | *niḥaḍḍar'lukum min elḥawâḍir: ʿêsh wegibn'è we-bêḍ wele'ben ḥâ-miḍ* |

| | | |
|---|---|---|
| Can you (plur.) not roast us a chicken and cook some eggs in butter? | mâ fîkon tishwûlna jâji (or ṭair jâj) utiklûlna baiḍât bsaman? | *mâ tirḍarûsh tishwûlina farkha wetiḳlûlina bêḍât' bisemn'?* |
| Hurry (plur.) with the supper, we are hungry | staʿjilu bilʿa'sha, niḥna jûʿânîn' | *istaʿgi'lu elʿa'she, iḥne gaʿânîn'* |
| Are you (plur.) sleepy? | ḥaḍrit'kon niʿsânîn'? | *ḥaḍarât'kum neʿsânîn'?* |
| 4 Will you go to bed (take your (plur.) rests)? | bitrîdu tâkhdu râḥat'kon? | *ʿâ=izîn'' tâkhudu râḥit'kum?* |
| We will talk a little | mnithâka shwaiyi | *nitḥâki shuwai'ye* |
| What is the name of this village (of this place)? | shû ism haḍḍai'ʿa (halba'lad[1])? | *ism elbe'led[1] dî ê?* |
| 7 Has it many inhabitants? | sukkânha ktâr? | *sukkânha ketîr?* |
| Of what religion are the people here? | min aina ṭâyifi[2] innâs haun? | *minânhi ṭâ=ife[2] ennâs hene?* |

---

[1] balad *beled* generally means a town, and that a small one, but sometimes it is used in a general sense for place, locality; e.g. shû (or wain) baladak *beledak ê* (or *fên beledak*) what (or where) is your town, i.e. where do you live?

[2] plur. ṭawâyif *ṭawâ=if*; it is properly 'sect' or 'community,' but actually has more a political than an ecclesiastical sense (just as the Turkish millet'), owing to the artfulness with which the Turks have at all times profited by the passions, especially by the lust of power of the ecclesiastical heads of the different religious communities. Hence the correctness of the current rendering of ṭâyifi *ṭâ=ife* by 'nation'; indeed the followers of the various religions in the Ottoman empire consider themselves throughout as 'nations'. Thus it is that the inhabitants of Syria have no feeling for, or understanding of, the prevailing unity in language, views, and customs: the Maronite is Maronite, the Orthodox is 'Greek,' etc.,

| | | |
|---|---|---|
| In what district is it? | min aina ḳaḍa?[1] | *minânhu ḳaḍa?*[1] |
| Is its ground fertile? | arḍha ṛallîli? | *arḍâha ṭaiyibe?* |
| What are its products? | shû hî maḥṣûlât'ha? | *maḥṣûlât'ha ê?* |
| 4 Is its climate good? | manâkh-ha ṭaiyib? | *hawâha ṭaiyib?* |
| There is no disease here | mâ bîṣîr' haun maraḍ | *mâ fîshi ʿaiya* |
| Is it (viz., the village, fem.) cold in winter? | bârdi fishshi'ti? | *bâride fishshi'te?* |
| 7 The temperature is medium, it neither gets very cold nor very warm | ilha'wa muʿtadil; mâ bîṣîr' bard ktîr ulâ shaub ktîr | *elha'wa muʿtadil; mâ yegîsh bardê ketîr welâ ḥarrê ketîr* |
| Is its water good? | moiyit'ha ṭaiybi? | *moiyet'ha ṭaiyibe?* |
| Is there (in it) a good spring? | fîha ʿain mlîḥa? | *fîha ʿên ṭaiyibe?* |
| 10 Are the inhabitants contented (Syr. with the worldly goods, Eg. with their condition)? | il=ahâli mabsûṭîn' fiddin'yi? | *el=ahâli mabsûṭîn' fî ḥâlhum?* |
| No, they are in debt | lâ, mitṛallbîn | *lâ, mitṛallibîn* |
| The harvests were bad the last two years | ilmwâsim mâḥli hassintain' | *elmewâsim baṭṭâle essenetên dôl* |
| 13 Is there a doctor in this place? | halba'lad fîha ḥakîm? | *elbe'led dî fîha ḥakîm?* |
| Are there any soldiers here? | fî ʿasker haun? | *fîh ʿasker hene?* |

---

and the Muslim who, just as all the others, talks Arabic, is in the eyes of his Christian countrymen a—Turk!

[1] A ḳaḍa is governed by a ḳâyimmaḳâm'; several ḳaḍa form (in Syria) a mutaṣarrifîyi (Turkish muteṣar'rifliḳ), and several of the latter constitute a wilâyi *wilâye* (Turkish wilayet'), province.

| | | |
|---|---|---|
| **These trousers got quite dirty on the road; take and wash them (Arab. sing.)** | halbanṭalûn twassakh fid-darb' kullo; khôd ṛasslo | *elbanṭalûn di itwas'sakh fid-darb' kullo; khod iṛsilo* |
| **The clothes got wet in the rain; spread them in the sun that they may dry quickly** | ittyâb tballalu mnilma'ṭar; inshur'hon fish-shams' tâ yinshafu ḳawâm | *elhudûm itbal'lu minennaṭar; inshur'hum fish-shems' ʿala shân yinshafu ḳawâm* |
| **These things have dried** | halawâʿi nishfu | *elḥawâ-ig dôl nishfet* |
| **4 We have prolonged our evening's entertainment (i.e., our conversation); I wish to sleep** | ṭauwal'na issah'-ra; baddi nâm | *ṭauwil'na essah'-ra; biddi anâm* |
| **Abdallah, prepare the bed** | yâ ʿabdal'la, dab-bir ilfar'shi | *yâ ʿabdal'la, ḥaḍ-ḍar elmarta'be* |
| **Do you sleep on the floor?** | bitnâm ʿalarḍ'? | *tenâm ʿalarḍ'?* |
| **7 I cannot sleep on the floor; it is summer, I am afraid of the fleas** | mâ biḳdir nâm ʿalarḍ'; iddin'yi ṣaif, bkhâf mnil-brâṛît' | *mâ aṛdarsh' anâm ʿalarḍ'; eddin'ye ṣêf, bakhâf min elbarâṛît'* |
| **Have you (plur.) no bedstead?** | mâfi ʿindkon takht? | *mâ fîsh ʿandu-kum serîr?* |
| **No, Sir** | khair, yâ sîdi | *lâ, yâ sîdi* |
| **10 Let them shake out the mats and sprinkle the floor and sweep it properly** | khallîhon ynaffi-ḍu ilḥuṣr' wiy-rish'shu ilarḍ' wiykannisûha mlîḥ | *khallîhum yenaf'-faḍu elḥuṣr' wa-yerush'shu el-arḍ' wayuknu-sûha ṭaiyib* |
| **It is winter (the rainy season); I fear the damp** | iddin'yi shiti; bkhâf mnirrṭûbi | *eddin'ye shite; bakhâf min erruṭûbe* |
| **Spread the oil-cloth (waterproof) cloak under the mattress** | ifrush kabbût ilmsham'maʿ taḥt ilfar'shi | *ifrish elkabbût elmusham'maʿ taḥt elmarta'be* |

| | | |
|---|---|---|
| **Are the sheets clean?** | ishshrâshif nḍîfi? | *elmilâyât' naḍîfe?* |
| **This cover is soiled** | ḥalmal'ḥafi wuskha | *elliḥâf di wisikh* |
| **Change these sheets** | ṛaiyir hashshrâshif | *ṛaiyar elmilâyât' dôl* |
| 4 **It is cold; bring me the woollen blanket** | iddin'yi bard; jibli ḥrâm iṣṣûf | *eddin'ye bard; hâtli elḥirâm eṣṣûf* |
| **Have you not a thicker coverlet than this?** | mâ ʿindak lḥâf atḳal min haida? | *mâ ʿandak'shi liḥâf atḳal min di?* |
| **Bring yet another coverlet** | jîb lḥâf tâni kamân | *hât liḥâf tâni kemân* |
| 7 **Bring me the travelling rug** | jibli ḥrâm issa'far | *hâtli ḥirâm essa'far* |
| **Spread it over the bed** | ifru'sho fauḳ ilfar'shi | *ifrisho fôḳ elmarta'be* |
| **Bring me my things out of the saddle-bags** | jibli awâʿî'yi mnilkhurj' | *hâtli ḥawâ≈igi min elkhurg'* |
| 10 **Give me the night-clothes** | aʿṭîni tyâb innaum' | *idîni hudûm ennôm* |
| **I forgot to wind up my watch** | nsît dauwir sâʿati | *nisît adau'war sâʿati* |
| **Give me the purse out of the trousers-pocket** | aʿṭîni jizdân ilmaṣâri min jaibit ilbanṭalûn | *eʿṭîni guzlân elfulûs min gêb elbanṭalûn* |
| 13 **It seems I have lost the watch-key** | mbaiyin ḍaiyaʿt' miftâḥ issâʿa | *elbai'yin ḍaiyaʿt'ê muftâḥ essâʿa* |
| **Ask the master of the house if he has a watch-key** | is≈al ṣâḥib ilbait' iza kân ʿindo miftâḥ sâʿa | *is≈al ṣâḥib elbêt iza kân ʿando muftâḥ sâʿa* |
| **Put out the light** | iṭfi iḍḍau' | *iṭfi ennûr* |
| 16 **Bring me some water** | jibli shwaiyi moiyi | *hâtli shuwai'ye moiye* |
| **Boy, get the horses ready** | yâ walad, dabbir ilkhail' | *yâ waled, ḥaḍḍar elkhêl* |
| **Did you feed them?** | ʿallaḳti'lon? | *ʿallaḳtu ʿalêhum?* |

| | | |
|---|---|---|
| **Did you water them?** | saḳait'hon | *sḳêthum?* |
| **Did you curry them?** | ḥassait'hon? | *masaḥ'tûhum?* |
| **Go, water them, feed and curry them** | rûḥ sḳîhon u'al-liḳ'lonuḥiss'hon | *rûḥ isḳîhum we 'al'laḳ 'alêhum weim'saḥ* |
| 4 **We will start in the cool (of the morning)** | baddna nsâfir'al-brûd | *biddina nesâfir 'alburûd* |
| **Saddle my horse and bridle him** | isruj ḥṣâni wil-ji'mo | *sarrag ḥuṣâni welaggi'mo* |
| **The mule is unshod and the horse has broken girths** | ilbarl' ḥifyân wil-hṣân mḳaṭṭa'a ḥzâmâ'to | *elbarl'a ḥafyâne walḥuṣân meḳaṭ'ṭa'a ḥizâmâ'to* |
| 7 **See if there is a farrier here who can shoe him (lit., who can put him a new shoe), and a saddler to repair the girths** | shûf yâ iza kân fî haun bîṭâr' yḥuṭṭlo na'l jdîd, wisrû-ji yṣalliḥ il-ḥizâmât' | *shûf iza kân hene bêṭâr' ye-ḥuṭ'ṭulo na'lê gedîd wasurûgi yi-ṣal'laḥ elḥizâmât'* |
| **My master, I have had the mule shod, but we found no saddler** | yâ m'allmi, il-barl' baiṭar'to, ulâkin srûji mâ lâḳai'na | *yâ sîdi, elbarl'a baiṭar'tâha, we-lâkin surûgi mâ leḳê'nâsh* |
| **What shall we do?** | kîf baddna na'-mil? | *ni'mil ê?* |
| 10 **The livery-man**[1] **has a packing-needle and pack-thread with him; he will repair the girths** | ilmkâri ma'o msalli ukhîṭân' maṣṣîṣ; bîḳaṭ'-ṭib ilḥizâmât' | *elmukâri mi'âh mesal'le wedu-bâre; yiḳaṭ'ṭab elḥizâmât'* |

[1] **Or the boy sent by him to accompany the travellers; Arabic** mukâri or mkâri *mukâri*, **the Europeans usually calling him 'mooker.'**

| | | |
|---|---|---|
| When we come to a village we will repair them properly or change them | mata wuṣul'na la-ba'lad minṣal-liḥ'hon mlîḥ yimma minṛai-yir'hon | *mata mâ wiṣil'na libe'led niṣal-laḥ'hum ṭaiyib walla niṛaiyar'-hum* |
| Get (plur.) us the breakfast ready | dabbrûlna ittir-wîḳa | *ḥaḍḍarûlna el-ṛa'da* |
| What will you have | shû bitrîd? | *'â=iz ê?* |
| 4 Boil (plur.) us some milk | fauwirûlna ḥalîb | *fauwarûlina le-ben* |
| Will you have some cheese and soft-boiled eggs? | bitrîd jibni u-baiḍ' brisht? | *'â=iz gibnê webêḍ birisht'?* |
| I want five, six hard-boiled eggs | baddi khamst, sitt baiḍât mas-lûḳin' mlîḥ | *biddi khamsa, sitte bêḍât' mas-lûḳîn' ṭaiyib* |
| 7 The breakfast is ready | ittirwîḳa ḥâḍra | *elṛa'da ḥâḍir* |
| How are you this morning, Sir (how did you enter on the morning to-day)? | yâ khawâja, kîf aṣbaḥt'ilyaum'? | *yâ khawâga, kêf mâ aṣbaḥt' en-nahar'da?* |
| I hope you have rested well | inshal'la irtaḥt' fî naumtak | *inshallâh ir-taḥt'ê fî nômak* |
| 10 Load up! | ḥammlu! | *ḥammilu!* |
| Gather the things and put them in the saddle-bags | limm ilawâ'i uḥuṭṭ'hon bil-khurj' | *limm elḥawâ=ig weḥuṭ'ṭuhum fil-khurg'* |
| Take care you lose nothing | û'a tḍaiyi' shî | *û'a tiḍai'ya' shê* |
| 13 Take provision with you | khôd zûwâ'di ma'ak | *khod zûwâ'de mi-'âk* |
| Do not forget the roast chicken and the boiled eggs | lâ tinsa ijjâji il-mishwîyi wil-baiḍât ilmas-lûḳin' | *mâ tinsâsh el-far'kha elmash-wîye walbêḍât' elmaslûḳîn'* |
| See if there is any fresh cheese | shûf iza kân fî jibni ṭarîyi | *shûf iza kân fîh gibne ṭâza* |
| 16 Take a bottle of Lebanon wine with you | khôd ma'ak ḳan-nînit nbîd ba-ladi | *khod mi'âk ḳizâ-zet nebîd beledi* |

| | | |
|---|---|---|
| **Have you paid for the fodder of the beasts?** | dafa't' 'alîḳ idd-wâbb? | *dafa't'ê 'alîḳ ed-dewâbb?* |
| **I wanted to pay, but they took nothing from me** | ritt idfa' lâkin mâ akhadu minni | *kuntê 'a=iz adfa' lâkin mâ akhadûsh minni* |
| **Give this to the servant** | a'ṭi haida liṣṣâni' | *idîh lilkhaddâm* |
| **4 Do not forget the blanket with which I covered myself last night** | lâ tinsa ilhrâm illi traṭṭait' fîh hallai'li | *mâ tinsâsh elhirâm elli itraṭṭêt fîh ellêle* |
| **We packed up all the things and loaded the mules** | ḍabbai'na ilawâ'i kullhon uḥammal'na ilbaṛl' | *lammêna elhawâ=ig kulluhum weḥammil'na elbaṛl'a* |
| **Go on, we will start** | yalla, nrûḥ | *yalla, nerûḥ* |

*On the March*

| | | |
|---|---|---|
| **7 We have started early; it is still cold** | bakkar'na; ba'd fî bard | *baddar'na; lissa fîh bard* |
| **I forgot to thicken my garment (i.e. to dress myself more warmly)** | nsît sammik malbûsi | *nisît ataḳḳal melbûsi* |
| **The weather has become warm** | difyit iddin'yi | *difyet eddin'ye* |
| **10 I feel the heat** | ḥassait' bish-[shaub'] | *ḥassêt bilḥarr'* |
| **I will take off my cloak** | baddi ishlaḥ kabbûti | *biddi aḳla' kabbûti* |
| **Take it, strap it to the saddle behind you** | khôd, sammṭo warâk | *khod, urbu'ṭo warâk* |
| **13 The weather has changed** | ṛaiyar ilha'wa | *itṛai'yar elha'wa* |
| **It will rain** | baddha tshatti | *râḥ tishti* |
| **Quick, give me the waterproof** | ḳawâm, a'ṭîni ilmsham'ma' | *ḳawâm, e'ṭîni elmusham'ma'* |
| **16 It is spitting with [rain]** | 'am bitnaḳ'ḳiṭ | *bitnad'da'* |

| | | |
|---|---|---|
| **It is raining** | 'am bitshat'ti or nizil ishshi'ti | *betish'ti* or *nizil eshshi'te* |
| **Ride quickly that we may reach the village before we get wet, otherwise we shall be drenched** | sûḳu tâ nûṣal lidḍai''a ḳabl mâ nitran'nakh willa minṣîr moi | *sûḳu nûṣal elbe'led ḳablê mâ nitran'nakh willa beḳêna moiye* |
| **What is the name of that place on the top of yonder hill (which lies at the foot of that mountain, on the ridge of the mountain, on the slope of this valley, in the bottom of this valley)?** | shû ism haidâk ilba'lad illi 'ala râs haidîk ittal'li (illi fî laḥf haidâk ijja'bal, 'ala ḍahr ijja'bal, 'ala kitf halwâdi, fî ka'b halwâdi)? | *ê ism elbe'led dikhâ elli 'ala râs ettall' dok-hâ (elli fîh safḥ egge'bel dok-hâ, 'ala ḍahr egge'bel, 'ala kitf elwâdi di, fî ka'b elwâdi di)?* |
| 4 **What is this building which (lies) before us?** | shû hal'amâra illi ḳuddâmna? | *êsh el'emâra dî elli ḳuddâmna?* |
| **To whom does this monastery belong?** | lamîn haddair'? | *limîn eddêr di?* |
| **Is this a monastery or a convent?** | haida dair ruhbân yimma dair râhbât'? | *di dêr ruhbân walla dêr rahibât?* |
| 7 **This is a school** | haida madrasi | *di medrese* |
| **What is the name of this tree?** | shû ism hashshaj'ra? | *ism eshsha'gara dî ê?* |
| **Does it bear (fruit)?** | btiḥmil? | *betiḥ'mil?* |
| 10 **Is its fruit edible?** | tamar'ha byittâkal? | *tamraha yitâkil?* |
| **Of what kind is its fruit, large or small?** | shû shikl tamar'ha, kbîr yimma zṛîr? | *minânhu shikl tamar'ha, kebîr walla zuṛai'yar?* |
| **Has it a kernel?** | ilo bizr? | *loh bizr?* |
| 13 **Fruit-tree** | fâkihâ'ni | *fâkihâ'ne* |
| **This is a tree that bears flowers only** | hai shajra btiḥmil zahr bass | *dî shagara betiḥ'mil zahrê bess* |

| | | |
|---|---|---|
| **What are those black tents?** | shû hiyi halkhi'yam issûd? | *êsh elkhiyâm dî essûd?* |
| **Those are Bedouin tents (a Bedouin camp)** | hai khiyam ʿarab (nazl ʿarab) | *dî khiyâm ʿarab* |
| **Of what tribe are these?** | mîn aina ḳabîli haudi? | *minânhi ḳabîle dôl?* |
| 4 **Who is the sheik of this tribe?** | mîn hû shaikh halḳabîli? | *mîn shêkh elḳabîle?* |
| **This valley is large; is there a river in it?** | halwâdi kbîr; fîhi nahr? | *elwâdi di kebîr; fîh nahr?* |
| **This valley is nothing but a channel; it carries (water) in winter and dries up at the end of spring** | halwâdi mâ hû illa sâḳiyi; btiḥmil fî îyâm' ishshi'ti ubitnash'shif fî âkhir irrbîʿ | *elwâdi di mâ húwe illa sâḳiye; betiḥ'mil fî aiyâm eshshi'te wabitnash'shiffi âkhir errebîʿ* |
| 7 **Whence does this river come?** | hannahr' mnain jâyi? | *ennahr'è di gâ-i min ên?* |
| **From the mountain which is opposite us** | mnijja'bal illi ḳbâlna | *min egge'bel elli ḳuṣṣâdna* |
| **Does it flow into the sea?** | bîṣubb' filbaḥr'? | *biṣubb' filbaḥr'?* |
| 10 **Is this mountain all rock (boulders) or are there any villages on it?** | hajja'bal kullo waʿr yimma fîh ḍiyaʿ? | *egge'bel di kullo waʿr walla fîh bilâd?* |
| **At its foot there are villages, in its middle there is an old building like a castle** | fî laḥfo fî ḍiyaʿ, fî wasṭo fî ʿamâr ḳadîm ka-in'no ḳalʿa | *fî safḥo beled, fî wuṣto ʿemâra ḳadîme ke-in'nâha ḳalʿa* |
| **On the eastern side all is inhabited** | fî jihit ishsharḳîyi kullo ʿamâr | *fî gihet eshsharḳîye kullo ʿamâr* |
| 13 **It seems we have come to a descending place (i.e. to a descent)** | mbaiyin wuṣul'na lamaṭ'raḥ nazli | *elbai'yin wiṣil'na limaṭ'raḥ nazle* |

| | | |
|---|---|---|
| **Can one ride along this road?** | iddarb' bitrak'-kib? | *yirtikib fiddarb'?* |
| **You can ride half-way (lit., to its half); when we reach the vicinity of the valley it becomes very steep** | bitrak'kib la-ḥadd' nuṣṣha; uma'ta wuṣul'na laḳurb' ilwâdi bîṣîr' daraj ktîr | *yirtikib liḥadd'ê nuṣṣɔ; wema'ta wiṣil'na liḳurb' elwâdi yidaḥrag ketîr* |
| **Then it is best to dismount** | fa=i'zan ilau'faḳ nḥauwil | *baḳa el=au'faḳ ninzil* |
| **4 Hold the horse that I may dismount** | haddi ilḥṣân tâ inzil | *imsik elḥuṣân ʿala shân anzil* |
| **Lead him on this slope** | ḳido fî hannaz'li | *ḳûdu finnazlâ di* |
| **This river is large** | hannahr' kbîr | *ennahr'ê di kebîr* |
| **7 Round it there are many bogs** | ḥawalaih' fî naʿṣ ktîr | *ḥauwalêh nazaz ketîr* |
| **The ground is miry** | ilarḍ' mûḥli | *elarḍ'ê muwaḥ'-ḥale* |
| **This bog seems deep** | mbaiyin hannaʿṣ' ḳawi (or ṛamîḳ) | *elbai'yin enna'zaz di ḳawi* (or *ṛa-mîḳ*) |
| **10 We cannot get along further here** | mâ fîna nrûḥ min haun | *mâ nirdar'shi nerûḥ min henc* |
| **Look for a better road** | iṭṭal'liʿ ʿala darb aḥsan | *dauwar ʿala darb aḥsan* |
| **We had better go back and make a detour** | ilau'faḳ nirjaʿ lawa'ra windûr iddau'ra | *el=au'faḳ nirgaʿ liwa'ra wane-liff'ê laffa* |
| **13 Where may one cross the river?** | mnain byinḳa'ṭiʿ innahr'? | *min ên ennâs ti-ʿaddi ennahr'?* |
| **Has it a ford or a bridge?** | ilo mukhâḍa yim-ma jisr? | *lo khôḍ walla gisr?* |
| **The ford is deep and long** | ilmukhâḍa ṛamî-ḳa uṭawîli | *elkhôḍ ṛamîḳ wa-ṭawîl* |
| **16 It seems this river is rapid** | mbaiyin hannahr' ʿazûm | *elbai'yin ennahr'ê di ṭaiyâr* |
| **One is afraid of the current** | byinkhâf mnis-sa'bali (or mnil-ḥâmû'li) | *khâ=ifîn min eṭ-ṭaiyâr* |

| | | |
|---|---|---|
| **I dare not pass through the water** | mâ bistar'ji iḳṭaʿ bilmoi' | *mâ bastag'ri afût filmoi'ye* |
| **We had better pass over the bridge** | aḥsan niḳṭaʿ ʿajjisr' | *aḥsan niʿaddi ʿaggisr'* |
| **Sir, the bridge is far; we must make a great turn in order to come to it** | yâ sîdi, ijjisr' bʿʿîd; lâzim ndûr daura kbîri tâ nûṣal laih | *yâ sîdi, eggisr' beʿîd; lâzim nedûr dôra kebîre ʿala shân nûṣal'lo* |
| 4 **Why expose oneself to danger?** | laish ilmukhâṭara? | *lê elmukhâṭara?* |
| **Before us there is a steep ascent** | ḳuddâmna ṭalʿa ḳawîyi | *ḳuddâmna ṭalʿa ḳawîye* |
| **Heavens! what a mountain!** | yâ laṭîf! milla ʿaḳabi! | *yâ salâm! milla ʿaḳabe!* |
| 7 **The horses will be suffocated in this heat** | ilkhail' baddha tifṭus bihashshaub' | *elkhêl lâzim tifṭas min elḥarr'ê di* |
| **Tighten the girths that the saddle does not slide down** | shidd ilḥizâm tâ mâ yiḳshuṭ issarj' | *shidd elḥizâm ʿala shân mâ yuḳaʿʿshi essarg'* |
| **Why is this horse lashing out?** | laish halḥṣân ʿam bîlab'biṭ? | *elḥuṣân di beyur'fuṣ lê?* |
| 10 **It is going to throw me** | raḥ bîwaḳḳiʿʿni | *râḥ yiwaḳḳaʿʿni* |
| **Look, the mooker has fallen off the mule** | shûf ilmkâri waḳaʿ mnilbaṛl' | *shûf elmukâri wiḳiʿ min ʿalbaṛl'a* |
| **Poor (boy), he has sprained his wrist** | yâ maskîn, infa'kashit îdo | *yâ maskîn, itfar'ki'shet îdo* |
| 13 **The bone is dislocated** | infakk' ilʿaḍm' | *infakk' elʿaḍm'* |
| **His foot too is wounded** | inja'raḥit kamân ijro | *inga'raḥet kemân riglo* |
| **Bandage it for him** | irbuṭ'lo yâha | *irbuṭhâlo* |
| 16 **Are we still far from the plain?** | lissâna bʿʿîdîn' ʿanissahl'? | *lissaḥ'na beʿîdîn' ʿanessahl'?* |

| | | |
|---|---|---|
| **In a quarter of an hour we shall come to a green meadow** | ba'd rub' sâ'a nû-ṣal lamarj' akh-ḍar | *ba'dê ruba' sâ'a nûṣal limarg' akhḍar* |
| **We are tired; we will take a little rest** | t'ibna; baddna nâkhud râḥa shwaiyi (or baddna nistrîḥ shwaiyi) | *ti'ib'na; biddina nâkhud râḥa shuwai'ye (or bid-dina nisterai'-yaḥ shuwai'ye)* |
| **We dismount at the spring which is in the middle of the meadow** | minḥau'wil 'al-'ain' illi fî nuṣṣ ilmarj' | *ninzil 'al'ên elli fî wusṭ elmarg'* |
| 4 **Its water is good and around it there is shade, and now is the time for the siesta** | moiyit'ha ṭaiybi wiḥwâlai'ha fai uhal'laḳ waḳt ilmisijor'no | *moiyet'ha ṭaiyi-be weḥauwalêha ḍill wedilwaḳt'i waḳt elmisigor'-no* |
| **Walk the horses up and down that their sweat may dry, and then water them** | mashshi ilkhail' tâ yinshaf 'a-raḳ'hon uba'dên sḳîhon | *mashshi elkhêl 'ala shân yin-shaf 'araḳ'hum weba'dên. isḳî-hum* |
| **We are hungry; give here (or bring here, come here), let us see what we have to eat** | ji'na; hait, tan-shûf shû fî ma'na lilakl' | *gu'na; hât, ne-shûf mi'âna lilakl' ê* |
| 7 **Go to that herds-man; perhaps he will give us some milk** | rûḥ la'and' hai-dâk irrâ'i; belki bya'ṭîna shwai-yit ḥalîb | *rûḥ 'and errâ'i dokhâ* (pron. *dok-hâ*); *belki yi'ṭîna shuwai'-yet leben* |
| **Put this bottle in the water** | ḥuṭṭ halḳannîni bilmoi' | *ḥuṭṭ elḳizâze dî filmoi'ye* |
| **I want to sleep a little** | baddi namli shwaiyi | *biddi anâm shu-wai'ye* |
| 10 **Bring the carpet and the cushion and cover me with the rug** | jîb issijjâdi wil-mukhad'di uraṭ-ṭîni bilḥrâm | *hât essiggâde wilmikhad'de weraṭṭîni bilḥi-râm* |

| | | |
|---|---|---|
| **Chase away the flies from me** | kishsh ʿanni iddibbân | *nishsh ʿanni eddubbân* |
| **Mind no snake or scorpion creeps on us** | iṣḥa tisraḥ ʿalai'na shî ḥaiyi yimma ʿaḳrabi | *iṣḥa tisraḥ ʿalêna shê ḥaiye walla ʿaḳrabe* |
| **Saddle (plur.) the horses and load (plur.) up** | shiddu ʿalkhail' uḥamm'lu | *shiddu ʿalkhêl weḥam'milu* |
| 4 **The time has passed (i.e., it is late); we can no longer reach the village by daylight** | maḍa ilwaḳt', mâ baḳa fîna nilḥaḳ iḍḍai'ʿa ʿala ḍau | *fât elwaḳt', mâ baḳênâsh' niḳdar nilḥaḳ elbe'led ʿala nûr* |
| **It is yet early** | lissa bakkîr | *lissa bedri* |
| **We have good horses** | khailna ṭaiybi | *khêlna ṭaiyibe* |
| 7 **Hurry on (plur.)** | rauwiju | *istaʿ'gilu* |
| **The weather is not safe** | iddin'yi mâ hî ṭaiybi | *elha'wa mush ṭaiyib* |
| **The wind has got up** | ṭiliʿ ilha'wa | *ṭiliʿ elha'wa* |
| 10 **Look at the dust** | shûf ilṛab'ra | *shûf elṛubâr* |
| **That is a storm, and we are in the open field** | haidi zaubaʿa uniḥ'na filbarrîyi | *di zôba'ʿa wiḥne filkhale* |
| **There is no place where we can enter (take shelter)** | mâ fî maṭraḥ nit=âwa (nulṭi) | *mâ fîsh maṭraḥ yi=wi* |
| 13 **The weather has cleared up; but one can no longer walk for mud** | ṣiḥyit iddin'yi; lâkin mâ baḳa yinmshi mnilwaḥl' | *ṣiḥyet eddin'ye; lâkin mâ baḳâsh yitmishi min elwaḥl'* |
| **Be that as it may, ride (plur.) quickly that we may reach some village, and rest** | kîf mâ kân, sûḳu, tâ nûṣal lashî ḍaiʿa unirtâḥ | *kêf mâ kân, sûḳu, ʿala shân nûṣal libe'led wenirtâḥ* |
| **I feel unwell** | ḥâsis mâli kêf | *ḥâsis mâlîsh' kêf* |
| 16 **My head is giddy** | râsi dâyikh | *râsi dâyikh* |

*Night's Quarters in a Tent*

| | | |
|---|---|---|
| **Do you alight at a house or shall we pitch the tent?** | btinzil fî bait yimma mnin-ṣub'lak iṣṣî-wân'? | *tinzil fî bêt wa-lla ninṣub'lak elkhêma?* |
| **Pitch (plur.) the tent; I have more freedom** | inṣu'bu iṣṣîwân'; bimluk ḥurrîyti aktar | *inṣu'bu elkhêma; bamlik ḥurrîyeti aktar* |
| **Look (plur.) for a dry place where there is not the least dampness** | fattshu 'ala maṭ-raḥ nâshif, mâ fîh rṭûbi aba-dan | *dauwaru 'ala maṭraḥ nâshif, mâ fîsh ruṭûbe ebeden* |
| 4 **This place is low; one cannot sleep here** | halmaṭ'raḥ wâṭi; mâ byinnâm haun | *elmaṭ'raḥ di wâṭi; mâ ninâmshi hene* |
| **The ground is damp, there is miasma in it; the air is foul** | ilarḍ' ruṭbi, fîha 'ufûni; ilha'wa mafsûd | *elar'ḍê riṭbe, fîha 'ufûne; elha'wa fâsid* |
| **Nobody sleeps here and keeps well** | mâ ḥada bînâm' haun ubîdamm' taiyib | *mâ ḥaddish bi-nâm hene weyib'-ka ṭaiyib* |
| 7 **Find (plur.) us a high place, some hill** | shûfûl'na maṭraḥ 'âli, shî talli | *shûfû'lina maṭ-raḥ 'âli, zêyi tall* |
| **Level the ground properly** | mahmid ilarḍ' mliḥ | *mahhia elarḍ'ê ṭaiyib* |
| **Sweep it** | kannis'ha | *uknusha* **(pron.** *uknus-ha)* |
| 10 **Bring me the little wallet** | jibli shanṭit izzrîri | *hâtli esh-han'ṭa ezzuṛai'yare* |
| **Take this key, open it (viz., the wallet, Arab. fem.) and take out the writing-book and the ink-stand** | khôd halmiftâḥ, iftaḥ'ha ushîl minha iddaf'tar widdawâyi | *khod elmuftâḥ di, iftaḥ'ha weshîl minha eddaf'tar waddewâye* |
| **Bring me the box in which are the instruments** | jibli il'ul'bi illi fîha ilâlât' | *hâtli el'il'be elli fîha elâlât'* |

| | | |
|---|---|---|
| Take the big trunk off the mule | nazzil ṣandûḳ il-kbîr mnilbaṛl' | *nazzil eṣṣandûḳ elkebîr min ʿal-baṛ'la* |
| Bring the trunk into the tent | fauwit iṣṣandûḳ liṣṣîwân' | *shîl eṣṣandûḳ fîlkhême* |
| Take the night-shirt and the slippers out of the trunk | shîl ḳamîṣ in-naum' wilban-tuflât mniṣṣan-dûḳ | *shîl ḳamîṣ en-nôm walbâbûg' min eṣṣandûḳ* |
| 4 My health is not yet (settled) restored | kêfi mâ jalas | *kêfi mâ raḳsh* |
| I caught a cold | akhatt' bard | *khatt bard* |
| A headache op-presses me | ḥakam'ni wajaʿ râs | *ḥakam'li wagaʿ râs* |
| 7 My stomach is out of order | miʿdeti mukhar'-baṭa | *miʿdeti melakh'-baṭa* |
| I feel a shivering cold as if I should get the fever | ḥâsis bṭashshât bard ka=in'no ṣâyir'li daur | *ḥâsis biraʿashân bard ke=in'no ga=yâli ḥimme* |
| Put the kettle on the fire and heat me some water | ḥuṭṭ irrak'wi ʿannâr usakh-khin'li shwaiyit moi | *ḥuṭṭ eṭṭâse ʿannâr wesakhkhan'li shuwai'yet moi-ye* |
| 10 Give me the medi-cine chest | aʿṭîni ṣandûḳit ilid'wyi | *eʿṭîni ṣandûḳ el-adwi'ye* |
| Hand me this powder | nâwil'ni hassfûf | *nâwil'ni essufûf dî* |
| Bring me half a glass of water that I may mix with it a few (a couple) of drops from this phial | jibli nuṣṣ kub-bâyit moi tâ naḳḳiṭ'li nuḳṭ-tain' min hal-khanjûr | *hâtli nuṣṣê kub-bâyet moiye ʿala shân ʿanaḳḳaṭ'li nuḳṭatên min el-ḳizâze dî* |
| 13 Cover me well that I may perspire | raṭṭîni ṭaiyib tâ iʿraḳ | *raṭṭîni ṭaiyib ʿa-la shân aʿraḳ* |
| A sudorific remedy | dawa muʿar'riḳ | *dawa muʿar'riḳ* |
| In perspiration; I am in perspiration | ʿirḳân ; ana khâ-yiḍ fî ʿaraḳi | *ʿarḳân ; ana khâ-yiḍ fî ʿaraḳe* |
| 16 Let no one come in to me | lâ tkhalli ḥada yfût laʿan'di | *mâ tikhallîsh ḥadd yekhush'-shê ʿandi* |

| | | |
|---|---|---|
| **Sir will you eat nothing?** | yâ sîdi, mâ btâkul shî? | *yâ sîdi, mâ tâkulsh'?* |
| **I cannot eat anything now** | hallaḳ mâ fîni âkul shî | *dilwaḳ'ti mâ ardarshi âkul shê* |
| **Tell the cook to make me some soup only** | ḳullo lil'ash'shi ya'mil'li shwaiyit shorba bass | *ḳul liṭṭabbâkh yi'mil'li shuwai'yet shorba bess* |
| **4 Let him bring the soup** | khallîh yjîb ishshor'ba | *khallîh yegîb eshshor'ba* |
| **I am better** | kêfi aḥsan | *kêfi aḥsan* |
| **I have recovered** | ṣaḥḥait' | *ṭibt* |
| **7 Call (plur.) me to-morrow morning early** | faiyḳûni bukra bakkîr | *ṣaḥḥûni bukra bedri* |
| **To-morrow early I hope we shall reach Baalbek, thence to the Cedars, and by the next steamer we start from Tripoli** | bukra nûṣal inshal'la bakkîr laba'al'bakk umin'ha lilarz' ufilwâbûr' ilḳâdim minsâfir min ṭrâblus | *bukra nûṣal inshallâh bedri liba'al'bekk wemin'ha lilerz' wefilwâbûr' elḳâdim nisâfir min ṭarâblus* |

# ENGLISH-ARABIC DICTIONARY

**By means of the subjoined vocabulary in smaller type numerous words and phrases may be referred to which are contained in the 'Phrases,' pp. 32 to 149. The first number indicates the page, the second the respective phrase on that page; for instance 97, 10 means: page 97, phrase (or group of words) 10; 95, 5.9 means the fifth and ninth sentences on page 95.**

**ability** ahlîyi *ahlîye*
**able to** .. ahl la... *ahl li...*, ḳâdir la... *ḳâdir li...*
**I am a...** byimkin'ni *yimkin'ni*, **lit., it is possible to me**
**ablution (religious)** wu'ḍû *tawaḍ'ḍi*
**to perform religious a...s** twaḍḍa *itwaḍ'ḍa*
**abode** makân, **pl.** amkine
**abolish** abṭal
**about (around)** ḥawalai' *ḥauwalê*
**(near to)** taḳrîban, takhmîn, ḥaraki **(the latter Syr. only)**
**(concerning)** bikhuṣûṣ
**a...ten pieces** ḥarakit ʿashra ḳiṭaʿ *yîgi ʿeshara ḳiṭaʿ*
**above** fauḳ *fôḳ*, fauḳ min *fôḳ min*
**a... all** ḳabl ilkull' *ḳabl [elkull']*
**from a...** min fauḳ *min fôḳ*
**abroad** fî blâd ajnabîyi *fî bilâd barra*
**absence** ṛaibi *ṛêbe*
**during my a...** bṛaibti *biṛêbeti* or *fî ṛiyâbi*
**absent (adj.)** ṛâyib *ṛâ-ib*
**to a... oneself from** .. ibta'ʿad ʿan .., tabâʿad ʿan .. *itbâʿad ʿan* ..
**abundance** ziyâdi *ziyâde*
**abundant** zâyid *zâ-id*
**abuse (insult)** shatm
**to a...** shatam
**Abyssinia** blâd ilḥa'besh *bilâd elḥa'besh*
**A...n** ḥabeshi, pl. ḥabesh

**a, an** 38,2; 103,1.3; 131,9
**abominable: that is a...** 60,6; 62,7
**about half an hour** 131,9
**a... what** 46,2

**acacia (coll.)** zinzilakht′
**(a single one)** zinzilakh′ti
**Nile acacia** *ṣunṭ*; **this is the thorned acacia (acacia nilotica) of the ancients, not the shady** lebbakh **(albizzia lebbek) which travellers, following a traditional error, generally mistake for it**
**accept** ḳibil
**accident (chance)** ṣudfi [*ṣudfe*]
**(mishap)** muṣîbi *muṣîbe*
**accompany** râfaḳ *rafaḳ*
**according** bmaujib *bimûgib*, ḥasab
**account** ḥisâb *ḥisâb*
**(a written one)** ḳâymit ilḥisâb *ḳâ-imet elḥisâb*
**on my a...** ʿala kîsi
**on a... of** bise′beb, li-ajl′ *li-agl′*, min shân ʿ*ala shân*
**see also news; reason**
**-book** daftar, **pl.** dfâtir *dafâtir*
**accuse somebody** ishta′ka ʿala *ishta′ka min*
**accustomed: to get a... to..** tʿauwad ʿala.. *itʿau′wad* [ʿ*ala..*]
**ache** wajaʿ *wagaʿ*
**to a...** wijiʿ *wigiʿ*
**my head a...s** râsi byûjaʿ′-ni *râsi betûgaʿ′ni*
**acid** ḥâmiḍ
**a...ity** ḥumûḍa
**acre (measure)** feddân; **in Syria = 734 square metres, in Egypt = 4200 sq. m.; see rod**
**across: to go a...** ʿ*abar*
**action (way of acting)** ʿamal, **pl.** aʿmâl
**(lawsuit)** daʿwa, **pl.** daʿâwi
**add** jamaʿ *gamaʿ*
**addition: in a... to this** *fauḳ* haida, ṛair zâlik *ṛêr zâlik*
**address (on an envelope)** ʿunwân, ʿulwân
**(allocution, speech)** khiṭâb
**see also note to 'bêk' in the Arabic Vocabulary, and top note on p. 32**
**adjust** sauwa
**administration** idâre
**administrator** mudîr
**admire: the Oriental very rarely admires; see wonder**
**admission (charge for same)** dukhûlî′yi *temen eddukhûl*
**adorn** zaiyan *zaiyin*
**a... oneself** jakhkh *gakhkh*
**a...ment** zîni *zîne*, zakhrafi *zakhrafe*
**advantage** fâida
**advertisement** iʿlân
**advice** mashwara
**to advise** shâwar *shâwir*
**affair** amr, **pl.** umûr
**afraid** fizʿân *fazʿân*
**to be a... of** khâf min
**I am a... we shall be late**

---

**accept this trifle** 54,8.10
**I a...** 86,12; 130,2
**account: detailed a...** 81,9
**accustomed: not a... to..** 99,1
**action: good a... (horse)** 120,1
**add (put)..to it** 91, 4
**adjure (entreat)** 53, 7
**advance: payment in a...** 86, 9
**affair: a strange a...** 59, 11
**afraid: one is a...** 143, 17

bkhâf nit=akh'khar *ba-khâf nit=akh'khar*
**I am afraid of the rain** ana fiz'ân mnishshi'ti *ana faz'ân min eshshi'te*
**don't be a...** lâ tkhâf *mâ tekhafsh'*, mâ 'alaik'
**Africa** ifrîki'ya
**A...n** ifrîki
**after (of time)** ba'd [warâ
**(behind)** khalf, khalf min,
**(according to)** biḥasb', bmaujib *bimûgib*
**a... four o'clock** ba'd sâ'a arb'a *ba'd essâ'a arba''a*
**run a... him!** irkuḍ *igri warâh!*
**-noon** ba'd iḍḍuhr' *ba'd eḍḍuhr'*; **(last part of it)**
**-wards** ba'dên ['aṣr
**again** 'âd, tâni marra *tâni marra*
**against** ḍidd, 'ala
**age** 'umr; see also old
**(old age)** shaikhûkha, kibr issinn' *kibr essinn'*
**(century, generation)** jîl *gîl*, pl. ijyâl *igyâl*
**agency** wakâle
**agent(representative)**wakîl, pl. wukala
**(manager of estates)**khauli
**ago: long a...** kabl min zamân *kabla min zemân*
**agree on something** itta'fak 'ala
**a... (consent) to something** riḍi bi.., kibil (**with acc.**)
**I a...** bikbal *bakbal*
**a...ment** ittifâk
**agriculture** zarâ'a
**aid**; see help
**ail: what ails you? are you ill?** shû bâk? *mâlak?*, mariḍ?
**air** hawa
**the a... is vitiated here** ilha'wa mafsûd haun *elha'wa mefsûd hene*
**(a tune)** laḥn, pl. alḥân
**Aleppo** ḥaleb
**Alexandretta**; see Scanderoon
**Alexandria** iliskandrîyi *iskenderîye*
**Algeria** ijjazâyir *elgezâ=ir*
**A...n** jezâyir'li *gezâ=ir'li*
**alight**; see descend [beh
**alike** mutashâbih *mutshâ-*
**alive** ḥai, ṭaiyib
**is your father still a...?** abûk ba'do *lissa* ṭaiyib?
**all** kull, jamî' *gamî'*; **(everything)**ilkull'*elkull'*, kullo
**above a... I must have ..** kabl ilkull' baddi .. *kabl elkull' biddi ..*
**all at once (at one time)** fard

---

after (in) three days 96, 6
afternoon: in the a... 68, 2; 85, 7
afterwards 99, 2
again: don't do it a... 52,18.19; 63, 9; bring this list a...96, 14
ago: a month, etc., a... 67,6
air-tight: not a... 103,5
airy 76,15; 86,1
alight: is the pipe a...? 47,15
(put up) 132,7; 147,1
where did you a...? 46,17
all these things 111,1
all that 96,10
all people (everybody) 97,4

marra, **(suddenly)** bil-mar'ra
**all the same (no matter)** mitl ba'ḍo *zê ba'ḍo*, ḳadd ba'ḍo [yalla !
**all right ! (march ! go on !)**
**allow (permit)** samaḥ
**(grant)** a'ṭa
**a... me** ismaḥ' li
**do you a... me ?** btismaḥ' li ? *betismaḥ' li ?*
**to be a...ed** jâz *gâz (yegûz)*
**a...ed (adj.)** jâyiz *gâ=iz*
**ally (a confederate)** ḥalîf, mut'âhid
**almond** lauz *lôz*
**(a single one)** lauzi *lôze*
**almost** illa ḳalîl *illa shu-wai'ye*
**alms** ḥasani *ḥasane*, iḥsân
**alone** wâḥid
**I, thou, he, she, etc. a... (by myself, etc.)** waḥdi, waḥdak, waḥdo, waḥdha *waḥdâha*, etc. [liṣ'ni
**let me a...** khallîni, khal-
**alphabet** hijâ *higâ*
**already : as a rule not expressed**
**also** kazâlik *kazâlik*, kamân *kemân, bard ;* **to the latter the suffixes are usually joined:** *bardi* **I too,** *bardak* **thou too,** *bardo* **he too, etc.**
**a... if** wa=in *wen*
**altar** madbaḥ, **pl.** medâbiḥ ; haikal *hêkal*, **pl.** hiyâkil *heyâkil*
**alter** ṛaiyar, baddal *baddil ;* **(be changed)** tṛaiyar *itṛai'yar*
**can this not be a...ed ?** haida mâ bîṣir' tiṛyîro ? *di mâ yimkinsh taṛyîro ?*
**a...ation** tibdîl *tabdîl*, tiṛyîr *taṛyîr* [ma'a in
**although** wa=in' *win* **or** *wen*,
**a... it is very difficult for me** ma'a inno ṣa'b ktîr 'alai'yi *ma'a inno ṣa'bê ketîr 'alêye*
**altitude** ertifâ'
**altogether** sawa
**always** dâyman *dâ=iman, tamalli* [eḍḍuhr'
**a.m.** ḳabl iḍḍuhr' *ḳabl*
**ambassador** safîr, iltshi
**amber** kahrubâ *kahramân*
**a... mouthpiece of a pipe** bizz min kahrubâ *fummê min kahramân*
**ambergris** 'anbar
**ameer ; same as emir**
**America** amê'rîkâ *amê'rikâ*, **or Turkish** yen'ḳî dû'nîa, **i.e. the New World**
**A...n** amîrîkâ'nî [sâ=in
**amiable** laṭîf, musâyir *mu-*
**amiss : to take a...** akhad 'ala khâṭro *khad 'ala khâṭro*

---

**all : of all kinds** 115,3
**that is all** 74,15
**under all these ..** 75,15
**no .. at all** 101,11
**no good at all** 107,14
**all together** 128,6
**alone : take me a...** 72,2
**the room a...** 79,3.4
**alter it** 114,3
**amiss : take it a...** 40,2 ; 49,11

**do not take it amiss** lâ twâkhid'na *mâ ti-âkhiznîsh'*
**ammunition** zakhîra *mûnet ʿaskar*
**among** bain *bên*
**a... the people** bain innâs *bên ennâs*
**a... other things** maʿa ṛairo *maʿa ṛêro*
**amount (sum of money)** mablaṛ, **pl.** mbâliṛ *mebâliṛ*
**amulet** ʿûzi *ḥigâb*; **the charm tied round the neck of children and animals, especially to prevent sore eyes, is**: ḥirz **or** *taḥwîṭa*; **see also remedy**
**amuse**; **see enjoy**
**a...ment** basṭ, kêf; **(with music and dancing)** fantazîa
**Anatolia**; **see Asia Minor**
**anchor (noun)** ḥadîd *mirse*
**ancient** ḳadîm, **pl.** ḳudm
**and: before a consonant which is followed by a vowel** w *wa* **or** u *we*; **before a consonant which is followed by another consonant** wi; **before vowels** w **or** wa *we*
**angel** malak *melek*, **pl.** mlâyiki *melâ-ike*
**anger** ṛaḍab
**angle (geom.)** zâwiyi *zâwye*
**angry with sby.** ziʿlân min **or** ʿala .. *zaʿlân min* **or** *ʿala* ..; ṛiḍbân *ṛaḍbân*
**to be a...** ziʿil
**animal** ḥaiwân *ḥêwân'*, **pl.** ḥaiwânât' *ḥewânât'*
**a wild a...** waḥsh, **pl.** wuḥûsh
**ankle** kaʿb, **pl.** kʿâb
**I have sprained my a...** infa'kashit ijri *itfa'raket rigli*
**annihilate** ʿadam
**announce** aʿlan
**annoy (vex)** kaddar
**a...ance** zaʿl *zaʿal*
**a...ed** ziʿlân *zaʿlân*
**anoint (with oil)** dahhan *dahhin*
**another** âkhar, **fem.** ukhra, **pl.** ukhar; ṛair *ṛêr*
**answer** jawâb *gawâb*, **pl.** ijwibi *agwibe*
**to a... (reply)** jâwab *gâwib*, radd jawâb *raddè gawâb*
**why do you not a... me?** laish mâ bitjâwib'ni? *mâ tigâwibnîsh' lê?*, laish mâ bitridd'li jawâb? *mâ tiruddilîsh gawâb lê?*
**(to be accountable for)** kafal
**ant** namli **or** nimli *nemle*, **pl.** naml **or** niml *neml*
**anterior part (of a thing)** muḳad'dam, auwal
**antimony (for painting the eyes)** kuḥl; **cf. Ezek. xxiii. 40**
**antique** antîka

---

**and** 128,5; 129,1; 133,17
**anew** 98,13
**angry: I am a... with you** 49,10
**annoying: that is a...** 60,4
**another knife, etc.** 80,4.5; 111,9
**a... time** 40,7
**answer me** 52,5
**anticipate** 56,9

**antiquities** antîkât'; see p. 114, note
**any** aḥad, ḥada *ḥadd*
**a... man you like** mînma kān *kân* or yekûn
**anything** ashma kān *kân* or yekûn
**ape**; see monkey
**apologise** i'ta'zar
**apoplectic fit** nukṭa
**apostle (and prophet)** rasûl, **pl.** rusul
**appear: so it a...s** mbaiyin haik *elbai'yin kide*
**appendix** zail *dêl* [*hîye*]
**appetite** ķâblî'yi *nafs, sha-*[?]
**I have no a...** mâli ķâblî'yi *mâlish' nafs*
**I have a good a...** ili ķâblî'yi ṭaiybi *lîye shahîye ṭaiyibe*
**apple** tiffâḥa, **coll.** *tiffâḥ*
**apply (ask)** ṭalab
**appointment (time and place)** mî'âd'; **(assignment, salary)** ta'yîn; **(command)** amr
**approach (to draw near)** ķarrab
**a...!** ķarrib! *ķarrab!*
**approval** istiḥsân, istiṣwâb
**approve** istaḥ'san *istaḥ'sin*, istaṣ'wab
**apricot** mishmishi *mishmi'she*, **coll.** mishmish
**April** nîsān' *abrîl*
**apron** fûṭa, wazri maryula
**aqua-fortis** moiyit ilfaḍ'ḍa *moiyet elfaḍ'ḍa*
**Arab** ibn 'arab, **pl.** ûlād' 'arab *ûlâd' 'arab*, **cf. p.** 127, note
**nomadic A...s** 'arab, 'urbân, badu **or** *bedwân*; **(a single one)** badawi *bedawi*
**Arabia** blād el'a'rab *bilâd el'a'rab*; **A...n** 'arabi
**Arabia Felix** yemen; **Arabia Petraea** ilḥijāz *elḥigâz*
**Arabic** 'arabi
**what is this called in A...?** shû ism haida bil'a'rabi? *ismo ê bil'a'rabi?*
**I speak only a little A...** mâ biḥki bil'a'rabi illa ķalîl *mâ aḥkîsh* **or** *akallim'she bil'a'rabi illa shuwaîye*; see also speak
**the A... written language** il'arabîyi *el'arabîye*
**arch (bridge)** ķanṭara, **pl.** ķanâṭir
**architect** muhan'dis. **This word also means builder, engineer, surveyor, and geometrician; the Oriental of to-day does not consider the architect an artist: he has no architects, and therefore no special name for same**
**ardor** ḥarâra
**argue** iḥtajj' *iḥtagg*

---

**any one** 95,3
**any one else** 71,7
**in any case** 109,9
**anything** 108,2
**I cannot eat a...** 149,2
**apartments** 85,1.2.3
**apparatus** 147,12
**appear: there a...s no sign** 118,1
**appointment** 41,12
**are**; see be

**I cannot argue with you** mâ akder aḥâjjak *mâ aḳder uḥâggek*
**arm (limb)** îd, **pl.** iyâdi *eyâdi;* drâ' *dirâ'*, **pl.** idru'; see yard
**(weapon)** silâḥ, **pl.** isliha *[aslihe]*
**armorer** ṣaikal
**armpit** bâṭ *ibâṭ*
**army** 'asker, **pl.** 'asâkir; jaish *gêsh*, **pl.** jiyûsh *giyûsh*
**A... Office**; see War Office
**around** ḥawalai' *ḥauwalê*
**arrange** rattab *rattib*
**arrest** ḥabs; **to a...** waḳḳaf
**arrival** wuṣûl
**arrive** wiṣil
**when shall we a... at ..?** aimta nûṣal la...? *imte nûṣal li...?*
**arrogant** mutekab'bir *mutkab'ber*
**arrow** sahm, nabl
**art (skill)** ṣan'a; fann, **pl.** fnûn *funûn [shûf]*
**artichoke** arḍeshôke *khar-[shûf]*
**artificial** maṣnû'
**artillery** ṭopjîyi *ṭôbgî'ye.* **This Turkish word is the plural of** ṭopji *ṭôbgi*, **an artilleryman; there is no word for 'artillery' in general**
**artisan** ṣanâ'i, **pl.** ṣanâ'i'yi *ṣanâ'i'ye*
**as (like, similar)** mitl *zê, [zeiy]*
**(conj. = since)** ḥais *ḥês*, bḥais *biḥês*
**as big, much as ..** ḳadd.. bittamâm *ḳadd..bittamâm [ḥadd'..]*
**as far as ..** laḥadd' *li-[ḥadd'..]*
**as for..** min yamm.., min jihit.. *min gihet..*
**as if** ka=in *ke=in*
**as long as** mâ dâm *mâ dâm*
**as soon as** auwil'ma *ḥâlan*
**Ascalon** 'asḳalân
**ascend** ṭili'
**Ascension-day** yaum iṣṣu'ûd *yôm eṣṣu'ûd*
**ascent** ṭulû', ṭal'a
**ashamed: to be a...** ista'ḥa
**are you not a...?** mâ btisthi? *mâ tistaḥîsh?*
**be a...!** isthi!, ista'ḥi!
**ashes** rimâd *rimâd*
**ash-holder (flat metal bowl)** manfaḍa
**ashore: go a..., I want to get out** rûḥ 'albarr', baddi iṭla' *rûḥ 'albarr', biddi aṭla'*

---

**Asia** blâd âsî'ya *bilâd âsî'ya*
**A... Minor** blâd ilanadôl *bilâd elanadôl* [ʿala]
**ask (question)** sa-al; **for** ʿan (**entreat**) trajja *itrag'ga*
(**demand**) ṭalab
**I ask you** bitrajjâk *batrag-gâk*; see also p. 53
**how much do you ask for it?** ḳaddaish' baddak fî haida? *kâm terîd ʿala shân di?*
**you ask too much** btiṭlub zyâdi *betiṭʿlub ziyâde*
**asleep: to fall a...** ṛifi, nâm *nâm*
**asparagus** halyûn *kishk almâs*
**aspect** manzar, pl. menâzir
**ass**; see donkey
**assist** sâʿad *sâʿid*
**a...ant (clerk)** muʿâwin
**association: in a... (i.e. together)** bilishtirâk
**astonished: to be a...** tʿajjab *itʿag'gib*
**I am greatly a...** bitʿaj'jib ktîr *batʿag'gib ketîr*
**at (in)** fî; (**near, by**) ʿind *ʿand*; (**with**) maʿ or maʿa
**at Paris** fî bârîzʿ
**at home** filbait' *filbêt*
**at a franc apiece** ilḳaṭ'ʿa bifrank' *elḳiṭ'ʿa bifrank'*
**at three o'clock** issâʿa tlâti *essâʿa telâte*
**at once** ḥâlan (**or, Syr. only:** hallaḳ)
**I was yesterday at your uncle's** kint mbâriḥ ʿind ʿammak *kunt embâreḥ ʿandê ʿammak*
**Athens** atîna
**atmosphere** falak *felek*, *gau*
**atonement** kaffâra
**attack on sby.** hujûm ʿala .. *hugûm ʿala..*
**to a... sby.** hajam ʿala .. *hagam ʿala ..*
**attention** intibâh
**to pay a... to..** dâr bâlo ʿala .. *khalla bâlo ʿala..*
**in future you must pay more a... to it** filmustaḳ'bal lâzim tdîr bâlak aktar ʿalaih' *filmustaḳ'bal lâzim tekhal'li bâlak aktar ʿalêh*
**attentive** mitnab'bih, muntabih
**attest** ṣaddaḳ ʿala
**auction** mazâd
**sale by a...** baiʿ bilmazâd *bêʿ bilmazâd*

---

**ask the..** 137,14
**ask him in** 36,18
**I ask permission** 42,10
**if I may ask** 133,11
**if any one asks for me** 95,3
**assure: be a...d** 55,6
**astonish: that is a...ing** 59,4
**at (where?)** 108,17
**at its foot** 142, 11
**at noon, at night** 68,1.4
**at what time?** 77,5
**at once** 39,3; 82,1; 95,7
**at his will** 121,11
**at the spring** 131,4
**look at your watch** 68,20
**atmosphere** 65,20
**attack of illness** 34,8
**attend to me** 51,15
**attendant** 99,6
**attention: pay a... (mind)** 80,11

**August** âb *aross'tos*
**aunt (on the father's side)** ʿammi ʿ*amme*
**(on the mother's side)** khâli [*khâle*
**Australia** austrâlya *ôstrâ'lya*
**Austria** austria, blâd innam'si *bilâd ennem'se*
**A...n** nimsâwi *nemsâwi*
**author** mual'lif, muṣan'nif
**authorities** ḥukûmi or ḥkûmi *ḥukûme*
**I shall complain to the a...** raḥ ishtki lilḥkûmi *râḥ ashtiki lilḥukûme*
**automobile** ôtômôbîl'
**autumn** kharîf
**avarice** bukhl
**avaricious** bakhîl, **pl.** bu-[khala
**aversion** kirha
**awake (adj.)** fâ=iḳ
**to a... (intr. = wake up)** fâḳ (yfîḳ) *ṣiḥi*
**(trans. = rouse)** faiyaḳ *ṣaḥḥa;* **see also call**
**awkward (unseemly)** simij *ṛalîẓ*
**(troublesome)** ṣaʿb
**awl** makhraz *mukhruz*
**awning** tende
**axe** ḳaddûm, balṭa, **(small one)** firrâʿa
**bachelor** aʿzab ʿ*âzib*

**back (the hinder part)** ḍahr
**there and b...** birrâyiḥ ubijjâyi *birrâ=iḥ wabiggâ=i*
**(mind) your b...!** ḍahrak!
**to come, go b...** rijiʿ *rigiʿ*
**backgammon** ṭawla
**backside** kafal
**(vulg.)** ṭîz
**backwards** lawa'ra *liwa'ra,* lakhalf' *likhalf'*
**bacon** shaḥm ilkhanzîr
**bad** radi, **pl.** irdyi *ardiye;* ʿâṭil; baṭṭâl; manḥûs
**(aching: of limbs)** bîwaj'jiʿ *beyûgaʿ*
**a bad man** insân radi *râgil* [*baṭṭâl*
**that's a bad thing!** haida shî radi! *di shê radi!*
**to go bad (of food)** ṣâr baṭṭâl
**badness** radâwi *radâwe,* khubs *khabs*
**bag** kîs, **pl.** ikyâs *ikyâs*
**skin-bag; see tube**
**baggage** ʿafsh
**bail (one who stands b...)** kafîl *kefîl* or *ḍâmin*
**(security)** kfâli *kefâle* or *ḍamâne*
**bake** khabaz
**b...r** khibbâz *khabbâz, farrân*
**bakhsheesh; see gratuity**

---

Austrian beer 102,16
A... post-office 82,8
authorities: we give the passport to the a... 75,14
avoid: it cannot be a...ed 75,3
awake: until I a... 80,10
away: go a... 52,8.9
take a... 52,11
Baalbek 149,8
back: bring b... the.. 96,13
take this.. b... 130,2
turn b... (trans.) 52,1
we had better go b... 143,12
bad: .. are bad 100,11; 135,12
bad habits (horse) 120,7
bake some eggs 134,1
baked meat 124,1
bakhsheesh 74,12

**balance (for weighing)** mîzân' *mîzân'*
**balcony** mamsha or balkûn *balakôn*. **In Egypt the porous cooling-vessels,** *kulle*, **which serve for the refrigeration of drinkable water are placed in those small open-worked, generally octagonal, upper fore-buildings called** *mashrebîye*
**bald** akra'
**ball (any round body)** killi, pl. kilal *kôra*, **pl.** *kuwal*
**(bullet)** rṣâṣ *ruṣâṣ*
**(dance)** ballu
**ballast** ṣâbû're
**balustrade** darbazîn
**bamboo** khaizarân
**banana** mauzi *môze*
**(coll.)** mauz *môz*
**band (ribbon)** shirîṭ *sherîṭ*
**(of musicians)** naubi *nôbe*
**English b...** mûsî'ka inglîzî'yi, **native b...** mûsî'ka ahlîyi
**bandage** 'iṣâbi *'iṣâbe*, ḍimâdi *ḍimâde*
**bank (for money)** bank, **pl.** bunûki *benûke*
**(of a river)** ḥaffi *ḥaffe*, ṭaraf
**banker** ṣirrâf *ṣarrâf*, bankêr
**bankrupt** miflis *mufel'lis*, munka'sir
**to become b...** aflas, fallas *fallis*, inka'sar
**b...cy** iflâs, inkisâr
**banquet** 'azîmi *'uzûme*, walîmi *welîme*
**Barbarian** berberi, **pl.** brâbri *barâbire* **or** *bara'bra*
**Barbary** blâd ilbrâbri *bilâd elbara'bra*
**barber** ḥillâk *mezai'yin*
**b...'s shop** dikkân ḥillâk *dukkân mezai'yin*; see also p. 100
**barefoot** ḥâfi **(or, Syr. only:** ḥifyân**)**
**bark (of a tree)** kishr
**to b... (of dogs)** 'awa
**barley** sha'îr
**b... water** moi sha'îr
**barn** ambar *shûne*
**barracks** kishli
**barrage** kanṭara, **pl.** kanâṭir
**barrel** barmîl, **pl.** barâmîl'
**barren land** bûr *bôr*
**Bashaw** bâsha
**basin (small tank)** birki *faskîye*, **pl.** burak *fesâki*
**(large one)** ḥawuz *ḥôḍ*
**(washhand-)** lakan *ṭisht*
**basket** selli *selle*, **pl.** *sellât*
**(large wicker-b...)** zambîl, kiffi *kuffe*
**bastard** bandûk, **pl.** bnâdîk' *ibnê zine*
**bat (animal)** waṭwâṭ, **pl.** waṭâwîṭ'
**bath** ḥammâm **or** ḥimmâm *ḥammâm*; see p. 98
**I wish to take a b...** baddi itḥam'mam *biddi astaḥam'mi*

**I wish to take a sea-bath** baddi itṛas'sal bilbaḥr' *biddi atṛas'sal bilbaḥr'*
**take me to a b...** dillni ʿala ḥammâm *dillini ʿala ḥammâm*
**Bath-chair**; see invalid carriage
**bathe (take a bath)** tṛassal *itṛas'sal*, tḥammam *istaḥam'ma*
**bath-wrapper** fûṭa, **pl.** fuwaṭ
**battle** ḳitâl, waḳaʿa, ḥarb
**bay (sea)** jûn *gûn*
**bayonet** ḥarbi *ḥarbe*
**be** kân *kân* (yekûn). **As an auxiliary it is mostly not translated, e.g. I am, thou art tired** ana, int tiʿbân *ana, inte taʿbân*
**how are you?** kîf ḥâlak? *ezai'yak?* **cf. pp. 33 to 35**
**When = must or shall, it is often expressed by the aorist with preceding** tâ, **e.g. the servant is to come** tâ yiji iṣṣâniʿ *yîgi el-khaddâm*
**what is that to me?** see care
**beach** shâṭi
**beads**; see rosary
**beak** minḳâr
**beam (of wood)** jisr *gisr*
**(ray of light)** shiʿâʿ, **pl.** ashiʿʿa

---


bay horse 119,8
be: I am 49,1 ff.
that I am not at home 95,3
I am better 149,5
is he at home? 82,5
is not hot, etc. 98,10; 100,6
is not (the size) 108,7
is there (danger)? 127,4
is this ..? 125,12; 141,6
is there no .. (here)? 103,15
is there water (here)? 87,6
he is better 35,17
here is, are .. 117,2.4.5.9
how is she? 35,18; 36,1
how is your wife? 35,4.5
it is (season, weather) 136,7.11; 137,4
it is still cold 149,7
it is Mr. .. 36,16
it is going to .. 144,10
she is quite well 35,8
that is .. 106,9; 112,12.13; 125,4
that is not .. 125,4.6
this is a .. 141,7
this is not his .. 130,4
this here is the .. 130,3
there is fear of .. 127,7
the wind is .. 66,6
(be) what is the matter? 34,2; 106,11
who is there? 132,3
we are (tired, etc.) 79,10; 133,6 134,2
here we are 132,1
are we still far from ..? 144,16
are you (plur.) sleepy? 134,3
are you (plur.) tired? 133,7
are you the ..? 95,11
how old are you? 46,6
how are you? 33,5
how are you this morning? 139,8
are not clean 99,11
of what .. are these? 142,3
the sleeves are too long 113,14
there are .. in it 129.3.4.5
these are .. 116,3; 117,3; 142,2
they are too .. 108,6.9
be that as it may 146,14
how many .. must there be? 85,4
it must be .. 94,10; 103,4
it will soon be .. 69,10
the .. must be .. 109,8; 111,5
(they) must be .. 77,6; 113,9.11
I was .. 34,7
with whom were you? 88,9

**bean: French b...s** lûbyi *lûbiya*, faṣûlya
**broad b...s** fûl
**bear (animal)** dubb *dibbe*, **pl.** dbâb **and** dubab *dibeb*
**bear (to carry)** ḥamal *shâl* (*yeshîl*)
**to b... (give birth to)** khal-[laf *wilid*]
**to b... (suffer, stand)** iḥta'-mal
**beard** daḳn, liḥyi *liḥye*
**beast (wild)** waḥsh, **pl.** wuḥûsh
**(horse, mule, ass)** dâbbi *rukûbe*, **pl.** dwâbb *rakâ:ib*
**beat (to hit, strike)** ḍarab
**(to thrash)** khabbaṭ, nizil fî
**to get a b...ing** akal'ha
**beautiful** kwaiyis *kuwai'yis*, jamîl *gamîl*
**beauty** jamâl *gamâl*
**because** la:in' *li:in'*, bḥais in *biḥês*
**b... of; see** account
**become (to be made)** ṣâr (yeṣîr)
**becoming (suitable)** mnâsib *munâsib*, lâyiḳ *lâ:iḳ*
**this is not b...** haida mush lâyiḳ *di mush lâ:iḳ*
**bed (to sleep in)** farshi *serîr*
**to go to b...** nâm *nâm* (ynâm *yenâm*)
**Bedouin** badawi *bedawi*, **pl.** badu **or** *bedwân* **or** ʿarab **or** ʿurbân; **see p. 127, note**
**B... girl, B... woman** badawî-yi *bedawîye*. **One of the best known and most popular Syrian songs has as refrain:** ilbadawîy-ilbadawîyiʿ **'the Bedouin girl, the Bedouin girl'**
**bedstead** takht *serîr*, **pl.** tukhûti *serâ:ir*
**bee** naḥli *naḥle*, **coll.** naḥl
**-house (= -hive)** kuwâra *khalâye*, **pl.** kawâyir *khalâyât*
**beef** laḥm baḳar; **see meat**
**beer** bîra
**beeswax** shamaʿ ʿasali
**beetle** jîz *gîz;* khunfusa *khunfuse*, **pl.** khanâfis
**beetroot** shmandar, sha-man'dar *bangar*
**befall (happen)** ʿaraḍ, ḥaṣal
**before (of place)** ḳuddâm
**(of time)** ḳabl, min ḳabl
**(conj.)** ḳabl mâ *ḳablê mâ*
**stand b... me** ûḳaf ḳuddâmi

---

**b... ten o'clock** ḳabl issâ a ʿashra *ḳabl essâʿa ʿashara*
**if you had come b...** lau kunt tiji ḳabl *lô kuntê tigi ḳabl*
**beg** shaḥad *shaḥat*
**Beg** ; see Bey
**beggar** shiḥḥâd *shaḥḥât* or *sâ=il*
**begin** ; see commence
**behave** salak
**behavior** taṣar'ruf
**behind (adv.)** min wara, min khalf [min ..
**(prep.)** wara min .., khalf]
**to remain b... (linger)** t=akhkhar *it=akh'khar*
**(the seat)** kafal, **(low)** ṭîz
**belch (verb)** tadash'sha *itkar'raʿ*
**belief** îmân' *îmân'*
**(opinion)** zann, fikr
**believe** ṣaddaḳ [ifta'kar
**(think, suppose)** zann,]
**(in God, etc.)** âman bi...
**b... me** ṣaddiḳ'ni *ṣaddaḳni*
**don't b... it** lâ tṣaddiḳ *mâ tiṣaddaḳ'shi*
**believer, believing** m=âmin *muâmin* [*agrâs*
**bell** jaras *garas*, **pl.** ijrâs]
**ring the b... !** duḳḳ ijja'ras ! *duḳḳ egga'ras !*
**the b... was ringing** indaḳḳ' ijja'ras *indaḳḳ' egga'ras*

**bellows** minfakh
**belly** baṭn
**belong** khaṣṣ ; **but generally expressed by the preposition** la *li* **only**
**this b...s to me** haida ili ana *di lîye ana*, haida bîkhuṣṣ'ni *di bikhuṣṣ'ini*
**to whom does this house b... ?** lamîn halḥâra? *limîn elbêt di ?*
**b...ing to** tabaʿ *betâʿ*, **fem.** *betâʿet*, **pl.** *betûʿ*
**below** taḥt
**bend (trans.)** lawa
**benefit (profit)** nafʿ
**(kindness)** maʿrûf, khair *khêr*
**to b... (trans.)** nafaʿ
**benevolent** khaiyir
**Berlin** barlîn
**berry** ḥabbi *ḥabbe*, **pl.** ḥabbât *ḥabbât* or ḥubûb
**(coll.)** ḥabb
**beside** jamb *gamb* **with or without** min..
**sit down b... me** uḳʿud jambi *uḳʿud gambi ;* jamb minni *gambê minni*
**b...s (over and above)** ṛair *ṛêr*
**besprinkle** rashsh
**best : the b...** ilaḥ'san *elaḥsan*
**b... man of a bridegroom** shibîn

---

beforehand (first) 111,7
begin ! 51,21
behind you 129,2; 140,12
believe : I b... you 48,5
who would have b...d that? 59,9

beseech : I b... you 53,6.7
besides (in addition to) 130,5
best : the b... 76,15 ; 82,12.13
the b... you have 112,3
the b... is you.. 85,2
it is b... to.. 143,3

**to do one's b...** ʿimil juhdo *ʿamal guhdo*
**I will do my b...** baʿmil kull juhdi *aʿmil kulli guhdi*
**bet (noun)** rahn
**to bet** *râhan*
**Bethany** ilʿâzârî'yi *elʿâzârî'ye*
**Bethlehem** bêtlaḥm'
**Beth-saida** bêt ṣaida
**betray** khân (yekhûn)
**betroth** khaṭṭab
**better** aḥsan or (Syr. only) aḥsin
**to get (grow) b...** iṣṭa'laḥ
**between** bain *bên*
**beverage** sharâb, pl. sharbāt
**bewailing (lamentation for the dead)** walwali *welwele*
**Bey** bêk, pl. bakawât *bêkawât'*; see note to 'bêk' in the Arabic Vocabulary
**beyond** fauḳ *fôḳ*, wara
**that is b... my patience** haida fauḳ ṭâḳati *di fôḳ ṭâḳati*
**Beyrout** bairût *bêrût'*
**Bible** ktāb ilmḳad'das *kitâb elmuḳad'das*
**bicycle** darrâje *ʿagele*
**big** kebîr (or, Syr. only: kbîr)
**bigger than..** akbar min
**bill**; see account, beak
**b... of exchange** kambya *kimbiyâle*
**bind (to tie)** rabaṭ
**(a book)** jallad *gallad*
**b...ing (of a book)** jîla *gild*
**bird** ṭair *ṭêr*, pl. ṭiyûr (or, Syr. only: ṭyûr)
**birth** wilādi *wilâde*, mîlād'
**biscuit** kaʿk *kaḥk*
**bit (a little)** shwaiyi *shuwai'ye*
**(of a horse)** ljām *ligâm*
**bitch** kalbi *kelbe*
**bite** ʿaḍḍ: **(sting of insects)** ʿaḳṣa
**to b...** ʿaḍḍ
**bitter** murr
**black** aswad *iswid*, fem. sauda *sôda*, pl. sûd
**Black Sea** baḥr bonṭus
**blacking** bûya
**blacksmith** ḥiddād *ḥaddâd*
**bladder (urinary vessel)** maṣâni *mesâne*
**blade (of a knife)** naṣli *naṣle*, pl. niṣâl

---

**blame** laum *lôm*
**, to b...** lâm (yelûm)
**blanket** ḥirâm or ḥrâm *ḥirâm*
**blasphemy** kufr
**blaze (noun)** lahîb
**bleed (open a vein, draw blood)** faṣad
**to have oneself bled** infa'ṣad
**it is b...ing** ṭili' iddamm' *kharr eddamm'*
**bless** bârak *bârik*
**God b... you!** Alla ybârik fîk! *Allâh yebârik fîk!*
**blessed** mubârak, mabrûk
**Blessed Virgin; see virgin**
**blessing** baraki *barake*
**blind (unable to see)** a'ma, pl. 'imyân *'imyân* or *'imi;* ḍarîr
**bliss: eternal b...** issa'âdit ilabadîyi *esse'âdet elebedîye*
**blister** baḳbûḳa *buḳbêḳa*
**blond; see fair**
**blood** damm
**blood-money (paid by a murderer to the survivors of the victim as atonement)** diyi *diye* [fâf-
**blotting-paper** waraḳa shaf-}
**blow (a stroke)** ḍarb, ḍarbi *ḍarbe*
**to b...** nafakh

**b... one's nose** tmakhkhaṭ *itmakh'khaṭ*
**blue** azraḳ, fem. zarḳa, pl. zurḳ
**blunderbuss; see gun**
**blunt (dull on the edge)** tilfân *talfân mutal'lim*
**blush (to become red)** iḥmarr'
**boar (a wild one)** khanzîr berri, ḥallûf
**board (plank)** lauḥa *lôḥa*, pl. alwâḥ; coll. lauḥ *lôḥ*
**(b... or side of a ship)** ṭaraf ilmar'kab *ṭaraf elmar'kib*
**(food)** ṭa'âm, akl
**b...ing-house** manzil, lukan'da *lokan'da*
**boat** filûkya or flûkya *felûke*, pl. flâyik *felâ-ik*
**(a bigger one)** shakhtûra
**large Nile-b...** *dahabîye*
**see also ship, steamer**
**body** beden, jism *gism*
**(main part)** wasṭ
**bog** na'ṣ *baṭîḥa*
**boil (trans.)** salaḳ
**(intr.)** ṛili
**boiled** maslûḳ
**boiler** dasti *dist*, khilḳîn
**boiling** ṛilyân *ṛâli*
**bold** jasûr *gasûr*, shajî' *shagî'*
**(impudent)** bilâ, ḥayâ
**b...ness** jasâra *gasâre*

---

**blame:** you are to b... 48,10
**bless:** God b... you 37,3
the b...ing has entered 37,2; 132,12
**blinds:** open the b... 51,13
**board (food)** 89,11
**boatman** 71,1
**boil (plur.)** us some milk 139.4
let it b... quickly 92.6
**boiled** 139,6.14
b... meat 124.3
**boisterous wind** 65.2

**bolt (of a door)** siḥḥâbi *saḥḥâbe*, dakkâra *tirbâs*
**to b... (fasten)** dakkar
**bone** ʿaḍm, **pl.** ʿidâm
**(of fish)** ḥaski *shôke*
**book (noun)** ktâb *kitâb*, **pl.** kutb **and** kutub
**bookbinder** mjallid *megal'-lid*
**booking-clerk** tazkarajî *taz-kargî*
**-office** maktab **or** maḥall' kaṭʿ ettezâkir
**bookseller** kutubi **or** *kutbi*
**boot: short b...s** lastîk *gazme*
**top-b...s** jazmi *shikârbe*
**to put on the b...s** libis illastîk *elgaz'me*
**to take off** shalaḥ *kalaʿ*
**'boots' (and porter)** khâdim lifatḥ' ilbâb *khaddâm kâʿet elôtîl'*
**border (edge)** ḥaffi *ḥaffe*, ṭaraf
**(boundary)** ḥadd, **pl.** ḥu-dûd
**bored by (tired of)** ziʿlân min .. *zaʿlân min* ..
**borer (gimlet)** khirbirr' *berîme*
**born** maulûd, khilkân
**borrow from** istaʿâr min ..
**both** ittnain' *eletnên*
**bother** ʿazâb *ʿazâb*
**to b...** ʿazzab *ʿazzib*
**bottle** kannîni *kizâze*, **pl.** kanâni *kizâzât'*; musau'-widi
**small b..., phial** ḥanjûr *ḥangûr*, **pl.** ḥanâjîr' *ḥa-nâgîr'*
**see also cooling vessel**
**bottom (of a vessel, box)** kaʿb *kaʿr*
**(foundation, basis)** asâs
**bow (to shoot with)** kaus *kôs*
**bowels; see intestines**
**bowl (drinking-)** kâsi *sul-ṭânî'ye*
**box (small one)** ʿulbi *ʿilbe*, **pl.** ʿulab *ʿilab*
**(big one)** ṣandûk, **pl.** ṣanâ-dîk'
**(plant)** baks
**(on the ear)** kaff
**I will box your ear** biḍ-rub'lak kaff
**boxing-day** tâni yaum ʿîd ilmîlâd' *tâni yôm ʿîd elmîlâd'* (bi-ingiltar'ra)
**box-maker** ʿulabı, **pl.** ʿu-labîyi
**boy** walad, **pl.** ûlâd' *ûlâd'*; ṣabi, **pl.** ṣibyân **(or, Syr. only:** ṣbaiyân**); see chap**
**bracelet** suwâri *iswîre*, **pl.** asâwîr' *asâwir*

---

bolt: horses must not b... 120,1
bone is dislocated 144,13
book-case, 109,12; 110,7
boots 108,1; my b... 80,11
these b... 108,17
a pair of b... 109,4.5
border: with a red b... 98,3
both: on b... sides, 101,9; 110,8
take them b... 84,6
bother the thing! 62, note 1
bottom: in the b... of the valley 141,3
boulders 142,10
bowl (basin) 79,13
(cup) 99,3
of a pipe, filled 104,5
box (small) 128,8; 129,1.3
boy (young man) 102,7

**braces (for trousers)** ḥammâl, pl. ḥammâlât' *ḥammâlât'*
**brain** dimâr̥, nukhâʿ *mukhkh*
**bran** nakhâli *nakhâle*
**branch (a big one)** ʿimd *farʿ*
(a thin one) shilḥ *ruṣn*
**brandy** [1] **(distilled from wine)** ʿarak̥ *ʿarak̥i*
**brass** nuḥâs aṣfar
**brave (adj.)** shajîʿ *shagîʿ*
**bravo!** brâwo! âfâ'rîm!
see also p. 62
**breach (opening)** khurk̥
**bread** khubz *ʿêsh*
**a piece of b...** shak̥fit khubz or khubzi *luk̥met ʿêsh*
**a loaf (or roll) of b...** rar̥îf, pl. irr̥ifi *arr̥ife*
**leavened b...** khubz *ʿêsh* khamîr [faṭîr]
**unleavened b...** khubz *ʿêsh*
**new b...** khubz ṭari or tâza *ʿêsh tâza*
**dry b...** khubz yâbis *ʿêsh ḥâ-*
**toasted b...** khubz mḥammaṣ *ʿêsh meḥam'mar*
**breadth** ʿarḍ, *ʿurḍ*
**break: at b... of day** ʿind ṭlûʿ iḍḍau' *ʿandê ṭulûʿ ennûr*
**to b...** kasar, kassar
**breakfast** tirwîk̥a *fuṭûr*
**to b...** faṭar
**breaking (a fracture)** kasr
**breast** ṣidr [*zaz*]
(female) bizz, pl. bzâz *bi-*
**breath** nafas *nefes*
**bribe** barṭîl, rishwi *rashwa*
**to b...** barṭal
**to receive a b...** tabar'ṭal
**bric-à-brac: dealer in b...** antak'ji *antîka'gi*
**brick** kirmîd
**Nile b...** *k̥âlib, ṭûb*
**clay b..., dried in the sun, as used by the peasants of the flat country** [2] libni *ṭûbe*, coll. libn *ṭûb*

[1] In Syria this liqueur is almost exclusively distilled from wine; in the towns it is frequently and considerably mixed with spirit, but in the mountains it is generally pure and of excellent quality. The most celebrated is that of Zûk, which place is also noted for its wool and silk industry (see p. 115, note). A small glass of ʿarak̥ poured into a glass of water produces a milk-white beverage, refreshing and cooling, and at the same time quite harmless.

[2] In the Syrian towns and in the mountains an easily-worked stone is generally used for building, or, as is the case in Damascus, for the substructure of the houses; in the latter case the remainder is of wood.

bread is not good 93,3
break: it will b... (tear) 121,9.
things that b... 129,3
before the b... of day 129,10
broken 84,10; 107,1.4.9; 138,6
break: that nothing is broken 72,13; 89,5
breakfast 139,2.7
with b... 79,3
at what time do they b...? 80,1

**bride** ʿarûs *ʿarûse*, **pl.** ʿarâyis *ʿarâ꞉is* [*ʿirsân*]
**-groom** ʿarîs, **pl.** ʿirsân
**bridal procession** zeffet il-ʿarûs *zeffet elʿarûse*
**bridge** jisr *ḳanṭara*, **pl.** jusûr *ḳanâṭir*
**bridle** ljâm *ligâm*
**to b...** lajam *laggim*
**brigand** ḥarâmi [naiyir]
**bright (shining)** lamiʿ, [naiyir]
**(of light color)** fâtiḥ *fâtiḥ*
**bring** jâb *gâb* (yjîb *yegîb*)
**b... me quickly ..** jibli ḳawâm .. *hâtli ḳawâm* or *idîni ḳawâm* .
**have they brought the things for me?** jâbu ilish'ya minshâni? *gâbu elish'ye ʿala shâni?*
**to b... in** fauwat *dakhkhal*
**to b... out** ṭailaʿ, ṭallaʿ
**broad** ʿarîḍ
**broken** maksûr
**broker (comm.)** samsâr, **pl.** semâsra
**bronze (noun)** nuḥâs aṣfar *naḥâs aṣfar*
**brook** moi *moiye*
**broom (besom)** miknsi *maḳash'she*, **pl.** mkânis *maḳashshât* [lahm]
**broth** markit laḥm *maraḳat* [lahm]
**brother** akh, **pl.** ikhwi *ikhwe* or ikhwân *ikhwân;* **with possessive adjectives see p. 16, top**
**brother-in-law** ṣahr *nasîb*
**(husband of a wife's sister)** silf
**brown: light b...** jauzi *gôzi*
**coffee-b...** binni *bunni*
**(of the human complexion)** asmar, **fem.** samra, **pl.** sumr; asmarâni
**bruise (noun)** raḍḍa
**b...ed** madḳûḳ
**brush** firshâyi *furshe*
**to b...** farrash **(or, Syr. only:** farsha)
**(to sweep)** kannas *kanas*
**b... the room!** kannis il-ûḍa! *uknus elûḍa!*
**bubble (a bladder, blister)** baḳbûḳa *buḳbêḳa*
**bucket** saṭl
**(well-b...)** dilu; **of leather:** *dilu*, **of wood:** *ardel*
**bucket-wheel** nâʿûʿra *sâḳiye*, tabût
**buckle (noun)** bukli, **pl.** bukal; *abzîm*
**buffalo** jâmûs' *gâmûs'*, **pl.** jawâmîs' *gawâmîs'*
**bug (coll.)** baḳḳ
**(the single one)** baḳḳa

---

**build** ʿammar *bana*
**b...er** miʿmâri
**b...ing (edifice)** ʿamâr, **pl.** ʿamârât′; bina *bine* or *bunye*, **pl.** ibnyi *abniye*
**Bulgaria** blâd ilbulṛâr *bilâd elbulṛâr*
**bull (animal)** taur *tôr*, **pl.** tîrân′ [ṣuḥbe]
**bunch of flowers** tishkîli
**b... of grapes, also cluster** ʿanḳûd [ḥiml]
**burden (also a camel's load)**
**burdensome** tḳîl *teḳîl*
**that is b... to me** haida tḳîl ʿalai′yi *di teḳîl ʿalêye*
**burn (trans.)** ḥaraḳ
**(intrans., become ignited)** shaʿal *walaʿ*
**(become consumed by fire)** iḥta′raḳ *itḥa′raḳ*
**the fire does not b...** innâr mâ shaʿalit *ennâr mâ walaʿet′shi*
**it won't b... (catch)** mâ baddo yishʿal *mâ btûlaʿsh′*
**the house b...t down** iḥta′raḳit ilḥâra *itḥa′raḳ elbêt*
**I b...t my finger** iḥta′raḳ iṣbaʿi *iḥta′raḳ ṣâbiʿi*
**b...t** maḥrûḳ, muḥta′riḳ
**burnoose** burnus **or** *barnûs*, **pl.** brânis *barânîs′*
**burst (intrans.)** infa′zar,
**bury** dafan [faḳaʿ]
**bush** ʿulʿai′ḳa *ʿullêḳa*, jubb *gubb*

**bushel: in Syria** kêli = 2 mudd; 1 mudd = 18 **litres**
**in Egypt:** *wêbe* = 4 *rubʿ*; 1 *rubʿ* = 8.25 **litres**; 6 *wêbe* = 1 *ardebb′*
**(1 bushel = 36.34 litres)**
**business** shuṛl, **pl.** ishṛâl
**(a single one)** shuṛli *shuṛle*, maṣlaḥa
**how is b...?** kîf ilishṛâl? *ezai′ elishṛâl?*
**that is my b...** haida kâri *di maṣlaḥ′ti*
**you have no b... here** mâ ilak shuṛl haun *mâlak shuṛlè hene*
**b...-place (shop or office)** maḥall′ ishshuṛl′ *maḥall′ eshshuṛl′*
**busy: I am b...** ana mashṛûl; see p. 41, 6-9
**but** amma, lâkin **or** lâken *lâkin*
**(except)** illa, ṛair *ṛêr*
**(only)** bass *bess*
**butcher (meat seller)** liḥḥâm *laḥḥâm*
**(slaughterman)** ḳiṣṣâb *gezzâr*
**butler** sâ′ḳî khamr *sufragî*
**butt (with the horns)** naṭaḥ
**butt-end (of gun)** kurnâfa
**butter (fresh)** zibdi *zibde*
**(for cooking)** samni *semne*
**butterfly** farfûr, farâsh
**button** zirr *zurâr*, **pl.** zrâr
**it wants a b... here** baddo zirr haun *biddo zurâr hene*

---

**business: that is your b...** 78,2
**busy: I am b...** 41, 6-9; 48,21
**but: any one else but ..** 52,16
**butter: cook in b...** 134,1

**the b... is torn off** inḳa'ṭa' izzirr' *inḳa'ṭa' ezzurâr*
**sew the b... on for me** khaiyiṭ'li izzirr' *khaiyaṭ'li ezzurâr*
**put the b... on securely** makkin izzirr' *makkin ezzurâr*
**to b...** bakkal *zarrar*
**-hole** ʿirwi *ʿirwe*
**buy** ishta'ra ; see p. 114, note
**where can I buy..?** wain biḳdir ishtri..? *fên baḳdar ashtiri..?*
**I want to buy a horse** baddi ishtri ḥṣân *biddi ashtiri ḥuṣân*
**buy me..** ishtrîli *ishtirîli..*
**by (near)** ʿind *ʿand*, jamb *gamb*
**(through)** bî, min, biwâsṭa
**by land** bilbarr'
**by water** bilbaḥr'
**by three o'clock** issâʿa tlâti *essâʿa telâte*
**by the life of the Prophet** wiḥyât inna'bi *waḥyât enne'bi* ; **by the life of Christ** wiḥyât ilmesîḥ *waḥyât elmesîḥ*
**by myself, thyself, etc.**; see alone
**cab** ʿarabîye
**cabbage** malfûf *korumb'*
**cabin** ḥujre *ḳamara*
**cactus** ṣubbair' *ṣubbêr* or *ṣabbâra*
**café** ḳahwi *ḳahwe*, pl. ḳahâwi
**caftan (for the summer)** ḳumbâz *ḳufṭân*, **(for the winter)** jubbi *gubbe*
**cage** ḳafaṣ
**Cairo** miṣr ilḳâhira *maṣr elḳâhira*
**Old C...** *maṣr elʿatîḳe*
**native of C..., Cairene** miṣri *maṣri*
**cake (in general)** ḥulu *ḥilw*
**pan-** maʿmûl
**biscuit** kaʿk *kaḥk*
**calamity** balîyi *belîye*
**calculate** ḥasab, ḥâsab *ḥâsib*
**calculation** ḥsâb *ḥisâb*
**calendar** ruznâmi, taḳwîm, maṭbûkh *netîge*
**calf (animal)** ʿijl *ʿigl*
**(of the leg)** baṭṭa *simmâne*
**calico (printed)** shît
**caliph**; see khalif
**call (a cry)** ṣirâkh, ṣîyâḥ
**(invitation to religion or food)** daʿwi
**(the call to pray)** azân
**to answer nature's c...**; see want
**to c...** nadah, nahar or ʿaiyaṭ *zaḳḳaʿ*
**(to awake)** faiyak *ṣaḥḥa*
**(to c... on, visit, q.v.)** zâr (yzûr)
**c... me a barber** indah'li shî ḥillâḳ *indah'li wâḥid mezai'yin*
**what is that man calling out?** shû biʿai'yiṭ harrijjâl? *errâgil di bizaḳḳaʿ ê?*

**buy the necessary** 89,7
**by the steamer** 77,2; 82,13
**time has slipped by** 41,15
**(by) obliged by your ..** 40,2.8
**call (plur.) me early** 149,7
**.. to c... me at six** 94,6

**they shall call me at five o'clock** lāzim yfaiyiḳûni issā'a khamsi *lâzim yeṣaḥḥûni essâ'a khamse*
**c... me to-morrow morning at .. o'clock** faiyiḳ'ni bukra 'ala bukra issā'a.. *ṣaḥḥîni bukra eṣṣubḥ' essâ'a ..*
**why did you not c... me?** laish mâ faiyaḳt'ni? *mâ ṣaḥḥêtinîsh' lêh ?*
**(to alight, stop)** ḥauwal; **for instance: does the vessel c... at Haifa?** il-mar'kab bîḥau'wil la-ḥai'fa? *elmar'kib yiḥau'-wil liḥai'fa?*
**what is this c...ed in Arabic?** kîf bîsammûh' haida bil'a'rabi? *ezai' bisam'mu di bil'a'rabi?* **or** shû ismo haida bil'a'rabi? *ismê di bil'a'rabi ê?*
**calm(ness)** hudu
**a c... (at sea)** ṛalîni *ṛalîne*
**(adj.)** hâdi, sākit *sâkit*
**to c...** hadda
**calumny** namîmi *nemîme iftî'ra*
**camel (for burdens)** jamal *gamal*, **pl.** jmāl *gimâl*
**(for riding)** dalûl *heǵîn*
**a female c...** nâḳa, **pl.** nûḳ
**-driver** jammāl *gammâl*
**camelopard**; **see giraffe**
**camomile** bâbû'nij *bâbû'nig*
**camphor** kâfûr'
**can (vessel)** kûz *ṣafîḥa*
**can (aux. verb)** ḳidir (yiḳ-dir *yiḳdar* **or** *yiṛdar*); **frequently expressed by 'to be possible,' e.g. I cannot = it is not possible for me** mâ byimkin'ni *mâ yimkinîsh*; **sometimes by the seventh of the derived forms (see p. 30), e.g. you, or one, cannot walk here** mâ byin-mashi haun *mâ yinmish-îsh hene* = **it walks itself not here, as in Italian:** non si va qui
**The English infinitive after 'can' is in Arabic expressed by the aorist, e.g. can you tell me whether..?** btiḳdir tḳulli iza..? *be-tiḳ'dar teḳul'li iza ..?*
**In the sense of 'to know how to do something' 'can' is expressed by** 'irif, **e.g. can you read?** bta'rif tiḳra? *beta''raf tiḳra?*
**where can (or may) that be?** wain baddo ykûn? *fên biddo yekûn?*

---

**Canaan** blâd kin'ân *bilâd ken'ân*
**canal** sâkiyi *tir'a*, **pl.** sawâki *tira'*
**candid (sincere)** khâliṣ
**speak c...ly** iḥki bilḥurrîyi *iḥke bilḥurrîye*
**candle** sham'a
**-stick** sham'adân
**cane (a reed)** ḳaṣab
**cannon** madfa' *medfa'*, **pl.** mdâfi' *medâfi'*
**c...eer** ṭopji *ṭôbgi*
**-shot** ṭop *ṭôb*
**cap (for the head)** ṭarbûsh, **pl.** ṭrâbîsh' *ṭarâbîsh'*
**cape (headland)** râs
**see also burnoose, collar**
**caper (fruit)** ûbâr', ḳubbâr
**Capernaum** kafr nâḥûm'
**capital (money)** rismâl *rasmâl*
**(town)** 'âṣimi *'âṣime*
**(adj. = excellent)** 'âl
**capitulations** imtiyâzât'
**capote** ḳabbû', **pl.** ḳabâbî' *kabbûd*
**captain (mil.)** kolaṛâsi
**(of a boat)** raiyis *re≈îs*
**c... of a harbor** raiyis ilmîna *re≈îs elmîna*
**captive** yasîr, **pl.** yusara
**caravan** karwân *ḳâfile*
**c...sary; see khan**
**carcase (dead body)** maiyti or jîfi *gîfe*, **pl.** jiyaf *giyef*
**card (of paper)** waraḳi *waraḳe*
**(visiting)** kartefezît
**c...s for playing** shaddi *waraḳ*
**a game at c...s** la'b ishshad'di *li'b elwa'raḳ*
**care (trouble, grief)** hamm
**to take c... of ..** dâr ilbâl 'ala .. *khalla elbâl 'ala ..*
**take c...!** dîr bâlak! *khalli bâlak!* û'a! twaḳḳa! *itwaḳ'ḳa!* **(threatening)** îyâk'! *îyâk'!*
**take c... nothing is forgotten** dîr bâlak inna mâ mninsa shî *khalli bâlak inna mâ beninsâsh ḥâge*
**I must take c... of myself** lâzim itwaḳ'ḳa *lâzim au'a 'ala nefsi*
**to c... about (give one's mind to)** .. dâr bâlo 'ala .. *khalla bâlo 'ala ..*
**what do I c...!** shû bîkhuṣṣ'ni! *ana mâli!*
**I don't c... (it is all one to me)** haida mâ hû shî 'indi *di mush ḥâge 'andi* or mitl ba'ḍo 'indi *zê ba'ḍo 'andi*
**careful (attentive)** mutnab'bih
**be c...!** îyâk'! *îyâk'!*
**Carmel: Mt. C...** jabal mâr ilyâs *gebel mâr elyâs*
**carnival** marfa'
**carob-tree (coll.)** kharrûb; **(a single one)** kharrûbi *kharrûbe*
**carpenter** nijjâr *naggâr*

---

candle: put the c... on .. 93,8
canter: does it c...? 123,3
capital! 102,3
care: take c...73,15; 128,7; 129,8
take good c... 72,13
careful: work them c...ly 109,8

**carpet** bsâṭ *busâṭ*, **pl.** busṭ; sijjâdi *saggâde;* see p. 116, note

**carriage (vehicle)** ʿarabâyi or ʿarabîyi *ʿarabîye;* karrûsa

**c... paid** khâliṣ ilij'ra *khâliṣ elug'ra*

**carrier (porter)** ʿittâl *shaiyâl*

**carrion;** see carcase

**carrot** jazar *gazar*

**carry** ḥamal *shâl (yeshîl)*

**will you c... this for me?** bitrîd tiḥmil'li haida? *b'trîd tiḥmil'li di?*

**c... my things upstairs** jîb awâʿî'yi lafauḳ' *shîl ḥawâ-igi lifôḳ*

**cart** karra *karro*, **pl.** karrât [*karrât*]

**cartridge** fashek *feshêk*

**Casa Blanca** dâr ilbai'ḍa *dâr elbêḍa*

**case (small box)** ʿulbi *ʿilbe*, **pl.** ʿulab *ʿilab*

**(big box)** ṣandûḳ, **pl.** ṣanâdîḳ' [*ṛulâf*]

**(cover, sheath)** muṛal'lif

**(cause in court)** daʿwa, **pl.** daʿâwi [aḥwâl]

**(state, condition)** ḥâl, **pl.**

**in this c...** iza kân haik *iza kân ʿala kide*

**cash (ready money)** naḳdîyi *naḳdîye;* the adverb is naḳdan (for cash)

**cask** barmîl, **pl.** barâmîl'

**cast (formed from a mould)** ḳâlib, **pl.** ḳwâlib *ḳawâlib*

**to c... (throw)** ṭaraḥ

**to c... up (add)** jamaʿ

**castanet** ifḳai'sha *sâge*, **pl.** *sâgât'*

**castle (fortified house)** ḳalʿa **(palace)** sarâya

**castor-oil** zait kharwaʿ *zêt kharwaʿ*

**cat** ḳuṭṭa, bsaini *besêbis*

**tom** bsain *besêbîs*, *ḳuṭṭ*

**catalogue** ḳâ-ime, fihrist'

**cataplasm** lazḳa; see also poultice

**cataract (waterfall)** shillâl *shalâl*

**(disease)** moi azraḳ *nuzûl el moiye*

**catarrh** nazli *nazle*

**catch (verb)** misik

**to c... a disease** inʿa'da, misik maraḍ

**caterpillar (coll.)** dûd

**(a single one)** dûdi *dûde*

**Catholic** kâtûlî'ki *kâtûlî'ke*, **pl.** kwâtli *katâlke*

**Roman C...** lâtî'ni; see Greek

**cattle (in general)** mawâshi

**(of the bovine genus)** baḳar

**Caucasus** ḳâf ḳâz

**cauliflower** ḳarnabîṭ

**cause (reason)** sabab *sebeb*

**what is the c...?** shû issa'bab? *esse'beb ê?*

**to c...** sabbab

---

**cautious** mutnab'bih
**cavalry** khîyâ'li *khaiyâle*
**cave** marâra, pl. murr **and** marâyir
**cease** (**of men**) baṭṭal ; (**of things**) inka'ṭa'
**cedar** arzi *erze*, **pl.** arz *erz*
**ceiling** sakf *sukf*
**celebrate** iḥta'fal
**celebrated** mashhûr
**celebration** iḥtifâl
(**of a marriage**) faraḥ
**celery** krafs *karafs*'
**cellar** kabu *kabwe*, **pl.** kawâbi *kubab*
**cemetery** tirbi *turbe*, makbara
**centre** wasṭ *wusṭ*; markaz *merkaz*, **pl.** marâkiz *merâkiz*
**century** jîl *gîl*, **pl.** ijyâl *igyâl*; karn, **pl.** kurûn
**cerastes** (**snake**) ḥaiyi bil kurûn
**certain** (**sure**) muak'kad, [akîd *ekîd*]
(**designated, fixed**) mu'ai'yan, mukad'dar
**c...ly!** bala shakk! ṣaḥîḥ! muak'kad! akîd! halbatt'!
**certificate** shihâdi *shihâde*, **pl.** shihâdât' *shihâdât'*
**certify** ṣaddak 'ala
**chaff** (**cut straw**) tibn
**chain** jinzîr *zengîr*, **pl.** jnâzîr' *zenâgîr'*; *silsile*
**watch-c...** kostak' *ustêk*
**Chain-Dome** (**in Jerusalem**) kubbet issil'sile
**chair** kursi, **pl.** krâsi *karâ'sî*
**chalk** ṭabâshîr'
**chamber**; see room
(**pot**) arḍîyi, musta''mali *kaṣrîye*
**chameleon** ḥirbâyi *ḥerbâye*
**chance** ṣudfi *ṣudfe*
**by c...** biṣṣud'fi *ḥâkim*
**change** (**alteration**) tiṛyîr *taṛyîr*
(**transposition**) tibdîl *tabdîl*
(**small money**) firâṭa, kiṭa'
**to c...** (**alter**) raiyar, baddal *baddil*
(**to exchange**) ṣaraf; p. 104
(**to be altered**) tṛaiyar *itṛai'yar*
**changeable** mutṛai'yir
**chap** (**young man**) ṛulâm, shâbb *waled*
**chapel** zâwyi *zâwiye*; khalwi [*khalwe*]

---

cease! 51,23
ceaseless (continuous) 39, note
ceremony: no c. between us 58,3
certain place 122,2
do you know this for c.? 45,20
I am c... 48,7
chair: offer the .. a c... 37,13
chamber: in the c... 88,15
change: where can I c... (money)? 83,1
c... me this (megeed) 106,8
c... (give others) 130,7
c... me this .. 80,3
(change) c... them 79,7
we will c... them 139,1
weather has c...d 140,13
give me the c... 118,15
changeable 66,4
channel (rill) 142,6
charge: at your c... 87,1
what is the c... for a telegram to ..? 82,15
c... the .. only 104,6
what have you c...d? 105,2
will be c...d 97,1
you c... too much 122,6

**character** (**personal qualities**) ṭabʿ
(**written**) shihâdi *shihâde*
**charcoal** faḥm
**charity** (**beneficence**) iḥsân
(**love**) maḥab'bi
**charm**; see remedy
**chase** (**to hunt**) ṣaiyad, iṣṭâd
(**to drive away**) dashshar *ṭarad*
**chaste** ʿafîf
**chat** (**to talk**) tḥâdas *itḥâdit*
**chauffeur** ûjâḳ'ji *wûgâḳ'gi*
**cheap** rakhîṣ, **pl.** rukhâṣ
**cheat** (**a fraud**) ṛishsh
**to c...** ṛashsh
**cheek** khadd, **pl.** khudûd [*khudud*]
**cheese** jibn *gibn*, jibni *gibne*
**chemist's shop**; see pharmacy
**cheque** shek
**chess** shaṭranj' *shaṭrang'*
**-board** ruḳʿit ishshaṭranj' *ruḳʿat eshshaṭrang'*
**king** shâh
**queen** wezîr
**castle** rukh
**bishop** fîl
**knight** faras
**pawn** bîyâ'di *baiyâde*
**man** ḥajar *ḥagar*
**square** bait *bêt*
**mate** mât *mât*
**checkmate** ishshâh mât *eshshâh mât*
**check to the king!** kishsh ishshâh! *kishsh eshshâh!*
**check to the queen!** kishsh ilwezîr! *kishsh elwezîr!*
**to take, beat** ḳatal
**we will play a game of c.** baddna nilʿab daḳḳ fishshaṭranj' *biddina nilʿab daḳḳ fishshaṭrang'*
**it is your move** luʿbak *liʿbak*
**chest** (**large box**) ṣandûḳ, **pl.** ṣanâdîḳ'
(**part of body**) ṣidr
**c... of drawers** bîro *barô*
**chestnut** kastani *abu farwe*
**chew** ʿalak *madaṛ*
**chibouque** ḳaṣabi *ḳaṣabe*, mâṣû'ra; see pipe
**chicken** farrûj *farrûg*, **pl.** frârîj' *farârîg'*
(**young one**) sûs *katkût*, **pl.** sîsân' *ketâkît'*
**chickpea** ḥummuṣ
**chief** (**captain**) ra-îs *re-îs*, raiyis
**chief judge** ra-îs ilḳuḍât *bâsh ḳâḍi*
**child** walad, **pl.** ûlâd' *ûlâd'*
(**small one**) ṭifl
**little children** ûlâd' zṛâr *ûlâd' zuṛâr*
**childishness, childish play** waldani *liʿb ezzuṛâr*
**chin** daḳn
**chisel** (**two-bevelled**) zmîl *zemîl* or *minḳâr*
**choice** (**selection**) intikhâb

---

**(charge) how much do you c...?** 97,2
**char-woman** 89,4
**chase away the flies** 146,1
**chest of drawers** 79,9; 110,5
**chill: I caught a c...** 34,3.4
**Chinese** 117,8.9
**choke: the horses will c...** 144,7

**cholera** hawa ilaṣ'far *hawa* [*elaṣ'far*]
**choose** inta'khab
**chrism** mairûn
**Christ**; see Jesus
**christen** ʿammad
 **c...ing** riṭâs
**christian** naṣrâni, pl. naṣâra; mesîḥi
 (=**infidel**) kâfir *kâfir*, pl. kuffâr
**Christmas** ʿid ilmilâd' *ʿîd elmîlâd'*
**church** knîsi *kenîse*, pl. knâyis *kenâ:is*
**cigar** sîgâ'ra franjîyi *sîgâ'ra ifrengî*
 **c...ette** sîgâ'ra
 **c...-holder** bizz *fumm*
**cinnamon** ḳurfi *ḳurfe*
**circle** dâyri *dâ:ire*, pl. dawâyir *dawâ:ir*
**circumcise** ṭahhar
 **c...sion** khitân, tiṭhîr *taṭhîr*, ṭuhûr
**circumstance** ḥâl; zarf, pl. zrûf *zurûf*
 **one must take account of the c...s** ilwâḥid lâzim bîrâʿʿi izzrûf *lâzim elwâḥid birâʿi elḥâl*
**cistern** maṣnaʿ *ṣahrîg*
**citadel** ḳalʿa

**city**; see town
**civil** (**political**) syâsi *siyâse*
 (**courteous**) mitwâḍiʿ
 **c... officer** ma:mûr mulkiy
**claim** (**right**) ḥaḳḳ
 (**pretension**) daʿwa, iddiʿâ
**class** ṭabaḳa, pl. ṭabaḳât
 (**school-**) ṣaff *firḳe*, pl. ṣufûf *firaḳ*
 **first-c...** brîmo
 **second-c...** sikon'do
**clay** trâb ilfikhkhâr *ṭîn*
**clean** (**adj.**) naḍîf or nḍîf
 **to c...** naḍḍaf, masaḥ
 **c... my boots at once** ḥâlan imsaḥ lastîki
 **c...liness** naḍâfi *naḍâfe*
**clear** (**adj.**) ṣâfi
 (**indisputable, distinct**) wâḍiḥ, zâhir
**cleave** (**to split**) shaḳḳ
**clergyman**; see priest
**clerk** kâtib *mistakh'dam*
**clever** mâhir, ḥâziḳ, shâṭir
**climate** manâkh *hawa*
**climb** (**up**) ṭiliʿ
**clipped** (**cut off**) maḳṣûṣ, [*maḥlûḳ*]
**cloak** kabbût, mashlaḥ
 (**peasant's, Bedouin's c...**) ʿabâyi *ʿabâye* or *zaʿbût*
 see also burnoose
**clock** sâʿa *sâʿa*; see pp. 68 to 70

---

choose! 84,5
 c... which you will 119,9
 let him c... 121,11
cigarette-paper 103,3
circumstances: what am I to do under all these c...s? 75,15
clean 79,5; 80,2; 99,11
 (hotel, village) 76,15; 126,10
 ..that everything is c... 89,5
 have you c...ed ..? 91,6.7

(clean) .. must be c...ed 80,11
 to c... a watch 107,3
clear the table 93,2
 .. has c...ed up 146,13
 it is c...ing up 64,15
 the sky is c... 64,16
clock: at 8 o'c... 77,6
 at .. punctually 81,1; 94,10
 for .. o'c... 94,9
 what o'c... is it? 68,19; 69,1

**close** (sultry) ḥarr, mufaṭ'ṭis
**c... (near) to..** ḳarîb.., jamb min..*gambê min..*
**c... by** bilḳurb'
**to c... (shut)** ṛalaḳ; **(to finish)** khatam
**closet**; **see cupboard**
**(w.c.)** mustarâḥ, bait il-moi' *bêt elmoi'ye, kenîf*
**cloth** jûkh *gûkh*; **see linen**
**clothing** libs, kiswi *kiswe*
**cloud** ṛaim *ṛêm*, **pl.** ṛyûm *ṛiyûm*
**clove** ḳurun'ful
**clover (white Egyptian)** *bersîm*
**club (stick)** nabbût, dabbûs, dabsi *dabse*
**clumsy** ṛashîm, **pl.** ṛushm
**clyster** ḥuḳni *ḥuḳne*
**coach** ʿarabâyi **or** ʿarabîyi *ʿarabîye*, karrûsa
**-greaser** *shaḥam'gi*
**-pusher** *ḳaṭar'gi*
**coachman** ʿaraba'ji, ʿarba'ji *ʿarba'gi*
**coal (char-)** faḥm
**mineral c...** faḥm ḥajar *faḥmê ḥagar*
**a live c...** jamra *gamra*, baṣṣit nâr
**-pan (stove)** kânûn', man-ḳal
**coarse (of stuff)** khishin, dûn
**(impolite)** simij *simig*, ṛalîz
**coast** shâṭi *shaṭṭ*
**(stretch along the c...** sâḥil, **pl.** sawâḥil
**coat** sitra *sitre*
**(a long one)** jubbi *gubbe*
**(a long, light summer c...)** ḳumbâz *ḳuftân*
**coax** lâṭaf, mallaḳ
**cobweb** ḥiyâk ilʿankabût *bêt elʿankabût*
**cock (bird)** dîk, **pl.** diyûk
**cockroach** ṣarṣûr
**coco-nut** jauz hindi *gôz hindi*
**cocoon (silk-)** sharnaḳa, **pl** shrânik *sharânik*
**code (law)** ḳânûn', **pl.** ḳa-wânîn'
**coffee (unground beans)** binn *bunn*
**(a single one)** binni *bunne*
**roasted c...** binn mḥammaṣ *bunn muḥam'maṣ*
**(the beverage and the c... house)** ḳahwi *ḳahwe*, **pl.** ḳahâwi
**-can (small tin can in which the Arabic c... is boiled)** rakwi *tanake, kanake*
**-cup** finjân *fingân*, **pl.** fnâjîn' *fenâgîn'*; **saucer** zarf
**-dregs** tifl *tanwa*

---

close the window 93,13
do the doors c... well? 84,9
this house is c... 85,10
follow me c...ly 51,6
cloth (serviette, etc.) 98,8.4
is too light, dark 113,3
give me the c...es 90,3
cloth dyed in the wool 112,7
clouds are dispersing 64,13
coach-house 86,3
coffee: cup of c... 102,10.11
c... with milk 81,1
bring me the c... 92,4
phrases of courtesy 39, note

**coffee-mill** ṭâḥûn′ ilḳah′wi *ṭâḥûn′ elḳah′we*
**-mortar**; see mortar
**keeper of a c... -house** ḳahwaji *ḳahwegi*
phrases; see pp. 39, 102-104
**coffin** tâbût′
**cognac** kunyâk
**coin (noun)** sikki *sikke*, ʿimli *ʿumle*
**coke** faḥm ḥajar maḥrûḳ *faḥmé mṣaffa*
**cold (the c...)** bard
**(catarrh)** rashḥ
**(adj.)** bârid *bârid*
**to have a c...** trashshaḥ *izzakam*
**I have a c...** ana murash′shaḥ *mazkûm*
**to take c...** akhad bard *khad bard* [*bardân*
**I am c...** ana birdân *ana*
**it is c...** iddin′yi bard *eddin′ye bard*
**it is very c... outdoors** fî bard ktîr barra *fîh bardé ketîr barra* [*rôsto bârid*
**c... roast-meat** rôsto bârid

**colic** ḳûlanj *maṛas*
**collar** ḳabbi *yâḳa*, **pl.** ḳabbât *yâḳât′* [*ṭôḳ*
**(necklace)** ʿiḳd *ʿuḳd, ṭauḳ*
**collect (trans.)** jamaʿ *gamaʿ*, lamm
**c...ively** ʿumûman
**college**; see school
**C... of Agriculture** madraset zirâʿa
**collyrium**; see antimony
**colonel** mîr âlây′
**colonise (populate and cultivate)** ʿammar
**color** laun *lôn*, **pl.** ilwân
**to c... (trans.)** lauwan, ṣabaṛ
**column** ʿâmûd′, **pl.** ʿawâmîd′
**comb** musht *miṣhṭ*
**to c...** mashshaṭ; **(one's hair)** tmashshaṭ *itmash′shaṭ*
**combat (noun)** muḳâtali *muḳâtale*, maʿraki *maʿ-rake*
**come** ija *gâ* or *gi*
**I came** jît *gît* [*gîti*
**you came** jît *gît*, **fem.** jîti
**c...!** taʿâl! *taʿâla!* **fem.** taʿâli!

---

coin of the country 104,12
cold water 79,12
it is still c.. 140,7
is it c... in winter? 135,6
make it c...(let in c...water) 99,9
I have a c... 34,3.4
I feel a shivering c... 148,8
colored cloth 112,2
c... embroidery 116,5
come: I came .. 38,6
he c...s 104,1
we have c... to .. 142,13
.. to which we c... 131,7
we shall c... to .. 145,1
when we c... to .. 139,1
you have just c... 40,10

(come) whence c... you? 45,11
whence does .. c...? 142,7
whence c... you (plur.)? 133,4
c... down 52,10
c... here 50,21
c... in 51,3
c... nearer 50,22
c... to me to-day 85,7
let him c... in 36,17
let no one c... in 148,16
I ask you to c... earlier 98,9
Mr. N. will c... presently 38,12
some one will c... 78,3
there is a wave coming 73,14
to c... to it 144,3
to c... (that I may c...) 42,2

**(come) coming** jâyi *gâ-i*
**I am coming** biji *bagi*
**you are coming** btiji *beti'gi*
see pp. 27, 28
**has no one c...?** mâ ija ḥada? *mâ ḥaddish gi?*
**when will you c... again?** aimta btiji tâni marra? *imte tigi tâni marra?* or aimta minshûfak? *imte neshûfak?*
**when will you c... back?** aimta btirja'? *tirga' imte*
**whence c... you?** minain jâyi? *min ên gâ-i?*
**she is to c... at 9 o'clock** tâ tiji issâ'a tis'a *tigi essâ'a tis'a*
**to c... in** fât (yfût) *khashsh;* **c... in!** fût! *khushsh!*
**to c... up** ṭili'
**to c... upon (learn) something** wakaf 'ala . .
**comet** nijmi ilha daneb *nigme liha deneb*
**comfort (ease)** kêf, irtiyâḥ, râḥa
**(consolation)** tasliyi or tislâyi *ta'zîye*
**to c... (console)** salla *'azza*
**comfortable (commodious, of things)** murai'yiḥ
**(of persons)** bîḥibb' irrâḥa *biḥibb' errâḥa;* mukai'yaf *mekai'yif;* **see note to kêf' in the Arabic Vocab.**
**command** amr, **pl.** awâmir *awâmir*
**to c...** amar [ḥâkim]
**commandant** ḳûmandân',
**commandment** waṣîyi
**the Ten C...s** ilwaṣâya il'ash'ra *elwaṣâya el'e'shara*
**commence** ibta'da **(or, Syr. only:** ballash)
**when do they (does one) c...?** aimta byibti'du? **or** aimta bîbal'lishu? *imte bibti'du?*
**commencement** ibtida, bidâyi **or** bdâyi *bedâye,* auwal
**where is the c...?** wain ilau'wal? *fên elau'wal?*
**at the c...** bilau'wal; fî bidâyit il... *fî bedâyet el...*
**before the c...** kabl bidâyit il... *kablê bedâyet el...*
**commerce** tijâra *tigâre*
**commercial tribunal** majlis tijâra *maglis ettigâre*
**common (low)** razîl, khabîs
**(usual)** 'âdi, i'tiyâdi
**(c... to all)** mushta'rak
**that is c... to all** haida shî maujûd 'ind ijjamî' *di shê maugûd 'and elgemî'*
**in c...** bilishtirâk, sawîyatan
**c...ly** ṛâliban
**communicate; see inform**
**company (somebody's c..., companionship)** mu'âshara
**(commercial)** shirki *shirke,* shirâki *shirâke*

---

**command: at c...** 49,13; 56.5
**(on my head)** 39,2
**what do you c...?** 45,12; 90,1
Commandaria-wine 124.1
commiseration 60,1 ff.
commission (agio) 105,2.3

**(party, society)** jam'îyi *gam'îye*, jamâ'a *gemâ'a*
**good c... (a person)** musâyir *musâ:ir* [ibri *ibre*
**compass (mariner's)** bûṣla,
**c...es** bîkâr'
**compassion** shafaḳa
**c...ate** ḥanûn
**complain of** ishta'ka, tshakka min *itshak'ka min*, shaka
**c... to me!** ishkîli!
**c...ant** mudda'i
**complaint** shakwa, shkâyi *shikâye*, da'wa
**I have a c... against him** ili da'wa 'alaih' *lîye da'wa 'alêh*
**complete (adj.)** kâmil *kâmil*
**to c...** akmal, kammal
**compliment: my c...s to Mr. ..** iḥtirâmâ'ti lilkhawâja .. *iḥtirâmâ'ti lilkhawâga ..* [kab *rakkib*
**compose (put together)** rak-
**(books)** allaf [*mu:el'lif*
**c...r (author)** mu:al'lif
**compulsory labor** sukhra
**conceal** khabba
**concern (verb)** khaṣṣ
**that does not c... you** haida mâ bîkhuṣ'ṣak *di mâ bikhuṣṣak'shi*
**as far as .. is c...ed** bikhuṣûṣ .., min yamm .., min jihit .. *min gihet ..*
**concert** konsêr
**conclude (trans. = finish)** kammal
**(intr. = infer)** istadall'
**condemn** ḥakam 'ala
**condition (state)** ḥâl, ḥâli, *ḥâle*
**(stipulation)** sharṭ, **pl.** shrûṭ **or** shurûṭ
**under the c... that ..** bisharṭ' in ..
**conduct (guidance)** hidâye
**a safe c...** amân
**to c...; see lead, behave**
**c...or; see railway; (of a concert)** marshed konsêr
**confectionery (sweetmeats)** ḥalâwi *ḥalâwe*, **pl.** ḥulwîyât' *ḥalâwîyât'*
**conference** mashware
**confess** ḳarr, i'ta'raf
**c...ion** iḳrâr; **see also creed**
**confirm (corroborate)** akkad, sabbat
**conflagration** ḥarîḳ *ḥarîḳe*
**congratulate** hanna
**c...tion** tahnîyi *tahnîye*; **see also pp. 43, 44**
**conjecture (imagination)** wahm
**to c...** khamman *khammin*
**conjurer** sâḥir, **pl.** su'ḥarâ; *ḥâwi*
**conquer** istau'la 'ala ..
**conscience** dimmi *dimme*

---

complete suit 113,7
c... suite, etc. 116,4; 121,5
compliments 35,12
compose yourself 52,13.14
concern: does not c... me 55,3
(concern) .. c...s you 123,2
condition: in good c... 87,2
condolence 60,1 ff.
conduct me to .. 82,4
congratulate: I c... you 61,8

**consent (verb) to something** riḍi bi .., ḳibil (**with acc.**)
**I c...** biḳbal *baḳbal*
**considerable** ʿazîm
**Constantinople** stambûl *istambûl*, ilâstâ'ni *elastâne*
**consul** ḳunṣul, pl. ḳanâṣil
**C... General** janarâl *ganarâl;* jannanâr *gananâr*
**Vice C...** ḳunṣul zṛîr *wakîl elḳun'ṣul*
**where does the British C... live?** wain bait ḳunṣul inglîzi? *fên bêt ḳunṣul ingelîzi?*
**I shall complain to the C...** baddi ishtki lilḳun'ṣul *biddi ashti'ki lilḳun'ṣul*
**Consular Court** maḥkamit ḳunṣlîye *magles ḳonṣolâto*
**consulate** ḳunṣlâto *ḳonṣolâto*, kinshlârî'yi *kanshellârî'ye*; see p. 82
**c...'s official (policeman)** ḳauwâṣ ilḳunṣlâto *ḳauwâṣ elḳonṣolâto*
**c...'s dragoman** tarjimân ilḳunṣlâto *turgemân elḳonṣolâto*
**consult (together) about..** tshâwar ʿala.. *itshâwir ʿala..*
**c...ation** mashwara, mushâwara
**consumption (med.)** sill
**contagious: to be c...** ʿada
**this disease is c...** halmaʿrad byiʿdi *elmaʿraḍ di biʿdi*
**contemptuous** ḥaḳîr
**content (adj.) with ..** mabsûṭ min.., râḍi bi..
**contents (of a book)** mauḍûʿ *môḍûʿ*
**continent (land)** barr
**continual** temel'li
**continue** kammal *kammil*
**contraband** tahrîb
**contract (agreement)** kuntrâtu
**c...or** meḳâwil
**contradict** ḍâdad *khâlif*
**contrary (opposite)** ḍidd
**that is c... to the arrangement** haida ḍidd ilittifâḳ *di ḍidd elittifâḳ*
**conversation** ḥadîs or *mukâlame*
**in the course of the c...** fî isnâ ilḥadîs *fî esnâ elḥadîs*
**convolvulus** liflâfi *laflâfe*
**cook (a male c...)** ʿashshi, pl. ʿashshîyi; ṭabbâkh, pl. *ṭabbâkhîn'*
**to c...** ṭabakh
**what can you c...?** shû btaʿrif tiṭbukh? *betaʿraf tiṭbukh ê?*

**cooked** maṭbûkh
**cooling-vessel** sharbi *ḳulle*
**coop (for poultry)** ḳafaṣ
**cooper; see box-maker; there are no special coopers in the Orient**
**copper** nuḥâs *naḥâs*
  **(boiler)** khilḳîn
**Copt** ḳibṭi, **pl.** iḳbâṭ
**copy** nuskha, **pl.** nusakh; ṣûra, **pl.** ṣuwar
  **to c...** nasakh
  **-book** daftar, **pl.** dfâtir *dafâtir*
**coral** mirjân *morgân*
**cord (a string)** ḥabl, marsa
**cork (tree or its bark)** fillîn *fill*
  **(a stopper)** fillîni *filli*
  **-screw** birrîni *berîme*
**corn (grain)** ḳamḥ **or** *ralle*
  **(a single one)** ḥabbi *ḥabbe*, **pl.** ḥubûb
  **(Indian c..., maize)** durra
  **(on the foot)** dimân
**cornelian (chalcedony)** ʻaḳîḳ
**corner** rukn, **pl.** arkân
  **(projecting point or edge)** ḳurni *ḳurne*
**corpse** maiyit, jîfi *gîfe*
**corpulent** jasîm *gasîm*
**Corpus Christi** ʻîd ijjaʼsad *ʻîd eggaʼsad*
**correct (adj.)** ṣaḥîḥ, maḍbûṭ *mazbûṭ*
  **to c...** ṣaḥḥaḥ
**correspondence** mukâtabi *mukâtabe*
**corvée** sukhra
**cost (price, value)** ḳîmi
  **(expenses)** maṣrûf
  **to c...** kallaf *kallif*
  **what does it c...?** bikâm, biḳaddaish'?
  **c...ly** tamîn, nafîs
**cotton** ḳuṭn
**cough (noun)** saʻli *saʻle*
  **to c...** saʻal *kaḥḥ*
**Council: Municipal C...** majlis beledîyi *meglis beledîye*
**count (to number)** ʻadd, ḥasab *ḥâsib*; **see rely upon**
**counting-house** maktab *mekteb*
**country (a c..., kingdom)** blâd *bilâd*, **pl.** bildân *buldân*
  **(region)** nâḥyi *naḥye*, **pl.** [nawâḥi]
  **in this c...** fî halblâd *fil-bilâd di*
  **c... man; see peasant**
**couple (noun)** jauz *gôz*; **also expressed by the dual of the substantives, e.g. a c... of piastres** ḳirshain' *ḳirshên*
**courage** jasâra *gasâre*, murûwi *murûwe*
  **I have no c... to do that** mâ ili ʻain aʻmil haida *mâlish ʻên aʻmil di*

---

cooking 88,19
cooking-apparatus 128,3
cool: I must c... off 102,5
  in the c... of the morning 138,4
corns: I have c... 109,7
correct: the account is c... 105,7
cost: how much does .. c...? 107,6; 118,10
cotton (thread) 94,8
couches (sofas) 110,6

**courageous** jasûr *gasûr*, shajî' *shagî'*
**courier** sâ'i *sâ'i*, barîd (**post c... as between Damascus and Bagdad**) tatar
**course** (**race**) sharaf ; (**race-ground**) mîdân' ; (**way**) ṭarîḳ
**Court of Justice** maḥkami *maḥkame*
**Criminal Court** maḥkami jinâyi *maḥkame ginâye*
**The Mixed Courts** *elmaḥâkim elmukhta'liṭa*, *elmagâlis elmukhta'liṭa*
**court-yard** ḥaush *ḥôsh*
**cousin** : **male c... (on father's side)** ibn il'amm' *ibn el'amm'* or ibn il'am'mi *ibn el'am'me*
**male c... (on mother's side)** ibn·ilkhâl *ibn elkhâl* or ibn·ilkhâli *ibn elkhâle*
**female c... ; see 'bint' in the Arabic Vocabulary**
**cover** (**a wrap**) ṛaṭa
(**for the bed**) liḥâf, **pl.** luḥuf
**to c...** ṛaṭṭa
**c...ing** ṛashâwi *ṛashâwe*
**covetous** ṭamî' *ṭammâ'*
**cow** baḳara
**cowardice** jabâni *gabâne*, ḳillit murûwi *ḳillet murûwe*
**cowardly** jabân *gabân*

**crab saraṭân, pl. sarâṭîn'** ; salṭa'aun', pl. *salâṭ'în'*
**crack** (**fissure**) shaḳḳ
**cradle** (**noun**) sarîr, marjûḥa *murgêḥa*
**craft** (**trade**) ṣan'a } [nuḳ'ṭa]
**cramps** (**epileptic**) dâ in }
**crawfish ; see crab**
**crawl** dabdab
**cream** ḳishṭa
**create** khalaḳ
**creation** khalḳ
**credit** (**noun, comm.**) krêdito
**I have something to my c... ; see owe**
**c...or** dâyin, ṣâḥib iddain' *ṣâḥib eddên*
**creed** (**confession of faith**), **of Christians** : kilmit ilîmân' *kilmet elimân*
**of Mussulmans** : kilmit ishshihâdi ; **it runs thus** : ashhadu an lâ ilâha illallâh ashhadu anna muḥam'madan rasûlullâh' **I testify that there is no God besides 'the God' (Allâh), I testify that Mohammed is the Apostle of God** ; or, lâ ilâha illallâh muḥam'madun rasûlullâh' **there is no God besides 'the God,' Mohammed is the Apostle of God**
**creep ; see crawl**

---

**course : of c... 123,4**
**courtesy 53,8**
**cousin : my (male) c... 87,10**
**cover for cushions 111,5**
**divan c...s 116,4**
**table c... 116,4 ; plur. 115,11**
**cover me well 148,13**
**c... me with the rug 145,10**
**with which I c...ed 140,4**
**c...ed buttons 113,9**
**crack(ed) 117,10 ; 118,1**
**creep : snake c...s on us 146,2**

**crescent** (the new moon) hilâl *hilâl*
**cress** jirjîr *gargîr*
**cricket** (insect) ṣarṣûr
**crier** (town-) munâdi
**crime** jinâyi *ginâye*
**crippled** mukar'saḥ *mukas'-saḥ*
**crocodile** timsâḥ *timsâḥ*, pl. tmâsîḥ' *temâsîḥ'*
**crooked** a'waj *a'wag*, fem. 'auja *'ôga*, pl. 'ûj *'ûg*
**crop** (gizzard) ḥûṣal'i *ḥuṣâle*
c...s (produce) maḥṣûl, ṛille *ṛalle*
**cross** (noun) ṣalîb, pl. ṣulbân
c... (angry) with .. zi'lân min or 'ala .. *za'lân min* or *'ala* .. ; see vexed
to c... (cancel) maḥa ; (a river) ḳaṭa' ; cf. pp. 143, 144
**crow** (bird) ḳâḳ, pl. ḳîḳân'
**crowd** (noun) zaḥmi *zaḥme* or *ziḥâm*, 'ajḳa
**crown** (diadem) tâj *tâg*, pl. tîjân' *tîgân'*
**crucifix** ṣalîb, pl. ṣulbân
**cruel** ḳâsi, zâlim
c...ty ḳasâwi *ḳasâwe*
**crush** (to pound) saḥan *dâs*
**crutch** 'ukkâzi *'ukkâze*, pl. 'akâkîz'
**cry** (an outcry) ṣiyâḥ, 'iyâṭ
to cry (call) ṣâḥ, 'aiyaṭ *zaḳḳa'*
(to weep) biki *'aiyaṭ*
**crystal** billôr

**cube** ka'b
**cubit**; see yard
**cucumber** khiyâr ; see squash
**cultivate** (plough) falaḥ
**cunning** (noun) ḥîli *ḥîle*, pl. ḥiyal ; ḥirfi, pl. ḥiraf
(adj.) khabîs *makkâr*
**cup** finjân *fingân*, pl. finâjîn' *fenâgîn'*
(tumbler) kâs *kâs*, pl. ku≈ûs *kâsât'*
(vase, also saucer) zarf ; (a European saucer is ṣaḥn ilfinjân *ṣaḥn elfingân*)
to cup (draw blood) ḥajam
**cupboard** khizâni *dûlâb'*, pl. khazâyin *dewâlîb'*
**cupola** ḳubbi *ḳubbe*
**cure** (healing and remedy) shifa
to c... (trans. = to heal) shafa, 'alaj *'alig*
**curiosities** antîkât'
dealer in c... antak'ji *antîka'gi*
**curry-comb** maḥas'si *maḥas'se*
**curse** (noun) la'ni or na'li *la'ne*
to c... sabb
God c... you Alla yil'anak
**cursed** mal'ûn
**curtain** birdâyi *sitâra*
**cushion** (of a sofa) masnid, pl. msânid *mesânid* ; (a smaller one) tikkâyi *tikkâye*

cross the bridge 144,2
c... the river 143,13
cuffs 98,11
cuisine (the cooking) 88,19
cup (bowl) 99,3
current (of a river) 143,17
curry (horses) 138,3
did you c... them? 138,2

**custom (usage)** ʿâdi *ʿâde*, **pl.** ʿâdât' **and** ʿawâyid *ʿawâ=id*
**that is the c...** hai ilʿâdi *elʿâde kide* [*âdi' ʿatti*]
**that is my c...** hai ʿâdeti
**c...er** zebûn
**customs (duties)** rasm
**custom-house** kumruk *gumruk*
**custom-officer** kumruk'shi *gumruk'gi*
**cut (slice)** ḳaṭʿa, **pl.** ḳiṭaʿ; **see also wound**
**to cut** ḳaṭaʿ, ḳaṣṣ
**to cut small, as tobacco, to hash meat** faram, farram
**I cut my finger** ḳaṣṣait' iṣbaʿi *ḳaṣṣêt ṣubâʿi*
**cut tobacco** dukhân mafrûm
**cutlet** barzûla *kastalêta*
**cwt.**; **see hundredweight**
**cypress** sarwi *sarwe* **pl.** sarw
**dagger (large)** khanjar *khangar*, **pl.** khanâjir *khanâgir*
**(small, two-edged)** shukrîyi *gembîye*
**daily (adj.)** yaumi *yômi*
**(adv.)** kull yaum *kulli yôm*
**daisy** iḥwân
**dam (a bank to confine water)** [sudd *gisr*]
**damage (harm done)** ḍarar
**to d...** ḍarr
**Damascus** ishshâm *eshshâm*
**of D..., Damascene** shâmi *shâmi*, **pl.** shwâm *shawâm*
**Damietta** dimyâṭ *dumyâṭ*
**damp (adj.)** ruṭib *riṭib*
**d...ness** ruṭûbi *ruṭûbe*
**dance** raḳṣ
**to d...** raḳaṣ; **(of dervishes)** [fatal]
**dancer (male)** raḳḳâṣ, râḳûṣ'
**(female)** raḳḳâṣa *râẓi'ye*, **pl.** *rawâzi*; **in Syria there are no special dancing-girls; the singers dance sometimes**
**danger** khaṭar, mukhâṭara
**is there any d... in it?** fî khaṭar fi haida? *fîh khaṭar fî di?*
**there is no d...** mâfi khaṭar *mâfîsh' khaṭar*
**dappled (spotted)** abrash
**dare (intr.)** tajâsar *itgâsar*, istar'ja *ista'gra*
**daring**; **see bold**
**dark (of color)** ramîḳ
**(obscure, dusk)** ʿitm *ḍilim*
**it has grown d...** ṣâr ʿatm eddun'ye *ḍilmet*

---

custom (habit) 86,11
custom-house 74,3.14 ff.; 77,7 ff.
cut the suit 113,8
cut the wick 93,7
cut me off .. 113,1
(razors) will not cut 90,17; 101,8
.. not to cut me 100,9
you have cut me 100,18
cut (wounded) horse 120,4
I want to have my hair cut 81,3
cut my hair short 101,7.9
Cyprus-wine 124,1
damage: to d... (spoil) 129,3
Damascus make 115,8; 117 note
damp room 84,7
danger: expose oneself 144,4
d... on the road 127,4
dare: I d... not .. 144,1
dark (lowering) 65,20
before it grows d... 131,10

**in the d...(ness)** bil'atm' *biddal'me*
**date (time)** târîkh' *târîkh'*
**(fruit)** balah *beleh*
**fresh d...** balah tari *beleh tâza;* **dried d...** tamr
**-liqueur** *'araki beleh*
**-stone** kalb balah *nawâye*
**-tree** nakhli *nakhle;* (coll.) nakhl
**daughter** bint, **pl.** bnât *banât*
**-in-law** kinni *mirât elibn'*
**David** dâ-ûd'
**dawn (noun)** fajr *fagr*
**day (of 24 hours)** yaum *yôm,* **pl.** îyâm' *îyâm'*
**(in opposition to night)** nhâr *nehâr*
**good d...;** see p. 33
**by, in the, day** binnhâr *binnehâr*
**by the, per, day** bilyaum' *bilyôm,* yaumîyi *yômî'ye*
**every day** kull yaum *kulli yôm*
**eight days (a week)** jum'a *gum'a, tamant îyâm'*
**to-day** ilyaum' **or** hannhâr *ennahar'da*
**day after to-morrow** ba'd-buk'ra *ba'dêbuk'ra*
**day before yesterday** au-wiltimbârih *auwal em-bâreh,* auwal ams
**the day has broken** tili' iddau' *tili' ennûr*
**at daybreak** 'ind tlû' iddau' *'andê tulû' ennûr*
**daybreak, dawn** fajr *fagr*
**it is daylight** fî dau *fîh nûr*
**dead** maiyit
**D... Sea;** see sea
**d...ly** bîmau'wit *bimau'wit*
**deaf** atrash
**dealer** bîyâ'' *baiyâ'*
**d... in second-hand goods** antak'ji *antîka'gi*
**dear (beloved)** mahbûb, 'azîz
**(costly)** râli [*di râli*]
**that is too d...** haida râli
**it seems you sell (to me) too d...** mbaiyin int bit-ral'li 'alai'yi *elbai'yin inte bitral'li 'alêye*
**my d...!** yâ 'aini! **see** '**'ain**' **in the Arabic Vocabulary**
**death** maut *môt*
**debt** dain *dên,* **pl.** dyûn *diyûn*
**debtor** madyûn
**deceit** rishsh
**d...ful** khaddâ'
**deceive** rashsh
**d...r;** **see juggler**
**December** kânûn' ilau'wal *dessem'ber*
**decide** hakam
**decision** hukm, **pl.** ahkâm

---

darn the socks 96,9
day: every day 68,14; 89,8
every other day 68,15
for a few days 78,7
in three days 96,6; 109,9
in these days 123,1
daylight: by d... 146,4
dear: that is d... 112,12
that is too d... 118,6
debt: in d... 135,11
decent (house, etc.) 76,15; 83,6
decisive 87,8

**deck-chair** kursi ḍahr il-mar'kab *kursi kuwer'ta*
**declare (testify)** shahad
**decorate** zaiyan *zaiyin*
**decoration (embellishment)** zakhrafi *zakhrafe;* **see also** order
**decorum** edeb
**decrease** tanḳîṣ
**to d... (trans.)** naḳḳaṣ; **(intr.)** niḳiṣ
**deep** ṛamîḳ *ṛawîṭ*
**defend** ḥâma ʿan, dâfaʿ ʿan
**defensive ally** ḥamîyi *ḥamîye*, **pl.** ḥamâya
**degree** daraji *darage*, **pl.** darajât *daragât*
**(rank)** rutbi *rutbe*
**delay** muhli *mihle*
**to d... (protract)** akhkhar, ʿauwaḳ; **(be protracted)** t=akhkhar *it=akh'khar*, tʿauwaḳ *itʿau'waḳ*
**Delta** iddel'ta *eddel'ta*
**deluge (noun)** ṭûfân'
**demand (noun)** ṭalab, maṭlûb
**to d...** ṭalab
**you d... too much** btiṭlub zyâdi *betiṭ'lub ziyâde*
**denial** inkâr
**deny** nakar *ankar*
**Department of Works** dâyret ilashṛâl *dîwân' elashṛâl*
**departure from** ṭulûʿ min, safar min
**depend; see rely**
**that does not d... on me** haida mush biyad'di ana *di mâ yiṭlaḥshi min îdi*
**depose (divest of office)** ʿazal
**d...d** maʿzûl
**to be d...d, removed** inʿa'zal
**(to testify)** afâd
**deposition (dethronement)** ʿazl
**(declaration)** ifâdi *afâde*
**deprive** ʿadam; **(of an office)** ʿazal
**depth** ṛumḳ
**derive from** akhad min *khad min*
**dervish** darwîsh *derwîsh*, **pl.** darâwîsh'
**-devotion with dance** zikr
**-monastery** tekkîyi *tekîye*
**descend** nizil **(or, Syr. only:** ḥauwal)
**to be d...d from: expressed by** aṣl **origin, e.g. he is d...d from an old family** aṣlo min bait ḳadîm *aṣlo min bêt ḳadîm*
**descent (declivity)** nazli
**(act of descending)** nizûl
**describe** waṣaf
**description** waṣf, ṣifa
**desert (wilderness)** shaul *khala*
**the African d...** ṣa'ḥrâ, **pl.** ṣaḥâra

---

(**adj.**) mustau'ḥish
**to d...** (**trans.**) tarak; (**intr.** =**flee**) harab
**deserve** istaḥaḳḳ'
**desire** shahwa, **pl.** shahawât
**to d...** ririb
**desk** ṭâwlet ktâbe *maktab*
**desolation** waḥshi *waḥshe*
**desperate** mai-ûs
**destiny** naṣîb
**destroy** rauwaḥ, kharrab, ['adam]
**detective** bulîs khafîya *bolîs sirri*
**devil** iblîs; shîṭân' *shêṭân'*, **pl.** shiyâṭîn' *sheyâṭîn'*
**dew** nidi *nide*
**dialect** lorat
**diamond** almâs
**diarrhœa** is-hâl *is-hâl* (see p. 3, No. 13), (or, **Syr. only:** jiryân)
**I have severe d...** mâshi baṭni ktîr *baṭni mâshi ketîr*, or ḥakam'ni jiryân ḳawi *ḥakam'ni is-hâl ḳawi*
**dictionary** ḳâmûs'
**die** (**cube**) ka'b
**to die** mât *mât* (yemût)

**difference** (**opposition**) khilâf *ikhtilâf*
**different** (**another**) rair *tâni*
**I will have this done d...ly** baddi haida rair shikl *biddi di shiklè tâni*
**difficult** ṣa'b
**I find it d...** ṣa'b 'alai'yi *ṣa'bè 'alêye*, byiṣ'ab 'alai'yi *biṣ'ab 'alêye*
**d...y** ṣu'ûbi *ṣa'ûbe*
**dig** ḥafar, bakhash
**digestion** haḍm
**dignified** mushar'raf
**diligence** ijtihâd *igtihâd*, shaṭâra
**diligent** mujtahid *mugtahid*, shâṭir
**dinner**[1] fuṭûr *rada*
**dip** (**trans.**) raṭṭaṣ
(**intr.**) raṭas, traṭṭas *itraṭ'ṭas*
**direct** (**adj.**) dugri *dôgru*
(**adv.** =**in a straight line**) dugri, râsan
**to d...** (**order**) amar, âmar
**to d... the telescope at..** dâr innaḍḍâra *ennaḍḍâra* 'ala..

---

[1] **At midday the Oriental eats but little, and he calls this meal** fuṭûr, **properly, breakfast(ing). The principal meal is taken after sunset, the time varying according to the season, usually at about 7 o'clock European time.**

---

**direct me to a doctor** dillni *dillini* ʿala ḥakîm
**direction (quarter)** naḥyi *naḥye*, ṣaub
**directly (soon)** ḳawâm *ḳawâm*
**(in answer to a call)** ḥâḍir **q.v. in the Ar. Voc.**
**director** mudîr, nâzer
**dirt** wasakh, wakhm
**(sweepings)** zibâli *zibâle*
**dirty** wusikh *wisikh*
**to make d...** wassakh
**to get d...** twassakh *itwas'sakh*
**disagree** takhâlaf *ikhta'laf*
**disappear** ṛâb *ikhta'fa*
**disaster** muṣîbi *muṣîbe*
**discharge (dismissal)** ʿazl
**to d... (dismiss)** dashshar *saiyib*
**discount**; see reduce
**discover** kashaf, ikta'shaf
**d...y** iktishâf
**disdain (verb)** iḥta'ḳar
**disembark (trans.)** nazzal *nazzil*, ṭallaʿ, ṭailaʿ, **all with** min ilmar'kab *min elmar'kib*
**(intr.)** nizil min ilmar'kab *nizil min elmar'kib*
**disengaged** fâḍi, muʿaṭ'ṭal *meʿaṭ'ṭal*
**disgust (noun)** ḳaraf
**to become, or be, d...ed with** .. ḳirif min .., istaḳ'raf min..
**dish (vessel)** ṣaḥn *sulṭânî'ye*
**(a large one)** jaṭ *ḳârib*
**(food)** shikl, **pl.** ishkâl *eshkâl*
**dishonest** mush mustaḳîm
**dismiss** ʿazal *ṭarad*
**d...al (deposition)** ʿazl
**disorder (=want of order)** ʿadem tirtîb *ʿadem tartîb*
**distance** buʿd
**from a d...** min bʿîd *min beʿîd*
**distant** bʿid *beʿîd*
**distinct** wâḍiḥ, zâhir
**distinguished** sharîf
**distrustful** muthim
**ditch** khandaḳ, **pl.** khanâ- [diḳ]
**divan** dîwân', **pl.** dawâwîn'
**dive (intr.)** ṛaṭas
**divide** ḳasam, ḳassam
**divine (adj.)** ilâhi *ilâhi*
**division** ḳismi *ḳisme*, tiḳsîm *taḳsîm*
**divorce: to get a d... from one's wife** ṭallaḳ **with acc.**

---

**do** ʿimil *ʿamal;* **for conjugation see pp. 23, 24**
**will you do this?** bitrîd taʿmil haida? *bitrîd tiʿmil di?*
**have you done it?** ʿimil'to? *ʿamal'to?*
**don't do it again!** lâ taʿmil'li haida tâni marra! *mâtiʿmil'she di tâni marra!* **or, threateningly:** îyâk' utaʿʿmlo tâni marra! *îyâk' wetiʿʿmilo tâni marra!*
**who did this?** mîn ʿimil haida? *mîn ʿamal di?*
**what shall I do?** shû baddi aʿmil? *aʿmil ê?*
**what shall I do with it?** shû baʿmil fîh? *baʿmil fîh ê?*
**well, I will (shall) do it** ṭaiyib, ana baʿmlo *ṭaiyib, ana aʿmi'lo*
**what shall we do (=nothing can be done)?** shû baddna naʿmil? *naʿmil ê?*
**what shall we do now?** shû mnaʿmil hallaḳ? *beniʿʿmil ê dilwaḳt'?*
**how do you do?** kîf ḥâlak? *ezai'yak?* **see pp. 33, 34**
**(to suffice)** kafa, kaffa
**doctor (also med.)** ṭabîb, **pl.** aṭib'ba; ḥakîm, **pl.** ḥukama
**take (lead) me to a d...** dillni ʿala ḥakîm *waddîni ʿandê ḥakîm*
**call me a d...** indah'li ḥakîm
**is there an English d... here?** fî haun ḥakîm inglîzi? *fîh hene ḥakîm inglîzi?*
**Doctors of Jurisprudence and Theology** ʿulama [*lâb*
**dog** kalb *kelb,* **pl.** klâb *ki-*
**bitch** kalbi *kelbe*
**doll** ulʿûbi, laʿʿûbi *ʿarûse*
**dollar** riyâl *riyâl*, mejidi **(coined under Sultan Abd-el-Majid)**
**dolphin** dilfîn *derfîl,* **pl.** dlâfîn' *derâfîl'*
**dome (cupola)** ḳubbi *ḳubbe*
**done (cooked)** muste'wi
**this is not d... yet** haida mush mustwi *di mush muste'wi,* haida baʿd mâ ista'wa *di lissa mâ istawâsh*

---


**do:** I do for you what I would not do for .. 56,11
I have much to do 41,7
I will do my utmost 96,7
I will have nothing to do with .. 122,4
what shall I do? 55,1
do it 107,11
do it quickly 107,7
don't do this 52,17
don't do it again 52,19
to whom does .. belong? 141,5
do not forget the .. 139,14
do you understand? 47,6
what do you say? 45,16
what shall we do? 138,9
did you .. ? 137,18; 138,1.2
what are you doing? 45,8
what have you done? 100,17
what are you going to do? 45,9
how could you do .. ? 63,1
why do you not do what? 95,8
you cannot do without!.. 127,3
it does not matter 50,19
that will not do 50,17.18; 54,13
will .. not do? 126,6

**donkey** ḥimâr or ḥmâr *ḥumâr*, pl. ḥamîr
**(a young one)** jaḥsh *gaḥsh*
**-driver** ḥimmâr *ḥammâr*
**door** bâb *bâb*, pl. ibwâb or bwâb *ibwâb*
**to open the d...** fataḥ ilbâb *fataḥ elbâb*; **to shut** ṛalaḳ *sakk*
**the d... won't open** ilbâb mâ byinfa'tiḥ *elbâb mâ yinfitiḥsh'*; **won't shut** byinsa'kir *yinsak'kish*
**to knock at the d...** daḳḳ ilbâb *daḳḳ elbâb*
**-keeper** bauwâb *bauwâb*
**dot** nuḳṭa, pl. nuḳaṭ
**double (adj.)** muḍâ'af, mijwiz *migwiz* [*zebûn*]
**doublet (garment)** mintân
**doubt** shakk
**no d...** bala shakk, min dûn shakk
**to d...** shakk, shakkak
**d...ful** mashkûk
**dough** 'ajîn *'agîn*
**to knead d...** 'ajjan *'aggin*
**dove** ḥamâmi *ḥamâme*; **coll.** *ḥamâm*
**down (prep. and adv.)** lataḥt' *taḥt*
**d...hill** binnâzil *binnâzil*
**d...ward (adj.)** nâzil *nâzil*
**d...wards** min fauḳ lataḥt' *min fôḳ litaḥt'*
**dowry** mahr, dûta
**doze (to drowse)** ṛifi
**drachm**; see dram
**drag (trans.)** saḥab, jarr
**dragoman**; see interpreter
**drah**; see ell
**drain (noun)** balû'a *ballâ'a*
**dram** dirhem, **pl.** drâhim *darâhim*, **in Syria = 3.2 grammes, in Egypt = 3.12 gr. (1 dram av. = 1.177 gr.); 400** drâhim = **1** oḳḳa; cf. pound
**drugs, gums, and oil of roses are sold by** misḳâl or mitḳâl = **4.8 gr.**
**draper** bayyâ' iljûkh *gû'khagî*
**draw (to pull)** saḥab, shadd
**(with a pencil)** rasam
**(a tooth)** ḳala'
**drawers (under-breeches)** lbâs or libâs *libâs*, shintyân
**chest of d...** bîro *barô*
**drawing-room** ṣâlya *ṣâle*, maḳ'ad; **see note to 'harîm' in the Arabic Vocabulary**
**dream** mnâm *manâm* or mnâmi *manâme*, **pl.** mnâmât' *manâmât'*

---

**to d...** baṣar bilmnām *shûf bilmanâm*
**I dreamt of you last night** hallai'li baṣar'tik bilmnām *ellêle di shuftik bilmanâm*
**dress (clothing)** libs
(**one**) taub *tôb*, **pl.** tyāb *tiyâb* [faṣâṭîn'
**ladies' d...**, **robe** fuṣṭân, **pl.**
**to d..., clothe (trans.)** labas, labbas *labbis;* (**intr.**) libis
**dressmaker** khîyâ'ṭa
**dried** munash'shaf, nāshif *nâshif*
**drink** shirb *shurb;* sharâb, **pl.** sharbāt
**to d...** shirib
**what is there here to d... ?** shû fî haun lishshirb'? *ê hene lishshurb'?*
**what have you to d...?** shû fî 'indak lishshirb'? *ê 'andak lishshurb'?*
**d...ing-cup** ḳadaḥ, **pl.** iḳdâḥ
**drive** sâḳ *yesûḳ*
**to d... a nail in the wall** daḳḳ mismâr bilḥaiṭ' *daḳḳ musmâr bilḥêṭ*
**driver** 'araba'ji *'arba'gi*
**dromedary** hajîn *hagîn*, **pl.** hujun *hugun*
**drop** nuḳṭa, **pl.** nuḳaṭ
**to d... (fall in d...s)** naḳḳaṭ
(**to fall**) waḳa' (yûḳa')
(**to let fall**) rama
**drown** ṛarraḳ
**to be d...ed** ṛiriḳ
**we shall be d...ed** raḥ niṛraḳ *ḥa niṛraḳ* **or** *râḥ niṛraḳ*
**druggist** 'aṭṭâr
**drum** ṭabl; dirbek'ki *darabuk'ka;* **see tambourine**
**to d...** ṭabbal; daḳḳ iṭṭabl' *daḳḳ eṭṭabl'*
**drummer** ṭabbâl
**drunk** sikrân *sakrân*
**d...ard** sikkîr, sikri
**d...enness** sikr
**Druse** durzi, **pl.** drûz *durûz*
**dry** yābis, nāshif *nâshif*
**to dry (trans.)** nashshaf *nashshif*
(**intr.**) yibis, nishif
**duck (fowl)** baṭṭa, **pl.** baṭṭâṭ; **coll.** baṭṭ
**due (proper)** wājib *wâgib*
**dulcimer (mus. instr.)** ḳânûn'
**dull** 'ikir
**dumb** akhras [yân *gâmid*
**durable** mākin *mâkin*, dai-
**dust (noun)** trâb *turâb*
**duty (obligation)** wājib *wâgib* **or** wājbi *wâgibe*, **pl.** wājbāt' *wâgibât'*
(**tax**) rasm *resm*, **pl.** rusûm
**to pay d...** dafa' irrasm' *dafa' erresm'*


dress more warmly 140,8
drink! 51,17
I will d... .. 102,10
water to d... 79,12
a d... of water 38,13
drive along! 131,5 and note
drop: mix a few d...s 148,12
it d...ped on the ground 106,13
dry: that they may dry 136,2
(dry) it dries up 142,6
that their sweat may dry 145,5
these things have dried 136,3
due (steamer) 77,3
dull (sky) 65,20
dust (the furniture) 89,2
dusty 79,9; (road) 66,2
dutiable 74,16
duty: that was my d... 58,4

**dwell**; **see live**
**dye (trans.)** ṣabaṛ, lauwan
**dyed** maṣbûṛ; **see p. 112**
**dyer** ṣabbâṛ
**each (adj.)** kull [*insân*
**e... man** kull insân *kulli*
**(used as subst.)** kullmîn, kull *kulli* wâḥid
**e... wants something different** kullmîn baddo shikl *kulli wâḥid biddo shikl* [*a'ḳibe*
**eagle** nisr *'uḳâb*, **pl.** nsûra
**ear** udn or daini *widn*, **pl.** dainât *ûidân'*
**(of corn)** sunbuli *sunbule*, **pl.** snâbil *senâbil*
**earlier** ḳabl
**if you had come e...** lau kunt tiji ḳabl *lô kunte tigi ḳabl*
**why did you not come e...?** laish mâ jît ḳabl? *lê mâ gêtish ḳabla?*
**early (not late)** bakkîr *bedri*
**(in the morning)** iṣṣubḥ' *eṣṣubḥ'*, 'ala bukra
**e... to-morrow morning** bukra bakkîr *bukra bedri*
**to get up e...** ḳâm bakkîr *ḳâm bedri*, bakkar
**it is yet much too e...** ba'd bakkîr ktîr *lissa bedri ketîr*
**earn** kisib ['*arbûn*
**earnest (-money)** ra'bûn
**(seriousness)** jadd *gadd*
**in e...** min jadd *min gadd*, 'an jadd *'an gadd*
**earring** ḥalḳa
**a pair of e...s** jauz ḥalaḳ *gôz ḥalaḳ*
**earth (which we inhabit)** arḍ, **pl.** arâḍi = **landed property**
**(mould, dust)** trâb *turâb*
**earthen-ware** fikhkhâr *fâkhûr'*
**earthquake** zalzali *zelzele*
**easily** bisuhûli *bisuhûle*
**east** sharḳ
**the E...** blâd ishsharḳ' *bilâd eshsharḳ'*
**eastern** sharḳi
**-wind** hawa sharḳi
**Easter** il'îd ilkbîr *el'îd elkebîr*, 'îd ilkbîr *'îd elkebîr*
**easy** sahil *sahl*, haiyin
**easier than ..** ashal (**pron.** as-hal) or ahwan min ..
**eat** akal *kal*, **conjug. p. 25**; tanâwal iṭṭa'âm *itnâwal eṭṭa'âm*
**what have you to eat?** shû fî 'indak lil-akl'? *fîh 'andak ê lil-akl'?*
**where can I get something to eat?** wain biḳdir lâḳi shî lil-akl'? *fên baḳdar altaḳi ḥâge lil-akl'?*
**eatables** mâkûlât' **pl.**
**ebbtide** jazr *gazr*

**echo (noun)** ṣada
**economise** waffar, ṣammad
**edge** ḥaffi *ḥaffe*, ṭaraf, **pl.** aṭrâf [*ṭâkil*
**edible** mâkûl′, mittâkil *mi-*
**edifice** ; see building
**educate** rabba *addib*
**educated** ribyân, mrabba *murab′bi* [*rab′ba*
**to become e...** trabba *it-*
**education** tirbyi, tirbâyi *tarbîye*
**eel** ḥinklîz *ti‘bân samak*
**effect (action)** fi‘l
**e...s (property)** mâl, **pl.** amwâl
**Effendi** ; see note to 'bêk' in the Arabic Vocabulary
**egg** baiḍa *bêḍa*, **pl.** baiḍât *bêḍât′* ; **coll.** baiḍ *bêḍ*
**soft boiled** brisht *birisht′*
**hard boiled** maslûk ṭaiyib
**fried** mishwi *mashwi*
**Egypt** blâd maṣr *bilâd maṣr*
**Lower E...** barr maṣr
**Upper E...** blâd iṣṣa‘îd *bilâd eṣṣa‘îd* [*maṣâwire*
**E...ian** maṣri, **pl.** maṣârwi
**eight** tmânyi **or** tmâni *te-man′ye* **or** *temen*
**eighth** tâmin *tâmin*, **fem.** tâmni *tamne*
**eighteen** tminṭa‘sh′ *te-mantâsher*
**eighty** tmânîn′ *temânîn′*
**eight hundred** tmänmîyi *tumnemîye*
**either (each)** kull
**e... .. or** yâ..yâ *yâ..weyâ*, yimma..yimma *yâmâ′.. weyâmâ′* [**etc.**) muraiṭ′
**elastic : gum e...** (**e... band,**
**elbow** kû‘, **pl.** kî‘ân′
**electric train** ḳaṭr kahra-bâye [*bâye*
**e... tram** tramwâi kahra-
**e...ity** kahrabâî′ya
**elephant** fîl, **pl.** ifyâl *ifyâl*
**e...'s tusk** sinn ilfîl *sinn elfîl*
**eleven** ḥda‘sh *ḥadâsher*
**ell** drâ‘ *dirâ‘*, **pl.** idru‘; see yard
**else (besides)** ṛair *ṛêr*
**elsewhere** ṛair maṭrah *ma-ṭrah tâni* [*isti′ha*
**embarrassment** tabash′lul
**embassy** safâra
**embrace (to hug)** ‘ânaḳ
**embroider** ṭarraz **or** *zarkash*
**e...y** zarkashi *zarkashe*
**emerald** zumur′rud
**emir** ; see 'bêk' in Ar. Vocab.
**emperor** imbaraṭûr *im-brâṭûr′*
**empire** imbarâṭûrî′yi ; dauli *dôle*, **pl.** duwal
**employ(ment)** istikhdâm, khadâmi *khidâme*
**to e...** istakh′dam
**employee** mistakh′dem
**employer** makhdûm
**empty (adj.)** fâriṛ, fâḍi
**to e...** farraṛ

---

**eggs: hard-boiled** 139,6.14
**Egyptian band** 104,3
**else: nothing e...** 74,6
**any one e... but** 52,16
**elsewhere** 40,3
**embroidery in gold** 116,1
**with colored e...** 116,5
**empty (the basin)** 91,14

**enamel** (noun) mîna
**encamp** khayyam
**enceinte** ḥibli *ḥible*
**enclose** (surround) aḥâṭ; (join) aḍâf ila
**end** (noun) nihâyi *nehâye* (appendix) zail *dêl*
**at the end** finnihâyi *finne-hâye*, bilâkhir *bilâkhir*
**at the end of** .. bi=âkhir il... *bi=âkhir el...*
**to end** (intr.) tamm; (trans.) khallaṣ
**endless** illi mâlo nihâyi *elli mâlôsh' nihâye*
**enemy** ʿadu, **pl.** aʿâdi; dushmân
**engaged : to become e... to a girl** khaṭab bint (**said of a woman :**) **to become e... to a man** inkha'-ṭabit *inkha'ṭabet*
**engine** (machine) âli *âle* (railw.) wâbûr'
**engineer** ; see architect
**England** ingiltar'ra, blâd ilinglîz *bilâd elingelîz*
**English, -man** inglîzi *in-gelîzi*, **pl.** inglîz *ingelîz*
**enjoy oneself** inba'saṭ; (**in Oriental fashion**) tkaiyaf *itkai'yif*
**enmity** ʿadâwi *ʿadâwe*, dashmani
**enough** ḥâji, bass *bess*, kfâyi *kifâye*
**I have e...** ḥâjti, byikfîni *bikfîni*, bîkaffî'ni *bikaf-fîni*
**to have had e...** (**food or drink**) shibiʿ; **have you e...?** shbiʿt? *shibiʿt'?*
**enter** dakhal, khashsh
**entertain** (guests) ḍaiyaf
**entire** kull, kâmil *kâmil*
**e...ly** bilkullîyi *bilkullîye*
**entrails** maṣârîn'
**entrance, entry** dukhûl
**e... hall** dihlîz
**enumerate** ʿadd; ḥasab
**envelope** muṛal'lif *ṛulâf* **or** *zarf*
**envious** ḥasûd
**envy** ḥasad
**Ephesus** ayaṣûluk' (**Turk.**)
**epilepsy** dâ innuk'ṭa **or** sâʿa *melbûse*
**epitaph** târîkh' *târîkh'*, **pl.** twârîkh' *tawârîkh'*. **The last verse or half-verse names the year of death in letters ; for the numerical value see pp. 1 to 5**
**equal** (adj.) mûsâ'wi *mû-sâ'we*
**equinox** iʿtidâl illail' win-nahâr *iʿtidâl ellêl wan-nehâr*
**equip** (arm) sallaḥ
**eradicate** kalaʿ
**erase** (efface) maḥa
**ere** ; see before

---

**English Consulate, etc.** 82,2.8
**enough** 48,19.20; 99,10; 101,14
**that is e...** 74,11
**that is not e...** 50,11
**enter** (take shelter) 146,12
(enter) **let no one e...** 95,2
**please to e...** 100,3
**blessing has e...ed** 37, 2; 132,12
**entertainment** (party) 136,4
**entirely** 115.9

**errand** mishwâr *mushwâr*, **pl.** mshâwîr' *meshâwîr'*
**will you do an e... for me?** bta'mil mishwâr minshâni? *beti''mil mushwâr 'ala shâni?*
**erroneous** ṛalaṭ
**error** ṛalaṭ
**to commit an e... in** ṛiliṭ fî
**eructate**; see belch
**escape (flight)** harîbi *firâr*
**to e...** harab, fall
**estate (property)** mulk, **pl.** imlâk *emlâk*
**esteem (noun)** i'tibâr, iḥtirâm
**all hold him in high e...** ilo iliḥtirâm izzâyid 'ind ijjamî' *loh eliḥtirâm ezzâ-id 'and eggamî'* (**properly: he has the highest e... with all**) **or, with a verbal construction:** ijjamî' byiḥtirimûh ktîr *eggamî' biḥtirimûh ketîr* (**properly: all e... him highly**)
**to e... (show regard to)** i'ta'bar, iḥta'ram
**estimate (a valuing)** ḥisâb *ḥisâb*
**to e...** tamman *tammin*
**eternal (without beginning)** azali
**(without end)** abadi
**(in general)** dâyim *dâ-im*
**eternity (without beginning)** azal
**(without end)** abad
**eucalyptus** kâfûr'
**Eucharist** ḳurbân
**eunuch** ṭawâshi
**Euphrates** ilfrât *elfurât*
**Europe** ûrob'ba, blâd ilfranj' *bilâd elifreng'*
**E...an** ûrubâ'wi *urubâwi*, franji *ifren'gi*
**even (adj. = level)** sahl
**(adv. = also)** ḥatta
**e... if** wa-in *wen*
**evening** masa *mise*, 'ashîyi ['ishe]
**good e...**; see p. 33
**in the e...** filma'sa **or** fil'ashîyi *el'i'she*
**-twilight** shafaḳ
**event** wâḳi'a *waḳ'a*, **pl.** waḳâyi' *waḳâ-i'*; ḥâdisi *ḥadse*, **pl.** ḥawâdis'
**eventually** ittifâḳan
**ever** abadan *ebeden*
**everlasting**; see eternal
**every** kull
**e...body** kullmîn, kull wâḥid *kulli wâḥid*
**evidence**; see testimony
**evident** zâher *bâyin*
**e...ly** ezzâher *zâhiran*
**evil (misfortune)** muṣîbi *muṣîbe*
**(wickedness)** sharr
**(adj.)** radi

---

**exact** (adj.) maḍbûṭ or mazbûṭ
**e...ly** tamâm *tamâm*
**exaggerate** bâlaṛ, ʿazzam
**exaggeration** mubâlaṛe
**examine** faḥaṣ, imta'ḥan
**examination** faḥṣ, imtiḥân
**example** matal *mesel*, **pl.** imtâl *emsâl*
**for e...** masalan *meselen*
**excellence** (goodness) faḍl, **pl.** afḍâl
**excellency** (title) saʿâdi *saʿâde* [*saʿâttak*]
(in the address) saʿâdtak
**except** (prep.) illa, minʿa'da
**e...** (conj.) **that .. ṛair in ..** *ṛêr in ..*
**exception** istisnâ
**excessive** zâyid *zâ:id*
**exchange** (place of e...) bursa
**to e...** baddal *baddil*, ṛaiyar
**excuse** (apology) maʿzira
(pretext) ʿuzr
**to e...** (trans.) ʿazar
**to e...** oneself iʿta'zar
**e... me** (don't take it amiss) lâ twâkhid'na *mâ ti:-âkhiznîsh'*
**execute** (put to death) ḳatal
(accomplish) kammal
**exist** wijid *wigid*, inwa'jad *itwa'gad*
**e...ence** wujûd *wugûd*
**exit** (way out) khurûj *khurûg*
**expect** istan'zar *inta'zar*, naṭar, istan'na
**expense** kilfi *kulfe;* maṣrûf, **pl.** maṣârîf'
**expensive** bîkal'lif *bikel'lif*
**experience** tijribi *tagribe*, **pl.** tjârîb' *tegârîb'*
**e...d** mujar'rib *mugar'rib*, shâṭir
**expert** ahl khibra *khabîr*
**explain** fassar
**e... this to me!** fassir'li haida! *fassar'li di!* fahhim'ni haida! *fahhim'ni di!*
**express messenger** sâʿi *sâʿi* makhṣûṣ
**e... train** ḳaṭr sarîʿ *ḳuṭâr eleksebriss'*
**to e...** (by language) **lafaz**
**external** barrâni
**e...ly** min khârij *min khârig*
**extinguish** ṭafa
**to become e...ed** inṭa'fa
**extract** (to draw out) ḳalaʿ
(to select) inta'khab
**extraordinary** fauḳ ilʿâdi *fôḳ elʿâde*
**extreme** âkhir *âkhir*, ṛâyi *ṛâye*
**e...ly** lilṛâyi *lilṛâye*

---

**eye** 'ain *'ên*, **pl.** 'ûyun or 'iyûn
**-brow** ḥâjib *ḥâgib*, **pl.** ḥwâjib *ḥawâgib*
**-lid** jifn *gifn*, **pl.** jifûn *gifûn*
**fable (instructive one)** matal *mesel*, **pl.** imtâl *emsâl*
**these are f...s (stories)** haida khurâfât' *di khurâfât'*
**face (noun)** wish
**fact (reality)** wâḳe' *ḥaḳîḳi*
**factory (manufactory)** karkhâni *fabrîka*
**fade**; see wither
**fagot** ḥuzme, **pl.** ḥuzam
**faint (verb)** ṛushi 'alaih' *ṛumia 'alêh*
**she f...ed** ṛushi 'alai'ha *ṛumia 'alêha*
**f...ing-fit** ṛashayân
**fair (market)** sûḳ, **pl.** iswâḳ; mausim *môsem*
**(clear)** ṣâfi
**(frank, just)** 'âdil
**(blond)** ashḳar, **fem.** shaḳra, **pl.** shuḳr
**(medium, middling)** mu'ta'dil, mutwas'siṭ
**fairy** jinnîyi *ginnîye*
**fairy-tale** ḥkâyi *ḥikâye*
**(nursery tale)** khurâfât'
**faith: testimony of f...**; see creed
**faithful** amîn
**fakir**; see dervish, monk; poor
**fall (a downfall)** waḳ'a
**to f...** waḳa' (yûḳa')
**fallen woman (girl)** bintilkha'ṭa *bintelkhaṭîye*
**(a low one)**; see rag
**false (counterfeit)** mazṛûl, falso
**(of persons)** kizzâb *kaddâb*, khâyin *khâ-in*
**falsify** zauwar
**family** ahl, ahlilbait' *ahlelbêt*; 'âyli *'â-ile*, **pl.** 'iyâl *'iyâl*
**fan** mirwaḥa *marwa'ḥa*, **pl.** marâwiḥ
**fanatic** mit'aṣ'ṣeb
**far (adj.)** b'îd *ba'îd*
**how far is it from here to ..?** ḳaddaish' b'îd min haun la...? *ḳaddi ê elmesâfe min hene li...?*
**how far is it to walk?** ḳaddaish' bilmâshi? *ḳaddi ê bilmâshi?* **.. to ride?** .. birrâkib? .. *birrâkib?*
**is it yet far?** ba'do b'îd? *lissa ba'îd?*
**far off** b'îd 'an *ba'îd 'an*
**far greater** akbar biktîr *akbar biketîr*
**far too little** ḳalîl ktîr *ḳalîl ketîr*
**far too much** ziyâdi biktîr *ziyâde biketîr*

---

eye: I did not close my eyes 34,10
facing us 142,8
f... the sea, the mountains 79,1
fade (color) 112,8
fail: I shall not f... 36,10
faith: of what f... 134,8
fall: dew is falling 65,18
.. has fallen 106,13; 144,11
that I may not f... 99,1
far: is .. far from here? 76,11
the .. is far 144,3
are we still far from ..? 74,2
so far off 73,6

**farce** maskhara
**fare (price)** ujret iṭṭarîḳ *ugra*
**what is the f...?** kâm ujret iṭṭarîḳ? *kâm elug'ra?*
**see passenger, food**
**farewell (noun)** ẇidâʿ
f...! maʿassalâmi! *maʿassalâme!*
**farm (estate)** rizḳ, **pl.** irzâḳ; *abʿâdî'ye*
**(hamlet)** mazraʿa, **pl.** mazâriʿ
**farrier** baiṭâr **(or, Syr. only:** bîṭâr')
**farthest** abʿad
**fashion (custom)** ʿâdi, **pl.** ʿawâyid
**(mode)** mûḍa, **pl.** muwaḍ
**fast (abstinence)** ṣiyâm, ṣaum *ṣôm*
**to f... (abstain)** ṣâm (yeṣûm), ḳaṭaʿ
**(adj. = firm)** mâkin *mâkin*, shedîd
**(quick)** sarîʿ
**(adv. = quickly)** ḳawâm *ḳawâm*, bilʿa'jel *bilʿa'gel* = **'on wheels'**
**to be or go f... (of a watch)** sabbaḳ
**to make f..., fasten** shadd
**fasting-month (the ninth of the Mohammedan months)** ramaḍân
**-tide** waḳt iṣṣaum' *waḳt eṣṣôm*
**fat (noun)** dihn, saman *semen*
**(adj.)** midhin; **(of living beings)** samîn
**fatal (deadly)** ḳâtil; **(destined)** muḳad'dar
**fate (destiny)** naṣîb
**father** ab (bai), **pl.** âbâ'; **with the possessive adjectives see pp. 15, 16**
**f...-in-law** ʿamm, **properly:** ḥamu
**fatigue (noun)** taʿb *taʿab*
**to f...** taʿab
**that is too fatiguing** haida mitʿib ktîr *di mitʿib ketîr*
**fatten (cram)** rabbaʿ
**fault (transgression, sin)** zamb, **pl.** zunûb; khaṭa **or** khaṭîyi *khaṭîye*, **pl.** khaṭâya
**(defect peculiar to a thing)** ʿaib *ʿêb*, **pl.** ʿiyûb
**that is not my f...** mâ hû zambi *mush zambi*, **or** mâli zamb, **or** mâ ʿalai'yi ḥaḳḳ *mâ ʿalêyash ḥaḳḳ*
**faulty (defective)** marlûṭ
**favor (noun)** maʿrûf, faḍl
**(gift)** niʿmi *niʿme*
**will you do me a f...?** bitrîd taʿmil'li maʿrûf? *terîd tiʿmil'li maʿrûf?*

---

**farewell! 42,13; 43,1**
**farrier: look for a f... 138,7**
**fashion: after the usual f... 113,8**
**fast: watch is f... 106,14**
**fat: I do not like fat 125,5**
**father (priest) 132,10**
**father: your f... 35,16**
**(his excellency) the f... 35,15**
**fault: it is your f... 48,10**
**it is not your f... 50,10**
**favor: do me the f... 52,20**
**if you will do me the f... 53,1**

**do me the f...** a'mil ma'i ma'rûf *i'mil ma'rûf*, **or** tfaḍḍal 'alai'yi *itfaḍ'ḍal 'alêye*
**favorite** muṣâḥib
**fear** khauf *khôf*
**to f... sby. or sthg.** khâf min ..
**to f... for sby.** khâf 'ala ..
**f... nothing** lâ tkhâf *mâ tekhafsh'*, mâ 'alaik'
**is there any f... of rain?** fî khauf mnishshi'ti? *fîh khôf min eshshi'te?*
**feast (festival)** 'îd or 'aid *'êd*, **pl.** i'yâd
**(banquet)** walîmi, **pl.** walâyim
**feather** rîshi *rîshe*, **pl.** riyash
**February** shbâṭ *febrâ-ir*
**feed (trans.)** ṭa''am, 'aiyash, 'allaḳ la *'allaḳ li*
**(intr.=eat)** akal *kal*; **see p. 25**
**f... the horses!** 'alliḳ lilkhail'! *'allaḳ lilkhêl!*
**feel** ḥass, istaḥass'
**(touch)** dass
**I do not f... well** ḥâsis mâli *mâlish kêf*
**f... it!** disso!
**feeling (noun)** lams
**felt** labbâd *libd*
**-carpet** labbâdi *labbâde*
**female (noun, of animals)** intâyi *entâye*
**(adj.)** mu-an'nas
**fence (enclosure)** ḥâ-iṭ
**to f... in (enclose)** aḥâṭ; **(with swords)** sâyaf
**fennel** shumre *ḥabbe sô'dâ*
**ferry** *ma'dîye*; **there are no ferries in Syria**
**-man** *ma'dâwi*
**festival** 'îd or 'aid *'êd*, **pl.** i'yâd
**congratulations; see p. 44**
**fetch (trans.)** jâb *gâb*, râḥ wara
**fever (in general)** ḥumma *ḥumme*, sukhûni *sukhûne*
**intermittent f...** daur *dôr*
**cold f...** bardîyi *bardîye*
**tertian f...** mtallati *mutal'late*
**I have an attack of f...** ḥakam'ni iddaur' *ḥakam'ni eddôr*
**few** ḳalîl
**a few** ba'ḍ, kam *kâm*; **also expressed by the dual of the substantive, e.g. a few piastres** ḳirshain' *ḳirshên* or ḳirshain' tlâti *ḳirshên telâte*, **properly; two to three piastres**
**fez (cap)** ṭarbûsh, **pl.** ṭrâbîsh' *ṭarâbîsh'*

---

**fear: there is f... of .. 127,7**
**f... nothing 100,10**
**I f... I am .. 41,13.14.15**
**I f... (am afraid of) .. 136,7.11**
**I f...ed that .. 38,5**
**feed them 133,3; 138,3**
**did you f... them? 137,18**
**feeding of the horse 122,4**
**feel: I f... the heat 140,10**
**(feel) how do you f...? 139,8**
**fertile ground 135,2**
**fetch 76,1; 93,3**
**f... him 88,1**
**you f... it then 75,14**
**why did you not f...? 92,5**
**fever 148,8**
**I have had a f... 34,6**
**I am f...ish 48,27; 49,1**

**Fez** (country) blâd fâs *bilâd fâs*
**fidelity** amâni, wafa
**field** ḥaḳli, pl. ḥuḳûl; ṛaiṭ *ṛêṭ*
**-watch** (pers.) nâṭûr′, pl. nawâṭîr′ [*mâra*
**fife** (instr.) zammâra *zum-*
**fifteen** khamsṭa‘sh′ *khamstâsher* [*khamse*
**fifth** khâmis, fem. khâmsi
**fifty** khamsîn
**fig** tîni *tîne*, pl. tînât′ coll. tîn
**fresh fig** tîn ṭari
**dried fig** tîn yâbis *tîn nâshif* [*tîn*
**-tree** shajrit tîn *shagarat*
**fight** (noun) ḳitâl
**to f...** ḳâtal, tḳâtal *itḳâtil*
**figure** (aspect, form) haiʼa, ḳâmi *ḳâme*
(picture) ṣûra, pl. ṣuwar
(arithm.) ‘adad *‘aded*
**file** (instr.) mabrad, pl. mbârid *mebârid*
(bundle) rabṭa
(row of soldiers) ṣaff ‘asker
**fill** (trans.) malla *mala*, talla, ‘abba
(to be filled) imtaʼla
**filled with** .. milyân .. *malyân* ..
**f... me the bottle with wine** ‘abbîli ilḳannîni nbîd *imlâli elḳizâze nebîd*
**filly** kurra, pl. kirâr
**film** (pellicle) ṛashâwi *ṛashâwe*
**find** (verb) lâḳa
(to f... sthg. nice, useful, etc.) shâf
**to be found** (exist, occur) wijid (yûjad) *wigid* (*yûgad*, inwaʼjad *itwaʼgad*, waḳa‘ *ḥaṣal*
**how do you f... this?** kîf bitshûf haida? *ezai′ bitshûf di?*
**did you not f... a ..?** mâ lâḳait′ ..? *mâ lâḳêt′shi ..?*
**where shall (may) I f... ..?** wain blâḳi ..? *fên baltiḳi ..?*
**fine** (noun = mulct) jaza naḳdi *geza naḳdi*
(adj. = not coarse) rafî‘ *rufaiʼya‘*, raḳîḳ
(pretty) jmîl *gemîl*
**finger** iṣba‘ *ṣubâ‘*, pl. aṣâbî‘′ or ṣâbî‘′ *ṣawâbi‘*
**fore-** sabbâbi *shâhid*
**middle-** ṭawîl or wasṭâni *wusṭâni*
**fourth-** binṣir or tâni
**little-** khanṣar

---

fie! 62,3
field: in the open f... 146,11
fill me a nargileh 103,4.11
filthy 92,3; 103,5; 121,7
final (decisive) 87,8
find (meet some one) 38,5.6
I cannot f... it 91,11
I have found .. 85,6
f... me (a house) 83,6; 85,3
find (plur.) us a .. 147,7
try to f... .. 128,4
do we f...? 126,9
we will f... 128,1
we found 138,8
you will f... 128,3
have you (plur.) found it? 72,9
fine: very f...! 59,2
there is nothing f...r 58,8

**thumb** bihâm **or** bâhim *kebîr*
**finish (trans.)** kammal, khallaṣ
(intr.) tamm
**fire** nâr (fem.)
(incendiary) ḥarîḳ *ḥarîḳe*
**light the f...!** sha''il innâr! *walla' ennâr!*
**the f... does not burn** mâ sha'alit innâr *mâ wala-'etsh' ennâr*
**the f... has gone out** inṭa'fit innâr *inṭa'fet ennâr*
**to f... off (a gun)** aṭlaḳ
**fire-place** ujâḳ *mauḳid*
**firm (solid)** mâkin *mâkin*
**f...ness** mikni *mukne*
**first (adj. and ord. number)** auwal **or** aulâ'nî *auwalâni*, **fem.** aulânî'yi *auwalânî'ye*
**(adv. = firstly)** bilau'wal, auwalan, ḳabl
**f... I want to know if ..** ḳabl baddi a'rif iza .. *ḳabla biddi a'raf iza ..*
**fish** samek *samak*
**(a single one)** samki *samake*, **pl.** samkât *semkât*
**to f...** ṣaiyad samek
**fisherman** ṣîyâd' samek *ṣaiyâd samek*
**fishing** ṣaid issa'mek *ṣêd esse'mek*
**fishmonger** sammâk

**fit (suitable)** mnâsib *munâsib* [just) sauwa]
**to fit (trans. = to suit, ad-]**
**this coat does not fit me** hassit'ra mâ btiji 'alai'yi *essit'ra di mâ betigîsh 'alêye* [yelîḳ]
**to be fit (becoming)** lâḳ
**five** khamsi *khamsa*
**five hundred** khamsmîyi *khumsemîye*
**flaccid** rakhu [dêra]
**flag (ensign)** bandai'ra *ban-*
**to hoist the f...** rafa' ilbandai'ra *rafa' elbandêra*
**to lower** nazzal *nazzil*
**flame (noun)** ḍau *ḍô*
**(a blazing one)** lahîb
**flannel** fanel'la
**flash (intr.)** baraḳ
**flat (level)** musal'ṭaḥ
**flatter** mallaḳ, ḍiḥik lawish' *ḍiḥik liwish'*
**f...y** timlîḳ *tamlîḳ*
**flax** kittân *kittân*
**flea** barrût, **pl.** brârît' *berârît'*
**flee** harab, fall
**fleet (navy)** 'amâra
**flesh** laḥm
**flight (fleeing)** harîbi *firâr*
**f... of the Prophet** hijra *higra*
**floor (story)** ṭabaḳa *dôr*
**(of a room)** arḍ; **(paved)** blâṭ *balâṭ*

---


finish, make haste 101,13
fire: light the f... 93,5
put .. on the f. . 92,6; 148,9
firm: with f... step 119,7
first(ly) 99,2; 109,12; 111,7
fit: does not fit me 108,7; 113,12
make it fit 114,3
fix tne price 94,11
flat (in a house) 85,1
floor: ground. top 85,1; 78,8.1

**flour (noun)** ṭaḥîn *daḳîḳ*
**flow (to run)** jara *gara*
**flower** zahra, **pl.** zahr **and** zhûr *zuhûr*
 **to f...** zahar
 **-pot** shaḳfi *shâliye*, **pl.** shiḳaf *shawâli*
**fluid** sâyil; mâyiʿ
**flute** shabbâbi *nai*
**fly (coll.)** dibbân *dubbân*
 **(a single one)** dibbâni *dubbâne*, **pl.** dibbânât′ *dubbânât′*
 **chase the flies from me** kishsh iddibbân ʿanni *kishsh eddubbân ʿanni*
 **to fly** ṭâr (yeṭîr)
 **to let fly** falat
**foal (noun)** muhr
**foam (noun)** raṛwi *raṛwe*
**fodder (food)** ʿalîḳ
**fog** ḍabâb *ḍabâb*
 **foggy** muṛai′yim
**fold (plait)** ṭawîyi *ṭawîye*
 **to f...** ṭawa *ṭawa*
**follow** tabaʿ, liḥiḳ
 **f... me from afar** ilḥaḳ′ni min bʿîd *ilḥaḳ′ni min baʿîd*, **.. closely ..** min ḳarîb
**food** ṭaʿâm, akl
 **cooked f...** ṭabkh, ṭabîkh
 **the f... is no good** il=akl′ mâ byiswa shî *el=akl′ê di mush ṭaiyib*
**fool, f...ish** majnûn *magnûn*, **pl.** mjânîn′ *megânîn′*; aḥmaḳ; balîd
**foot** ijr **or** rijl *rigl*, **pl.** irjul *argul*
 **(mind) your f...!** rijlak! *[riglak!]*
 **fore-f... of an animal** îd
 **on f...** mâshi *mâshi*
 **my feet ache** ijrai′yi byûjaʿû′ni *riglêye betûgaʿ′ni*
 **I sprained my f...** infa′kashit ijri *itfa′raket rigli*
 **my feet are swollen** ijrai′yi wârmîn′ *riglêye warmîn*
**foot-ball** laʿb ilkûra *liʿb elkôra*
 **-path** ḳâdûmî′yi
 **-soldier** ʿaskeri
 **-stool** skamli *targîl*
**fop (coxcomb)** ṛandûr
**for (conj.)** fa=inn′
 **(prep. = in favor of)** min shân *ʿala shân*, **la** *li*
 **(in place of)** ʿiwaḍ, bdâl *bidâl*

---

**is that for me?** haida ili? *di lîye?* haida minshâni? *di 'alashâni?*
**for what reason?** li-ai' sabab? *li-ai'yi sebeb?*
**what is this for?** minshân êsh haida? *di 'ala shân ê?*
**I fear for him** ana fiz'ân 'alaih' *ana faz'ân 'alêh*
**forage (noun)** 'alîk, 'alaf
**forbid** mana', harram
**forbidden** harâm
**force (strength)** kûwi *kûwe*
**by f...** bilrasb'
**to f...** ajbar
**ford (noun)** mukhâda *khôd*
**to f...** khauwad
**forehead** jibîn *gibîn,* jibîni *gibîne* **or** *gubhe*
**foreign** ajnabi *agnabi,* **pl.** ajânib *agânib* [*edduhr'*]
**forenoon** kabl idduhr' *kabl*
**forerunner** migri *sâ-is*
**forge (to counterfeit)** zauwar
**forger** mzauwir *mezau'wir*
**forget** nisi
**forgive** sâmah
**f... me** sâmih'ni
**I cannot f... you** mâ bikdir sâmhak *mâ ardarsh' asâmihak*
**fork** furtai'ki **or** shanki *shôke,* **pl.** shuwak
**form (a mould)** kâlib, **pl.** kwâlib *kawâlib*
**former (adj.)** sâbik *sâbik*
**f...ly** sâbikan
**fort** istihkâm
**fortress** kal'a
**fortune (good)** hazz
**(wealth)** rina
**forty** arb'în *arba'în*
**forward(s)** lakuddâm *likuddâm*
**to f... (send)** wadda
**foul (immoral)** fâhish, dinis
**found (establish)** assas *assis*
**f...ation** asâs
**fountain** naufara *nôfara, faskîye*
**four** arb'a *arba'* **and** *arba'a*
**f... hundred** arb'amîyi *rub-'êmîye*
**fourteen** arbata'sh' *arba'-tâsher*
**fourth** râbi', **fem.** râb'a *rab'a*; **fourth part** rub', **pl.** erbâ'
**fowl; see chicken, hen**
**fox** ta'lab, **pl.** ta'âlib; bû husain'
**fraction** kasr, **pl.** ksûr *kusûr*
**fragrant** rîhto taiybi *rîhto taiyibe*
**frame** birwâz, **pl.** barâwîz'

---

**franc** (coin) frank *ferank'*
**France** fransa *feran'sa*
**frank** (sincere) ṣâdiḳ
**free** (being at liberty) ḥurr, pl. aḥrâr
(permitted) jâyiz *gâ-iz*
**freedom** ḥurrîyi
**freight** (cargo) wasḳ
(the price) nâulûn'
**French, F...man** frinsâwi *feransâwi*, pl. frinsâwî'yi *feransâwî'ye*
**fresh** ṭari; see also new, sweet
**Friday** yaum ijjum'ʿa *yôm eggum'ʿa*
**friend** ṣâḥib, pl. iṣḥâb or ṣḥâb *aṣḥâb*
lady f... ṣâḥbi *ṣaḥbe*
he is a great f... of mine hû ṣâḥbi ktîr *hûwe ṣaḥbi ketîr*
f...ship ṣuḥbi, ulfi, maḥab'bi *maḥab'be*
**fright** fazaʿ, khauf *khôf*
of f... mnilfa'zaʿ *min el-fa'zaʿ*
**frog** ḍifdaʿ *ḍufdaʿ*, pl. ḍafâdiʿ
**from** min
f.... to min .. la *min .. li*
f... here to .. min haun laḥadd' .. *min hene liḥadd'* ..
**front** (noun) wij, muḳad'dam
in f... ḳuddâm, min ḳuddâm
to place in f... ḳaddam *ḳaddim*
**frontier** ḥadd, pl. ḥudûd
**frost** (also hoar-f...) ṣaḳʿa, ṣuḳʿa
**froth** rar̤wi *rar̤we*
**fruit** samra, pl. ismâr
(of trees) fâkiha, pl. fuâki *fewâkih*
**fry** ḳala
**fugitive** (adj.) hirbân *harbân*
**full** (adj.) milyân *malyân*
f... moon badr *bedr*
**fumigate** bakhkhar
**funeral** dafn, jinâzi *genâze* or *mashhad*
**fur** farwi *kurk*
**furious** (wrathful) raḍbân
**furnished** (as a room) mafrûsh

---

**furrow (noun)** tilm *ḥart*
**further behind** ba'd lawa'ra *lissa wara*
**f... in front** ba'd lakuddâm *lissa kuddâm*
**fury (rage)** ṛaḍab
**(madness)** junûn *gunûn*
**future (noun)** mustak'bal *mustak'bil*
**(adj., in f..)** bilmustak'bal
**gain (noun)** makseb, kasb
**to g...** kisib, ribiḥ
**gaiter** ṭmâk *ṭimâk*, **pl.** ṭmâkât' *ṭimâkât'*
**gale** zauba'a *zôba'a*, nau *nô*
**Galilee (in the Arabic translations of the Bible)** ijjalîl *eggalîl;* **the modern** mutesar'riflik **'akka covers about the ancient Galilee**
**gall** ṣafra, marâri *marâre*
**gallop** khiyûli *ramḥ*
**to g...** khaiyal *ramaḥ*
**gallows** mashnaka, **pl.** mshânik *meshânik*
**galoche** gâlosh'
**game (play)** la'b *li'b*
**g... at cards** la'b ishshad'di *li'b elwa'rak*
**g... of hazard** la'b ilkumâr *li'b elkumâr*
**(animals hunted)** ṣaid *ṣêd*
**garden (orchard)** bustân *bustân*, **pl.** bsâtîn' *besâtîn'*
**(flower g...)** jnaini *genêne*, **pl.** jnainât *genênât'*
**gardener** jnaināti *ganâ-ini*

**garlic** tûm
**garment; see dress**
**loose g... for throwing over a lady's dress (white linen)** izâr, **pl.** uzr or yizr; **(colored)** mlâyi *milâye*
**gas** kâz
**gate** bauwâbi *bauwâbe*
**-keeper** bauwâb *bauwâb*
**gather (bring together)** jama' *gama'*, lamm
**g...ing (of people)** maukib, **pl.** mwâkib *mewâkib*
**gay** farḥân
**gazelle (male)** ṛazâl, **(fem.)** ṛazâli *ṛazâle*, **pl.** ṛizlân
**gazette** jarîda *gurnâl*
**gehenna; see hell**
**gender** jins *gins*
**general (mil.)** ṣâri **'askar;** jananâr *gananâr*
**adj.=common** 'umûmi
**in g...** 'umûman, ṛâliban
**generous** karîm, khaiyir
**Genesareth: Lake of G...** baḥr ṭabarai'ya
**gentleman** saiyid, sîd
**genuine (real)** khâliṣ, ṣaḥîḥ
**genus** jins *gins*
**geography** jigrâfya *gogrâfiya*
**George** jirji *girgi*
**Georgia** gurjistân
**German** almâni
**(language)** nimsâwi *nemsâwi*, **properly: 'Austrian'**
**G...y** almânya

---

further: we cannot get f. 143,10
future: in f... 93,3
gallop 123,3.4
g...! (plur.) 131,5

gather the things 139,11
generally 105,3
generosity 54,3
gentlemen! 102,8

**get**; see arrive, become, fetch, find, gain, have, obtain, receive, turn, win, etc.
**get a bottle of good wine** dabbir ḳannînit nbîd ṭaiyib *shûf waḥde ḳizâze nebîd ṭaiyib*
**get away!** imshi! tḳalla'!
**to get back** (recover) ḥaṣṣal
**to get down** (alight) nizil, (or, Syr. only: ḥauwal)
**we will get down** (dismount) baddna nḥauwil *biddina ninzil*
**get down!** inzil! (or, Syr. only: ḥauwil!)
**do we get there by daylight or after dark?** innûṣal binnhâr yimma billail'? *nûṣal binnehâr wala billêl?*
**to get up** (rise) ḳâm (ye-[ḳûm])
**Gethsemane** jizmânî'yi
**ghost** (apparition) jinni *ginne*, pl. jinn *ginn*
**the Holy Ghost** irrûḥ ilḳu'dus *errûḥ elḳu'dus*
**giaur**; see unbeliever
**Gibeon** ijjîb *eggîb*
**Gibraltar** jabal *gebel* ṭâriḳ
**giddiness** daukha *dôkha*
**giddy** daukhân *dôkhân'*
**my head is g...** râsi dâyikh *râsi dâ=ikh*
**gift** 'aṭîyi *'aṭa*; hadiyi *hedîye*, pl. hadâya
**gilt** mudah'hab
**gimlet** khirbirr' *berîme*
**ginger** zinjfîl *ganzabîl*
**gipsy** (coll.) nawar
(**a single one**) nawari *nûri*
**giraffe** zarâfi *zarâfe*
**girdle** zinnâr *ḥizâm*, pl. znânîr' *ḥizâmât'*
**girl** ṣabîyi *ṣabîye*, pl. ṣbaiyât *ṣabâye*; bint, pl. bnât *banât*
**girth** (of a saddle) ḥizâm *ḥizâm*, pl. ḥizâmât' *ḥizâmât'* or ḥuzm
**give** 'aṭa or *adâ*
**g... me** .. a'ṭîni .. or *idîni* ..
**can you g... it to me?** btiḳdir ta'ṭîni yâh? *tiḳdar tedîh'li?*
**I g... nothing** mâ ba'ṭi shî *mâ adîsh ḥâge*
**I g... no more** mâ ba'ṭi aktar *mâ adîsh ziyâde*

---

**(to pay)** dafa'
**I do not g... (pay) more than that** aktar min haik mâ bidfa' *aktar min di mâ adfaḥsh'*
**I will g... (pay) you .. for it** bidfa''lak fîh .. *badfa''-lak fîh ..*
**do they g... bakhsheesh?** bya'ṭu bakhshîsh? *yidu bakshîsh?*
**I have given it to you** a'ṭai'-tak yâh *idêtuh'lak*
**to g... a gratuity** bakhshash
**I g... you this** haida bakh-shish'lak yâh *adîlak di*
**to g... back** radd
**to g... in (consent)** sallam
**glad** masrûr, firḥân *farḥân*
**to be g...** firiḥ, insarr'
**glass** ḳizâz *ḳizâz* [*bâye*]
**(water-g...)** kubbâyi *kub-*
**(wine-g...)** ḳadaḥ, pl. iḳdâḥ
**looking-g...** mirâyi or mrâyi *mirâye*
**a g... of water** kubbâyit moi *kubbâyet moiye*
**dealer in g...** ḳizâzi
**glasses**; see spectacles
**glitter (verb)** limi'
**globe**; see ball, world
**glory (noun)** iftikhâr, fakhr
**gloves** kufûf *eldiwân*
**glue** ṛiri *ṛirâye*
**to g...** lazzaḳ bilṛi'ri *lazzaḳ bilṛirâye*
**gnat** nâmûs', barṛash
**gnaw** ḳaraṣ
**go** râḥ (yerûḥ)
**we will go** baddna nrûḥ *biddina nerûḥ*
**let us go!** tanrûḥ! *nerûḥ!*
**where are you going?** la-wain' râyiḥ? *'ala fên râ=iḥ?*
**go! rûḥ! (clear out)** imshi! rûḥ min haun! *rûḥ min hene!* tḳalla'!
**I will go to-morrow** baddi rûḥ bukra *biddi arûḥ bukra*
**is the boat gone?** râḥit il-flûkya? *râḥet elfelûke?*
**to go down (as the sun)** ṛarab
**to go for a walk, a ride, a drive** shamm ilha'wa *shamm elha'wa*

---

**(go) what is there going on (happening)?** shû ṣâyir haunîk? *elkha'bar ê henâk?*
**to go out** ṭili‘, ḍahar; **(become extinguished)** inṭa'fa; see fire
**go out!** iṭla‘! iḍhar!
**goat** ma‘zi *mi‘ze*, **pl.** ma‘z
**a he-g...** tais *tês*, **pl.** tyûs [*tiyûs*]
**a kid** jidi *gidi*
**God** Allâh, Alla, Allâh ta‘âla
congratulations, etc. see p. 43
**God!** yalla! yâ rabb! yâ laṭîf! yâ sattâr!
**would to God!** yâ rait! *yâ rêt!*
**godfather** shibîn [diheb]
**gold** dahab (or, **Syr. only:**
**pure g...** dahab khâliṣ
**g... coin** dahab (or, **Syr.** only: diheb), lîra or rîla
**goldsmith** ṣâyiṛ *ṣâ=iṛ*, **pl.** ṣâṛe
**g...s bazaar (in Cairo)** *sûḳ eṣṣâ=iṛ*
**golf** la‘b iṣṣûlajân' *ṣôlagân'*
**Golgotha** ijjul'jula *eggul'gula*
**gonorrhœa** ta‘ḳîbi
**good** ṭaiyib, mlîḥ *melîḥ*
**better** aḥsan, aḥsin
**the best** ilaḥ'san *elaḥ'san*
**the g... (welfare, prosperity, a g... thing)** khair *khêr*
**g... morning, etc.**; pp. 32, 33
**g...!** ṭaiyib! mlîḥ! *melîḥ!*
**will you be so g... as to tell me?** iza kân bitrîd ḳulli? min faḍlak ḳulli?
**to be g... to one (profit him)** nafa‘ **with acc.**; **that is no g... to me** haida mâ byinfa‘'ni *di mâ binfa‘nîsh*
**much g... may it do you!** il‘âfyi! *bishshi'fe wel‘âfiye!* **Answer:** Alla y‘âfîk' *Allâh yi‘âfîk'*; **with water, lemonade, etc.,** hanîyan; see p. 39 note
**good-for-nothing (scamp)** ‘arsa *falâti*
**Good Friday** jum‘it ilḥazînî *gum‘at elḥazîne*
**goods** baḍâ‘a; mâl, **pl.** amwâl; mulk, **pl.** amlâk
**goose (coll.)** wazz *wizz*
**a single one** wazzi *wizze*, **pl.** wazzât *wizzât*

---

**Gospel** injîl *ingîl*
**gout** nuḳrus
**government** ḥukûmı or ḥkûmi *ḥukûme*
**g...official** ma-mûr iddau'li *me-mûr eddôle*
**governor (in general)** ḥâkim, pl. ḥukkâm
**(of a district)** ḳâyimmaḳâm'
**(of a** mutaṣarrifîyi **consisting of several districts)** mutaṣar'rif
**(of a province)** wâli *wâli*, **pl.** wulât *wulât*
**g...ate** mutaṣarrifîyi *muḥâfza*
**gown (lady's, white linen)** izâr, **pl.** uzr or yizr; **(colored)** mlâyi *milâye*
**grace (favor)** ni'mi *ni'me*, **pl.** ni'am
**graciously** biluṭf'
**gradually** bittidrîj *bittedrîg*
**graft (verb)** ṭa''am [ḳamḥ]
**grain (corn collectively)**
**(a single one)** ḥabbi *ḥabbe*, **pl.** ḥubûb
**g... magazine** ḥâṣil, **pl.** ḥawâṣil
**gramophone** âlet naḳl iṣṣaut' *âle linaḳl' eṣṣôt*
**grand** 'azîm
**grand-daughter (daughter of a son)** bint ilibn' *bint elibn'*; **(daughter of a daughter)** bint ilbint' *bint elbint'*
**-father** jidd *gidd*, **pl.** ijdâd [*igdâd*]
**-mother** sitt
**-son (son of a son)** ibn ilibn' *ibn elibn'*, ḥafîd; **(son of a daughter)** ibn ilbint' *ibn elbint'*, ḥafîd
**grant (as a prayer)** istajâb *istagâb*
**grapes** 'inib or 'ineb *'aneb*
**grass** ḥashîsh, 'ishb
**gratis** bilâsh *balâsh*, bala taman *bilâ temen*, majjânan *maggânan*
**gratuity**; see gift, present
**(to waiters, coachmen, etc.)** bakhshîsh *baḳshîsh*
**if I am satisfied with you I will give you a good g...** iza kunt mabsûṭ minnak ba'ṭîk bakhshîsh ṭaiyib
**grave (sepulchre q.v.)** ḳabr, **pl.** ḳubûr
**gravity** tiḳl
**gravy** marḳit laḥm *maraḳat laḥm*
**grease** duhn *shaḥm*
**to g...** dahan
**great** kebîr (or, **Syr. only:** kbîr)
**G... Britain** birîṭâ'niya il'uz'ma
**g...er than ..** akbar min ..
**g...ness** kibr *kubr*
**Greece** blâd ilyûnân' *bilâd elyûnân'*
**greedy**; see covetous

---

gown (robe) 98,1
grain (weight) 105,14
grapes 125,18
grass: on the green 122,7
gratis 118,7
gratitude 54,10
grazing-land 122,7
great longing 37,7
very g... 53,9; (too g...) 53,8
greatest (at the most) 37,8

**Greek** rûmi, yûnă'ni *yûnâ'ni*
  **G... Orthodox**[1] rûm
  **G... Catholic** rûm kătûlîk'
**green** akhḍar, **fem.** khaḍra, **pl.** khuḍr
**greet**; see salute
**grey** rimădi *rumâdi*
**grief** asaf, ṛamm
**grieve (trans.)** ṛamm
  **to g... at** .. t=assaf ʿala .. *it=as'sif ʿala* ..
**grind (to sharpen)** sann
  **(to pulverise)** ṭaḥan, ṭaḥḥan
**grocer** ʿaṭṭâr
**groom** săyis *sâ=is*
**gross (unrefined)** khishin
  **(fat, thick)** samîn
**grotto** maṛâra, **pl.** muṛr or maṛâyir *maṛâ=ir*
**ground (surface of land)** arḍ, **pl.** arâḍi
  **(foundation)** asâs
  **(reason)** aṣl
  **-tax** werko, yerko
  **-work** asâs
**grow (intr.)** kibir
  **(trans. = to raise)** rabba
**growl (verb)** ʿawa
**guarantee (noun)** kfăli *ḍamâne*
  **to g...** tkaffal ʿan .. *itkaf'fal ʿan* .., ḍaman li ..
**guard (sentinel)** ṛafîr; see railway
  **to be on one's g...** waʿa, twakka *itwak'ka*
  **to g...** sahar ʿala, ḥaras
  **-house** karakûn *karakôl*
**guardian (of an orphan)** waṣi
**guess (verb)** ḥazar
**guest** ḍaif *ḍêf*, **pl.** ḍiyûf

---

[1] **This is the Russo-Greek Church, the established religion of Russia and Greece, sometimes wrongly called Greek Catholic; its official name in Russia is the Orthodox Catholic Faith; in the Orient it is simply called 'Greek.' The 'Greek-Catholic' Church on the contrary forms a branch of the great Catholic Church, recognises the Pope, and is distinguished from the Roman Catholic religion only by a few insignificant questions of rite and dogma; in affairs connected with the home department she is, however, like the Maronite Church, independent of Rome, and she jealously guards this internal independence against the attacks of the Latin priesthood, which is represented in Beyrout by a nuncio for Syria.**

---

**guide** (person) dālûl' *dalîl*, pl. dwālîl' *dulala*
**guilt** zamb, pl. zunûb
**guilty** miznib
**not g...** bala zamb
**guitar** gîtâ'ra, ʿûd
**gulf** (bay) jûn *gûn*
**gum** (Arabic) ṣamṛ
(of juniper, etc.) ʿilk
(of teeth) liset il-asnân
**gun** bârû'di *bunduḳîye*, pl. bwārîd' *banâdiḳa*; see cannon
**double-barrelled gun** jift *gift*, pl. jifûti *gifûte*
**to load** dakk
**to discharge the gun** aṭlaḳ ilbârû'di *aṭlaḳ elbunduḳîye*
**gunsmith** ṣâneʿ asliḥa *tufakshî*
**gut** (intestine) miṣrân, pl. maṣârîn'
**gutter** (noun) mizrâb
**gypsum** jefsîn *gibs*
**haberdasher** khurda'ji
**habit**; see custom, dress
**hail** (frozen drops) barad
**it is h...ing** ʿam byinzil barad *beyin'zil barad*
**hair** shaʿr
(a single one) shaʿra
**I want my h... cut** baddi ḳuṣṣ shaʿri *biddi aḳuṣṣ shaʿri*; see also pp. 100, 101
**half** nuṣṣ
**h... moon** hilāl *hilâl*
**hall** ḳâʿa, dâr (fem.)
**-porter** bauwāb ilḳâʿa *bauwâb ḳâʿet elôtîl'*
**halter** ḥabl
**ham** jambûn *gambûn*
**hammer** shâkûsh'
**hand** yadd or îd, pl. iyādi or daiyāt *ayâdi*
**God bless your h...s!** (returning thanks) Alla ysallim daiyātak! **Answer:** udaiyātak!
(of a clock) ʿaḳrab sâʿa
**to h...** (sthg. to sby.) nâwal with double acc.
**h... me the fruit, please** nâwil'ni ilfuâki iza kān bitrîd *nâwîl'ni elfewâkih iza kuntè terîd*
**a h...ful** kamshi *kabshe*
**handkerchief** maḥrami *mendîl*, pl. maḥârim *menâdîl'*
**handle** (of a basket, knife) miski ʿ*ullâka*
(of a door) saḳḳâṭa *suḳḳâṭa*

---

guides (horsemen) 127,8; 129,6
habit: bad h...s (horse) 120,7
haggle 112,14; 118,11
hail! 33,4
hair: cut my h... 101,7.9
.. one's h... stand on end 61;2
hairdresser 100,2
half an hour 131,9
h... past twelve 70,6
1½ .. 109,4; 110,3
(half) 2½ francs 72,1
27½ piastres 112,17
in h... an hour 92,12
h... an hour before .. 129,10
for the last h... year 67,5
one h... .. and the other h... 104,12; 106,6
halfway 143,2
hand me the .. 125,18; 137,10.12
you must h... over the .. 87,2

**handwriting** kitâbet îd *khaṭṭ*
**hang** (**trans.** = **to tie sthg. to**) ʿallaḳ; (**execute sby.**) shanaḳ
(**intr.** = **be suspended**) tʿallaḳ *itʿal'laḳ*
**hangman** gallâd *jellâd*
**happen** waḳaʿ *wiḳiʿ*, ḥadas *ḥaṣal*, ṣâr (yeṣîr)
**happiness** saʿd, bakht, ḥazz or ḥaḍḍ
**happy** saʿîd, misʿad
**harbinger**; **see forerunner**
**harbor** mîna, **pl.** miyan; eskeli *eskele*
**does the vessel remain off the h...?** byibḳa ilmar'kab barrât ilmîna? *tibḳa el-mar'kib khârig elmîna?*
**-master**; **see captain**
**hard** ḳâsi, shedîd
(**fig.**: **h... for sby.**) ṣaʿb ʿala
**to be h... towards** shadd (yeshidd')
**h... by** ḳarîb
**harden** ḳawwa
**hardly** anjaḳ *yâ dûb*
(**with difficulty**) bizzûr
**hardship** zulm; ṣuʿûbe
**hare** arneb
**harem** ḥarîm; **see note to same in the Ar. Voc.**
**hark!** ismaʿ!
**harm** ḍarar; **to h...** ḍarr
**I do myself h...** binḍarr' *banḍarr'*
**that does me h...** haida biḍurr'ni *di biḍurr'ini*
**there is no h...** mâfi ḍarar *mâfîsh'* ḍarar, **or** mâ bîsâ'yil *mâ yiḍurr'ish*
**harness** ṭaḳm
**to h...** ʿallaḳ
**harp** ʿûd
**harrow** mislafe
**to h...** salaf
**harvest** (**h...ing, cutting**) ḥaṣîdi *ḥaṣîde*
(**time, crop**) mausim *môsem*, **pl.** mwâsim *mewâsim*; ṛille *ṛalle*, **pl.** ṛlâl *ṛilâl*, **especially that which is reaped**
**hasheesh** (**narcotic, somewhat acrid, gum-resin prepared from hemp**) ḥashîsh
**h... smoker** ḥashshâsh
**to smoke h...** shirib ḥashîsh
**haste** (**noun**) ʿajal *ʿagel*
**hat** burnai'ṭa *burnêṭa*, **pl.** barânîṭ'
**hatch** (**eggs**) farrakhat
**hatchet** (**large**) balṭa
(**small**) firrâʿa
**hate** (**hatred**) burḍ
**to h...** baraḍ
**that is something which I h... to the uttermost degree** haida shî bibṛḍo fî âkhir idda'raji *di shê abṛabḍo fî âkhir edda'rage*
**hated, hateful** mamkût
**haughtiness** kibriya
**haughty** mutkab'bir *muta-kab'bir*

---

**happen: what has h...ed?** 46,3
**hard condition** 86,10
**h...-boiled eggs** 139,6
(**hard**) **the bed is h...** 94,1
**harness of the horse** 121,5
**haste: make h...** 101,13

**have (to possess)** malak; **as a rule simply expressed by the dative of the possessor: I have** ili *li*, **thou hast** ilak *lak*, **he has** ilo *lo* **etc., or by** 'ind *'and*: **has he money?** 'indo maṣâri? *'ando fulûs?* **I had** kân ili *kân li* **or** 'indi *'andi* **etc.**
**I should like to h...** .. baddi .. *biddi* ..
**I h... to do** .. 'alai'yi .. *'alêye* ..; **thou hast to do** .. 'alaik' .. *'alêk* ..
**to be had**; see there
**havoc** takhrîb
**to make h...** kharab
**hawk (falcon)** bâr
**hay** ḥashîsh
**hazard (danger)** khaṭar
(**game**) la'b ilḳumâr *li'b elḳumâr*
**hazardous** mukhûf
**head** râs, **pl.** ru꞊ûs
(**a chief**) ra꞊îs *re꞊îs*, raiyis
**headache** waja' râs *waga' râs*
**my head aches** râsi byûja''ni *râsi betûga''ni*
**head-band (for the head-kerchief)** 'uḳâl
**-kerchief (of men)** kaffîyi *kuffîye*; **(of women)** ṭarḥa
**-land** râs
**-long** mutahaw'wir
**-man of a village** shaikh ilba'lad *shêkh elbe'led*
**-master** ra꞊îs madrasi *bâsh ma'lem*
**-quarters (of an army)** ur'dî
**-waiter** ra꞊îs ilkhaddâmîn' *bâsh khaddâm*
**heal (trans.)** shafa
**(intr.)** shifi, ṣaḥḥ
**health** ṣaḥḥa, salâmi *salâme*, 'âfyi *'âfiye*
**your h...!** sirrak! **Answer:** ṣaḥḥtain'! see also good
**healthy** sâlim *sâlim*
**to be h...** ta'âfa
**heap (noun)** kaumi *kôme*

---

**hear** simiʿ; **from** .. ʿan ..
 **I heard** smiʿt *simiʿt'*
 **I do not h... well** mâ bismaʿ *asmaʿ'shi* ṭaiyib
**heart** ḳalb, **pl.** ḳulûb
 **beating of the h...** khafaḳân ilḳalb' *khafaḳân elḳalb'*
**heat (noun)** ḥarr, shaub *shôb*
 **to h... (trans.)** sakhkhan; **(intr.)** sakhan
**heaven** sama, **pl.** samawât
**heavy** taḳîl, **pl.** tiḳâl
**hedgehog** ḳunfud
**heel (noun)** kaʿb
**height** ʿulûw *ʿilwâye*
**heir** wâris *wâris*, **pl.** warasi *warase* [**(fem.)**
**hell** jahan'nam *gahan'nam*
**helmsman** dûman'ji *dûman'gi*
**help (noun)** musâʿadi *musâʿade*
 **with God's h...** biʿaunillâh *biʿônillâh'*
 **h...!** meded meded!
 **to h...** sâʿad *sâʿid*
**hem (edge)** kfâfi *kefâfe*
 **to hem** kaff *kaffif*
 **hemmed** makfûf
**hemorrhoids** bawâsîr'
**hemp** ḳinneb *ḳinnib*, kittân
 **-seed** bizr ilḳin'neb *bizr elḳin'nib, kittân*
**hen** jâji *farkha*
**henceforth** min hallaḳ urâyiḥ *min dilwaḳt' werâ-iḥ*
**herbage** ḥashîsh
**herd (noun)** ḳaṭîʿ
 **herdsman** râʿi, **pl.** raʿyân
**here** haun *hene*
 **(hither)** lahaun' *hene*
 **is he h... or there?** hû haun yimma haunîk? *hûwe hene wala henâk?*
 **h..., take!** khôd! *khod!*
**heritage** irs, mîrâs', taraki *tirke*, wirti *wirâse*
**hide (trans.)** khabba
 **(intr.)** tkhabba *itkhab'ba*
 **hiding-place** mikhbâyi *mikhbâye*
**high** ʿâli; **higher** aʿla
 **how h... is this mountain?** ḳaddaish' ʿâli hajja'bal? *ḳaddi ê ʿâli egge'bel di?*
 **where is the highest point, spot?** wain ilmaṭ'raḥ ilaʿ'la mâ ykûn? *fên elmaṭ'raḥ elaʿ'la mâ yekûn?*

---

**high-water** madd
**hill** tall *tell*, talli *telle*, **pl.** tlâl *tulûl*
**hind-part** khalf
**hip (flank)** khâṣra, khaṣr
**hippopotamus** ḥṣân ilbaḥr' *huṣân elbaḥr'*, faras ilnahr'
**hire (noun)** kiri *kire*
**on h...** bilki'ri, bilij'ra *bilug'ra* [*ista-'gar*]
**to h...** istak'ra, istâjar
**history** târîkh', **pl.** tawârîkh'
**hitherto** lil-ân *liḥadd' el-ân*
**hoarse** mabḥûḥ
**hoist**; see flag
**hold (to grasp)** misik
**(contain)** sâ' (yesâ')
**(last, be strong)** ḍâyan, misik
**h... tight!** imsik! **or** msîk!
**h... my hand** imsik îdi
**hole** bukhsh, **pl.** ibkhâsh **or** bikhûsh *ḥufra*, *ḥarḳ*
**holidays** fasḥa *fusḥa*
**Holland** blâd ilfalamank' *bilâd elfalamank'*
**hollow (empty)** fâriṛ, fâḍi
**holy** muḳad'das
**Holy Land**; see Palestine
**home** waṭan; see also house
**(whither?) h...** lilbait' *lilbêt*
**(where?) at h...** filbait' *filbêt*
**honest** amîn *emîn*, **musta**ḳîm
**honey** 'asal
**honor** sharaf
**to h...** karram, iḥta'ram
**h...able, h...ed** mukar'ram
**hoof** ḥâfir [*khuṭṭâf*]
**hook** shankal, **pl.** shanâkil;
**(a large one)** *kullâb*
**hookah**; see pipe
**hope** amal [*it-am'mal*]
**to h...** ammal, t-ammal
**I h..., let us h...** inshal'la *inshallâh*
**horizon** ufḳ
**horn** ḳarn, **pl.** ḳurûn
**h...ed cattle** baḳar
**horse-power** ḳûwet ḥuṣân
**-race** sibâḳ ilkhail' *elkhêl*
**horses (coll.)** khail *khêl*; see stallion, mare; also pp. 118 to 123

---

**horse-shoe** na'l
**hospice**; see monastery
**hospitably**: **to receive h**... daiyaf
**hospital** mustash'fa, khastakhâne, isbitâlya
**h...ity** ḍiyâfa
**host**; see army, landlord
**(wafer)** birshâni *burshâne*
**hot** sukhn
**(of weather)** shaub *shôb*, ḥarr; see p. 64
**(spiced)** ḥadd
**I am very hot** ana mshau'wib ktîr *ana mushau'wib ketîr*
**hotel** hôtel'lo *ôtîl'*
**hour** sâ'a *sâ'a*, **pl.** sâ'ât' *sâ'ât'*
**in (after) an h**... ba'd sâ'a *ba'dê sâ'a*
**for an h**... lasâ'a *lisâ'a*, minshân sâ'a *'ala shân sâ'a waḥde*
**a quarter of, half, three quarters of, an h**... rub', nuṣṣ, tlât rbâ' issâ'a *ruba', nuṣṣ, telat irbâ' essâ'a*
**an h... and a half** sâ'a unuṣṣ' *sâ'a wenuṣṣ'*
**house** bait *bêt*, **pl.** biyût; ḥâra, pl. ḥârât'; dâr
**-boat** ḳârab bkhaimi *ḳârib bkhême*
**-rent** ṛille *ṛalle*
**-tax** ḍarîba
**how** kîf *kêf* **or** *ezai'*
**how do you do?** see p. 33
**how long does it take to get to ..?** ḳaddaish' baddo ilwâḥid tâ yûṣal la...? *ḳaddî ê biddo elwâḥid 'ala shân yûṣal li...?*
**how much** ḳaddaish' *ḳaddî ê*, kâm *kâm*
**however** ma'a zâlik *ma'a zâlik*
**howl (verb)** 'awa
**huge (great, grand)** 'azîm
**human (not divine)** bashari
**(not animal)** insâni *insâni*
**humanity** insânî'yi *insânî'ye*
**(kindness)** ma'rûf
**humble (adj.)** mitwâḍi'
**humility** tawâḍu'
**humbug (swindler)** ṛashshash; see nonsense
**hump** ḥadbi *ḥadbe*
**(of a camel)** sanam
**hundred** mîyi *mîye*
**h...weight** ḳanṭâr; **the Syrian** ḳanṭâr = **256 kilogrammes, the Egyptian = 45 kilogrammes, the Alexandrian = 140 kilogrammes; 1** ḳanṭâr = **100** roṭl

---

**hunger (noun)** jûʿ *gûʿ*
**hungry** jûʿân′ *giʿân* or *gîʿân′*
**I am h...** ana jûʿân′ *ana giʿân*
**hunt (verb)** ṣaiyad, iṣṭâd
**hunter** ṣîyâd′ *ṣaiyâd*
**hunting** ṣaid *ṣêd*
**hurricane** zaubaʿa shedîde
**hurry (noun)** ʿajal *ʿagel*
**hurt : it hurts (smarts)** yûjaʿ *yûgaʿ*
**(injured)** maḍrûr
**husband** jauz *gôz*
**h...man ; see peasant**
**hush !** iskut !
**hut** khuṣṣ *ʿishshe*
**hydrophobia** kalab
**hyena** ḍabʿ, **pl.** ḍibâʿ
**hymn** tartîl
**-book** ktâb *kitâb* tartîl
**hypocrisy** nifâḳ, munâfaḳa
**hypocrite** munâfiḳ
**ibis** *herêz, abu mingal*
**ice** jalîd *gelîd*
**ichneumon** nims
**idea** fikr, **pl.** ifkâr
**idiot** mahbûl *ʿabîṭ*
**idol** ṣanam, **pl.** aṣnâm
**idolator ; see worshipper**
**if (with indic.)** iza, **generally followed by the pret., e.g. if you do that** iza ʿimilt′ haik *iza ʿamaltê kide*
**(with subj.)** lau *lô*, lû, **e.g. if it were so** lau kân haik *lô kân kide*
**if not** iza mâ, lau mâ *lô′lâ in*
**ignorant** jâhil *gâhil*
**ill (sick, ailing)** mariḍ, ḍaʿîf or ḍʿîf *ʿaiyân*
**to be ill** miriḍ, ḍiʿif
**illness** maraḍ, **pl.** imrâḍ
**illegitimate** bandûḳ, **pl.** bnâdîḳ′ ; *ibnê zine*
**imitate** ḳallad *ḳallid*
**imitation** tiḳlîd *taḳlîd*
**immoderate** mufriṭ
**immoral** fâḥish, dinis
**immortal** dâyim *dâ-im*
**impartial** mâlo ɣaraḍ *mâ-lôsh′ ɣaraḍ*
**i...ly** bala ɣaraḍ
**impatient** ḳalîl iṣṣabr′ *ḳalîl eṣṣabr′*
**implements** ʿiddi *ʿidde*
**impolite** khishin
**important** muhimm′
**impose on** ɣashsh

---

**hungry : are you h... ? 46,7**
**we are h... 134,2 ; 145,6**
**hurry ! 51,5 ; 79,10 ; 134,2 ; 146,7**
**we must h... 131,10**
**in a h... 41,5**
**hurt : they h... my .. 108,10**
**I am 48,21.24 ff. ; 49,1 ff.**
**I pay you the difference 107,14**
**I will pay what you like 107,12**
**I want .. 83,9**
**it is I 48,3 ; see also me**
**ice (for eating) 102,9**
**if he has .. 137,14**
**if I may ask 133,11**
**if it is .. 96,13**
**if there is .. 138,7 ; 139,15**
**as if 148,8**
**if (that, or because) you 53,3.4**
**if any one asks 95,3**
**if in need (if necessary) 128,1**
**if you .. 95,9 ; 99,7**
**if you (deny) 53,3**
**if you do not .. 126.7**
**if you will .. you will .. 53,1**
**if Allah wills 42,6**
**implore : I i... you 53,6**

**impossibility** imtinâʿ
**impossible** mush mimkin, muḥâl, mustaḥîl
**imprison** sijn *ḥabas*
**improve (trans.)** ṣaḥḥaḥ **(intr.)** tḥassan *itḥas'san*
**i...ment** tiṣḥîḥ *taṣḥîḥ*, tiṣlîḥ *taṣlîḥ*
**impudent** ḳalîl ilḥa'ya *ḳalîl elḥai'ya*
**impure** nijis *nigis*
**in (within)** jûwa *gûwa*
**(where ?=at)** fi
**(whither ?=into)** la *li*, fî
**when determining time it is often not translated, e.g. in the evening** ilma'sa **or** ʿashîyi *elʿi'she*
**incapable for ..** ʿâjiz ʿan .. *ʿâgiz ʿan ..*
**incense (noun)** bakhûr
**inch** iṣbaʿ **(lit., finger)=2.82 centimetres; 1** iṣbaʿ **= 6** ḥabbi shaʿîr **barley-corns**
**inclination (wish, mind)** khâṭir
**inclined: I feel very much i... to go for a walk** ili khâṭir ktîr shimm ilha'wa *lîye khâṭir ketîr ashimm' elha'wa*
**I don't feel at all i...** mâ ili khâṭir abadan *mâ fish khâṭir ebeden*
**income** îrâd', madkhûl, dakhl
**increase** izdiyâd
**to i...(trans.)** kattar; **(intr.)** keber
**indecent** fâḥish, razîl
**indeed (in truth)** bilḥaḳîḳa
**i... ! (yes !)** aina'ʿam
**indemnify (sby.)** ʿauwaḍ ʿala.. *ʿauwaḍ li...*
**India** blâd ilhind' *bilâd elhind'*; hindustân
**indigo** nîl
**indisposition (especially indigestion)** tukhmi *tukhme*
**infant (suckling)** ṭifl
**infantry** rijjâli *raggâle*, mushât
**infidel** kâfir *kâfir*, **pl.** kuffâr
**infinite** illi mâlo nihâyi *elli mâlôsh' nihâye*
**inflammation** iltihâb *iltihâb*
**i... of the eye (Egyptian ophthalmia)** ramad

---

inform khabbar *khabbir,*
akhbar
  I shall i... the consul, the
  authorities ana bkhabbir
  ilḳun ṣul, ilḥkûmi *ana
  akhbir elḳun'ṣul, elḥu-*
  i...ation khaber    *[kûmi*
inhabitant sâkin, pl. sukkân *sukkân;* aḥâli
ink ḥibr, ḥabr    *[wâyeṭ*
  -bottle, -stand dawâyi *de-*
inn manzil *menzil,* pl.
  mnâzil *menâzil;* luḳan'da
  *loḳan'da*
  (of the lowest class) khân
inner jûwâ'ni *gúwá'ni*
innkeeper (landlord of a
  khan) khânâ'ti *khânâ'te*
innocent (not guilty) bala
  zamb    *[yuḥṣa*
innumerable lâ yu'add', *lâi*
inquest taḥar'ɪ î *taḥkîḳ*
inquire after .. istakh'bar
  'an .., faḥas ..
inquiry istikhbâr, istifḥâm
inscription ktiḇi *kitâbe*
insects ḥasharât
inside (noun) bâṭin
  (adv.) jûwa *gúwa*
insight into iṭṭilâ' 'ala ..,
  wuḳûf 'ala ..
  to get an i... into waḳaf 'ala
insolent ḳalîl ilḥai'ya *ḳalîl
  elḥai'ye*

inspector mufat'tesh
instance ; see example
instead 'iwaḍ, bdâl *bidâl*
instrument âli *âle*
insult (verb) 'azzar *shatam*
intend ḳaṣad
  I i... to ; see intention
intention ḳaṣd, nîyi *nîye,*
  mrâd *murâd,* maḳṣûd,
  marâm
  that is not my i... haida
  mush mrâdi *di mush
  murâdi*
  I have the i... of .. nîyti
  in .. *nîyeti in ..*
interest (concern) nafʿ ; ṣâliḥ, pl. ṣawâliḥ
  (premium) fâyiz *fâɜiz* or
  *faraḍ*
  I have no i... in this affair
  mâ ili ṣâliḥ bihashshî
  *mâ lîsh ṣâliḥ bishshê di*
  to i... (excite) rarrab fî ..
interpreter tarjimân *turgemân,* pl. trâjmîn *terâgime*
intestines maṣârîn'
into la *li,* fî
intoxicated ; see drunk
introduce dakhkhal, jalab
  *galab*
invalid-carriage 'arabiyet
  naḳl il'ayyanîn
inveigh (against) 'aiyaṭ,
  'azzar *shatam*

**invent** ikhta'ra'
**invention** ikhtirâ'
**investigate ; see examine**
**invite** 'azam
**Ireland** irlânda
**iron (noun)** ḥadîd
**(adj. = of i...)** min ḥadîd
**to i... (linen)** kawa
**ironmonger** ḥaddâd
**irrigate** saḳa
**i...d** misḳi *maski*
**irrigation** sikâyi *siḳâye*
**-channel** sâḳiyi *tir'a*, **pl.** sawâḳi *tira'*
**-wheel** nâ'û'ra *sâḳiye* **or** *tâbût'*, **pl.** nawâ'ir' *sawâḳi* **or** *tawâbît'*
**is there ; see there**
**island** jazîri *gezîre*, **pl.** jazâyir *gezâ-ir*
**Italian** ṭilyâni *iṭalyâni*
**Italy** aṭâlya
**itch (noun)** jarab *garab*
**ivory** sinn ilfîl *sinn elfîl*; 'âj
**(adj. = of i...)** min 'âj
**jackal** wâwi
**jacket** kubarân **or** kubrân *demîr, salṭa*
**ladies' j...** salṭa

**Jaffa** yâfa *yâfa*
**jam (preserve)** mirab'ba
**January** kânûn' ittâni *kânûn' ettâni* **or** *yanâ-ir*
**Japan** jâbûnîa *yâbân'*
**J...ese** jâbû'ni *yâbâ'nî*
**jasmine** yâsimîn', fill *full*
**jaundice** rîḳân'
**javelin** ḥarbi *ḥarbe*
**jealous** ṛaiyûr
**jealousy** ṛîri *ṛîre*
**jerboa (animal resembling the dormouse)** yarbû'a *yerbû'a*
**Jericho** irrîḥa *errîḥa*
**Jerusalem** ilkuds' *elkuds'* **(the Holy)**; baitilmaḳ'dis *bêt elmaḳ'dis* **(Holy Place)**; ilḳuds' ishsherîf *elḳuds' eshsherîf* **(the Celebrated)**
**man from J...** ḳudsi
**J... pilgrim** ḥajj
**jest (noun)** mazih, mazâḥ *hizâr*
**to j...** mazaḥ *hazzar*
**Jesus (the Christians say)** yesû'; **J... Christ** yesû' ilmesîḥ *yesû' elmesîḥ*
**(the Muslims say)** saiyidna 'îsa : **our Lord Jesus**

---

invite him (to enter) 36,18
I am i...d 40,3
irak : raki 124,1
iron (clothes) 95,10 ; 96,1
i...ed 98,12
is : see be
it 50,19 ; 59,3-6 ; 86,5 ; 96,13
it is .. 106,2
it is I 48,3 ; that is it 48,4
it is raining 64,8 ; 140,16 ; 141,1
of it 47,4
any part in it 107,13
put (the matches) on it 93,8
(it) .. do you want it? 86,5
to come to it 144,3
what is the matter with it? 106,11
do it quickly 107,7
give it 102,13.14
look for it 72,8
let it boil 92,6
put it in .. 51,19
take it to the .. 77,7
wash it 92,3
its (air, etc.) 84,7 ; 135,3.8 ; 145,4
its (watch spring) 107,4

**Jew, Jewish** yahûdi
**Jews** yahûd
**jewel** jauhar *gôhar*, **pl.** jawâhir *gawâhir*
**jeweller** jauhar'ji *gôhar'gi*
**John** ḥanna
**J... the Baptist** yûḥan'na ilma'madân *yûḥan'na elma'madân*
**St. J... (the Apostle)** ilkaddîs yûḥan'na *elkaddîs yûḥan'na*
**join** waṣal ; laḥam
**joined** mawṣûl
**joke (fun)** mazḥ, ḍiḥk *hazar*
**(something witty)** sakhâni'yi *sukhrîye*
**to j...** mazaḥ *hazzar*
**jolly (merry)** mabsûṭ
**Jordan** ishsherî'a *eshsherî'a*
**Joseph** yûsuf *yûsif*
**journal** jurnâl *gurnâl*
**journey (the travelling)** safar, siyâḥa
**(a single j...)** safra
**how many days does the j... to .. take?** safar kam yaum la...? *safar kâm yôm li...?*
**joy** surûr, basṭ, faraḥ
**Judea (in the Arabic translations of the Bible)** ilyahûdi'yi *elyahûdî'ye;* **the modern** muteṣar'riflik ilḳuds' **'province of Jerusalem' covers about the ancient Judea**
**judge (noun)** ḳâḍi
**to j... over** ḥakam ('ala)
**judicial adviser** mushâwer ḳaḍâyi *mushâwer ḥuḳûḳ*
**jug (big one)** jarra *ballâse*, **pl.** jrâr *ballâsât'*
**(small one)** brîḳ *ebrîḳ*, **pl.** bârîḳ' *ebârîḳ'*
**earthen water-jug** sharbi **or** na'âra *ḳulle*
**juggler** muza''bir **or** muza'bir'ji *ḥâwi*
**juice** zûm *'aṣîr*
**juicy** zaki
**jujube (fruit)** 'unnâb
**July** tammûz *yûliye* **or** *lûliye*
**jump (noun)** naṭṭa, **fazzi** *fezzè*
**to j...** naṭṭ, fazz
**junction** waṣl
**June** ḥazîrân' *yûniye*
**jurisdiction** ḥukm *ikhtiṣâṣ*
**jurisprudence** 'ilm ilfikh'
**just (adj.)** minṣif, 'âdil
**(adv. = this moment)** hallaḳ *dilwaḳt'*
**justice (righteousness)** 'adl, inṣâf; **see also judge**
**court of j...** maḥkami *maḥkame*, majlis *meglis*
**international court of j...** *ḥaḳḳâni'ye*
**jutty (in a building)** kishk *kushk* **or** *kharge*; **see balcony**
**Kabyle** ḳabîli *ḳabîle*, **pl.** ḳabâyil *ḳabâ-il*
**kauwas; see consulate's official**

---

jobmaster (livery-man) 119,1
journey: for this j... 126,4
returned from the j... 34,12
(journey) let for the j... 122,2
jump: I cannot j... 73.6
horses must not j... 120,1

**keep (to retain)** ḥafaz *ḥafaḍ*
**(to hold)** misik
**to k... far from, k... aloof** ibta‘‘ad ‘an.., tabâ‘ad ‘an .. *itbâ‘ad ‘an ..*
**kernel** bizr, bizri *bizre*, **pl.** buzûr [*eggôz*
**(of a nut)** ḳalb ijjauz′ *ḳalb*
**kerosene** zaitilkâz *zêt batrôl*
**key** miftâḥ *muftâḥ*, **pl.** mfâtîḥ′ *mefâtîḥ′*
**khalif** khalîfi *khalîfe*, amîr ilmu≈minîn *emîr elmu≈minîn*
**khan (inn of the lowest description ; in large towns, at the same time shop and warehouse)** khân **or** *wukâle*, **pl.** khanât *khanât* **or** *wakâ≈il*
**Khartoum** elkharṭûm **(elephant's trunk)**
**khedive ; see viceroy**
**kick** rafse ; **to k...** rafas
**kid (male)** jidi *gidi*
**(female)** ‘anâḳ
**kidney** kilwi *kilwe*
**kill** ḳatal, mauwat
**(to slaughter)** dabaḥ
**(applied to many)** dabbaḥ
**kiln** furn, **pl.** afrân
**kilogramme** kîlô
**kilometre** kîlômitr′
**kind (sort, class)** nau‘ *nô‘*, **pl.** inwâ‘ ; jins *gins*, **pl.** ijnâs *ignâs ;* shikl, **pl.** ishkâl *ishkâl*
**of this k...** min hajjins′ *mineggins′ê di*, min hashshikl′ *min eshshikl′ê di*
**of that k...** min haidâk ijjins′ *min eggins′ê dikhâ* **(pron.** *dik-hâ***)** [*zarîf*
**(adj.)** laṭif, anîs, âdemi
**kindle ; see fire**
**kindness** faḍl, **pl.** afḍâl
**we thank you for your k...** nishkur afḍâlak
**to have the k...** tfaḍḍal *itfaḍ′ḍal*
**have the k !** tfaḍḍalu ! *itfaḍ′ḍalu !*
**kine-pox ; see vaccinate**
**king** malik, **pl.** mulûk
**King of England** malik ingiltar′ra
**kingdom** mamlaki *memleke*
**kiosk** kishk [*bûse*
**kiss (noun)** bausi *bôse*, bûsi
**to k...** ḳabbal[1] *bâs*, bauwas

1 bîḳab′bil iyâdîk′ **or** daiyâtak *biḳab′bil ayâdîk′* **'he kisses your hands' is the Arab's reply when a superior has inquired after the health of an inferior.**


keep ; God k... you 43,10
.. k... up with you 131,3
nobody k...s well 147,6
I k... my passport 75,11
kettle 148,9
kind : of each k... 108,4
of one k... 116,5
(kind) of what k... is .. ? 141,11
of all k...s 115,3 ; 117,5
various k...s 124,1
kindle the fire 93,5
kindness : have the k... 52,21
I shall not forget your k... 54,6
your k... is very great 53,8.9

**kitchen** maṭbakh
**kite (bird)** ḥidâi
(toy) ṭîyâ'ra *ṭaiyâra*
**knead** ʿajjan *ʿaggin*
**knee** rikbi *rukbe*, **pl.** rikbât *rukab*
to **kneel** rakaʿ
**knife** sikkîn, sikkîni *sikkîne*, **pl.** skâkîn' *sekâkîn'*
**butcher's k...** sa'ṭûr, **pl.** sawâ'ṭîr
**pen-k...** mi'brâ
**knit** ḥayyak
**knock (to beat)** khabaṭ
**to k... at the door** ḍakk ilbâb *elbâb*
**who is there?** mîn?
**knot** ʿukdi *ʿukde*
**to k... (tie)** ʿakad
**know** ʿirif; conjug. see 23, 24
**I should like to k... when, how, if** baddi aʿrif aimta, kîf, izá *biddi aʿraf imte, kêf, iza*
**do you k... English?** btaʿrif inglîzi? *betaʿraf ingelîzi?*
**do you (plur.) k... whether, what, where?** btaʿrfu iza, shû, wain? *betaʿra'fu iza, ê, fên?*
**I k... nothing about it (khabar=news, knowledge)** mâ ʿindi khabar ʿanno *mâ ʿandîsh khabar ʿanno*
**it is known to you (plur.) that ..** maʿlûmkon in .. *maʿlûmkum in ..*
**knowledge** maʿrifi *maʿrife*, **pl.** maʿârif; ʿilm, **pl.** ʿulûm
**knuckle (noun)** kaʿb, ḳâḥil
**kohl**; see antimony
**Koran** ilḳur=ân *elḳur=ân*
**label** waraḳe; **(for marking the price)** raḳam
**labor** shurl, **pl.** ishrâl
**without l...** bilâ taʿab
**laboratory** dâr ilʿamalîyât' *maʿmal kîmîâ'wi*
**lacerate** khazzaḳ
**lace-work (galloon)** sharâyiṭ *sharâ=iṭ*
**lad** walad
**ladder** sullam *sellim* **(fem.)**, **pl.** slâlîm' *selâ'lîm*
**ladle** kafkîr
**lady** sitt
**lake (water)** baḥra, buḥai'ra [*beḥêra*]
**lamb** ranmi *kharûf*
**lame (adj.)** aʿraj *aʿrag*
**lameness** ʿarj *ʿarg*
**lament** nâḥ *yenûḥ*
**l...ation**; see bewailing
**lamp** ḳandîl *lamda*, **pl.** ḳnâdîl' *lumad*
**(earthen)** sirâj *sirâg*, **pl.** surj *surg*
**lampoon (satire)** haju *hagu*
**lance** rumḥ, **pl.** rmâḥ *rimâḥ*; *ḥarbe*, **pl.** *ḥurab*

---

knock at the door 80,10
some one is k...ing 36,12
know: I k... 53,8
I do not know 50,5
what do I k...! 50,6
you k... this for certain? 45,20
do you k... (Arabic)? 47,6
(know) do you k... how to ..? 88,13; 96,1
tell me what you k... 88,14
I k... how to .. 88,15
I k... only 88,19
labor: how great l... 74,10
lady (wife) 35,4

**land (surface, real estate)** arḍ, pl. arâḍi
**(continent, shore)** barr
**arable l...** ḥaḳli
**see also country**
**do you see l...?** bitshûf ilbarr'?
**to l...** ṭili' 'albarr'; **see also call, disembark**
**where shall we l...?** wain niṭla' 'albarr'? *fên niṭla' 'albarr'?*
**landau** 'arabîyet lan'dô
**landing-stage** iskilat innuzûl lilbarr'
**landlord (of a house)** ṣâḥib ilbait' *ṣâḥib elbêt*, **pl.** aṣḥâb ilbait' *aṣḥâb elbêt*
**(of an hotel)** ṣâḥib illukan'da *ṣâḥib ellokan'da*; **see also innkeeper**
**lane (narrow street)** zuḳâḳ, **pl.** aziḳ'ḳi; zârûb', **pl.** zawârîb'; *khuṭṭ*
**language (speech, words)** kalâm *kelâm*
**(of a people)** lisân *lisân*, **pl.** ilsini *alsine;* luṛa, **pl.** luṛât
**lantern (of glass)** fânûs'
**(of paper)** fanâr
**lap (also bosom)** ḥuḍn
**large** kebîr **(or, Syr. only:** kbîr), 'arîḍ
**last (adj.)** âkhir *âkhir*
**l... night** mbârḥa *embâreḥ fillêl*
**l... year** sint ilmâḍyi **or** sint ilma'ḍit *esse'ne elli fâtet*, 'âm ilau'wil *'am enau'wal*
**at l...** binnihâyi *nehai'to*
**to l...** dâm (yedûm)
**to l... long** ṭauwal **or** *ṛâb*
**how long will it l...?** ḳaddaish' baddo yṭauwil? *ḳaddê yeṭau'wil* **or** *ḳaddê yeṛîb?*
**latch (of a door)** saḳḳâṭa *suḳḳâṭa*
**late** laḳḳîs *wakhri*
**(speaking of one dead)** marḥûm
**to be l... (delay)** t=akhkhar *it=akh'khar*
**I fear we shall be l...** bkhâf nit=akh'khar *bakhâf nit=akh'khar*, **or** bkhâf mâ mnûṣal 'ala waḳt *bakhâf mâ nûṣalshi 'ala waḳt*
**it is already l...** ṣâr laḳḳîs *ṣâr wakhri*, fât ilwaḳt' *fât elwaḳt'*
**I will call (ask) again later on** 'âd is=al ba'dên *arga' as=al ba'dên*
**at the latest at 8 o'clock** 'alktîr issâ'a tmânyi *'alketîr essâ'a teman'ye*
**lately** akhîran
**laugh (noun)** ḍiḥk
**to l...** ḍiḥik; **at** 'ala
**laurel (-shrub)** shajrit ilṛâr *shagarat elṛâr*

landlord of a house 137,14
lash out (horse) 120,1; 144,9
last two years 135,12
late: I am l... 41,3.4
(late) I fear I am l... 41,13.15
it is l... 40,14; 146,4
sooner or l...r 68,17
at the l...st 70,7

**lavatory**; see closet
**law** (rule, act) ḳânûn′, pl. ḳawânîn′; nazâm, pl. nazâmât′
(code, body of laws) sharî‘a
the Mohammedan law ishsharî‘at ilislâmî′yi *eshsharî‘a elislâmî′ye*, shar‘i sherîf
**law-court**; see justice
**lawful** shar‘i
**lawyer** mutfaḳ′ḳih, faḳîh
**lay** (to put) waḍa‘
(lay down) naiyam *naiyim*
**lazy** kislân *kaslân* or *kasûl*, tembel
laziness kasal
**lead** (metal) rṣâṣ *ruṣâṣ*
**lead** (to conduct) ḳâd (yeḳîd), wadda
where does this road l... to? lawain′ bitwad′di haddarb′? *‘ala fên yiwad′di eddarb′ê di?*
**lead-pencil** ḳalam rṣâṣ *ḳalem ruṣâṣ*
**leaf** waraḳa or warḳa, pl. ûrâḳ′ *aurâḳ*; coll. waraḳ
(of a book) ṣaḥifi *ṣaḥîfe*, pl. ṣaḥâyif *ṣaḥâ=if*
**leak** dalf
to l... wakaf *nazz*
**lean** naḥîf
(thin) rafî‘ *rufai′ya‘*
l... meat ḥabr
**learn** t‘allam *it‘al′lim*
(to hear) simi‘, istakh′bar
l...ed ‘âlim, pl. ‘ulama
l...ing (science) ‘ilm
**lease** (of a house) kiri *kire*
on l... bilki′ri, bil=ij′ra *bil=ug′ra*
**least** il=akall′ *el=aḳall′*
at l... bil=akall′, aḳall′ mâ yekûn, bilḳalîli *bilḳalîle*
**leather** (noun) jild *gild*
(a piece) jildi *gilde*
(adj., of l...) min jild *min gild*
**leave** (of absence) izn, istîzân′ *istîzân*
to take l... ista=′zan *ista=′zin*
(farewell) widâ‘
to take l... of wadda‘, auda‘ with acc.
to l... (trans.) tarak, khalla, dashshar *saiyib*
(to start) sâfar *sâfir*
the mail leaves Beyrout at 6 o'clock ilbus′ṭa bitsâfir min bairût issâ‘a sitti *elbus′ṭa bitsâfir min bêrût′ essâ‘a sitte*

---

lay the cloth 93,1
you have not laid .. 124,7
laziness continues 95,9
lead him 143,5
l...ing to the garden 78,10
lean (meat) 124,3
least: not the l... 147,3
leather (boot-) 109,3
leave: by your l... 42,8
I beg l... 42,10
with your master's l... 38,13
leave .. only 101,5
l... the light here 94,2
l... (plur.) nothing in .. 74,5
l... off! 63,4
if you l... the house 95,1
.. cannot l... the house 96,4
(steamer) l...s for .. 77,3; 82,13
why did you l... your ..? 88,10
I did not l... him 88,11
you are l...ing us? 40,9
I have no .. left 96,8

**leave) to l... off (of persons)** baṭṭal; **(of things)** inḳa'ṭa'
**when will you l... off lying (telling falsehoods)?** aimta tbaṭṭil tikzib? *imte tebaṭ'ṭal tikdib?*
**the rain has left off** inḳa'ṭa' ilma'ṭar *inḳa'ṭa' elma'ṭar*
**Lebanon : Mt. L...** jabal libnân *gebel libnân*
**lecturer (Mohammedan)** khaṭîb [*dûde*
**leech** 'alaḳa, **pl.** 'alaḳât ;
**(coll.)** 'alaḳ **or** *dûd*
**left (opp. right)** shmâl *shemâl* [*shemâlak !*
**(mind) your l... (in Cairo) !**
**on the l... hand** 'ala îdak ishshmâl *'ala îdak eshshemâl*
**leg** sâḳ, **pl.** sîḳân'
**(the thigh of an animal)** fakhd, **e.g. leg of mutton** fakhd ṛanam
**legal** shar'i
**legation** safara
**lemon** laimûni *lamûne*; **coll.** laimûn *lamûn*
**l...ade** laimûnâ'ḍa *lêmû-* [*nâ'ta*
**lend** 'âr (ye'îr)
**(money)** daiyan
**length** ṭûl
**lentil** 'adsi *'adse* · **coll.** 'ads **or** 'ades
**pillau with l...s (dish)** mjaddara
**leprosy (white)** baraṣ
**leprous, leper** abraṣ
**less than ..** aḳall' min ..
**lesson** dars, **pl.** durûs
**(task)** mtîli *metîle*, **pl.** mtâyil *metâ-il*
**let (a house, etc.)** kara, âjar *âgar*
**(to permit)** khalla
**let alone or let go, quit** dashshar *saiyib*, tarak
**letter (character)** ḥarf, **pl.** ḥurûf **or** aḥruf
**(a note)** maktûb *gawâb*, **pl.** mkâtîb' *gawâbât'*
**lettuce** khass
**leucoderma (white leprosy)** baraṣ
**Levant**; see Orient
**levée** istiḳbâl (ilma'lik lizâyirih ras'mîyan)
**level (noun and adj.)** sahl
**to l...** sauwa
**lexicon** ḳamûs
**liar** kizzâb *keddâb*
**a big l...** kizzâb mutbar'bik *keddâb mu-ar'ram*
**liberal (adj.)** karîm, sakhi
**l...ity** karam, sakhâwi *sakhâwe*
**library** maktabi *maktabe*, kutubkhâne

---

Lebanon-wine 124,1 ; 139,16
leisure : at our l... 102,2
length : of .. in l... 110,3
let him bring the .. 149,4
let him come in 36,17
let no one enter 95,2
let it boil 92,6
let them shake the .. 136,10
let us (enter, see) 106,10 ; 145,6
have you .. to let ? 78,5 ; 119,2
how do you let your .. ? 122,2
they tell me you have .. to let 83,7
the apartment to let 84,2
I cannot let it for less 86,7
level the ground 147,8

lick (to lap) liḥis *laḥas*

licorice sûs

lid ṛaṭa

lie (falsehood) kizb, kizib, *kidb;* a single one kizbi kidbe [*kidiḥ*]

to lie (tell a lie) kizib

(to rest extended, of persons) nâm *nâm* (yenâm)

(to be situated, as of things) generally not expressed, sometimes rendered by the past part. of ḥaṭṭ to lay where lies ..? wain ..? *fên ..?*

the book lies on the table ilktâb ʿaṭṭau'li or ilktâb maḥṭûṭ ʿaṭṭau'li *elkitâb ʿaṭṭarabéze*

lieutenant mlâzim *melâzim*

life ʿumr, ḥayât

in the whole of my l... kull îyâm' ʿumri *kull îyâm' ʿumri*

lifeless jâmid *gâmid*

lift (passenger, etc.) mâkina râfʿa

to l... (raise) rafaʿ

light (noun) ḍau *nûr*

(a candle) shamʿa

kindle the l...! ishʿal iḍḍau'! *walla' ennûr!*

put out the l..! iṭfi iḍḍau'! *iṭfi ennûr!*

(bright, of color) fâtiḥ *fátiḥ*

it is l... (day-l...) fî ḍau *fîh nûr*

(not heavy) khafîf

l... railway sikke ḥaḍîdiye *khafîfe*

(easy) sahil *sahl*

l...er than .. ashal (pron. as-hal) min .., (of weight) akhaff' min ..

to l... the fire shaʿʿal innâr *walla' ennâr*

to give l... to ḍauwa *nauwar*

light-hearted farḥân

lighthouse fanâr

lightness khiffe

lightning barḳ

it was lightening baraḳit *baraḳet,* with or without iddin'yi or iddi'ni *eddin'ye*

like (similar, as) mitl zê, *zeiy*

to l... ḥabb

I l... this better than .. haida bhibbo aktar min .. *di baḥib'bo aktar min ..*

I l.. that very much ana ktîr mabsûṭ min haida *ana mabsûṭ ketîr min di*

I should l... to know ana bhibb ktîr aʿrif *ana baḥib'bé ketîr aʿraf*

see also inclined

**(like) I should l... is also expressed by** baddi *biddi*, **thou shouldst l...** baddak *biddak*, **he should l...** baddo *biddo*, **etc.**
**I don't l... that** mâ baddi haida *mâ biddîsh di*, **or** mâ brîd haida *mâ aḥib'-bish di*
**as you l...** mitl mâ bitrîd *zê mâ terîd*
**likewise** kazâlik *kezâlik*
**liking: that is to my l...** haida 'ala khâṭri *di 'ala khâṭri*
**limb** 'aḍu, **pl.** a'ḍa
**lime (stone)** kils *gîr*
**to dress or plaster with l...** kallas *baiyaḍ*
**see also lemon**
**limp (flexile)** laiyin
**to l...** 'araj *'arag*
**limping** a'raj *a'rag*
**line (stroke, stripe)** khaṭṭ
**(in a book)** saṭr, **pl.** asṭur
**(row)** ṣaff, **pl.** ṣufûf
**(thread, rope)** ḥabl
**to range in a l...** ṣaff, ṣaffaf
**to l... (clothes)** baṭṭan
**lined** mubaṭ'ṭan
**linen (noun)** kittân *kittân*
**(adj.)** min kittân
**see also washing**
**lining (of clothes)** baṭâni *baṭâne*
**lion** saba'
**lip** shiffi *shiffe*, **pl.** shiffât *shafâ=if*
**liqueur; see brandy**
**liquid (noun and adj.)** mâyi'
**listen (hearken)** tsamma' *ista'ma'*
**(to grant)** istajâb *istagâb*
**l... to (hear) me** isma''ni
**literal** ḥarfi; **l...ly** ḥarfîyan
**litre; cf. bushel**
**little (small)** zṛîr *zuṛai'yar*, **pl.** zṛâr *zuṛaiyerîn* **or** *zuṛâr*
**(not much)** ḳalîl *shuwai'ye*
**l... by l...** bittidrîj *bittedrîg*
**a l...** shwaiyi *shuwai'ye*
**l... was wanting that .. (a l... more and ..)** biḳi shî ḳalîl ḥatta .. *baḳa shî ḳalîl ḥatta ..*
**live** 'âsh (ye'îsh)
**(to dwell)** ḳa'ad, sakan; **for the present tense the participle** sâkin *sâkin* **is generally used; I, etc. l...** ana, **etc.** sâkin *sâkin*, **we etc. l...** niḥna *iḥne*, **etc.** sâknîn' *saknîn*
**have you lived there a long time?** ḳa'adt' ktîr haunîk? *ḳa'adt'ăketîr henâk?*
**lively** nishîṭ
**liver** kibdi *kibde*, ḳaṣbi sauda *ḳaṣbe sôda*

---

**lizard** (small one) sakkâyi *sehlîye* [dûn] (bigger one) hirdaun' *har-*
**load** (noun) hamli *hamle*
**to l...** (a gun) dakk (to freight) hammal *hammil*
**loaded** (gun) madkûk
**loaf** (bread) rarîf, pl. irrifi *arrife*
**loam** (lute, marl) tîn
**loan** (of money) kard
**lobster** saratân ilbahr'
**lock** (for doors) râl, pl. râlât'; *kâlûn'*
(padlock) kufl *kifl*
**to l...** sakkar *sakk*; (with a padlock) kafal
**l...ed** musak'kar, makfûl
**locksmith** (and blacksmith) hiddâd *haddâd*
**locust** (insect) jarâd *garâd*
**London** londra
**loneliness** wahdâni'yi *wahdânî'ye*, wahdi *wahde*
**lonely** wahdâni
**long** (adj.) tawîl, pl. tuwâl
(of time) zamân tawîl *zemân tawîl*, ktîr *ketîr*
**to be or last l...** tauwal
**this lasts a l... time** haida bîtau'wil *di bitau'wal*
**don't be l...** lâ ttauwil *mâ titauwalsh'*
**for a l... time** (since l...) min zamân *min zemân*
**l... before** kabl min zamân *kabla min zemân*
**as l... (time) as** kaddma *kaddi mâ*, or mâ dâm *mâ dâm*
**longer than** .. (measure) atwal min .., (time) aktar min ..
**I can wait no longer** mâ bikdir istan'zir aktar *mâ ardarsh' astan'na aktar*
**how much longer will it last?** kaddaish' bîtau'wil ba'd? *kaddi ê bitau'wal lissa?*
**to l... for** ishtâk la... *ishtâk li...*
**I l... greatly for you** ana ktîr mushtâk lêk *ana mushtâk lak ketîr*
**longboat** kârib
**longing** (ardent desire) shauk *shôk*, ishtyâk *ishtiyâk*
**look** (glance) nazar, pl. anzâr

---

load the baggage 77,7
l...! 139,10; 146,3
we have l...ed 140,5
lock the house 95,4
long (space) 143,15
too l... 113,14; 130,9
make them l...er 130,8
(time) for how l...? 86,5
for a l... time 37,4
it is l... since .. 48,15
do not keep me waiting l... 96,8
not l... ago 48,16
I shall not stay here l... 80,8
so l... as that? 34,13
longing: the greatest l... 37,9
look at it 51,18
l... at this watch 106,11
l... at your watch 68,20
l... (plur.) for .. 72,8; 147,3.7
l... for a better road 143,11
l... for a woman 89,4
l... if there is .. 139,15
I will go to l... 114,4
to l... after (keep ready) 129,10
(coin) l...s bad 105.10
for whom, what are you l...ing? 47,2.3
I am l...ing for some one 88,3

**look (appearance, aspect)** hai-a, shaufi *shôfe*
**to l... (see)** shâf *shâf* (yeshûf)
**(to appear) expressed by** shaufi *shôfe*, **which means 'the appearance': I look, thou lookest, he looks, etc. ill** shaufti, shauftak **m.,** shauftik **f.,** shaufto, **etc.** marîḍ *shôfti, shôftak* **m.,** *shôftik* **f.,** *shôfto,* **etc.** *'aiyân*
**to l... after (attend to) ..** dâr ilbâl 'ala .. *khalla elbâl 'ala ..*
**to l... for (seek) ..** dauwar 'ala .., fattash *fattish* 'ala ..
**what are you looking for?** 'ala aish bitfat'tish? *bitfat'tish 'ala'ê?*
**to l... like**; see resemble, seem
**l... out!** û'a! ḍahrak!
**looker-on** nâzir, **pl.** nuzzâr
**looking-glass** mirâyi **or** mrâyi *mirâye*
**loom (weaver's)** naul *nôl*, **pl.** inwâl
**lord** saiyid, ṣâḥib
**(God): our Lord** rabbina
**lose** ḍaiya'
**(not win or gain)** khisir
**I lost my purse** ḍaiya't' kîsi **or** ḍaiya't' kîs ilmaṣâri *ḍaiya'tê kîs elfulûs*
**I lost (at a speculation, at play, etc.)** ana khisrân *ana khasrân*
**to l... one's way** ḍâ' (yeḍî') *tâh*
**loss** khasâra *khusâra*
**at a l... (embarrassed)** mutbash'lil
**lost (ring, etc.)** ḍâyi'
**lot (luck, chance)** naṣîb
**(share)** ḳism, **pl.** aḳsâm
**by lot** bilḳur''a
**lottery** yâ naṣîb
**lotus-tree** ḥandaḳûḳ
**loudly** bil'âli
**louse** ḳamli *ḳamle;* **coll.** ḳaml
**love (noun)** maḥab'bi *maḥab'be*, ḥubb
**(amorousness)** 'ishḳ, hawa, ṛarâm
**in l... with** muṛram fî
**to l...** ḥabb
**lover** muḥibb'
**low (not high)** wâṭi
**(mean)** razîl, khabîs
**lower (placed beneath)** tiḥtâni *taḥtâni*
**luck (good l...)** ḥazz **or** ḥaḍḍ
**(chance)** naṣîb
**luggage** 'afsh, awâ'i, labash
**l... examination** teftîsh il'afsh'
**l... office** maḥall' il'afsh'
**l... porter** 'ittâl *shaiyâl*
**l... ticket** waraḳit il'afsh'

---

look: by the l... 120,7
loosen his reins 121,1
lose: mind you l. nothing 139,12
loud: knock l...ly 80,10
love: out of l... to me 54,9
lower the curtain 92,8
lowering (dull) 65,20
lucifer-matches 79,8; 93,8
luck: Oh my l...! 61,5
what l...! 61,9

**lukewarm** fâtir *fâtir*
**lunch (taken at noon)** fuṭûr *ṛada;* see dinner
**to l...** faṭar
**lung** rîa
**lupine** turmus
**lustration** tiṭhîr *taṭhîr*
**lute (cithern)** ʿûd
**machine** mâkina, âle
**mad** majnûn *magnûn*
**(of dogs, etc.)** kilbân *kalbân*
**madam!** yâ mʿallim'ti! *yâ meʿallim'ti!*
**magazine** makhzin *makhzan*, **pl.** mkhâzin *makhâzin*
**maggot (coll.)** dûd
**(a single one)** dûdi *dûde*
**magian** majûs *magûs*
**magistrate (police)** ḳâḍi
**magnanimous** kerîm
**magnet** maṛnaṭîs
**maize** durra
**Majesty** jalâli *galâle*
**H.M. the King of England** jalâlit malik ingiltar'ra *galâlet malek elingelîz*
**H.M. the Queen** jalâlit il-ma'liki *galâlet elma'like*
**major (mil.)** bimbashi
**m... general** amîr *mîr* liwâ
**make (verb)** ʿimil
**m... me ..** aʿmil'li *iʿmil'li ..*
**m... haste!** rauwij! *istaʿʿgil!*
**to m... a fire** shaʿʿal innâr *wallaʿ ennâr*

**male (noun and adj.)** dakar, **pl.** dukûra
**mallow** khibbêzi *khubbêze*
**Malta** mâlṭa
**Maltese** mâlṭi'
**mamaluke** mamlûk, **pl.** mamâlîk
**man** rijjâl *râgil*, **pl.** rjâl *rigâle*
**(man in general, mankind)** insân *insân*, **pl.** nâs *nâs;* ibn âdam, **pl.** bani âdam
**manage (to control)** dâr (yedîr), dabbar
**manager** mudîr
**(of estates)** khauli
**mandate;** see command
**mange** jarab *garab*
**mangy** jirbân *garbân*
**manifest (adj.)** zâhir, wâḍiḥ
**mankind** bâshar
**manners: good m...** edeb
**manure (noun)** zbâli *zibl*
**manuscript** ktâb khaṭṭ *kitâb khaṭṭ*, **pl.** kutub khaṭṭ
**many** ktîr *ketîr*
**m... people** nâs ktîr *nâs ketîr*
**how m...** ḳaddaish' *ḳaddi ê*, kâm *kâm*
**map** kharṭa
**marble (noun)** rukhâm
**march** mushwâr
**to m...** masha
**March** adâr *mârs*
**mare** faras, **pl.** afrâs

---

lunch (verb) 40,1
mail (post) 82,12.13
make me .. 110,2.3.4.5.7
m... haste 101,13 107,7
m... me a nargileh 103,4.11
tell him to m... me .. 149,3
make the bed 92,7; 136,5
you must m... me .. 108,15
what m... are these? 115,7 ff.
man (a person) 122,1; 123,2
many inhabitants 134,7
marble slab 110,5

**mark** (**token, sign**) 'alâmi *'alâme*
**market** sûk, pl. iswâk; bâzâr'
**m...-place** sâha
**Maronite** mârû'ni or mûrâ'ni (**the latter more vulgar**), pl. mwârni *muwârne*
**marriage** ziwâj *zewâg*, jêzi *gawâz*
**married** mutjau'wiz *mitgau'wiz*
**marrow** mukhkh
**vegetable m...** kûsa
**marry** (**trans.**) zauwaj *zauwig*
(**intr.**) tjauwaz *itgau'wiz*
**martyr** shahîd, pl. shuhada
**Mary** maryam
**masher** (**dandy**) randûr
**mass** (**liturgy**) kaddâs, pl. kadâdîs'
**mast** (**in a ship**) sâri, pl. sawâri
**master** (**also teacher**) m'allim *me'al'lim*
**my m...!** (**inferiors addressing superiors**) yâ m'allmi! *yâ sîdi!*
**mat** (**straw-**) hasîri *hasîre*, pl. husr
**match** (**lucifer**) shihhâta **or** shahhai'ta *kibrît*
**matter: what is the m... with you?** shû bâk? *mâlak?*
**see also nothing**
**mattress** farshi, firâsh *martabe, tarrâhe*
**Maundy-Thursday** khamîs ilrusl' *khamîs elrusl'*, khamîs ilkbîr *khamîs elkebîr*
**may is generally expressed by** kidir '**to be possible,**' **e.g. may one here ..?** byikdir ilwâhid haun ..? *bikdir elwâhid hene ..?* **sometimes by** jâz *gâz* '**to be permitted**'
**where may that be?** wain baddo ykûn? *fên biddo yekûn?*
**May** iyâr' or nûwâr' *mâ'yô*
**mayor** raiyis ilbaladîyi *re'îs elbeledîye*
**Mazagan** iljadîda *elgedîda*
**meadow** marj *merg*, pl. mrûj *murûg*
**meal** (**repast**) rada, [akli *akle*]

---

mean (central) wastâni *wus-ṭâni*
(vile) razîl, pl. arâzîl'
to m... (imagine) zann
(to signify) generally expressed by the noun 'meaning,' e.g. what does that m...? shû ma'nâh or shû ma'nâto? *ma'nâh ê?*
meaning ma'na, pl. ma'âni
meanness rizâli *rezâle*
means (expedient) wâsṭa, pl. wasâyiṭ *wasâ=iṭ*
(income) mâl, pl. amwâl
by m... of bwâsṭit *biwâsi-ṭat*
by all m... hais kân, bikull' ilihwâl *bikull' elâhwâl*
measles dashîshi *deshîshe*
measure (that which m...s) ḳyâs *ḳiyâs*; see yard, rod
to m... ḳâs (yeḳìs)
meat (coll.) laḥm
(a single lump or piece) laḥmi *laḥme*
a piece of m... shaḳfît laḥm *ḥiṭṭet laḥm*
beef laḥm baḳar
mutton laḥm ṛanam, laḥm ḍâni
pork laḥm khanzîr
veal laḥm 'ijl *laḥmè 'igl*
boiled m... laḥm maslûk
roast m... laḥm miḳli, rôsto
fresh m... laḥm ṭari
fat m... laḥm midhin

Mecca mekki *mekke*, frequently with the addition ilmukar'rami *elmukar'rame* 'the honored'
M... and Medinailḥaramain *elḥaramên* ('the two forbidden or sacred ones')
M... pilgrim ḥajj
mechanic(ian) makinistî
Medical Department dâyrit ittibb' *diwân' eṭṭibbiya*
medicine (science) ṭibb
(physic) dawa, pl. idwyi *adwiye*
Medina ilmdîni *elmedîne*, frequently with the addition ilmunau'wara *elmunau'wara* 'the enlightened'

Mediterranean; see sea
medlar, -tree za'rûr
meek laṭîf [ḳâbil
meet (verb) lâḳa, ilta'ḳa
(each other) talâḳa *itḳâbil*
to go to m... (solemnly) istaḳ'bal
to be met with (exist) wijid *wigid* (yûjad *yûgad*), inwa'jad *itwa'gad*
meeting (assembly) majlis *meglis*, pl. mjâlis *megâlis*
(solemn reception) istiḳbâl
melody laḥn, pl. alḥân
melon (water-) baṭṭîkh aḥmar
(musk-) baṭṭîkh aṣfar *shamâme*

**melt** dâb (yedûb)
**member** ʿaḍu, **pl.** aʿḍa
**Memlook** memlûk, **pl.** memâlîk'
**memory** ḥâfiza
**Memphis: the ruins of M... are generally named after the village of** sakkâra, **which is not far off**
**menace** tihdîd
**to m...** haddad, khauwaf
**mention** zikr
**to m...** zakar, jâb sîrit *gâb sîret*
**merchandise** baḍâʿa *buḍâʿa*
**merchant** tâjir *tâgir*, **pl.** tujjâr *tuggâr*
**merciful: the M... (God)** irraḥmân *erraḥmân*
**mercury (quicksilver)** zaibaḳ *zêbaḳ*
**mercy** raḥmi *raḥme*
**to ask for m...** istar'ḥam
**merriment** surûr, faraḥ
**merry** farḥân
**messenger** raṣûl, barîd
**metal** maʿdin, **pl.** maʿâdin
**metre** mitr *metr*
**midday** ḍuhr
**middle (noun)** wasṭ *wusṭ*
**(adj.)** wasṭâni *wusṭâni*
**in the m...** fî wasṭ *fî wusṭ*
**midnight** nuṣṣ lail *nuṣṣ ellêl*
**midwife** dâyi *dâye* **or** *ḳable*
**mild** laṭîf, laiyin

**mile** mîl, **pl.** amyâl
**milk** ḥalîb *leben*
**curdled, sour m...** laban *leben ḥâmiḍ*
**to m...** ḥalab
**mill** ṭâḥûn' **fem., pl.** ṭawâḥîn'
**hand-m..., quern** jârûsh' *raḥâye*
**press-m... (for oil, etc.)** maʿṣara
**millet** dukhn, dura baiḍa *durra bêḍa*
**milliner** bayyâʿat lawâzim ilkhîyâ'ṭe *tâger adawât khaiyâṭa*
**million** milyûn, **pl.** mlâyîn' *melâyîn'*
**minaret** mâdni *mâdne*, **pl.** meâdin
**m...-warder (who chants the call to prayers)** mu-ez'zin *mu-ed'din*
**mind (noun)** ʿaḳl
**never m... (it does not matter)** lâ ba-s, mâ bîsâ'yil *mâ yiḍur'rish*
**m... your right! (in the streets of Cairo)** *guar'da! ôâ! yemînak!* **your left!** *shemâlak!*
**mine (pit)** laram
**(pron.);** **see p. 16, line 15**
**minister (of the State)** wazîr *nâzir*

---

melt: the snow is m...ing 65,19
mend the socks 90,8
mention: don't m... it 58,1
not worth m...ing 57,9
mephitis 147,5
mere water 125,13
miasma 147,5
midday-rest 145,4
middle: in the m... 110,8; 145,3
in its m... 142,11
milk: coffee with m... 81,1
mind (take care) 51,24; 80,11
m... (look out) 146,2
m... not to .. 100,9

**Ministry** wazâra
**M... of Finance** nazâret ilmâlî'ye *wazâret elmâlî'ya*
**M... of the Interior** nazâret iddâkhilî'ye *wazâret eddâkhlî'ya*
**M... of Justice** nazâret il-ʿadlîye *wazâret elḥakkânî'ya*
**M... of Public Instruction** nazâretilmaʿârefilʿumûmî'ye *wazâret elmaʿâref*
**M... of Public Works** nazâret innâfʿa *wazâret elishrâl*
**minute** daḳîḳa, **pl.** daḳâyiḳ *daḳâ=iḳ*
**miracle** ʿajîbi *ʿagîbe*
**misfortune** muṣîbi *muṣîbe*
**Miss**; see note to 'bêk'
**miss (to lose, lack)** faḳad
**missing (wanting)** nâḳiṣ
**one of the trunks, a package of my luggage, is m...** nâḳiṣ wâḥid mniṣṣanâdîḳ' *min eṣṣanâdîḳ'*, ḳiṭʿa min ʿafshi
**missionary** mubash'shir
**mistake** ṛalaṭ, ṛalṭa
**to make a m... in** ṛiliṭ fî
**did you not make a m...?** manak ṛilṭân? *mantish ṛalṭân?*
**you made a m...** ṛliṭṭ *ṛiliṭṭ'*, akhṭît
**excuse me, it was my m...** lâ twâkhid'ni, kân ṛalaṭ minni *mâ ti=âkhiznîsh'*, *kân ṛalaṭ minni*
**you are mistaken** intṛilṭân *inte ṛa'ṭân*
**by m...** bilṛa'laṭ
**I mistook my way** ḍiʿt ʿan iṭṭarîḳ *ḍiʿt ʿan eṭṭarîḳ*, **or** *tuht*
**Mister N. N. (of Christians)** ilkhawâja .. *elkhawâga* ..
**(of Mohammedans)** issai'yid .. *essai'yid* ..
**mistress** mʿallmi *meʿal'lime*
**Mrs. N. N.** issitt' .. *essitt'* ..; cf. note to 'bêk'
**(love)** maḥbûbe
**mistrust (noun)** tuhmi *tuhme*
**mix (trans.)** khalaṭ
**mixed** makhlûṭ
**Mixed Tribunal** *maḥkame mukhta'liṭe* [mutwas'siṭ]
**moderate (adj.)** muʿta'dil,
**modest (bashful)** mustaḥi
**Mohammedan** muslim, islâmi *islâmi*
**mole (the quadruped, coll.)** khuld; **(a single one)** khuldi *khulde* [*shâme*]
**(upon the skin)** shâmi
**moment** daḳîḳa, laḥza
**monastery** dair *dêr*, **pl.** idyuri **or** dyûra *diyûr*; see dervish

**Monday** yaum ittnain' *yôm eletnên* **or** *letnên*
**money** maṣâri, fulûs **or** flûs, ʿimli *ʿumle*; **see also** pp. 104 to 166
**silver** faḍḍa
**copper** nuḥâs *naḥâs*
**gold** dahab (**or, Syr. only**: diheb)
**ready m..., cash** naḳdîyi *naḳdîye*
**small m..., change** firâṭa, ḳiṭaʿ
**is this piece good?** halḳiṭʿa ṣaḥîḥa? *elḳiṭʿa di ṣaḥîḥe?*
**don't they take it here?** mâ byiḳbaḍûha haidi haun? *mâ yakhdûsh di hene?*
**can you give me change?** btiḳdir tiṣruf'li? *betiḳ'dar tiṣruf'li?* **or, when the difference is to be returned**: btiḳdir tkammil'li? *betiḳ'dar tikammil'li?*
**moneychanger** ṣirrâf *ṣarrâf*, banker
**moneylender** musal'lef flûs *musal'lef darâhem*
**monk** râhib, **pl.** ruhbân *ruhbân*
**monkey** ḳird, **pl.** ḳurûd; saʿdân **or** nisnâs *nisnâs*
**monster** masîkh
**month** shahr, **pl.** ishhur **or** shhûr; **see pp. 66, 67**
**the first ten days** awâyil, **the second ten days** awâsiṭ, **the last ten days** [awâkhir]
**monthly** shahri
**moon** ḳamar
**full m...** badr
**new m..., crescent** hilâl
**eclipse of the m...** khusûf ilḳa'mar *khusûf elḳa'mar*
**Moor (also slave, negro)** ʿabd, **pl.** ʿabîd
**(Magrebian = western)** maṛribi, **pl.** *mṛârbi*
**Moorish** marâkischî'yi, marâk'shî
**more than ..** aktar min ..
**(added, something else)** kamân *kemân*
**the m... .. the m... ..** kullma .. kullma, ḳaddma .. ḳaddma [*marra*]
**once m...** tâni marra *tâni*
**morning** ṣubḥ, ṣabâḥ
**good m...**; see p. 32
**in the m...** ʿaṣṣubḥ', ʿala bukra
**this m...** ilyaum' ʿala bukra *ennahar'di eṣṣubḥ'*
**to-morrow m...** bukra ʿala bukra *eṣṣubḥ'*
**Morocco** ilmaṛ'reb ilaḳ'ṣa
**(town)** marâkîsh' *marâkesh*
**morocco leather** sakhtiyân

---

**mortar** (stone basin) jurn *gurn*
(iron basin) hiwân *hawân*
**mortgage** rahn
to m... rahan
**mosque** jâmiʿ *gâmiʿ*, pl. jawâmiʿ *gawâmiʿ*
(a small one) masjid *masgid*, pl. msâjid *mesâgid*
**mosquitoes** (coll.) nâmûs'
m...-net nâmûsî'yi
**most** aktar
m... men aktar innâs *aktar ennâs*
**mostly** bilaṛ'lab, ṛâliban
**mother** umm, pl. ummhât *ummahât*; wâldi *wâlide*
m...-in-law ḥamât
m...-of-pearl ṣadaf, ṣafad
**motor** (moving power) ḳûwe muḥar'rike
m...-car ʿaraba bukhârî'ya *ôtômôbîl*
-cycle darrâja bukhârî'ya *darrâget bukhâr*
**mould** (matrix) ḳâlib, pl. ḳwâlib *kawâlib*
**Mount Lebanon** jabal libnân *gebel libnân*
**Mount Sion** jabal ṣahyûn *gebel ṣahyûn*
**mount** (to ascend) ṭiliʿ
(to get on a horse) rikib
(to paste) laṣaḳ
**mountain** jabal *gebel*, pl. jibâl *gibâl*
**mourning** (grief and dress) ḥidâd *ḥidâd*
m...-woman niddâbi *neddâbe*
**mouse** fâra *sîsî*, pl. firân' *sîsiyât*; see also jerboa
**moustache** shwârib *shawârib* or *shenab*
**mouth** tumm or timm *fumm* or *ḥanak*
(of animals) bûz
m...piece of a pipe bizz *fumm*
**move** (trans.) ḥarrak
(intr.) tḥarrak *itḥar'rak*
(out of a house) naḳal *ʿazal*
**mow** (verb) ḥaṣad
**much** ktîr *ketîr*; see how m...
too m... ktîr *ketîr*, ziyâdi *ziyâde*
very m... ktîr ktîr *ketîr khâliṣ*, ktîr jiddan *ketîr giddan*
m... more aktar biktîr *aktar biketîr*
far too m... ziyâdi biktîr *ziyâde biketîr*
m... money maṣâri ktîr *fulûs ketîr*
as m... as ḳaddma *ḳaddima*
**mud** tîn, waḥl
**muezzin**; see minaret-warder
**mulberry-tree** (coll.) tût
(a single one) shajrit ittût *shagarat ettût*, tûti *tûte*

---

mosquito-curtain 92,8
mother: your m... 35,18
move into a house 84,12
Mr. N. N. (European) 82,6
much: that is m... 48,22
that is far too m... 71,6
there is too m... water 106,13
(much) do not cut off m... 101,2
do not use m... .. 101,10
you are making it too m. 122,6
mud in the streets 66,7
quite full of mud 90,4
cannot walk for mud 146,13
muddy (miry) 143,8

**mule** (coll.) baṛl
(**a single one**) baṛli *baṛle* **pl.** ibṛâl
**multiply** (**arithm.**) ḍarab
**municipality** baladîyi *be-ledîye*
**murder** ḳatl
**to m...** ḳatal
**m...ed** ḳatîl
**a traveller has been m...ed** wâḥid mnissûwâḥ' ḳitil **or** wâḥid mnissûwâḥ' râḥ ḳatîl *wâḥid min essûwâḥ' râḥ ḳatîl*
**m...er** ḳâtil
**muscle** ʿaḍali *ʿaḍale*
**museum** dâr ittu'ḥaf *antîḳ-khâ'na*
**mushroom** fuṭr
**music** mûsî'ḳa
**m...-hall** ḳâʿet mûsî'ḳa
**musician** mûsî'ḳaji *mûzi-ḳâ'ti*
**musk** misk; **a piece** miske
**muslin** shesh *shâsh*
**must** (**aux. verb**) **generally rendered by** lâzim *lâzim* **'necessary' with following aorist, or by** wâjib ʿala .. *wâgib ʿala* .. **'it is duty for ..' with following in and aorist**
**I m... start now** lâzim sâfir hallaḳ *lâzim asâfir dil-waḳt'*
**you m... do that, it is your duty** wâjib ʿalaik' innak taʿmil haida *wâgib ʿalêk tiʿmil di*
**you m... not do that** mâ lâzim taʿmil haik *mush lâzim tiʿmil kide*
**mustard** khardal *mustarda*
**mutilate** ʿawwar
**m...d** muʿaw'war
**mutton** laḥm ṛanam, laḥm ḍâni
**muzzle** (**of a gun**) tumm *fumm*
**myrrh** murr
**myrtle** rîḥân'
**myself** ana nafsi *ana nefsi*
**mystic** ṣûfi
**nail** mismâr *musmâr*, **pl.** msâmîr' *mesâmîr'*
(**finger n...**) ḍifr *ḍufr*, **pl.** aḍâfîr' *ḍawâfir*
**to n...** masmar
**naked** ʿiryân *ʿaryân*, mu-zal'laṭ, bizzalṭ'

---

**name** ism, pl. asmâ or asâmi *asámi*

  **your honored n...?** ilism' ilkarîm? *elism' elkerîm?*

  **in the n...** of God bismillâhi

  **to n...** samma

**namely** ya'ni

**naphtha** naft

**narcissus** narjis *nargis*

**narrow** (adj.) ḍaiyik

**nasty** (dirty) wakhim (infamous) ḳabîḥ

**native country** blâd *bilâd*, waṭan

  **N... Court** maḥkame ahlíye

**natural** (adj.) ṭabî'i

**nature** ṭabî'a

  **to ease n...;** see necessary

**naught** (nothing) mâ shî *mush hâge*

  **(zero)** ṣifr

**navel** surra, zabr, zubb

**Nazareen** nâṣiri

**Nazareth** innâṣira *ennâṣira*

**near** ḳarîb

  **n... ..** jamb min .. *gambê min ..*

**nearer than ..** aḳrab min ..

**nearly** ḳarîb *ḳurai'yib*

**neat** (dainty) zarîf, nâzik'

**necessary** lâzim *lâzim*

  **to do the n...** (answer nature's call) ḳaḍa ḥâji *ḳaḍa ḥâge;* see also water

**necessity** luzûm

**neck** 'unḳ, raḳbi *raḳaba*, nuḳra

**neckerchief: the silk head-kerchiefs** (q.v.) **and hand-kerchiefs** (q.v.) **serve for same**

**necklace** 'iḳd *'uḳd,* ṭauḳ ṭôḳ   ['âze

**need** (narrow means) 'âzi

  **to n...** 'az, i'tâz, iḥtâj iḥtâg

**needle** ibri *ibre,* pl. ibar

  **packing-n...** msalli *mesal'le* or *mêbar*

  **Cleopatra's n...** msallit klîubat'ra *mesal'let keli-ubat'ra*   [fal

**negligent** mutraf fil *muṛaṛ*-ʃ

**negotiate** dabbar

**negro** 'abd

**negress** 'abdi *'abde*

---

**neigh** (verb) ṣahal, ḥamḥam
**neighbor** jâr *gâr*, pl. jîrân' *gîrân'*
**n...hood** (environs) ḍawâḥî
**neither** .. **nor** lâ .. ulâ *lâ .. walâ*
**n... one nor the other** (n... **this nor that**) lâ haida ulâ haida *lâ di walâ di*
**n... so .. nor so** .. lâ haik .. ulâ haik *lâ kide .. walâ kide*
**nephew** (son of one's brother) ibn ilakh' *ibn elakh'*
(son of one's sister) ibn ilukht' *ibn elukht'*
**nerves** a'ṣâb
**nest** 'ishsh, wikr
**net** (noun) shabaki *shabake*
**never** abadan *ebeden*
**new** jdîd *gedîd*, pl. jdâd *gudâd* or judud *gudud*
**news** khabar jdîd *khabar gedîd*, pl. akhbâr jdîdi *akhbâr gedîde*
**what is the n...?** shû fî jdîd? *ê fîh gedîd?*
**New Year** râs issi'ni *râs esse'ne*; wishes, see p. 44
**nice** kwaiyis *kuwai'yis*, zarîf
**niece** (daughter of one's brother) bint ilakh' *bint elakh'*
(daughter of one's sister) bint ilukht' *bint elukht'*
**nigger**; see negro
**night** lail *lêl*, laili *lêle*, pl. lyâli *leyâlî*
**in the n..., at n...-time** billail' *billêl* [ellêle
**to-n...** illai'li or hallai'li
**it has become n...** ṣâr lail *ṣâr lêl*
**to pass the n...** nizil, bât (ybât) *bât* (*yebât*)
**can one pass the n... here?** mnikdir nbât haun? *nikdar nebât hene?* see pp. 131 to 140
**nightingale** bulbul
**Nile** baḥr innîl *baḥr ennîl, elbaḥr'*
**White N...** *baḥr elab'yaḍ*
**Blue N...** *baḥr elaz'rak*
**N... boat** *dahabîye*
**the N... valley** wâdi innîl *wâdi ennîl*
**nilometer** *mikyâs*
**nine** tis'a
**nine hundred** tis'mîyi *tus'emîye* [tâshen
**nineteen** tisaṭa'sh' *tis'a-*
**ninety** tis'în
**ninth** tâsi' *tâsi'*, fem. tâs'a *tas'e*
**nitre**; see saltpetre

---

**no** lâ
**have you no ..?** mâfi ʿindak *mâfîsh' ʿandak ..?*
**no one** mâ ḥada *mâ ḥaddish*
**no (without) doubt** bala shakk
**no ceremony** min dûn tiklîf
**nobility** sharaf
**noble** sharîf
**noise** ṣaut *ṣôt*, ṛaushi *ṛôshe*
**noiselessly** bilwâṭi
**nominate** ʿaiyan *ʿaiyin*
**to be n...d** tʿaiyan *itʿai'yin*, tsamma *itsam'ma*
**none** mâ ḥada *mâ ḥaddish*
**nonsense** kalâm fâreṛ, hals
**to speak n...** takal'lam bala maʿna
**nor I** ulâ ana *welâ ana*
**north** shmâl *shemâl*
**northern** shmâli *shemâli*
**north wind** hawa shmâli or hawa smâwi *hawa baḥri*
**nose** minkhâr, pl. manâkhîr'
**nosegay** tishkîli *ṣuḥbe*
**nose-ring (of a camel)** khizâm
**not** mâ, mush
**(with a prohibition)** lâ *mâ-sh*
**in order not to (with inf.)** tâ mâ (with aorist)
**is there not any one here who could get (procure) me ..?** mâfi haun ulâ wâḥid byiḳdir ydabbir'li ..? *mâfîsh' hene walâ wâḥid yeshûfli ..?*
**not at all** abadan *ebeden*, ḳaṭʿan
**notable (distinguished)** wajîh *ʿumde*
**note-paper** waraḳ mkâtîb' *waraḳ mekâtîb'*
**nothing** mâ shî or mâshi *mush ḥâge*
**for n...** bilâsh *balâsh*
**as good as n...** ka-in'no mâshi *ke-in'no mush ḥâge*
**that is n... (it does not matter)** mâ hû shî *mush ḥâge*, mâ bîsâ'yil *mâ ʿalêsh*
**notify**; see inform

---

**notwithstanding** faḍlan 'an
**November** tishrîn ittâni *nôvem'ber*
**now** halwakt' or hallak or halkait' or issa *dilwakt'*
**now then (come on, go on)!** yalla!
**now and then** iḥyân, ba'ḍ ilûkât' *ba'ḍ elaukât*
**now one way, now another** sâ'a haik sâ'a haik *sâ'a kide sâ'a kide*
**Nubia, etc.**; see Barbary
**number** 'adad *'aded*, numro
**to n...** 'add
**nun** râhibi *râhibe*, **pl.** râhbât' *rahbât*
**nurse (who tends a child)** dâ'dâ
**sick-n...** khaddâmi
**to n... (attend)** khadam
**(to suckle)** raḍa'
**nut (coll.)** jauz *gôz*
**(a single one)** jauzi *gôze*
**nutmeg** jauzit iṭṭîb *gôz eṭṭîb*
**O! Oh!** yâ!
**oar** mikdâf, **pl.** maḳâdîf'
**oasis** wâḥ
**oath** yamîn *yemîn*; see curse
**to take the o...** ḥalaf yamîn *ḥilif yemîn*
**by God** wallâh *wallâhi*
**by your life** wiḥyâtak *waḥyâtak*
**by your eyes** wiḥyât 'aintênak *waḥyât 'ênêk'*
**oats**: **grow wild only in Syria, in Egypt not at all**
**obedience** ṭâ'a
**obedient** muṭî'
**obelisk** msalli *mesal'le*
**obey** ṭâwa'
**objection**: **there is no o...** mâ fîsh mâni'
**oblige (to compel)** ṛaṣab
**(to gratify)** ṣaiyar mamnûn *ṣaiyar memnûn*
**much o...d** mamnûn ktîr *memnûn ketîr*
**o...d (compelled)** malzûm, majbûr *magbûr*
**obscene** fâḥish, dinis
**observatory** dâr irra'ṣad *raṣadkhâna*
**observe (to remark)** lâḥaz *lâḥiz*
**obstacle** mâni' *mâni'*, **pl.** [*mawâni'*]
**obstinacy** 'inâd *'inâd*
**obstinate** mu'ânid, 'anîd
**obstruct** sadd (yesudd')
**obtain** nâl (ynîl) *nâl (yenîl)*, ḥaṣal 'ala *itḥaṣ'ṣal 'ala*, ḥaṣṣal
**occasion (opportunity)** furṣa, **pl.** furaṣ
**(need, reason)** sabab, **pl.** isbâb *asbâb*
**occident** maṛrib
**occur (to happen)** ṣâr (yeṣîr) *gara*
**ocean** baḥr ilmuḥîṭ
**October** tishrîn ilau'wal *oktôber*

---

**nowadays** 123,1
**obey**: you must o... me 95,7
**objects** (Oriental) 114,4
**obliged** 40,2.8
(obliged) I am o... to you 49,7
I shall be o... to you 54,4
we are o... for your .. 37,10
you will greatly oblige me 53,1

**odd: an odd (single) one** fard
**at the end of a large number, instead of the units, when the latter are of little importance or when they cannot at once be stated:** uksûr or wiksûr *wakusûr*, **e.g. 250 odd** mîtain' ukhamsîn wiksûr *mîtên' wakhamsîn wakusûr*
**odor: unpleasant o...** rîḥa keriha
**of** min
**off, far off** ba'îd
**off!** rûḥ!
**offence (insult)** ihâni *ahâne*; **see also crime**
**to offend** hân *hân*
**offer (price bidden)** dafa'
**to o...** kaddam *kaddim*
**(to bid for)** dafa' fî
**what can I o... you?** shû bikdir kaddim'lak? *akaddim'lak ê?*
**I o... you .. for it** bidfa''lak fîh .. *badfa''lak fîh ..*
**office (charge, function)** wazîfi *wazîfe*, **pl.** wazâyif *wazâ:if*; ma:mûrî'yi *me:mûrî'ye*
**(place of business)** maktab *mekteb*
**officer** zâbiṭ, **pl.** zubbâṭ
**official (employee)** mâmûr *ma:mûr*
**often** ktîr *ketîr*, amrâr ktîri *imrâr ketîre*
**Oh!** yâ!
**Oh that ..!** yâ rait ..! *yâ rêt ..!*
**oil (sweet)** zait *zêt*; **see petrol, sesame oil**
**oil-cloth** musham'ma' (**or, Syr. only:** mshamma')
**ointment** marham, **pl.** marâhim; duhûn
**old (not young)** ikhtyâr, **fem.** ikhtyâra, **pl.** ikhtyârî'yi *ikhtiyârî'ye*; kbîr *kebîr*
**(not new)** kadîm, **pl.** kudm
**(ancient)** 'atîk, **pl.** 'itik
**(not fresh)** bâyit *bâ:it*
**old man** shaikh *shêkh*
**old woman, old lady** 'ajûz *'agûz*, **pl.** 'ajâyiz *'agâ:iz*
**old age** shaikhûkha *shêkhû'kha*
**how old are you?** kaddaish' 'umrak? *ê 'umrak?* ibn kam sini int? *ibnê kâm sene inte?*
**oleander** difl
**olive, -tree** zaitûni *zêtû'ne*, **coll.** zaitûn *zêtûn'*
**Mt. of Olives (at Jerusalem)** jabal iṭṭûr *gebel eṭṭûr*

---

of 500 francs each 104,10
of 20 words 82,15
of wool 114,4
fear of thieves 127,7
I am dying of thirst 102,4
off the mule 144,11
clear off! 51,9
offended: I am o. with you 49,11
offer a chair 37,13
I o... it to you 54,12
I do not know what to o... 54,7
oil: put in more oil 98,7
oil-colors 129,4
old swords 117,1

**omnibus** omnibus
**on** fauḳ *fôḳ*, ʿala ; **the latter is contracted with the following article, e.g.** ʿalkur'si **on the chair, for** ʿala ilkur'si *ʿala elkur'si*
**once** marra **or** *nôbe*
**(one single time)** marra wâḥdi *marra waḥde*
**(formerly)** filḳadîm, filmâḍi
**all at o... (suddenly)** bilmar'ra ; **(at one time, at one draught, etc.)** fard marra
**o... more ; see more**
**one** wâḥid, **fem.** wâḥdi *wâḥde*
**one after the other** wara baʿḍhon *wara baʿḍûhum*
**one another : we, you, they .. one another** baʿḍina, baʿḍkon *baʿḍûkum*, baʿḍhon *baʿḍûhum*
**one by one** wâḥidan wâḥidan, fardan fardan
**one-eyed** aʿwar, **fem.** ʿaura, **pl.** ʿûr
**onion (coll.)** baṣal
**(a single one)** baṣli *baṣale*
**only (adj. = single)** wâḥid
**(adv. = but)** faḳaṭ', **lâkin** *lâkin*
**open (adj.)** maftûḥ
**in the o... land** filbarrîyi *filkha'le*
**to o...** fataḥ ; **(intr., to be opened)** infa'taḥ *itfa'taḥ*
**o... to me !** iftaḥ'li !
**speak openly ! see candid**
**operations of an army** ḥarakât ilʿas'ker
**ophthalmia (Egyptian)** ramad
**opinion** zunn *zann*, fikr
**what is your o... ?** shû fikrak ? *fikrak ê?* mâ ḳaulak ? **or** shû ḳaulak ? *ḳôlak ê ?* shû râyak ? *râyak ê ?*
**opium** afyûn
**o... smoker** ḥashshâsh
**opponent** khaṣm, **pl.** ikhṣâm
**oppose** khâlaf
**opposite** ḳibâl
**oppression (injustice)** zulm
**or** yâ, yimma, willa *wala*
**orange** burdḳâni *bortuḳâne*; **coll.** burdḳân *bortuḳân*
**orchestra** jamâʿat mûsî'ḳa *gamâʿat mûsî'ḳa*

---

**order (arrangement, trimness)** tirtîb *tartîb*
(**command**) amr, **pl.** awâmir *awâmir* [*tauṣîye*
(**an o... for goods**) tûṣyi
(**decoration**) nîshân' *nîshân'*, **pl.** niyâshîn' *niyâshîn'* [*rahbâne*
(**a religious one**) rahbani
**to o...** (**to command**) amar
(**to o... goods**) waṣṣa; **o... me ..** waṣṣîli ..
(**to put in o...**) rattab *rattib*
**in o... that** liajl' *lagl*, min shân ta *min shân* **or** *'ala shân*, ḥatta, tâ
**ordinance** (**rule**) sharî'a *sunna* [yâdi
**ordinary** (**usual**) 'âdi, i'ti-
**organ** (**mus. instr.**) urgun
**orient** blâd ishshark' *bilâd eshshark'*
**o...al** sharki
**origin, o...al** (**noun**) aṣl
**o...al** (**adj.**) aṣli
**o...ally** mnilaṣl' *min elaṣl'*
**orphan** yatîm, **pl.** îtâm'
**ostrich** na'âmi *na'âme*
**-egg** baiḍit na'âm *bêḍat na'âm*
**-feather** rîshit na'âm *rîshet na'âm*
**other** âkhar, **fem.** ukhra **pl.** ukhar
**the o... day** haidâk ilyaum' *ennahâr dok-hâ*
**otherwise** willa
**ought: he o... to be here** kân lâzim inno ykûn haun *kân lâzim yekûn hene*; **see also must**
**ounce** *wukîye* = **37.08 gr.; (1 oz. troy = 31.10 gr., av. = 28.34 gr.)**
**the Syrian** wukîyi = **213 gr.**
**the Egyptian** *wuḳîye* = **12** *darâhim*, **the Syrian = 66⅔; cf. dram**
**out** (**where?**) barra
(**whither?**) labar'ra *barra*
**the fire is out; see fire, burn**
**outer** (**external**) barrâni
**outside** khârij *khârig*
**from o...** min barra
**oven** furn
**over** fauk *fôk*, fauk min *fôk min*, 'ala [*elbâb*
**o... the door** fauk ilbâb *fôk*
**put it o... it** ḥuṭṭo fauk minno *ḥuṭṭo fôk minno*

---

order: in o... (arranged) 89,5
in o... to arrive 131,10
out of o... (spoiled) 106,16; (stomach) 148,7
ordinary chairs 110,6
oriental objects 114,4
other people 72,1
every o... day 68,15
the o... half 104,12
bring o...s 79,6; 99,12
and others (etc.) 114,4
another piece of .. 125,8
otherwise 84,1; 141,2
our 38,11; 126,9; 132,10 note
out of the house 95,1
out of the bag 137,9
out of the pocket 137,12
bring (plur.) out .. 74,4
go out 51,4
take .. out 147,11
take this .. out 95,6
over: pass o... the bridge 144.2
overclouded 64,17
overlooking 79,1

**over (more than) five hours** aktar min khams sâ'ât' *aktar min khamas sâ'ât'*
**o... hither (on this side)** lahaşşaub' *linnaḥyâ di*
**(remaining)** bâķi, fâḍil
**to be o... (remain)** biķi, fiḍil
**to be o... (be complete, have finished)** tamm
**overcome (to vanquish)** ŗalab
**overseer**; see superintendent
**overtake (also to follow)** liḥiķ
**owe: how much do I owe you (paraphrased: how much to you on me or with me)?** ķaddaish' ilak 'alai'yi or 'indi? *kâm lak 'alêye* or *'andi?*
**in a similar manner: you still owe me something** ba'do ili ma'ak (or 'indak) shî *lissa lîye mi'âk* (or *'andak*) *shê*
**owl** bûmi *bûme*, **coll.** bûm
**owner** mâlik, şâḥib
**ox** taur *tôr*, **pl.** tîrân
**pace (manner of walking)** mashi, mashyi
**pack (verb)** ḥazam, ḍabb *şarr*
**p... up the things!** ḍabb ilawâ'i *şurr elḥawâ-ig*
**pack-saddle** jlâl *gilâl*
**padlock (noun)** ķufl *ķifl*
**page (of a book)** wajh *şaḥîfa*
**pail** saṭl
**pain** waja' *waga'*
**to have, be in, p...** twajja' *itwag'ga'*
**to p...** wiji' *wigi'*
**painful** alîm, bîwaj'ji' *bi-wag'gi'*
**paint (also for the face)** duhûn
**(rouge)** ḥamra
**(for the eyes)** kuḥl
**to p...** şauwar; **(one's face)** dahan
**painter** muşau'wir *meşau-warâti*
**(house-decorator)** dihhân *naķķâsh*
**painting (picture)** şûra, **pl.** şuwar
**pair (noun)** jauz *gôz*
**palate** ḥulķûm
**Palestine** filisṭîn
**palm (date-tree)** nakhli *nakhle*, **coll.** nakhl
**palma-christi** kharwa'; see castor-oil
**palsy** fâlûj' *fâlûg'*
**pane (of glass)** ķizâz *ķizâz*
**pants (under-breeches)** lbâs *libâs*, shintyân *shintyân*
**paper** waraķ
**sheet of p...** waraķa, **pl.** ûrâķ' *aurâķ*
**Paradise** janni *ganne*
**paraffin** kâz *ŗâz* or *gâz*

---

**paralysed** mukar'sah *mekas'sah*, maflûj *maflûg*
**paralysis** fâlûj' *fâlûg'*
**parasite (also intruder)** ṭufai'li *ṭufêli*
**parcel** rizmi *ruzme*
**p... post** ṭrûdet busṭa *ṭurûd busṭa*
**parchment** rakk
**pardon (noun)** 'afu
**to ask p...** istar'far
**to p...; see forgive**
**parents** ilwâldain' *elwâlidên'*
**Paris** bârîz' [*barân*
**parrot** babarâ, babrâl *ba-*
**parsee; see worshipper of fire**
**parsley** bakdûnis
**part (a share)** kism, **pl.** aksâm; **see also side**
**to p... (trans.); see divide, separate**
**(intr. = to be separated)** tafar'rak
**partial (biassed)** yitrar'raḍ
**partisan (follower)** tâbi', **pl.** taba'a [shuraka
**partner (comm.)** sharîk, **pl.**
**p...ship** shirka *mushâraka*
**partridge** ḥajal *ḥagal*
**party (company, troop)** jamâ'a *gemâ'a*
**(partisans)** ḥizb, **pl.** iḥzâb *aḥzâb*
**(soirée)** sahra
**pasha** bâsha; **see note to 'bêk'**
**pass (mountain)** borâz
**(passport)** tizkiri **or** tizkri *tezkire*, bazabort'; **see p. 75**
**to p... (go or walk past)** marak min **or** min 'ind *min 'and*; **fât** *fât*
**(come to p...)** ḥaṣal
**(p... through, cross)** kaṭa'
**(hand, transfer); see hand**
**(p... the night); see night**
**passage (way)** zârûb', **pl.** zawârîb'; *zukâk*
**passenger** râkib, **pl.** rukkâb *rukkâb*
**passion (affection, love)** hawa
**(desire)** shahwa, **pl.** shahawât
**Passion Week** jum'it ilḥazîni *gum'at elḥazîne* = **the sorrowful week**
**past (gone by)** mâḍi
**paste** 'ajîn *'agîn*
**to p...** laṣak
**patch** ruk'a, **pl.** ruka'
**to p... (sew)** kaṭṭab
**patched** murak'ka'
**patent (noun)** farmân
**path-sweeper** kannâs iṭṭarîk *kanâs eṭṭarîk*
**patience** ṣabr
**patient (adj.)** ṣabûr
**(a sick person)** marîḍ

**patriarch** baṭrak, pl. baṭârki *baṭârike*

**patrol** ṭauf *ṭôf* [moṣṭra]

**pattern** 'ainiyi *'ainiye,* Paul bûlus

**pavement** blâṭ *balâṭ*

**pay (wages, salary)** ijra *ugra*
  **to pay** dafa'
  **how much have I to pay?**
  kaddaish' lâzim idfa'? *ḳaddê 'âiz minni?* kaddaish' 'alai'yi? *kâm 'aléye?*
  **I want to pay what I owe** baddi idfa' illi 'alai'yi *biddi adfa' elli 'aléye*
  **I have paid** dafa't' ana
  **I shall pay on receipt** bidfa' waḳt ittislîm *adfa' waḳt etteslîm*
  **to whom have I to pay that?** lamîn baddi idfa' haida? *limîn adfa' di?*

**payment** dafa'

**pea** bázel'la *bisil'la*
  **chick (grey) pea** ḥummuṣ
  **roasted chick pea** kaḍâmi *ḥummuṣ megôhar*

**peace** silm, ṣulḥ

**peach (coll.)** durrâk *khôkh*

**peacock** ṭâwûs'

**pear** njâṣ *kummit'ra*
  **prickly p... ; see cactus**

**pearl** lûlu

**peasant** fallâḥ *fellâḥ,* pl. fallâhîn' *fellâhîn'*
  **p...'s wife** fallâḥa *fellâḥa,* pl. fallâhât' *fellâhât'*

**pebble (small stone)** baḥṣa *ḥaṣwa*

**pedestrian** mâshi *mâshi*

**peel** kishr; **to p...** kashshar

**peg (pin, pole)** wated, pl. autâd

**pen: steel-** rîshit ḥadîd *rîshet ḥadîd*
  **reed-** ḳalam, pl. aḳlâm

**penis** ḳaḍîb, pl. ḳuḍbân

**penknife** 'uwaisîyi, mûs *maṭwa*

**pension** ma'âsh

**people (nation, tribe)** sha'b, pl. shu'ûb; ummi *umme* pl. umam
  **(persons in general)** nâs *nâs* [ketîr]
  **many p...** nâs ktir *nâs*

**pepper (noun)** filfil, bahâr

**per cent** bilmîyi *bilmîye*

**perfect (adj.)** kâmil *kâmil*

**performance (theatr.)** tish-khîṣ *tashkhîṣ*

---

**perfume** (noun) ʿiṭr
**perhaps** belki, rubbama
**(in questions)** yâtara *yâ halta'ra*
**peril** khaṭar
**p...ous** mukhaw'wif
**perjurer** shâhid zûr
**perjury** yamîn zûr
**permission** izn, rukhṣa
**with your p...** bi-iz'nak, bil-izn'
**have you received p...?** akhatt' izn?
**to ask p...** ista-'zan *ista-'zin*
**with your p... (if I might venture to say, no offence!)** min ṛair mwâkhidi *min ṛêr mu-âkhaze*
**to permit**; see allow
**Persia** blâd ilʿa'jam *bilâd elʿa'gam*
**Persian (adj. and noun)** ʿajami *ʿagemi*
**(of the language)** farsi
**person** shakhṣ, pl. ashkhâṣ
**your noble (or honored) p...age** zâtkon ilkarîmi *zâtkum elkerîme*; see p. 14, bottom
**p...al** shakhṣi, zâti
**perspiration** ʿaraḳ
**in p... (perspiring)** ʿirḳân *ʿarḳân*
**I am quite in a p...** ana ʿirḳân ktîr *ana ʿarḳân ketîr*
**perspire** ʿiriḳ
**I wish to p... well this night** baddi iʿraḳ mlîḥ hallai'li *biddi aʿraḳ ṭaiyib ellêle di*
**pest**; see plague
**Peter** buṭrus
**petition** (noun) ʿarḍuḥâl
**petrol** batrûl, kâz *ṛâz* or *gâz*
**petticoat** tannûra
**Pharaoh** firʿaun' *farʿôn*
**pharmacy** farmashîyi or ijzâ-î'yi *egzakhâne*
**phial** ḥanjûr *ḥangûr*, pl. ḥanâjîr' *ḥanâgîr'*
**philosopher** failasûf *fêlasûf'*, pl. flâsfi *felâsife*
**philosophy** falsafa
**phlegm** bizâḳ *balṛam*
**photograph** rasm foṭoṛrâf *ṣûra*
**to ph...** rasam bishshams' *ṣawwar*
**ph...er** foṭôṛrafî *muṣawwerâtî*
**phthisis** sill
**physician**; see doctor
**piastre** ḳirsh, pl. ḳurûsh
**pick (to pluck, gather)** ḳaṭaf
**p... out (select)** inta'khab, naḳḳa
**p... up (lift)** ḳâm (yeḳîm)
**p... it up!** ḳimo! *shîlo!*
**pickles** ṭurshe *ṭurshi*
**pickpocket** nashshâl
**picture** ṣûra, pl. ṣuwar

---

perhaps 84,6
p... it is full of .. 107,16
perish (go to ruin) 129,3
permission: with p. 38,13; 42,9
(permission) I ask p... 42,10
petticoats 98,2
piastre: for a p... 76,8
twelve, ten p...s 97,3.4

**piece** shaḳfi *ḥiṭṭe*, **pl.** shiḳaf; ḳaṭ'a, **pl.** ḳiṭa'
**pig** khanzîr
**pigeon** ḥamâmi *ḥamâme*; **coll.** ḥamâm
**pilgrim (of Jerusalem or Mecca), p...age** ḥajj
**p...'s dress** iḥrâm
**place of p...age** mezâr
**pill** ḥabbi *ḥabbe*
**pillar** 'âmûd', **pl.** 'awâmîd'
**pillow** mukhad'di *makhad'de* [*khudêdî'ye*]
**(a small one)** khudaidîyi
**pilot (noun)** ḳilâwuz', dû-man'ji *dûman'gi*
**pin (of wire, etc.)** dabbûsi *dabbûse*; **see also peg**
**pincers** kimmâshi *kammâshe*, malḳaṭ
**pinch (to squeeze)** ḳaraṣ
**pine (tree)** ṣnaubar *ṣanôbar*
**pink (flower)** ḳurun'ful
**pious** taḳi, **pl.** itḳya; mut-dai'yin
**pipe (tube)** ḳasṭar, **pl.** ḳasâ-ṭir; *mâsû're*
**(mus. instr.)** zammâra *zummâra*
**(long Turkish tobacco p...)**[1] ḳaṣabi *ḳaṣabe*, mâsû'ra
**(hookah p...)**[1] argîli or ar-kîli, **pl.** arâkîl'; *shîshe* **pl.** *shîshât'*
**bowl** râs ilarkîli *râs esh-shîshe*
**mouthpiece** bizz *fumm*
**flexible tube** nabrîj *lai*
**pistachio (nut)** fustuḳ
**-tree** shajrit ilfus'tuḳ *shagarat elfus'tuḳ*
**pistol** ṭaban'ja *ṭaban'ga*

---

[1] **The hookah pipe is in the Orient not sold in a complete form. The glass vessel, without exception European make, mostly coming from Bohemian glass-works, is bought at the glass-merchant's** (ḳizâzi); **the metal top with the stem passing into the water and the little bent side stem into which the flexible tube is put, is bought at the hardware-dealer's** (khurda'ji); **the tube, at the tube-merchant's** (nebârî'ji); **and the bowl of burnt clay, at the bowl-seller's** (bîyâ' ruûs arkîli.)**—The long-stemmed 'chibouque', or 'chib,' is in Syria nowadays but rarely used, but it plays an important part in Egypt. Stems of jasmine or rose-wood as well as bowls of burnt clay, and mouthpieces, can be had at the pipe-seller's** (mewâsî'ri **or** bîyâ' mewâsîr')**.—The lower classes in Syria as well as in Egypt smoke out of a** jauze *gôze* **coconut-shell.**

---

piece 118,4; 124,6; 125,6.7
pillow 111,4
-cases 98,8; 111,5
pinch (hurt) 108,11
pins 94,8
pistols 117,6

**pit (hole)** jûra *gûra*
**pitch (of tar)** zift
**pity** shafaka, raḥmi *raḥme*
**to p..., have p... on** riḥim
**what a p...!** ḥarâm! *yâ khasâra!*
**place** maṭraḥ, **pl.** maṭâriḥ; maḥall', **pl.** maḥallât *maḥallât;* mauḍa' *môḍa'*
**(large open p...)** mîdân' *mêdân'*
**(to give p... to)**; see turn aside
**plague (epidemic)** ṭâ'ûn'
**plain (level ground, also adj. =smooth)** sahl **or** sahli *sahle*, **pl.** suhûl
**(clear)** zâhir, ṣâfi
**plait (of hair)** jdîli *gedîle*, **pl.** jdâyil *gedâ-il*
**to p... (hair)** jaddal *gaddil*
**plan (drawing, trace)** rasm
**plane (tool)** fâra *mabra-i*
**(level surface)** sahl
**planet** nijmi sîyâ'ra *nigme saiyâra*
**plane-tree** dilbi *dulbe*
**plank** lauḥa min khashab *lôḥ khashab*
**plant** nabât *nabât*
**to p...** ṛaras
**plaster (cataplasm)** lazka
**(for walls, etc.)** ṭîn
**plate (dish)** ṣaḥn, **pl.** ṣuḥûn
**platform (of wood)** raṣîf (khashab)
**play** la'b *li'b*; **to p...** li'ib
**plea** ḥijji *ḥugge*
**plead (a cause)** ḥâma 'an
**pleasant** makbûl, laṭîf
**please** 'ajab *'agab*
**that p...s me very much** haida bya'jib'ni ktîr *di bi'gib'ni ketîr*
**(in order) to p... you** min shân khâṭrak *'ala shân khâṭrak*
**p... to enter** tfaḍḍal fût *itfaḍ'ḍal khushsh*
**as you p...** 'ala kêfak, 'ala khâṭrak, bkhâṭrak *bi-khâṭrak*
**pleased (glad)** masrûr
**to be p...** insarr', firiḥ, inba'saṭ [*bisirr'*]
**pleasing (gratifying)** bîsirr'
**pleasure** ḥazz
see also amusement
**with the greatest p...** bimazîd issurûr *bimezîd es-surûr*, 'arrâs wil'ain' *'arrâs wal'ên*, 'al'uyûn
**I travel for p...** ana musâfir lashamm' ilha'wa *ana musâfir lishamm' elha'wa*
**what is your p...?** na'am?
see note on p. 45

---

**pledge** rahn
**(earnest, in an agreement)** ra'bûn *'arbûn*
**to p...** rahan
**plenty** kitri *kutr*
**plough** sikki *mihrât*
**to p...** ḥarat, falaḥ
**plum (coll.)** khaukh *berḳûḳ*
**plunder** nahîb
**to p...** nahab, salab
**p.m.** ba'd iḍḍuhr' *ba'd eḍḍuhr'*
**pocket** jaib *gêb*, jaibi *gêbe*
**to put in the p...** ḥaṭṭ bij-jai'bi *ḥaṭṭ biggêbe*
**pocket-handkerchief;** see handkerchief
**pod (husk)** ḳishr
**poem** ḳaṣîdi *ḳaṣîde*, **pl.** ḳa-ṣâyid; shi'r, **pl.** ish'âr
**poet** shâ'ir, **pl.** shu'ara
**poetry** shi'r
**point (dot)** nuḳṭa, **pl.** nuḳaṭ
**(sharp end)** râs, **pl.** ru꞊ûs
**to p... the gun at ..** dâr ilbârû'di *elbârû'de* 'ala..
**p...ed** murau'was *masnûn*
**poison** samm, simm
**to p...** sammam
**p...ous** musimm', sammi
**Poland** bulûniya
**Pole, Polish** bulûni
**pole (stick)** ḳaḍîb, **pl.** ḳuḍ-bân
**(a long one)** *nâbûṭ'*
**(measure)** *ḳaṣabe* **(prop., 'reed')=3.55 metres; (1 pole=5 metres)**
**police, p... soldier** zabṭîyi *zabṭîye*
**p... (and consulate) -constable** ḳauwâṣ, **pl.** ḳau-wâṣa
**p...inspector and magistrate** raiyis izzabṭîyi *re꞊îs ez-zabṭîye, elḥâkim*
**p...man** (nafar) bôlîs'
**polish (verb)** jala *gala*
**polite** laṭîf
**politics** syâsi *siyâse*
**pollution (filth)** nijâsi *ne-gâse*
**polytechnic school** madrasit 'ulûm mukhta'lifi *medreset 'ulûm mukhta'life*
**pomatum** bûmâ'ḍa
**pomegranate (coll.)** rummân *rummân*
**(a single one)** rummâni *rummâne*
**pond** ṛadîr *birke*
**poor** faḳîr, **pl.** fuḳara; ṭifrân *mufel'lis;* maskîn *meskîn*, **pl.** msâkîn' *me-sâkîn'*
**pope** bâ'bâ
**poplar** ḥaur *ḥôr*
**porcelain** ṣîni
**porcupine** ḳunfud
**port;** see harbor
**at what p...s does the vessel call?** lawain' bîḥau'wil ilmar'kab? *'ala fên ti-ḥau'wud elmar'kib?*
**Port Sudan** saṛr issûdân' *bôr sûdân'*

---

**plenty:** use p... of .. 100,15
**pocket:** put it in your p... 51,19
the p...s must be .. 113,11
**pole** (wooden rod) 111,8
**policeman** (mounted) 127,8.9
**porcelain** 117,8

**Porte : the Sublime P...** ilbâb il'âli *elbâb el'âlı*
**porter (carrier)** 'ittâl *shaiyâl* **(doorkeeper)** bauwâb *bauwâb*
**portion (part)** ḳism, **pl.** aḳsâm ; see also dowry
**portmanteau** ṣandûḳ, **pl.** ṣanâdîḳ'
**portrait** ṣûra, **pl.** ṣuwar
**Port Said** burt (bunt) sa'îd
**Portugal** borturâl
**position** mauḍi'
**possession** mulk
**p...s, landed property** rizḳ, **pl.** arzâḳ
**possible** mimkin
**post (for letters, etc.)** busṭa **(mil. station)** karakûn *karakôl ;* see also situation
**postage** ijrit maktûb *ugrat mektûb*
**p... stamp** bûl
**post-card** tazkaret busṭa
**Post-office** maktab busṭa
**Post-office order** ḥawâlet busṭa or ḥawâle 'ala il-bus'ṭa
**postpaid** khâliṣ ilij'ra *khâliṣ elug'ra*
**pot** tanjara *tangara,* **pl.** tnâjir *tenâgir;* ḳidri *ḳidre*
**potato** buṭâṭa *baṭâṭis*
**potsherd** shaḳfit fikhkhâr *shaḳfit fukhâr*
**potter** fâkhû'ri
**poultice** lazḳa
**to apply cold p...s** 'imil labkhât bârdi *'amal labkhât bâride*
**pound (weight)** nuṣṣ oḳḳa, **i.e. half an** oḳḳa **; the Syrian** oḳḳa **= 1.28 kilogramme, the Egyptian = 1.24 kilogramme**
**in Syria : 2** oḳḳa **= 1** roṭl, **therefore 1** roṭl **= 2.56 kilogrammes**
**in Egypt : 1** *roṭl* **= 449 grammes, or nearly 1 lb.**
**1 lb. = 454 grammes; cf. ounce (20 sh.)** lîra *ginê*
**to p... (crush)** saḥan *dâs*
**pour in** ṣabb
**p... out (i.e. away)** kabb
**p... me out a glass of ..** ṣubbli kubbâyit .. *ṣubbilı kubbâyet ..*
**poverty** faḳr
**powder** sufûf, bôdra
**gun-p...** bârûd'
**power** ḳudra
**(authority, etc.)** ḥukm
**the intellectual p...** ḳûwat mudrikat
**that is not in my p...** haida mâ hû biyad'di *di mâ yiṭlaḥ'shê min îdi*
**powerful** ḳâdir, 'azîm
**a p... man** ṣâḥib ḳudrat

---

**praise** madḥ ; **(of God)** ḥamd
**to p...** madaḥ ; **(God)** ḥamad
**to p... oneself up** madaḥ nafso *madaḥ nefso*
**God be praised** ilḥam'dilla *elḥam'do lillâh*
**p...worthy** ḥamîd, maḥmûd
**pray** ṣalla
**(for someone)** da'a la... *da'a li...*
**prayer** ṣala, **pl.** ṣalawât
**a p... for someone** du'a
**to say one's p...s** ṣalla
**preach** wa'az
**preacher (general)** wâ'iz
**(Moham.)** khaṭîb
**preaching** wa'z
**precaution** iḥtiyâṭ
**as a p...** liliḥtiyâṭ
**precede (in rank)** taḳad'dam
**(in time)** sabaḳ
**precious** tamîn, nafîs
**p... stone** jauhar *gôhar*, almâs
**prefer** faḍḍal ; **to** 'an **or** 'ala
**pregnancy** ḥabl
**pregnant** ḥibli *ḥible*
**prepare** sauwa
**prescription** waṣf, ritshet'ta
**presence** ḥaḍar
**present(gift)** hadîyi *hadîye*, **pl.** hadâya
**(adj.)** ḥâḍir
**to be p...** ḥiḍir *ḥaḍar*
**the p... time** ilwaḳt' ilḥâḍir *elwaḳt' elḥâḍir*
**at the p... time** hallaḳ ilḥâḍir **or** bilwaḳt' ilḥâḍir *dilwaḳt'*
**presently: I am coming p...** hallaḳ biji *ḥâlan agi*
**preserve** ḥafaz
**(fruit, etc. in vinegar)** kabas, kabbas
**preserved fruit** murab'ba, **pl.** murabbayât *murabbât*
**p... in vinegar (of cucumbers, etc.)** makbûs, **pl.** makbûsât' *mukhal'lal*
**preserves in vinegar** ṭurshe *ṭurshi*
**president** ra-is *re-is*, raiyis
**press (for oil, wine, etc.)** ma'ṣara, **pl.** ma'âṣir
**(printing-)** mâkina
**to p...** 'aṣar, kabas, shadd (yeshidd')
**pretension (claim)** da'wa, iddi'â
**pretty** kwaiyis *kuwai'yis*, zarîf [khalla
**prevent** 'auwaḳ, mana', mâ
**price** taman *temen*, ḥaḳḳ
**set p..., as of shares** si'r
**cost p...** rismâl *rasmâl*
**what is the p...?** kâm tamano? *kâm temeno?* ḳaddaish' ḥaḳḳo? *ḳaddi ê ḥaḳḳo?*
**that is an excessive p...** haida taman fâḥish *di temen fâḥish*

---

prance (horse) 120,1
pray 37,11
I p... you to excuse me 40,4
prepare everything 52,12
p... the bed 136,5
price (cost, hire) 86,12; 94,11
(sale) the lowest p... 112,13
let us settle the p... 118,3
what is the p...? 47,11; 118,4
its p... is .. 118,5.11

**have you it not at a cheaper p...?** mâ 'indak minno bita'man arkhaṣ? *mâ 'andak'shi minno bite'-men arkhaṣ?*
**pride (noun)** kibriya
**priest (Christian, secular)** khûri *kassîs*, **pl.** khawârni *kusus*
**(Christian, regular, member of a religious order)** kassîs, **pl.** kasâkisi
**(Protestant)** kassîs
**(Jewish)** khâkhâm', khîkhâm'
**(Mohammedan, who recites the prayers)** mubal'lir
see also p. 132, note
**prince** amîr, **pl.** umara; see note to 'bêk'
**princess** amîri *emîre*
**principal (head)** raiyis *re:îs*
**(adj.)** aṣli, akbar
**p...ly** bilakhaṣṣ'
**print (verb)** ṭaba'
**printer (typographer, compositor)** ṭabbâ'
**(proprietor)** ṣâḥib maṭba'a
**printing-press** âlet ṭibâ'a *mâkinet ṭab'*
**prison** ḥabs, sijn *sign*
**p...er** maḥbûs; **yasîr, pl.** yusara
**probable** ilar'lab *elar'lab*
**probe (to examine)** faḥaṣ
**procession (and benediction with the Holy Sacrament)** zîyâḥ' *ashâre*
**proclamation** manshûr
**procure** dabbar *shâf*
**can you no ip... me ..?** mâ btikdir tdabbir'li..? *mâ tirdarsh' teshûfli ..?*
**procurer (pimp)** 'akrût *me-'ar'raṣ*
**profession of the faith of Islam**; see creed
**professor** ustâz *ustâd*
**programme** brûrrâm
**promise** wa'd; **to p...** wa'ad
**promissory note** sanad
**promotion** tarak'ki
**pronunciation** talaf'fuz, lafz
**property (possession, fortune)** mâl, mulk
**prophet** nabi *nebi*, **pl.** imbyi *ambiya*
**by (the life of) the P...!** wanna'bi! *wanne'bi!* wiḥyât inna'bi! *waḥyât enne'bi!*
**proportion: in p... to ..** bi kadr' .. *kaddê ma ..*
**p...al, p...ate** munâsib *munâsib*
**propriety** edeb
**prose** nes
**prostitute**; see fallen woman
**protect (sby.)** ḥâma 'an
**p...ion** ḥimâyi *ḥimâye*

---

procure me some .. 119,6
p... us some .. 121,13
to p... you an apartment 85,2
products 135,3
promenades 81,11
promise: I p... you that .. 48,11
prompt; see ready
properly (well) 147,8
proprietor of the house 85,8
of the hotel 78,4; 88,2
of the carriage 94,11
prosper: God p... you 39,8

**protest (verb) against ..** ḳâm ilḥij'ji ʿala .. *ḳâm elḥig'ge ʿala ..*, ʿ*amal elberotes'to ʿala ..*
**proud** mutkab'bir *mutakab'bir*
**prove** shâhid, **pl.** shawâhid
**to p...** asbat
**provender-bag** mikhlâyi *mikhle*, pl. makhâli
**provide oneself with** akhad maʿa
**provided (supposing) that ..** iftaraḍ'na in .. *nifriḍ in ..*
**province** wilâyi *mudîrî'ye*
**provisions** mûni *mûne*, zûwâ'di *zûwâ'de*
**proximity** ḳurb
**Prussia** brûsiya *berus'yâ*
**P...n** brusyâni *berusyâwi*
**psalm** mizmâr, **pl.** mzâmîr' *mezâmîr'*
**public (adj.)** ʿumûmi
**p... house** mîkhâ'neh *khammâre*
**p...ly, before the p...** ḳuddâm innâs *ḳuddâm ennâs*
**pull (verb)** shadd
**p... out (extract)** ḳalaʿ
**pulpit** mimbar *mambar*
**pulse** nabḍ
**to feel the p...** dass innabḍ' *dass ennabḍ'*
**pump (noun)** trumba
**pumpkin** yaḳṭîni *ḳarʿa;* **(coll.)** yaḳṭîn *ḳarʿ*
**p...-cucumber** kûsa ʿ*agûr;* see squash
**punish** jâza *gâza*, ḳâṣaṣ
**p...ment** jaza *gaza*
**pupil** talmîz, **pl.** talam'za or talâmîz'
**purchase** shiri **or** shrâyi *shirâye*, mushtara
**sale and p...** baiʿ ushi'ri *bêʿ weshi're*
**I acquired this by p...** haida akhat'to bishshi'ri *di akhat'to bishshi're*
**to p...**; see buy
**pure** naḍîf *nḍîf*, ṣâfi
**purgative (a purge)** mishil **(pron. mis-hil), sharbi** *sharbe*
**purity** naḍâfi *naḍâfe*
**purple (adj.)** urjuwâni *urguwâni*
**purpose** ḳaṣd
**on p...** makhṣûṣ, ḳaṣdan
**purse** kîs, **pl.** ikyâs *akyâs;* ṣurra; jizdân ilmaṣâri *guzlân elfulûs;* **or, Syr. only:** frâra
see also 'kîs' in the Arabic Vocabulary
**purslane (plant)** baḳli *rigle*
**push** dafshi *zaḳḳe*
**to p...** dafash *zaḳḳ*

---

**put (to place, lay)** ḥaṭṭ
**put away (lay up, hide)** khabba
**put by** ḥafaz
**put off (defer)** amhal
**put on one's clothes** libis
**put out (a candle)** ṭafa; **see** light
**put up with** iḥta'mal
**I cannot put up with that** mâ fîni iḥmal haida *mâ ardarsh' aḥmil di*
**pyramid** haram, **pl.** ahrâm
**quail** sumni *samâne*, **pl.** sm̃min *semâmin*
**qualification** ittiṣâf
**qualified** muwâfiḳ
**quality** jins *gins;* shikl; ṣifa, **pl.** ṣifât; khaṣli *khaṣle* **especially bad qu...**
**the best qu...** jins il'âl *gins el'âl*
**quantity** miḳdâr
**what qu...; see** how much
**quarantine** karantîna
**quarrel** khiṣâm, nizâ' *khinâḳe*
**(fight)** muḳâtali *muḳâtale*
**to q...** 'imil kalâm *'amal kalâm*
**quart (measure): liquids are generally weighed; in Egypt a** *ḳadeḥ* **(prop., 'cup') = 2.06 litres; 1 quart = 1.14 litres; cf.** bushel
**quarter (a fourth part)** rub', **pl.** erbâ'
**a q... of a town** ḥai *ḥâra*
**quay** raṣîf
**queen** maliki *malike;* **see** Majesty
**question** su:âl *su:âl*, **pl.** is:ili *as:ile*
**(that which has been qu...ed)** mas:ili *mes:ele*
**that is the qu...** haida il-mas':ili *di elmes':ele*
**to q...** sa:al
**quick (adj.)** sarî'
**quickly** ḳawâm *ḳawâm*, bil'a'jel *bil'a'gel*
**qu... (go on)!** yalla!
**quick-sand** rumêle
**quicksilver** zîbaḳ
**quiet (adj.)** hâdi, sâkit *sâkit*
**be qu...!** irtâḥ! uskut!
**quince** safar'jal *safar'gal*
**quinine** kîna
**quite** bilkhâliṣ *khâliṣ*
**rabbi** khâkhâm', khîkhâm,

---

**rabbit** arnab, pl. arânib
**radish** fijl *figl* [*ifren'gi*]
**(small one)** fijl franji *figl*
**raft (float used on the Tigris, consisting of inflated skins)** kelek
**rag** sharṭûṭa *sharmûṭa*,[1] pl. sharâṭîṭ' *sharâmîṭ'*; khirḳa, pl. khiraḳ
**rage (noun)** ṛaḍab
**rail of a railway** ḳaḍîb sikket ilḥadîd, pl. ḳuḍbân sikket ilḥadîd
**railing (and trellis-work)** sha'rîyi *silk*
**railway** sikket ilḥadîd
**-carriage** 'arabîye, pl. 'arabîyât'
**-guard** komsâri; **(chief)** re=îs ilḳaṭr'
**-inspector** mufet'tish
**-station** maḥaṭ'ṭe
**rain** shiti *shite*, maṭar
**to r...** shatta *naṭar*
**it has been raining** shattit iddin'yi *shatet eddin'ye*
**it is raining** 'am bitshat'ti
**it is now going to r...** hallaḳ raḥ tshatti *dilwaḳt' râḥ tishti*
**it is pouring down** iddin'yi kâbsi *eddin'ye kulliha naṭar*
**it is raining in slow drops** 'am bitnaḳ'ḳiṭ *bitnad'da'*
**rainbow** ḳaus ḳaḍaḥ *ḳôs ḳazaḥ*
**raisin** zbîb *zebîb*
**ram** kabsh *kebsh*
**Ram Castle (in Cairo)** *ḳal'ât elkebsh'*
**ramadan**; **see fasting-month**
**rampart** sûr
**rank (station, dignity)** rutbi *rutbe*
**rare** nâdir *nâdir*, ḳalîl ilwujûd *ḳalîl elwugûd*
**rash (fickle)** ṭâyish, jahlân *gahlân*
**rat** jirdaun' *girdôn*, pl. jarâdîn' *garâdîn'*; fâr, pl. fîrân'
**rate of exchange** si'r
**raven** ṛurâb, pl. aṛribi *arribe*
**raw** nai
**razor** mûs, pl. mwâs *imwâs*
**read** ḳiri *ḳara*
**can you r...?** bta'rif tiḳra? *beta'raf tiḳra?*
**reading (noun)** ḳrâyi *ḳirâye*

---

[1] **Do not misapply the two words** sharṭûṭa **and** sharmûṭa; sharṭûṭa **is in Syria a rag**; sharmûṭa **in Egypt, rag, but in Syria, prostitute.**

---

**ready** ḥâḍir, khâliṣ
**r...!** khalâṣ!
**to be r...** khalaṣ
**to get r... (finish, trans.)** khallaṣ, kammal *kammil*
**real (genuine)** ṣaḥîḥ
**rear(-guard)** daneb *deneb*
**reason (faculty)** ʿaḳl
**(cause)** sabab *sebeb*, **pl.** isbâb *asbâb*
**for what r...?** liai' sabab? *liai'yi sebeb?*
**reasonable** ʿâḳil
**recall; see remember**
**receipt for ..** waṣl ʿala or ʿan..
**acknowledge (acquaint me with the) r...** ʿarrif'ni ʿan ilwuṣûl *ʿarraf'ni ʿan el-wuṣûl*
**give me a r...** aʿṭîni waṣl or *idîni waṣl*
**to r...** aʿṭa waṣl
**receive (accept, take)** akhad or *khad*
**(a visitor, guest)** ḳibil, **(kindly)** ḳâbal *ḳâbil*
**(find, get)** lâḳa; **frequently expressed by 'to reach,' e.g. I r...d your letter** wiṣil'li maktûbak = **your .. letter reached me**
**reception (solemn)** istiḳbâl
**recipe** waṣf, ritshet'ta
**reciter of prayers (before the congregation of the Mohammedans)** mubal'liṛ
**reckon** ḥasab, ḥâsab *ḥâsib*
**how do you r... that?** kîf btiḥsub haida? *ezai' betiḥ'sib di?*
**recluse** ḥabîs, **pl.** ḥubasa
**recognise** ʿirif
**recommend** waṣṣa
**can you r... me a good servant?** btiḳdir twaṣṣîni ʿala ṣâniʿ mlîḥ? *betiḳ'dar tewaṣṣîli ʿala khaddâm yekûn ṭaiyib?*
**have you a r...ation?** maʿak tûṣyi? *miʿâk tausiye?*
**reconciled: to be r...** tṣâlaḥ *iṣṭa'laḥ*
**reconciliation** muṣâlaha, ṣulḥ [ṣaḥḥ]
**recover (become healthy)** **(to rest)** irtâḥ *isterai'yaḥ*
**(to get back)** ḥaṣṣal
**r...y (from sickness)** shifa
**red** aḥmar, **fem.** ḥamra, **pl.** ḥumr
**Red Sea; see sea**
**Red Sea Province** wilâyit ilbaḥr' ilaḥ'mar *mudîrî'-yet elbaḥr' elaḥ'mar*
**reddish** aḥmarâni

---

**ready: get them r... 109,9**
**get the horses r... 133,14; 137,17**
**get (plur.) us the .. r... 139,2**
**have you everything r...? 73,3**
**have you anything r...? 108,2**
**I have nothing r... 110,1**
**is .. r...? 129,7**
**must be r... 92,12**
**(ready) what is r...? 133,17**
**r... (made) 111,1**
**really? 59,12**
**recently 48,16**
**reception-room; see drawing-r.**
**reckon on; see rely**
**recommend me a good .. 87,9**
**recovered (health) 149,6**

**reduce (price)** nazzal *nazzil*
**reduction** khaṣm
**reed** ḳaṣab fārsi *bûs*
**writing r...; see pen**
**r... pipe (instr.)** zammâra *zummâra* [*barrad*
**refresh** raṭṭab or baurad
**r...ment (drinks, etc.)** shî mubar'rid *shê muraṭ'ṭab*, **pl.** mubarridât
**refuse (verb)** rafaḍ, imta'naʿ ʿan
**regard; see esteem**
**regiment** âlây'
**region (country, direction)** nâḥyi *naḥye*, **pl.** nawâḥi
**register (book)** daftar, **pl.** dfâtir *defâtir*
**r...ed (post)** musau'kir
**regret (verb)** tᵋassaf ʿala *itᵋas'sif ʿala*
**regular** ḳiyâsi *ḳiyâsi*, ʿal-ḳyâs *ʿalḳiyâs*
**regulation** nizâm *uṣûl*
**reign (verb)** ḥakam
**rein** ljâm *ligâm*, *surʿ*
**related, a relation, relative** ḳarîb, **pl.** ḳarâyib *ḳarâᵋib*
**reliable** amîn
**relic** ḍakhîri *ḍakhîre*
**religion** dîn, dyâni *diyâne*
**religious** dîni
**rely on** itta'kal ʿala *iʿta'mad ʿala*
**I rely on you** bitta'kil ʿalaik' *baʿta'mid ʿalêk*
**remain** biḳi, ḍall, fiḍil
**r...der** baḳîya *bâ'ḳî*
**remark** mulâḥaza
**to r...** lâḥaz *lâḥiz*
**remedy (physic); see medicine**
**to r...; see repair**
**secret r..., consisting of scraps of papers with unmeaning dicta or letters which are worn on the body or, when torn into small pieces, taken in water, and such like** ḥâjib *ḥâgib*, **pl.** ḥujub *ḥugub*
**remember** ifta'kar, tzakkar *itzak'kar*, fâḳ, waʿa
**I cannot r... his name** mâ bitzak'kar ismo *mush mutazak'kir ismo*, mâ bfîḳ ʿala ismo *mânish fâkir ismo*
**r... me to all your family** sallim'li ktîr ʿala jamîʿ ahl baitak *sallim'li ketîr ʿala gemîʿ ahlê bêtak*; see p. 35
**remembrance: in r...** lilis-tizkâr
**remind** fakkar
**r... me of ..** fakkir'ni fî .. *fakkar'ni* **with acc.**
**remove (a tooth)** ḳalaʿ
**(out of a house)** naḳal *ʿazal*

---

refreshing: something r... 102,6
refuse: I cannot r... 56,8
I must r... your request 55,5
regret: I r... it 60,3.5
I r... that I must .. 55,5
reins 120,10; 121,1.9
religion: of what r... are ..? 134,8 and note 2
rely on me 56,7
I can r... on you 54,5
remove the cloth 93,2
r... (raise) the curtain 92,8

**renegade** murtadd′
**renew** jaddad *gaddad*
**rent** kiri *kire*, kiritilbait′ *is-kirwet elbêt* [*ta*=′*gar*
**to r...** istak′ra, istâjar *is-*}
**repair** tiṣlîḥ *taṣlîḥ*
**to r...** (**mend**) ṣallaḥ
**repeat** karrar
**repent sthg.** nidim ʿala .., tnaddam ʿala .. *itnad′-dim ʿala* ..
**r...ance** nidâmi *nedâme*
**reply** radd, **pl.** rudûd
**to r...** radd
**represent (a play, etc.)** ḳad-dam, shakhkhaṣ
**r...ation** tishkhîṣ *tashkhîṣ*
**reproach (noun)** ʿitâb
**repugnance** kirha
**reputation** ṣît
**request**; see demand, ask
**resemble** shâbah *ashbah*
**resign** istaʿfa
**r...ation (retirement)** istiʿfâ
**resist** khâlaf *khâlif*, ḍâdad
**r...ance** mukhâlafi *mukhâ-lafe*, ḍiddîyi *ḍiddîye*
**respect**; see esteem
**with respect to (as for)** .. min jihit.. *min gihet* ..
**respiration** nafas
**respite (delay)** muhli *mihle*
**to r...** amhal
**rest (remainder)** bâḳi **or** baḳîyi *baḳîye*
**(quiet)** râḥa
**I want r...** btilzam′ni râḥa *ana ʿâ*=*iz râḥa*
**I wish to have a long night's r...; (see) that no one comes to-morrow morning to wake me** baddi ishbaʿ mninnaum′, tâ mâ yiji ḥada bukra ʿala bukra bîfaiyiḳ′ni *biddi astau′fa ennôm, mâ ḥaddish yîgi bukra eṣṣubḥ′ yiṣaḥḥîni*
**to r...** istarâḥ, irtâḥ
**we will r... a little** baddna nistrîḥ shwaiyi *biddina nisterai′yaḥ shuwai′ye*
**restore** ṣallaḥ
**resurrection: Church of the R...** knîsi ilḳiyâmi *kenîset elḳiyâme*
**retailer** bîyâʿ *baiyâʿ*

---

render a service 56,10
rent of this house 86,4; of the room 79,2.3
I will r... the room 79,4
repair: in good r... 87,2
r...s at your charge 87,1
r... this watch 107,5
you r... it thoroughly 107,12
you must r... it 84,10
have .. r...ed 87,3
until .. is r...ed 84,11
all that needs r...ing 96,10
a saddler who r...s 138,7
he will r... the girths 138,10
.. must be r...ed 96,10; 107,2
replace it 107,13
reply: a decisive r... 87,8
repose; see rest
repugnant: that is r... 60,6
require: what you r... 110,1
respect: my r...s 35,12
reside: does the consul r. ..? 82,3
rest a little 37,11
have you r...ed well? 139,9
that I may r... 99,2
that we may r... 146,14
we will take a r... 145,2
restaurant 123,7.8
restive (horse) 120,9
restored (health) 148,4

**return** (**coming back**) rujûʿ *rugûʿ*
(**restoration, reply**) radd
**to r...** (**go, come back**) rijiʿ *rigiʿ*
(**give back**) radd
**I r... to England to-morrow** bukra birjaʿ la-ingiltar'ra *bukra argaʿ li-ingiltar'ra*
**r...-ticket** warakit rauḥa warujûʿ *warugûʿ*
**revenge** târ, intikâm
**to take r...** akhad târo
**revenue**; see income
**reverend** mukar'ram
**revolver** riwol'wer
**rheumatism** dâ ilmafâṣil *dâ elmafâṣil*
**rhinoceros** karkadann'
**rhubarb** râwend'
**rhyme** ḳâfiyi *ḳâfiye*, **pl.** ḳawâfi
**rib** ḍilʿ, **pl.** ḍulûʿ
**ribbon** shirîṭ *sherîṭ*
**rice** ruzz, rizz
**rich** ṛani, **pl.** iṛnya *aṛnîye*; zenkîl, **pl.** zanâkîl'
**riddle** (**enigma**) laṛz *luṛz*, **pl.** ilṛâz
**ride** mishwâr *mushwâr*, **pl.** mshâwîr' *meshâwîr'*
**to r...** rikib
**in a carriage** bilʿarabîyi *bilʿarabîye*, bilkarrûsa
**ridicule** hagu *hagu*, ḍiḥk
**to r...** ḍiḥik ʿala ..
**ridiculous** ḍuḥka *maskhara*
**right** (**justice, claim**), ḥaḳḳ, **pl.** ḥuḳûḳ
**the r... hand** yamîn
(**correct, true**) ṣaḥîḥ
(**straight, sincere**) mustaḳîm
**r... on the top** fauḳ khâliṣ *fôḳ khâliṣ*
**on the r...** ʿalyamîn
**on your r... hand** ʿala îdak ilyamîn *ʿala îdak elyamîn*
**quite r...!** tamâm! *tamâm!*
**you are r...** ilḥaḳḳ' maʿak *elḥaḳḳ'ê miʿâk*, ilḥaḳḳ' fî îdak **or** bûdak
**you have no r... to act thus** mâ ilak ḥaḳḳ taʿmil haik *mâlak'shi ḥaḳḳê tiʿmil kide*
**I will look after my r...** ana bshûf ḥaḳḳi *ana ashûf ḥaḳḳi*
**to make r...** (**adjust**) sauwa
**rigid** shedîd
**rim** (**border**) kanâr
**rind** ḳishr

---

return: I r...ed from .. 34,12
until I r... 94,13
you must r... this list 96,14
reward: God will r... you 54,1.2
God r... you 57,5
how I shall r... you 57,4
ride quickly! (plur.) 131,5
I will r... 94,12; 118,17
(ride) can one r...? 143,1
you can r... halfway 143,2
.. to r... on it 121,8
I will go for a r... 118,17
riding on it is bad 130,5
right: that is r... (true) 48,1
that I have the r... 86,12
you are not r... 50,8

**ring (circle, also knocker)** ḥalaḳ [ḥalḳa
**earrings**
**finger-r..., plain, without anything set in** maḥbis; **with a stone, seal, etc.** khâtim, **pl.** khawâtim
**nose-r...** khizâm
see also bell
**ripe** mustawi (**or, Syr. only:** mistwi)
**to ripen (intr.)** ista'wa
**rise (to stand, get up)** ḳâm (yeḳûm)
**(of the sun, moon)** ṭiliʿ
**when does the sun r...?** aimta tiṭlaʿ ishshams'? *imte tiṭlaʿ eshshems'?*
**when does the moon r...?** aimta byiṭlaʿ ilḳa'mar? *imte yiṭlaʿ elḳa'mar?*
**the Nile has r...n** *ennîl zâd*
**river** nahr, **pl.** inhur; **the Nile (q.v.) makes an exception**
see also pp. 142 to 144
**rivulet** moi *moiye*
**road** darb; **see street, way**
**does this r... lead to ..?** bitwad'di haddarb' la...? *biwad'di eddarb' di li...?*
**roast meat** mishwi **or** *rôsto;*
see pp. 123 to 125
**to r... (meat) shawa; (coffee)** ḥammaṣ
**r... me a chicken** ishwîli jâji *ishwîli farkha*
**roasted** mishwi *mashwi;* **(coffee)** muḥam'maṣ
**rob (plunder)** nahab; **(steal)** saraḳ
**robber** luṣṣ, **pl.** liṣâṣ; *ḥarâmi*, **pl.** *ḥarâmî'ye*
**robe of honor** khilʿa
**religious robe** libâs ruhbâ'nîyi
**rock (stone)** ṣakhr, **pl.** ṣukhûr **or** ṣkhûr
**rocket** sarûkh, **pl.** sawârîkh'
**rod (measure)** *ḳaṣabe murab'baʿa* **= 12.6 square metres;** see acre
**rogue** naṣṣâb
**roll along** daḥraj *daḥrag*
**(wrap)** laff
**Rome** rûmîye
**roof (flat one)** saṭḥ
**room (apartment)** ûḍa, **pl.** [uwaḍ
**rooster** dîk, **pl.** diyûk
**root** shirsh *gidr*, **pl.** shurûsh *gudûr*

---

**rope** ḥabl, **pl.** ḥibâl
**-maker** ḥabbâl
**rosary (rel.)** masbaḥa
**rose (coll.)** ward
**(a single one)** wardi *warde*
**Rosetta** reshîd
**rotten** mut'af'fin
**rouge**; see paint
**rough (coarse, rude)** khishin
**round (adj.)** mudau'war
**(around)** ḥawalaih' *ḥauwalê*, dâyir mindâr *dâ=ir mindâr*
**r... the town** dâyir mindâr ilba'lad *dâ=ir elbe'led*
**row (line)** ṣaff, **pl.** ṣufûf
see also quarrel
**to row** ḳaddaf *ḳaddif*
**royal** mulûki
**rub (verb)** farak
**rubber** lastik
**rubbish (as of buildings)** [radm]
**rudder** daffi *deffe*
**rude** simij *simig*, ṛalîz
**ruin (destruction)** kharâb
**to r... (demolish)** kharrab
**ruins (remains)** khirbi *khirbe*, **pl.** khirab
**rule (principle, usage)** ḳânûn'; ḳâ'idi *ḳâ'ide*, **pl.** ḳawâ'id
**(command)** ḥukm
**to r... over** ḥakam 'ala
**ruler (governor)** ḥâkim, **pl.** ḥukkâm
**(female)** ḥâkimi *ḥâkime*
**(instr.)** musṭra *masṭa'ra*
**run (verb)** rakaḍ *gara*
**run!** irkuḍ or rkûḍ! *igri!*
**to run away** fall *hirib*
**running water** moi jâriyi *moiye garye*
**ruse** ḥîle, **pl.** ḥiyal
**rushes** ḥalfa
**Russia** rûsî'ya, blâd ilmis'kob *bilâd elmoskôf*
**R...an** miskôbi *moskôfi*
**rust (noun)** ṣidi *ṣada*
**sabre** saif *sêf*, **pl.** siyûf **(or, Syr. only:** syûf)
**sack** kîs, **pl.** ikyâs *ikyâs*
**(a big one for coals, potatoes, etc.)** 'adîli *zekîbe*
**a s... of coals** 'adîlit faḥm
see plunder
**Sacrament, the Holy** ilḳurbân ilmuḳad'das *elḳurbân elmuḳad'das*
**sacrifice (offering)** ḳurbân
**sad** ḥazîn, msaudin *musau'dan*, mkaddar *mekad'dar*, zi'lân *za'lân*
**saddle** sarj *sarg*, **pl.** srûj *surûg*
**pack-** jlâl *gilâl*
**to s...** saraj *sarrag*, shadd 'ala
**s... the horses** isruj ilkhail' *sarrag elkhêl*, shidd 'alkhail' *shidd 'alkhêl*

---

rotten 130,6
round: around it 143,7
roundabout way 143,12; 144,3
row (pull)! 73,8
rub me down 99,6
rub it on the .. 105,16
rug 72,12; 137,7
cover me with the rug 145,10
saddle the horses! 146,3
is my horse s...d? 129,7
-bag 128,8; 129,2; 137,9
-horses 122,1.3; 126,4

**saddle-bag** khurj *khurg;* see p. 128, note
**saddle-cloth** ḳamîṣ *barda'a*
**(of felt)** libbâdi *labbâde*
**saddler** surûji *surûgi*
**safe ;** see box (big), cupboard
**(trustworthy)** amîn
**(free from danger)** sâlim
**safety** amnîyi *emnîye*
**saffron** za'farân, kurkum
**sail** ḳala', **pl.** ḳulû'
**sailing-ship** markab ḳulû'i *markib ḳilâ'i*
**sailor** baḥri, **pl.** baḥrîyi *baḥrîye*
**saint (adj.)** mâr
**St. Joseph, etc.** mâr yûsuf, **etc.**
**a s... (Christian)** ḳaddîs, **pl.** ḳadâdîs'; **(Mohammedan)** weli, **pl.** ûliya
**image of a s...** ṣûrit ḳaddîs *ṣûret ḳaddîs,* îko'nî
**sainted** muḳad'das
**sakieh** sâḳiye, **pl.** sawâ'ḳî
**salad** salaṭa *salâṭa*
**(lettuce and other green s...)** khass
**salamander** saman'dar
**sal-ammoniac** milḥ innushâdir *malḥ ennashâdir*
**spirits of s...** rûḥ innushâdir *rûḥ ennashâdir*
**salary (wages)** ijra *ugra*
**monthly s...** shahrîyi *shahrîye,* mâhî'yi *mâhî'ye*
**sale** bai' *bê'*
**is this for s... (for purchase)?** haida lishshi'ri? *di lishshi're?*
**saloon** ḳâ'a
**salt (noun)** milḥ *malḥ*
**(adj.)** mumal'laḥ
**to s...** mallaḥ
**-cellar** mamlaḥa *mallâḥe*
**saltpetre** milḥ *malḥê* bârûd'
**salty** mâliḥ *mâliḥ*
**salutation** salâm ; pp. 43, 44
**to salute sby.** sallam *sallim* 'ala ..
**same : that is not the s...** haida mush mitl ba'ḍo *di mush zê ba'ḍo*
**it is all the s... to me** kullo 'indi sawa *kullo 'andi zê ba'ḍo*
**sample** mosṭra, **pl.** masâṭir ; *'aiyine*
**sand** raml
**sandal** nu'âl
**sandal-wood** ṣandal
**sanitary** ṣiḥḥî
**sap (noun)** zûm *'aṣîr*
**Satan** shîṭân' *shêṭân',* **pl.** shiyâṭîn' *sheyâṭîn'*
**satin** aṭlas
**satisfied with ..** râḍi bi .., mabsûṭ min ..
**(satiated with food or drink)** shib'ân *shab'ân*
**to be s...** riḍi ; **(with food)** shibi'

safe : not s... (weather) 146,8
is the road s...? 127,5
safety : arrive in s... 43,6
salutation : 35,12 ; 36,8
sample : bring me a s... 111,7
sandals (wooden) 99,1
satisfy the mind of .. 78,1
that satisfies me 48,20 ; 89,1
I am satisfied 49,9
are they satisfied? 135,10

**Saturday** yaum issabt' *yôm essabt'*
**sauce** marḳa, salsa
**saucepan** ṭanjra *kasarôla*
**saucer** zarf
(**a European one**) ṣaḥn il-finjân *ṣaḥn elfingân*
**sausage** salsîsa
**small s...s** maḳânik
**savage (a man)** berberi, **pl.** brâbri *barabra;* mut-waḥ'ḥish
**save (to rescue)** khallaṣ, najja *nagga*
(**to spare, economise**) waf-far, ṣammad
**God s... you!** Alla ysall-mak! *Allâh yisal'limak!*
**savory** ṭa'mto ṭaiybi *ṭa'me-to ṭaiyibe*
**saw** minshâr; **to saw** nashar
**sawdust** nishâre
**say** ḳâl (yḳûl)
**what did you say?** shû ḳult? *ḳult ê?*
**what does one (do they) say in Arabic for ..?** kîf bîḳû'lu bil'a'rabi 'an ..? *ê biḳûlu bil'a'rabi 'an ..?*
**that is to say (viz.)** ya'ni
'**he (she) is said to ..**' **rendered by** bîḳû'lu *bi-ḳûlu*
**scales (balance)** mîzân' *mîzân'*
**scandal (noun)** faḍîḥa, jursa *gursa*
**Scanderoon** iskenderûni *is-kenderûne*
**scarab (beetle)** khunfusa *gu'rân*
**scarcely** anjaḳ *yâ dûb*
(**with difficulty**) bizzûr
**s... had we arrived** auwal mâ wiṣil'na
**scarecrow** takhwîf
**scholar (learned man)** 'âlim
(**pupil**) tilmîz, **pl.** tlâmîz' *telâmîz'*
**school (elementary)** maktab, kuttâb *kuttâb*
(**academy, college**) madrasi *medrese*, **pl.** mdâris *me-dâris*
**-boy**; see scholar
**-master** faḳîh *fiḳîh*
**science** 'ilm, **pl.** 'ulûm
**scissors** maḳaṣṣ
**scold sby.** 'aiyaṭ 'ala .. *ṭauwal 'ala ..*
**scorpion** 'aḳrab
**Scotland** iskut'landa
**scratch (verb)** ḥakk
(**of the cat**) kharbash
**screw** barmi **or** birrîni *berîme*
**to s... (fasten with s...s)** ḍabaṭ bibar'rî
**screwdriver** mufakk'(bar'rî)
**scribe** kâtib *kâtib*, **pl.** kut-tâb *kuttâb*
**Scriptures: the Holy S...** ilktâb ilmuḳad'das *elki-tâb elmuḳad'das*

---

**save: God save you** 36,11; 43,2
**say no more** 63,11
**what are you saying?** 45,15
**what are they saying?** 46,2
(**say**) **how did you say?** 45,14
**what do you say to it?** 45,16
**they said nothing to me** 38,7
**scrub the house** 89,3.4

**sea** baḥr, **pl.** bḥûr *biḥâr*
**the Dead Sea** baḥr *lûṭ*
**the Mediterranean Sea** baḥr ilmutwas'siṭ *baḥr elmutawas'siṭ*
**the Red Sea** baḥr ilaḥ'mar *baḥr elaḥ'mar*
**sea-captain** raiyis ilmar'kab *re=îs elmar'kib*
**seal (the engraved signet)** khâtim
**(the impression)** khatm
**sealing-wax** shama' aḥmar
**seaman** baḥri
**seamstress** khîyâ'ṭa *khaiyâṭa*
**search sthg.** fattash **'ala ..** *fattish 'ala ..*
**season (of the year)** faṣl, **pl.** fuṣûl; **(in Cairo, London, etc.)** mausim *môsim*
**seat (place)** maṭraḥ
**(of a government, etc.)** markaz *merkaz*
**(bench)** takht, **pl.** tukhûti *[tukhat]*
**see also chair, sit**
**sea-weed** ḳashsh franji *ḳashsh ifren'gi*
**second; see p. 20**
**secret** sirr, **pl.** isrâr
**(adj.)** mukhfi
**faithful to a s...** ṣâḥib **sirr**
**secretly** bilmukh'fi
**secretary** kâtib *sekretêr*
**security; see safety, bail**
**sedan-chair** takhtrawân *takhtêrawân*
**seduce** ṛarr
**see** shâf *shâf* (yeshûf), ḳasha'
**do you see the .. there?** bitshûf haunîk ..? *bitshûf henâk ..?*
**I do not see it** mâ bshûfo *mâ bashûfuhsh'*
**I see nothing** ana mâ bshûf shî *ana manish shâ=if ḥâge*
**have you seen ..?** shuft or shift ..?
**when can I come (can I honor myself) to see you (plur.)?** aimta biḳdir itshar'raf la'and'kon? *imte aṛdar atshar'raf 'andukum?*
**why do you (plur.) not come to see us oftener?** laish mâ bitsharr'fu la'and'na aktar? *lê mâ tisharrifûsh 'andina aktar?* **see also visit**

---

**seed** bizâr, zarî'a, bizr
**(what is sown)** mazrû'a
**(s... of animals)** shahwi *shahwe*
**seek for** dauwar 'ala
**seem** baiyan, tbaiyan *it-bai'yin*
**it s...s so** mbaiyin haik *elbai'yin kide*, izzâhir haik *ezzâhir kide*
**'it s...s to me' expressed by: 'I think'** biftkir *baf-tikir*
**seize** misik
**self** nafs *nefs*, zât *zât*; **or Syr. only:** ḥâl
**I myself** ana nafsi *ana nefsi*, **thou thyself** int nafsak *inte nefsak*, **etc.**
**sell sthg. to sby.** bâ' (yebî') **with acc. of thing and person**
**seller** bîyâ'' *baiyâ'*
**send** arsal, wadda, ba'at
**s... me ..** waddîli .., ib'at'li ..
**I wish to s... some one to .., to Mr. ..** baddi waddi wâḥid la..., la'and' il-khawâja.. *biddi ashaiya' wâḥid li...*, *'and elkhawâga ..*
**to s... for** wadda wara, râḥ wara, istaḥ'ḍar
**s... for ..** rûḥ wara .., ib'at wara .. **or** khallihon yjîbu .. *khallîhum yegîbu* .. **=let them bring**
**sense (intellect, understanding)** 'aḳl, zakâwi *zakâwe*
**(meaning)** ma'na
**the five s...s** ilḥawâss ilkham'si *elḥawâss elkham'se*
**sensible (reasonable)** 'âḳil
**sentinel** ṛafîr
**separate (adj.)** lawaḥ'do, laḥâlo *liwaḥ'do*
**to s... (trans.)** farraḳ **(intr.)** infa'ṣal
**September** ailûl *êlûl'* **or** *sebtem'ber*
**sepulchre** ḳabr, **pl.** ḳubûr
**the Holy S... (at Jerusalem)** ilḳabr' ilmuḳad'das *elḳabr' elmuḳad'das*
**serene** râyiḳ *râ-iḳ*, ṣâḥi
**sergeant (police constable)** ḳauwâṣ, **pl.** ḳauwâṣa
**sermon** wa'z
**servant** khâdim *khaddâm*; ṣâni', **pl.** ṣunnâ'
**female s...** khâdmi, khaddâmi *khaddâme*; ṣâni'a
**will you stay with me as s...?** bitrîd tiḳ'ud 'indi ṣâni' *'andi khaddâm?* **or**

---


**seek:** go s... to hire, etc. 128,4
**seem:** he s...s well 36,6
it s...s I have .. 137,13
it s...s to be .. 117,10
**send for ..** 80,7; 81,3; 85,8; 113,5
.. s... with us 122,1; 123,2
.. s...s it to .. 75,14
to request .. to s... 77,9
**send them ready into the house** 111,1
I sent for you 113,6
**separate room** 98,17
**serious:** speaking s...ly? 46,16
**servant** 87,9; 88,2
for the s.. 121,10; your 126,5
give this to the s... 140,3

**(to a female s...):** bitrîdi tiḳʿudi ʿindi ṣâniʿa *ʿandi khaddâme?*
**serve (trans.)** khadam
**what does this s... for?** minshân êsh haida? *di ʿala shân ê?*
**service** khidmi *khidme*, khadâmi *khidâme*
**(I am) at your s...** taḥt il-amr' *taḥt el-amr'*, amrak, ḥâḍir
**service-berry** ṛabîra
**serviette** fûṭa, **pl.** fuwaṭ; *beshkîr*
**sesame** simsim
**-oil** zait simsim *zêt simsim*
**set (to put, place)** waḍaʿ
**(as the sun, the moon do)** ṛarab, ṛâb (yeṛîb)
**setting (of the sun)** ṛurûb, ṛyâb *ṛiyâb*
**settle (down, to sink, intr.)** rasab
**s... an a/c with** ḥâsab *ḥâsib* **with acc.**
**I want to s... with you** baddi ḥâsbak *biddi aḥâsibak*
**we will s... between us** baddna nitḥâsab *biddina nitḥâsib*
**seven** sabʿa
**s... hundred** sabʿmîyi *subʿêmîye*
**seventeen** sabaṭaʿsh' *sabaʿtâsher*
**seventh** sâbiʿ *sâbiʿ*, **fem.** sâbʿa *sabʿa*
**seventy** sabʿîn
**several** jimli *gumle*, sirbi
**s... people** sirbit nâs *gumlet nâs*
**severe** ḳâsi
**sew** khaiyaṭ; **see button**
**sex** jins *gins*
**shade (noun)** fai *ḍill*
**a shadow thrown by some object** khayâl
**a shady place** maṭraḥ fîh fai *maṭraḥ fîh ḍill*
**to sit in the shade** ista'ḍal or ista'zal
**shake (trans.)** hazz, khaḍḍ; **(clothes, etc.)** naffaḍ
**(intr.)** irta'ʿash
**shake the stuff (garments, etc.) well!** naffiḍ ilawâʿi mlîḥ! *naffaḍ elhudûm ṭaiyib!*
**shall; see must, and p. 22, No. 4**
**shall I speak?** hal lâzim *lâzim* aḥki?
**shall I do this?** baddi aʿmil haik? *aʿmil kide?*

---

**serve 88,13.15**
**s... me (the coffee) 81,1**
**to s... me 88,3; you 58,5**
**have you s...d in a ..? 88,12**
**he s...s well 87,10**
**service: at your s... 39,2; 100,5**
**have you been in s...? 88,8**
**I would render you a s... 56,10**
**(service) I am at your s... 49,12**
**settle the price 94,11; 118,3**
**s... the gratuities 100,1**
**sew this button 94,7; 96,9**
**shake the clothes 89,6**
**did you not s... 90,4**
**let them s... out 136,10**
**shall we bring them? 119,5**

**shame (honest sh..., modesty)** ḥaya
**(disgrace)** ʿaib *ʿêb*, ʿâr; cf. p. 62, note 2.
**sh... (be ashamed)!** istḥi! istaʼḥi!
**shape (noun)** hai=a
**share (portion)** naṣîb, pl. anṣibe; *ḥiṣṣa*, pl. *ḥiṣaṣ*
**sharp (adj.)** ḳawi, ḳâsi, mâdi
**a sh... wind** hawa ḳawi, rîḥ ḳawîyi *rîḥ ḳawîye*
**to sharpen** sann
**shave** ḥalaḳ; see pp. 100,101
**I wish to be shaved** baddi iḥluḳ *biddi aḥlaḳ*
**shawl** shâl *shâl*
**sheath** mural'lif *ṛulâf*
**sheep** ṛanmi *ṛaname*, naʿji *naʿge*
**sheet (of paper)** ṭalḥîyi or ṭarḥîyi *farkh*
**(linen-)** milâye
**sheet-iron** tanek *ṣafîḥ*
**sheik** shaikh *shêkh*; see also note to 'bêk'
**shell (concha)** ṣafad, ṣadaf
**(bomb)** killi *ḳunbule*
**to shell (with balls)** ḍarab birruṣâṣ
**shepherd** râʿi
**sherbet** sharbât *sharbât*; cf. drink, smoke
**shield (buckler)** turs, tirs
**shilling** shlîn *shilin*
**shine (to flash)** limiʿ
**shining (a gleam)** lamaʿân, raunaḳ
**(adj.)** lamîʿ, naiyir
**ship** markab *markib*, pl. mrâkib *merâkib*; **sefîni** *sefîne*, pl. sufun
**steam-** wâbûr', pl. wâbûrât'
**war-** markab ḥarbi *markib ḥarbi*, bêlik' *dunanma*
**see also boat**
**ship's captain** raiyis ilmar'kab *re=îs elmar'kib*
**shirt** ḳamîṣ, pl. ḳumṣân
**peasant's shirt (cotton)** *tôb*
**shoe (European)** kundra *gazma*
**(oriental)** sirmâyi *ṣarma* or *bâbûg'*
**peasant's shoe** medâs *balṛa*
**women's light house-shoe (of one piece)** sarmûji *sarmûge*
**horse-shoe** naʿl
**to shoe a horse** baiṭar or *ṭabbaḳ*

---

**shoemaker** kundur'ji or kunder'ji *gazmâti* ; see tailor
**shoesmith** ḥiddâd *ḥaddâd*
**shoot (sprout)** farkh
**to shoot** ḳauwas *ḍarab*
**shooting-star** nijm zârik *nigmè zârik*
**shop (small one, also stall)** dikkân *dukkân*, **pl.** dkâkîn' *dekâkîn'*
**(big one, store)** makhzin *makhzan*, **pl.** mkhâzin *makhâzin*
**shore** shaṭṭ, shâṭi [ḳuṣâr}
**short** ḳaṣîr *ḳuṣai'yar*, **pl.**}
**there is one s...** ; see missing
**to shorten** ḳaṣṣar
**shorthand** kitâbet ishâra *kitâbe mukhta'ṣara*
**shortly (soon)** sur'atan
**shot (the act, discharge)** ḍarbi *ḍarbe*
**(small bullets)** khurduk
**shoulder** kitf, **pl.** iktâf *iktâf*
**shout (noun)** ṣaut *ṣôt*, ṣiyâḥ, 'iyâṭ
**s... of joy (on solemn occasions)** zalṛûṭ *zarṛûṭa*, **pl.** zalâṛîṭ' *zarâṛîṭ'*
**to shout** ṣâḥ, 'aiyaṭ *zaḳḳa'*
**shovel (noun)** mijrafi *magrafe*
**show (trans.)** farja, warra
**show me** farjîni, warrîni
**to show the way** dall
**is there any one who could show me the way?** fî ḥada bîdill'ni? *fîh ḥaddi yidil'lini?*
**shriek** ṣarkha ; **to s...** ṣâḥ
**shrimp** ḳraydîs
**shrink (as flannel)** inkamash *kashsh*
**shrovetide** ; see fasting-tide
**shut (trans.)** ṛalaḳ ; **(the eyes)** ṛammaḍ
**(intr.)** inṛa'laḳ
**to shut in** ḥabas
see also lock
**shutter** darfi *darfe*
**shy (adj.)** yijfil *yigfil*
**to shy** jafal *gafal*
**sick** ; see ill
**I feel s...** ili tukhmi *'andi tukhme* [*tukhme*}
**sickness (nausea)** tukhmi}
**sickle** manjili *mangale*
**side** jamb *gamb*, jânib *gânib*, ṣaub *naḥye*
**on this s...** fî haṣṣaub' *binnaḥ'ye di*
**on that s...** fî haidâk iṣṣaub' *binnaḥ'ye dik-hâ*
**to this s...** lahaṣṣaub' *linnaḥyâ di*
**go on the other s...** rûḥ lahaidâk iṣṣaub' *rûḥ linnaḥ'ye dik-hâ*

---

**(side) at, or on, the s...** ʿaj-ja'neb *ʿalalgamb'*
**on my s...** ʿala jambi *ʿala gambi*
**Sidon** ṣaida
**sieve** ṛirbâl *ṛurbâl*
**to sift** ṛarbal
**sigh (noun)** tnahhud *tanah'-hud*
**to s...** tnahhad *itnah'hid*
**sight (vision, seeing)** baṣar
**(spectacle, aspect)** manzar, pl. menâzir
**sign (token, mark)** ʿalâmi *ʿalâme*, pl. ʿalâmât'
**to s...(a paper, etc.)** waḳḳaʿ, amḍa
**signal**; see sign
**signature** imḍâ *firma*
**signify**; see mean
**it does not s...** haida mâ hû shî *di mush ḥâge*, mâ bîsâ'yil *mâ ʿalêsh*
**silence (noun)** sukût
**to s...** sakkit
**silent: to be s...** sakat *sukut*
**be s...!** uskut! sus! *ḥûs!*
**silk** ḥarîr; **raw s...** ḳazz
**of s..., silken** min ḥarîr
**s...s, s... stuff** ḳumâsh ḥarîr
**-factory** kerkhânit ḥarîr *meftel* or *fabrîkat ḥarîr*
**-worm** dûd ilḥarîr *dûd elḥarîr*, dûd ilḳazz' *dûd elḳazz'*
**silly** sakhîf, khasîf; **(of persons)** aḥmaḳ, balîd *belîd*, mahlûl; **the last word is the strongest and most vulgar one**
**silver** fiḍḍa *faḍḍa*
**silversmith**; see goldsmith
**similar** mshâbih *mushbih*
**simple** basîṭ
**simplicity** basâṭe
**simply (solely)** faḳaṭ
**sin** khaṭîyi *khaṭîye*, **pl.** khaṭâya
**to sin** khaṭa, akhṭa
**Sinai** jabal mûsa *gebel mûsa*, ṭûr sîna
**since (adv. = since that time)** min haidâk ilwaḳt' *min elwaḳt'ê dik-hâ*
**(conj. = since the time when)** min waḳt illi *min waḳtê mâ*
**(inasmuch as)** min ḥais *min ḥês*
**s... when?** min aimta? *min imte?* [*sene*]
**a year s...** min sini *mini*
**some time s...** min middi *min mudde*
**sincere** mustaḳîm
**s...ly** bikul' ikhlâṣ
**sincerity** ṣadâḳe or ṣidḳ
**sinew (also root)** shilsh, **pl.** shlûsh *shulûsh*
**sing** ṛanna

**singer** muṛan'ni
**female s...** muṛannîyi *muṛannîye*, pl. maṛâ'nî
**singing (act of)** ṛina
**single (not double)** mufrad, munfi'rid *munfa'rid*
**(not married)** a'zab *'âzib*
**singly** waḥdo, laḥâlo *binef'so*
**sink (in a kitchen, etc.)** mizrâb
**to s...** nizil; **(in the water)** ṛiriḳ
**Sir!** yâ sîdi! yâ khawâja! *yâ khawâga!* **see note to 'bêk' in the Ar. Voc.**
**(an inferior addressing his superior)** yâ m'allmi! *yâ sîdi!*
**Sirdar** ra-îs 'asâker *sirdâr*
**sirocco** shlûḳ *samûm* or *shard*
**sister** ukht, **pl.** akhawât or khaiyât *ukhwât*
**s...-in-law** silfi *silfe*
**sit, sit down** ḳa'ad
**sit down!** u'ḳud!
**situation (place)** mauḍi'
**six** sitti *sitte*
**six hundred** sittmîyi *sut-[têmîye]*
**sixteen** siṭṭa'sh' *sittâsher*
**sixth** sâdis *sâdis*, **fem.** sâdsi *sadse*
**sixty** sittîn
**skin** jild *gild*
**water-s...** ḳirbi *ḳirbe*
**skull** jimjimi *gimgime*, **pl.** jamâjim *gemâgim*
**sky** sama, **pl.** samawât
**(firmament, atmosphere)** falak *felek*
**slab (of stone)** blâṭ *balâṭ*
**slack (loose)** rakhu
**slanting** a'waj *a'wag*
**slave** 'abd
**female s...** 'abdi *'abde*
**-dealer** bîyâ'' il'abîd *baiyâ' el'abîd, gallâb*
**-market** bâzâr' il'abîd *bâzâr' el'abîd*
**sleep** naum *nôm*, naumi *nôme*
**to s...** nâm *nâm* (ynâm *yenâm*)
**to fall asleep** ṛifi
**I am tired, I should like to s...** ana ti'bân, baddi nâm *ana ta'bân, biddi anâm*
**I have not slept the whole night** mâ nimt ṭûl illail' *mâ nimtish ṭûl ellêl*
**I have not yet slept enough** ba'd mâ shbi't mnin-naum' *lissa mâ istaufêtshi ennôm*

---

single sole (on boot) 109,4
Sir! 47,18; 89,10; 115,1
sit down 37,12
will you not sit down? 38,2
situate: well s...d 83,6
highly s...d 76,15; 147,7
size 107,10; 108,4
skirts (lady's) 98,1
sky is clear 64,16
sky is lowering 65,20
sky is overclouded 64,17
sleep: I cannot s...136,7
I wish to s... 136,4
do you s...? 136,6
one cannot s... here 147,4
nobody s...s here 147,6
we want to s... 79,10
have you slept well? 139,9

**(sleep) I wish to s... late** baddi nâm ktîr *biddi anâm ketîr*; **see also rest**
**how did you s...?** kîf aṣbaḥt' ilyaum'? *kêf mâ aṣbaḥt' ennahar'da?*
**sleepy** ni'sân *na'sân*
**I am s...** n'ist *ni'ist'*
**sleeve** kimmi *kumm*, **pl.** kmâm *ikmâm*
**slender** raḳîḳ, raḳîḳâ'ni
**sling (for throwing stones)** miḳlâ'
**slip of paper** waraḳa
**s... of the pen** sahu ḳalam
**to s... (slide)** zalaḳ
**slipper** bantuf'li *bâbûg'*, **pl.** bantuflât *bawâbîg'*; ḳaltshîn; sarmûji *sarma* **(ladies')** bâbûj'
**slow** 'almahl' *bishwêsh*
**my watch is s...** sâ'ati bit=akh'khir *sâ'ati mit=akh'khare*
**slowly!** 'ala mahlak! shwai shwai! *shuwai'ye shuwai'ye!*
**small** zṛîr *zuṛai'yar*, **pl.** zṛâr *zuṛaiyerîn* **or** *zuṛâr*
**smaller than ..** azṛar min ..
**smallpox** jidri *gidre*
**small shot** khurduḳ
**smear (with pomatum)** dahhan *dahhin*
**smell** rîḥa, **pl.** rawâyiḥ *rawâ=iḥ*
**(sense of s...)** shamm
**bad s...** rîḥa kerîha
**this flower has a very pretty s...** hazzah'ra ilha rîḥa jamîli ktîr *ezzah'ra di liha rîḥa gemîle ḳawi*
**to s... (trans.)** shamm
**(intr.) rendered by 'to have a smell'; see above**
**it smells badly here** haun fî rîḥa mush ṭaiybi *hene fîh rîḥa mush ṭaiyibe*
**smile (verb)** tbassam *itbas'sam*
**smoke** dukhân
**to s... (tobacco)** shirib dukhân
**I am very fond of smoking** ana bḥibb ktîr shirb id-dukhân *ana baḥibb' ketîr shurb eddukhân*
**this tobacco is not fit to s...** haddukhânât' mâ byinshi'ribu *eddukhân di mâ binshiribsh'*
**the stove smokes** ilkânûn' bîdakh'khin *elkânûn' bidakh'khan*
**smokeless** mâ fîhi dukhân
**smoker** shirrîb dukhân
**smoky** mudakh'khan
**smooth (adj.)** mâlis *mâlis*, amlas, laiyin, nâ'im

---

**smuggle** harrab
**s...d tobacco** dukhân mu-har'rab
**Smyrna** izmîr
**snail** bazzâka
**snake** ḥaiyi *ḥaiye* **or** *ta'bân*
**-charmer (in Egypt)** *ḥâwi*
**-tamer** *rifâ'i*, **pl.** *rifâ'î'ye*
**sneeze (verb)** 'aṭas *'aṭṭas*
**snipe** jâjit ilarḍ' *degâget elarḍ'*
**snore (verb)** shakhar *shakh-khar*
**snout (of beasts)** bûz
**snow** talj *telg*, **pl.** tlûj *tulûg*
**it is snowing** 'am btitlij iddin'yi, nâzil talj *nâzil telg*
**snuff (powdered tobacco)** 'aṭûs, anfîyi *nushûk*
**to s... (tobacco)** shamm 'aṭûs *itnash'shak*
**so** haik *kide*
**so much the better!** aḥsan'-lak! **(or, Syr. only:** aḥsin'lak!**)**
**soap** ṣâbûn'
**sofa** dîwân'
**soft** nâ'im
**soil (earth, ground)** trâb *turâb*, arḍ
**Nile s...** *ṭîn*
**to s...(make dirty)** wassakh
**soiled** wusikh *wisikh*
**solder (verb)** laḥam
**soldier** 'askeri
**sole (of a shoe)** na'l
**solicitor** wakîl da'âwi *wa-kîl ashrâl*
**solitude** waḥshi *waḥshe*
**some days** kam yaum *kâm yôm*
**s... people** ba'ḍ innâs *ba'ḍ ennâs*
**s... fifty, etc.**; see odd
**somebody** aḥad, wâḥid
**something** shî *shê* **or** *ḥâge*, shwaiyi *shuwai'ye*
**somewhere else** ṛair maṭraḥ *maṭraḥ tâni*
**son** ibn, walad
**in the address:** maḥrûs **or** 'arîs, **e.g. how are your sons?** kîf ḥâl ilmaḥrûsîn' **or** 'irsânak? *ezai' el-maḥrûsîn'* **or** *el'irsân?*
**song** uṛnîyi, **pl.** aṛâni; mûwâl' *mauwâl*
**son-in-law** ṣahr *ṣihr*
**soon** karîb, ba'd shwaiyi *ba'dê shuwai'ye*
**as s... as possible** biak'rab wakt
**as s... as ..** auwil'ma .. *ḥâlan ..*
**sorcerer** sâḥir, saḥḥâr
**sorcery** siḥr

---

**sorrel** (plant) mulûkhî'yi *humêda*
**sorrow** ġamm *huzn*
**sorry** (sorrowful) ḥazîn
**to feel s... for**; see repent
**sort**; see kind
**soul** nafs *nefs* (fem.), pl. infus; nasami
**sound** (voice, cry, noise) ṣaut *ṣôt*
(healthy, valid, whole) ṣaḥîḥ
**to s...** (search) faḥaṣ; (make a noise) ṣauwat
**soup** (noun) shorba or shaurba
**sour** ḥâmiḍ
**south** junûb *gunûb*, ḳibli *ḳible*
**south wind** hawa ḳibli
(hot) shard; see wind
**sovereign** (ruler) ḥâkim, pl. ḥukkâm
(coin) lîra *ginê*
**sow** (to scatter seed) zaraʿ
**space** (noun) wusʿa
**Spain** sbânya *isbânye*
**span** shibr; (with forefinger) fitr
**Spaniard, Spanish** sbanyôli *isbanyôli*
**spark** sharâri *sharâre*
**sparrow** ʿuṣfûr, pl. ʿaṣâfîr'
**speak** tkallam *kallim, itkal'lim*, ḥaka
**I s... Arabic only as far as I can read it off this book** ana mâ biḥki bilʿa'rabi illa ḳaddma biḳdir iḳrâh min halktâb *ana mâ baḥkîsh bilʿa'rabi illa ḳaddêma baḳdar aḳrâh min elkitâb di*
**you s... too quickly; s... very slowly that I may understand you** int bitrau'wij ktîr bilḥa'ki; iḥki shwai shwai tâ ifhamak *inte betistaʿ'gil ketîr bilḥa'ki; iḥki shuwai'ye shuwai'ye ʿala shân afha'mak*
**is there any one here who speaks English?** fî ḥada haun yiḥki inglîzi? *fî ḥaddi hene yiḥki ingelîzi?*
**I wish to s... to Mr. ..** baddi kallim ilkhawâja .. *biddi akal'lim elkhawâga ..*
**speaker** (orator, lecturer) khaṭîb
**spear** ḥarbi *ḥarbe*
**special** khâṣṣatan, khuṣûṣan
**spectacles** ʿuwai'nat (sing.), naḍâra (sing.)
**speech** (language, words) kalâm *kelâm*
(a discourse) khiṭâb
**speed** (quickness) surʿa, ʿajal *ʿagala*

---

**sorry**: I am s... 34,1; 55,1; 60,3
I shall be s... 53,3.4
we are s... 38,11
**sort**: what s...? 106,5; 111,11
of the same s... 116,5
**speak** to me 52,6
do you s... .. 47,7
I wish to s... to .. 78,4
**special room** 98,17
**specie**: in s... (hard cash) 118,9

**spend (money, etc.)** ṣaraf
**sphinx** abulhaul' *abulhôl*
**spice** bahâr, **pl.** bahârât'
**-dealer** ʿaṭṭâr
**spider (small one)** ʿankabût
**(big black one)** rutai'li *abû shebet*
**-web**; see cobweb
**spin (cocoons)** ḥall
**spinach** sbânikh *sabânikh*
**spirit** rûḥ (**fem.**), **pl.** irwâḥ
**the Holy S...** irrûḥ ilḳu'dus *errûḥ elku'dus*
**(liquor)** sbîrto *isbîrto*
**spirited (horse)** nishiṭ
**spiritual** rûḥâ'ni
**spit (for roasting)** sîkh, **pl.** syâkh *siyâkh*
**to s... (spittle)** bazaḳ *taff*
**spittle** bizâḳ
**split (trans.)** shaḳḳ
**spoil (to pervert, impair)** fassad, nazaʿ, rauwaḥ
**to get spoiled** inta'zaʿ, fisid, infa'sad *tilif*
**spoiled** manzûʿ, minfa'sid, mafsûd, fâsid
**spoke (of wheel)** bakret iddûlâb' *bârmak*
**sponge (noun)** sfinj *isfing'*
**(a single one)** sfinji *isfin'ge*
**spoon** malʿaḳa **or** maʿlaḳa, **pl.** maʿâliḳ
**spot (stain)** dibr *zafar*
**(locality)** maḥall', maṭraḥ
**spotted (dappled)** abrash
**spouse (husband)** jauz *gôz*
**(wife)** jauzi *gôze*
**spread (trans.)** madd, farash
**spring (season)** rabîʿ
**(fountain)** ʿain *ên*, **pl.** ʿuyûn **or** ʿiyûn; naba', **pl.** unbûʿa
**(of carriage)** yây, **pl.** yâyât'
**(leap)**; see jump
**sprinkle (verb)** rashsh
**spur (goad)** mihmâz *mahmûz*
**spy (noun)** jâsûs' *gâsûs'*
**square (noun and adj.)** murab'baʿ
**(public place)** sâḥa
**s... metre** mitr murab'baʿ *metr murab'baʿ*
**s... cubit, in Syria only,** drâʿ murab'baʿ = **4590 s... centimetres**
**squash (cucurbitaceous plant)** kûsa *ʿagûr*
**stuffed s...es (favorite dish)** kùsa miḥshîyi *kûsa maḥshi*
**squint-eyed** aḥwal, **fem.** ḥaula *ḥôla*
**stable (noun)** yâkhûr', yâkhor *iṣṭabl'*
**staff-officers** arkân ilḥarb' *arkân elḥarb'*
**stain**; see spot
**stairs** daraj *darag*, sullam *sellim* **fem.**

---

spend the night 126,8
spiteful 63,2
split the difference 112,17
spoil (damage) 129,3
s...ed (out of order) 106,16
sprained 144,12
spread the clothes 136,2
s... the waterproof 136,12
s... it 137,8
spring (watch-) 107,4
sprinkle water 92,11; 136,10
squeeze out 103,10

**stake (for empaling)** khâzûḳ′
**stalk (stem)** sâḳ
**(of reed)** ḳasbi *ḳasbe*
**to s... (walk)** fashakh *it-fa′shakh*
**stallion** ḥṣân *ḥuṣân*, **pl.** iḥṣini or ḥuṣn *aḥṣine*
**stamp (postage)** bûl busṭa, waraḳ busṭa
**stand (verb)** waḳaf
**(to s... up)** ḳâm (yeḳûm)
**(to bear)** iḥta′mal
**s... !** ûḳaf ! [*nugûm*]
**star** nijmi *nigme*, **pl.** njûm
**constellation** kaukab; burj *burg*, **pl.** brûj *burûg*
**starling** zurzûr *zarzûr*
**start (to set out)** sâfar *sâfir*
**state (condition)** ḥâl, ḥâli *ḥâle*
**(body politic)** dauli *dôle*
**station (railw.)** maḥaṭ′ṭe
**-master** wekîl ilmaḥaṭ′ṭe
**statue** timsâl, haikal
**stature** ḳâmi *ḳâme*
**stay (abode, sojourn)** iḳâme
**to s... (intr.)** biḳi, ḍall, fiḍil, tamm (damm *dann*)
**s... here until I come back** khallîk haun ḥatta tâ irjaʿ *khallîk hene lamma argaʿ*
**we will s... at this place two or three days** baddna niksir fî halba′lad yaumain′ tlâti *biddina nifḍal filbe′led di yômên′ telâte*
**steal** saraḳ
**steam-engine** âle bukhârî′ye
**steamer** wâbûr′, **pl.** wâbûrât′; see p. 77
**steam-roller** maḥdla bukhârî′ye
**steel** bûlâd′ *bûlâd′*
**step (one move of the foot)** fashkha *khaṭwa*
**(gradation)** daraji *darage*
**step-son** rebîb
**steward (agent)** wakîl kharj
**stew-pan** ṭanjara *ṭangara*, **pl.** ṭnâjir *ṭenâgir*
**stick (slender branch)** ḳaḍîb, **pl.** ḳuḍbân
**a long s...** khashbe ṭawîle
**walking-s...** ʿaṣâyi *ʿaṣâye*, **pl.** ʿiṣi
**to s... (trans.)** lazzaḳ
**(intr.)** tlazzaḳ *itlaz′zaḳ*
**still (yet)** lissa, kamân *kemân*, baʿd
**(nevertheless)** maʿa zâlik *maʿa zâlik*
**are you s... ill ?** baʿdak marîḍ ? *lissa ʿaiyân ?*
**(silent)** sâkit *sâkit*

---

**stilts (wooden stilt-shoes)** ḳabḳâb, pl. ḳabâḳîb′
**sting (of insects)** ʿaḳṣa
**to s...** shakk, ʿaḳaṣ, nakhas *ḳaras*
**stink**; see smell
**stirrup** rikâb *rikâb*, pl. rikâbât′ *rikâbât′*
**stock (goods, store)** makhzin *makhzan*, pl. mkhâzin *makhâzin*
see also capital, cattle, share
**stockings** kilsât *shûrâbât′*
**stolen** masrûḳ
**stomach** miʿdi *miʿde*
**a disordered s...** miʿdi mukhar′baṭa *miʿde mulakh′-baṭa*
**stone** ḥajar *ḥagar*, pl. ḥjâra or aḥjâr *aḥgâr*
**stool (seat without a back)** skamli *targil*
**stop (.)** nuḳṭa, pl. nuḳaṭ
**to s...** waḳḳaf
**s...!** waḳḳif! ʿindak! *ʿandak!*
**my watch has stopped** waḳḳafit sâʿati *wiḳfet sâʿati*
see also leave off
**stopped up (closed)** masdûd
**stopper** fillîni *filli*
**store**; see shop
**-room** bait ilmûni *kerâr*
**storey** ṭabaḳa *dôr*
**stork** laḳlaḳ **(storks are numerous in the beḳâʿ, the fertile valley between the Lebanon and the Anti-lebanon)**
**storm** zaubaʿa *zôbaʿa*, nau *nô*
**story (narrative)** ḥikâyi or ḥkâyi *ḥikâye*; ḳiṣṣa, pl. ḳiṣaṣ
**story-teller (Oriental)** ḥakawâti *shâʿir* or *muhad′dit*
**straight** mustaḳîm
**s... on!** dôgru! dugri! ʿala sawa! sawa sawa!
**straits (channel)** boṛâz
**the Straits of Gibraltar** izzuḳâḳ *ezzuḳâḳ*
**strand (beach)** shâṭi
**strangle** khanaḳ
**strap (of leather)** jildi *gilde*
**straw (long)** ḳashsh
**(chaff)** tibn
**blade of s...** ḳashshi *ḳashshe*
**street** darb; ṭarîḳ, pl. ṭuruḳ or ṭurḳât; sikki *sikke*
**principal s... in a town** darb *shâriʿ*
**strength** ḳûwi *ḳuwe*
**(s... to endure something)** ṭâḳa

---

**stretch (trans.)** madd (**intr.**) imtadd' *itmadd'*; see p. 30, No. VIII
**strike (to make a blow)** ḍarab
**to s... work** ʻaṭal
**the lightning has struck** nizlit zâʻiḳa *nizilet ṣaḥḳa*
**string (pack-thread)** maṣṣîṣ *dubâra*; ḳîṭân', **pl.** ḳiyâṭîn'
**strip (to rob)** shallaḥ
**they stripped him totally** shallaḥûh tishlîḥ
**striped** muḳal'lam, âlâ'ja *âlâ'ga*
**stroke (blow)** ḍarbi *ḍarbe* (**line**) chaṭṭ, zîḥ
**to s... (rub and press)** farak
**strong** ḳawi, shedîd
**stubble** baḳîyet ilḥiṣâd *ḳashsh ezzarʻ*
**stud (button)** zirr ḳamîṣ *zurâr ḳamîṣ*
**student** ṭâlib ʻilm *talmîz*
**stuff (material, linen, also rubbish)** ḳumâsh *ḳumâsh*, **pl.** aḳmishi *aḳmishe*
**a stuffed chicken** jâji miḥshîyi *degâge maḥshîye*
**stumble (to trip)** tfarkash *itfar'kish*
**stupid** ṛashîm
**stutter (verb)** ladaṛ
**subject (one ruled, a follower)** raʻiyi *raʻîye*, **pl.** raʻâya; tâbiʻ, **pl.** tabaʻa
(**matter, theme**) mauḍûʻ, **pl.** mawâḍîʻ
**what s... are you?** min tabaʻa mîn int? *min tabaʻa mîn inte?*
**are you an Ottoman, Greek, Italian, British, German s...?** int min tabaʻit ilʻos-man'li, ilyûnân', îṭâl'ya, ingiltar'ra, almânya? *inte min tabaʻat elʻos-man'li, elyûnân', îṭâl'ya, ingiltar'ra, almânya?*
**submission (obedience)** ṭâʻa (**surrender**) taslîm
**submissive** mutwâḍiʻ
**subtract** ṭaraḥ, khairaj
**successive** mittâbiʻ
**s...ly, bit by bit** bittâbiʻ *bitadrîg*
**such** haik *kide*
**s.. a one** falân *felân*
**suck** maṣṣ; (**as a child does, at the breast**) riḍiʻ
**to suckle** raḍḍaʻ
**suckling (infant)** ṭifl
**Sudan** issûdân' *essûdân'*
**Sudanese** sûdâ'nî
**suddenly** ʻalfaur' *ʻalfôr*, ʻal-ṛaf'li *ʻa'ṛaf'le*, bilmar'ra

---

**stretch: they will s...** 108,12
**strike: it is striking** 69,3
**it will soon s...** 69,11
**it has struck** 70,1
**that it does not s...** 107,15
**strong** 119,7; 121,2
**s... horses** 119,6.10
(strong) of s... cloth 113,11
stronghold (castle) 142,11
study (room) 91,13
stuffed (mattress) 111,9
sub-district 135, note
such as 129,4
**s... is the law** 75,2

**Suez Canal** khalîj issuês *tir'at essuês* or *kenâl essuês*
**suffer** iḥta'mal, ṭâḳ (yeṭîḳ)
**sufficient** kâfi *kâfi*
**suffocate (trans.)** khanaḳ, faṭṭas
(**intr.**) fiṭis
**sugar** sukkar
**water with s... in it** moi bsukkar *moiye bisuk'kar*
**-cane** ḳaṣab maṣṣ
**suicide (the act)** intiḥâr
**(the person)** ḳâtil nafsahu
**suit of clothes** ṭaḳm, **pl.** ṭḳûmi *ṭuḳûme*
**to have a new s... made** ḳaṣṣ ṭaḳm jdîd *ḳaṣṣê ṭaḳmê gedîd*
**lawsuit** da'wa, **pl.** da'âwi
**to s... (accord with)** wâfaḳ
**that does not s... (please) me** haida mâ bîwâfiḳ'ni *di mâ yiwâfiḳnîsh'*
**this (dress, etc ) suits you well** haida yilbuḳ'lak *di yilbaḳ'lak*
**does the hat s... me?** btilbuḳ'li ilburnai'ṭa? *betilbaḳ'li elburnêṭa?*
see also fit
**suitable** munâsib, musta'idd'
**sulphur** kibrît
**sultry** mufaṭ'ṭis
**sum (the total)** jimli *gumle*
**(amount of money)** mablaṛ, **pl.** mbâliṛ *mebâliṛ*
**to sum** jama'
**summer** ṣaif *ṣêf*
**summit** râs, **pl.** ru:ûs
**summon (to the law-court)** jalab *ṭalab* (lilmaḥ'kame)
**summons** 'ilme ṭalab, or i'lâm
**sun** shams *shems* **fem.**
**the sun is very hot to-day** ishshams' ilyaum' ḥârra ktîr *eshshems' ennahar' da ḥârra ketîr*
**to walk, to sit in the sun** mishi, ḳa'ad bishshams' *bishshems'*
**what time does the sun rise?** aimta btiṭla' ishshams'? *imte tiṭla' eshshems'?* or aimta ṭlû' ishshams'? *imte ṭulû' eshshems'?*
**what time does the sun set?** aimta bitṛîb, or ṛurûb, ishshams'? *imte teṛîb,* or *ṛurûb, eshshems'?*
**before, at, after sunrise** ḳabl, 'ind, ba'd ṭlû' ishshams' *ḳablê, 'andê, ba'dê ṭulû' eshshems'*
**sunbeam** shi'â', **pl.** ashi''a
**Sunday** yaum ila'ḥad or ilḥadd' *yôm elḥadd'*

---

**suffice: it s...s** 48,19
that s...s me 89,1
the necessary s...s me 83,12
**sufficiently: not s...** 98,11
**suffocate: they will be s...d** 144,7
this house is suffocating 85,10
**suit of clothes** 113,6.7.8
coat does not s... me 113,13
**suite of furniture** 116,4
**summer: it is s...** 136,7
for the s... 111,9
s... fruit 125,17

**sun-dial** sâ'a shamsîyi *sâ'a shemsîye*
**sunset** ṛurûb ishshams' *ṛurûb eshshems'*
**(time of s...)** maṛrib
**-glow** shafaḳ
**sunshade** shamsîyi *shemsîye*
**sunstroke : I had a s...** khadni ishshams' *eshshems'*
**superintendence** nazar, munâzara
**superintendent** nâzir, munâzir
**supper (principal meal)** 'asha *'ishe;* see p. 187, note
**supply (provisions)** mûni *mûne*
**to s...** dabbar *dabbir*
**supposing that ..** faraḍan .., faraḍ'na in ..
**surgeon (in its original meaning, i.e. one whose profession is to cure injuries, as wounds or cuts, by manual operation)** jarrâḥ *garrâḥ;* see doctor
**surmise (to conjecture)** khamman *khammin*
**surprised : to be s... at** t'ajjab 'ala *it'ag'gib 'ala*
**surveyor (inspector)** ma-mûr
**suspected** mutham
**suspicion** tuhmi *tuhme*
**I have my s...s of this one** tuhmti 'ala haida *tuhmeti 'ala di*
**swallow (bird)** snûnu
**swear (take an oath)** ḥilif
**(at sby., revile)** sabb
**sweat ;** see perspiration
**sweep (to brush)** kannas *kanas*
**sweepings (dirt)** zibâli *zibâle*
**sweet (adj.)** ḥulu, ḥilu
**sweets ;** see confectionery
**sweet-scented** rîḥto ṭaiybi *rîḥto ṭaiyibe*
**swell (intr.)** wirim
**(trans.)** warram
**swim (verb)** sabaḥ
**can you s... ?** bta'rif tisbaḥ? *beta''raf tisbaḥ?*
**my head swims ;** see giddy
**swindler** ṛashshâsh
**swing (apparatus)** marjûḥa *murgêḥa,* 'anzûḳa
**Swiss** min swîsera *min iswîsera*
**switch (railw.)** muftâḥ
**Switzerland** blâd swîsera *bilâd iswîsera*
**swollen** wârim *wârim*
**sword** saif *sêf,* **pl.** siyûf **(or, Syr. only :** syûf**)**
**-cutter** siyûfi
**sycamore** jimmêzi *gimmêze,* **pl.** jamâmîz' *gamâmîz'*
**syphilis** ḥabb franji *ḥabb ifren'gi*
**Syria** ishshâm *eshshâm*
**S...c, S...n** shâmi *shâmi,* ibn 'arab ; cf. p. 127, note

---

**sunrise :** before s... 129,10
**sup :** will you sup ? 133,16
**sweat :** if you will s... 99,7
**sweated** (of coins) 105,9
**sweep** it 147,9
(sweep) let them s... it 136,10
you will s... the house 89,2
why did you not s... ? 92,9
**sweet,** please (coffee) 102,13
s...s (pastry) 124,1

**syringe** miḥḳan
**to s...** ḥaḳan
**system** tartîb, ḳiyâs
**s...atic** ḳiyâsi
**table** ṭauli *ṭarabêze*, **pl.** ṭaulât *ṭarabêzât'*; lauḥ *lôḥ*, **pl.** alwâḥ
**dining-** sufra
**-cloth** maddit sufra *sufra*
**tablet** lawḥ
**tail** daneb or dambi *dêl*
**tailor** khîyâṭ' *khaiyâṭ*
**is there a t... here?** fî khîyâṭ' haun? *fîh khaiyâṭ hene?*
**let the t... come here, to me** khalli ilkhîyât' yiji la-haun', la'an'di *khalli el-khaiyâṭ yigi hene, 'andi*
**where does the t... live?** waino sâkin ilkhîyâṭ'? *elkhaiyâṭ sâkin fên?*
**taint (verb)** 'ada
**take** akhad *khad*; **see p. 25**
**t...!** khôd! *khod!*
**to t... in**; **see bring in, cheat**
**t... my things**; **see carry**
**t... me to a ..**; **see direct**
**tale** ḳiṣṣa, **pl.** ḳiṣaṣ
**(malignant)** si'âye
**talent** isti'dâd *isti'dâd*
**talisman** ṭilsim, **pl.** ṭalâsim
**talk (idle)** fishâr *hezeyân*
**to t...** takal'lam, ḥaka; **(idly)** fashar
**this man talks too much** halinsân byiḥki ktîr *el-insân di biḥki ketîr*
**talkative** mutakal'lim
**talker (silly)** 'illâk *'allâk*
**tall** ṭawîl
**tallow** shaḥm
**Talmud** talmûd
**tamarind** tamar hindi

---

**table: lay the t... 93,1**
**clear the t... 93,2**
**to serve at t... 88,15**
**(put it) on the t... 51,20**
**(it is) on the t... 91,13**
**dining- 110,5**
**kitchen- 110,5**
**writing- 110,8**
**-cover 116,4; plur. 115,11**
**-wine 125,12**
**take it (Ar. masc.) 54,9; (Ar. fem.) 107,14**
**t... me to .. 83,4**
**t... me into .. 98,17; 99,2**
**t... the luggage 77,7**
**t... the measure 108,16**
**t... this .. back 130.2**
**t... this (gratuity) 75,6; 100,1**
**t... (plur.) this 72,12; 74,13**
**t... this letter 52,16**
**t... me ashore 71,1.7**
**t... us to .. 132,9**
**t... away 52,11; out 147,11; 148,3**
**take off (clothes) 98,17; 109,1 140,11**
**t... off the cover 93,11**
**t... off the saddle 120,4**
**t... the trunk off 148,1**
**do you t... medicine? 34,14**
**how much do you t... for 97,2**
**if you t... no .. 126,7**
**I will not t... it 84,1**
**I will t... them 84,6**
**I will t... something 102,6**
**that you may t... my .. 113,6**
**you must t... no .. 72,1**
**must we t... .. with us? 128,2**
**we must t... .. with us 127,2**
**they took nothing 140,2**
**why will you t... it? 75,12**
**I want some one to t... me 81,12**
**the 'taking there' 122 note 1**
**talk: we will t... 102,2; 134,5**
**what are they t...ing about? 46.2**
**what kind of t...? 63,7**

**tamarisk** ṭarfa
**tambourine (with little bells)** daff or dâyiri *rekk*
**(hemispheric t...)** naḳḳâra
**Tangier** ṭanja *ṭanga*
**tanner** dabbâr
**tape-worm** dûd
**remedy against the t...** dawa liddûd
**to expel** rauwaḥ
**tar (pitch)** ḳuṭrân *ḳaṭrân*
**tariff** ta'rîfi *ta'rîfe*
**tassel** shirrâbi *shurrâbe*
**taste (which something has)** ṭa'mi *ṭa'me*
**(which somebody has)** zauḳ *zôḳ*
**that has a good, bad, strange t...** haida ṭa'mto ṭaiybi, radîyi, rarîbi *di ṭa'meto ṭaiyibe, baṭṭâle, rarîbe*
**that is not to my t...** haida mush 'ala khâṭri *di mush 'ala khâṭri*
**to t...** dâḳ (yedûḳ), is-taṭ''am; **but generally rendered by the noun**
**it tastes like ..** haida ṭa'mto .. *di ṭa'meto ..* .
**that tastes bad** haida ilo ṭa'mi radîyi *di lo ṭa'me baṭṭâle*
**tattoo (verb)** washsham il-ba'dan bil-ib'ra *daḳḳ elba'dan*
**tavern (wine-house)** kham-mâra
**tax** rasm, **pl.** rusûm
**ground-** werko, yerko
**income-** tamat'tu' *firḍe*
**tea** shai *shây*
**teach** 'allam *'allim*
**teacher** m'allim *me'al'lim*
**teaching (instruction)** ti'lîm *ta'lîm*
**tear (from the eye)** dam'a, **pl.** dmû' *dumû'*
**tear (to lacerate)** ḳaṭa', khazzaḳ *sharmaṭ*
**to be torn** inkha'zaḳ
**tedious** bîza''il *bîza''al*
**tedium** za'l *za'al*
**telegram, telegraph** telegrâf **(or, Syr. only :** tilgrâf)
**to send off a t...** wadda or ḍarab tilgrâf *wadda, ḍarab* or *katab telegrâf*
**telegraph-post** 'umûd it-tilgrâf *'amûd ettelegrâf*
**-wire** shirîṭ ittilgrâf *sherîṭ ettelegrâf*
**telescope** naḍḍâra
**tell** ḳâl (yḳûl), ḥaka, aḥka
**if you please, t... me whether, how, when, where ..** iza kân bitrîd ḳulli iza, kîf *kêf*, aimta *imte*, wain *fên* ..
**can you not t... me ?** mâ btiḳdir tḳulli? *mâ betiḳ-darsh' teḳul'li?*

---

**tell him to come** ḳullo tâ yiji *ḳullo yigi*
**they have told me of it** aḥkûli ʿanno
**t... me the story from the beginning to the end** iḥkîli ilḳiṣ'ṣa mnilau'wal lilâkhir *iḥkîli elḥikâye min elau'wal lilâkhir*
**temper (disposition)** ṭabʿ
**(anger)** zaʿl or zaʿle
**temple (edifice)** maʿbad, **pl.** maʿâbid
**(of the head)** maṣdaṛ, **pl.** maṣâdiṛ
**ten** ʿashra *ʿashara*
**tenant** musta='jir *musta='ger*
**tender (adj.)** ṭari ; see offer
**tent** khaimi *khême*, **pl.** khiyam ; ṣîwân', **pl.** ṣawâwîn'
**tenth** ʿâshir, **fem.** ʿâshra *ʿashra*
**terrace** saṭḥ
**testament: the Old T...** ilʿahd' ilʿatîḳ *elʿahd' elʿatîḳ*
**the New T...** ilʿahd ijjdîd *elʿahd' eggedîd*
see also will
**testicle** baiḍa *bêḍa*
**testimony** shihâdi *shihâde*, **pl.** shihâdât' *shihâdât'*
**text** matn, aṣl
**texture** nasaj *nasag*, nasîji *nesîge*
**than** min
**thank (verb)** shakar, tshakkar *itshak'kar* ; see p. 57
**thankful** shakûr, shâkir
**thanks** shukr
**that (pron.)**; see pp. 16, 17
**(conj.)** in, **before vowels:** inn
**that I, thou, he, she; we, you, they** inni, innak, inno, inha *innâha;* inna, inkon *innûkum*, inhon *innûhum*
**in order that** tâ, ḥatta, min shân *ʿala shân*
**the (article)**; see p. 7
**the..the** kullma..kullma
**theatre** tiâtro
**theft** sirḳa

---


tembek 103, note
temperature 135,7
temporary (passing) 34,16
tend: to t... the beasts 122,1
the t...ing of the horse 122,4
tent: pitch the t... 147,1.2
Bedouin t...s 142,2
than: thicker than this 137,5
thanks 57,1; other expressions 39,5.6
(obliged) 35,3; for your .. 40,8
we thank God 33,8
that (dem. pron.) 60,4.5.6
that is a .. shop 106,9
that is beyond comprehension 59,13
that is he, it 48,4
of that 141,3; to that 145,7
what is that? 59,7
all that (which) is necessary 89,7; 96.10
nothing that you require 110,1
that which 82,13
(in order that) 73,5; 88,1; 131,1.10
that I am not .. 95,3
that I was not .. 38,10
that I might not .. 38,5

**then** haidâk ilwakt' *dok-halwakt'*
**theology** ʻilm illâhût' *ʻilm ellâhût'*
**there** haunîk or hunâk [*henâk*]
**there, take!** khôd! *khod!*
**there he is** hai hû *âho'*
**there she is** hai hî *âhi'*
**there and back** birrâyiḥ ubijjâyi *birrâ=iḥ wa-biggâ=i*
**is there .. here?** fî haun ..? *fîh hene ..?* byûjad haun ..? *yûgad hene ..?* **the third pers. sing. of the preterite of this last verb is** wijid *wigid* **'to exist'**
**what is there to eat?** shû fî lilakl'? *êsh fîh lilakl'?*
**therefore** fa=i'zan *baka*
**thereupon** baʻdo, baʻd minno, baʻdên
**thick** takhîn, smîk, ḍakhm
**thickness** sumk, tukhn
**thief** ḥarâmi, **pl.** ḥaramîyi *ḥaramîye*
**thigh** fakhd, **pl.** afkhâd
**thimble** kishtbân *kustebân*
**thin** rafîʻ *rufai'yaʻ*, naḥîf
**(flowing, fluid)** sâyil
**(not numerous)** ḳalîl
**thing** shî *shê*, **pl.** ishya *ashye;* ḥâji *ḥâge*, **pl.** ḥawâyij *ḥâgât'*
**(matter, affair, business)** amr, **pl.** umûr
**things (effects)** awâʻi, ḥawâyij *ḥawâ=ig*
**(luggage)** ʻafsh
**take my things upstairs** waddi awâʻî'yi lafauk' *waddi ḥawâ=igi lifôk;* **to the hotel** lillukan'da *lillokan'da;* **to the ship** lilmar'kab *lilmar'kib*
**these are my things, three packages** hai awâʻî'yi tlât kitaʻ *di ḥawâ=igi telâte kitaʻ*
**who will clean my things?** mîn bînaḍ'dif awâʻî'yi? *mîn yinaḍ'ḍaf ḥawâ=igi?*

---


their (value) 104,11
them: to see them 119,5
I will try them on 108,5
I cannot walk in them 108,13
shall we bring them 119,5
that we may inspect them 75,1
feed them 133,3
mend them 90,8
wash them 96,3
then: since then 34,13
(in this case) 127,2; 143,3
hence to .. 149,8
there is no .. 146,12
there is (are) .. 104,2.3; 123,8
there is nothing 49,18
there will be (a storm) 65,14
are there not ... 126,8
(there) take me there 82,9
is there ..? 135,13; 142,5
are there any ..? 81,4.11
from there 75,14; 149,8
what is there? 81,10
who is there? 132,3
thermometer (measure of heat and cold) 129,4
these 108,17; 116,2; 117,3
they are .. 108,6.9
they took nothing 140,2
they said nothing 38,7
thicker coverlet 137,5
thin (cloth) 112,9
thing: these t...s 84,1; 111,1
of the t...s 97,1
there are t...s in it 129,3

**think** ifta'kar
**I think** biftkir *baftikir*
**third** tâlit *tâlit*, **fem.** tâlti *talte*
**thirst (noun)** ʿaṭash
**I am very thirsty** ana ʿiṭshân ktîr *anâ ʿaṭshân ketîr*
**thirteen** tlaṭṭaʿsh' *telatâsher*
**thirty** tlâtîn' *telâtîn'*
**this** ; see p. 16
**this day** ilyaum' or hannhâr *ennahar'da*
**this evening** ilʿashîyi *elmi'se*
**this morning** ilyaum' ʿala bukra *ennahar'di eṣṣubḥ'*
**thistle** shauk *shôk*
**thorn** shauki *shôke*
**(coll.)** shauk *shôk*
**thou** ; see p. 13
**though** maʿa in
**thought** fikr, **pl.** ifkâr
**thoughtful** mutafak'kir
**thousand** alf
**thread** khaiṭ *khêṭ*, **pl.** khîṭân'
**a ball of t...** bakarit khîṭân' *bakaret khêṭ*
**threaten** haddad, **khauwaf**
**threatening letter** maktûb tahdîd
**three** tlâti *telâte* **or** *talât*
**three hundred** tlâtmî'yi *tultèmîye*
**threshold** ʿatabi *ʿatabe*
**throat** zlâʿîm' *zôr*
**throne** takht, **serîr**
**through** min, bi
**(by one's instrumentality)** biwâsṭa
**throughout the week** ṭûl ijjum'ʿa *ṭûl eggum'ʿa*
**throw (verb)** rama, **warra**, zaṭṭ
**(noun)** rami **or** ramye, ṭarḥ
**thumb** ; see finger
**thunder (noun)** raʿd
**it is t...ing** iddin'yi ʿam btirʿad *eddin'ye betir'ʿad*
**t... storm** zaubaʿa, nau
**Thursday** yaum ilkhamîs *yôm elkhamîs*
**thus** haik *kide*
**ticket (of admission, railw.)** tizkri *tezkire*, **pl.** tzâkir *tezâkir*; warka, **pl.** ûrâḳ' *aurâḳ*

---

**think : what do you t...? 47,4**
**what are you t...ing of? 47,5**
**who would have thought that 59,9**
**thirst : I am dying of t... 102,4**
**thirsty : are you t...? 46,8**
**this evening 67,15 ; town 76,15**
**this soap 100,16 ; waistcoat 98,11 ; year 68,7**
**this house 85,10 ; road 127,6 ; village 134,6**
**this tube (pipe) 103,5**
**this cloth 112,6 ; pair 108,7 ; soup 124,2**
**this is leather 125,4**
**this is a .. 120,5**
**this is the .. 130,3**
**this is not well .. 98,12**
**this one (Arab. fem.) 105,13**
**only this ? 74,9**
**take this 100,1**
**take (plur.) this ! 74,13**
**thicker than this 137,5**
**who is this? (masc.) 45,3 (fem.) 45,4**
**thought : my t...s 56,9**
**thread (cotton) 94,8**
**throw (off the horse) 144,10**

**tickle (verb)** zakzak *zarzar*
**to be ticklish** rår *yerår*
**I am very ticklish** ana brâr ktîr *ana barîr ketîr*
**tie (verb)** rabaṭ, ʿaḳad
**to tie to, hang on** ʿallaḳ
**(noun)** rubâṭ, **pl.** rubâṭât'
**tiger** nimr
**tight (drawn, etc.)** mashdûd, shdîd
**(narrow)** ḍaiyiḳ
**hold t...!** imsik ṭaiyib!
**Tigris** nahr iddij'li *nahr eddig'le*
**till (conj., until)** ḥatta, ḥatta tâ, tâ *lamma*
**to t... (the soil)** ḥarat, falaḥ
**time** waḳt, zamân *zemân*
**(with reference to repetition: turn, blow, etc.)** marra, **pl.** marrât; ṭrîḳ, **pl.** ṭurḳ; **see** Adverbial Numbers, p. 20
**t... for the accomplishment of a promise, payment, etc.** waʿdi *mîʿad*
**it is t... to go** ṣâr ilwaḳt' tanrûḥ *âho' elwaḳt' nerûḥ*
**have you t...?** ilak waḳt? *miʿâk waḳt?*
**we still have t...** baʿd maʿna waḳt *lissa miʿâna waḳt*, baʿd mâ ṣâr ilwaḳt' *lissa mâ gâsh elwaḳt'*
**shall we arrive in t...?** nûṣal baʿd ʿala waḳt? *nûṣal lissa filwaḳt'?*
**for a long t... (long since)** min zamân *min zemân*
**at times** aḥyânan
**one, two at a t...; see p. 20**
**time-table** jadwal auḳât issa'far *gedwal ôḳât' essa'far*
**timid** khajûl *misthi*
**tin** ḳazdîr *ḳazzîr*, tanek *ṣafîḥ*
**a tin plate, tin vessel** tanki *ṣafîḥa*
**tinker** sankari
**tip (point)** awj *awg*
**see also gratuity**
**tire (trans.)** taʿab *atʿab*
**(intr., to get tired)** tiʿib
**tired** tiʿbân *taʿbân*
**tired of (annoyed with)** ziʿlân min *zaʿlân min*
**that is very tiring** haida shî yitʿib ktîr *di shê yitʿib ketîr*
**title; see 'bêk' in the Ar. Voc.**

---

**to (noting motion)** la *li*, ila, lahadd' *lihadd'*
**in order to (with infin.)** tâ **(with aorist)**
**from .. to** min .. la *min .. l i*
**from two to three** tnain tlâti *etnên telâte*
**go to the doctor** rûh la'and' ilhakîm *rûh 'and elha-kîm*
**up to ten pieces** lahadd' il'ash'ra kita' *lihadd' el'a'shara kita'*
**how far is it yet to .. ?** kaddaish' fî ba'd la .. ? *kaddi ê lissa li .. ?*
**toast**; see bread
**tobacco** dukhân, tutun
**(for the hookah pipe)** timbek, tambak *tumbâk*
**tobacconist** bîyâ' dukhân *baiyâ' dukhân*, titnâti *dakhakh'ni*
**to-day** ilyaum' **or** hannhâr *ennahar'da*
**toe** isba' ilijr' *subâ' errigl'*, **pl.** sâbî' ilijr' *sawâbi' errigl'*
**together** sawa
**toilet (dress)** libs
**(table)** bishtakh'ta *bash-takh'ta*
**tolerate** ihta'mal, tâk yetîk
**I cannot t... that** mâ fîni tîk haida *mâ ardarsh' atîk di*
**why do you t... that?** laish tihmal haida? *tihmil di lê?*
**tomato** banadûra *kûta*
**tomb** tirbi *turbe*, darîh; see also epitaph
**to-morrow** bukra, rada **or** radi
**t... morning** bukra 'ala bukra *essubh'*
**tongs** malkat *mâshe*, **pl.** melâkit *mâshât'*; kimmâshi *kammâshe*
**tongue** lisân *lisân*
**to-night** illai'li *ellêle*, hallai'li *ellêlâ' di*
**too: I too** ana kamân *ana kemân*; see also also
**too big, too small: generally rendered by the simple 'big,' 'small'; sometimes** bizzyâdi *bizziyâde* **is added**
**one franc too much** ziyâdi bifrank' *ziyâde bifrank'*

to him 82,4
to me 85,7; 148,16
to a (doctor, etc.) 83,4; 145,7
to a (hotel, etc.) 76,15; 116,6
from .. to .. 131,8; 149,8
to him 106,10; to us 132,5
to a certain place 122,2
to the hotel, village 76,5; 131,6
to which we come 131,7
shall we bring .. to you? 119,5
to-day 85,7
until to-day 88,9
together with 72,11
toil (noun) 74,10
to-night 67,15
token of gratitude 54,10
too hot 91,3; 99,8
too little 71,8; 99,16
too much 71,6; 103,13
too wide, too tight 108,6.9
(=likewise) 84,12

**tools** ʿiddi *ʿidde*
**tooth** sinn, **pl.** snân *isnân;* ḍirs, **pl.** aḍrâs
**I have a decayed t...** li ḍirs musau'was *musau'wis*
**who draws a t... most skilfully?** mîn ilash'ṭar mâ ykûn laḳa'laʿ ḍirs? *mîn elash'ṭar liḳa'laʿ ḍirs?*
**my teeth ache dreadfully** snâni byûjaʿû'ni ktîr *isnâni bûgaʿû'ni ketîr*
**tooth-pick (of feathers)** rîshi *rîshe*, **pl.** riyash
**top** râs, **pl.** ru=ûs
**torch** mishʿal *mash'ʿale*, **pl.** mshâʿil *mashâʿîl'*
**torment** ʿazâb *ʿazâb*
**to t...** ʿazzab *ʿazzib*
**torn** mukhaz'zaḳ **(or, Syr. only:** mkhazzaḳ)
**tortoise** zilḥifi *ziḥli'fe*
**Egyptian t...** tirsa
**-shell** ḳishr izzil'ḥafi *bâṛa*
**torture**; see torment
**total** kullîye; **(adj.)** kull
**towel** minshifi *manshife*, **pl.** mnâshif *menâshif;* fûṭa, **pl.** fuwaṭ
**tower** burj *burga*, **pl.** ibrâj *ibrâg*
**(fort)** ḳalʿa
**town** balad *beled;* mdîni *medîne*, **pl.** mudn

**trade (commerce)** tijâra *tigâre*
**(occupation)** ṣanʿa, kâr
**traffic (movement)** ḥarake
**train (railw.)** ḳaṭr
**to t... (educate)** rabba
**traitor** khâyin *khâ=in*
**translate** tarjam *targim*
**translation** tarjimi *targame*
**transport** naḳl
**to t...** naḳal, ḥauwal
**trap (snare)** fakhkh, **pl.** fkhâkh *fukhûkh*
**travel** safra; see journey
**to t...** sâfar *sâfir* [sûwâḥ' **pl.**] 
**traveller** sâyiḥ *sâ=iḥ*
**travelling-companion** rafîḳ. **Proverb:** irrafîḳ ḳabl iṭṭarîḳ *errafîḳ ḳabl eṭṭarîḳ* **the t... before the journey! i.e. you should provide yourself with a brave and honest t... before you start**
**tread (verb)** daʿas *dâs*
**treasure** kinz, **pl.** kunûz
**treasury** khazni *khazne*
**treatment (med.)** muʿâlaji *muʿâlage*
**treaty** muʿâhadi *muʿâhade*
**tree** shajra *shagara*, **pl.** shajrât *shagarât* **or** ishjâr *ashgâr*
**(coll.)** shajar *shagar*

---

**tremble** rijif *irta'‘ash*
**trial (experiment)** tijribi *tagribe*; **(judicial)** taḥkîk
**tribe (people)** ḳaum *ḳôm*
**(of Bedouins)** ḳabîli *ḳabîle*, **pl.** ḳabâyil *ḳabâ=il*
**tribunal** maḥkami *maḥkame*, majlis *meglis*
**tribute** mâlmî'ri
**tricycle** darrâjet bitlātit dwālîb' *darrâga bitalât ‘agalât*
**trifle (noun)** shî jiz=i *shê ḳalîl*
**trifling** zahîd, jiz=i *guz=i*, ṭafîf
**trip**; see stumble, journey
**Tripoli** ṭrâblus *ṭarâblus*
**trooper** khîyāl' *khaiyâl*
**trouble (noun)** hamm
**to t... (trans.)** kallaf *kallif*, kallaf khâṭir .. *kallif khâṭir* ..
**to t... oneself** ijta'had *igta'had*, ‘imil juhdo *‘amal guhdo*
**do not t... yourself** lâ ti‘tal hamm, lâ tsharṛil fikrak *mâ tisharṛil'she fikrak*
**trousers** shirwāl *shirwâl*
**(European t...)** banṭalûn
**true** ṣaḥîḥ
**truly! (it is so)** ḥakkan; **(as oath)** wallâhi!
**trumpet (noun)** nafîr
**trunk (of a tree)** ḳurmi or ḳurmîyi *ḳurme*, **pl.** ḳarâmi
**elephant's t...** kharṭûm
see also chest
**trust (noun)** ittikâl, i‘timâd
**to t... in** twakkal ‘ala *itwak'kal ‘ala*, i‘ta'mad [‘ala
**trustworthy** amîn
**truth** ḥakîka
**in t...** bilḥakîka, ḥakkan
**try (verb)** jarrab *garrab*
**tub** marṭas
**tube (of leather)** ḳirbi *ḳirbe*; ḍarf, **pl.** ḍurûf
**(of the hookah)** nabrîj *lai*
**-dealer** nebârî'ji
**Tuesday** yaum ittlāti *yôm ettalât*
**tumor** dumli *dimmil*, **pl.** [dumal *demâmil*
**Tunis** tûnis
**turban** ‘amāmi *‘imme*, **pl.** ‘amâyim *‘imam*
**Turk** turk, atrâk; ‘osman'li (**sing. and pl.**)
**Turkey** blād il‘osman'li *bilâd el‘osman'li*
**Turkish** turki

---

tribe: of what t...? 143,3
of this t... 142,4
tricks: stupid t... 62,8
trim my beard 101,6
t... the wick 93,7
trot (horse) 123,3
trouble: excuse the t... 57,8
to have caused the t... 57,7
what great t... 74,10
trousers 113,7; plur. 90,6
trousers-pocket 137,12
true: that is t... 48,1
try to find .. 128,4
I will try them on 108,5
that I may try him 120,3
which I tried 130,2
we have tried 123,3
we will try .. 106,1; 120,8
tumbler 125,2
Turkish post-office 82,8
T... slippers 90,10
£ Turkish 104,13

**turkey-cock** dîk ḥabesh *dindi* **or** *farkha rûmi*
**turn (a t..., a rotation)** daur *dôr*
**now your t... has come** hallaḳ ija daurak *dil-waḳ'ti ga dôrak*
**to t... (trans.)** dauwar; **(intr.)** dâr (yedûr)
**(to shape on a lathe)** kharaṭ
**to t... red** iḥmarr'
**t... round ! (intr.)** dûr!
**t... round ! (trans.)** dauwir! *dauwar!*
**to t... aside (make way for sby.)** ḥaiyad **or** ḥâyad *ḥauwad;* **e.g.** ḥaiyid **or** ḥâyid ʿan iṭṭarîḳ ḥatta imruḳ! *ḥauwad* **or** *ḥau-wud ʿan eṭṭarîḳ ḥatta amruḳ!* **t... away from the road until I pass !**
**to t... back (intr.)** rijiʿ *rigiʿ*
**to t... over (trans.)** ḳalab; **(intr.)** inḳa'lab
**turnip** lift
**twelve** ṭnaʿsh *etnâsher*
**twenty** ʿishrîn *ʿeshrîn*
**twist (to plait, as a rope)** baram [tain' *etnên*
**two** tnain *etnên*, **fem.** tin-
**two hundred** mîtain' *mîtên'*
**typewriter (machine)** âlet kitâbe *âle lilkitâba*
**typhus** tîfûs
**tyranny** zulm
**tyrant** zâlim, mustabidd'
**ugly** shnîʿ *shenîʿ*, bishiʿ, wiḥish
**ulemas (learned persons)** ʿulamâ, **plur. of** ʿâlim
**umbrella** shamsîyi *shemsîye*
**unbelief** kufr
**unbeliever** kâfir *kâfir* **(prop. concealer), pl.** kuffâr
**uncle (father's brother)** ʿamm, **pl.** ʿumûmi *aʿmâm*
**(mother's brother)** khâl, [pl. akhwâl
**uncooked** nai
**under (prep.)** taḥt
**(adj.)** tiḥtâni *taḥtâni*
**u... the table** taḥt iṭṭau'li *taḥt eṭṭarabêze* [wakîl
**U...-Secretary** mustashâr
**underneath** min taḥt
**understand** fihim
**did you u... me ?** fhimt ʿalai'yi ? *fihimt' ?*
**I u... but little Arabic** mâ bifham ʿarabi illa ḳalîl *mâ afham'she ʿarabi illa ḳalîl*
**I do not u... you** mâ fhimtak *mâ fihim'tish*
**is there any one here that u...s English ?** fî ḥada haun yifham inglîzi? *fîh ḥaddi hene yifham ingelîzi?*

**undone : to come u...** **(to be opened)** infa'taḥ *itfa'taḥ*
**undress (trans.)** shallaḥ
**(intr.)** shalaḥ
**unfortunate** mankûd il-ḥazz'; maskîn, **pl.** msâ-kîn' *mesâkîn'*; **cf.** fallen
**u...ly I have none** lisû ḥazzi mâ ma'i *lisû ḥazzi mâ ma'ish*
**uniform (official suit of clothes)** badali rasmîyi *badle resmîye*, forma
**uninhabited** mâḥa'da ṣâ-kin fîh *mâ ḥaddish ṣâkin fîh*
**unite (trans.)** jama', waṣal
**United States of America** il-wilâyât' ilmutta'ḥida ilamîrikî'ye
**unjust** zâlim
**unknown** mush ma'rûf, majhûl *maghûl*
**unlawful** ḥarâm
**unnecessary** mush lâzim *mush lâzim*
**unoccupied** fâḍi, mu'aṭ'ṭal *me'aṭ'ṭal, baṭṭâl*
**unripe** fijj *'agr*
**unscrew** fakk ilbar'ṛî *ḥall elbarrîme*
**untie** fakk
**until (prep.)** laḥadd' *liḥadd'*
**(conj.)** ḥatta, ḥatta tâ
**untrue** ṛair ṣaḥîḥ *kidb*
**up** fauḳ *fôḳ*
**(noting motion)** lafauḳ' *fôḳ*
**uphill** biṭṭâli'
**upper** fûḳâ'ni *fôḳâ'ni*
**Upper Egypt** blâd iṣṣa'îd *iḳlîm eṣṣa'îd* = **the happy land or province**
**upset (to turn over, trans.)** ḳalab [*mshaḳlab*]
**upside down** munḳa'lib
**urchin; see hedgehog**
**urinal** âbdestkhâ'ni *adab-khâne*
**urinate** bauwal *shakhkh*, ṭaiyar moi *saiyib moiye*
**urine** baul *bôl, shukhâkh*
**use (utility)** nafa', fâyidi *fâ:ide*
**(habit)** 'âdi *'âde*, **pl.** 'âdât' **and** 'awâyid *'awâ:id*
**(employment, usage)** isti'-mâl
**to use (employ)** ista''mal
**used to ..** mut'au'wid 'ala .. *mit'au'wid 'ala ..*; **see also accustomed**
**useful** nâfi' *nâfi'*, mufîd
**useless** mush nâfi' *mush nâfi'*

**usual** musta'‘mal, ‘âdatan, ‘alrâlib, ilar'lab
**as u...** ḥasab il‘âdi *ḥasab el‘âde*
**utmost** râyi *râye*, âkhir *âkhir*
**at the u...** lilrâyi *lilrâye*
**at the u... ten minutes** bil-ktîr ‘ashr daḳâyiḳ *bil-ketîr ‘eshara daḳâ=iḳ*
**vaccinate with the cow-pox** ṭa‘‘am ijjid'ri *ṭa‘‘am eggid're*
**vagabond** hâshil *hâshil*
**vain** mutkab'bir *muta-keb'bir*
**in v...** bilâsh *balâsh*, bala fâyidi *bala fâ=ide*, bala nafa‘
**all in v...!** kullo bilâsh! *kullo balâsh!*
**valet** khaddâm (lilmalbûs)
**valid** mu‘ta'bir
**valley** wâdi *wâdi*, **pl.** wid-yân *widyân*
**value (noun)** ḳîmi *ḳîme*
**vanguard** ṭalî‘a
**vanquish** ralab
**varnish** jilâ *gilâ*, duhn
**to v...** ṭala *gala*, dahan
**vault (arch)** ḳubbi *ḳubbe*
**vegetables** khuḍra *khuḍâr* **(sing.)**
**veil** mandîl or mindîl, **pl.** mnâdîl' *menâdîl'*; *bur-ḳu‘*, **pl.** *berâḳi‘*
**(a long one)** ṭarḥa
**vein (blood-vessel)** ‘irḳ, **pl.** ‘urûḳ
**velvet (noun)** makhmal, mukhmal *ḳaṭîfe*
**venerable** muḥta'ram
**vertebra** faḳârit iḍḍahr' *faḳârat eḍḍahr'*
**very (adv.)** ktîr *ketîr*, jiddan *giddan* **(always following)**
**vessel** wu‘a, firâr, firâra; **see also ship**
**vestibule** dihlîz
**vetch** mâsh *mâsh*
**vexed: to be v...** zi‘il
**I am much v... about that** ana ktîr zi‘lân min haida *ana za‘lân ḳawi min di*
**vice (depravity of manners)** ‘aib *‘êb*, **pl.** ‘iyûb
**Vice-Consul; see consul**
**Viceroy** wakîl ilma'lik *wekîl elme'lik*
**V... of Egypt** *khidîw mṣr*, **by the natives simply called** *efendîna*: **'our master'**
**victor** râlib; **v...y** naṣr
**victoria (carriage)** ‘arabîyit ḥanṭûr *ḥanṭûr*
**village** ḍai‘a, **pl.** ḍiya‘; *kafr* **or** *beled*

---

usual fashion 113,8
utmost: at the u... 71,7
I will do my u... 42,2
vase (flower-) 117,9
vegetables 124,1
vessel of earthenware 114,4
vexed: I am v... 60,8
I shall be v... 53,8
vicinity 143,2
village: in the first v... 131,7
that we may reach the v... 141,2; some v... 146,14
in the v...s 126,10
go (plur.) to the v... 131,6
to the first v... 131,8
when we come to a v... 139,1

**vine** dâlyi *dâlye*
**-dresser** karrâm
**vinegar** khall
**vineyard** karm, **pl.** kurûm
**violent** shedîd, ḳawi
**violet** bnafsaj *binaf'sag*
**violin (the two-stringed one, the sounding - body of which consists of a coco-nut shell)** kaman'ja *ke-men'ge*
**(the one-stringed one of the Bedouins, with a square body)** rebâbi *rebâbe*
**viper** af'a, **pl.** afâ'ʿî
**virgin** bint, bikr
**the Blessed V...** il'ad'ra, issai'yidi *essai'yide*
**virtue** faḍîli *faḍîle*, **pl.** faḍâyil *faḍâ:il*
**virtuous** fâḍil
**visible** yinshâf *yinshâf*
**visit**[1] ziyâra
**to v...** zâr (yzûr), ija la'and' *gi* **or** *ga 'and*, râḥ la'and' *râḥ 'and*
**(=to honor)** sharraf **with acc. or with** la'and' *'and*
**(=to honor oneself)** tsharraf la'and' *it-shar'raf 'and*; **see see**
**I want to v... Mr. N. N.** baddi zûr ilkhawâja .. *biddi azûr elkhawâga* .., **or** baddi rûḥ la'and' il-khawâja .. *biddi arûḥ 'and elkhawâga* ..
**vitriol** zâj *zâg*
**viz.** ya'ni
**vizier ; see minister**
**vocabulary** ḳâmûs'
**voice** ṣaut *ṣôt*, ḥiss
**he has a nice v...** ḥisso kwaiyis *ḥisso kuwai'yis*
**volcano** jabal nâr *gebel nâr*
**volume (tome)** mjallad *megal'lad*
**voluntary** ikhtiyâ'rî
**vomit (verb)** istafraṛ, nataḳ *istan'taḳ*
**vow** nadr, **pl.** nudûra
**to vow** nadar
**vulture (white-headed one)** nisr
**bearded v..., in Egypt only** *big*
**carrion v...** rakham
**wafer, also the consecrated one,** birshâni *burshâne*
**wages** ijra *ugra*, kiri *kirwe*
**waist-belt ; see girdle**
**waistcoat** ṣidrîyi *ṣidêri*

---

[1] **If the speaker wishes to be polite he uses, for the visit paid to him by the person addressed, the word** tishrîf *teshrîf*, **honoring, homage—from** sharraf **to honor—and for the visit paid by himself to the person addressed, the word** tsharruf *tashar'ruf*—**from reflexive** tsharraf *itshar'raf*.

---

**visit : obliged for your v...** 37,10 ; 40,8
**visitors of an hotel** 80,1
**wages : from your w...** 95,9

**wait** istan'zar, istan'na, naṭar, ṣabar
**to w...** on khadam
**w... a little** uṣbur shwaiyi *istan'na shuwai'ye*
**how long shall I w... for you?** ḳaddaish' baddi inṭuraḳ? *ḳaddî ê astannâk?*
**I have been waiting a quarter of an hour** ṣarli rub' sâ'a nâṭir *ruba' sâ'a mustan'ni*
**I cannot w... any longer** mâ biḳdir istan'zir (or istan'ni) aktar *mâ arḍarsh' astan'na aktar*
**he keeps us waiting a long time (properly: he tarries much)** hû biṭau'wil ktîr *hûwe biṭau'wil ketîr*
**w... for me below the American church** inṭur'ni taḥt ilknîsit ilamârîkânî'yi *istannâni taḥt elkenîse elamêrikânî'ye*
**waiter (at an hotel)** sufraji *sufragi*
**wake up (trans.)** faiyaḳ *ṣaḥḥa*
**(awake, intr.)** fâḳ (yfîḳ) *ṣiḥi*
**wali**; see governor
**walk (gait)** mashi, mashyi
**(ramble, a w...)** mishwâr *mushwâr*, **pl.** mshâwîr *meshâwîr*
**to w...** mishi
**walking (pres. part.), on foot** mâshi *mâshi*
**I w... (in opp. to ride)** ana brûḥ mâshi *ana mâshi 'ala rigli*
**you w... too fast (properly: you are very quick)** bitrau'wij ktîr *betista''gil ketîr*
**you w... too slowly** btimshi 'ala mahlak ktîr *betim'shi bishwêsh ketîr*
**are you a good w...er?** btimshi ṭaiyib? *betim'shi ṭaiyib?*
**wall (in a room)** ḥaiṭ *ḥêṭ*, **pl.** ḥîṭân'
**(round a town)** sûr
**(round a garden)** tiṣwîni
**wallflower** ḳurun'ful
**walnut (coll.)** jauz *gôz*
**(a single one)** jauze *gôze*
**wander** dâr
**want (scarcity) of..** ḳillit .. *ḳillet ..*
**(narrow means)** 'âzi *'âze*

---

**(necessity)** ḥâji *ḥâge*, luzûm
**to do one's w...** ḳaḍa ḥâji *ḳaḍa ḥâge*; **see also water**
**to w... (wish)** riṛib, râd (yerîd), ʿâz (yeʿûz), badd *bidd*
**what do you w...?** shû bitrîd? *ʿâ-iz ê?* **or** shû baddak? *biddak ê?*
**I still w...** baʿd baddi *lissa biddi*, baʿdni ʿâyiz *lissa ana ʿâ-iz*
**war** ḥarb, **pl.** ḥurûb
**Holy War** jihâd *gihâd*
**warm (adj.)** ḥâmi, dâfi *dâfi*
**to w...** daffa
**to get (intr.) w...** difi
**warming** mudaf'fi
**warmth** shaub *shôb, dafa*
**War-Office** nazâret ilḥarbîya *nazâret elgihâdî'ye*
**war-vessel** bailik', bêlik' *dunan'ma*
**wash (trans.)** ṛasal, ṛassal
**to w... oneself** tṛassal *itṛas'sal*
**I should like to w... myself** baddi itṛas'sal *biddi atṛas'sal*, **or** baddi ṛassil *biddi aṛas'sil*
**bring me water, soap, and a towel, that I may w... myself** jibli moi, ṣâbûn' umin'shifi tâ itṛas'sal *hâtli moiye, ṣâbûn' wamen'shife ʿala shân atṛas'sal*
**washerwoman** ṛissâli *ṛassâle*
**washhand - basin** lakan, ṭusht *ṭisht*
**washing (clothes washed)** ṛasîl; **see pp. 95 to 98**
**count the linen** ʿidd ilṛasîl *ʿidd elṛasîl*
**how many pieces are there?** kam ḳaṭʿa ṭiliʿu? *kâm ḳiṭʿa ṭiliʿu?*
**washing-blue** nîl
**wasp** dabbûr, **pl.** dbâbîr' *debâbîr'*
**watch (timepiece)** sâʿa *sâʿa;* **see foot of p. 68**
**to w... over** sahar ʿala, ḥaras
**watch-chain** jinzîr sâʿa *kattîna*

---


(want) we w... (need) 121,12; (wish to have) 79,10; 121,10
how much do you w...? 71,4; 89,9; 122,4; (plur.) 76,2
I hear that you w... .. 88,2
what sort do you w...? 106,5; 111,11
ware: china ware 117,8
warm: I am w... 49,6
it is (very) w... 64,2.3
it does not get very w... 135,7
it has become w... 140,9
w... some water 79,13
see also hot
was: I was 34,7; see also be
wash: I will w... my .. 79,13
I must have my .. w...ed 80,8
I have .. to be w...ed 96,2
do you know how to w...? 96,1
bring water for w...ing 90,11
w... it 92,3; 98,13; 136,1
w... them 96,3
w... my head 101,12
who w...es well 95.10
material that will w... 113,4
washing (linen) 80,8; 96,2
(what has been washed) 96,4
-bill 97,6; -stand 110,5
watch: I forgot to wind my w... 137,11

**watchmaker** sâ'â'ti *sâ'â'ti*; see pp. 106, 107
**watchman** ḥâris
**water** moi (properly: mwai), moiyi *moiye*
**a glass of w...** kubbâyit moi *kubbâyet moiye*
**bring w... quickly** ḳawâm jîb moi *ḳawâm hât moiye*
**high w...** madd
**low w...** jazr *gazr*
**to make w...** ṭaiyar moi *saiyar moiye*
**I want to make w...** baddi ṭaiyir moi *biddi asai'yar moiye*
**to w...** saḳa *iska*
**w... the horses** isḳi ilkhail' *isḳi elkhêl*
**water-closet**; see closet
**waterfall** shillâl *shalâl*
**watering-can** marash'shi
**water-jug (with a long narrow neck)** sharbi *ḳulle*
**waterproof** musham'ma'
**water-seller** saḳ'ḳâ
**water - wheel (hydraulic machine)**; see irrigation-wheel
**wax (noun)** shama'
**wax matches** kibrît shama'
**way** darb fem., pl. durûb; ṭarîḳ, pl. ṭuruḳ or ṭurḳât; *sikke*, pl. *sikak*
**(manner)** ṭarîḳa
**is this the right way to ..?** haidi iddarb' la...? *di eddarb' li...?*
**where does this way lead to?** lawain' bitwad'di haddarb'? *'ala fên yiwad'di eddarb' di?*
**the first road on the left** auwal darb bitridd' 'ashshmâl *auwal darb 'ashshemâl*
**which is the best way to ..?** aina hî aḥsan darb la...? *enhû aḥsan darb li...?*
**how is the road to ..?** kîf iddarb' la...? *ezai'eddarb' li...?*
**is the road dry, fit to ride on, very steep?** iddarb' nâshfi, bitrak'kib, daraj ktîr? *eddarb' nâshif, bitrak'kib, darag ketîr?*
**to lose one's way** ḍâ' (yeḍî') *tâh*
**a long way off** b'îd *be'îd*
**make way for me**; see turn aside
**way out** khurûj *khurûg*, ṭulû'
**where is the exit?** mnain iṭṭlû'? *min ên eṭṭulû'?* wain ilbâb? *fên elbâb?*

---

**weak** ḍ'if *ḍa''if*, **pl.** ḍ'âf *ḍu'âf*
**to weaken** ḍa''af
**weakness** ḍu'f
**wealth** ṛina
**weapon** silâḥ, **pl.** isliḥa *asliḥe*
**wear (to put on, as clothes)** libis
**he wore Arab, European clothes** kân lâbis 'arabi, franji *kân lâbis 'arabi, ifren'gi*
**weary (adj.)** ti'bân *ta'bân*
**weasel** ibn 'irs
**weather** hawa, ṭaḳs ; **see pp. 63 to 66**
**weave** ḥaiyak
**weaver** ḥîyâk' *ḥaiyâk*
**wedding** 'irs *farah*
**-procession** zaffi *zeffe*
**wedge (noun)** sefîn
**Wednesday** yaum ilar'ba'a *yôm elarba''a* **or** *larba'*
**week** jum'a *gum'a*, **pl.** jmâ' *gimâ'*; usbû'a, **pl.** *esâbî'*
**in the course of the w... (i.e. on one day of the w...)** fî 'arḍiyit ijjum''a *fî baḥr eggum''a*
**weigh (trans.)** zân **(yezîn)** *wazan*
**(intr.) rendered by** wazn
**weight: what does it w...?** ḳaddaish' wazno? *kâm wazno?*
**weight** wazn, tiḳl *tuḳl*; **see pound**
**a w... (a stone)** wazni *wazne*
**welcome!** ahlan wasahlan!
**welfare** khair *khêr*
**well (spring)** bîr, **pl.** biyâr
**a public fountain** sebîl
**to dig a w...** ḥafar bîr
**(adj. and adv.)** ṭaiyib
**(in health)** sâlim *sâlim*
**I as w...** ana kamân *ana kemân* **or** *bardi*
**as w... as** mitl
**to get, grow w...** shifi
**w...! (come! go on! etc.)** yalla
**well-bred** zarîf
**west** ṛarb, maṛrib
**-wind** hawa ṛarbi
**wet (noun)** ruṭûbi *ruṭûbe*
**(adj.)** mablûl
**to wet** ball
**wether** kharûf
**wet-nurse** murḍi'a

---

**wharf** ma'bar
**what** shû or aish *êsh* or *ê*
**what is that?** shû haida? *di ê* or *di ê di?*
**what sort of .. is that?** mîn hal ..? shû hal ..? *êsh di ..?*
**what is there? what is the matter?** shûfi? *khabar ê?*
**what must we do now (what is now to be done)?** shû baddna na'mil hallaḳ? *ni'mil ê dilwaḳt'?*
**what am I to do with it?** shû baddi fîh? *ba'mil fîh ê?*
**what did you say?** kîf ḳult? *ḳult ê?*
**what is your pleasure?** na'am? see p. 45, note
**what for?** laish? *'ala shân ê?* or *lê?*
**what is the time?** see p. 68
**what is the price?** see how much, cost
**wheat** ḥinṭa *ḳamḥ*
**wheaten bread** khubz ḥinṭa *'êsh ḳamḥi*
**wheel** dûlâb' *'agele*, pl. dwâlîb' *'agel*
**when** aimta *imte*, limma *lamma*
**when can it be seen?** aimta mniḳdir nshûf haida? *imte neshûf di?*
**since when?** min aimta? mnaimta? *min imte?*
**whenever it may be possible** lamma yakmin
**where** ain or wain or fain *fên*
(=**whither**) lawain' *'ala fên*
**where are you?** wainak? *fênak?*

---

what are they talking about? 46,2
what are those ..? 142,1
what are you doing? 45,8
what are you going to do? 45,9
what are you looking for? 47,3
what are you saying? 45,15
what are you thinking of? 47,5
what for? 144,4
what (fruit) have you? 125,16
what (talk) is this? 63,7
what (laziness) is this! 91,8
what kind? 141,11
what sort? 106,5; 111,11
what has happened to you? 46,3
what have you to ..? 123,9
what (as much as) you will 89,10
what (how much) ..? 104,4
what is that? 59,7
what is the matter with you? 46,5
what is the matter with it (Arab. fem.)? 106,11
what is the question? 46,1
what is your town? 134, note 1
what is yours? 118,15
(from) what is ready 138,17
of what religion? 134,8
of what tribe? 142,3
that is what .. 49,15
.. what I tell you 95,8
whatever is missing 97,1
whence come you? 45,11
whence does it come? 142,7
whence do they come? 115,7
where are you going? 45,10; (plur.) 133,5
where do you live? 134, note 1
where were you? 46,21
from where are you coming? 45,11
place where (in which) 126,8; 132,4; 147,3

**where do I find .. ?** wain blâḳi ..? *fên altiḳi ..?*
**where is there .. ?** wain fî ..? *fên ..?*
**where shall we meet (come together)?** wain nitlâḳa? *fên nitlâḳa?*
**where does .. live?** wain sâkin ..? *fên sâkin ..?*
**where do you want (intend) to go?** lawain' ḳâṣid? *'ala fên ḳâṣid?*
**where is .. coming from?** mnain jâyi ..? *min ên gâ=i ..?*
**whether**; see if
**whetstone** misann'
**whey** maṣl *shirsh elgib'na*
**which**; see p. 17, and below
**whilst** mâ dâm
**whim** hawa
**whimsical** suwai'âti *ḥâlâ'ti*
**whip (noun)** karbâj *kurbâg*, ḳamshi *ḳamshe*
**whirlpool** ṛamr
**whirlwind** zauba'a *zôba'a*
**whisper (verb)** washwash
**whistle (verb)** ṣafar, ṣaufar *ṣôfar*
**white** abyaḍ, **fem.** baiḍa *bêḍa*, **pl.** biḍ
**whitish** abyaḍâni
**whitewash (verb)** kallas *baiyaḍ*
**Whitsuntide** 'îd il'an'ṣara
**whoever it may be** mînma kân *kân* or yekûn
**whole** kull
**the whole house** kull ilbait' *kull elbêt* or ilbait' kullo *elbêt kullo*
**as a whole (altogether)** bilkullîyi *bilkullîye*, jamî'an *gamî'an*
**why** laish, li=ai' sabab *li=ai'yi sebeb*, lê, lêh *'ala shân ê*
**wick** fitîl
**wicked** sharîr
**wickedness** fasâd, shar
**wide** wâsi' *wâsi'*
**widow** armili *ermile*
**widower** armil *ermil*
**widowhood** taram'mul
**width** 'arḍ, 'urḍ

---

**wife** jauzi *gôze;* mara *mar-a* **and** *imra-a*, **pl.** nisa **and** niswân *niswân;* **see also 'bêk' in the Ar. Voc.**
**how is your w...?** kîf ḥâl martak *ezai' mirâtak* **or** bint 'ammak **or** baitak *bêtak* **or** maḍâmtak? **or, more politely:** kîf ḥâl jinâb issitt'? *kêf ḥâl genâb essitt'?* **=how is the lady?**
**wild (not tame)** shmûs *shamûs;* **see also savage**
**(as a country)** barr, barri
**wilful** 'anîd
**wilfully** bi'inâd
**will, wish (noun)** irâdi *arâde*
**(testament)** waṣîyi *waṣîye*
**I w...** brîd *'â-iz* **or** baddi *biddi*
**I w... not** mâ brîd *mush 'â-iz* **or** mâ baddi *mâ biddîsh*
**for radical forms of these verbs see wish (next page)**
**willingly (certainly)!** tikram! 'ala râsi!
**willingness** riḍâ
**willow** ṣafṣâf
**win** kisib, ribiḥ
**I have won** ana kisbân *ana kasbân*, ana ribḥân *ana rabḥân*
**wind** hawa; rîḥ **fem., pl.** aryâḥ; **see pp. 63 to 66**
**hot hurricane-like w... (in Egypt of frequent occurrence from the middle of February to the middle of June)** shlûḳ *samûm;* **if carrying fine dust:** *shard*
**windlass** manjanîḳ *manganîḳ*
**window** ṭâḳa, **pl.** ṭuwâḳ; shubbâk *shibbâk*, **pl.** shbâbîk' *shebâbîk'*
**open the w...** iftaḥ ishshubbâk *eshshibbâk;* **close** sakkir
**leave the w... and the door open** khalli ishshubbâk wilbâb maftûḥîn' *khalli eshshibbâk walbâb maftûḥîn'*
**wine** nbîd *nebîd*
**-grower** karrâm
**-house** khammâra
**-press** ma'ṣara, **pl.** ma'âṣir
**wing** jinâḥ *ganâḥ*, **pl.** ijniḥi *agniḥe*

**winter** shiti *shite*
**wire** shirîṭ ḥadîd *silk*
**wisdom** ḥikmi *ḥikme*
**wise (adj.)** ʿâlim, shâṭir
**wish (noun)** raṛbi *raṛbe*
**to w...** riṛib, râd (yerîd), badd *bidd* **or** ʿâz (*yeʿûz*)
**as you wish** mitl mâ bitrîd *zê mâ terîd*
**is this what you wished for?** haida marṛûbak? *di marṛûbak?*
**with** maʿ or maʿa, ʿind ʿ*and*
**with me** maʿi *miʿâye;* **with you** maʿak *miʿâk;* **with him** maʿo *miʿâh*, etc.
**(instrumentally)** bi, **e.g. with the hand** bil-îd
**without** bala, min ṛair *min ṛêr*, min dûn
**witness** shâhid, **pl.** shhûd *shuhûd*
**to w...** shahad
**wolf** dîb, **pl.** dyâb *diyâb*
**woman** mara *mar-a* **and** *imra-a*, **pl.** nisa **and** niswân *niswân;* ḥurmi
**wonder** ʿajîbi ʿ*agîbe*, uʿjûbi
**w...ful** ʿajîb ʿ*agîb*
**wood** khashab
**fire-w...** ḥaṭab
**(forest)** ḥirsh, **pl.** aḥrâsh
**wool** ṣûf
**word** kilmi *kilme*, **pl.** kilmât *kilmât*
**work** shuṛl, **pl.** ishṛâl **(or, Syr. only:** shṛâl)
**to w...** ishtaʿṛal *ishtiʿṛil*
**w...shop** karkhâna *warsha*
**world** dinyi **or** dini *dunye*
**worm (coll.)** dûd
**(a single one)** dûdi *dûde*
**wormwood** ṣabr
**worse than ..** arda min ..
**worshipper of idols** ʿâbid ilaṣnâm ʿ*âbid elaṣnâm*, **pl.** ʿabadit ilaṣnâm ʿ*abadet elaṣnâm*
**w... of fire** majûs *magûs*
**worth (price)** ḳîmi *ḳîme*
**to be w... sawa; or rendered by the noun**
**worthless** baṭṭâl, mâlo ḳîmi *mâlôsh ḳîme*

---

**would to God!** yâ rait *yârêt!*
**wound (noun)** jurḥ *gurḥ*, jurḥa *gurḥa*
**wrap up in** .. laff bi...
**wrap it up in paper, in a rag** liffo biwar'ḳa, bishartûṭa *liffo biwa'raḳa, bisharmûṭa*; see rag (note)
**wretched (mean)** ḥakîr
**write** katab; **(books)** allaf
**writer (scribe)** kâtib *kâtib*, **pl.** kuttâb *kuttâb*
**(author)** mu-al'lif *mu-el'lif*
**writing (caligraphy, document)** ktîbi *kitâbe*
**(letter, etc.)** taḥrîr
**(hand-w...)** khaṭṭ
**in w...** bilktîbi *bilkitâbe*
**wrong (news, road, etc.)** mush ṣaḥîḥ
**yard (court)** ḥaush *ḥôsh*
**(measure)** drâʿ *dirâʿ*, **pl.** idruʿ; **properly 'arm,' 'cubit'; in Syria = 68 centimetres, in Egypt = 58 cm.**
**yawn (verb)** tâwab *titâwib*
**year** sini *sene*, **pl.** sinîn **or** sanawât; ʿâm; p. 66, note
**this y...** issi'ni **or** hassi'ni *essenâ di*
**last y...** ʿâm ilau'wal **or** ʿamlau'wal *ʿamenau'wal*
**next y...** sint ijjâyi *esse'ne eggâ-iye*
**yearly (adj.)** sanawi
**(adv.)** kull sini *kulli sene*
**yellow** aṣfar, **fem.** ṣafra, **pl.** [ṣufr]
**yes** aiwa, bala
**yes, certainly** naʿam
**oh yes** aina'ʿam
**yesterday** ams **or** mbâriḥ *embâreḥ*
**the day before y...**; see day
**yet** kamân *kemân*, lissa
**(nevertheless)** maʿa zâlik *maʿa zâlik*
**yoke (for drawing)** nîr *nâf*
**young** zṛîr *zuṛai'yar* (filʿumr')
**a y... man** shabb **or** shbaib *shebêb*, **pl.** shubbân **or** shibâb; *gedaʿ*, **pl.** *gidʿân*
**a y... girl** ṣabîyi, **pl.** ṣabâya **or** ṣbaiyât *ṣibaiyât*
**younger** azṛar
**zero** ṣifr
**zinc** tûtya
**zoological garden** bustân ilḥaiwânât' *bustân elḥêwânât'*

---


**wound: (his foot) is w...ed 144,14**
**not w...ed 119,10; 120,4**
**write: can you w...? 47,9**
**I cannot w... 50,14**
**writing-case 147,11; -table 110,8**
**wrong: you are w... (in error) 48,8**
**you are in the w... 48,9**
**yet: it has (is) not yet .. 70,1.2**
**why have you not yet .. ? 91,7**
**you, your (polite form) 32, note**
**ho there! you! 71,1**
**(you) before you (plur.) 131,2**
**with you (plur.) 131,3**
**I will give you 87,8; 89,11**
**I have not seen you 37,4**
**what I tell you 95,8**
**behind you 129,2**
**for you 37,7; 85,6; 126,5**
**your .. 46,18; 78,2; 88,10**
**what is y... name? 88,4**
**yours: what is y... 118,15**
**Zûk 115, note**

# ARABIC-ENGLISH VOCABULARY

**Note.—The Arabic words appear here mostly in the Syrian form, from which the Egyptian deviates according to rules on page 6; the following correspond therefore as a rule:**

| **Egyptian** | **Syrian** |
|---|---|
| *â* . . . . . . . . . | ă̂ |
| *â=i* . . . . . . . . | âyi, ă̂yi |
| *e* **initial or in the interior** | a |
| *e* **at the end** . . . . . | i |
| *ê* . . . . . . . . . | ai |
| *ô* . . . . . . . . . | au |
| *g* . . . . . . . . . | j |
| *gg* . . . . . . . . . | jj |

**Egyptian words showing other deviations have been included in this Vocabulary, likewise such to which, in Syrian, words of a different derivation correspond. If the same word has different meanings in the two dialects it is also indicated.**

**After some practice the tourist or student making use of this book will be able to find out the verbal roots after detaching the servile letters, i.e. those which serve to form the different moods, tenses, numbers, and persons (see pp. 21 to 31); also the singular forms of the broken plurals (see p. 9). The vowels in parenthesis, after the verbs, refer to the formation of the aorist, e.g.** katab (i) **forms** yiktib, ṣâr (i) **forms** yeṣîr, biḳi (a) **forms** yibḳa.

a'âdi pl. of 'adu
ab father
âb August (the month)
abadan *ebeden* eternally, for ever and ever; (with a negation and by itself, as a reply:) never! at no time!
'abâyi cloak of peasants and Bedouins
'abba to fill; pack up
'abd, pl. 'abîd slave
'abes impossible
abraṣ, pl. burṣ leprous
*abrîl* April
abûna our father; yâ abuna, see p. 132 note
abyaḍ, fem. bêḍa white
'âd (ye'ûd) to return, come back, do again
'âd (adv.) again, once more, yet
*ada* (*yidi*) to give
'ada to infect, be contagious
'ada (prep.) except, besides
adab, pl. âdâb' good breeding, courtesy
adabkhâni closet, privy
'adad number
'adâli righteousness, justice
adâr March
'adâwi enmity, malice
'add (i) to count
'aḍḍ (u) to bite
adeb'ta privy, closet
'adem want, non-existence
âdemi, pl. awâdim humane, decent, worthy
'ades '*ads* lentils
'âdi, pl. 'awâyid custom, habit
adîb decent
'âdil just, righteous
'*adîle* large bag or sack
adil'li pl. of dalîl
'adl righteousness
'aḍm, pl. 'iḍâm bone
'adra, il'ad'ra the Blessed Virgin
'adu, pl. 'ida or a'âdi enemy
a'ḍu, pl. a'ḍa member, limb
*adwiye* pl. of dawa
'â'fâ to restore to, or preserve in, health
'*afârim!* bravo!
afḍâl (pl. of faḍl) favors, proofs of kindness
'âfiyi, 'âfyi health
afkâr pl. of fikr
afkhâd pl. of fakhd
afrâs pl. of faras
'afsh (small) luggage
'afshîka of bad quality, inferior
'afu pardon
'*agele* wheel
'*agem* Persian (coll.)
aḥad one, any one
yaum el-aḥad Sunday
ahâli inhabitant
'ahd treaty
aḥjâr *aḥgâr* pl. of ḥajar
ahl inhabitant (coll.), family, household; ahlilbait' family, housewife; ahl la .. *ahl li* .. fit for .., worthy of ..
ahlan wasah'lan! welcome!
aḥmaḳ foolish, stupid
aḥmar, fem. ḥamra, pl. ḥumr red
aḥruf pl. of ḥarf

aḥsan, aḥsin **better, more;** aḥsan'lak, aḥsin'lak **it is better for you, so much the better!**
aḥwâl **pl. of** ḥâl
ai **that is to say, namely**
'aib *'êb* **shame;** 'aib 'alaik' **it is a disgrace to you! be ashamed of yourself!**
yâ 'aib ishshûm! **what a shame! expression of confusion and shame, or excuse, when a visitor or guest cannot be duly received**
'â=ile **family**
ailûl *êlûl'* **September**
aimta? *imte?* **when?**
ain? *ên?* **where?**
'ain *'ên,* **pl.** 'uyûn *'iyûn* **eye; spring, fountain; gold piece, in specie, e.g.** tlât lîrât''ain **three pounds in gold;** yâ 'aini! yâ 'uyûni! *yâ 'iyûni!* **my eye! my eyes! (words of endearment)**
aina? **which? what? see p. 17, e.g.** min aina jins **or** min aina shikl? **of what sort, kind?**
aish? *ê?* **what?** *ê* **is always placed after the verb or subject, e.g. what do you want?** aish bitrîd? *bitrîd ê?*
aiy, **fem.** aiye? **which? what?** see p. 17
*aiyâm* **pl. of** yaum
*'aiyân* **ill, unwell, weak**
*'aiyaṭ* **to cry**
*'aiyâṭ* **screams, cries**
'ajab *'agab* (*i*) **to please**
'ajam *'agem* **Persian (coll.);** blâd il'a'jam **Persia;** 'ajami **Persian (a single one)**
ajânib **pl. of** ajnabi *agânib*
'ajâyib (**pl. of** 'ajîbi) *'âga=ib* **strange things; strange!**
'ajel 'ajâli' *'agel 'agale* **haste, urgency**
'ajîb *'agîb* **wonderful, strange**
'ajîbi *'agîbe* **anything extraordinary; (adv.) strangely;** see 'ajâyib
'âjiz *'âgiz* **weak, impotent, exhausted**
'ajjaz *'aggiz* **to render one weak; disturb**
ajmal *agmal* (min) **nicer, more beautiful (than)**
ajnabi *agnabi,* **pl.** ajânib **strange(r), foreign(er)**
ajnâs *agnâs* **pl. of** jins
'ajûz *'agûze,* **pl.** 'ajâyiz **old woman**
'aḳad (u) **to knot**
akal *kal* (*u*) **to eat**
akbar (min) **greater, bigger (than)**
'aḳd **knot, treaty**
aḳdâḥ **pl. of** ḳadaḥ
akh, **pl.** ikhwi **or** ikhwân **brother**
akhad *khad* (*u*) **to take;** akhad 'ala khâṭro **to take amiss;** akhad bard **to catch cold**
âkhar, **fem.** ukhra, **pl.** ukhar **the other, another**
akhbâr, **pl. of** khabar

akhḍar, **fem.** khaḍra, **pl.** khuḍr **green**
âkhir **last**
bilâkhir **at last, at the end**
akhîran' **lastly, at last, later**
*akhôr* **stable**
akhras, **fem.** ḳarsa **dumb**
akîd **certain, sure**
'âḳil **intelligent, prudent, quiet, rational**
akkad *akkiā* **to assure**
akl **food**
'aḳl **mind, intellect**
*akle* **meal**
'aḳrab **scorpion; hand of a clock**
'akrût **procurer (favorite insult)**
'aks **contrary, reverse**
aktar (min) **more (than)**
aḳwa **stronger**
aḳwas **finer, more beautiful**
'al **for** 'ala il **on the, e.g.** 'alkur'si = 'ala ilkur'si **on the chair**
'âl **excellent, capital; e.g.** min jins il'âl **of the best quality**
'ala **(prep.) on, upon**
'ala mahlak ! **slowly !**
'ala râsi **properly: on my head, e.g. as you may command me**
'ala mahlak ! **slowly !**
*'ala shân* **for**
'alaḳ **leech**
âlây' **regiment**
*aldiwân*, **plur.** *-ât* **glove**
alf, **plur.** alâf **thousand**
'alfaur' **suddenly**

'âli **high;** 'âli 'an .. bi .. **high over .. by .., i.e. higher than .. by ..**
âli, **pl.** âlât' **instrument**
'âlim **wise; learned man**
'alîm Allâh ! **God knows! (asseveration)**
'alḳiyâs **in proportion to, analogically**
Allâh, Alla **God;** Alla ysallmak, Alla yiḥfazak **God keep you;** Alla yin'im 'alaik' **God prosper you;** Alla ya'ṭîk, Alla yib'at'-lak **God give you; see also pp. 43, 44, nd notes on pp. 32, 33, 39**
Allâhu a'lam ! **or** Allâhu il'alîm ! **God knows it best ! God knows !**
'allaḳ **to suspend, hang up;** 'allaḳ 'ala **to feed (cattle)**
'allam *'allim* **to teach**
almâni **German**
almânya **Germany**
almâs **diamond; also a female proper name**
*alsine* **plur. of** lisân
alwâḥ **pl. of** lauḥ
alwân **pl. of** laun
'alyamîn **on, or to, the right**
'am, 'amma, 'ammâl **particle; placed before the aorist it forms the present; e.g.** 'am biktub **I am writing**
'âm **year;** 'âm ilau'wal **or** 'amlau'wal *'âmenau'wal* **last year**
'âm (u) **to swim**

a'ma, pl. 'umyân blind
amal hope
'amal (i) to do ; an action
amân protection, safety ; pardon ; help ; bi=amânillâh' ! or fil=amân ! adieu ! God be with you !
amâni safety; trust, charge ; object deposited with somebody for safety
amar, âmar (u) to command, order
'amâr '*imâra*, pl. 'amâr building, edifice
'amâra fleet, squadron
*ambiya* pl. of nabi
amîn sure, faithful, reliable
amîr or mîr *emîr* prince ; see 'bêk,' note
amkan to be possible ; amkan'ni it was possible for me, I have been able to
'amm pl. 'umûmi uncle, father-in-law
amma but, however
'amma ; see 'am
ammal to hope
'ammâl ; see 'am
'ammar to build
amr, pl. umûr thing, affair, business
amr, pl. awâmir order, decree
'amr life ; yikta' 'amro prop. : may his life be cut off (favorite malediction)
ams yesterday
'âmûd', pl. 'awâmîd' column, pillar
'an (prep.) of, from, for, on
ana I
an'am 'ala . . to grant a favor to .
'and (prep.) with, by ; la'and' to
'*aneb* ; see 'inib
'ankabût spider
ankar to deny
'anṣara Whitsuntide ; 'îd il'an'ṣara feast of Pentecost
ant thou (masc.)
anti thou (fem.)
*antikagi* dealer in antiquities
antîkât' antiquities
*anwâ'* pl. of nau'
anwâr pl. of nûr
anzâr (pl. of nazar) looks, countenance ; bi=anzârak, b=anzârak, taḥt il=anzâr under your looks, under your kind regard (viz. I am well ; reply to the inquiry after the health); see p. 83, No. 8
'âr shame, disgrace
'arab Arab (coll.), implying, however, nomadic Arabs (Bedouins) only ; the peasant and townsman calls himself ibn 'arab (prop., son of the Arab), pl. ûlâd' il'a'rab, fem. bint 'arab, fem. pl. bnât 'arab
'araba'ji '*araba'gi* coachman
'arabâyi '*arabîye* coach, cab, carriage
'arabi, fem. 'arabîyi Arab, Arabic, Arabian ; il'a'rabi the Arabic language (in general); il'arabîyi the Arabic written language

ʿaraḍ (u) to present, show, bring before; tâ aʿruḍ'lak (prop.: that I may submit to you; a polite form for:) allow me to inform you
arâ'ḍî (pl. of arḍ) landed property
ʿaraḍi accidental, casual
ʿaraḍîyi a passing indisposition
ʿaraj *ʿarag* to limp
aʿraj *aʿrag* limping, lame
ʿarak̇ sweat; (= ʿarak̇i) raki, a liqueur distilled from wine
arâkîl' (pl. of argîli) hookah-pipes
ʿarâyis pl. of ʿarûs
arâzîl' pl. of razîl
arbʿa four; yaum il=ar'baʿ Wednesday
ʿarbaji coachman
*ʿarbûn* earnest-money
arḍ (fem.) earth, land; see arâ'ḍî
ʿarḍ breadth, latitude
*ardebb'* a dry measure; see bushel, p. 168
*arḍêḥâl* petition
arḍîyi *k̇aṣrîye* chamber-utensil
ʿarḍîyi: biʿarḍîyit ijjum'ʿa in the course of the week
ʿarḍuḥâl petition, memorial
argîli, arkîli *shîshe* hookah; pl. arâkîl'
ʿarîḍ broad
ʿarîs, pl. ʿirsân bridegroom; marriageable son
arjûk I ask you
arkhaṣ min cheaper than
ʿark̇îyi cap for perspiration
aṛlab overcoming, preponderating; bil=aṛ'lab mostly
*armâḥ* pl. of rumḥ
armal widower, armale widow
arnab, arneb hare
*aṛos'ṭos*, August (month)
ʿarraf *ʿarrif* to make known, let know, acquaint; ʿarrif'ni ʿan..let me know, inform me of ..; shû biʿarrif'ni! what do I know!
arrakh to date, fix the date
ʿarras to take a nap towards the end of the night; lead a loose life
aṛribi pl. of ṛurâb
aṛrife pl. of raṛîf
ʿarsa a loose-living man
ʿarûs *ʿarûse*, pl. ʿarâyis marriageable young lady, fiancée, bride, young wife until the first confinement
arz *erz* (coll.) cedars; arzi cedar (a single one)
ʿaṣab, pl. aʿṣâb nerve
asad, pl. usûd or usud lion
ʿaṣâfîr' pl. of ʿaṣfûr
ʿasal, ʿasel honey
asâmi pl. of ism
asar, pl. âsâr' trace, vestige effect; pl. monuments
ʿaṣar to press, squeeze
*asbâb* pl. of sabab
aṣfar, fem. ṣafra, pl. ṣufr yellow
ʿaṣfûr, pl. ʿaṣâfîr' little bird
ʿâsh (yeʿîsh) to live

ʿasha *ʿashe* supper
*aṣḥab*; see ṣâḥib
*ʿashara* ten
ʿashîyi *ʿishe* evening; fil ʿashîyi or min ʿashîyi in the evening
ashḳar, ashḳarâni light red, fair, blonde
ʿashra *ʿashara* ten
ashrâf pl. of sharîf
*ashṛâl* (pl. of shuṛl) affairs
ʿashshi cook
ʿâ'ṣî refractory, rebellious
*as-ili* pl. of *su-âl*
aṣîr captive
ʿasker (coll.) army, soldiers
ʿaskeri soldier (a single one)
aṣl, pl. uṣûl origin, root, element
aṣlan original, radical, thorough
asmâ pl. of ism
asmar, fem. samra, pl. sumr brown, brunette
asmarâni brownish
ʿaṣr late afternoon, last part of the day
assar fî to have effect, make an impression on
aswad *iswid*, fem. sauda, pl. sûd black
*aswak* pl. of sûḳ
aṣwât pl. of ṣaut
aʿṭa (i) to give
atar trace; see asar
ʿaṭas (a) to sneeze
ʿaṭash thirst
ʿatîḳ, pl. ʿutuḳ old
ʿâṭil bad, damaged
ʿaṭl interest
ʿatm darkness, duskiness
aṭrâf pl. of ṭaraf
ʿaṭrash, fem. ṭarsha deaf
*ʿaṭshân*; see ʿitshân
ʿaṭṭal to leave unemployed, hinder, spoil, destroy
ʿattam to grow dusk; ʿattamit iddin'yi (or iddi'ni) it has got dark
ʿaṭṭâr druggist, perfumer
audaʿ: audaʿnâk! goodbye!
auḥasht'na prop.: you left us lonely, i.e. we have felt your absence, we have missed you; see p. 37, No. 5
ʿauja fem. of aʿwaj
auḳât or ûḳât' (pl. of waḳt) times; auḳâtak saʿîdi (reply: yisʿid auḳâtak) good day; baʿḍ ilauḳât sometimes, at times, now and then
*aulâd*; see ûlâd' and walad
aulâni or ûlâ'ni first
ʿauwad to return, turn back (adv.) again; after all, yet
ʿauwaḍ to make up for, compensate
auwal, auwil *auwalâni*, fem. ûla *auwalânî'ye* first bilau'wal at first, in the beginning
auwal embâriḥ the day before yesterday
ʿauzi need, want
ʿawa (i) to howl
ʿawâfi, ilʿawâfi! health! hail! greeting!
aʿwaj *aʿwag*, fem. ʿauja, pl. ʿûj crooked
ʿawâmîd' pl. of ʿâmûd'

awâmir **pl. of** amr
aʿwar **one-eyed**
ʿawâyid **pl. of** ʿâdi
ayâdi **pl. of** yadd
ʿâyiz **being in need of**; ana (int, hû, **etc.**) ʿâyiz maṣâri **I (thou, he, etc.) need money i.e. have none; in Egypt it often means 'desiring, wanting' only, e.g.** *ana* (*int*, **etc.**) *ʿâ:iz arûḥ* **I (thou, etc.) will (wilt, etc.) go, I wish to go, etc.**
aʿzab **unmarried, single (said of a man)**
ʿazâb **pain, torment**
ʿazal (i) **to dismiss, displace (from office)**
ʿazam (i) **to invite**
aʿzam **bigger, greater**
azan (i) **to permit**
azân **call to prayer**
ʿazar (i) **to excuse, accept one's excuse**
ʿazîz **dear, honored**
azraḳ, **fem.** zarḳa, **pl.** zurḳ **[blue]**
*azrire* ; see zirr
ʿazza **to condole with one**
ʿazzab **to torment**
ʿazzal **to clear and clean out**
bâʿ (yebîʿ) **to sell**
baʿat **to send**
bâb, **pl.** ibwâb **door; chapter;** ilbâb ilʿâ'lî **the Sublime Porte**
*bâbûg'*, **pl.** *bawâbîg'* **slipper**
bâbû'nij **camomile**
baʿd **(prep.) after**
**(adv.) yet**
baʿḍ **some, a few;** baʿḍ innâs **some people, many people**
badal **(prep.) instead of**
badan **body, trunk**
badawi, **pl.** badu *bedwân* **Arab, Bedouin**
badd *bidd* **to wish, be willing:** baddi, baddak, baddo, baddha (badda), baddna, baddkon, baddhon **I, thou, he, she, we, you, they will**
baʿdên **afterwards**
badr **full moon**
*badri* **early**
bahâ **beauty**
bahâr **spice, pepper**
bahdal **to insult, scoff, despise**
bahdali **insult, derision**
baḥr **sea;** baḥr innîl *baḥr ennîl* **or** *elbaḥr'* **the Nile**
baḥri **sailor, seaman**
baḥs **discussion**
bai **father**
baiḍ *bêḍ* **eggs (coll.)**
baiḍa **egg (a single one)**
baʿîd, bʿîd **far, distant**
ilbaʿîd **prop.: the remote one; when invectives are said this is interjected in the speech in order to exclude the person addressed**
baʿîd ʿannak **prop.: far from you (viz. be it!); it is interjected in the speech when an accident, an illness, a death, etc. are mentioned**
bain *bên* **(prep.) between**
bait *bêt*, **pl.** byût **house; housewife (with the Muslims)**

baiṭar to shoe (a horse)
baiṭâr *bêṭâr'* farrier
baitilmâ, baitilfa'ḍa privy, closet
baiyâ' seller
baiyaḍ to whiten; baiyaḍ wishsh .., properly: to whiten some one's face, i.e. to justify some one
baiyan *baiyin* to explain
baiyin distinct, clear; il-bai'yin it seems
bak, bâk with you, in you; shû bâk? what is the matter with you?
baḳa at last; yet
frequently untranslatable, used when beginning a sentence = for the rest, by the by, now, finally
bakar roll, ball
baḳar (coll.) cattle
baḳara cow (a single one)
baḳdûnis parsley
bakhîl, pl. bukhala miserly, stingy
bakhkhar to fumigate
bakhshîsh *baḳshîsh* gratuity, tip
bakhûr incense
baḳḳ bugs
baḳḳâl greengrocer
bakkar to be early, get up early
bakkîr early, too early
bâl mind, thought, memory; see also dâr, dîr, râḥ
bala (adv.) yes! yea!
bala (prep.) without
bala shakk without doubt
bala' (a) to swallow

balad *beled* place, town; district, country
baladi native, of the country; (and therefore) noble, superior, e.g. ma'z baladi high-class (blood) goat; nbîd baladi Lebanon wine
balaḥ dates
bal'am to devour
balaṛ (u) to reach, attain
*balâsh* in vain, to no purpose
balâṭ pavement, flag-stone
balîd dull, stupid
balîyi calamity, misfortune
ball (i) to wet
ballaṛ to cause to attain, convey, bring
ballash to begin
ballaṭ to pave
ballûṭ oak
balwa misfortune, affliction
*banât* pl. of bint
bandai'ra *bandêra* flag, banner
banṭalûn trousers
bantuf'li slipper
b-anzârak under your regards; see anzâr
barad hail, hail-stone
baraḍ to hate, detest
baraḳ to lighten, flash
bâraḳ to bless
baraki blessing; see p. 37
barânîs' pl. of burnus
barâniṭ' pl. of burnai'ṭa
baraṣ leprosy
barâwîz' pl. of birwâz
bard cold, coldness
bardîyi cold fever
*barîd* I will

bârid cold, frosty; (of people) indifferent, dull
bârîk pl. of brîk
bark lightning, flash
barl (coll.) mules
 barli mule (a single one)
barmi turn, twist, loop
barmîl cask
barr land, continent (in opp. to bahr sea)
barra outside; min barra from outside; labar'ra out, thither, hither
barrad to cool, make cool, refresh
barrak to congratulate, invoke benediction
barrâni outer, external; (adv.) direct
barrash (coll.) gnats
barrât (prep.) outside
barrîyi open country (in opp. to town, village); desert; bilbarrîyi, filbarrîyi in the open land
barrût, pl. bararît flea
bartal (a) to bribe
bârûd' gunpowder
bârû'di, pl. bwârîd' or bawârîd' gun, musket
ba-s: lâ ba-s it does not matter
bâs (u) to kiss
basal onions
basar (trans.) to see
basar (noun) sight, vision
bâsha; see bêk, note
bashar mankind; bani bashar human beings (prop.: children of the flesh, in opp. to superior beings)
bashûsh friendly, affable
basît simple
bass only; enough!
bast gladness, amusement
bât armpit, shoulder
bât (yebât) to pass the night
batâni lining (of clothes)
batâta *batâtis* (coll.) potatoes
batîha bog
bâtıl void, vain
batn belly
batrak, pl. batârki patriarch
batt (coll.) ducks
 batta duck (a single one)
batta calf (of the leg)
battal to stop (doing something), be disinclined to do something
battâl useless, bad
battan to line (clothes)
battîkh melon; battîkh ahmar *battîkh* watermelon; battîkh asfar *kâwûn'* or *shammâm* sweet melon
baurad to cool
bausi *bôse* kiss
bauwâb door-keeper, gatekeeper
bauwâbi gate, gateway
bauwal to urinate
bauwas to kiss
bawârîd' pl. of bârû'di
bazabort' passport
bâzâr' market
bâzel'la (coll.) green peas
bazzâka snail
bdâl *bidâl* (prep.) instead of

bdâyi *bidâye* beginning; bilbdâyi, filbdâyi in the beginning
bdûn *bidûn* (prep.) without
bêʿ sale
*bêḍ* eggs (coll.)
*bêḍa* an egg
*bedle* suit, clothes
bedri early
*bedwân* pl. of badawi
bêk[1] Bey

---

[1] Effendi is any one who can read and write; Bey, pronounced bê by the Turks, bêk by the Arabs, and Pasha, Arabic bâsha, are titles conferred by the Porte. The title Bey is, however, often wrongfully assumed (somewhat like the Austrian 'baron'), and almost every young Turkish fop claims to be addressed by it. But after all, these titles have nothing to do with the dignity: there are mutessarrifs, i.e. governors, and what is more, state ministers, who after their names have simply the title of Effendi. Nor does the religion make any difference: there are in Turkey a good many Christian Effendis, Beys, and Pashas. In Syria and Egypt the title Effendi is restricted to government officials and influential private persons; it is always placed after the name, that is to say, it is inserted between the first name and the family name; but the word corresponding to our 'Mr.' is with Christians khawâja *khawâga*, and with Muslims saiyid, or, when they have made the pilgrimage, ḥajj *ḥagg*. In the address these titles are, as in English, used without the article, but the person is generally accosted by the first name only: Mr. George! yâ khawâja jirji! *yâ khawâga girgi!* Mr. Omar! yâ saiyid ʿomar! or yâ ḥajj ʿomar! *yâ ḥagg ʿomar!* If, however, a person is mentioned who is absent or not spoken to, the khawâja *khawâga*, saiyid or ḥajj *ḥagg* must be preceded by the article, e.g. have you seen Mr. George? shuft ilkhawâja jirji *shuft elkhawâga girgi*, have you seen Mr. Omar? shuft issai'yid ʿomar? *essai'yid ʿomar?* or ilḥajj' ʿomar? *elḥagg' ʿomar?* Neither in the address nor at the mention of a person are these titles used if, instead of his usual name, the honorary name, i.e. the name after the first-born son, is employed, e.g. abu selîm 'Selim's father.' In the same way 'Mrs.' and 'Miss' in the direct address are rendered by sitt, but at the mention of the ladies by issitt' *essitt'*; married ladies

bela (adv.) yes
bela (prep.) without
bêlik' a small war vessel
*berîme* screw, corkscrew
*berḳûḳ* plum
bess only; enough!
*betâ'*, fem. *betâ-a(t)*, pl. *butû'* property (serves for expressing possession)
bi (prep.) with, by, through
b'îd far
*bidâl* instead
*bidâye* beginning
*bidd* to wish, be willing
*bidûn* without
*bikâm*; see kam, kâm
*bikhêr* in good
biki (i) to weep, cry
biḳi (a) to remain, last
bikr virgin
bilâ (prep.) without
*bilâd* land
bil-ak'tar more, still more
bilâsh *balâsh* in vain; for nothing; unnecessary!
bilkfâyi sufficiently, enough
billâh! by God! billâh 'alaik'! for God's sake! (viz. I implore you!)
bilmîyi per cent.

---

are as a rule simply called after the name of their first son, e.g. umm selîm 'Selim's mother,' without sitt.

The title Bey is sometimes conferred by the Porte on influential Syrians as a title of honor, and for a political purpose. The title of Pasha, Arabic bâsha, is but seldom obtained by Syrians, and then only when they are in the service of the Porte.

Upon the whole, all these Turkish titles are little respected by the Syrian people; not much more so, except in some parts of the mountains, is the native nobility of the Lebanon; there are two classes of it: (1) shaikh *shêkh* is the name given to those of the gentry: chief of a Bedouin tribe or clan (not to be confounded with shaikh *shêkh* 'aged man, teacher, professor,' also title given to learned men); (2) emîr or mîr, originally a commander, generally rendered by 'prince,' of which, indeed, it was formerly the equivalent.

With a few exceptions the nobility, especially that of the Druses, has lost its wealth, influence, and respect. Display and the maintenance of great hospitality are the only cares of the Syrian noble families, but they take no pains to provide the wherewithal, and therefore are continually declining, and you may find 'emirs' as privates in the Lebanon militia, and 'emiresses' as maidservants.

bimbashi **major**
bina **building, edifice**
binâ-an ʿala .. **in virtue of, on the ground of ..**
binaf'saj *binaf'sag* **violet**
binn *bunn* **coffee in berries (coll.)**; binni *bunne* **coffee-berry (a single one)**
bint *binte*, **pl.** bnât *banât* **daughter, girl**
bint ʿarab, **pl.** bnât ʿarab *banât ʿarab* **settled, domiciled Arab, Egyptian, Syrian woman**; see p. 127 note
bint ʿammi, ʿammti **daughter of my uncle, of my aunt on father's side; also: my wife (corruption of** bint ḥami **daughter of my father-in-law)**
bint khâli, khalti **daughter of my uncle, of my aunt on mother's side**
bintilkha'ṭa, bintilḥarâm **daughter of sin, prostitute**
bintu **(from Italian 'venti') twenty-franc piece, French pound**
binye, **pl.** binan **bodily structure**
bîr **well, spring**
bîra **beer**
birdâyi **curtain**
birêbeti **in my absence**
birîd **I will**
birki, **pl.** burak **basin, pond**
birrîni *berîme* **screw, cork-screw**
birwâz, **pl.** barâwîz' **frame**
bishiʿ **ugly**
*bishwêsh* **slow**
bîṭâr' **veterinary surgeon, farrier**
bitrîd **you will; will you? shû** bitrîd? **what do you want?**
bizr **seed; kernel**
bizz, **pl.** bzâz **breast (female)**
bizzyâdi **too much**
bkhair *bikhêr* **in the good, in prosperity, in happiness**; cf. pp. 43, 44
bkhûsh **pl. of** bukhsh
blâd *bilâd* **country**; blâd ilʿa'jam **Persia**; blâd ilinglîz **England**; blâd ilmis'kob *elmos'kob* **Russia**
blâṭ **pavement; square-stone**
blâṭa **stone slab**
bnât **pl. of** bint
bôdra **powder (except: gunpowder)**
*bolîs* **police**
*bortuḳân* **oranges**
*bôse* **kiss**
brîd *barîd* **I will**
brîḳ or ibrîḳ *ebrîḳ*, **pl.** *bârîḳ'* **jug**
brisht **soft boiled (of eggs)**
brûd **coolness, morning freshness**
brûsiya **Prussia**
bsaini *bsêne* **cat**
bsâṭ, **pl.** busṭ *busâṭ* **cover, carpet**
bsâtîn' **pl. of** bustân
bshâra **good news**
buʿd **distance**
buḍâʿa, **pl.** baḍâʿi **ware, merchandise**
bukhala **pl. of** bakhîl
bukhl **avarice**

bukhsh, pl. bkhûsh hole
bukra morning, to-morrow
'ala or 'an bukra, 'abbuk'ra early in the morning
bulbul nightingale
bûmâ'ḍa pomatum
bûmi owl
*bunn, bunne* coffee in berries
burak pl. of birki
buṛâz pass (mountain), straits
burḍ hatred, disgust
burdkân *bortuḳân* oranges (coll.)
burdkâni *bortuḳâne* orange (a single one)
burnai'ṭa *burnêṭa*, pl. barânîṭ' hat
burnus, pl. barânîs' silk cloak
burṣ pl. of abraṣ
burûd freshness (of the morning)
*busâṭ* cover, carpet
bûsi kiss
busṭ, pl. of bsâṭ
busṭa post, post-office
bustân, pl. bsâtîn' garden, orchard
bûz snout, muzzle
bwârîd' pl. of bârû'di
byût pl. of bait
bzâz pl. of bizz
*da* this; see p. 16
dâ illness, disease; dâ innuk'ṭa epilepsy; dâ ilmulûk gout; dâ izzuh'ra or dâ ilmubârek syphilis
ḍâ' (yeḍî') to be lost
da'âwi pl. of da'wa
dâb (ydûb) to melt, dissolve
ḍab' hyena
ḍabâb fog
dabâbîs' pl. of dabbûs
dabaḥ (a) to kill, slaughter
ḍabb to pack together
dabbar to procure; manage
dabbâṛ tanner
dâbbi *rukûbe*, pl. dawâbb or dwâbb beast, horse, mule, ass
dabbûs, pl. dabâbîs' pin
dafa' (a) to push back, ward off; to pay, give
ḍafâdi' pl. of ḍifda'
dafan (i) to bury
daff *reḳḳ*, pl. dfûf tambour; tambourine, with small bells
daffa to make warm
dâfi warm
ḍâfîr' pl. of ḍifr
daftar, pl. dafâtir or dfâtir *defâtir* account book, register; pl. archives
dahab gold
*dahabîye* Nile-boat
dahan (i) to smear
ḍahar to go out
dahhan to smear
dahr time, age; world
ḍahr back (hinder part)
ḍai'a, pl. ḍiya' village
ḍaif *ḍêf*, pl. ḍuyûf or ḍiyûf guest
ḍa'îf weak, ill; thin
dâi-kh giddy
dain *dên*, pl. dyûn *diyûn* debt; 'alai'yi dain I have debts
daini ear

dair *dêr*, pl. idyura or dyûra *diyûr* convent, abbey
daiya' to lose
daiyât (pl. of îd) hands; Alla ysallim daiyâtak! thanks! (prop.: God save you your hands!)
ḍaiyiḳ *ḍaiyaḳ* narrow, strait
dâḳ (u) to taste
ḍâḳ (yḍîḳ) to be narrow
ḍaḳal to prevent
dakar male
daḳâyiḳ pl. of daḳîḳa
dâkh (u) to become giddy
dakhal (u) to enter, go in
dâkhil in, inside, within
dakhîlak or dakhlak I beg you, implore you
dakhkhal to let come in, introduce, bring in
daḳîḳa, pl. daḳâyiḳ minute, moment
dakk (u) to load (a gun)
daḳḳ (u) to beat, strike (also of a clock)
daḳn beard; chin
dalîl, pl. adil'li or dalâyil proof (in Egypt: guide)
dall (i, u) to direct, guide, show the way; dall 'ala.. to direct to some one
ḍall to remain, stay
dallâl crier, auctioneer
dâlûl' guide
dâlyi vine
dam blood
dâm (u) to last
dam'a, pl. dumû' tear; drop
ḍamâne security, bail
ḍâmin or ḍammân surety
ḍamîr interior, secret thought
damm to remain
ḍâni or laḥm ḍâni mutton
dâr in Egypt, house; in Syria, the inner hall of a house, generally covered, around which the rooms are situated without being connected with one another
dâr (yedûr) to go or turn round, be going; (yedîr) to make or cause to move round, turn round, direct, control, set agoing; dâr ilbâl 'ala to pay attention to
dâ'râ to tend, take care of
ḍarab (a) to beat, hit
darabuk'ka; see dirbek'ki
daraje *darage*, pl. -ât degree, step
ḍarar damage
daras to study, learn
darb, pl. durûb or drûb way, road, street
ḍarb blow, hit
ḍarbi blow, misfortune
darfi wing (of a door, window, etc.)
ḍarîr blind
ḍarr (u) to injure, hurt
darras to teach
dars, pl. durûs or drûs lesson, instruction
dashar to run or walk about loose
dâshir loose, roaming about
dashshar to chase away; to let alone, quit
dass to touch, feel

dastûr! **permission!**
ḍau **light, day, daylight**
dauḳ *dôḳ* **taste**
dauli *dôle*, **pl.** duwal **empire, realm, power**
daur *dôr* **fever; turn, period;** iddaur' ʿala mîn? **whose turn is it?** ija daurak **your turn has come**
daura *dôra* **round-about way; rotation**
ḍauwa **to kindle, light**
dauwar **to turn (trans.)**
ḍauwi! **kindle! light!**
dauwir! **turn round! turn back! (trans.)**
dawa, **pl.** idwiyi **or** idwyi *adwiye* **medicine, remedy**
daʿwa, **pl.** daʿâwi **pretension, claim; lawsuit**
dawābb **pl. of** dābbi
dâwam ʿala.. **to persevere in.., pursue steadily..**
dawâwîn' **pl. of** dîwân'
daʿwi **invitation; matter, affair;** shû iddaʿ'wi? *eddaʿ'we ê?* **what is the matter? what is the point in question?**
ḍâyan **to endure, last, wear (well, etc.)**
dāyi **midwife**
dāyim *dâ=im* **everlasting, continual**
dāyiman *dâ=iman* **or** dāyman **always**
dâyir mindâr **round about**
*defâtir* **pl. of** daftar
*ḍêl*, **pl.** *ḍiyûl* **tail**
deneb **tail**
derwîsh, **pl.** derâwîsh' **dervish**
*desem'ber* **December**
dfûf **pl. of** daff
*di*, **fem.** *dî* **this;** **see p. 16**
dîb, **pl.** diyâb **wolf**
dibbān **(coll.) fly**
dibbāni **fly (a single one)**
dibḥ **(the) slaughtering; something slaughtered**
ḍidd **against, contrary, contrarily**
ḍifdaʿ, **pl.** ḍafâdiʿ **frog**
ḍiji **to get warm, warm oneself**
ḍifr, **pl.** aḍâfîr' **or** ḍâfîr' **finger-nail**
diheb **gold**
ḍiḥik (a) **to laugh**
dihn **grease, fat**
ḍiʿif (a) **to become ill, weak; to grow thin**
dîk, **pl.** diyûk **or** dyûk **cock, rooster;** dîk ḥabesh **turkey-cock**
ḍîḳ **narrowness, need**
*dik-ha* **that, yon (fem.)**
dikkān, **pl.** dkākîn' **shop**
ḍilim **dark, obscure**
ḍill **shade**
dillāl **auctioneer, crier**
dimâr **brain, head**
dimmi **conscience**
dîn **religion, creed, religiousness**
dinyi, dini **world, the present world; (weather)** **see pp. 64 to 66**
dîr bālak! **look out! mind!**
dirbek'ki **or** darabuk'ka **drum-like instrument**
dirhem, **pl.** derâhim **drachm**
diri (i) **to know**

ḍirs, pl. aḍrâs molar, grinder
dîwân′, pl. dawâwîn′ Turkish sofa; collection of poems (of a particular poet)
ḍiyaʿ pl. of ḍaiʿa
*diyâne* religion
ḍiyûf pl. of ḍaif
*diyûn* pl. of dain
*diyûr* pl. of dair
dôgri, dôgru straight, correct; straight on!
*dôḳ* taste
*doḳ-ha*, fem. *diḳ-ha* yon, that
drâʿ, pl. idruʿ arm, forearm; cubit
drûb or durûb pl. of darb
du′ʿâ prayer, wish
du꞊âf sudden death
dubb, pl. dubab bear (animal)
dubbân same as dibbân
dûd (coll.) worm; dûd ilḥarîr or dûd ilḳazz′ the silkworm
dûdi worm (a single one)
duʿf weakness
dûfân′ deadly poison
ḍufr finger-nail
*dugâg* poultry
ḍuhr noon, midday
dukhân smoke, tobacco
dukkân shop
dûlâb′, pl. dawâlîb′ or dwâlîb′ wheel; cupboard
dumli tumor
dûn low, common
dûr! turn round! (intr.)
durr pearls; durra a pearl
durra maize; durra bêḍa millet
durrâḳ *khôkh* peaches (coll.)
durûb pl. of darb
ḍurûra necessity, need
ḍurûri necessary
durûs pl. of dars
durzi Druse
duwal pl. of dauli
ḍuyûf pl. of ḍaif
dwâbb pl. of dâbbi
dyâni *diyâne* religion, faith
dyûra pl. of dair
ê (adv.) that is viz.
*ê?* what?
*ebeden*; see abadan
*ebrîḳ* jug
effendi; see p. 317, note
*el*; see il
*embâriḥ* yesterday
*emîr*; see amîr
*emlâk* pl. of mulk
*emsâl*; see matal
en′hû, fem. en′hî, pl. enhum which? what? see p. 17
*enti* thou (fem.)
*es-hâm* pl. of sâhm
ʿeshara ten
*eshkâl* pl. of shikl
*eshrâl* pl. of shurl
*esnân* pl. of sinn
*etnên* two; *yôm eletnên* Monday
faḍḍa silver, para
fâḍi empty; unoccupied
faḍîḥa shame, disgrace
faḍl, pl. afḍâl pre-eminence; preference; benefit, favor; kullo min faḍlak all through your favor, everything is owing to you
faḥaṣ (a) to examine, investigate

fahham *fakhim* (with double accus.) to make some one understand sthg., explain
fâḥish foul, low, obscene; taman fâḥish an excessive price
fâḥishi, pl. fawâḥish abandoned woman
fahm understanding, intelligence
faḥm (coll.) coal; faḥm ḥajar mineral coal, pit coal
faḥṣ examination, investigation
fâʿil day-laborer, workman
failasûf, pl. flâsfi *felâsife* philosopher
fain? *fên?* where?
faiyaḳ to awake, waken
fajj *figg* unripe (of fruit)
fajr *fagr* morning flush
fâḳ (yfîḳ) to wake up; fâḳ ʿala .. to recollect
faḳaʿ to burst, pop
faḳaṭ' only, but
fakhd, pl. afkhâd thigh; leg (of mutton, etc.)
*fâkhûr'* earthen vessel
fâkiha a fruit (of trees); pl. fuâki *fewâkih* fruit
faḳîr, pl. fuḳara poor
fakk (u) to untie, loose
fakkar to remind
faḳr poverty
falaḥ (a) to plough
falân a certain person, so and so, Mr. what's his name
fall, pl. fulûl fissure, notch
fallâḥ *fellâḥ* peasant
fallâḥa peasant woman
fallas to become bankrupt, have no money
falsafe philosophy
fanâr lighthouse, paper or stuff lantern
fânel'la flannel
fânûs' glass lantern
fâr, pl. fîrân' mouse; in Egypt, also: rat
faraḥ joy, festival, occasion of a marriage
farak to rub (and press)
faraḳ to separate, distinguish; mâ btifriḳ maʿi it makes no difference to me, that is the same to me
faras, pl. afrâs mare
farash (u, i) to spread on the floor, prepare the bed
farâsh butterfly, moth
fard single, one, unique; fard marra a single time, at one time, all at once
fard pistol
farḍ, pl. furûḍ statute, command, duty; farḍ ʿalai'yi a duty upon me, it is my duty
farḥân glad
fâriṛ empty
farḳ separation, difference
farkha offset, shoot; in Egypt: hen
farmashîyi pharmacy
farraḳ to separate
farraṛ to empty, pour out
farsh bedding, bed-clothes
farshi mattress
farṭ small money
farwi fur, fur coat
fâs hatchet

fasâḥa **eloquence**
fashak, fashki *fashûka* **cartridge; rocket**
fashkha **step, pace**
fashr! **ah! aha! psh!**
*fashûka*; **see fashak**
fâsid **spoiled, ruined**
fasîḥ **eloquent, intelligible**
faskîye **fountain**
fasl, **pl.** fuṣûl **section, chapter; difference; stupid trick;** shû hal faṣl? **what a silly thing is this?** wallâhi faṣl! **that is by Allah a strange thing!**
fassar **to comment, explain**
faṣûlya **French beans**
fât (yfût) **to go by, pass, elapse;** fât ilwakt' **it has got late**
fataḥ (a) **to open**
faṭar (i, a) **to breakfast**
fâtir **lukewarm, tepid**
fattash ʿala .. **to look for**
fatwa **legal decision; answer to a question of (Mohammedan) law**
fauk *fôk* **above, upstairs;** fauk min (**prep.**) **over, upon**
fawâḥish **pl. of** fâḥishı
fawâyid *fawâ=id* **pl. of** fâyidi
fâyidi *fâ=ide*, **pl.** fawâyid **advantage, useful remark**
fâyiz *fâ=iz* **interest (on money)**
fazaʿ **fright, terror**
fazîʿ **terrible**
fazzaʿ **to frighten**
*febrâ=ir* **February**
felâsife; **see failasûf**
feddân **feddan, acre (734 square metres)**
*fellâḥ* **farmer**
*felûke* **boat, barge**
feshêk; **see fashak**
*fewâkih* **fruit (coll.)**
fî (**prep.**) **in, with, in comparison with, upon; conjunction with the pers. pron., p. 14**
fiḍi (a) **to be empty, unoccupied**
fiḍil (a) **to be left, remain**
*figg* **unripe**
fihim (a) **to understand**
fijl *figl* **radish;** fijl franji *figl ifren'gi* **or** *figl rûmi* **small cultivated radishes**
fikh **jurisprudence**
fikhkhâr *fûkhûr'* **earthenware, clay**
fikr, **pl.** afkâr **thought, idea**
fîl **elephant**
fiʿl, **pl.** fiʿâl **deed, act**
filfil **pepper**
fill (**coll.**) **a species of jasmine, double jasmine, in Egypt: cork**
filli **jasmine-plant, in Egypt: a cork stopper**
fillîn *fill* **cork**
fillîni *filli* **a cork stopper**
filûkya flûkya *felûke* **boat, barge**
finjân *fingân* **or** *fingâl* **cup, coffee-cup**
fîrân' **pl. of** fâr
firâṛa **bag, purse**
firḥân **merry, joyful**
firiḥ (a) **to rejoice, be merry**
firiṛ (a) **to be empty**
firshâyi *furshe* **brush**

fisid to spoil, ruin
fizi' to get frightened, be afraid
flûkya boat, barge
flûs, fulûs money
*fôk* above, upstairs
franj *ifreng'* (coll.) Europeans
franji *ifren'gi* European
fransa France
fransâwi French
fransîs French (coll.)
frâṭa small money
ftîl wick
fuâd heart
fuâki pl. of fâkiha
fuḳara pl. of faḳîr
fûl (coll.) broad bean
fulûs money
furn oven
furṣa opportunity
*furshe* brush
furtai'ki fork
furûḍ pl. of farḍ
fustuḳ pistachio-nut
fuṣûl pl. of faṣl
fût ! come in ! enter !
fûṭa, pl. fuwaṭ napkin, serviette
fuṭur in Syria : the meal at noon; in Egypt : first meal in the morning
*gâ* or *gî*, *gi*, *igi* (*yigi*) to come
*gâ'* (*u*) to be hungry
*ga'al* (*a*) to make
*ga'ân* hungry
*gâb* (*yegîb*) to bring
*gabal* mountain
*gabân* cowardly
*gabar* to compel
*gada'*, pl. *gid'ân* young chap
*gadd* earnestness; grandfather
*gafal* (*i*) to shy
*gahal* to know nothing, be ignorant
*gahhiz* to equip, fit out
*gâhil* not knowing, thoughtless
*gahlân* frivolous, acting foolishly
*galab* (*i*) to bring, import
*gallid* to bind (a book)
*gama'* (*a*) to unite
*gamâ'a* party, company
*gamal* camel
*gamâl* beauty
*gamb* beside, near
*gamî'* all, every, quite
*gâmid* hard, fast
*gam'îye* society
*gamîl* beautiful
*gammêz*, pl. *gamâzîz'* sycamore
*gâmûs'* buffalo
*ganân* veil; darkness; harem
*ganâze* funeral
*gânib* side
*gann* to go mad
*gâr*, pl. *gîrân'* neighbor
*gara* (*i*) to flow, run; occur
*gâra*, pl. *gârât'* female neighbor
*garâd* grasshoppers (coll.)
*garaḥ* (*a*) to wound
*garas* bell
*garḥ*, pl. *gurûḥ* wound
*gâri* running, current
*gâriye*, pl. *gawâri* female slave, servant
*garr* (*u*) to draw, pull

*garra* big jug
*garrib* to try, taste
*gau* atmosphere
*gauḳ* troop, legion
*gauwiz* to give in marriage
*gawâb* letter, reply
*gawâz* marriage
*gâwib* to reply
*gâz* paraffin oil, gas
*gazme* long-legged boots
*gazr* ebb
*gazzâr* butcher
*gêb* pocket
*gedd* grandfather
*gedde* grandmother
*gedîd* new
*gelîd* ice ; frozen
*gemâl* beauty
*gemîl* beautiful
*genaḥ* wing
*genâze* funeral
*genênâ'ti* gardener
*genêne*, pl. *genâ⸗in* garden
*gêsh* army
*gezîre*, pl. *gezâ⸗ir* island
*gibn* cheese
*gidri* smallpox
*gifn* eyelid
*gild*, pl. *gulûd* skin, leather
*gimgime* skull
*gindi* soldier
*gins*, pl. *agnâs* kind, species
*giri* to run
*gism*, pl. *agsâm* body
*gisr*, pl. *gusûr* dam, bridge
*gôhar*, pl. *gawâhir* precious stone
*gôhargi* jeweller
*gôz* pair ; husband ; nuts
*gôze* wife ; nut
*gû*ʿ hunger
*guhd* zeal
*gûkh* cloth
*gumʿa* week ; *yôm elgum'ʿa* Friday
*gumruk* custom-house
*gunûb* south
*gunûn* madness
*gurn* stone-mortar
*gurnâl* journal
*gûwa* inside, in
*guz*, pl. *agzâ* portion, part
*guz⸗i* trivial
*guzlân* purse
*ḥa* expresses the future, e.g. *ḥayik'tib* he will write
ḥabak to weave ; connect
ḥabas (i) to imprison
ḥabb (coll.), pl. ḥubûb corn, seed-corn
ḥabb franji syphilis
ḥabbi corn, grain (a single one) ; berry
ḥabb (i) to love, like
ḥabesh Abyssinia
ḥabîb beloved, dear ; yâ ḥabîbi ! O my dear !
ḥabs imprisonment, prison
hâda, fem. hâdi, pl. haudi or hadôl this
ḥada a, any
hadâk, fem. hadîk, pl. hadolîk or haudik that
haḍam (i) to digest
ḥaḍar (a) to be present
ḥadd (adj.) sharp, trenchant (prep.) beside, near (noun), pl. ḥudûd boundary
hadda to stop, halt (trans.); last (as a garment)
haddad to threaten
ḥaddâd blacksmith

ḥaḍḍar to prepare, get ready (trans.)
ḥaddi a, any
ḥâdi quiet
ḥadîd iron; anchor
ḥâḍir ready, prepared; at command! at once![1]
ḥadîs (adj.) new
(noun) event, novelty; conversation, tradition (particularly of the Prophet)
hadîyi, pl. hadâya present, gift
ḥaḍrtak properly: your presence (used instead of the personal pronoun when addressing a person)
ḥâdsi, pl. ḥawâdis event, occurrence; chance, accident
ḥadûr steep declivity, slope
ḥafaḍ: biḥa'faḍ Allâh! *biḥifzillah'!* God guard you!
ḥafar (u) to dig, bore
ḥafaz (a) to guard, keep, preserve; learn or know by heart
ḥaffi edge, border
ḥâfi barefoot
*ḥâgeti* I have enough
haia form, shape
haida same as hâda
haidāk same as hadāk
haik so, thus
ḥais *ḥês*, ḥais inn inasmuch as, since
hait bring here, give here
ḥaiṭ *ḥêṭ*, pl. ḥîṭân' wall
ḥaiwân, pl. -ât animal
ḥaiyi snake
haiyin easy
ḥajal *ḥagal* partridge
ḥajar *ḥagar*, pl. aḥjâr stone
ḥâji *ḥâge* want, need; in Egypt generally implying 'thing,' 'something,' a diminutive or slighted object, and often added to the speech without any particular meaning (something or other)
(adv.) enough
hajîn *hagîn* dromedary
ḥajj *ḥagg* pilgrimage; pilgrim
ḥâjti *ḥâgeti* I have enough
ḥaka (i) to speak, tell, narrate
ḥakam (u) to decide, judge; ḥakam 'ala .. to sentence
ḥakawâti story-teller, narrator
ḥaḳiḳ true
ḥaḳîḳa truth, certainty; bilḥaḳîḳa in truth, for certain
ḥâkim, pl. ḥukkâm judge, magistrate, ruler
ḥakîm, wise, sage; doctor
ḥaḳîr mean; humble

---

[1] This is one of the favorite expressions of Oriental servants; it is always on their lips when ordered to fetch anything, but by no means implies prompt service. It is well to wean them as soon as possible from this word as well as from the inshal'la (please God! let us hope!).

ḥakk, pl. ḥuḳûḳ right, claim; price; ilḥaḳḳ' ma'o elḥaḳḳ' mi'áh or ilḥaḳḳ' bi-ído he is right; ilḥaḳḳ' 'alaih' he is wrong

hal particle, sometimes placed in front of a question, e.g. hal ra-ai'to? have you seen him?

ḥâl, pl. aḥwâl condition, circumstance

ḥalaf (i) to swear

ḥalaḳ (a) to shave; get shaved

ḥalaḳ rings, earrings

ḥalâl lawful, allowable

ḥâlan at once, instantaneously

ḥalâwi sweetness, sweetmeat

ḥâli condition, state

ḥalîb milk

ḥalḳ gullet; palate

ḥalḳa circle, ring, earring

ḥall to loosen, solve; spin cocoons; put up, reside, encamp

ḥallaḳ, halwaḳt this moment, now

ḥallûf wild boar

ḥamad (a) to praise, speak well of

ḥamaḍ to be sour

ḥamal (i) to carry, bear

ḥamâm pigeons, doves (coll.)

ḥamâmi a pigeon

ḥamd praise, reward

ḥâmi hot, glowing; ardent

ḥâmiḍ sour, acid; lemon

ḥamîr pl. of ḥimâr

ḥamli load, burden

hamm care

ḥammal ḥammil to load; bear

ḥammâm bath (a hot one); ḥammâm ilbaḥr' sea-bath

ḥammâr donkey-driver

ḥammil to load

ḥammil! load! pack up!

ḥamra fem. of aḥmar

ḥanafîyi tap, stop-cock

hanîyan! may it do you good!

hanna to congratulate; Alla yhannîk or hannâk Allâh may God prosper you (answer to: hanîyan; see p 39, note)

ḥâra, pl. ḥârât' ward of a town

harab to flee

ḥârab to wage war against, fight

ḥarak to move

ḥaraḳ (a) to burn (trans.)

ḥaraki movement

ḥaram, pl. ahrâm pyramid

ḥarâm unlawful, forbidden; sin, theft; a pity! yâ ḥarâm expression of pity, sometimes of tenderness ibn ḥarâm bad, worthless fellow

ḥarâmi, pl. ḥaramîyi thief

ḥarâra heat; heat pimple

ḥarat (i) to plough

ḥaraz (i); to be worth, be worth the while

ḥarb, pl. ḥurûb war

ḥarbân fugitive

ḥarbi, javelin, bayonet

ḥardaun' lizard

ḥarf, pl. ḥurûf or aḥruf letter, type
ḥarfîyan literally
ḥarîḳa fire, conflagration
ḥarîm [1] harem
ḥarîr silk
ḥâris watchman, guard
ḥarr hot; heat
ḥarrak *ḥarrik* to move, shake (trans.)
ḥasab (i) to reckon, count
ḥâsab (with acc.) to settle an account with ..
ḥaṣad (i) to mow
ḥaṣal (u) to happen, gain, result; ḥasal ʿala to attain, get
ḥasani good action; alms
ḥasb (prep.) according to; ḥasb ilʿâdi after the custom
ḥashîsh grass, hay; the well-known hemp preparation
ḥâṣil resulting; ilḥâṣil, wilḥâṣil *walḥâṣil* in short, in a word
ḥâṣil, pl. ḥawâṣil magazine, warehouse
ḥaṣîri, pl. ḥuṣr straw mat, reed mat
ḥasra; yâ ḥasrti! alas! O my misfortune! woe is me! see p. 60, note 3
ḥaṣṣal to obtain, acquire, exact, reach
ḥasûd envious
ḥât! give!
ḥaṭab firewood
ḥatîki shame, dishonor
ḥaṭṭ (u) to put, place
ḥatta, ḥatta tâ that. in order to, until
ḥauḍ *ḥôḍ*, pl. aḥwâḍ basin
ḥaudi pl. of hâda, hâdi
haudîk pl. of hadâk
haun *hene* here
haunîk there
ḥaush *ḥôsh* farm; wooden enclosure for cattle; see hôsh
ḥauwal *ḥauwil* to descend, alight, get down; endorse (a bill), transfer, assign
hawa air, weather; hawa ilaṣ'far the cholera
ḥawâdis pl. of ḥâdsi
*ḥawalê* round about
ḥawâli endorsement; order, assignment
ḥawâṣil pl. of ḥâṣil
ḥâwi snake-charmer
ḥaya honest shame
ḥayât life
ḥazam (i) to tie, pack together
ḥazîrân' June
ḥazz good luck; pleasure

[1] In a wide sense, all the female members of a house; in particular, lawful wife (or wives, of which the Muslim may have four); in the latter meaning the word is sometimes used by Christians also: ḥarîmi my wife; in the figurative sense it implies the women's apartments, and these comprise in most Mohammedan houses all the rooms except the selâmlik' (drawing-room).

*hene* here
*ḥês, biḥês'* because
*ḥêṭ* wall
hezl jest, joke
hî, hîyi she
ḥibr ink
ḥifyân barefoot; unshod
ḥijji *ḥugge* proof; document, title deed; pretext
hijra *higra* flight of the Prophet from Mecca to Medina (A.D. 622)
hilâl new moon
ḥillâḳ barber
ḥilm, pl. aḥlâm dream
ḥilu sweet
ḥimâr, pl. ḥamîr donkey
ḥiml load, burden
ḥimma *ḥimme* hot fever; ḥimma tîfûsî'yi typhoid fever
ḥinṭa wheat
ḥirâm woollen blanket, travelling rug
hirbân *harbân* fugitive
ḥirzân worth the while, worth talking about
ḥisâb, ḥsâb account
ḥiṣân, ḥṣân, ḥuṣân, pl. iḥṣini or ḥuṣn horse, stallion
ḥiss voice
ḥîṭân' pl. of ḥaiṭ
hîyi she
ḥizâm belly-band of a horse
ḥizb party, partisans
ḥkûmi government
ḥmâr donkey
*ḥôsh* open hall, or court of a house
ḥsâb account
ḥṣân horse, stallion
ḥubb dear, beloved one
ḥubûb pl. of ḥabb
ḥudûd pl. of ḥadd
hudûm clothes
ḥudûr presence, appearance
ḥufra pit, hole
*ḥugge* proof; title-deed; pretext
ḥukkâm pl. of ḥâkim
ḥukm jurisdiction, judgment, sentence
ḥuḳûḳ pl. of ḥaḳḳ
ḥukûmi authorities, government
ḥulḳûm throat
ḥulu sweet
hum *huma* they
ḥumâr donkey
ḥummuṣ (coll.) chick-pease
ḥumr pl. of aḥmar
ḥurmi wife
ḥurr free frank
ḥurrîyi liberty, freedom
ḥurûb pl. of ḥarb
ḥurûf pl. of ḥarf
ḥuṣân horse, stallion
ḥuṣn pl. of ḥiṣân
ḥuṣr pl. of ḥaṣîri
ḥuṭṭ! put! place!
huwa he
ibn son
ibn 'arab, pl. ûlâd' 'arab, *aulâd 'arab* domiciled, resident Arab, Egyptian, Syrian; (see p. 127, note)
ibn ḥalâl a decent, good fellow; ibn ḥarâm a bad man
ibri *ibre*, pl. ibar needle
ibta'da to begin
ibtida beginning
ibwâb pl. of bâb

*ibzîm* buckle
îd, pl. ayādi or daiyāt hand
ʻîd feast, festival; ʻîd izzṛîr *ʻîd ezzuṛai'yar* the little Bairam (on the 1st of Shauwâl, immediately after the fasting-month); ʻîd ilkbîr *ʻîd elkebîr* the great or Kurban Bairam (six weeks after the little one)
ʻida pl. of ʻadu
ʻiḍâm pl. of ʻaḍm
idruʻ pl. of drâʻ
idwiyi pl. of dawa
ifranj' *ifreng'*, *ifren'gi*, ifran'ji same as franj
ʻifrît demon; villain
ifta'kar *ifti'kir* to think, consider
ihāni insult, offence
iḥbāb pl. friends
ihda! stop! compose yourself!
iḥki! talk! speak!
iḥmarr' to turn red
iḥṣini pl. of ḥiṣân
iḥta'mal *iḥtimil* to bear, endure
iḥta'ram *iḥti'rim* to esteem, venerate
iḥtirâm esteem, veneration, respect
ija *igi* to come; conj. p. 27 ff.
ʻijji *ʻugge* pancake
ʻijl *ʻigl* calf (animal)
ijniḥi *agniḥa* pl. of jnâḥ
ijr foot
ijra *ugra* wages, pay, salary; ijrit maktûb postage
ijta'maʻ *igta'maʻ* to unite, come together
ijzâ=i *egzâ=i* chemist
ijzâ=î'yi *egzâ=i'ye* pharmacy
iḳbal accept, take
ikhta'raʻ to invent
ikhta'sha to be afraid, shy
ikhtirâʻ invention
ikhtyâr, fem. and pl. ikhtyârî'yi old
ikhwân, ikhwi (pl. of akh) brothers (and sisters)
îko'nî image of a saint (of Greek orthodox Christians)
iḳsām pl. of ḳism
ikta'sab *ikti'sib* to earn, acquire
ikyās pl. of kîs
il *el* the; see p. 7
ila to
ilak to you
il=ān *el=ân* now, in this moment
ilfi company, friendship
ilḥaḳ to follow; ilḥaḳ'ni follow me, go behind me
ili *lî* to me
ʻilim to know
ʻilk silly talk; piece of mastic, a resin used by the women as a chewing-gum; in Egypt: scoundrel
illa (prep.) besides (adv.) of course
illai'li *ellêle* this night, tonight
ʻillāk talker
illi which, who
ʻilm science, knowledge
ilsini pl. of lisān
ilta'hab to flare up, be inflamed
ilta'ḳa to find; meet

ilta'zam *ilti'zim* to be obliged, be bound, take upon
  oneself; take a tenancy,
  lease (from the government)
iltihâb inflammation
iltizâm tenancy, lease
iltshi envoy, ambassador
ilyaum'*ennahar'da* to-day
imâm he that recites the
  prayers before the congregation; mosque-priest
îmân' faith, belief
'imâra building
imbârih *embârih* yesterday
imbyi pl. of nabi
'imil to do, make
imkân possibility; biḳadr'
  ilimkân as much as one
  (you, etc.) can
imlâk pl. of mulk
imm *umm* mother
imrâḍ pl. of maraḍ
imshi! go! march on! off!
imsik! hold! seize!
imta'han to examine, test
imtâl pl. of matal
*imte?* when?
imtihân examination, test
imwâs pl. of maus
in that, to (conj.)
in'a'zal to be deposed, dis-
  missed
inba'saṭ to be merry, amused,
  cheerful, content

'ind with, by, at
'indak! stop! (said to the
  coachman)
indaḳḳ' to be beaten, struck
'ineb *'aneb* grapes (coll.)
infus pl. of nafs
inglîzi English; btiḥki inglîzi? do you speak English?                [self up]
inha'jab to veil, wrap one-
inhur pl. of nahr
'inib *'aneb* grapes (coll.)
injîl *ingîl* Gospel
inka'sar *inki'sir* to break
  (intr.); become bankrupt
inkha'jal *inkha'gal* to be
  ashamed
inkha'ṭab to be, become
  engaged (said of a girl)
inkisâr ruin, bankruptcy
inni, innak, inno, inha,
  inna, inkon, inhon that
  I, thou, he, she, we, you,
  they
inramm' to grieve, be sorry
insân, pl. nâs man
inṣa'raf to turn away, run
  away; be settled (of dis-
  putes)
insarr' to rejoice, be de-
  lighted
inshal'la, inshallâh![1] if it
  please God! I hope! let
  us hope!

1 A favorite word of the Oriental, which he pronounces
at every possible, suitable or unsuitable, opportunity, but
with which he generally simply cloaks his innate laziness
and indolence, frequently also his ill-will. As the European
by hearing this inshal'la always pronounced with the
same nugatory, often even ironical tone, is at last reduced

int *inte* thou (masc.)
inṭa'fa to be extinguished, go out
inta'khab to choose
inti *enti* thou (fem.)
intiḳâl emigration; death
inwâʿ *anwâʿ* pl. of nauʿ
inwa'jad *inwa'gad* to be found, occur
inzil! descend! come down! go down!
ʿirḍ honor; bʿirḍak *biʿir'ḍak* by your honor (I implore you)
ʿirif to know
irmâḥ *armâḥ* pl. of rumḥ
irṛifi pl. of raṛîf
ʿirs wedding
ʿirsân pl. of ʿarîs
irtâḥ to take repose, compose oneself
ʿiryân naked
iṣbaʿ *ṣubâʿ*, pl. ṣâbiʿ *ṣawâbiʿ* finger
isbâb *asbâb* pl. of sabab
iṣḥa! take care! mind!
iṣḥâb *aṣḥâb* pl. of ṣâḥib
is-hâl diarrhœa
is-hâm *es-hâm* pl. of sahm
ishâra sign, token
ʿ*ishe* evening
ishhur *ushhur* pl. of shahr
ishkâl *eshkâl* pl. of shikl
ishrab! drink!
ishshâm Syria, Damascus
ʿisht! bravo!
ishta'ka *ishti'ki* to complain, bring forth an accusation
ishta'ra *ishti'ri* to buy
ishta'ṛal to work, make great exertions
ishtiṛâl occupation
ism, pl. asmâ or asâmi name
ismal'la properly: name of God; exclamation by which, according to the belief of the Arabs, the evil eye is warded off cattle and children
ismaʿ! listen! hark!
isrâr pl. of sirr
issa now, just now; still
ista'ḥa to be ashamed
istaʿ'jal *istaʿ'gil* to hurry, lose no time
istaʿ'jil! make haste!
istak'tir bkhairak I give you many thanks
iṣṭa'laḥ to improve, get in order (intr.)
istan'na to wait
istan'zar to wait; expect
istarâḥ *istarai'yiḥ* to rest, take repose
istaṛfrallâh properly: I ask God pardon: for the use of this expression see p. 58, note 1
ista'wa to get ripe, become done (cooked)

---

to sheer despair, he will do well to break his companion of it as soon as possible. The Muslims only should not be interfered with, because the Koran prescribes to them the continuous use of this showy phrase.

ista-'zan to ask permission, take leave
istrîḥ! rest! take a seat!
iswâk̦ *aswâk̦* pl. of sûk̦
*iswid* black
i'ta'raf to admit, confess, go to confession
i'ta'zar to excuse oneself
iṭla'! (go) out!
'itm dark, dusky
'iṭr perfume, scent
'iṭshân *'aṭshân* thirsty
itta'kal 'ala.. to rest, rely on..
'ittâl carrier, porter
iṭṭal'la' to see, regard, look about
ittifâk̦ coincidence, concurrence
'iwaḍ (with or without 'an) instead of
îyâm' pl. of yaum
îyâr' May
'iyâṭ *'aiyâṭ* outcry, clamor
'*iyûn*; see 'ain
iza if
izâr, pl. uzr or izr or yizr broad veil of white linen in which the Syrian women wrap themselves when outside the house
izn permission; bi-iz'nak, bil-izn' with your permission! especially when implying: I beg to take leave (viz. with your permission)
jâ *gâ, igi* (yiji *yigi*) (rare form for ija) to come
jâ' (yjû') *gâ'* (*u*) to be hungry
ja'al *ga'al* (*a*) to make, do
jâb *gâb* (yjîb) to bring
jabal *gabal*, pl. jibâl mountain(s)
jabân *gabân* cowardly
jabar *gabar* to set (a broken bone); to compel
jadd *gadd* earnestness
jahal *gahal* to ignore, not to know
jahan'nam *gahan'nam* hell
jahd *gahd* effort, zeal
jâhil *gâhil* not knowing; ignorant, foolish
jahlân *gahlân* frivolous, acting foolishly
jaib, jaibi *gêb*, pl. juyûb pocket
jaish *gêsh* army
jâj *dugâg* (coll.) poultry
jâji hen
jakhkh *gakhkh* to adorn oneself, be adorned
jala, jalla *gala, galla* to trim, polish, wash up (kitchen utensils)
jalab *galab* (*i*) to bring, attract, summon to appear
jallad *gallid* to bind (a book)
jama' *gama'* (*a*) to unite, bring together
jamâ'a *gamâ'a* party, company; people, community
jamal *gamal* camel
jamb *gamb* (with or without min) beside, at the side of
jambîyi *gambîye* bag for hanging round the shoulders
jamî' *gamî'* all every; jamî' ahl baitak all your family
jâmid *gâmid* hard, congealed; without life
jam'îyi *gam'îye* society

jaâyin *ganâ=in* pl. of jnaini
jann *gann* to go mad
janni *ganne* paradise
jâr *gâr* neighbor
jâra female neighbor
jara *gara* (*i*) to flow; occur, happen
jarâdîn' *garâdîn'* pl. of jirdaun'
jaras *garas* bell
jarayân *garayân* running, course; diarrhœa
jâri *gâri* running, current (adj.); ijjâri the current month
jarra *garra* big water-jug
jarrab *garrib* to try, taste
jarras to dishonor, take away some one's character
jâryi *gâriye* female slave, servant
jau *gô* atmosphere
jau'ân *ga'ân* hungry
jauhar *gôhar*, pl. jawâhir *gawâhir* precious stone; substance, quintessence
jauwaz *gauwiz* to perform a marriage, marry (a daughter, etc.)
jauz *gôz* (coll.) nut; husband
jauzi nut (a single one), nut-tree; wife
jawâb *gawâb* answer
jâwab *gâwib* (with acc.) to answer
jawâhir pl. of jauhar
jâyi *gâ=i* coming, future
jâyiz *gâ=iz* passing; permissible
jâz *gâz* (yjûz) to pass; be permitted
jazr *gazr* ebb; madd ujazr' flux and reflux
jdîd *gedîd* new
ji'ân' *ga'ân* hungry
jibn *gibn* (coll.) cheese
jibni a cheese
jidd *gidd*, *gadd* grandfather
jiddan *giddan* very, very much
jidri *gidri* smallpox
jifil *gafal* (*i*) to shy (horse)
jifn *gifn* eyelid
jift *gift* double-barrelled gun
jild *gild* hide, skin; binding (of a book)
jimâ' *gimâ'* copulation, pairing
jindi *gindi* soldier
jins *gins*, pl. ajnâs kind, species
jirâd *garâd* (coll.) locusts
jirdaun' *girdôn*, pl. jarâdîn' rat
jism *gism* body
jisr *gisr*, pl. juṣûr beam (of wood); bridge; dam
jît *gît* I have come, thou (masc.) hast come
jîti thou (fem.) hast come
jîtu you have come
jiz *guz* part, portion
jîz *gîz* beetle
jizdân *guzlân* letter-case, pocket-book; purse
jîzi *gîze* marriage, matrimony
jlâl pack-saddle
jlîd *gelîd* ice; frozen
jmâl, jmâl *gemâl* beauty; also pl. of jmîl
jmî' *gemî'* all, entire

jmîl *gemîl* **beautiful**
jnâḥ *genâḥ*, **pl.** ijniḥi *agniḥa* **wing**
jnainâti *genênâ'ti* **gardener**
jnaini *genêne*, **pl.** janâyin **flower-garden**
jnâzi *genâze* **funeral**
jûʿ *gûʿ* **hunger**
jûʿân' *guʿân* **hungry**
jubbi *gubbe* **long overcoat, caftan**
juhd *guhd* **zeal, effort**; baʿmil kull juhdi **I will do all that is in my power**
jukhkh *gukhkh* **adornment, pomposity**
jumʿa *gumʿa*, **pl.** jmâʿ **week**; yaum ijjumʿʿa *yôm elgumʿʿa* **Friday**
jumli *gumle* **sum, total, the whole**; bijjum'li **on the whole, taken altogether**
junûn *gunûn* **madness, insanity**
jûra *gûra* **deep hole, precipice**
jurd **high bare mountain, high mountain-chain**
jurn *gurn* **mortar, stone basin**
jusûr *gusûr* **pl. of** jisr
jûwa *gûwa* **inside, in**
juz *guz* **portion, part**
ḳâʿa **large room, drawing-room**
ḳaʿad (u) **to sit, sit down**
kaʿb **heel, ankle; the lowest, bottom**
ḳabaḍ (a) **to seize, take hold of; receive, cash**
ḳâbal *ḳâbil* **to meet**
ḳabar **to bury**
kabas (i) **to press, preserve (fruit)**
kabb (u) **to pour out**
ḳabbal **to kiss**
kabbût **cloak, capote**
kabid **liver**; yâ kabidi! **a word of endearment (properly: Oh my liver!)**
ḳabîḍ **constipated**
ḳabîḥ **ugly, common**
ḳâbil **capable of ..**
ḳabîle, **pl.** ḳabâ꞊il **tribe (of Bedouins)**
ḳâbilî'yi **appetite**
ḳâbis; iddin'yi kâbsi **it is raining in torrents**
ḳabḳâb, **pl.** ḳabâḳîb **wooden shoe**
ḳabl (**adv.**) **before, formerly (prep.) in front of**
ḳabr, **pl.** ḳubûr **grave, tomb**
*kabshe* **handful**
ḳabṭân **captain**
ḳabu, **pl.** ḳawâbi **subterranean vault, cellar**
ḳabûl **acceptance**
ḳabûlî'ye **receipt**
ḳâd (u) **to guide**
ḳaḍa (i) (**trans.**) **to accomplish, execute; judge, decide**
ḳaḍa **district governed by a** ḳâyimmaḳâm'; **jurisdiction, office of a cadi, judge**
ḳadâdîs' **pl. of** ḳaddâs
ḳadaḥ, **pl.** aḳdâḥ **cup, glass**
ḳadd **measure; as, just as, just like**
kaddab, kaddâb; **see kazzab, kezzâb**

ḳaddaish'? *ḳaddêsh?* how much?
ḳaddam *ḳaddim* to offer, present; step in front, go on before
kaddar *kaddir* to grieve
ḳaddar *ḳaddir* to value, estimate; Allâh lâ yḳaddir may God not preordain it [liturgy]
ḳaddâs, pl. ḳadâdîs' mass, [liturgy]
ḳaddim! step in front! come nearer!
ḳaddîs saint
ḳaddma in proportion to; ḳaddma .. ḳaddma the .. the
ḳaddûm axe, chopper
ḳâḍi judge
ḳadîm old (not new), ancient
ḳâdir able to, capable of ..
ḳadr measure; destiny, providence
kafa (i) to suffice
kâfa to reward, recompense
kafal to stand security for
ḳafal (i) to shut
ḳafaṣ cage
kaff palm of the hand; hand
kaffa to suffice
kaffal to make one stand security for another
kaffîyi man's kerchief for the head (as a protection against sun and wind)
kâfi sufficient
kâfîl' one who stands bail
ḳâfile caravan
kâfir, pl. kuffâr unbeliever
kafr village, hamlet
kâfûr' camphor
ḳahar (a) to force, overcome; maltreat, annoy
*kaḥḥ (u)* to cough
ḳahr compulsion; spite, anger
kahrabâ-i electric
kahrabâ-î'ye electricity
ḳahwaji *ḳahwegi* coffee-house keeper
ḳahwi coffee; coffee-house
ḳâ'idi, pl. ḳawâ'id rule
kaif *kêf* as, like
*ḳâ-ime* list, catalogue, note, bill; pocket-book; Turkish banknote
*ḳa-immaḳâm* lieutenant-colonel; in Syria: ḳâyimmaḳâm' governor of a district (ḳaḍa)
kaiyal to measure (corn and other dry goods)
ka'k biscuit
*kal (u)* to eat
kâl (ykîl) to measure (corn, etc.)
ḳâl (yḳûl) to say
*ḳala' (a)* to take off (clothes)
ḳal'a fortress, castle
ḳalab (i) to turn (trans.)
ḳalam reed, reed-pen; ḳalam ḥadîd steel-pen; ḳalam riṣâṣ lead pencil
kalâm speech; words
kalb *kelb*, pl. kilâb or klâb dog
ḳalb, pl. ḳulûb heart
ḳalîl little, paltry; ḳalîl ilḥai'ya impertinent, shameless
ḳallad *ḳallid* to imitate

kallaf *kallif* **to impose a difficult matter upon, trouble**; kallif khâṭrak! **be so kind!** kallaft' il-khâṭir! **or** kallaf'na il-khâṭir! **best thanks!**
kallal *kallil* **to marry, unite in marriage (said of the clergyman)**
kallam *kallim* **to speak**
kalsât **stockings**
ḳaltshîn **house-shoe, slipper**
kam? kām? **how much?** bkām? *bikâm?* **(properly: for how much?) how much is ..?**
ḳâm (yḳûm) **to rise, stand up**; (yḳîm) **to raise, set up, take away**
kamâl **perfection**
kamān **also, too**
ḳamar **moon**
kambyāli *kimbiyâle* **bill of exchange**
kāmil **perfect, complete**
ḳamîṣ, **pl.** ḳumṣân **or** ḳimṣân **shirt**
ḳaml **lice (coll.)**
ḳamli **louse (a single one)**
kammal **to complete, perfect**
kammil! **finish! go on!**
ḳamshi **whip**
ḳâmûs' **dictionary**
kān (ykûn) **to be**
*kanas* (*u*) **to sweep**
ḳanâṣil **pl. of** ḳunṣul
ḳandîl, **pl.** ḳanâdîl' **lamp**
kaníf **closet, privy**
kannas **to sweep (the house)**
ḳannîni, **pl.** ḳanâyin **or** ḳanâni **bottle**
ḳanṭâr **hundredweight**
ḳanṭara, ḳanṭra, **pl.** ḳanâṭir **vault, arch; in Egypt: bridge**
kânûn' **charcoal-pan, stove**
kânûn' ilau'wal **December**
kânûn' ittāni **January**
ḳânûn', **pl.** ḳawânîn' **rule, norm, law; dulcimer (mus. stringed instrument)**
kâr **business, trade; gain**
kara (i) **to let, hire out**
ḳara (a) **to read**
ḳarâbe **relationship**
ḳaraf **disgust**
karakûn **watch, watch-house**
karam **kindness, liberality**
ḳaran **to tie, join**
karantîna **quarantine**
karâsi **pl. of** kursi
ḳarâyib **relatives**
karbâj *kurbâg* **whip**
ḳarfaṣ **to squat, cower (with the hands joined in front of the knees)**
ḳarîb **near, soon**
karîh **detestable, repugnant**
karîm **kind, liberal**
*ḳarîye* **chamber-utensil**
karkhâni **factory; silk-spinning establishment; public building; in Egypt implying the latter only**
ḳarn, **pl.** ḳurûn **horn**
ḳarnabîṭ **cauliflower**
ḳarr **to confess, admit**
ḳarrab **to bring near; approach**
ḳarraf **to excite disgust**
karram *karrim* **to honor**
ḳarrib! **come near!**

karrûsa, pl. karrûsât' or karârîs' carriage, coach
ḳaryi village, hamlet
kâs cup, bowl
ḳaṣa breed; pipe; thread of gold, embroidery in gold
ḳaṣab maṣṣ sugar cane
ḳaṣad (u) to intend
ḳasâḳisi pl. of ḳassîs
kasal (intr.) to be lazy
kasal (noun) laziness
ḳasam (i) to divide
kasar (i) to break (trans.)
ḳaṣar (u) to be short, fall short of, lag behind
kasb gain, earnings
ḳaṣd intention
kashaf (i) to uncover, reveal; look into (as a window)
ḳashsh straw; ḳashsh franji sea-weed
ḳashshar to peel, rind
ḳâsi hard
kâsi bowl, cup
ḳaṣîdi, pl. ḳaṣâyid a (long) poem
ḳaṣîr short
kaslân lazy
kasr crack, breaking
ḳaṣr, pl. ḳuṣûr palace
*ḳaṣrîye* chamber-utensil
ḳass (u) to cut
kassar to break to pieces (trans.)
ḳaṣṣar to shorten; to be negligent
ḳassîs, pl. ḳasâḳisi *ḳusasa* Catholic priest who is a member of a religious order; Protestant clergyman
ḳaṭaʿ to cut; yiḳṭaʿʿamrak an imprecation
ḳaṭʿa, pl. ḳiṭaʿ piece
katab (i) to write
kâtab (with acc.) to write to some one [off
ḳaṭaf to pick, pluck, take
ḳatal (i, u) to kill
ḳâtal to fight, try to kill
kâtib scribe, writer
ḳatîl murdered; râḥ ḳatîl he has been murdered
ḳatl murder, homicide
ḳaṭr railway train
kattaf to tie, gag
ḳaṭṭaf *ḳaṭṭif* to pick, pluck
kattar *kattir* to do often, overdo
kattir khairak! many thanks! cf. p. 57
ḳaum *ḳôm* people, multitude
kaumi *kôme* heap, stack
ḳaus *ḳôs* arch, bow
ḳaus ilḳa'daḥ rainbow
kauwam *kauwim* to heap up
ḳauwas to shoot
ḳauwâṣ, pl. ḳauwâṣa archer, hunter; consulate-officer, policeman
kauwâyi woman-ironer
kawa (i) to iron (linen)
ḳawâbi pl. of ḳabu
ḳawâʿid pl. of ḳâʿidi
ḳawâm (adv.) fast, quickly
ḳawânîn' pl. of ḳânûn'
kawi the ironing; bala kawi unironed
ḳawi strong
*ḳawûn* sweet melon
kazâlik likewise

kazzab *kazzib* to give the lie to, accuse of lying
kbîr *kebîr* great, big
*kêf* how, in what way
kêf[1] good humor, comfort, excitement from opium, carouse
*kelb* dog
kemâl perfection
*kerâr* larder
*ketîr* much, very
kezzâb liar
kfâli bail, surety
kfâyi sufficiency
kfûf pl. gloves
khabar, pl. akhbâr, news, information; mâ 'indi khabar I know nothing about it
khabarîyi news, tale, story
khabaṭ (a) to beat, strike
khabbar *khabbir* (with acc. of the person and 'an of the thing) to inform some one of sthg., to tell
khabbas to do bad things; to be careless
khabbâs scoundrel
khabbaṭ to beat, beat about
khabbaz to bake (bread)
khabbâz baker
*khabbir* to inform
khabîs bad, low
khabîṭ blow, cudgel
*khad* to take
khadam (i) to serve
khadâmi service; kull khadâmi tilzam (prop.: every service is obligatory) I am at your service in everything
khadd, pl. khudûd cheek
khaddâm, khâdim servant
khâdimi, khâdmi female servant
khaḍra fem. of akhḍar
khâf (ykhâf) min .. to be afraid of ..
khafîf light (of weight)
khai brother; khaiyi, khaiyak, khaiyo, khaiha, etc. my, thy, his, her, etc. brother

[1] When the Arab wishes to express 'comfortable' in the sense of 'enjoying or feeling comfort,' he uses the participle mukai'yaf *mekai'yif*, which properly means: 'placed in the state of kêf, i.e. of comfort, of good humor.' But to him comfort and amusement, especially his kind of amusement, coincide: kêf is therefore every amusement that places in the state of comfort, especially drink: 'imil kêf or tkaiyaf *itkai'yaf* 'to do a kêf,' means: to get tipsy, to carouse, and mukai'yaf *mekai'yaf* is 'comfortable' as well as 'fuddled.' When in its proper sense the word 'comfortable' can be expressed differently: are you comfortable? int fî kêfak haik? *inte fî kêfak kide?* yes, I feel quite comfortable! aiwa, ana fî kêfi bittamâm! *aiwa, ana fî kêfi bittamâm!*

khail *khēl* (coll.) **horses**
khaimi *khême*, **pl.** khiyam *khiyâm* **tent**
khair *khêr* **better ; the good, welfare** ; see also bkhair
khair (**adv.**) **no**
khaiṭ *khêṭ* **thread**
khaiyâl **horseman, mounted policeman**
khaiyaṭ **to sew**
khaiyâṭ **tailor**
khaiyâṭa **dressmaker**
khaiyir **liberal, generous**
khajal *khagal* **shame, bashfulness**
khajjal *khaggal* **to put to shame, cause to blush**
khâkhâm' **rabbi** ; khâkhâm'bashi **chief rabbi**
khâl **uncle on maternal side**
*khala* **the open air, outside**
khalaḳ (a) **to create**
khalaṣ *khiliṣ* (*a*) **to be finished, be at an end** ; baddna nikhlaṣ or ikhlaṣ or khlâṣ or ikhlaṣ'ya ! **finish ! come to an end !**
*khalâṣ!* **ready !**
khalaṭ (u) **to mix; to confuse**
khalf (**adv.**) **behind** ; khalf min (**prep.**) **behind**
khalfâni **being or coming behind**
khâli **aunt on maternal side**
khalîfe, **pl.** khulafa **khalif**
khâliṣ, **ready. finished ; no, not** ; bilkhâliṣ **at all, altogether**
khall **vinegar**
khalla **to let, permit**
khallaf **to leave behind ; bear, beget (children), bring forth (young)**
khallaṣ **to get ready (trans.); rescue, deliver** ; khalliṣ'ni **leave me, let me go**
khallaṭ **to throw into confusion**
*khamastâsher* **fifteen**
khâmis **fifth**
khamîs : yaum ilkhamîs **Thursday**
khamman **to estimate ; surmise, think**
khams, khamsi **five**
khamsṭa'sh', khamsṭa''-shar *khamastâsher* **fifteen**
khân (u) **to betray**
khân **inn**
khandaḳ **moat, ditch**
khanjar *khangar* **dagger, short sword**
khanzîr **pig**
khanzîr berri **wild boar**
khara **dung, excrement**
kharaj *kharag* (*u*) **to go out, come out**
kharaḳ (u) **to pierce**
kharbaṭ **to spoil (trans.), put out of order**
kharîf **autumn**
*kharḳ*, **pl.** *khurûḳ* **hole**
kharrab **to spoil (trans.), ruin**
kharraj *kharrag* **to take out**
kharrûb (**coll.**) **carob-tree ;** kharrûbi **a single carob-tree**
khârûf, **pl.** khawârîf **sheep, wether**
khaṣam **to deduct**

khâṣam (with acc.) to quarrel with
khasâra *khusâra* loss
khashab wood, timber
khashbi a piece of wood
*khashsh* (*u*) to enter
khaṣm adversary, antagonist
khass lettuce
khastakhâni hospital
khaṭa sin
khaṭab (u) to become engaged (in marriage, said of a man)
khatam (i) to seal, affix one's seal to
khaṭar peril, danger
khaṭîb preacher, orator
khaṭib engaged (in marriage, said of a man), fiancé
khaṭîbi engaged (said of a girl), fiancée
khâtim, pl. khawâtim stone, seal; seal-ring
khâṭir mind; khâṭrak *khâṭirak* adieu! good bye! ʿala khâṭrak *ʿala khâṭirak* according to your choice, as you will; kîf khâṭrak? *kêf khâṭirak?* how are you?
khaṭîyi, pl. khaṭâya sin
khatm seal, impression
khaṭra time, turn, once; khaṭrtain′ *khaṭratên* twice
khaṭṭ, pl. khuṭûṭ line, handwriting
khaṭwa, pl. khaṭawât pace, step
khauf *khôf* fear
khaukh *berḳûḳ* plum (coll.) in Egypt the corresponding *khôkh* means peach
khaukhi *khôkhe* a single plum; in Egypt, a single peach
khauwaf *khauwif* to frighten
khawâja *khawâga*, pl. -â Mr., Sir (of Christians)
khawârîf′ pl. of khârûf′
khawârni pl. of khûri
khawâtim pl. of khâtim
khâyif afraid
khibra experience
*khidîw* Khedive
khidmi service
khîkhâm′ rabbi
khilik to be born
khiliṣ to be ready
khilḳa face
khilḳân born
khirbân ruined, destroyed
khirbi ruin, deserted place
khirib to go to ruin, fall into ruins
khirḳa, pl. khiraḳ rag, patch
khishin rough, coarse
khiṭâb address, speech
khîyâl′, pl. khîyâ′li horseman, mounted policeman
khiyâr cucumber
khîyâṭ′ tailor
khîyâ′ṭa dressmaker
khiyâṭa sewing, tailoring; ʿulbit ilkhiyâṭa workbox
khizâni cupboard
khôd! take! there, take!
*khôge*, pl. *-ât* teacher

khubz (coll.) bread
khubzi a piece of bread
khuḍâr green stuff; greens; vegetation; see akhḍar
khuḍar'ji *khuḍari* vegetable-seller, greengrocer
khudi! take! (fem.)
khuḍr pl. of akhḍar
khudu! take! (plur.)
khudûd pl. of khadd
khums fifth part
khûri, pl. khawârni clergyman
khurj *khurg* saddle-bag; cf. p. 128, note
*khusâra* loss
*yâ khusâra!* a pity!
khuṣṣ booth of reeds, branches and foliage (especially for rearing silkworms)
khuṣûṣ relation; peculiarity
khuṣûṣan, 'alkhuṣûṣ especially
ḳibâl *kuṣṣâd* opposite, vis-à-vis
kibdi liver
ḳibil (a) to accept, take
kibir (a) to become great, grow, grow old
ḳibli side towards which one turns in prayer (towards Mecca); south; southern
kibr *kubr* greatness, largeness; old age
*kibrît* matches
kibriya pride
*ḳibṭ* Copts, *ḳibṭi* a Copt
ḳiddâs mass, liturgy
*ḳide* thus, so
ḳidir (a) can, to be able
ḳidri pot
kîf? how?
kifâli surety, bail
ḳil', pl. ḳilâ' or ḳulû' sail
kilâb pl. of kalb
kilfi trouble; ceremony; costs, expenses
kill, etc., same as kull, etc.
kilmi word
kils lime (stone)
kilsât stockings
ḳîmi value
kimil to be or become complete, perfect, finished
kimmi, pl. kimâm or kmâm sleeve
ḳimṣân pl. of ḳamîṣ
*kinîse* church
kinwi, kinyi (family-) name
ḳirâyi reading (noun)
ḳirba pipe, tube
kirh disgusting
kiri wages, pay, house-rent
kirih (a) to detest, abhor
kirmâl in honor of, e.g. kirmâlak or kirmâli khâṭrak to honor you, to please you
ḳirsh, pl. ḳurûsh piastre
kîs, pl. ikyâs bag, purse; sum of five pounds Turkish (now rarely met with)
kisbân winning; ana kisbân I have won
ḳishli barracks
ḳishr skin, rind, peel
ḳishṭa cream
kishtbân *kustubân* thimble
kisib (i) to win
kislân lazy, idle
ḳism, pl. iḳsâm portion, part

*kiswe* dress
ḳiṭʿa, pl ḳiṭaʿ piece; see ḳaṭʿa
*kitâb* book
*kitâbet îd* handwriting
*kitâbet eshâra* shorthand
kitf, pl. aktâf shoulder
kitîbi writing (noun); bil-kitîbi in writing
ḳitil to get killed, murdered
kitri plenty, great number
kittân linen
ḳizâz glass, pane, window
*ḳizâze* (Eg.) bottle
kizb lie, falsehood
kizib (i) (intr.) to lie, tell a lie
kizib (noun) lie, falsehood
kizzâb liar
klâb pl. of kalb
kmâm pl. of kimmi
knîsi *kinîse*, pl. knâyis church
kôl! eat!
*komsâri* (railway) conductor
krâsi pl. of kursi
ktâb *kitâb*, pl. kutub book; ktâb ilmuḳad'das *kitâb elmuḳad'das* the Holy Scriptures
ktâb tartîl hymn-book
ktîbi writing (noun)
ktîr *ketîr*, pl. ktâr much
kubbâyi tumbler, glass
kubbi a Syrian national dish consisting of soaked and roasted wheat-grains, rice, and minced meat
ḳubbi vault, cupola
kubr greatness; (old) age
ḳubrus Cyprus
ḳubûr pl. of ḳabr
ḳuddâm (prep.) in front of (adv.) min ḳuddâm before

ḳuds, ḳudsishsharîf Jerusalem
kuffâr pl. of kâfir
ḳuffi basket
ḳufl lock, padlock
kufr unbelief, ingratitude
ḳuftân caftan of thin stuff (for the summer)
kuḥl, kuḥli antimony for blacking the eyes
kull whole, all; kullo everything
*ḳulle* water-jug
kullîyi totality; kullîyan and bilkullîyi entirely, all; kullîto everything
ḳulûʿ pl. of ḳilʿ
ḳulûb pl. of ḳalb
ḳumâr game of chance
ḳumâsh, pl. aḳmishe stuff, cloth
ḳumbâz thin caftan for the summer
*kummit'ra* pear
kumruk custom, duty custom-house
ḳumṣân pl. of ḳamîṣ
ḳunṣul, pl. ḳanâṣil consul
ḳur-ân Koran
ḳurb nearness, vicinity
*ḳurbâg* whip
ḳurni corner
kursi, pl. karâsi or krâsi chair
ḳurûn pl. of ḳarn
ḳurun'ful cloves; clove-pink
ḳurûsh pl. of ḳirsh
kûsa squash (a cucumber-like fruit) marrow
*ḳuṣai'yar* short
*ḳusasa* pl. of ḳassîs

*kuṣṣâd* opposite
*kustubân* thimble
ḳuṭn cotton
ḳuṭṭ tom-cat
ḳuṭṭi cat, she-cat
kutubi bookseller
ḳûwet ḥuṣân horse-power
ḳûwi power, strength
ḳûz can, tin vessel
kwaiyis beautiful, fine
ḳyâs measure
la *li* (prep.) to; indication of the dative
lâ no; not (prohibitive particle)
phrases with lâ: lâ sîyamâ' especially, much less, still more
lâ twâkhid'ni don't take it amiss, excuse me
laʿb play, sport
laban curdled, sour milk; in Egypt: fresh, sweet milk
labash luggage
labbas *labbis* to dress (trans.)
lâbis dressed, clad
laff (i) to wrap up, envelop
laffi turban
laḥadd' (prep.) to, as far as, till
laḥm meat
laḥza moment
lail, laili *lêl, lêle* night
laimûn *lêmûn'* (coll.) lemon
laimûni a single lemon
la=inn' because
laish? *lêh?* why? what for?
lajam *laggim* to bridle
lak to you
lâḳ (ylîḳ) to be becoming, fit
lâ'ḳâ to find
lâkin but, nevertheless
laḳḳîs late
lâm (u) to blame
*lamba* lamp
lamîʿ shining, sparkling
lamm (i) to gather
lamma as, till
lastîk boot
laṭîf pleasant, amiable, delicate, thin; yâ laṭîf! oh dear! good gracious!
lauḥ *lôḥ*, pl. alwâḥ board, plank
laum *lôm* blame
laun *lôn*, pl. alwân color
lauz *lôz* (coll.) almond
lauzi almond (a single one), almond-tree
lawain'? where (to)?
lâyiḳ *lâ=iḳ* becoming, fit
lâzim necessary
lazḳa cataplasm
lbâs pants
*lêh?* why?
*lêl, lêle* night
lezze (material) pleasure
*li* to
*lî* to me
*libâs* pants, drawers
libis (i) to put on, dress
libs clothing, dress
lift turnip
liḥâf, pl. luḥuf quilt
liḥḥâm butcher
liḥiḳ to come up to, follow
liḥis (a) to lick (with the tongue)
liḥyi beard
liʿib (a) to play
lijâm *ligâm* bridle
lil=ân hitherto
lîra a pound

lisā̂n, pl. ilsini *alsine* tongue, language
lissa now, till now; yet
lîwân′ room in the back of a house
liziḳ to stick
lizim (a) to be necessary
*lôḥ* board, plank
*lôm* blame
*lôn* color
*lôz* almonds
lûbiyi *lûbye* French beans (coll.)
luḥuf pl. of liḥâf
lujj *lugge* high sea
lukan′da inn
luḳme bit, mouthful
lûlu pearl
lûmân′ galley
luṭf kindness
luzûm need, necessity
mâ not; mâ baʿrif I do not know; mâ maʿi maṣâri *mâ miʿâye maṣâri* I have no money with me; mâ ti=âkhiz′ni don't take it amiss, excuse me
maʿ with
maʿassalā̂mi! farewell! (said to one taking leave; p. 43)
mablaṛ amount
mabsûṭ content, pleased; well, healthy
madaḥ (a) to praise
madbaṛa tannery
madd (i) (trans.) to stretch out, spread; (issuf′ra) to lay (the cloth)
madd (noun) flux, high water; madd ujazr′ high and low water
madfaʿ, pl. mdā̂fiʿ or madâfiʿ cannon
mâḍi past, gone
madrasi *medrese*, pl. mdā̂ris *medâris* academy, high school
madyûn in debt; debtor
mafrûm hashed, minced
maftûḥ opened, open
maḥa to blot out, efface, erase
maḥab′bi love
maḥall′ place; abode; firm, business house
maḥbûb beloved, dear
maḥbûl idiot
maḥbûs captive
mâhî′yi monthly salary, wages
maḥkami, pl. maḥâkim law-court
maḥrami, pl. maḥârim handkerchief
maḥrûs guarded, protected; son
maidân *mîdân′* open place, arena; ilmaidân name of a quarter in Damascus
mail *mêl* inclination
maiyit dead
majdûb *magdûb* silly, idiotic
majjânan *maggânan* gratis
majlis *meglis*, pl. majâlis, mjā̂lis session, board, commission, council; majlis idâra council of administration; majlis tijâra commercial tribunal
majnûn *magnûn*, pl. majânîn′ idiotic, mad
maḳâm place; place of pilgrimage; sanctuary
makânis pl. of miknisi

maḳbara burying-place
maḳbûl accepted; acceptable, agreeable
makhdûm employer
makhlûṭ mixed
makhnaḳ hot room for stifling silkworms contained in the cocoons
makhṣûṣ (adj.) special, peculiar, particular (adv.) especially, extra
makhtûm sealed
makhzin, pl. mkhâzin or makhâzin shop
mâkin fast, solid, durable
makkan to fasten
makrûh abhorrent; detested; legally inadmissible
maksûr broken
maktab school; office, counting-house
maktabi library; writing-table
maktûb, pl. mkâtîb' *mekâtîb'* letter
mâl, pl. amwâl fortune, property
*mala* (*a*) to fill
mâlak? what is the matter with you?
ma'laḳa and mal'aḳa spoon
malfûf cabbage
*malḥ* salt
mâliḥ salted, salt
malik, pl. mulûk or mlûk king
malkaṭ fire-tongs
malla to fill
m'allim *mu'al'lim* teacher, master; yâ m'allmi! my master! Sir! (an inferior addressing his superior)
ma'lûm known; data (adv.) of course!
malyân full
mamlaḥa salt-cellar
mâmûr' official, officer
ma'na, pl. ma'âni sense, meaning; shû ma'nâto? what is the meaning of it? what do you call it?
mana' (a) to prevent, hinder
*ma'nâh ê?* what is the meaning of it?
manâkhîr' nose
manfa''a advantage, profit
mâni' preventing, obstructive; pl. mawâni' obstacle
manẓar view, sight
mara, pl. nisa or niswân woman
maraḍ, pl. imrâḍ illness
maraḳ (min or 'ala) to pass, go past, go through
maraḳa, marḳa gravy, sauce
marâkiz pl. of markaz
maṛâra, pl. maṛâyir or muṛr den, cave
maṛas colic
marfa' carnival
mar'ḥabâ or marḥabâbak hail! greeting! (answer: marḥabtain')
marîḍ ill, sick
markab *markib*, pl. mrâkib *merâkib* ship
markaz, pl. marâkiz centre; headquarters; station; seat (of an official, of the authorities)
marḳûḳ large round loaf of bread of Syrian peasants (very thin and flat)

marlûb **conquered, beaten, overcome, wronged**
marr (u) **to go past**
marra **time, turn, once**; fard marra **at once, all at once**; marritlukh'ra **another time**
marrib **west**; ilmar'rib **the Mohammedan countries of North Africa exclusive of Egypt**
marribi, **pl.** mrârbi **Magrebian, from Northern Africa**
*mârs* **March**
ma'rûf **known, acknowledged; famous; complaisance**
masa **evening**; masalkhair'! **good evening!**
masâfi **distance**
masaḥ (a) **to wipe, dust**
masal; **see matal**
masalan **for instance**
masal'li **packing-needle; obelisk**
maṣâri **money**; **see** miṣrîyi
maṣârîf' **expenses, costs**
masâṭir **pl. of** mosṭra
masdûd **stopped, closed up**
mashâyikh **pl. of** shaikh
mashhûr **known, celebrated**
mashi, mashyi **gait, manner of walking**
mâshi **walking, on foot**; bilmâshi **on foot**
mashnaḳ **gallows**
mashshaṭ **to comb**
mashshi! **go! march on! go on! be gone!**
mashwara **consultation, council**
masjid *mesgid* **(small) mosque**
maskîn, **pl.** msâkîn' **or** masâkîn' **poor, unfortunate**; yâ maskîn! **poor (boy, man, etc.)!**
maṣlaḥa, **pl.** maṣâliḥ **business, interest**
maslûḳ **boiled**
masmar **to nail**
maṣna' **cistern**
masnid, **pl.** msânid **or** masânid **cushion, pillow, bolster**
maṣr **Egypt**; **see** miṣr
maṣrûf, **pl.** maṣârîf' **expense**
masrûḳ **stolen; robbed**
masrûr **glad, pleased**
mass (i) **to touch**
maṣṭaba **raised ledge in front of a house; seat of the salesman**
mâsû'ra, **pl.** mawâsîr' **long Turkish pipe, chibouque**
mât (u) **to die**
matal, masal, **pl.** imtâl *emsâl* **instance, example, proverb**; Alla ykattir min imtâlak! **bravo!**
maṭar (u) **to rain**
maṭar **rain**
maṭba'a **printing-house, printing-office**
maṭbakh **kitchen**
maṭḥani, **pl.** maṭâḥin **mill**
maṭlûb **demand, claim**
maṭraḥ, **pl.** maṭâriḥ **place**; mâ fî maṭraḥ ba'd? **is there still any room?** mâ 'âd fî maṭraḥ **there is no more room**

maṭrân, pl. maṭârîn' archbishop
*maṭwa* penknife
mauḍi', pl. mawâḍi' place, locality, site
mauj *môg*, pl. amwâj wave
maus, pl. imwâs knife, penknife, razor
mausim *môsem*, pl. mwâsim or mawâsim harvest; fair, market
maut *môt* death
mauwat *mauwit* to murder; mauwitak! mauwtak! I'll kill you! (a threat)
mauz *môz* (coll.) bananas
mauzi banana (a single one)
mawâḍi' pl. of mauḍi'
mawâni' pl. of mâni'
mawâsir' pl. of mâsû'ra
*mâ'yô* May
ma'z (coll.) goats
ma'zi goat (a single one)
mazâd auction
mazîd augmentation, excess; bimazîd .. with the greatest (pleasure, etc.)
ma'zira excuse, apology
mazra'a, pl. mazâri' hamlet; with the article: ilmaz'ra'a, but without any other addition, it frequently is the name of a village [it seems]
mbaiyin clear, distinct;
mbârak *mubârak* blessed
mbârḥa last night
mbâriḥ *embâriḥ* yesterday
mdâfi' pl. of madfa'
mdâris *medâris* pl. of madrasi
medîne, pl. medâ-in and mudun town
*mekai'yif*; see mukai'yaf
mekân place, locality
*mekâtîb'*; see maktûb
meḳâwil contractor
*mêl* inclination
memnûn obliged, thanks
menâm sleep, dream
mendîl pocket-handkerchief
*merâkib*; see markab
*mesâmîr'*; see mismâr
*mesgid* (small) mosque
*meshâ'il'*; see mish'al
*meshâwîr'*; see mishwâr
*mezai'yin* barber
*mezâmîr'*; see mizmâr
mîdân' open place, arena
mi'di stomach
midwam continual, everlasting
mijwiz double; double piece (of money), especially the double silver-piastre or double bargut, but also the half-megeed piece (as a double quarter)
miḳdâr mass, amount, quantity
mikhâneh public-house
mikhfi concealed, clandestine; bilmikh'fi secretly
mikhlâyî *mikhle* provender-bag
miknisi, miknsi, pl. mkânis or makânis broom, besom
mikwâyi flat-iron
mikwi ironed (as linen)
milâye sheet, cloth; see also mlâyi

milḥ *malḥ* salt; milḥ bârûd′ saltpetre
mille nation, creed
miʿmâri builder, bricklayer
mimkin possible
min from, out of
after comparatives: than
minʿa′da except, with the exception of
minfauḳ′ from above
minjadd′ in earnest, seriously
minja′ra for ..'s sake
minshân (prep.) on account of, for; (conj.) that, in order that
mintaḥt′ from beneath
mintaḥt′ râs on account of, for the sake of
minzmân *min zemân* for a long time past
mîn? who?
mînmakân′ whoever (it may be)
mîna enamel
minfakh bellows
minkhâr nose
mintin stinking
mîr prince; see amîr
mîrâlây′ colonel of a regiment
mirwaḥa fan
*mise*; see masa
miṣfâyi sieve (a fine one)
mishʿal *mishʿâl*, pl. mshâʿil *meshâʿil* torch
mishi (i) to go, walk, march
mishmish; see mushmush
mishwâr, pl. mshâwîr′ *meshâwîr′* walk, errand; ramble
mishwi baked
misik (i) to seize, hold, last, be durable
misk musk
miskîn same as maskîn
mislâṭ bolt; the bit of key
mismâr *musmâr*, pl. msâmîr′ *mesâmîr′* nail
miṣr Cairo; see maṣr
miṣrîyi, pl. maṣâri smallest Turkish coin, para
mistakh′dem employee
mistwi ripe, done (cooked)
mitʿaṣ′ṣeb fanatic
mitʿib fatiguing
mitl as, like, similar; mitl baʿḍo it is just the same
mitr metre
mîye hundred
mîzân′ balance, scales
mizmâr, pl. mzâmîr′ *mezâmîr′* psalm
mjaddara Syrian national dish of lentils, rice, and onions
mjallad *mugal′lad* volume, binding
mjallid *mugal′lid* bookbinder
mkânis pl. of miknisi
mkâri *mukâri* livery-man, jobmaster; mule-driver
mkâtîb′ *mekâtîb′* pl. of maktûb
mlâyi *milâye* long and loose colored garment of silk as worn by Mohammedan ladies in Syria
mlûk *mulûk* pl. of malik
mnâsib *munâsib* fit, suitable, becoming
*môg* wave

moi or moiyi water
moiytilward rose-water
moizahr blossom - water (essence of orange - blossoms)
*môsem* harvest, season
mostra, pl. msâtir or ma-sâtir pattern
*môt* death
*môz* bananas
mrabba' *murab'ba'* square (adj. and noun); mitr mrabba' a square metre
mrâkib *merâkib* pl. of markab
mrallif, cover, sheath, envelope
mrârbi pl. of marribi
mratta *murat'ta* covered
mrauwij speedy, quick
msâkîn' pl. of maskîn
msâmîr' pl. of mismâr
msânid pl. of masnid
msâtir pl. of mostra
msauwir painter, photographer
mshâ'il pl. of mish'al
mshauwib heated, in a heat
mshâwîr' pl. of mishwâr
mtîli, pl. matâyil lesson, task
mu'ad'dal middle, proportional, average; 'ala hal-mu'ad'dal in this proportion
mu'af'fin rotting, decaying
*mu:âkhaze*; see muwâkhadi
*mu'al'lim* teacher, master
muaz'zin he who summons the people to prayer in a mosque
*mubârak* blessed
mubash'shir missionary
mudâ'af doubled, double
mudau'war *mudau'wir* round, circular
mudd a corn-measure
mudîr director; administrator of a nâhiyi (subdivision of a kada i.e. district)
mufakk' burri screwdriver
mufet'tish inspector, controller
muflis bankrupt
mufrad single
mufti jurisconsult, an official expounder of Mohammedan law; his opinion, decree, is called fatwa
*mugal'lad* binding, cover
*mugal'lid* bookbinder
muhâl impossible
muhan'dis engineer, surveyor
muhta'ram honored, respected
mujad'dara same as mjaddara
mukai'yaf *mekai'yif* comfortable; see note on p. 339
*mukâri* livery - man, job-master; mule-driver
mukhkh head, skull
mukhta'sar abridgment, abbreviation; compendium
mukhtir dangerous
mulk, pl. imlâk *emlâk* property; pl. goods, landed estates
*mulûk* pl. of malik
mumkin possible
*munâsib* suitable, appropriate

murab'ba **preserved (in sugar)**; murabbayât **preserved fruits**
*murab'ba'* **square**
muraiṭ' **India-rubber, elastic**
*muraṭ'ṭa* **covered**
murḍi'a **wet-nurse**
mûristân' **lunatic asylum**
murr **bitter**
muṛr **pl. of maṛâra**
murûwi **manliness**
mûs, **pl.** mwâs **penknife, razor**
mûsâ'wi **equal, parallel**
mush **not**
muṣḥaf, **pl.** muṣâḥif **a copy of the Koran**
musham'ma' **oil-cloth**
mushîr **chief military dignitary; commander of an army corps**
mushmush, mishmish **(coll.) apricots**
mushmushi **apricot (a single one); apricot-tree**
mushṭ **comb**
*musmâr* **nail**
mustaḥi **ashamed, bashful**
mustaḥîl **impossible**
musta''jil *musta''gil* **hasty**
mustaḳ'bal *mustaḳ'bil* **future**; bilmustaḳ'bal **in future**
mustaḳîm **straight; sincere, honest**
mustawi **ripe, done (cooked)**
mutaṣarrifîyi **province**
mutashâbih **alike**
mut'au'wad *mut'au'wid* **('ala) accustomed (to)**
muṭî' **obedient**

mutjau'wiz *mutĝgau'wiz* **married**
mutkab'bir **haughty, proud**
mutḳad'dim **advanced**
mutrab'ba **educated, well-bred**
mutwâḍi' **modest, humble, submissive**
mutwaḥ'ḥish **uncivilised, wild, rough**
muwâkhadi, mwâkhadi *mu-âkhaze* **the act of finding fault, of taking amiss**; bidûn muwâkhadi! *min ṛêr mu-âkhaze!* **no offence!**
mwâs **pl. of** mûs
mwâsim **pl. of** mausim
*mzaiyin* **barber**
mzâmîr' **pl. of** mizmâr
na'am **yes**; na'am yâ sîdi **yes, Sir; if pronounced with a strongly interrogative accentuation it means: what is your pleasure, Sir?**
naba', **pl.** unbû'a **source, spring**
nabaḥ **to bark**
nabât **plant, vegetation**
nabbah **to inform**
nabḍ **pulse**
nabi, **pl.** imbyi *ambiya* **prophet**; inna'bi **or** nabîyullâh' **the Prophet, the Prophet of God, i.e. Mohammed**
naḍâfi **cleanliness, purity**
naḍḍaf **to clean**
naḍḍâra **telescope**
naḍîf **clean**
nadîm **fellow-boarder, mess-mate**

nâdir **rare**
nafʿ **profit, use;** shû nafʿo? *nefʿo ê?* **what is the use of it? i.e. it is no good**
nafaʿ (a) **to profit, be useful**
nafad (i) **to penetrate; be effective, have influence and thus arrive at one's purpose**
nafakh (u) **to blow (with the mouth)**
nafar **common soldier**
nafas **breath; the bowl of the nargileh filled with tembek** (p. 103 note)
naffad **to cause to pierce; carry out, conclude; flow into**
naffad **to shake (clothes), clean (furniture)**
nâfiʿ **useful**
nafs, **pl.** nufûs **or** infus **soul; person; self;** nafsi, nafsak, **etc., I myself, thou thyself, etc.**
nahab **to rob, plunder**
nahâr, nhâr **day;** nhârak saʿîd! nhârak mbârak! **good day!**
nahîb **robbery, plunder**
naḥl **(coll.) bees**
naḥli **bee (a single one)**
nahr, **pl.** inhur **river**
naḥu **the Arabic syntax; grammar**
(adv.) **about, nearly**
nai **raw, underdone**
najaḥ *nagaḥ* (a) **to suceeed**
najjâr *naggâr* **joiner, carpenter**
naḳal (u) **to transport, remove, change one's abode**
nakar (i) **to deny**
naḳaṣ (a) **to be short of, be missing, diminish (intr.)**
naḳd **ready money**
nakhli **palm-tree**
nâḳiṣ **missing, short; imperfect**
naḳḳaṣ **to lessen, make light of, diminish (trans. and intr.)**
naḳḳaṭ **to trickle**
nâl (a) **to obtain**
naʿl **sole; horseshoe**
nâm (a) **to sleep**
namsa **(always with the article):** innam'sa **Austria**
nâmûs' **(coll.) small gnats, mosquitoes**
nâmûsî'yi **mosquito curtain**
nâr **fire**
nargîle **nargileh**
nâs **(pl. of** insân**) men, people**
nasakh **to copy, transcribe**
naṣâra **pl. of** naṣrâni
nâshif **dry; (of persons:) austere, unkind**
nashshaf **to dry (trans.)**
naṣîḥa **(good) advice**
naṣr **victory**
naṣrâni, **pl.** naṣâra **Christian**
natîji *natîge* **consequence; (Eg.) calendar**
naṭṭ (u) **to jump**
nauʿ, **pl.** inwâʿ *anwâʿ* **kind, species**
nauar **(coll.) gipsies**
naubi **band, orchestra; music**
naulûn **freight**
naum *nôm* **sleep**

nâ'û'ra **bucket-wheel, water-wheel**
nauwal *nauwil* **to hand, give**
nauwar **to enlighten**
nâwal **(with a double acc.) to hand sthg. to sby.**
nazar (u) **to look at, see**
nazar, **pl.** anzâr **look; see anzâr**
nâzir **superintendent, inspector, minister**
nazli **alighting, descent; cold, catarrh**
nazzal *nazzil* **to cause to descend, bring down, take down**
nebîd **wine**
*nef'o ê?* **what is the use?**
nehai'to **at last, finally**
*nemsâwi* **pl. of** nimsâwi
*neyâshîn'*; **see** nîshân'
nhâr **day**
ni'am **pl. of** ni'mi
nidim (a) **to repent**
nidir **to be or become rare**
nidmân **repentant, contrite**
nidr **vow; anything consecrated to God**
nihâye **end**
nijâsi *nigâse* **dung, filth**
nijis *nigis* **dirty, impure**
nîl **indigo, Nile-blue**
ni'mi, **pl.** ni'am **favor, grace**
niml **(coll.) ants**
nimli **ant (a single one)**
nimr **tiger, leopard**
nimsâwi *nemsâwi* **Austrian; (of the language:) German**
nisa **pl. of** mara
nîsân' **April**
ni'sân **sleepy**
nisbe **proportion, relation**
nîshân', **pl.** niyâshîn' *neyâshîn'* **order, decoration; target, aim**
nishif (a) **to dry (intr.)**
nisi (a) **to forget**
nisr, **pl.** nusûra **eagle, vulture**
niswân **pl. of** mara
nitin, nitn **stinking**
niyâshîn' **pl. of** nîshân'
nîyi **intention**
nizâ' **dispute**
nizâm **law, regulation; regular (active) soldiers**
nizil (i) **to alight, go down;** nizil fî **to fly out at one, come down on, drub, fight**
*nôm* **sleep**
*novem'ber* **November**
nufûs **pl. of** nafs
nufûz **influence**
nuḥâs **copper;** nuḥâs aṣfar **brass**
nukṣân **diminution; defect**
nuḳṭa, **pl.** nuḳaṭ **drop; dot; apoplectic fit;** dâ innuḳ'ṭa **epilepsy**
nûr, **pl.** anwâr **light, brightness**
nuskha **copy**
nuṣṣ **half (noun and adj.)**
nusûra **pl. of** nisr
nûwâr' **May**
oḳiyâ'nûs **ocean**
oḳḳa **okka (1.236 kilogr.)**
*oktôber* **October**
ra'ad (a) **to thunder;** 'am btir'ad **it is thundering**
ṛâb (i) **to be absent**
rabaṭ (u) **to tie up, bind;** rabat iṭṭariḳ **to bar the way (said of robbers)**

**rabb** lord, The Lord; yâ rabb! yâ rabbi! my lord! (frequent exclamation, especially of workmen when they start on work)
rabba to bring up, educate
rabîʿ spring (season); verdure, fresh grass in spring; rabîʿ ilau'wal and rabîʿ ittâni the third and fourth months of the Mohammedan year
rabṭa tie, cravat
raʿbûn *ʿarbûn* pledge; earnest money
ṛad morrow; nahâr ilṛad' to-morrow
râd (yerîd) to will, wish
raʿd thunder
ṛada meal; dinner; cf. ṛadi
raḍaʿ (a) to suck (breast)
ṛaḍab anger, wrath
radd (u) to turn or give back, send away; radd jawâb to answer
ṛaḍḍ (u) inna'zar ʿan .. prop.: to cast down the look (or eyes) on, i.e. to overlook, be indulgent towards ..
radda bruise, contusion
ṛadda (with acc.) to give food to, feed
radi bad
ṛadi or ṛada to-morrow
râḍi content, satisfied
rafaʿ (a) to raise, lift; take away
**rafaḍ** to leave, let go
**râfaḳ** *râfiḳ* to accompany
raff shelf on the upper wall to stand vessels on
rafîʿ fine, thin
rafîḳ companion
ṛâfil negligent
ṛafîr watchman, sentinel
rafrâf shed, roof, awning
rafsh large shovel
raftîyi permit, written order for passing goods from the custom-house
*râgil* man
râḥ (yrûḥ) to go; râḥ min bâli to forget
râḥa rest, repose [bet]
rahan (a) to pawn; lend;
râhib, pl. ruhbân monk
râhibi nun
rahn pledge
ṛâ=ib absent
ṛaibi *ṛêbe* absence; bṛaibti *biṛêbeti* during my absence
ṛaim *ṛêm* clouds
ṛair *ṛêr* other, another; (prep.) except, but
ṛair shikl otherwise, differently
ṛair inn .. except that ..
ra=îs same as raiyis
raiyaḥ to tranquilise; raiyiḥ bâlak! make your mind easy!
ṛaiyar *ṛaiyir* to alter (trans.)
raiyis *re=îs* president, chief; captain
raiyisi, raiysi, raisi *re=îse* lady superior
rajjaʿ *raggaʿ* to return, restore
*raḳaba* neck

rakaḍ (u) to run, gallop
raḳaṣ (u) to dance
raḳbi neck
rakhîṣ cheap
rakhkham to lay out with marble
rakhu loose, soft, slack, flaccid
râkib, pl. rukkâb rider, passenger
raḳîḳ thin, fine, meagre
raḳḳaʿ to mend, patch
rakkab to let a horse for riding; put one thing on another; compose, sew on
rakwi small kettle, can for making coffee
ṛala dearness
ṛalab (i) to overcome, vanquish
ṛalaṭ mistake, error
ṛâ'lî dear, expensive
ṛâlib overcoming, prevalent
ṛâliban, ilṛâlib mostly; probably
ṛalṭa mistake, fault
rama (i) to throw
ramaḍân (Musl.) fast-month
raml (coll.) sand
ramli a grain of sand; a sand-heap
ṛamm sorrow
ṛanam wether
ṛa'nî rich
ṛaras to plant
ṛarb west; ilṛarb' the Mohammedan countries of North-western Africa
ṛarîb strange, wonderful
ṛarîf, pl. irṛifi *arṛife* loaf of bread
ṛaṛwi foam, froth
râs, pl. ru-ûs head
ṛasal (i) to wash
ṛaṣb compulsion; bilṛaṣb' by force; in spite of (one)
ṛaṣban ʿan .. in spite of ..
ṛashâwi cover; film
ṛashîm stupid, inexperienced, clumsy
rashsh (u) to sprinkle, scatter in drops
ṛashsh (u) to deceive
raṣîf paved road; quay
rasm drawing, sketch
rasmâl capital, stock
rasmi official (adj.)
ṛassal to wash
ṛassâle laundress
rasûl, pl. rusul messenger, envoy; prophet
ṛaṭa, ṛaṭâyi cover, veil
raṭib damp
raṭl pound (445 grammes)
ṛaṭṭa to cover
rattab *rattib* to put in order, arrange
rauwaḥ to let go away; use up; spoil, injure, destroy; in Egypt also: to go
rauwaḳ to clear, settle; (of persons:) compose oneself
rawâyiḥ pl. of rîḥa
ṛâyi extreme, extremity, utmost; end; biṛâyit il .. with the greatest ..; lilṛâyi in the extreme
ṛâyib absent
râyiḳ clear, light; (of persons:) composed, quiet
ṛâz gas; paraffin oil
ṛazal (i) to spin
ṛazâle gazelle

razîl, pl. arâzîl' common, low; scamp
*ṛâziye*, pl. *ṛawâzi* Egyptian dancing-girl
*re-îs* chief; captain
*reḳḳ* tambourine
*ṛêm* clouds
*ṛêr* other
ribḥân winning; ana ribḥân I have won, made a profit
ribi to be or become educated
ribyân brought up
ribiḥ (a) to win, profit
riḍi (a) to be content
riḍiʿ (a) to suck (breast)
rifâʿi snake-tamer
rîḥ wind; flatulency
rîḥa, pl. rawâyiḥ smell, odor
rîḥân' myrtle
rijiʿ *rigiʿ* to return, go back
rijjâl, pl. rijâl man
rijl *rigl* foot
rîḳân' jaundice
rikbi knee
rikib (a) to ride, mount
ṛili to become dear
ṛ:li to boil (intr.)
ṛilib to be overcome, succumb
ṛilli harvest, that which has been harvested, corn
ṛilṭân mistaken
rimâd ashes
rimâdi ashy (in color)
ṛiriḳ (a) to be drowned
risâli epistle, essay
*riṣâṣ* lead (metal)
rîsh (coll.) feathers
rîshi feather, pen; toothpick, quill
ṛishsh fraud, deception
rismâl capital, money
riwâyi tradition, recital; play (theatr.)
ṛiyâb absence; sunset
rizâli meanness, villainy
rizḳ, pl. erzâḳ livelihood
rizmi *ruzme* parcel, bundle
rizz rice
rôsto roast meat
rṣâṣ *riṣâṣ* lead (metal)
rubʿ quarter, fourth part
*ṛubâr* dust
rubḥ gain, profit
rûḥ spirit, soul
rûḥ! go! [back]
rujûʿ *rugûʿ* return, coming
ruḳʿa label, ticket
*rukbe* knee
rukhâm marble
rukhṣa permission
rukûbe saddle-horse, mule, ass
rumḥ, pl. irmâḥ or rmâḥ *armâḥ* lance, spear
rummân (coll.) pomegranates
rummâni pomegranate (a single one)
ṛurâb, pl. aṛribi raven
ṛurbi absence in foreign parts
ṛurûb sunset
*ruṣâṣ* lead (metal)
rusul pl. of rasûl
rutbi rank, degree
ruṭib damp, humid
ruṭûbi dampness
ru-ûs pl. of râs
*ruzme* parcel
ruzz rice
sâʿa hour, moment; sâʿato, sâʿit'ha at that hour, in that moment
sâʿad to help

sa'âdi **happiness, beatitude**
sa'âdtak **your Excellency**
sa-al (a) **to ask, question**
sa'al (a) **to cough**
ṣa'b **difficult**; ṣa'b 'alai'yi **it is hard for me**
sab', saba' **lion**
sab'a **seven**
sabab, **pl.** isbâb *asbâb* **reason, cause**
ṣabâḥ **morning**; ṣabâḥ il-khair' ! **good morning !**
ṣabar (a) **to wait, be patient**
ṣabaṛ (u) **to dye, color**
ṣabb (u) **to pour, pour in**
sabbab **to cause**
ṣabbaḥ **to wish a good morning**
ṣabi, **pl.** ṣibyân **boy**
sâbi' *sâbi'* **seventh**
ṣâbi' **pl. of** iṣba'
sâbiḳan **previously, formerly**
sabîl **public well, drinking fountain**
sâbit **at rest, stationary, energetic**
ṣabîyi **girl**
ṣabr **patience**; **wormwood**
sabt : yaum issabt' **Saturday**
ṣabûn **soap**
ṣabûra **ballast**
ṣâd (yṣîd) **to hunt, shoot**
sa'd **good fortune**; **happiness**
ṣadaḳa **alms, charity**
sa'dân **monkey**
sadd (i, u) **to fill up, close**
ṣaddaḳ **to believe, consider truthful**
ṣâdiḳ **sincere**
ṣadîḳ, **pl.** aṣdiḳa **friend**
sâdis **sixth**
*ṣadr* **chest, breast**
safar **journey**
sâfar **to travel, start (on a journey)**
safâra **embassy**
safar'jal *safar'gal* **quince**
ṣaff **to range in a line, array**
ṣaff, **pl.** ṣfûf **line, row, class (in a school)**
ṣaffaf *ṣaffif* **to range in a line**
ṣâfi **clear, pure**
safîr **ambassador**
safra **journey**
ṣafra **gall, bile** ; see also aṣfar
sâḥa **open, public place**
saḥab (a) **to drag along, hoist (a flag)**
ṣâḥab **(with acc.) to make friends with, associate with**
ṣaḥḥ (a) **to be healthy, sound, true, valid**
ṣaḥḥa **health**
ṣaḥḥaḥ **to make healthy; correct, rectify**
ṣâḥib, **pl.** iṣḥâb *aṣḥâb* **friend ; master, owner**
ṣaḥîḥ **healthy, sound, true, valid**
sahil **easy**
sâḥil, **pl.** sawâḥil **sea-coast, shore**
sâḥir, **pl.** su'ḥarâ **conjurer**
sahl **plain, level**
sahli **plain, level tract of country**
sahm, **pl.** ishâm *eshâm* **(pron.** is-hâm *es-hâm*) **arrow ; lottery - ticket, share**

ṣaḥn plate (tray)
sahra evening party, soirée
ṣaḥra desert, waste
ṣahrij *ṣahrig* cistern, tank; canal
sahûle facility, ease
sâ'i runner, messenger, courier
ṣaid *ṣêd* hunt, chase, shooting
sa'îd happy, lucky
ṣa'îd Upper Egypt
saif *sêf*, pl. siyûf sword
ṣaif summer
*sâ-iḥ* traveller
ṣâ'iḳa thunderbolt, striking lightning
ṣaiyad to hunt, chase
ṣaiyâd huntsman, fisher
saiyid master, lord; yâ saiyidi! or yâ sîdi! Sir!
sàiydi *saiyidi* lady, madam
sâḳ, pl. sîḳân' leg, shank
sâḳ (ysûḳ) to drive, urge on; gallop, ride quickly
saḳa (i) to water (cattle)
ṣaḳ'a intenseness of cold, frost
sakan (u) to dwell, live
sakat (u) to be silent
saḳaṭ (u) to fall, drop
saḳaṭ damaged, defective, in two, asunder
saḳf roof, ceiling
sâkhin ill (feverish)
ṣakhr, pl. ṣukhûr or ṣkhûr rock, cliff
ṣaḳî' hoar-frost
sâkin, pl. sukkân inhabitant
sâkit silent
sâḳiye, pl. sawâ'ḳî sakieh, canal
saḳḳâ water-seller
saḳḳâṭa, saḳḳûṭa wooden or iron latch-bolt
sâko cloak, mantle
sakt silence
ṣala prayer, divine service
salab to plunder, rob
salâm safety (from all faults and defects of body and soul), salutation; salâmun 'alaik'! hail (peace) be on you! Answer: wa-'alaik' issalâm! and on you hail (peace)! This greeting is, however, used by Muslims only; towards and by Christians it is never employed. — *yâ salâm!* Oh Allrighteous! exclamation of surprise with the Egyptians; *salâm* is in this instance one of the beautiful names of God
salâmi safety, soundness, well-being; ma'assalâmi! farewell!
ṣalât, pl. ṣalawât prayer, divine service
ṣalaṭa salad
sa'li cough
ṣâliḥ, pl. ṣawâliḥ interest, good, welfare
sâlim well, healthy
ṣalla to pray, say one's prayers
ṣallaḥ to repair, put right
sallam 'ala to greet
salli *selle* (market-) basket
sallim! greet! remember (me to ..)!

saltane Sultanate, Lordship
ṣâm (yṣûm) to fast
sama heaven, sky
samaḥ (a) to grant, permit
sâmaḥ to pardon
saman *samn* fat, cooking-butter
samek (coll.) fishes
sâmiḥ'ni pardon me
*samîk* thick
samîn fat, plump
samki fish (a single one); see samek
samm, simm poison
sammâk fishmonger
sammam *sammim* to poison
sammar *sammir* to nail
*samn*; see saman
samni fat, cooking-butter
ṣamr gum; ṣamr ʿarabi gum Arabic
samra fem. of asmar
samsâr broker, agent
*samûm* simoom
ṣanaʿ (a) to make
ṣanʿa, ṣanâʿa craft, trade
sanad support, prop; deed, document, note
ṣandûk, pl. ṣanâdîk' case, box
ṣâniʿ, pl. ṣunnâʿ steward, servant
ṣâniʿa female head servant
ṣanîyi tray, pedlar's box
ṣâr (i) to become
ṣâr of full weight (coin)
ṣaraf (i) to spend, give out; to change
sarak (a) to steal
ṣarakh (a) to shout, cry
ṣâri, pl. ṣawâri mast, flag-staff
sârik thief
sarj *sarg* saddle
sarmûji slipper
ṣarraf *ṣarrif* to change (trans.)
ṣarrâf money-changer, banker
satar to cover
saṭḥ flat roof
saṭl bucket, pail
ṣauban to wash (with soap)
ṣaʿûbe difficulty
ṣaum *ṣôm* fasting, abstinence
ṣaut *ṣôt*, pl. aṣwât sound, noise
sauwa to make equal, adjust, arrange
sauwad *sauwid* to blacken
ṣauwar *ṣauwir* to paint
ṣauwat to produce a sound, make a noise
sawa equal, even; sawa sawa straight on; together; ʿassa'wa straight on
sâwa to be equal to worth as much as ..
*ṣawâbiʿ* pl. of *ṣubâʿ*
sawâḥil pl. of sâḥi
ṣawâliḥ pl. of ṣâliḥ
ṣawâri pl. of ṣâri
ṣawâwîn' pl. of ṣiwân'
sawîyi equally, in the same way
sâyiḥ *sâ:iḥ*, pl. sûwâḥ' traveller, tourist
ṣâyiṛ *ṣâ:iṛ* goldsmith
sâyis *sâ:is* groom, horse boy
*sebtem'ber* September
*ṣêd* chase, shooting
*sêf* sword
*ṣêf* summer

*seger*, *segere;* see shajar
*selle* basket
*sellim* ladder, stairs
*sene* year
*serîr* bed
ṣfûf pl. of ṣaff
shaʿal to light, kindle
shabake net
shabb, pl. shbāb young man
shâf (u) to see
shahad (a) to bear witness, testify; shahad la *shahad li* to testify in favor of; shahad ʿala to testify against
shaḥad to beg (alms)
shahâde evidence
shaḥaṭ to draw a line
shaḥḥâd beggar
shaḥḥaṭ to drive away
shaḥḥâṭa lucifer-match
shâhid, pl. shuhûd or shhûd witness, eye-witness
shaḥm fat, suet
shahr, pl. shuhûr or ishhur *ushhur* month
shahrîyi monthly salary
shaḥrûr blackbird
shai tea
shaikh *shêkh*, pl. shuyûkh or mashâyikh old man, teacher, professor; chief, one of the gentry; see bêk
shâʿil burning, on fire
shaʿîr barley
shaiyâl porter, carrier
shajâʿa. *shagâʿa* courage, valor [(coll.)
shajar *shagar*, *seger* trees
shajra *shagare*, *segere* tree (a single one)

shakar (u) to thank
shakhkh to make water
shakhkhaṣ to represent (a drama), act (a part)
shakhṣ person, individual
shakhtûra large boat
shakk (u) to doubt
shakk doubt; bala shakk, bdûn shakk without doubt
shaḳḳ (u) to split; visit
shaḳḳ cleft
shaḳshaḳîḳ anemone, daisy
shâkûsh′ hammer
shāl (yshîl) to take away, lift up, deduct; carry
shalaḥ (a) (Syr. only) to undress (oneself)
shallaḥ to make one undress himself; plunder, rob
shām: ishshām Syria; Damascus
shamʿa wax; taper, candle; shamʿa ḥamra sealing-wax
shamʿadān candlestick
shâmi Syrian
shamm (i) to smell
shammâm sweet melon
shân: min shân *ʿala shân* for, in order to
shanta portmanteau, bag
shaʿr (coll.) hair
shaʿra hair (a single one)
sharʿ or sharʿi sherîf the Mohammedan law (system of law)
sharaf honor
sharaḥ (a) to expound, comment on
sharâmîṭ′ pl. of sharmûṭa

sharânik̩ pl. of sharnak̩a

sharâṭîṭ' pl. of sharṭûṭa

sharbi drink, draught; purge; in Syria also: water-jug

sharḥ, sharḥo commentary, exposition, explanation

*shâri'*, pl. *shawâri'* road, street

shar'i legal

sharî'a law (as a system; especially the Mohammedan law)

sharîf, pl. ashrâf noble, high-born; descendant of the Prophet

sharîk, pl. shuraka partner, associate ; farmer, peasant

shark̩ east

shark̩i oriental

sharmûṭa, pl. sharâmîṭ' in Syria: low woman ; in Egypt: rag

sharnak̩a, pl. shrânik̩ or sharânik̩ cocoon of the silkworm   [visit]

sharraf *sharrif* to honor,

sharral to occupy, work (trans.)

sharṭ, pl. shrûṭ *shurûṭ* condition, stipulation

sharṭûṭa, pl. sharâṭîṭ' in Syria : rag; in Egypt : low woman

shatam (i) to insult

shaṭâra cunning, cleverness

shâṭi or shaṭṭ coast, shore

shatime insult

shâṭir cunning, clever

shatta to rain

shaub heat

shauk (coll.) thorns

shauki thorn (a single one), sting ; fork

shâwar to consult ; to advise

*shawâri'* pl. of shâri'

*shawârib* moustache

shbâb *shebâb* (pl. of shabb) young people ; youth

shbâbîk' *shebâbîk'* pl. of shubbâk

shbâṭ February

shbîn godfather, sponsor

shdîd *shedîd* firm, hard

shê thing, object

*shebâb* young people ; youth

*shebâbîk'* pl. of shubbâk

shebbi alum

*shedîd* hard, fast

shefâyif pl. of shiffi

shêkh old man, teacher

shelâl cataract

shemâl left side, north

shems sun

*sheneb* moustache

sheshmi closet, privy

*shêṭân'* devil, Satan

shhûd *shuhûd* pl. of shâhid

shî *shê* thing, object; shî âkhar another thing

shibi' (a) to satisfy one's hunger

shidde vehemence, need

shifa healing, cure

shiffi, pl. shefâyif lip

shifi to recover, be healed

shi'il (a) to be kindled, burn

shikl, pl. ishkâl *eshkâl* kind, species ; dish (food)

shilḥ branch

shilsh, pl. shlûsh *shulûsh* root, sinew

shintyān *shintyân* **pants, drawers**
shiʿr **poetry**
shirb **drink, draught; the drinking**
shiri **purchase**
shirib (a) **to drink, smoke**
shirîṭ **ribbon, thread; telegraph-wire**
shirki **society, company**
shirwāl **wide trousers, trunk-breeches**
*shîshe* **hookah**
shît **printed calico**
shiti **winter, rain**
shlikki **strumpet**
shlûḳ **hot wind, sirocco**
shlûsh **pl. of** shilsh
shmāl **north**
shmāli **northern**
shnîʿ **ugly**
*shôḳ* **longing, desire**
*shôke* **fork**
shorba **soup**
shrâki **society, company**
shṛâl *eshṛâl* **pl. of** shuṛl
shrānik **pl. of** sharnaḳa
shrāyi **purchase**
shrîṭ **same as** shirîṭ
shrûṭ *shurûṭ* **pl. of** sharṭ
shû? **what?**
shû bāk? **what is the matter with you? what ails you?**
shû bitrîd? **what do you want?**
shû miftkir? **what do you think?**
shulhkāyi? shulmas'ʿali? shû iddaʿwa? **what is the matter? what is up?**
shubbāk, **pl.** shbābîk' *shebâbîk'* **window**
*shuhûd* **pl. of** shâhid
shuhûr **pl. of** shahr
shukr **thanks, thankfulness**
shukrîyi **dagger, knife**
*shulûsh* **pl. of** shilsh
shûm: yâ ʿaib ishshûm! **what a shame!**
*shûrâb'*, **pl.** *shûrâbât'* **stocking**
shuraka **pl. of** sharîk
shuṛl, **pl.** shṛâl *eshṛâl* **work, business**
shurûḳ **sunset**
*shurûṭ* **pl. of** sharṭ
shuyûkh **pl. of** shaikh
shwai *shuwai'* **a little;** shwai shwai! *shuwai'ye shuwai'ye!* **slowly!**
shwaiyi *shuwai'ye* **a little;** shwaiyit lukhra **a little later, a little more**
shwārib *shawârib* **moustache**
sibâḳ ilkhail' *elkhêl* **horse-race**
sibb **curse, the reviling**
ṣibyân **pl. of** ṣabi
sîd **master, lord;** yâ sîdi **Sir**
ṣidr *ṣadr* **chest, breast**
ṣidrîyi **waistcoat**
ṣifr **zero**
sîgâ'ra **cigarette;** sîgâ'ra franjîyi **cigar**
*sign* **prison**
ṣihhî **sanitary**
sijjâdi *siggâde* **(prayer-) carpet**
sijn *sign* **prison**
sîkân' **pl. of** sâḳ
sîkh, **pl.** syākh *siyâkh* **spit (for roasting)**
sikir **to get drunk**

sikit **to be silent**
sikki **street, way, road; plough**; die (for coining), **Mint**; sikkit ilḥadîd **railway**
sikkîn, sikkîni **knife**
siḳli **burden, charge**
sikr **intoxication, carouse**
sikrân **drunk, tipsy**
silâḥ, **pl.** as'liḥa **weapon**
silk **wire**
sill **phthisis**
silsile **chain**
simi' (a) **to hear**
simm **poison**
sini *sene*, **pl.** snîn **year**
ṣî'nî **china, porcelain**
ṣînî'yi **tray, pedlar's box**
sinn, **pl.** snân *esnân* **tooth**
sinn ilfîl **ivory**
sintilma'ḍa, sintilma'ḍit **last year**
si'r **price, set price, rate**
sirḳa **theft**
sirr, **pl.** isrâr **secret, mystery**
sitâre **curtain**
sitri **(European) coat**
sitt **lady, woman, grandmother**; yâ sitti **madam**
sitt, sitti **six**
sitta'sh' *sittâsher* **sixteen**
sittîn **sixty**; sittîn sini! *sittîn sene!* **prop.: sixty years! i.e. what do I care! I don't care! what's that to me!**
siwa **except, other than**; siwâ꞉an .. an .. **may it .. or .., whether it .. or ..**
ṣîwân', **pl.** ṣawâwîn' **tent**
siwi **to be worth, cost**
ṣîyâd' **hunter, fisher**
*siyâkh* **pl. of** sîkh
ṣiyâm **abstinence, fasting**
siyûf **pl. of** saif
ṣkhûr **pl. of** ṣakhr
slâlim **pl. of** sullam
smâwi **northern**
smîk **thick**
smîn **fat, plump**
snân **pl. of** sinn
ṣnaubar **pine-tree**
snîn **pl. of** sini
snûnu **swallow (bird)**
*ṣôt* **voice, sound**
sû **evil, calamity, the being vicious; un-, mis-, dis-, ill-**
su꞉âl, **pl.** as꞉ili **question**
sub' **seventh part**
*ṣubâ'* **finger**
subḥ **morning**
sûd **pl. of** aswad
sûdân' **Soudan**
ṣudfi **chance, incident**
suds **sixth part**
ṣûf **wool**
ṣufr **pl. of** aṣfar
sufra **(dining-) table**
sufraji *sufragi* **attendant at table**
ṣuḥbi **friendship**
suhûli **facility, ease**
sûḳ, **pl.** iswaḳ *aswâḳ* **market, market-place**
sukhn **hot**
sukhra **compulsory labor, villanage**
sukhûni **heat, hot fever**
ṣukhûr **pl. of** ṣakhr
sukkar **sugar**
ṣulḥ **peace**

sullam *sellim* fem., pl. slâlim stairs, ladder
sulṭân, pl. salâṭîn' Sultan
sumk thickness
sumr pl. of asmar
ṣunnâ' pl. of ṣâni'
sûr wall
sûra, pl. suwar chapter of the Koran
ṣûra, pl. ṣuwar picture, portrait; copy
surûr joy, gladness
ṣu'ûbi difficulty
sûwâḥ' pl. of sâyiḥ
suwâri, pl. asâwîr' bracelet
syâkh pl. of sîkh
syâsi politics, policy
ta, tâ that, in order that; when standing alone before the aorist it imparts to the latter the meaning of an invitation, a challenge: tanrûḥ! we will go! let us go!
tâ ḳullak! I wish to tell you!
ta'a! come (masc. sing.)! come on!
ṭâ'a obedience
ta'ab to fatigue, jade
ta'âl! ta'âla! ta'âli! come (fem. sing.)! come on!
ta'âlu! come (plur.) on!
ṭa''am to feed, give food to
ṭa'âm food
ta'b fatigue, weariness
ṭab' nature, disposition, character
taba' expresses the relation of the genitive (pp. 10, 16); taba'i mine, taba'ak thine, etc.
ṭaba' (a) to print
ṭabaḳa class; story (floor); layer, shelves
ṭabakh (u) to cook, bake
ta'bân tired
ṭaban'ja *ṭaban'ga* pistol
ṭabbâkh cook
ṭabî'a nature
ṭabîb doctor, physician
ṭabî'i natural
ṭabîkh the cooking; decoction
ṭabl drum
tâbût' trunk, chest, coffin
ṭafa (i) to extinguish
ṭafrân poor
*tagribe* trial, test
ṭaḥan (a), ṭaḥḥan to grind, crush
ṭahhar to clip, lop
ṭaḥîn flour
ṭâhir clean, without stain
taḥt under(neath)
ṭâḥûn', ṭâḥû'ni mill
ṭaila' to bring out
ṭair *ṭêr*, pl. ṭyûra *ṭiyûr* bird
ṭaiyar to let fly; ṭaiyar moi to make water
*ṭaiyâra* kite (toy)
ṭaiyib good
tâjir *tâgir*, pl. tujjâr merchant
t'ajjab *it:ag'gab* to wonder
takhîn thick, coarse
t:akhkhar *it:akhkhar* to be late, come too late
takhmîn estimate, conjecture
(adv.) about, perhaps
*takhte* bench, seat
taḳîl, pl. tiḳâl *tuḳâl* heavy
takkîye dervish monastery

ṭakm, pl. ṭkûmi *ṭukûme* suit (of clothes), harness, set
ṭâl (u) to be or become long
ṭalab (u) to demand, ask
ṭalab demand, request
ta'lab fox
ṭalâk separation, divorce
talâte three
tâlit third
talj *telg* snow
tall, talli hill
talla to fill
ṭalla' to bring out
ṭallak, to divorce, dismiss a wife
ṭama' covetousness, greed
ṭa'ma to feed, give food to
tamâm perfect, complete, ready; tamâm! or bit-tamâm! (adv.) quite right! right! bravo! enough!
taman value, price
tambak Persian tobacco for a hookah pipe
ṭamî' covetous, greedy
tâmin eighth
tamm (i) to be perfect, be complete, be over; stay
t=ammal *it=am'mal* to hope
t=ammul (the) hoping, hope
tammûz July
tamr (coll.) dried dates
*tanâbile* pl. of tembel
tâni second; tâni marra for the second time
tanjara *tangara*, pl. tnâjir stewpan
târ revenge; akhad târo to take one's revenge
ṭâr (yṭîr) to fly
*ṭarabêze* table
ṭarad (u) to expel, drive out
ṭaraf, pl. aṭrâf edge, side
ṭaraḥ (a) to cast, throw, have an abortion
tarak (u) to leave, quit
ṭarash to whitewash (a wall)
ṭarbûsh fez
ṭarḥa long veil of light stuff, trimmed with lace, and hanging down to the ground at the back
ṭari fresh, tender
ṭarîk, pl. ṭuruk or ṭurkât road, street
târîkh', pl. twârîkh' *tawârîkh'* history, chronicle
tarjam to translate
tarjimi translation
tarjimân *tergumân*, pl. trâjmîn' *terâgimîn'* interpreter, dragoman; travelling-marshal
ṭarrâḥa small square mattress, placed on the floor, and serving as a seat; in Egypt: mattress in general
ṭarsh whitewash, the white-washing; cattle
t'ashsha *it'ash'sha* to sup, have supper
ṭâsi porringer of copper
tâsi' ninth
taslîyi amusement, conversation
ṭauf *ṭôf* night patrol
ṭauli *ṭarabêze* table
taur *tôr* bull, ox
taurât the Law of Moses, the Old Testament
t'auwad *it'au'wid* 'ala to get accustomed to
ṭawa (i) to fold, bend
ṭâwa' to obey

tawaffa to die
*tawârîkh'* pl. of târîkh'
ṭawâshi eunuch
ṭawîl, pl. ṭwâl *ṭuwâl* long; ṭawîlî ʿala rakbitak! *ṭawîle ʿala rakbetak!* go and be hanged!
ṭawîyi fold
tâze fresh
*teglîd* (the) binding, cover of a book
telg snow
tembel, pl. tnâbil *tanâbile* lazy
temel'li without intermission, continued, as usual
tenek, teneki tin (vessel)
*ṭêr* bird
*tergumân, terâgimîn'* interpreter
*tezkire* ticket, passport
tḥâdas *itḥâdis* to converse (among one another), talk (together)
tḥammam *itḥam'mam* to take a bath, bathe oneself
tiʿbân tired
tifl dregs, grounds (of coffee, etc.)
ṭifrân poor, without means
tifsîr explanation; commentary to the Koran
tihdîd threat
tiʿib to be tired, become wearied
tijâra *tigâra* trade, commerce
tijlîd *teglîd* binding (of a book)
tijribi *tagribe* trial, test
tiḳâl pl. of taḳîl
tiḳl weight
tiklîf burden, trouble, ceremony, etiquette; mâfi tiklîf! no ceremony!
tikram! willingly! answer to a request or demand
ṭiliʿ (a) to go out, come out; put forth (as a plant); rise (as the sun)
tilt third part
timbek tobacco for the hookah-pipe
timbîh admonition; note, annotation
timsâḥ crocodile
timsâl statue
tîn (coll.) figs
tîni fig (a single one); fig-tree
ṭîn loam, clayey soil
tirbi tomb
tirsa Egyptian tortoise
tirwîḳa breakfast
tisʿa nine
ṭisht wash-hand basin
tislâyi amusement
tiṣwîra picture
ṭiyâ'ra kite (toy)
*ṭiyûr* pl. of ṭair
ṭîz hindmost, backpart
tizkiri, tizkri *tezkire* ticket, passport
tjauwaz to marry, get married
tḳîl heavy
ṭḳûmi pl. of ṭaḳm
tmanye eight
tmashsha *itmash'sha* to go for a walk, walk up and down
tmashshaṭ *itmash'shaṭ* to comb oneself
tnâbil pl. of tembel
tnaḍḍaf *itnaḍ'ḍaf* to cleanse oneself, be purified

tnâjir pl. of tanjara
tnaṣṣat *itnaṣ'ṣat* to hearken
tnâwal *itnâwil* to partake of, take, receive
tôb garment
trâb *turâb* earth, dust
tṛadda *itṛad'da* to take food, breakfast
trajja *itrag'ga* to beg, ask
trâjmîn' pl. of tarjimân
tṛassal *itṛas'sal* to wash, bathe oneself
trumba pump
tsalla *itsal'la* to console oneself, be consoled; amuse oneself, spend a pleasant time
tṣauban *itṣau'ban* to wash (one's hands with soap)
tṣauwar *itṣau'war* to imagine; be imagined, be painted, have one's photo taken
tshakka *itshak'ka* to complain
tshakkar *itshak'kar* to [thank]
tsharraf *itshar'raf* to be honored, honor oneself; to visit
tuffâḥ (coll.) apples
tuffâḥa apple (a single one); apple tree
ṭuhûr purity; circumcision
tujjâr pl. of tâjir
*tuḳâl* pl. of taḳîl
tukhn thickness
*ṭuḳûme* pl. of ṭaḳm
ṭûl length; throughout the ..., during the whole ..., e.g. ṭûl illail' throughout the night
tult third part
ṭulûʿ ascent
ṭulum'ba pump, fire-engine
tûm garlic
tumn eighth part
*turâb* earth, dust
turbi, tirbi tomb, chapel, mausoleum, cemetery
ṭurrâḥa same as ṭarrâḥa
ṭuruḳ, ṭurḳât pl. of ṭarîḳ
ṭusht basin, wash-hand basin
tût, tûti mulberry-tree
tutun tobacco
tûtya zinc, tutty
*ṭuwâl* pl. of ṭawîl
twâḍuʿ modesty, humility
ṭwâl pl. of ṭawîl
twârîkh' pl. of târîkh'
ṭyûra pl. of ṭair
tzakkar *itzak'kar* to recollect, remember
u and
ûʿa! take care! mind!
ʿufûni putridity; miasma
ʿ*ugge* pancake
*ugra* wages, salary
ʿûj ʿ*ûg* pl. of aʿwaj
ûḳaf! stop! stand up!
ʿuḳâl string
ûḳât' collateral form of auḳât
ʿuḳdi knot
ukhar, ukhra; see âkhar
ûla; see auwal
ûlâd' *aulâd* (pl. of walad) sons, children; ûlâd' ʿarab *aulâd ʿarab* prop.: sons of Arabs, i.e. domiciled Arabs, Egyptians, Syrians; see p. 127, note

ûlâ'ni collateral form of aulâni [box
ʻulbi pl. of ʻulab little case,
ulfi friendship
ulʻûbi toy, doll
ʻulûm sciences
ʻulwân title, address
*umm* mother
umm ḳêḳ lich-owl, brown owlet
ʻumr life
ʻumûm generality, public, people; bilʻumûm, ʻumûman in general
ʻumûmi public, general
ʻumûmi pl. of ʻamm
umûr pl. of amr
ʻumyân pl. of aʻma
unbûʻa pl. of nabaʻ
ʻunwân title, address
ʻurbân Bedouins
urdu army corps
ʻurwi buttonhole
uṣbur! wait!
*ushhur* pl. of shahr
usûd, usud pl. of asad
uṣûl pl. of aṣl
ʻutuḳ pl. of ʻatiḳ
ʻuwaisîyi pocket-knife, penknife
ʻuyûn pl. of ʻain
uzr pl. of izâr
ʻuzr excuse, apology
wa *we* and
waʻa to awake; keep in mind, recall
waʻad (yûʻid) to promise
waʻaz (yûʻaz) exhort, preach
wâbûr' steamer
waʻd promise
waḍaʻ (yûḍaʻ) to lay, put
wadda to conduct, send
waddaʻ to take leave
wâdi, pl. widyân river, valley
waʻdi set term, fixed day, day or period on which a bill, etc. falls due
wâḍiḥ clear, manifest, distinct
wâfaḳ to agree with, befit
waffar *waffir* to save, lay up
*wâgib* necessary; duty
*wâḥ*, pl. *wâḥât'* oasis
*waḥayât* or *waḥyât;* see wiḥyât
waḥd .., waḥdi, waḥdak, waḥdo, etc., I alone (I by myself), thou alone, he alone, etc.
waḥîsh ugly, rough, rude
waḥl dirt, ordure
waḥsh wild beast; wild, rude
wâʻiz preacher
wajaʻ *wagaʻ* (yûjaʻ) to pain
wajaʻ *wagaʻ* pain
wajad *wagad* (yajid) to find
wâjbât' *wâgibât'* compliments, respects
wâjbi *wâgibe* duty
wâjib *wâgib* necessary; obligation
waḳaʻ (yûḳaʻ) to fall, befall, occur
waḳʻa, pl. waḳâʻi event
waḳaf (yûḳaf) to stand, stand up; stop
waḳf, pl. auḳâf pious legacy
waḳfe pause, rest
wakhm dirt, mud
*wakhri* late

wâḳif standing; stopping
*wâkil* eating
wakîl, pl. wukala substitute, agent
wakîl daʿâwi solicitor
waḳḳaf to bring to a standstill, stop, make to halt
waḳḳif! stand! stop! halt!
waḳt, pl. auḳât or ûḳât' time
walad (yûlid) to beget
walad *waled*, pl. ûlâd' *aulâd* son, boy
walâyim *walâ=im* pl. of walîmi
wâldain' *wâlidên'* parents
wâldi *wâlide* mother
wâli governor, governor-general of a province
wâlid father
walîmi, pl. walâyim *walâ=im* entertainment, banquet
walla or
walwali bewailing, lamentation for the dead
wara behind (adv.); min wara .., wara min .. behind ..
waraḳ (coll.) leaves of paper
warḳa *waraka*, pl. aurâḳ leaf (a single one)
waram *yûram* to swell, be swollen
ward (coll.) roses
wardi rose (a single one)
wârim swollen
wâris, pl. warasi heir
warra to show
wasakh dirt
wasaṭ central, middling
wâsiʿ wide, large
*wâsiṭa* means
waṣl receipt, acknowledgment
waṣṣa to recommend
wassakh to soil, dirty
waṣṣal *waṣṣil* to conduct
wasṭ centre, middle
wâsṭa *wâsiṭa* means, expedient
wasṭâni central
waṭan home, native place
wâṭi low, common; low, not loud; bilwâṭi gently, softly
waṭwâṭ bat (animal)
*waya* with
waʿz preaching, admonition
wazan (yûzin) to weigh
wazâra ministry
wazîfe office
wazîr, pl. wuzara vizier, minister
wazn weight
wazz *wizz* (coll.) geese
wazzi goose (a single one)
*we* and
widâʿ leave, farewell
widn, pl. yudân ear
widyân pl. of wâdi
wiḥish ugly, rude, uncivilised
wiḥyât! *waḥayât* or *waḥyât!* by the life of ..!
wij *wishsh* face; cover
wijid *wigid* to exist, be found, find oneself
wiḳif (yûḳaf) to stand, stand up, draw up
wilâyi government of a province; province, Wilayet
wilid (yûlid) to bear, give birth to

wirs, wirti heritage
*wishsh* face; cover
wisi' (yûsa') to be wide
wisikh dirty
wiṣil (yûṣal) to arrive
wîṭwâṭ' bat (animal)
wizâre ministry
*wizz* (coll.) geese
wuḍûḥ clearness; evidence
wuḥâd one at a time
wukâh Christian church-warden
wukala pl. of wakîl
wukiyi ounce; see p. 245
wuķû', pl. wuķû'ât' (the) falling, fall; occurrence
wusikh dirty
wusṭ same as wasṭ
wuṣûl arrival; receipt, acknowledgment
yâ vocative particle; yâ khawâja, yâ sîdi! Sir! yâ m'allmi! my master!
yâbis dry
yadd, pl. ayâdi or daiyât hand
yahûd Jews
yahûdi Jewish, a Jew
yalla! all right! go on! off!
yamîn oath
yamîn zûr perjury
yamîn right (in opp. to left)
'alyamîn on the right
*yanâ=ir* January
ya'ni that is to say, viz.
yâtara perhaps
yaum *yôm*, pl. îyâm' *aiyâm* day
yimma or
*yôm* day
yudân pl. of widn
*yûlih* or *yûliye* July
*yûnih* or *yûniye* June
yuzbashi lieutenant
zâbiṭ officer (mil.)
zabṭîyi police, police-soldier
zâd provision, provender
zâd (yzîd) to be over, be too much; to increase, add
zahar (a) to shine; to appear, become manifest
zâhir manifest; izzâhir evidently, it seems
zaḥme crowd(ing)
zahr (coll.) flowers
zahra, pl. zuhûr flower (a single one)
zai, zaiy *zê* as, like, just like; zai ba'ḍo *zê ba'ḍo* it is the same, it is equal
zaibaķ *zêbaķ* quicksilver
zait *zêt* oil
zaitûn *zêtûn'* (coll.) olives
zaitûni olive (a single one)
zaiyan *zaiyin* to decorate, illuminate
zakhîra ammunition
zakhraf to decorate, adorn, embellish
zakhrafi decoration, embellishment
zakzak to tickle
za'l vexation, sorrow, ennui
zalami, pl. zulm person, fellow; foot-soldier
zâlim unjust; oppressor, tyrant
zalrûṭ, pl. zalâriṭ' shout of joy (of women, at weddings, etc.)
zalzali earthquake
zamân time; min zamân a long time since, for a long time
zamb, pl. zunûb fault, sin

zambil large basket
zann (u) to believe, think
zann belief, opinion
zâr (yzûr) to visit, make a pilgrimage to
zara' (a) to sow
zarf saucer ; envelope
zarî'a seed
*zarîf* amiable
zarḳa fem. of azraḳ
za'rûr medlar tree
zât, pl. zawât person, a high personage ; cf. foot of p. 14
*zât yôm* or *yôm min zât el-iyâm'* some day, once
zaṭṭ to throw
zauba'a *zôba'a* storm
zauj *zôg* husband
zauji *zôge* wife
zauḳ *zôḳ* taste
zauwaj *zauwig* to marry to, couple with
zawât pl. of zât
zâwyi *zâwiye*, pl. zawâya corner, nook
zâyid *zâ-id* more, too much, over, superfluous
zbîb *zebîb* (coll.) raisins
*zê* as
*zekîbe* sack
*zenânîr'* pl. of zinnâr
zenkîl, pl. znâkîl' rich
*zêt*, *zêtûn'* oil, olives
zîbaḳ quicksilver
zibdi table-butter
zift pitch, tar
zi'il to be angry, be sorry, want pastime
zikr remembrance, memory ; religious function of the Mohammedans
zi'lân angry, sorry, bored, tired
zilḥifi tortoise
zîni decoration, embellishment ; illumination
zinjfîl *ganzabîl* ginger
zinnâr, pl. znânîr' *zenânîr'* girth, waist-belt
zinzilakht' acacia
zirr *zurâr*, pl. zrâr *azrire* button
ziyâdi abundance ; too much
zîyâḥ' procession
znâkîl' pl. of zenkîl
*zôba'a* storm
*zôg* husband
*zôḳ* taste
zṛaiyir *zuṛai'yar* little, small
zṛîr little, small
zuhûr pl. of zahra
zujâj *zugâg* glass
zuḳâḳ lane
*zukâm* cold in the head, catarrh
zulm pl. of zalami
zunûb pl. of zamb
zûr compelled; yamîn zûr perjury ; bizzûr hardly, with difficulty
*zuṛai'yar* small
*zurâr* button
zurḳ pl. of azraḳ
zûwâ'di provision, provender
zyâdi abundance ; too much

# NEW WORDS

## A

**accident insurance** *n.* ta-mîn ḥawâdes *ta-mîn ḥawâdis*
**aggression** *n.* eʿ-tidâʹ *eʿ-tidâʹ*
**air base** *n.* ḳâʿidé jau-wiʾyé *ḳâʿida gau-wiʾya*
**air conditioner** *n.* mu-kaiʾifʾ hawâʾ *mukaiʾif hawâʾ*
**aircraft carrier** *n.* ḥâmi-latʹ ṭai-yarât *ḥâmilatʹ ṭâ-irât*
**airfield** *n.* maṭâr *maṭâr*
**air liner** *n.* ṭai-yaretʹ rukʾ-kâb *ṭaiʹyâretʹ rukʾ-kâb*
**airmail** *n.* barîd jau-wî *barîd gau-wî*
**airplane** *n.* ṭai-yara *ṭâira*
**airport** *n.* maṭâr *maṭâr*
**air-raid shelter** *n.* malʹ-jaʹ ṛârât jau-wi-yet *malʹgaʹ ṛârât*
**allergic** *a.* ḥas-sâs *ḥas-sâs*
**allergy** *n.* ferṭ ḥas-sa-siê *ferṭ ḥas-sa-sia*
**amplifier** *n.* mukab-birʹ ṣaut *mukab-birʹ ṣôt*
**anesthetic** *n.* binj *bing*
**appetizer** *n.* muḳab-bilʾ *muʹshahʹ-hi*
**atom bomb** *n.* ḳunbulatʹ zar-ri-yatʹ *ḳunbula zarʹ-ri-ya*
**atomic fission** *n.* tafâʿulʹ zarʾ-ri *tafâʿulʹ zarʾ-ri*

## B

**black list** *n.* ḳâʹîmat saudâʹ *ḳâʹîmat saudâʹ*
**black market** *n.* sûḳ saudâʹ *sûḳ saudâʹ*
**blowup** *n.* (photo) takʾ-bîr (sûra) *takʾ-bîr* (*sûra*)
**blow up** *v.* (photo) yû-kabʾ-bir (sûra) *yekabʾ-bir* (*sûra*)
**bulletin board** *n.* lauḥ iʿlanât *lôḥ iʿlanât*
**bus station** *n.* maḥaṭ-et buṣ-ṣât *maḥaṭat otobîs*
**bus stop** *n.* mauḳef buṣ-ṣât *mauḳef otobîs*

## C

**cablegram** *n.* teleṛ'râf *teleṛ'râf*
**camera** *n.* âlat' taṣ'wïr *âlat' taṣwîr*
**canned meat** *n.* laḥm maḥfûz *laḥma maḥfûza*
**can opener** *n.* fat'-taḥat 'elab *fat'-taḥat 'elab*
**ceiling price** *n.* si'r muḥad-dad' *taman muḥad-dad'*
**checkroom** *n.* ṛurfat el-malâbis *ṛorfat el badlât*
**classified ad** *n.* i'lân mubau'ab' *i'lân mubau'ab'*

## D

**day-letter** *n.* kitâb Yaumî *kitâb yau-mî*
**dial** *v.* Udau-wir'*yidau-wir'*
**dial telephone** *n.* telefôn ôtomatîkî *telefôn ôtomatîkî*
**driver's license** *n.* rokhsat' Sewâḳa *rokhsat' sewâ'ḳa*
**driving lesson** *n.* dars sewâḳa *dars sewâ'ḳa*

## E

**electrician** *n.* kahrabâ'-î *kahrabâ'-î*
**electrification** *n.* kahrabat *kahraba*
**elevated railway** *n.* sik'-kit' ḥadîd marfu'a *sik'-kat' ḥadîd ṣaṭ'ḥia*
**elevator** *n.* miṣ''ad' *meṣ''ad'*
**emergency brake** *n.* farmalat' ṭawâri' *farmalat' ṭawâri'*
**emergency landing** *n.* hubûṭ ṭawâri' *hubûṭ ṭawâri'*
**employment agency** *n.* wikâlet' tauẓîf *wikâlet' tauẓîf*
**escalator** *n.* mar'ḳa *mar'ḳa*
**excess baggage** *n.* 'afsh zäyed *'afsh zâ-id*
**exhaust pipe** *n.* (auto) mâsurat' el 'âdim' *shak'mân*
**extension telephone** *n.* waṣlat' telefôn *tauṣîlat' telifôn*

## F

**filling station** *n.* mḥaṭ'it' benzîn *maḥaṭ'tet' banzîn*
**film roll** *n.* (photo) bakarat' film *bakarat' film*
**flashlight** *n.* baṭ'ṭariyê *baṭ'ṭari-ya*
**forced landing** *n.* hubûṭ iṭ'ṭirârî *hubûṭ iî'ṭirârî*
**foreign exchange control** *n.* murâkabat' an'naḳd *marâḳ'bet' el'nakd*
**fountain pen** *n.* alam ḥibr *alam abanôs'*
**fuse** *n.* kaubes *kobes*
**fuselage** *n.* haikal' eṭ'ṭayâra *hai'kal eṭ-ṭaiyâra*

## G

**gas chamber** *n.* ḥujrat' el gâz *ḥugrat' el gâz*
**gas mask** *n.* ḳinâ' wâḳî *ḳinâ' elwâḳî*
**general delivery** *n.* taślîm 'âm *taślîm 'âm*

## H

**hand brake** *n.* farmalet' yad' *farmalet' yad'*

## I

**ice box** *n.* bar'râd *tal'lâg*
**ice-cream parlor** *n.* maḥal' bûza *maḥal jilatî*
**identification card** *n.* bitâḳat' hawi'at' *kart' taḥ'ḳîḳ el shakh'si'-ya*
**ignition** *n.* (auto) maf'lat' el kah'raba *muf'lat' el kah'raba*
**inflation** *n.* intifâkh *nafkh*

## J

**jet plane** *n.* ṭai-yâra jet *ṭai-yâra jet*
**juke box** *n.* ṣandu' mûsi-a *ṣandûḳ mûsika*

## L

**labor union** *n.* nikabat′ ‘um′ mâl *nikabat′ ‘um′ mâl*
**landing field** *n.* maṭâr *maṭâr*
**landing gear** *n.* daf’fet′ hubûṭ *daf’fat′ hubûṭ*
**license plate** *n.* numret′ ôtombîl *nimret′ ôtombîl*
**lipstick** *n.* ḥumret′ shifâf *aḥ’mar′ shafâ′yef′*
**local call** *n.* mukâlamê maḥal′liê *mukâlama maḥal′liya*
**long-distance call** *n.* mukâlamê khârîjiê *mukâlama khârîgiya*
**loudspeaker** *n.* mukab′ bir′ *mukab′bir’*
**lubricating oil** *n.* zait taz′yît *zêt tash′ḥîm*

## M

**make-up** *n.* twâlet′ *twâlet′*
**microphone** *n.* mikrofôn *mikrofôn*
**mileage** *n.* ‘ad′dâd el am′iâl *‘ad′dâd el amyâl*
**military police** *n.* bolîs el jêsh *bolîs gêsh*
**mimeograph** *n.* mimiogrâf *mimiogrâf*
**money order** *n.* ḥawâlet′ bôsṭa *hiwâlet′ bôsṭa*
**motion picture** *n.* sûwar mutaḥar′rikê *sûwar mutaḥar′rika*
**motorbike** *n.* môtôsîkl *môtôsîkl*
**motorboat** *n.* mar′kab′ bûkhârî *markeb′ bûkhârî*
**motorcycle** *n.* môtôsîkl *môtôsîkl*
**motorist** *n.* sûw′wa′ *saw′wâḳ*
**mudgard** *n.* (auto) raf’raf′ *raf’raf’*

## N

**negative** *n.* (photo) sâlib′ iṣ-Ṣûra *‘afrît′*
**network** *n.* shabakê *shabaka*
**newsreel** *n.* akh′bâr mûsaw′wara *akhbâr sînama′îya*
**non-aggression pact** *n.* hilf′ ‘adam’i‘tidâ′ *ḥilf′ ‘adam′i‘tidâ′*

## O

**operator** *n.* 'âmelet' tele fôn *'âm'let' telifôn*

## P

**packaged tour** *n.* raḥlê kâmlê *riḥla kâmla*
**parachute** *n.* mazal'lê *mizal'la*
**pay station** *n.* (telephone) telefôn ij'ra *telifôn agâr*
**phonograph record** *n.* isṭ'wânet' fônogrâf *asṭawâ'na*
**photogenic** *a.* ḥasan it'taṣwîr *mustagîb it'taṣwîr*
**plainclothes man** *n.* bolîs sir'rî *mokh'bir' sir'rî*
**planned economy** *n.* iḳ'tiṣâdiê munaz'zamê *iḳ'tisâdiy'ya munaz'zama*
**police station** *n.* noḳ'ṭet' elbolîs *noḳṭet' elbolîs*
**post office box** *n.* ṣandû' barîd *sondûḳ barîd*
**pressure cooking** *n.* ṭabkh biḍ'ḍarṭ *ṭabkh biḍ'ḍarṭ*
**preventive war** *n.* ḥarb'wikâyê *ḥarb wikâ'iya*
**psychiatrist** *n.* ṭabîb' nif'sânî *mohal'lil' naf'sânî*
**psychiatry** *n.* 'ilâj nif'sânî *'ilâg naf'sânî*
**psychoanalysis** *n.* taḥ'lîl nif'sânî *taḥ'lîl naf'sânî*
**psychopath** *n.* moṭ'ṭarib' el'nafs *moṭ'ṭarib al'nafs*

## Q

**questionnaire** *n.* âymet' as-ilê *ḳai'mat' as-ila*

## R

**radar** *n.* radâr *radâr*
**radiator** *n.* mad'fa-a *mid'fa-a*
**radio commentator** *n.* mu'al'lik' radio *mu'al'lik' radio*
**radio transmitter** *n.* mḥaṭ'ṭet' irsâl *maḥaṭ'ṭet' irsâl*
**receiver** *n.* mḥaṭ'ṭet' istilâm *maḥaṭ'et' istilâm*

**record changer** *n.* âlet′ taṛyîr ist′wanât *âlit′ taṛ′yîr astowanât*
**recorded music** *n.* mûsî′-a msaj′jalê *mûsîka musag′galâ*
**refugee** *n.* lâji′- *lâgi′*
**refrigerator** *n.* til′lâj *tal′-lâg*
**registered letter** *n.* mak'-tûb msaj′jal' *gawâb musag′gal′*
**release the clutch** *v.* falat' il′kluṭsh *falat' il′kluṭsh*
**rental library** *n.* kutub' bil′ijra *kutub′ bil′og′ra*
**remote control** *n.* aḍ-ḍabṭ il' ba'îd *aḍ-ḍabṭ il′ba'îd*
**rocket** *n.* ṣarûkh *ṣârukh*
**roomette** *n.* (rail) ûda ṣṛîrê *oda wâgon-lit′*

S

**sales tax** *n.* ḍarîbet' bê' *ḍarîbat' bê'*
**service station** *n.* mḥaṭ′-ṭet′ benzîn *maḥaṭ′ṭat banzîn*
**short circuit** *n.* ḳuṣr *ḳuṣr*
**short wave** *n.* maujê aṣîrê *moga ḳasîra*
**sleeper** *n.* (train) ûda ṣṛîrê lin′nôm *oda wâ-gon-lit′*
**smoker** *n.* (rail) ṛurfit′ tid′khîn *masmûḥ tad-khîn*
**social security** *n.* ḍamân ijtimâ'î *ḍamân igtimâ'î*
**spare parts** *n.* pl. uṭa'′ ṛiyâr *ḥitat′ ṛiyâr*
**spare tire** *n.* dûlâb zi-yâdê *'agala ziyâda*
**speed limit** *n.* ḥad′ lis′-sir'a *ḥad′ lis′sur'a*
**sponsor** *n.* (radio) mu-mawil′ radio *mumawil′ radio*
**standard of living** *n.* mustawal-ma'îshê *mus-tawa ma'îsha*
**steam shovel** *n.* maj′-rafê Bûkharîê *mag′rafa Bûkhari′-ya*
**stickup** *n.* sir′=a *sirḳa*
**stock market** *n.* bôrṣa *bôrṣa*
**station wagon** *n.* 'arabat' *'arabat'*
**stratosphere** *n.* iṭ′ṭaba′=al' jaw el'alawîê *ṭaba-ḳaṭ al'gau al′ 'alawiya*
**streamlined** *a.* ḥadîth (sound of th) *ḥadîth (sound of th)*
**subway** *n.* ḳiṭâr en′na-fak′ *aṭr taḥt′ el′arḍ*
**swimming pool** *n.* bir′kit′ sbâḥa *ḥam′mâm sibâḥa*

## T

**tabloid** *n.* jirnâl *gornâl*
**take a photograph** *v.* khôd ṣûra *khud ṣûra*
**take a drive** *v.* (auto) ÿet′naz′zah' bil' ôtombîl *yit'fas′saḥ' fil' ôtombîl*
**take off** *v.* ala' (clothes) or ṭâra (plane) *same*
**take out insurance** *v.* yâkhud bolîset′ te′mînyâkhud *bolîsat' ta′mîn*
**telecast** *n.* yezî'bil′televizion *yizî'bil′televizion*
**telegraph blank** *n.* fôrmet' tel′leṛ′râf *fôrmet′ teleṛ'râf*
**telegraph office** *n.* maktab′ et′tel′leṛrâf *maktab′ teleṛrâf*
**telephone booth** *n.* kishk′el telefôn *kôshk′ telifôn*
**telephone call** *n.* mûkâlamê telefonîê *mukâlama telifôni′ya*
**telephone directory** *n.* dalîl el-telefôn *daf′tar′ telifôn*
**teletype** *n.* âlit' tel′leṛ′râf *âlet′ teleṛrâf*
**television** *n.* televizion *televizion*
**ticket window** *n.* shib′bâk et′tazâkir' *shob′bâk et′tazâkir'*
**traffic jam** *n.* ḥashd *ḥashd*
**traffic light** *n.* ḍau el' murûr *nûr murûr*
**traffic officer** *n.* zâbit' el murûr *zâbit′ murûr*
**traffic violation** *n.* mûkhâlafet′ el murûr *mûkhâlafat′ murûr*
**trolley car** *n.* trâmway *trol′lî*
**truck** *n.* 'arabit' na≠el' *'arabat naḳl′*
**turn on the radio** *v.* if′taḥ il radio *if′taḥ il radio*
**turnstile** *n.* bâb dûwâr *bâb dawâr*
**typewriter** *n.* âlê kâtbê *âla kâtiba*
**typist** *n.* kâtib′ 'alal′âlê elkâtbê *kâteb′ 'alal′âla el kâtiba*

## U

**United Nations** *n.* al′u mam′ el mu′taḥidê *al′umam′ el mut′taḥida*

## V

**vacuum cleaner** *n.* âlet′ tin'dîf' kah′rabâ-iyê *âlat′ tanẓîf kahrabâ'iya*

## W

**washing machine** *n.* âlet′ ṛasîl kah′rabâ′iyê *âlat′ ṛasil kah′rabâ'iya*

**wavelength** *n.* maujê *môga*

**weather forecast** *n.* bayân it′ta′=es' *bayân it′-ta′=es'*

**weekly magazine** *n.* ma-jal'lê isbû'îyê *magal'la usbû'îya*

**windshield wiper** *n.* mamsaḥet′ izâz el ôtombîl *mamsahat′ izâz el-ôtombîl*

**wireless** *n.* lâsil′kî *lâ-sil′kî*

## Z

**zipper** *n.* ziper *ziper*

# NEW PHRASES

## Traveling by Car

| | es'-safar'bil' ôtmobîl | *es-safar'bil ôtmobîl* |
|---|---|---|
| **Can I rent a car?** | bi=dir istajir' ôtombîl' | *a=dar a=agar liôtombîl* |
| **For a day, a week, per hour?** | le-yaum, le-jim'a, bis'sa'a | *yôm. ligom'a, bis'sa'a* |
| **How much will it cost?** | ad'dêsh bikal'-lif' | *yekal'lif'kâm* |
| **Is it a late model?** | hayda môdel' jdîd | *hûwa môdel' gedîd'* |
| **Are American or British cars more popular here?** | el-ôtombîlât el-Amerkâniyê yemma el-Englizîyê mashhûra ak-ter'hôn | *elôtombîlât el-inglizî as'har' wal'la elamir-kânî* |
| **Will I need a permit?** | biḥtâj le-rukhṣa | *lâzim' agîb taṣrîḥ* |
| **I prefer to drive myself** | bfaḍ'ḍil 'sû'= bnaf'sî | *afaḍ'ḍal asu'-bnaf'sî* |
| **I would like to hire a driver** | bḥib' ista=jir' shôfer | *aḥib' agîb sawa'-* |
| **Can women drive here?** | bti=dir' en='nis'-wân tsu'- hôn | *te=dar' es-set-tât tsu hena* |
| **I'd like a small car, a convertible, a four-door sedan** | bḥib' ôtombîl ṣrîr, mak'shûf, bi=arba' bwâb | *'a'yez ôtombîl soṛa'yar', ôtom-bîl maf'tûḥ, ki-bîr* |
| **How are the roads?** | kîf-ţ-ţurât | *ṭurug kwai'yîsa* |

| | | |
|---|---|---|
| **How is the traffic in the city?** | kîf z'zaḥmê bil'-mdinê | *izâi' elmurûr fil'madîna* |
| **Do cars drive on the right or left?** | bit'sû'-el-ôtom-bîlât 'al yamîn yemma 'ash-mâl | *elôtombîlâ btim-shî 'alal'yimîn walal'shimâl* |
| **Where is the nearest gas station?** | wâyn a=rab' mḥaṭet' benzîn | *fên a=rab maḥa-ṭet' banzîn* |
| **Do they sell by the gallon or quart?** | bîbî'o bil'galôn yemma bit'-tankî | *bî-bî'u bil'galun walla bir'-rob'* |
| **Give me ten** | 'ṭinî 'ashra | *id'dînî 'ashara* |
| **Fill'er up** | mal'li'-tank' | *im'la el-khazzân* |
| **The windshield needs wiping** | el-ezâz bad'do masḥ | *el-izaz 'âyiz' tan'dîf* |
| **Can I get a road map?** | bi=dir jîb khârṭa liṭ'ṭarî' | *a=dar agîb khâ-riṭa li'sikka* |
| **I hope there is a spare tire** | inshal'la yekûn fî dûlâb ziâdê | *inshal'la yukûn fî'agala ziyâ'da* |
| **How far is the next town?** | ad'-dêsh btib-'ud' il-balad' il-ba'd haydî | *a=rab' madîna bu'daha kâm* |
| **What's the best road?** | ay-yâha aḥsan ṭarî' | *el aḥsan sik'ka* |
| **Is there a speed limit?** | fî ḥad'lis'sir'a | *fî hâd' liś-sur'a* |
| **I have a flat tire** | ṣâr ma'î ben-shar' | *ḥadas' ma'î ben-shar* |
| **Can you change it?** | bte=dir' tṛai-ro | *te=dar teṛai'-yaru* |
| **Is there a garage, a mechanic around?** | fî karâj- mîka-nîkî bhal'jih'-hât | *fî garâj au mo-han'dis'* |
| **The car is not running well** | el-ôtombîl' ma byimshî mlîḥ' | *elôtombîl met'aṭ'-ṭal* |

| | | |
|---|---|---|
| **Check the brakes, the spark plugs, the headlights** | ifḥaṣ il fremât (al-brikât) al-bôjiât, wil iḍwiyê | *shûf elfarmala, elbujî, wil anwâr* |
| **I don't want to have an accident** | ma bad′dî a‘mel′ iṣtidâm | *mish′ ‘ayiz yeḥṣal′lî ḥâ′dis′* |
| **We were in a bad smash-up last year** | sâr ma‘na iṣtidâm fazi‘ issenê il-maḍiyê | *haṣal′lina ḥâdis′ fazî‘ es′sana il′lî fâtit′* |
| **The car stalls** | ôtombîl biwa=if′ | *el-ôtombîl biyû′=af′ ‘alaraf′la* |
| **We had a breakdown two miles out** | t‘aṭ′ṭal’ ma‘na ‘ala bi‘d mîlên | *it‘aṭ′ṭalna ba‘d masâ′fit′ mîlên′* |
| **The car had to be towed in** | iltazamna n-jur′ el-ôtombîl′ | *wiḍ-ṭar′rêna negur′el-ôtombîl* |
| **Turn left, right, at the next crossroads** | ilfut′ shmâl, yamîn,‘ind msal′lab′ ṭuru′ it′tânî | *khud shimâ′lak′, yamî′nak′ ‘ala ta=a′ṭu′ il′turug el′gaî* |
| **A good mountain highway** | ṭarî′ -il jabaliyê kwaysê | *tarîg gabalî kuwai′yis′* |
| **The bridge is not far** | el′ jisr mish’ b‘îd | *el′kob′rî mish′ bi‘îd′* |
| **The car needs new parts** | el-ôtombîl′ bad′du′ shi=af′ jdîdê | *elôtombîl ‘ayiz ḥitat′ ṛiyâr* |
| **How long will it take to fix?** | ad′dêsh biṭa′wil’ tislîhu | *el′taślîḥ yâkhud ad′-êh* |
| **Can you fix it quickly?** | bti=dir′ tṣalḥu bî‘ajalê (AWÄM) | *te=dar teṣal′laḥu awâm* |
| **The battery is dead** | el′-biṭ′ṭarî′yê maitê | *el′baṭ′ṭarîya mayeta* |
| **Send for a spare part** | ib‘at′ jîb iṭ′‘it′ ṛiâr | *eb‘at′ uṭlub′ ḥitat′ṛiyâr* |

| | | |
|---|---|---|
| **W'ell wait for it.** | mnintizera | *ḥanintizerha* |
| **The roads are dusty, in bad condition, well kept** | ṭurât mṛab-'barê, 'idmânê, bḥalî kwaysê | *el'ṭurug' mal'-yana ṭurâb, weḥ'ala awî, mu'tana biha* |
| **We went 60 miles an hour** | riḥna bsir'a sit'-tîn mîl bis'sa'a | *sur'na si'tîn mîl fis'sa'a* |
| **Go slow; curves ahead; hairpin curve** | su' 'ala mah-lak-, kûrbât amamak', min-'ataf' ḥâd | *su' bish'wêsh, elḥawadayât' gay'ya, ḥawa-da'ya sa'ba awî* |
| **Dead end; detour; road under repair** | âkhir ṭarî', in-ḥarif', ṭarî' taḥt'til'-tiṣ'liḥ | *nihay'it' el'tarîg, sik'ka ganibiy'-ya tar'mîmât* |
| **Thirty miles to the border** | tlâtîn mîl lil'-ḥudûd | *talatîn mîl lil' ḥudûd* |

## Traveling by Air

| | Es-safar' bit-ṭayara | *es-safar' bit-ṭayara* |
|---|---|---|
| **We save four hours by plane** | min'waf'fir' arba' sa'ât bit'ṭayâra | *nuwafar' arba' sa'ât bit-ṭayâra* |
| **Is there plane service to Damascus?** | maujûd mḥaṭ'-ṭit' ṭayarân ila-shâm | *fî khaṭ gawî lidi-mashq'* |
| **What time should we be at the airport?** | ay wa=it lâzim' nkûn fil'maṭâr | *lâzim' nikûn fil'maṭâr es-sa'a kâm* |
| **The plane leaves at 4: 15** | ṭayâra btit' ruk' is-sa 'a arba'a we rub' | *eṭ'ṭayâra misa-fra es-sa'a ar-ba'a wirib'* |

| | | |
|---|---|---|
| **Where do we pick up our tickets?** | min′ fên mnish′-tirî tazâkir | *fên nistelem′ ta-zâkerna* |
| **How much luggage am I allowed?** | ad'-desh byes-maḥu lî ‘afsh | *a=dar âkhud ad′ê ‘afsh* |
| **What are the extra charges?** | shû it-takâlîf iz-zaydê | *bikâm el′ ‘âfsh ez-ziyâda* |
| **I want to go to the airport** | bed'-dî rûḥ lil′-maṭâr | *‘ayiz arûḥ el-maṭâr* |
| **How many passengers does the plane take?** | kam râkib ’btiḥ-mul′ iṭ-ṭayâra | *eṭ-ṭayâra tâkhud kâm musâfer′* |
| **Do they serve meals?** | bi=admu akl′ | *bi-ademu akl′* |
| **Steward, stewardess, do I have a window seat?** | mûdîf, mûdifat′, ma=‘adî ḥad′-dil′ shebâk | *ḥadret′ elmûdîf, elmûdîfa, maṭ′-raḥî gamb eshub′bâk* |
| **I never get airsick** | ma bdûkh bij′-jau | *‘omrî ma at‘ab′ fil′ tayâra* |
| **Fasten your safety belts** | ḥakmo ḥzamât il′najât | *orbotû el-aḥzima* |
| **The safety belt is stuck** | ilḥizâm mash-bûk | *elḥizâm khasrân* |
| **Chewing gum relieves pressure on the ears** | maḍr-il′ ‘ilk bî-khafif′ iḍ′ḍarṭ ‘ala iznân | *el′lebân yikal′lil′ eldarṭ ‘ala el-widân* |
| **We are taking off** | raḥ nṭîr | *ebtadena neṭîr* |
| **Smooth, bumpy flight** | raḥlê sahlê, bit-khuḍ | *reḥla sahla, sa‘ba* |
| **How fast are we going?** | ad′dêsh is=sir‘a il′li′ raiḥîn fîha | *sur‘et′ eṭ-ṭaiyâra kâm* |
| **Jet planes go faster** | ṭayarât il jet′ bit′rûḥ asra‘ | *eṭ′ṭaiyarâ el′naf′-fatha teṭîr asra‘* |

| | | |
|---|---|---|
| **We're above the clouds** | niḥna fô' ilṛaym | *iḥna fô'elṛaym* |
| **How high are we flying?** | ad-dêsh niḥna 'alyîn | *eṭ'ṭaiyâra 'ala irtifa'kâm* |
| **We land in an hour** | mnûṣal' ba'd sa'a | *ḥanûṣal ba'd sa'a* |
| **Do you enjoy flying?** | bitḥib' is-safar' bij'jau | *inta biṭ'hib' eṭ'-ṭaiyarân* |
| **I always travel by air** | daiman' bsâfir' bij'jau | *ana ṭawâl'lî asâ-fir biṭ'ṭaiyâra* |
| **I like flying** | bḥib' iṭ'ṭayarân | *ana aḥeb es'sa-far' biṭ'ṭaiyâra* |
| **He owns a private plane** | 'indô ṭayâra khṣûṣiê | *huwa 'andu tai-yâra khaṣ'ṣa* |
| **Can we charter a plane?** | mni=dir' nista=jir' ṭayâra | *mumkin' ne=ag'-gar' ṭaiyâra* |
| **We need an experienced licensed pilot** | mniḥtâj liṭa'yâr khabîr ma'ô rukhṣa | *neḥtâg' ela ṭai-yâr mutama-ren' wi'andu rokhṣa* |
| **I've had ten hours of instruction** | ana ṭayart' 'ashr sa'ât drâsî | *ana 'andi 'ashâr sa'ât ṭaiyâran* |
| **The co-pilot took over** | musâ'id' iṭ'-ṭa-yâr istalam | *musa'id' eṭ'ṭai-yâr bîy'su'* |
| **Night flying, blind flying** | ṭayarân bil'lail', ṭayarân bidûn irshâd | *ṭaiyarân bil'lel, ṭaiyarân a''ma* |
| **Coming in for a landing** | ar'rab'na 'al'-hubût | *ar'rab' yinzil'* |

## Using the Telephone

| | isti mal et′telefon | *isti mal et′telefon* |
|---|---|---|
| **Operator, will you please get me . . .** | min′ faḍ′lik′ ‘ṭeenî . . . | *min′fad′lik′ id′-dînî . . .* |
| **Hello, may I speak to . . .** | halô-mumkin′ iḥkî ma‘ | *hello, a′=dar a-kal′lim′ . . .* |
| **This is Mr. Andrews** | ana mister′ ândrûs | *ana mister′ an-drews* |
| **Who's calling?** | mîn byeḥkî | *mîn elmutakal′-lim′* |
| **He's not in** | hû mish hôn | *huwa mesh mau′-gûd* |
| **When will he be back?** | aymta byer′ja‘ | *ḥayerga‘ emta′* |
| **I'll call again** | bit′iṣil′ ma’u mar′ra tân-yê | *ḥa-aḍ′rab′ tânî* |
| **Would you please give him a message?** | bta‘mil′ ma‘rûf balṛu risâltî | *min′fad′lak′ ol′-lo . . .* |
| **Please ask him to call back** | khal′lî ye’tiṣil′ ma‘î bit′tele-fôn | *min′fad′lak′ teṭ′-lub′ men′nu yeḍ′rab’* |
| **He can reach me at the Hotel** | biye′=dir′ yet′-tiṣil′ ma‘î bil′-hotel′ | *ye′=dar yed′rab′-lî fil′hotel* |
| **Goodbye, and thank you** | ash′kurak′ we-bkhâṭrak′ | *sa‘î′da, kat′tar′k* |
| **His phone is out of order** | telefôno m‘aṭ′ ṭal′ | *telifôno kharbân* |
| **Operator, I got the wrong number** | ‘ṭaitînî numra ṛalaṭ′ | *edetînî nemra ṛalaṭ′* |

| | | |
|---|---|---|
| **Long distance, please** | elkhaṭ′ el khârijî min′ fad′-lik′ | *mukâlama kharigî′ya min′-fad′lik′* |
| **I want to call Cairo, person-to-person** | brîd it′tiṣil′ bîma′sr, shakh′-sian′ | *'a′yiz aka'lim′ elkahira mukalama shakhsîya* |
| **What are the rates?** | ad′dêsh bîkal′lif' | *bikâm el mukâlama* |
| **Is there a public telephone?** | fî telefôn 'umûmî | *fî telifôn 'umûmî* |
| **May I have some change, please** | fîk ta'ṭînî srafê min′ fad′lak′ | *'andak′ fak′ka min′fad′lak′* |
| **May I use your telephone?** | bi=dir′ ista'mil′ telefônak' | *a′=dar asta'mil telifônak′* |
| **Please speak louder** | arjûk′ irfa' ṣauṭak′ | *min′fad′lak 'al′lî sôṭak′* |
| **I am sorry, I didn't get that** | mit′=as′sif′ ma fhimt′ shû elt′ | *muta=as′sif′masme'tesh âkher kelma* |
| **Will you please repeat that** | râji' il-jim′lê min′ faḍ′lak′ | *min′fad′lak,'îd elgomla* |
| **What is your phone number?** | shû hi′-yê num′-rit′ telefônak′ | *nimret′telifônak kâm* |
| **Did anyone call me?** | ḥada ḍarab′lî telefôn | *ḥad ḍarab′lî telifôn* |
| **Any telephone messages?** | ijânî risalât telefôniê | *fî m′ukâlama telifôni-ya* |
| **They can't get through to Cairo** | ma idru yet′-tiṣ′lu bimasr | *mish âdrîn yet′-teṣlu bil′kahira* |
| **The lines are down temporarily** | ilkhuṭûṭ′ m'aṭ′-ṭali mauwa=at' | *el-khaṭ met′ 'at′-tal′ muwaḳ′ḳatan* |
| **The line is busy** | ilkhaṭ′ mashṛûl | *el-khaṭ mashṛul* |
| **Will you please** | jar′rbî in-num′- | *min′fad′lik' gar′* |

| | | |
|---|---|---|
| **try that number again?** | ra mar′ra tânyê min′ faḍ′lik′ | *ribî en′nemra dî tânî* |
| **I'll call you back later** | bit′tiṣil′ fîk ba‘dän | *ḥadrab′lak' telifôn ba‘dên* |
| **I was disconnected** | aṭa‘û ‘alai′yê il-khaṭ′ | *elkhaṭ′ in-aṭa‘* |
| **Information, please** | maktab' il-isti‘lamât min′ faḍ′lik′ | *iste‘lamât min′fad′lik′* |
| **An extension phone, a French phone** | telefôn îḍafî, telefôn frin′sawî | *telifôn îḍafî, telifôn fransawî* |
| **Is there a telephone directory?** | maujûd dalîl lil′telefôn | *fî daf′tar′ telifôn* |

## Traveling with a Camera

| | es-safar′ ma ‘kamera | *es-safar′ ma‘kamera* |
|---|---|---|
| **I have a reflex camera, a box camera, a folding camera, a 35 mm. camera** | ‘indî kamira reflex, san'doo′ btiṭ‘wî khamsê witlâtîn mil′limetre | *‘andî reflex camera, box, folding, khamsa wtalâtîn mm.* |
| **I brought some extra rolls of film with me** | jibt′ ma‘î aflâm ziadê | *gebt aflâm ziâda ma‘aya* |
| **Color and black-and-white** | mlawanê wa-aswad′wa-abyaḍ' | *aflâm mulou′wana, wi ab′yad′ wi eswed'* |
| **Is film obtainable at the Hotel, in the shops?** | maujûd aflâm fil′hotel′, fid′dakakîn | *maugûd aflâm fil′hotel, fil′ dakakîn* |

| | | |
|---|---|---|
| **How much is it?** | shû si'ra | *tamanhum kâm* |
| **Can I have films developed here, or should I take them home with me?** | byeṭba'u-aflâm haun, au lâzim' âkhud'hun'-ma'î 'al' bilâd | *a=dar aḥam'-maḍ' aflâm hena wal'la âkhudhum elbêt ma'aya* |
| **When can I pick them up?** | imtîn bi=dir' âkhudhun' | *emta agî âkhud'-hum* |
| **Are they reliable? I don't want these rolls spoiled** | bi=dir' it'tikell' 'alaihun', ma brîd tintizi'-il aflâm | *mumkin' waḥid' yit'takel' 'alehum' mish' 'a-yiz elaflâm dî tekhsar'* |
| **They are irreplaceable** | mish' mimkin' ta'wîḍun' | *ma=darsh a'a-waḍ'hum* |
| **Please develop them on glossy, dull (matte) finish** (print) **paper** | min' fad'lak' iṭba' hun' 'ala wara' lam'mî' wara' nâshif' | *min'fad'lak' iṭ-ba'hum 'ala wara' lami', wara' kheshin'* |
| **I'd like this enlarged** | be'dî haydî mkab'bara | *aḥib akab'bar'dî* |
| **One print of each** | ṣûra min'kil' wâḥdî | *ṣûra waḥda min' kul' 'afrît'* |
| **The strap on my case broke. Can you repair it?** | in=aṭa'-le'=shâṭ yellî 'ala maḥ-fazṭî, bti=dir'-tṣalḥu | *ed-elkîs etkas'-saret te=dar' teṣalaḥ'ḥa* |
| **How much is a new one?** | ad'dêsh si'r-el jedîd | *kâm taman waḥ-da gedîda* |
| **I got some good shots of the town from the balcony** | akhazt' ṣûwar kwaysê lil'-balad' min-el bal'kôn | *akhadt ṣûwar kuwai'yisa lil' madîna minil' balcôna* |

| | | |
|---|---|---|
| **A very picturesque place** | makân jamîl lit′tiṣ′wîr | *balad gamîl awî* |
| **Will they pose for us?** | biûafu ḥat′ta' nṣawer′hun′ | *yesmaḥulna nâkhud′ ṣuret′-hum′* |
| **I have to change the roll first** | lăzim' ṛayir' il film bil′awal' | *lâzem aṛai′yar elfilm el′auel′* |
| **I've already used up six shots** | is′ta‘malt′ minil film sit′ ṣûwar | *akhadt sit′ ṣuwar* |
| **She is very photogenic. I photograph badly** | btâkhud ṣûwar min′ kil′ jih′ha ma ba‘rif′ ṣawer kwayis' | *hey′ya teṭ′la‘ kuwai′yisa fil′ ṣûwar, ana aṣawar ‘âtel′* |
| **Is it all right to take movies of the ceremony?** | bi=dir' âkhud′ ṣûwar mit′ḥarkê lil′haflê | *masmûh waḥid′ yakhud′ ṣu′war lil′ ḥafla* |
| **Can I get some close-ups?** | bi=dir' âkhûd ṣûwar arîbê | *min′urai′yeb′* |
| **It is all right to take pictures** | masmûh akhid′ ṣûwar | *masmuḥ waḥid′ yakhud′ ṣu′war* |
| **No pictures allowed** | mamnû‘ et-tiṣ′wîr | *mish′ masmûḥ* |
| **I saw that in the newsreels** | shif′to bîfilm il-akhbâr | *shuft′ el′ manzar da fil′ cinema* |
| **Will you please take a picture of us? Thank you** | min′ faḍ′lak′ tâkhud′ ṣûret-na, mamnûnîn | *min′fad′lak′ tâkhud′ ṣuret′na, kat′tar′ kherak′* |
| **Just press the lever down until yuo hear a click** | iḍraṭ′ ‘al′kib′bâs ḥat′ta tis'ma‘ ṭa=a | *dus ‘ala′zir'leḥad ma tesma‘sôt* |
| **Do you know how to adjust the camera?** | bta‘rif′ t‘ad′dil′ il kamera | *te‘raf′ testa‘mil′ el kamera* |

| | | |
|---|---|---|
| **You're standing too close** | wâ=if'arîb ktîr | *enta wa'=f arai'-yib' khaliṣ'* |
| **That's better** | hayda aḥ'san' | *ay'wa keda aḥsan* |
| **I forgot to turn the roll** (of film) | nsît ub'rum' il' film | *nesît adaw'war el' film* |
| **We'll have a double exposure** | byiṭla' ṣûrtain 'ala waḥdî | *ḥa yeṭla'û ṣurtên 'ala ba'ḍ* |
| **Will we stop for pictures on the way?** | fîk twa=if' lanâ-khud' ṣûwar 'aṭ'ṭarî' | *ḥa nu'=af nâ-khud' ṣuwar 'alasik'ka* |
| **I like candid shots** | bḥib' is-ṣûwar iṭ'ṭabî 'ie | *aḥib' el ṣuwer el-ṭabî'ya* |
| **I saw a good buy in a new camera, a used camera** | shift' kamera jdîdê, shar'wî kamera mus'-ta'malê | *shuft' kamera rikhiṣa, kamera musta'mala* |
| **Will I have to pay duty on this when I return home?** | lâzim' id'fa' kum'ruk' 'alai-ha lam'ma bir'ja' | *lâzim adfa' gom-rok'aleha lam'-ma arga'* |
| **This one is an American-made camera** | haydî kamera shuṛl America | *dî kamera amîr-kânî* |
| **I'll send you a print if it turns out well** | bib'at' lak' ṣûra iza ṭil' 'it' mlîha | *ḥa ab'atlâlak' ṣura iza ṭel'et kuwai'yisa* |